AMANDA'S QUEST

KINGDOM OF TORRENCE

BY D.M. STODDARD

Kingdom of Torrence
Reno Nevada

KingdomOfTorrence.com
DMStoddard.com

ACKNOWLEDGEMENTS

I would like to thank my family and friends for their support and encouragement for me to complete this story that I offer for your reading pleasure. Special thanks to my wife and children from whom I stole time to complete this book.

As an author I enjoy creating worlds and storylines for readers, but it can become confusing in terms of grammar, logic, consistency, and many other important parts needed to deliver a story. For this, I have beta readers who read my drafts, helping me remain logical and consistent while reassuring me that what I am creating continues to be entertaining. My editor, who was so flexible and supportive during some very strenuous times, gave me guidance on grammar, structure, vocabulary, and other components that make meaningful words, sentences, paragraphs, pages, chapters, and ultimately this book. When you write, when you create a story, you do not necessarily concentrate on the proper word or format. These are the people who have attempted to keep me honest:

Editor	Beta Readers
Toni Rakestraw	C.V. Stoddard, H.K. Gilbert,
Rakestraw Book Design	E.M. McCuskey, and D.R. Bagley

I am glad to publish Amanda's Quest for your enjoyment.

Special Acknowledgements

In honor and memory of his namesake, Prince Garrett faces unforeseen challenges and, just when things appear to be at their worst, he is thrown from his horse in the midst of battle. As his men race to gather around him the prince continues to battle on, facing his own, personal Goliath.

Inspiration to write, just like inspiration to push through life's challenges, comes from a variety of sources. To the latter, when life's challenges have become overly burdensome and I have thought I could take no more, I have found inspiration from the personal battles of others who have faced far greater adversities. Thinking to myself if they have such strength and determination then I must certainly be able to conquer my day. Thank you for showing me the way.

In Memory of

Christina Maria Miarecki
May 8, 1965 – May 1, 2015

Garrett Allen
August 8, 1999 – April 24, 2015

Note from the Author

I should confess that I choose to use the word "Elve" rather than "Elf" despite my editor's advice; every time I read "Elf" I envision a Christmas character rather than a fantasy character from the forest. I also struggle with the term "teleport" or "teleportation." When I read the word "teleport" I immediately think of some space craft waiting to beam the character off the surface of Dendür. So, magical properties project rather than transport or teleport. Please grant me a little creative license as I paint a picture of the world of Dendür for your entertainment.

By D.M. Stoddard

TABLE OF CONTENTS

PROLOGUE

H*ad it really been a year?* Reginald thought to himself as they walked down the cobblestone street towards the Minstrel's Inn.

The elderly bard struggled more than he had the year before to take the small steps that carried him towards the joviality that awaited them. The music of so many bards who were awaiting his arrival was echoing up the street through the cool fall air. Reginald anticipated their welcoming applause.

Once again it was the last night of the Bards' Festival. Remembering that on this night a year ago he had promised the brethren he would return to play 'Amanda's Quest' for them, he approached the inn. He could hear the brethren singing 'The Legend of Jerrod' together, refreshing their memories about the heroes of Torrence in preparation for the second song to be sung by the Master of Bards.

The ballad, 'The Legend of Jerrod,' was about Jerrod and his comrades who had sought a secret treasure. On the road to fame and fortune, Jerrod had become the focus of many people's attention. Guided by a witch, Jerrod found a magical sword. His first and closest friend was Amanda, a beautiful warrior who he learned was so much more than he had imagined. Together they met Drin. He was slightly older, in his early twenties, and pursuing knighthood in the Order of One. After becoming close friends, the three had promised to protect the wizard, Nathanial, on an adventure to recover the lost treasure of Terrace Xul. They tried to prepare secretly, but the week before they left Torrence a mysterious sage, Fraum, invited himself to join their adventure.

It was not until they had reached the Plateau of Kronese that they met the druid princess, Rhonda, and her Elven guardian, Imelrinn.

Pursued by mercenaries, the group entered the Black Forest under the protection of the druid princess from Lithlillia, but it had not gone well. When Rhonda was critically wounded and healing-priests of Asclepius had refused to treat a non-believing druid, Amanda went to the Guild of the Crimson Pommel for help in persuading the priests. Because of Amanda's respectable status as a guild member, the guild was more than willing to apply the appropriate persuasions, for a price. Amanda had sworn to undertake a blood-debt. 'The Ballad of Amanda's Quest' memorialized her efforts and the consequences arising from saving Rhonda's life.

When they reached the Minstrel's Inn, Lawrence helped the legendary bard step into the inn from the street while James held the heavy oak door open for his master and the master's protégé. James' head was slightly cocked to the left as he stared down at the floor of the door frame, not looking at the others. The long, open curls of James' dirty blond hair partially obscured his slightly deformed face.

As Reginald stepped through the door, the frame illuminated ever so slightly, such that the conscious mind might not perceive the change. The mysterious light helped the master see the doorway steps more clearly, causing a smile to cross Reginald's face as he stepped through.

Lawrence had not noticed. It was not that Lawrence was indifferent, egotistical, or pompous. He focused on Reginald to a fault. Nothing came before his master. Stepping through right behind his mentor, Lawrence's rapier bounced under his purple cavalier cape.

As always, the festive bards were dressed in colorful cotton shirts, leather vests or jerkins, and tight pants partially covered with knee high boots. They wore various caps ornamented with ostrich or pheasant feathers. Here and there a female bard wore a bodice or waist cincher, some with ankle height boots replacing the more traditional knee high boots, consorted with her peers. Long daggers and swords were hanging from wide, leather belts like the bards of old, but the weapons had become more of an ornamental hand rest.

Silence fell over the crowd as Reginald Rhinestone appeared in the doorway. Leaning on Lawrence more than he had the year before, Reginald walked to the middle of the large room. His hands had more of a quiver. Although he still wore the warmer layers of clothing, the fire in the stone fireplace gave him comfort. The light from the fire momentarily glistened in the tiger's eye ring on his little finger.

"He looks older," someone whispered beyond Reginald's hearing.

"There are more brethren than last year," Reginald spoke softly over his shoulder to Lawrence.

James did not have to scurry far to find a stool. A nearby bard quickly rose, offering up his seat for the Master of Bards. Shuttling the stool back to Reginald, James offered the master's beautifully crafted mandolin to him.

"Thank you, James," Reginald said compassionately before turning to the crowd.

"Good evening. It's a pleasure to be here with you, my family, again. Each and every one of you, bards in your own right. It's truly an honor to sing for you." Reginald paused to take a cup from James.

Sipping from the cup, the cool water quenched his thirst and moistened his mouth so he could more easily sing.

"This is my protégé, Lawrence," Reginald said loudly, introducing the much younger man. "He is going to play a moment while I settle in."

Surprising Lawrence by the announcement, the young protégé humbly accepted the Master's mandolin. Lawrence could feel his square jaw tightening as his nerves tensed in anticipation. He removed his purple cape and handed it to James, then pushed his rapier aside with his free hand to sit down on the stool meant for his Master.

"Thank you, Master Reginald," Lawrence said as his fingernails began to pluck the strings of the magnificent instrument.

Lawrence's dark, shoulder length hair contrasting against his face made him seem paler than he really was, but it was the focus of his eyes that made him seem so intense. He fit the expectations of a young nobleman, as the rumors suggested. He was as lost in the community of minstrels as he was in the court of noblemen to which his father and older brother were so much more accustomed. Being the great grandnephew of a count and the second son of his father left him an empty title that he never used.

"Let me play an instrumental for you. As I play imagine starting on the Coast of Semanie, up the Torrence River, over Limerin Falls, and on to the high mountain lake of Almandee surrounded by the Crispten Mountains. You will pass over much of the land that Jerrod traveled with his companions so long ago."

Lawrence's enchanted music, sweeping over the brethren like the warmth of a fire spreading out into a room, created a vision of the trip. No one was sipping their drinks as Lawrence played on. Those standing swayed with the tempo of the mandolin. The walls seemed to disappear as the magical music carried them from rocky shores where sea water crashed over their heads to a high mountain meadow near a waterfall before racing through a forest as though they were all deer leaping over fallen trees. The cold, fresh water of Lake Almandee and the shadows of the snow-capped mountains chilling the brethren so much that some pulled upon their jackets, seeking warmth. They could sense the salty sea water of the fjord, the cool mountain air, and the beating heart of the deer.

The bards' music was the last of the magic known to a world where dragons and wizards, druids and Elves, no longer existed. And Lawrence's music was exceptional, even for a bard. Perhaps not quite as exceptional as Reginald's, but still beyond that of any other of the brethren.

As the last frames of the music diminished, the images faded.

While Lawrence played, Reginald had gone to the bar to get a glass of warm red wine. The patrons had quietly stepped aside to allow him to pass while their attention focused on Lawrence's music. They were captivated. At the bar, Reginald turned around and watched the crowd. A soft smile grew on his old face as he observed his protégé successfully completing his debut. The crowd's silence was an achievement beyond the complementary joining in to sing alone.

I remember when my music first silenced the brethren, Reginald reflected.

A sense of happiness filled the patrons, who immediately called for more spirits. The bar maidens leapt to business. The innkeeper, already rendered into happiness by Lawrence's music, wore a broad smile as coins exchanged hands from bards to the maidens. The innkeeper loved the festival and this night above all others.

"He's a money maker," the innkeeper said to the maiden tending the bar.

Reginald stepped towards the center of the room, softly clapping his shaking hands. He exchanged places with Lawrence and, resting the dark, brownish-red instrument with its white, delicately inlaid face on his thigh. The silver inlay reflected the dim light of the inn's tavern.

I remember when I sat with the brethren listening to the master. The room. The lights. How many generations have I watch come and go? Reginald asked himself.

"Brethren," Lawrence commanded their attention. "Reginald Rhinestone!" Lawrence said after the dramatic pause.

Lawrence retreated to mingle with the others, observing the rustic atmosphere that non-bards never had a chance to experience. They all knew Reginald. They all knew his physical appearance was not an indication of his musical and magical abilities. Last year's rendition of 'The Legend of Jerrod' had been magnificent despite the signs of his old age. The brethren, holding their breath in anticipation, patiently awaited Reginald's next word.

"Lawrence of Cipper, ladies and gents. Let's give him another hand," Reginald said, causing the crowd to erupt into a roar.

"It is always an honor and a pleasure to play for you. Last year I sang of Jerrod," Reginald started when the bards quieted again.

Reginald picked at the strings, his fingers sliding over the silver frets on the nearly black neck. As he was warming up he spoke of Jerrod's desperate desire to be more than a miller. That desire had led Jerrod into an adventure fraught with battles of steel and magic against mythical beasts, but the battles were not Jerrod's greatest challenge. Nor was his growing love for Amanda and Rhonda. Like the others, Jerrod was trapped in the blood-debt that had finally torn their group apart and sent Amanda on an adventure of her own while the others were left facing treachery without her.

The trials of Amanda's quest were not altogether uncommon to her. She had grown up relying upon guile and her ability to "recover lost items." To save Rhonda she had promised to "retrieve" the Horn of Valhalla within the year. The horn was in the northern kingdom of Haithenbeurn, where the followers of Asgard dwelled. The looming deadline to return the horn to the Guild of the Crimson Pommel did not bother Amanda as much as leaving Jerrod with Rhonda, the beautiful druid princess and priestess-daughter of Lithlillia.

Reginald stopped picking the strings for a moment. Taking his last sip of wine as he looked around the audience of bards, he savored the moment. How he loved that instance before a song, when the beginning first captivated the audience.

"And now, as promised, I will play 'Amanda's Quest,'" he announced.

CHAPTER 1

NEW BEGINNING

Amanda stood at the bow of the ship, her long blonde hair blowing freely in the wind, her feet solidly planted on the deck as it rose and fell beneath her, and her hands grasping the rail as the water of the winter sea sprayed up into the air each time the bow dove into the next wave. Her journey had begun.

She was enjoying the salty mist of the ocean spray as she reflected on the events that had set her on the voyage to Ornholtz alone. She felt refreshed and empowered, and somehow the ominous quest before her seemed more achievable.

It had started months before with a promise that had ensured Rhonda's wounds would be treated. But with only a year to complete the blood debt, she had to go on alone while her friends ascended Terrace Xul. As if returning the Horn of Valhalla to the Grand Thief in Torrence within the year was not challenging enough, traveling through the Crispten Mountains in the winter had been slow and now she was behind.

If I don't acquire the horn within the year, the guild will kill us all, she thought.

The Crimson Pommel was the strongest guild in Torrence. Nothing lay outside of their influence. There was no place the guild could not reach except maybe the Order of One. Even the outlawed magical scholars known as the Triad were wary of the guild's influence. Amanda knew the guild's strengths and weaknesses all too well. She was, after all, their greatest thief. But not even Amanda was fully aware of the extent of the guild's power. As she stood at the rail she wondered if their influence reached into the northern kingdom of

Haithenbeurn. The ship hit another wave, causing her to take a step in order to regain her balance.

If the guild had someone in Haithenbeurn they would have used them to acquire the horn. Instead they are forcing me to 'recover' it, she concluded as the spray washed over her again.

The smell of the salty water was refreshing, but the bearskin she wrapped over her black leather jacket and tight pants was getting soaked by the sticky water of the fjord.

It can't be that difficult, she decided.

Leaving Jerrod had not been easy for her. He was her first and only love. She knew his life was in danger as long as they traveled with Nathanial, but she counted on the hope that, together with their friends, they could all survive Nathanial's treachery.

That morning she had remained hidden in the cargo hold while her friends frantically searched for her. She heard their voices calling for her until they accepted that she was gone, and then she heard the horses being offloaded as her friends prepared to ascend the Steps of Terrace Xul. Once the ship began moving forward, Amanda pulled her hair back into a ponytail in anticipation of trouble before slipping out of her hiding place to find the captain.

The crew, who was rushing about setting the ship in motion for the wind to catch the sail, had not noticed the sound of Amanda's kneehigh boots stepping on the thick wood deck as she moved towards the stairs up to the main deck with cat-like motion.

When Amanda stepped up on to the maindeck the crew was busy adjusting the sail, tying off rope, or at the helm guiding the course of the ship while the captain pondered over a nautical chart. Amanda chuckled to herself when no one paid attention to her moving towards the captain.

Captain Grogan was a burly man. He was tall and muscular with shoulder length hair and a thick beard. His hands were callused from pulling at oars and, in his earlier years before becoming a merchant sailor, pulling at fishing nets. His calculating mannerisms, developed over years of bartering furs for supplies between Ornholtz, Dorindril, and the other cities on the fjord, influenced every action he took.

He had sailed the Fjord of Menduran all of his life, but he had never set passengers off at the pier below Mount Thoradan. He wanted to ensure their course was set directly for Ornholtz and had not noticed Amanda walking up beside him.

With one hand resting on the crimson pommel of the dagger hanging from her belt, Amanda reached out to touch Grogan's shoulder.

"Captain," Amanda addressed the older man.

Grogan pulled back slightly, startled by Amanda's presence on his ship.

"Good morning, Captain. I require passage to Ornholtz and I'm willing to pay my way."

Amanda had taken a small bag of coins and gems out of the inner pocket of her leather jacket and began tossing the bag up and down playfully. The coins inside the bag made an enticing sound. She smiled coyly as her chilling blue eyes fixated on the much older man.

"You were gone?" the Captain responded with a puzzled look on his bearded face. "Your friends were looking for you. What are you doing here? How did you get on my ship?"

"I stayed aboard, but that shouldn't matter to you. I need to go on to Ornholtz as soon as possible and I can pay," Amanda answered, still playing with the bag of coins.

"What was it you said? You wanted nothing to do with Terrace Xul. Nor do I," she continued.

Your companions will have to face the wizard without you. Take care who you travel with. That one has a dark soul that brings death, Amanda recalled the witch's warning.

It was Grogan's gruff voice that brought her attention back to their conversation.

"And what is it worth to you?" he asked.

They bartered over several small gems before Amanda had gone to the bow to watch as the ship sailed north-by-northeast across the great fjord. Grogan watched as Amanda undid her ponytail, allowing her long blonde hair to blow in the breeze.

Not the wife of a sailor, he thought, admiring the curves of her athletic build.

Now, standing alone at the bow, Amanda's thoughts turned to the peaceful, moonlit nights in Torrence when she sat alone on the rooftops listening to the city's sounds and pondering what was going on below her skyline perch. Sitting there calculating the best ways to enter various establishments, she had been a distant observer, safely out of reach of the kingdom's affairs. Nothing could touch her. At the bow of Grogon's ship the feeling that nothing could touch her had returned, calming her mind.

Amanda pulled the bearskin Lady Lieisa had given her tight around her shoulders, fondly remembering their visit to Lithlillia, but her thoughts quickly returned to the task at hand. Haithenbeurn. An obscure northern kingdom rumored to be barbaric. Other than knowing that Ornholtz would be her entry point, she really knew nothing about the kingdom along the Nasdrawuen coast.

If I fail my friends will die, if Terrace Xul doesn't kill them first, the anxiety crashed back into her consciousness.

Is that you, my love? Are you watching us sail away? Or am I just imagining it? Amanda thought as she stared forward, into the wind, into the adventure lying before her as if she were trying to see through the darkness of the night. *Good bye my love.*

By the time her friends had reached the mountainside cottage along the steps of Terrace Xul, the ship and its stowaway had sailed to the middle of the fjord, a day and a half away from Ornholtz.

Grogan took pleasure watching Amanda standing at the bow of his ship. He wondered what she was thinking as she stared across the waves.

When Amanda had smiled at him while bartering for passage, she had completely disarmed him. At that point she could have had anything she wanted with her secretive nature, her fair skin, and full lips.

And those chilling blue eyes. She is more woman than any other living on the fjord, or in Haithenbeurn, for that matter. More than a king's wife, I'll wager. Definitely worth giving up the sea for if she were willing to sleep warmly at your side, but no sailor would be able keep her, he thought.

The dangling scabbard of Amanda's long sword caught Grogon's eye. He noted that the scabbard hung from a *frog*, two smaller belts that looped down from her belt attaching to the scabbard at the top and a little further down.

Not one to be trifled with, either. That blade isn't hanging there as an ornament.

The captain committed to memory that she rigged her sword as if she were an experienced warrior.

Why have you left your friends to climb Mount Thoradan alone while you sail to Ornholtz, little one? Perhaps you are less the fool. The thought made him chuckle.

But why travel alone into the northern kingdom? Her decision to secretly continue on without letting her friends know was curious.

"Make sure the crew knows to give Amanda a wide berth. I think anyone who crosses her course will come away the lesser for it," Captain Grogon ordered, looking at his First Mate.

The sooner I land her safely at Ornholtz the better for all of us.

✳   ✳   ✳   ✳   ✳

In the warmth of her cottage, Felicia had watched the image of Amanda reflecting on the surface of the oil in the brass basin sitting on the table before her. As she watched the image, she stroked the black cat sleeping on a pillow next to her. She had not been surprised by Amanda's secret departure from Terrace Xul. She stirred the oil with a long fingernail and the image shifted to Jerrod as he glanced over his shoulder looking down towards the fjord, while he wondered about Amanda.

Felicia was intrigued. Jerrod's longest love had sailed on a ship to Ornholtz in order to pay a blood-debt while his newest love rode next to him. And the thought that the wizard, Nathanial, rode with them made her chuckle aloud. Felicia knew Jerrod would be tempted by the Fates and that delighted her even more, but in the end, he would stand alone.

"There is no stopping Nathanial now, Sasha," Felicia said softly.

We shall see, the familiar thought back to her. *We shall see.*

"Do you think you know more than me?" Felicia questioned the cat aloud.

I think humans are resilient and love is triumphant, Sasha thought as the black cat changed into a panther. *I would not underestimate Jerrod or dismiss his love for Amanda.*

"But what about the druid princess?" Felicia teased.

✳   ✳   ✳   ✳   ✳

Far above the Fjord of Menduran and far enough away not to be seen, the winged horses had taken turns watching for signs of Rhonda, the druid princess of Lithlillia and the half-Elven daughter of Lady Lieisa. While the wizard's dragon circled above Mount Thoradan they had not been able to move closer.

The dragon had protected her master diligently and her need for food caused her to circle relentlessly.

When the winged herd sent their report to Lady Lieisa, they had only been able to offer that Rhonda had most likely entered Terrace Xul. They had assumed she was safely with her companions, but they had not been able to reach her mind. Rhonda was too far away. Consequently, their report had offered little information and less comfort.

✻   ✻   ✻   ✻   ✻

As Amanda undressed in the confines of the small cabin, a strange series of feelings washed over her. Thoughts of her love for Jerrod, her promise to complete the blood-debt, and her determination to finish that quest within the remainder of the year in order to protect everyone from the wrath of the Crimson Pommel twisted in her mind. Fraum, her recent mentor, desired she refrain from thievery, or at least, for her to stay out of "trouble" as he put it. The question whether her friends would survive Nathanial's treachery tormented her conscience.

Stop it! Focus on the tasks at hand, she thought as she pulled on a clean pair of black leather pants and hung the sea-soaked pants she had been wearing out to dry.

Amanda knew if she allowed herself to become distracted she might give herself or her intentions away at a crucial moment. She was on her own in a foreign kingdom without a friend. Too far away to expect assistance from anyone.

After changing, Amanda went through her pack, checking her possessions. The treasures she had collected on the journey from Torrence were all still there. She pulled her thieves' tools and climbing gear out of the pack to dry and then turned her attention to her bow and quiver of arrows. With great care, she began oiling her sword and daggers. The dagger with the crimson pommel, the jeweled dagger she found in Tilhelm Keep, and the silver dagger the witch, Felicia, had given her.

When she was finished she paused to twirl her dagger in her hands. Playing with the silver-colored blade of the crimson pommeled dagger, she contemplated her life. For the first time she found herself questioning her position in the guild.

What does being the best thief in the guild offer me? I answer to the Grand

Thief. I do his bidding. My past accomplishments for the guild were not enough to buy care for Rhonda. I had to agree to this blood debt, Amanda pondered.

And I am alone.

She felt sure the crew was too scared of Captain Grogan to enter her cabin or rummage through her belongings. He had accepted her as a passenger and taken her money, which ensured her safety and and that of her belongings. Nathanial had paid handsomely for their group to travel in a large cabin from Dorindril to the Steps of Terrace Xul beneath the shadow of Mount Thoradan. She paid less and got less, but the smaller quarters suited her fine.

Putting her dagger away, Amanda began practicing the dance-like exercises that Fraum had started teaching her on their journey. Like her master, at times she moved slowly. When she did, her muscles trembled with strength. The next moment she exploded through a series of rapid strikes, blocks, and kicks. In the months that she had practiced with the monk, Amanda's speed had quickened.

When she was done with her exercises she sat down and picked up the dagger she had "recovered" from Tilhelm Keep. It was the first opportunity she had had to examine the ornamental dagger. Semi-precious stones were embedded on either side of the hilt. From her experience dealing with such items, Amanda concluded the dagger was used primarily for meals. She had seen similar weapons on the belts of wealthy merchants at banquets. She appraised the gems as marginally valuable.

Everyone wants to wear a weapon. It makes them feel powerful, important. This is the least valuable of my collection, she concluded.

After partially repacking her bag, Amanda stuck it in the corner under the climbing gear. Then she leaned her bow and quiver of arrows in front of both. When she was done, the pile of her belongings seemed unremarkable. After spreading her wet bearskin out to dry, she laid down for her first night's sleep alone in many months, her sword lying at her side.

The next morning was crisp and cold. The sky was clear, the pale blue color of winter, as the wind steadily pushed their vessel onward. The crew pointed out another hump of a sea creature which breached the surface once, but the monster, whether it was a giant barracuda or serpent, did not come any closer.

"Praise Aegir," Grogon mumbled the prayer to the Asgardian god of the sea under his breath.

Amanda remembered the devastation of the attack as she watched for the creature to return. Silently, Amanda wished Rhonda was present to communicate with the creature, to steer it away from a confrontation. The absence of a druid on board bothered her, but to the merchant sailors it was a normal risk. Amanda wondered how well the sailors could fight off an attack, but when she asked Grogon, his answer was disheartening. More ships were lost than survived encounters with such monsters.

As dusk fell upon the fjord, the lights of Ornholtz came into view. The lamps of the city went up the hill away from the shore line. The shadows of the Ragnaugh Mountains and Mount Ornholtz loomed behind the city. Amanda could just see the pine forest on the lower ridges. It was long after nightfall when the ship finally eased up to the pier. Very few men from Ornholtz came to assist the late arriving vessel in mooring to the bollards.

"By the Fates," Amanda whispered.

The captain, who knew his crew was unsettled from the voyage, allowed them to go ashore for the night in celebration of another safe arrival. He knew it would mean a late start offloading the cargo in the morning, but that would give him time to negotiate the sale of his cargo and barter for goods to sell on the return journey. He would also be able to spend some time finding a jeweler to sell the gems Nathanial had paid him without the crew waiting impatiently for his return. The more time he had, the better price he should get for the stones.

Grogan had decided to keep the gems Amanda had paid for himself. He seldom held out from the crew, but as he grew older he tried to store away a savings for his retirement. When the ship was securely moored he released the crew, leaving the ship nearly empty, and sat down at his desk for some sailors' grog.

Outside, in the shadow of the night, the silhouette of a woman in tight black leather slipped over the side of his ship and onto the pier. She moved like a mountain lion, swift and strong, fierce yet agile. Her long, blonde hair pulled back into a pony tail held in place with a leather headband, bounced as she moved straight into the shadows of Ornholtz and disappeared into the city. Only her foot prints in the snow indicated she had passed, but there was no one lingering in the cold winter night to notice.

The warehouse district, and its inns and taverns, were considered the less savory part of the city. During daylight the pier commerce mixed merchants with passengers. Warehouses, where traders did business with the ship captains and local merchants, were built down as close to the pier edge as possible, but anyone wishing to travel by sea had to approach each ship and ask to speak with the captain to barter passage. Unlike Dorindril, the city lord did not involve himself with the business. But at night, only the drunk sailors in nearby taverns occupied the less savory district.

Amanda had learned on the voyage that in Ornholtz women rarely traveled alone, particularly at night, but the adventure made her feel at home. She felt exuberant, sneaking through the city unnoticed. For a moment it was as though she wandered Torrence, secretly observing the city she felt she owned.

She moved from doorway to doorway, listening at each to the drunken banter of the men in the tavern. It was a mixture of sailors and dock workers drinking away the frustrations of a long voyage or the demands of family life. Amanda could hear patrons inside the taverns boasting of great feats and toasting at the end of magnificent stories. When cheering erupted, Amanda envisioned the brutes inside in an arm wrestling contest. Perhaps there were games of dagger throwing.

She watched the few passersby from the shadows. Bearded men, most of them overweight, passed from tavern to tavern, their heavy fur boots trudging through the snow. They wore pants, shirts, and furs pulled over their shoulders and tucked into wide leather belts to keep them warm.

Even in a peaceful surrounding the men of Orholtz carried heavy swords they called *langsax*. The weapon, which was shorter than the long swords from Torrence, seemed slightly wider with flat pommels and short cross guards. Amanda was more interested in the single-sided axes with eight inch long, curving blades that some men carried in place of the *langsax*. The axe blades were flat along the top, but on the bottom curved back towards a two foot long handle, ideal for throwing.

She already knew she could not enter into the taverns or conduct business dressed in thieves' leather armor and carrying a long sword. To reach the king's city of Theasendür she would need to blend into the culture around her. She would have to become a citizen of Haithenbeurn. So, before returning to Grogan's ship, she went deeper into the city where she found a merchant district. And there, Amanda broke into a store to steal some traditional women's clothing.

In the store she saw mostly yak furs, but there were a few bearskins and an occasional wolf-skin. She had not seen a yak before and wondered what the animal looked like, but from the size and shape of the fur she assumed it was similar to the cattle in Torrence. She also found large, square bags with a single woven strap long enough to hang from a woman's shoulder. Amanda packed a bag with local clothing before leaving a gem on the counter and stealing back into the shadows of the street.

By the early morning hours the inn taverns quieted and the sailors returned to Grogan's ship to sleep off their drunkenness. It was easy for Amanda to return to her cabin with her spoils without being noticed, so easy she was able to take the gangway back onboard without being observed. Like everyone in the city, the ship's crew was asleep.

After sunrise, as the captain was preparing to go sell his cargo, there was a knock on his door.

"Come in," Grogan barked.

A local woman stepped through the door. She was ordinary looking, nothing remarkable. The heavy yak-wool sweater and skirt with gray leggings concealed Amanda's figure. Her long hair, pushed up under the colorful striped knitted cap, did not give away her identity. Had it not been for a golden dagger with a crimson pommel on her belt and the bow and quiver, Grogan never would have guessed her identity.

"Amanda?" he asked, not yet certain who he was looking at.

"I wanted to thank you for your hospitality and discretion, Captain," Amanda responded, pleased that her disguise had worked so well on someone who knew her. "I trust my arrival on your ship will remain a secret."

The captain nodded yes.

Amanda held her bow and quiver out to the burly, older man.

"I want you to have my bow," she started. "They will raise unwanted attention to me where I am going. They have provided me good service. I hope they will do the same for you. I have also left a few things in my cabin. Mostly rope. Do what you want with it."

After saying their goodbyes, Grogan watched her pick up a long bedroll and a large wool travel bag. Watching Amanda walk up the stairs to the main deck, he realized that she was leaving as mysteriously as she had arrived. He really knew nothing about her or her intentions but he would always remember the image of her at the bow of his ship, the wind blowing through her long blonde hair.

"Urd, keep her safe. She is a good person and deserves your watchful eye," Grogan prayed quietly to the Asgardian goddess of fate.

Amanda headed into Ornholtz. She had discovered that, beyond the wharf district that had been built along the sea-line, there were inns, shops, and the beginnings of homes. The buildings were bigger, and the farther they lay from the wharf district, the better they were kept. The best shops and inns appeared to be near the center of the city.

Amanda decided to visit shops in the richer district with the intent of obtaining a room nearby. As she walked through the city observing how the inhabitants, particularly the women, behaved, she learned their ways so she could mimic their habits. The relaxed atmosphere in the streets made her integration into their culture easier.

She observed strong men who were fighters, hunters, soldiers, sailors, blacksmiths, and dock-men. There were a few weaker men, too. Men who apparently made a living managing liveries, warehouses, and the few businesses needed to run a city. When the stronger men interacted with those appearing weaker, the stronger men always dominated the encounter.

Most of the women she observed were those venturing out alone to shop. And there were lesser women who worked in the taverns passing out the ale and inevitably ending up on some man's lap. The lesser women were exploited for their looks and the men's pleasure, and discarded later when they lost their looks to age with less consideration than dogs turned out to feed upon scraps.

The taverns served ale. There was no wine or mead, nor any other drink that might be considered manly. They ate pork, yak, chicken, and fish served mostly with potatoes. Dairy, such as butter and cheese was also available, but milk, which was also available, was never served to the men in a tavern. The only women eating in the taverns were accompanied by husbands, brothers, or their fathers, and children always accompanied them.

The sight reminded Amanda of Horis and his city. They too were chauvinistic. The men of Dorindril had angered her, but she had been able to restrain herself from striking them down and liberating the women. Amanda took a deep breath. Now, she was faced with an entire kingdom of chauvinists and what appeared would be many weeks of travel.

Near the center of Ornholtz Amanda found a lapidary. When she was the only one in the shop, she showed the merchant a few of the gems she was carrying, bartering a sale to obtain some local money. The money would not draw unnecessary attention to her during her quest. She repeated similar sales twice more to obtain a modest amount of local coins that would cover the anticipated cost of her trip.

According to the Crimson Pommel, she would find the Horn of Valhalla in the king's lodge in Theasendür. Her best guess was that she would need to pay for travel, rooms, and food before reaching the king's city. The primary form of winter travel between the cities was by ship along the Coast of Nasdrawuen.

It would be easier to just ride into the cities. There are no walls so my entry and departure would not have been noted, but it's winter. Now I will undoubtedly be seen getting off the ship. But I think this disguise will suffice, Amanda concluded.

Immersing herself into the community, Amanda waited for Grogan's ship to sail. Once he departed there would be no evidence where she had come from, making it more certain her new identity would remain intact. Until that time she needed a room where she could eat and stay without raising suspicion. There were several modest inns nearby that promised to provide a suitable hideaway.

As she neared the first suitable inn a large man grabbed her arm and pulled her into an alleyway. The bearded brute towered over her. In his large hand was a double edged dagger with a blade that was nearly a foot long and two inches wide. The steel blade was thicker in the middle, tapering gradually down to the outer edge.

Sturdy but cumbersome, constructed for the battle field rather than single combat, Amanda concluded.

Her sword would have easily overpowered the dagger, but even in the alley, the risk of drawing unwanted attention was too great. As the brute pulled her farther into the alley, Amanda allowed Fraum's teachings to take control of her reaction. She submitted, letting him pull her in. When they passed out of sight of the street, Amanda stepped past the man, using his weight and momentum to pull him off balance. Grabbing his wrist as she passed, Amanda pushed the back of his upper arm with her free hand, causing the already off-balanced man to tumble face first into the alley wall.

The would-be thief hit the wall and then stumbled back towards the center of the alley as he tried to regain his balance. Like the continuing motion of the dancers at a festival, without hesitating Amanda brought her knee up towards his chest and then snapped her foot outward, driving the ball of her foot deep into his chest. The large man flew backward, striking the wall a second time. Jumping forward and thrusting the side of her foot into his chest, Amanda's movements continued as the smooth flow of a choreographed dance. Under her foot her assailant's ribs sounded like saplings breaking under the great stress of being bent to the ground. The man slid down the wall to rest on the alley floor.

"I don't want any trouble from you," Amanda warned.

"I'm going to break you in half and leave you dying in the snow," the assailant growled in anger, struggling to push himself to his knees.

He drew his *langsax* as he stood up, leaning against the wall as a crutch. When he swung the sword at her chest, Amanda dropped to one knee, letting the blade pass over her as she drew her dagger from her belt. She plunged the point of the dagger deep into his groin next to his leg and then jumped back as the man fell to his knees. The tip of his sword fell to the dirt as he stared up into her cold eyes.

Amanda looked down on the helpless brut, considering that she could not afford to let the man live to identify her as a foreign warrior. Worse yet, she could not afford to be pursued for assaulting the would-be thief. If word spread of a search for his assailant it would most likely increase the vigilance of those who guarded the horn.

It's best if you die here, Amanda thought.

Jumping around her large attacker, Amanda covered his mouth with her free hand, and pulling his chin to the side, exposing his neck, she drove the dagger upward into his skull behind his ear. The man's body went limp instantly and he fell face first to the ground.

Blood from the carotid artery began spurting out of his neck in pulses with the last beats of his heart as blood from the iliac artery finished gushing down his pant leg. Amanda stepped back, watching his death.

I'm not an assassin. This should not have been necessary. Your death is on the guild, she thought.

Removing her blood-soaked wool sweater, Amanda grabbed the bearskin from the ground and pulled it around her shoulders. After wiping her dagger off on the bloody sweater, she threw the soiled clothing over the man's face and left the alley in the other direction.

Moving back into the stream of shoppers, Amanda assumed the walking speed of the surrounding crowd. In the first store she came to she bought an olive-drab sweater and a new knit cap. She also bought a couple of wooden bracelets to accent her disguise. She shopped casually, but before returning to the street Amanda carefully observed the crowd.

Women took their time shopping at vendor's carts with their children while others stepped in and out of the shops. Here or there a gruff, bearded man pushed through the street, but there were no soldiers racing to the nearby alley. No alarm or panic indicating the body had been found. As a small group passed by the doorway, Amanda stepped out into the street, immediately blending in. She traveled through the crowd, moving from one group to the next without raising suspicion.

Two corners down from the sweater shop, Amanda stopped to buy some ale and cooked meat in a tavern. She was hungry. The male patrons seemed to ignore her, but the innkeeper's scowling expression indicated his disapproval. As she sat waiting for her meal she listened to the gossip. The conversations around her varied greatly, but she learned the overland road between Ornholtz and Morganwray, which was typically very difficult to travel in the deep winter snow, had been closed for days. Others spoke of how the shipping had slowed for the winter. From what she heard, Amanda finalized her plan to barter passage along the Coast of Nasdrawuen to Theasendür.

A winter voyage seems to be in my destiny. The thought nearly made her giggle.

After finishing her meal she worked her way up the street towards a local inn. Avoiding the largest inns, where a perception that she was wealthy might cause staff to scrutinize her comings and goings in the name of better customer service, Amanda found a modest sized inn to obtain lodging. The sign of the inn read Odin's Hytte.

Odin's Hytte, meaning Odin's Cottage, was a two-story inn with windows and two entrances. The kitchen was near the back entrance. A large stone fireplace split the tavern from the kitchen. The front entrance was on the other side of the tavern. A split-log staircase opposite the fireplace led up to the preferred, second floor guest rooms, but Amanda did not want to risk being cornered upstairs. There were only a couple of guest rooms on the first floor. The rooms, near the back entrance across from the kitchen, were typically used for patrons who had become too drunk to stumble home. The sounds from the kitchen and tavern filled the rooms, but they suited Amanda's needs perfectly.

This will do nicely, Amanda thought, satisfied with her find.

✻   ✻   ✻   ✻   ✻

Jerrod had not told anyone when Amanda disappeared into the night, but waited for the morning when his companions discovered she was gone. He felt it was her place to tell them if she had wanted them to know, but she had snuck off in the darkness of night, just like the thief Nathanial had accused her of being. Jerrod was not really certain he even understood her reasoning. Before she left she had warned him about Nathanial, but none of them could have anticipated Nathanial's treachery.

They had gone into the Lost Kingdom without her in hopes of finding the treasure Nathanial had promised. Now a small portion of that treasure lay strewn across the white marble floor of Agganon. Only a moment before they had been sealed in a secret treasure room, deep in Terrace Xul, but the instance Jerrod moved the silver dial of the beautifully polished, mossy-green artifact, they had appeared in the middle of the octagonal building.

Agganon, the portal of the Olympian gods, was empty, void of other life. Around them white marble columns with veins of gray supported heavy marble beams that held up the stone ceiling above. Between the columns and the outer marble wall a hallway circled the room. In every other side of the outer walls were double doors made of heavy dark wood inlaid with gold. Despite the lack of life, the polished floor looked as though it had just been cleaned. The room was brightly lit by golden lamps that extended from the outer walls and from four golden lamps that were placed near the center of the floor, but there was no one there to light them or refill the oil. The strange, empty room was breathtaking.

"Agganon!" Fraum gasped.

For fifteen feet around them gold coins, gems, golden statues, goblets, and other treasure spread across the cold floor. The two golden braziers they had been sitting between in Terrace Xul were also there. The braziers' flames still burned as they as though they still sat in the secret treasure room of the Lost Kingdom, but the cavernous walls of the secret treasure room were gone, replaced by the lavish marble of the temple.

Fraum, Jerrod, and Drin stood up while Rhonda continued sitting, but she paused from treating Imelrinn. Fraum's light brown monk's robe was marked with burns from the forks of lightning that had arched from Nathanial's staff. Drin's white tunic that covered his chain mail was similarly singed. Even Jerrod's chain mail showed scorch marks where a fork of the magical lightning had struck him, but the fire that had nearly killed Imelrinn had not scorched him. Rhonda was the only one who had not been struck by the lightning or burned by fire.

She tried to comfort her Elven guardian as he lay on the floor. His burns were severe. Most of his clothing was burned. His exposed skin was blackened and charred, and much of his blond hair had been burned away. His pointed ears and high cheeks were like white ash where they were not already covered with blisters.

"Agganon," Fraum repeated again as he turned around slowly.

The light and temperature of the room was welcoming, but the lack of any sound was eerie. It was so quiet they could hear each other breathing. Time seemed to freeze as the reality they were no longer in the Lost Kingdom of Terrace Xul set into their minds. Relief that they were no longer trapped by the Rahjin slowly gave way to anxiety over their unknown surroundings.

"By the Fates," Jerrod whispered, causing Drin to shoot a disapproving glance at him.

Jerrod was caught up in the moment. He had entered a strange environment using a magical artifact. Vast wealth lay at his feet. His first thought was to share the moment with Amanda, but she was gone. As he imagined Amanda's coy little smile, he looked down into Rhonda's pleasant, half-Elven eyes, confusing him more than ever.

While the others began adjusting, Fraum took in the majesty of the structure surrounding them, and then he glanced back at his companions. He began to realize they did not recognize the name, Agganon.

"This is the ancient gateway to the gods of Olympus. Through those eastern doors the gods came and went from our world." Fraum's scholarly excitement resonated through his voice.

Drin quickly glanced around the room, his eyes snapping from door to door as his square jaw began to tighten. He was obviously uncomfortable with the knowledge he was in an Olympian temple. Rhonda's gaze was far less panicked as she slowly looked around. But Jerrod was not interested in the room. He looked down at the artifact he held in his hand and then he looked up at the others. They shared a look of bewilderment before Fraum reached out, taking the green stone from Jerrod.

"I'll hold this for safe keeping. Maybe the scrolls in the monastery have some history on the artifact," Fraum explained.

Once again reality pressed on them like the eddies of a swift river. The wealth around them was more than they could ever spend. Jerrod's dream of fame and fortune, and the answer to Drin's knighthood had been secured.

"And what of all this?" Drin gestured towards the assorted treasure.

"One thing at a time. We are in the Anacoztiel Mountains far to the east of the Plains of Demeter. Let's figure out our food and water first. We'll have time for the treasure later," Fraum suggested.

"We should not be here. This is not the place for me. The Order would not approve!" The powerful jaw line of Drin's square face locked.

They all turned to look at him. The young Initiate of the Order of One, hoping to be a knight at the end of their adventure, was uncommonly shaken by the surroundings. His heavy, thick eyebrows were raised into an arch above his dark, widely opened eyes.

"I am not sure we have much of a choice," Jerrod pointed out, trying to calm his older friend.

"This is a place of worship for the misguided who have not yet accepted our teachings. It is an unholy place." Drin looked around as if anticipating some hidden attack to strike at him.

Rhonda rose from Imelrinn's side, stepping towards Drin.

"And where does that leave druids who worship nature and not one of the flatlanders' gods?" she challenged.

"You are lost," Drin snapped with a sense of superiority in his voice. "I pray for you nightly, but yours is not a true religion." He looked down at her over the high bridge of his olive colored nose.

"That is a lot of compassion for someone with such contempt for non-believers," Rhonda said angrily.

"If you hate us so much, why did you save me in the Black Forest in the first place?"

"You are human," he paused, realizing Rhonda was half-Elven.

He realized his mistake immediately, but it was too late. The words were out. He had spoken as thoughtlessly as a child angered by his playmates.

"You deserved help and you are my friend." Drin tried to overcome his thoughtless words.

"Whom you apparently don't approve of!" she whipped back in anger as her green eyes began to glow.

A small breeze began to rise, swirling around inside the octagonal building. Rhonda's light brown hair began to lift from her shoulders as the temperature in the room began to drop.

The vivid image of Rhonda in the battle of Sismin Summit rushed into Jerrod's consciousness. The scene had been permanently etched in his mind. Rhonda's slightly thin body floating in the air before a field of dead giants was unforgettable. Her awesome power scared him. Imelrinn was the only other person to have seen the devastation.

Jerrod stepped between Rhonda and Drin.

"Let's not start a religious war in front of the gates of Olympus," Jerrod said to her as he gently grabbed her waist. "We don't need Ares descending from Olympus to answer a call to war," he urged, looking back and forth between Rhonda and Drin,

"If such a man even exists," Drin said in disgust, not thinking his comment might further antagonize the situation.

"It takes all types," Fraum said calmly as he laid a hand on Drin's shoulder.

The young Initiate took a step back, looking intently at the older man. Fraum's skeletal face was expressionless.

"For the part of life's journey that we have shared over the last few months you have witnessed many things that no one would have believed. Dead trolls getting up out of the dirt to attack again. A dragon killing a beast with its will..." Fraum stopped.

The monk, who they had first known as a scholar, once again observed his three younger companions. Years of study in the monastery's library had made him wise. Years of meditation had made him peaceful.

"Wouldn't it be better to keep an open mind about our friends? Life would certainly be boring if we were all the same." Fraum chuckled.

Drin looked at the older man. His bald head and sparkling, almond-shaped eyes calmed his soul. The monk's sense of peace was contagious. Drin did not resist Fraum taking him by the shoulder to turn him towards the western doors.

"Let's see what's outside," Fraum said softly.

They walked together across the room. When they reached the western doors, Fraum put his back against the door and turned to face Drin.

"The wonderful thing about a new door," Fraum paused as he began to push the door open with his back, "is that it opens new opportunities."

The door swung open, exposing a spectacular, panoramic view. From the mountain top where Agganon was built on the western side of the Anacoztiel Mountains they could see a lower range of foothills to the west. Beyond the foothills stretched the great basin. Everything was covered in white snow. In the distance a great, icy blue river seemed to stand still, reflecting the blue winter sky like the reflection of a mirror as the river flowed south through the eastern edge of the great basin.

Fraum and Drin stepped out of the octagonal building into the snow. Behind them the jagged peaks of the Anacoztiel Mountains loomed upward. Valleys of deep blue and cold gray scratched away the mountainside channeling the chilling, winter air downward to press against their chests. Their laborious breath created gray clouds each time they exhaled. Fraum ignored the cold, enjoying the view for a moment before he turned to his young friend.

"If it is snowing in Torrence, are you having a good day?" Fraum asked.

Drin looked at the old man, puzzled by his question. "What?"

"Why let something out of your control affect you? We are here together. All of us. We have saved each other over and over again. We have risked our lives for each other so many times. Standing in a building with friends will not jeopardize your beliefs." Fraum paused to look again at the mountains. "Aren't they beautiful?" the monk said, nearly whispering.

Drin relaxed as his lungs took in the cold mountain air. He reflected on the covenant of the Order. Their intention to convert everyone, one village at a time, to their belief was working. In Torrence the Order was already larger than all the other temples combined, even the temple of Zeus, and they were beginning to influence the king. How could his presence in a pagan temple deter their goal?

"You are a hero, Drin. We will all be called heroes," Fraum said as he tucked his hands into the sleeves of his light brown robe.

Drin contemplated the thought as Fraum watched him. Being watched had never bothered him before, but somehow Fraum's examination of his life in that moment of time made him question his own beliefs.

He is truly wise, the young knight-to-be reflected.

"We have fought beasts and recovered great wealth. Others will praise our success for more than it is." Fraum waited again, allowing Drin to digest thoughts one piece at a time.

I have completed a gallant quest defeating horrible beasts and I am returning unimaginable riches in order to be deemed worthy of knighthood, Drin reflected.

"Yes, I suppose," Drin answered softly as he stared to the west, overlooking the vast emptiness of the great, snow-covered basin.

"Keep in mind that it is more important what we do afterward," Fraum advised.

Drin looked at Fraum again.

There is only the Order, he thought.

"What are you suggesting?" Drin asked.

Fraum looked back through the open door to where Rhonda knelt next to Imelrinn. Jerrod squatted nearby, trying to comfort both of them.

"Compassion and patience are also virtues of a hero," Fraum counseled.

"The Order may not tolerate other religious beliefs but they are your friends," Fraum said, nodding towards the group inside. "Nothing is absolute. To fully accept them you must also accept their beliefs, and respect both. It is our compassion that defines us as humans." The older man stared into Drin's soul.

＊　　＊　　＊　　＊　　＊

Inside, Jerrod and Rhonda turned their attention to Imelrinn. The Mountain Wood Elve was badly burned, causing him great pain. Rhonda's fretting over her guardian was apparent.

There will be scarring, Rhonda thought.

"I don't know what herbs may grow around here, particularly during winter," Rhonda said aloud, trying to calm down.

She glanced up at Jerrod, the fire returning to her eyes as she relived Drin's statement. Rhonda shook her head slightly before refocusing on Imelrinn.

"I don't know if I can heal him!" Rhonda said as she looked up at Jerrod again, tears swelling in her eyes.

For the first time since he had known her, Jerrod sensed panic in Rhonda's voice.

"I will see what I can find. Please stay with him," Rhonda begged.

Jerrod watched as Rhonda rushed towards the northern doors and then he sat down with Imelrinn. Jerrod reached out and gently touched the Elve's burnt shoulder.

"How are you, my friend?" he asked.

A strange sensation swept through Jerrod's body. He could feel his touch gently warming Imelrinn's shoulder.

At first the warmth burned nearly as bad as the fire Nathanial had cast upon him, causing Imelrinn to wince, but the pain quickly subsided. As it did, the damaged skin burnt off, igniting the remnants of his shirt, which smoldered and fell away. The fine ash drifted away like glitter thrown into a light breeze.

The ancient Elve looked at the young flatlander in amazement. Something was different. Jerrod's silver hair still curled around the back of his ears and the base of his neck. His round face, button nose, and shiny azure-blue eyes were still the same as those of the eighteen year old boy he had met on the Plateau of Kronese, but the heart and soul of the boy were not the same. It was not just a man of Torrence who sat next to him.

You are developing some extraordinary powers, Imelrinn thought.

"I don't know," Jerrod answered the unasked question as if he had heard the Elve's thoughts.

Imelrinn watched him speechlessly.

"Things are starting to happen. I don't even think about it. It's more like my desires are answered before I realize what is happening," Jerrod tried to explain.

"That's like the connection druids have with nature. Their connection draws upon the powers of nature. It is not really magic. It is a channeling of the power of nature through their bodies," Imelrinn responded.

It was Jerrod's turn to stare. Magic was still a wonder. Jerrod had seen Nathanial's wizardry and illusion magic. He had also seen Rhonda's druid "magic." To him Rhonda was just as powerful, just as threatening, when she was surrounded by nature as Nathanial was at the onset of a battle.

"Unlike wizards, druids call upon natural phenomena, plants, storms, lightning, or worse. Wizards have to study their magic spells. Some magic even requires components for spells. Have you ever studied magic?" the Elve asked.

Jerrod innocently shook his head no.

Jerrod continued healing Imelrinn's remaining wounds, not knowing how he was accomplishing the task. Each time he touched the guardian Jerrod grew more tired and the ancient Elve grew healthier.

When Rhonda returned, the only evidence Imelrinn had ever been injured was his lack of clothes and his burnt hair. He stood shirtless in his leather pants and boots. His shirt and riding robe had burnt away. His once long, braided hair had been burned down to almost nothing. Imelrinn moved as though nothing had ever happened, but Jerrod slept on the floor with his head resting on his riding cloak. She watched Imelrinn pick up his fur and slide it over his shoulders.

"What happened to your wounds?" Rhonda asked in bewilderment.

Imelrinn nodded towards Jerrod.

"I don't understand. What happened?" she pressed.

"It's Jerrod. He healed me. He doesn't know how and I don't know what to tell you," Imelrinn answered softly.

When the others returned, Imelrinn dismissed his wounds as having been fleeting due to the quick recovery of Elven metabolism. The answer satisfied Drin, but Fraum looked at him quizzically.

Later, when they were able to speak privately, Jerrod and Imelrinn decided to keep the secret of his growing power between themselves.

CHAPTER 2
THE VOYAGE

Outside in the streets of Ornholtz, soldiers scurried towards the richer district. Unlike the uniformed soldiers of Torrence, the northern warriors wore a variety of clothes and armor ranging from leather, to large rings attached to leather, to metal breast plates. Most of them wore simple, pot-like helmets over their braided, shoulder-length hair.

They advanced through the street more like a pack of wolves than an army squad. Many of the large bearded men struggled towards the alley. As they trotted, their spears beat against their round wooden shields. Those that did not carry spears held axes in their free hand as they "ran" onward.

The body of Amanda's assailant had been found, but there was no evidence of the killer. The soldiers could not tell whether he was the aggressor or had just been in the wrong place at the wrong time. And to the uneducated, the fact the victim still had his coin purse went unnoticed, to the benefit of the undertaker. The soldiers' search of the immediate area had been brief while they waited for the undertaker to cart the body away.

"No one will miss this weak fool," one of the soldiers remarked.

Ornholtz had little interest in the body of a man who held little importance. He had not been a chieftain, a soldier, nor a wealthy business man. He had held no position of respect, such as a sailor, dockworker, or muleskinner. Apparently he was only slightly more important than a woman—only because he was male—and that alone did not raise enough concern to investigate further.

Amanda spent the next two days watching the pier for Captain Grogan's ship to sail. She waited to ensure no one would be available to answer questions on how she had arrived in Ornholtz or to challenge her new persona. During the day she wandered the city, picking up customs by observing the merchants and their customers. As she slowly immersed herself into the Haithenbeurn culture, she confirmed her fear. The women were, in fact, second-class citizens. Amanda submitted to their custom of waiting for the men as they concluded their business. To complete her persona, she adopted a Haithenbeurn name she had overheard while shopping.

"I am Estrianna," she answered without looking up.

✻   ✻   ✻   ✻   ✻

The day after Grogan sailed, Amanda went to the pier and found a ship willing to take a single Haithenbeurn woman as a passenger to Theasendür. Captain Vendal negotiated "Estrianna's" passage at the end of the gangway onto his ship. To Amanda he seemed like a mixture of the seagoing merchant-fishermen from Dorindril and the barbarian warriors of the north.

This ship could easily be configured into a war vessel, Amanda thought as she observed the crew's interactions.

The ship was constructed like the large cargo ships from Dorindril. It had a pointed bow and stern like the ships of the south with large carvings rising above each point, but there were two masts for the large, square sails needed on the ocean voyages. The taller main mast rose up near the center of the ship. The shorter foremast was halfway between the main mast and the bow.

An open hold was accessible from the center of the main deck, or weather deck. Large cargo could be lowered through the two upper decks down to the third level. The hole was walled off on the upper deck, but open on the middle and lower deck.

Unlike the ships of the south, the ships of Haithenbeurn were longer and wider with an additional deck. The captain's cabin was at the stern. A door across from the captain's cabin closed off the stairs leading down to the middle deck. The remaining part of the deck was divided for passengers' quarters by thick wooden walls that added to the stability of the ship and muffled the constant noise.

The middle deck had open crew quarters in the bow and benches for the oarsmen in the middle of the ship. Portals in the hull along the benches allowed oars to be put into the water for rowing when it became necessary. There was also a kitchen in the stern and stairs leading up to serve food to the guests, and down to accesses supplies from the lowest deck. Unlike the upper deck, there was a large, open hole amid-ship where the crew could lower cargo down to the bottom deck.

The lowest deck was an open hold for cargo and ship's supplies. Cargo, supply boxes, and barrels could be tied down for a safer ocean voyage. When fully loaded the ship rode deeper in the water and was more stable, rocking less from the waves than the ships from Dorindril. But when the ship was empty or carried mostly passengers, it bounced about on the waves like a child's toy boat being beaten around as it bobbled down a wild, spring creek, a condition that challenged even the most seaworthy sailor from becoming seasick.

There were already several other passengers on the ship when Amanda boarded. A family of three, a family of four, two men, and a group of three other men had also booked passage and were already in their cabins.

As the ship pushed away from the pier, the southwesterly wind caught the sails, causing the wood decks to creak as they began to ease into the fjord. The ship began picking up speed as she tacked in a close haul or beating point of sail, cutting forty-five degrees across the course of the wind. As they cleared the harbor, half the sailors dropped oars into the water to help pick up speed, rowing to the steady beat of a drum. The bow rose then crashed down into the winter waves of the fjord as the ship began its westerly course.

In her cabin, Amanda prayed to Zeus for good weather and to Poseidon for fair seas. Her prayers reminded her of Rhonda calming the sea as they had sailed north towards Terrace Xul.

How can Rhonda control the weather if the weather was under a god's control? The question surged into her mind like the incoming tide slowly covering the beach.

The thought of Rhonda led her back to Jerrod. Rhonda had him with her. Amanda recalled Rhonda's sweet, innocent face, and the image of the kiss she had shared with Jerrod.

How can I lose Jerrod? she thought. *No, I can't think of them right now. Drin. What about Drin and the Order of One?* She frantically tried to distract herself.

The Order seemed to challenge everyone. They openly defied the gods' power and authority. They claimed to be the only true religion. Even the Guild of the Crimson Pommel was becoming concerned about the Order's growing strength.

Amanda did not feel the excitement of her new adventure or the anxiety of the unknown. She did not feel the calming peace of someone who had submitted to their destiny. Her thoughts bothered her more than she cared to admit. Her thoughts of Jerrod still distracted her from the blood-debt she was undertaking.

Stop it! her mind screamed.

Unlike the voyage into Ornholtz where she wandered the deck openly, Amanda planned to isolate herself in the privacy of her cabin. She reasoned that seclusion was more appropriate for a Haithenbeurn woman traveling alone. She tried to practice the dance-like exercises that Fraum had taught her, but the constant movement of the cabin as the ship rocked on the wild winter sea quickly overcame her.

"I have to get fresh air!" she said aloud to herself.

As Amanda made her way to the weather deck where she could see the coast and breathe the fresh air, the mid-day sun cast a small shadow of the mast in the middle of the deck, but from the low angle of the sun over the southern horizon she could tell the ship had turned north towards the mouth of the Fjord of Menduran. They ran in a broad reach, one hundred thirty-five degrees from the point of the wind. It was the fastest point of sail for Haithenbeurn vessels and the oarsmen had pulled the oars out of the water, relying on the ship to pick up wind speed as they continued north.

Amanda spent most of the afternoon watching the water beat against the cliffs along the passage at the mouth of the fjord. Just before the evening meal Amanda went below to the galley, where she introduced herself as Estrianna and quietly sat at the far end of the table with the two women and their children. The three quickly became friendly as they spoke quietly, carefully avoiding anything which might disturb the men.

The family of three was traveling to Morganwray to visit the father's family. They were apparently some sort of minor nobility with a large home and two dozen men at arms. The family had some land on the outskirts of town with oxen and timber, which they cut and sold for construction and firewood. Their son was going to meet his grandparents for the first time.

The family of four was traveling to Theasendür. The father had lost his ability to care for his family and was traveling home in disgrace. He was a proud man going home to work in the family coal mine, which was apparently one of the lowest positions in Haithenbeurn. He would mine coal in the Rhinefjell, the mountains east of Theasendür, only coming home to see his son on the weekends. His wife and their children would live with his mother.

After the meal, Amanda went back on deck for more fresh air. She was feeling the confinement of the small cabin. By the time she returned to the weather deck, the ship had rounded the Cape of Bestla and was sailing east, still in a broad reach, but they were sailing with the waves, which reduced the motion caused from crashing through the sea. The fresh night air and open sky eased her churning stomach.

The two full moons hid behind a thin layer of clouds, creating the glow of a double witches' moon. Amanda looked past Questil, the larger, green moon resting lower in the night's sky, focusing on the smaller purple moon, Dori. Dori was higher and to the right, partially obscured by Questil and somehow a little more mystical.

Perhaps it's the purple color that is more alluring? Amanda thought.

Parts of the clouds glowed green or purple while other parts, where the moonbeams mixed, were a dark greenish-brown creating a spectacular, eerie sight. Amanda acknowledged the colorful display of nature. Her mind cleared the thoughts from her consciousness as she stared into the vast emptiness of the sea, but her eyes focused ahead, to the north, on a silhouette in the middle of a rocky island that was not much bigger than the river-island of Torrence. She could not see a beach, just large boulders, many of which appeared as large as their ship. The flat, snow-covered plain beyond the rocks was undisturbed.

A single tower loomed upward in the middle of the island. It was at least twice the height of the king's towers in Torrence, rising over a hundred feet into the air. The massive structure was out of place, but even more out of place was the solitary light at the top that captivated Amanda's attention.

A tower without people. No footprints in the snow. No roads. Nothing. She assessed the image silently.

It would have been easy to sail by, overlooking the lack of a tower entrance. How the light got there and how it continued to burn began to nag at Amanda's curiosity. She was too far and it was too dark to see the type of stone and mortar or how well the blocks fit together, but she reassured herself that she could climb it.

Tighter fitting blocks just make it more challenging. I can climb anything, she reassured herself.

She envisioned the challenge of the icy surface making the sight that much more appealing. She had never found a surface she could not climb. Climbing an icy pinnacle just to say she had done what others might not dare tempted her. The only thing that kept her from stealing away to the island was the pressing deadline of the blood-debt.

Standing at the rail she yearned to escape, but she was uncertain whether it was the confines of the rocking ship or the responsibility for the debt that had been pressed upon her from which she sought release. After one last look at the tower she turned to go to her cabin, finding herself face to face with Captain Vendal.

"Estrianna, it is cold out here. It could be dangerous. The waves break over the side. It gets wet and icy. You could slip," the captain said with a heavy, gruff voice. "Go below."

"Yes. I was just going," she responded meekly, her hand resting innocently on the pommel of her dagger. "Captain, what is that tower?"

"We use it as a beacon to navigate by at night and through storms," Vendal growled.

"Who built it?"

"I don't know. No one knows. We call it Balder's Tower in tribute to the god of light. It has been there since time began. Go below. Get out of this weather."

"Yes, Captain," Amanda answered without looking up as she turned to walk away.

"Estrianna," he commanded.

Amanda stopped, looking partially over her shoulder.

"If something happened, no one would find you."

* * * * *

The next day passed in much the same manner with Amanda spending most of her time in her cabin and joining the others just before the meals. Amanda played the part of a dutiful Haithenbeurn woman, returning to her cabin alone after the meal, where she practiced Fraum's teachings. Afterward Amanda lay in her bunk, trying to find that deep sleep which would carry her through an uneventful night, but her desire to escape was growing into anxiety.

By mid-morning of the second day the ship sailed into Morganwray's harbor. The familiar rocking motion of the ship as it bumped into the pier every time another wave rolled in was nauseating. Captain Vendal told the through passengers they could go ashore while cargo was exchanged, but they were to be back before the evening meal.

When the passengers for Morganwray departed the vessel, Amanda quickly took up the Captain's offer to disembark. Wanting to clear her head of the motion sickness, she decided to take a quick walk around Morganwray. Despite being numb from the seasickness, Amanda's power of observation was unconstrained. She noted the similarities to the larger city of Ornholtz. The city was laid out the same, a dock area with warehouses, a merchant area, and then residence. Like Ornholtz, the city did not have a surrounding wall and the city leader apparently lived in a garrison near the center of the city.

The primary purpose of the city appeared to be the port, shipping lumber and supplies up and down the coast. The city was the closest stop to the Cape, offering relief that was particularly important to ships hoping to escape the winter storms, but all of the ships visited her port, ensuring Morganwray's prosperity.

Before it was time for the evening meal, the dockworkers saw a woman dressed in yak-wool, thick fur boots, and heavy wool jacket approach and board the ship. Estrianna's mannerisms, her walk, her posture, had become no different than any other Haithenbeurn woman. Nothing special. Nothing remarkable. She went straight up the plank and down the stairs to her cabin without acknowledging anyone.

While the men and boys sat at their end of the table, Amanda sat with the remaining woman and her daughter at the far end. They spoke in whispers so their conversation would not disturb the men, who were already being served. The men's tankards of ale were being refilled as the females at the table were just being served.

The men shared tales of battles and heroes, talking loudly without regard for the conversation at the other end of the table. They spoke of the continual war along the "southern wall" as Amanda listened intently.

"Estrianna? Estrianna!" the young girl's voice broke Amanda's focus from the men's discussion.

"I'm sorry, little one. What is it?" Amanda mimicked the local mannerisms.

"Where are you from?" the girl asked quietly while her mother listened closely.

Amanda looked at her kindly, wishing she could tell the girl of all the wonders that she had seen. Her stories of fighting trolls and vespree, riding centaurs, and listening to a bard play under the stars, of dragons, and of Jerrod. But at that moment Amanda wished most of all that she could show the young girl that women could be independent.

"My home is in the Ragnaugh Mountains," Amanda responded, drawing from information she had overheard in Ornholtz.

"Why are you alone? Women don't travel alone," the girl continued with a puzzled look on her face.

"My parents died," Amanda replied without missing a beat. The lie saddened her. She wanted to be truthful, but the lie was necessary to preserve her disguise. "I am going to Theasendür to live with my cousin and his family until I can marry," Amanda explained.

After the meal Amanda returned to her cabin and dutifully practiced Fraum's teachings. But when she went to her bed, the lie began pounding in her mind. Her anxiety over being cooped up on the ship immediately compounded the problem until she was ready to scream. Then the thoughts of Jerrod and the others rushed in, intensifying her agony.

"Athena?" Amanda called upon the goddess of wisdom and heroism. "Isn't it enough I must endure this quest, this blood-debt? Must I be confined amidst such masculine arrogance?"

But the little room she slept in remained silent. Slowly, her mind began to wander away from her troubles and the sounds of the creaking wood around her drew her attention. The ship. What did she know of the ship and her captain?

Amanda's curiosity had taken control. Later that night, dressed in black leather, she slipped into the dimly lit passageway beyond her door. Behind the doors she passed without making a sound, the other passengers were sleeping. Most of the crew slept as well. Only a couple of the crew stood watch above, ensuring no one boarded the ship in the night.

Amanda paused a moment at the stern before opening the door across from the captain's quarters and quietly walking down the stairs. She moved like a cat carefully descending stairs in pursuit of prey. Amanda could hear men snoring below.

The open space of the second deck was darker, with a few hanging oil lamps providing the minimal light necessary for the crewmen remaining awake. The darkness also provided her cover as she passed between the canvas bunks that hung in the open space near the bow of the ship.

Beginning to relax as she passed unnoticed between the crew members,

Amanda circled through the sleeping men, pausing briefly to inspect their belongings but taking nothing. When she had inspected all the sleeping crew, she moved to the middle of the deck and stopped at the edge of the large hole leading down into the cargo hold. Grabbing the edge of the hole and sliding her legs around, she lowered herself down into the darkness. Hanging from the deck a moment, Amanda let go, dropping a few feet to the deck below.

She landed in a crouched position and paused. The darkness of the lowest deck engulfed her, making it difficult to see the cargo. After moving towards the side of the ship, Amanda pulled a candle, flint, and steel from her jacket. The ship rocked against the pier as she moved through the cargo hold with the faint candle light.

The cargo was not remarkable. Furs from the south, bolts of wool and great spools of wool yarn from Ornholtz, and lumber from Morganwray filled about half the space. Three barrels of serpent oil were roped together. There were some crates of food and barrels of ale as well, but nothing satisfied her curiosity. She passed by the ship's supplies as she moved to the stern and began to take the stairs upward.

The sound of a passing crewman somewhere close on the middle deck caused her to pause a moment, but the footsteps passed by quickly and Amanda was very soon back on the upper passenger deck. Her curiosity still unsatisfied, Amanda considered her only remaining options. The passenger cabins, half of which were empty, and the captain's cabin remained unchecked. She could hear Fraum's voice in her mind, warning her to stay out of trouble as she began to open the captain's door.

The room was lit by a hanging oil lamp that burned low, providing just enough light to see that Vendal slept in his wooden bunk. There was a table in the middle of the room and a sea chest at the foot of the bunk. As her eyes adjusted to the dark, allowing her to see the shelf along the captain's wall, a loud knock hit the other side of the door.

"Captain?" a crewman called out.

Amanda dove under the wooden bunk without hesitation. Her hand instinctively came to rest on the pommel of her dagger as she lay quietly, hardly breathing.

"Captain?" the crewman called again.

"What is it?" Vendal yelled as he rolled over, opening his eyes, trying to see his door.

"You're needed on deck, sir. Something about late cargo."

Vendal kicked his legs out of bed, sat up, and reached for his boots before he rose.

"I'll be right there."

His callused hand grabbed his jacket from the foot of the bed as he stood up. After blowing the lamp out, Vendal found his way to the door, leaving Amanda alone in the dark.

Amanda smiled as she rolled onto her back to rest a moment. Her hand slipped from the dagger's pommel as she reached for the candle again.

Good to be prepared. She nearly chuckled.

Pulling the thief's tools from the inside of her jacket, she wasted no time picking the lock on the captain's chest. Inside the chest Amanda found a leather pouch amongst the clothes and personal belongings. She untied the leather strap closing the pouch and let the contents slide into her open hand. Even in the dim light of her candle, she could see the jeweled amulet that fell from the pouch was far more valuable than a common sea captain should own.

After taking a moment to appreciate the beauty of the amulet, Amanda slid the jewel back into the pouch, closed the chest, and slipped out of Vendal's cabin without encountering anyone. As she entered her cabin she thought of Fraum again.

See? I can stay out of trouble. She smiled as she pulled the ponytail from her long, blonde hair.

✵   ✵   ✵   ✵   ✵

As soon as things had settled with Imelrinn, Rhonda went back outside to send word to her mother. Standing in the snow, she let her body slip into a meditative state as her mind reached out, trying to find a suitable courier, perhaps a hawk, a falcon, even a dove who could carry her message more swiftly. What she found was a crow.

In her experience crows seemed to be less reliable than other species. However, it was hard to find birds in the winter months. Rhonda gave the crow a simple message, "We are safe in Agganon," providing just enough information to let her parents know where she was without overloading the crow's mind.

Rhonda watched the large black bird fly away before returning to the Olympian temple. The crow quickly found a hawk who, after some deliberation as the two birds spun and danced in the air while the crow avoided being eaten, promised to carry the message on. The hawk, in turn, found a Peregrine falcon who ultimately sped towards Lithlillia on the druid princess' errand.

Lady Lieisa reacted quickly to the message. Within an hour winged horses carrying Elven guards and supplies needed for the journey home flew towards Agganon. Lieisa knew there was not a chance her daughter would leave her friends behind, so she did not send one of the winged steeds to simply ferry her home.

It's a long journey from Agganon back to Lithlillia. Imelrinn would give his life for Rhonda, but I feel better knowing there will be more Elven guards with them, Lady Lieisa thought as she watched the horses fly away.

Elves lived for hundreds of years and even into Lieisa's mother's time the gods of Olympia had not returned to the mystical Temple of Agganon.

Still, it will be good for them to depart Agganon as quickly as possible. E'fretté, watch over them, the druid queen prayed.

*   *   *   *   *

The morning after their arrival at Agganon, Jerrod, Drin, Fraum, Rhonda, and Imelrinn began working on plans to return to Torrence and Lithlillia. The discussion about the treasure did not last long. The Elves knew the importance of the treasure to the young warriors, but they struggled with the flatlanders' determination not to abandon their spoils. Recovering the secret treasure from the Lost Kingdom had been, after all, the purpose of their journey, but it was Fraum, who never showed much interest in treasure, who suggested the solution.

"A wagon. We can construct a wagon on skis. Rhonda, can't you use your druid magic to warp and shape the wood of dead trees?" Fraum suggested.

"What can't be shaped, we can cut with our swords," Jerrod said, thinking aloud.

"We can use rope or wooden pegs to fasten planks on beams like in my father's fishing village," Drin added.

Jerrod and Drin searched the evergreen forest and dragged the fallen trees to the southern steps of Agganon, where they began constructing a wagon, while Jerrod started making the basic cuts, sizing the wood down with his sword. Fraum and Rhonda worked together laying out the frame, and then Rhonda began shaping larger pieces while Fraum whittled the pegs. While the others worked, Imelrinn hunted.

As the afternoon sunlight warmed the edges of mountains, the ridge appeared to be illuminated in brilliant silver light. Jerrod stopped to observe the mountains west of them.

"It's magnificent, isn't it?" Rhonda asked.

"I have never appreciated nature more," Jerrod answered, his silver hair catching the light of the sun.

"The peace of life in the magnitude of the solitary mountains. It is man who brings chaos into the world," Fraum interjected.

"You're a warrior and a philosopher," Rhonda teased.

"I am simply a sage who studies at the White Fist Monastery." Fraum smiled.

"Right. And I am Sir Michael," Drin added, a smile crossing his face above his cleft chin.

After dark they all sat inside weaving twine from fibrous plants and bark they found in the forest. The temple was warmer than being out in the winter night, but the cold marble floor was uncomfortable, particularly without blankets. After weaving some twine they stopped to eat roasted venison and drank herbal tea in golden goblets pulled from their treasure.

"I will return my share to the Order," Drin stated factually in hopes of easing his discomfort.

"I'm sure that will be enough for you to be knighted. What will you do with your share, Jerrod?" Fraum asked, sitting cross-legged with his hands tucked into his monk's sleeves.

The young warrior glanced at Rhonda before answering.

"I will build a castle and lead my own men to do good when and where it is needed," Jerrod answered.

Rhonda squeezed his hand gently and smiled at him. Curious about the flatlanders' preoccupation with wealth, she turned to Fraum.

"And what will you do with your share, Fraum?" she asked.

"Whatever is mine will go to the monastery. Perhaps we will build an addition to our library. It will be up to our wise Master to determine what the best use for the treasure is," Fraum answered humbly.

"Where can we store all this treasure?" Jerrod asked.

"I must take my share to the Prophet," Drin answered before anyone else could speak.

"I guess we should take our share to Lithlillia. We can use it to purchase flatlander goods and materials from the innkeeper for a very long time," Rhonda said thoughtfully.

"What of Amanda's share? She should have a share of the treasure even though she was not in the treasure room at the end. She saved us many times," Jerrod asked.

"She deserves a portion," Drin agreed.

"No argument from me. I owe her my life," Rhonda added.

"I can hold her share at the monastery if no one objects," Fraum said, looking between his companions.

"Could you also hold mine? I don't have anywhere large enough or safe enough to hold my share of this wealth," Jerrod stated, waving his hands over the treasure on the marble floor.

When they were finished talking, they laid back on the few evergreen branches they harvested from live trees after a great deal of prayer. They had hoped the branches would soften the floor and block some of the cold, but they proved not to be very good mattresses.

✶   ✶   ✶   ✶   ✶

When the Elven guards arrived with the supplies they put up tents and moved out of the Olympian's gateway. They smoked the remaining while continuing to work on the wagon. The smoked venison would allow them to spend more time traveling and less time hunting.

They melted snow to store water in bags brought by the Elves and in golden jugs mixed in with the treasure. Rhonda collected herbs for tea while the others scraped the hide collected from Imelrinn's hunt. After the hide was salted and dried, removing all the flesh from the skin, it could be beaten into softness to be used for warmth. More hids would be quickly collected to protect them from the cold. Each time a creature gave his life for their protection, the Elves would offer a quiet prayer.

Rhonda and Imelrinn shared one tent brought from Lithlillia. Rhonda preferred her Elven guardian close by and Imelrinn would have insisted anyway. Jerrod, Drin, and Fraum shared a tent, leaving the last one for the Elven guards. A collection of blankets and furs were used in the tents for additional warmth.

During the days that followed, Jerrod and Rhonda began taking walks together. They shared their dreams. It was the first time they had really spoken about random topics. Previously, their conversations had focused on obtaining the lost treasure of Terrace Xul. Now, while they walked safely in the shadows of the Anacoztiel Mountains, their discussions inevitably led to the topic of love, commitment, and religion.

"We are not animals, having sex as often as possible with any partner we can find. Our ceremonies are pure of heart and intent. Like many of nature's creatures, druids mate for life. After we mate we are inseparable," Rhonda explained defensively.

What's gotten into her? Jerrod thought.

"I hadn't heard anything about your rituals," Jerrod voice was quiet.

"We're commonly accused of things witches do," Rhonda's tone was sharp.

"Witches?" Jerrod asked with concern.

"I understand their rituals often include sexual acts. Some witches are better than others, but you should be cautious of all witches," Rhonda responded indignantly.

"How can you tell a good witch from a bad one?" Jerrod asked.

"You can't. That is part of the reason they are so dangerous. Whether they are good or evil is not apparent until they have given you a charm or curse, and by then it is too late," Rhonda answered.

"The witch in the forest," Jerrod spoke softly, not quite a whisper.

"What did she do?" Rhonda questioned.

"She warned Nathanial that Jacob was coming for us. And she warned Amanda about Nathanial." Jerrod paused. "And she gave me this," he continued, pulling a small vial from behind his belt, where he had tucked it away months ago.

The vial was made of bluish clay with a cork top. It was small enough to fit in the palm of Jerrod's hand as he lifted it higher for Rhonda to see.

"She said it would save me," Jerrod added.

"Save you? From what?" Rhonda grew concerned.

Jerrod no longer looked like a boy growing into manhood, but she realized there was still so much that he did not know. She watched him looking at her in bewilderment.

You're still so innocent, she thought.

"She didn't say," Jerrod answered.

"Jerrod, you have to be careful about witches' gifts. You can never tell if they are good or evil and they are always given for a reason that benefits the witch," Rhonda warned.

✱   ✱   ✱   ✱   ✱

The winter solstice came as they prepared to depart Agganon. That night both Questil and Dori were full and partially hiding behind a cloudy sky. The drifting clouds stretched across the moons' faces, obscuring their round bodies as their colors reflected through the clouds. Questil's green and Dori's purple mixed to create a beautiful collage.

E'fretté, your beauty is magnificent tonight, Rhonda thought, giving thanks to the power of nature.

The winter solstice was a druidic religious holiday, but it was special to have a double full moon. The condition occurred once every three years. The solstice, which occurred between the end of one year and the beginning of the next, was one of the most spiritual days for the druids.

"Lithlillia is having a great banquet in the Pavilion tonight," Rhonda said to Imelrinn.

"Your mother will lead everyone to the forest altar afterward for the ritual. We should offer prayer, too," the guardian Elve responded.

Rhonda directed the Elves to construct a bonfire away from their campsite. Jerrod happily helped them plant twelve logs in the ground surrounding the pyre. His growing love for Rhonda and his friendship with Imelrinn motivated his enthusiasm. Even Fraum, who was eager to learn about the druids and their worship, helped. The monastery libraries had very little information on druids and nothing about their rituals, but before he was allowed to participate, Rhonda made him swear he would not share what he witnessed.

Although Lady Lieisa had declared Drin a Friend of Lithlillia, he was obviously uncomfortable about the religious preparations. Out of respect, Rhonda excluded him from participation and arranged for him to guard the camp after dusk in hopes of easing his discomfort.

She knew their beliefs, which Drin thought paganistic, disgusted him. While their celebration of the winter's solstice went into the night, Drin stayed in his tent, praying as though he wished to ward off some evil that might come from the nearby druid worship. He pushed his great two handed sword into the ground before him, where he knelt in reverence to the One.

At dusk, the Elves lit the bonfire and they all ate and drank together after Rhonda offered thanks to nature and the natural force that bound all things together. By midnight the bonfire had burned down to glowing embers. Rhonda stood up and led them into the middle of the tree-trunk columns. Imelrinn, Jerrod, Fraum, and the other Elves gathered around the edge of the circle, just in front of the wood trunks.

Rhonda began the druid ceremony by laying her long sword and dagger on the ground. The Elves followed suit, causing Jerrod to do the same, by placing the Sword of Trisdale on the ground before him. She began praying in Elvish, glittering with a pale, green light. The light radiated out to the others, who glowed with the green light of druid magic, but when the green light reached Jerrod, nothing happened.

This is really odd, Rhonda thought.

Jerrod felt the unfamiliar sensation he had experienced when he healed Imelrinn surging through his body. It was accompanied with a warm feeling as a silvery white light began pulsating around him.

The light was dim at first, but as the ceremony continued the light grew brighter and brighter. Its pulsing increased until a single burst of light radiated from him, knocking everyone except Rhonda to the ground, where they lay temporarily blinded. Rhonda stood in the center of the druid circle staring at Jerrod.

"In the name of E'fretté! What did you do?" Rhonda asked calmly.

Like Drin, her mother had declared Fraum and Jerrod to be "Friends of Lithlillia," so she had let them partake in the secret druid ritual.

"Nothing, I swear to Apollo." Jerrod called upon the god of truth.

"Never in druid history has anyone reacted to a druid ceremony this way, Jerrod," Rhonda said slowly.

Never had another light been generated from anyone other than the priestess leading the ceremony, nor had another light ever overtaken the druid magic. Not from another priestess. Not from another magical being. And certainly not from a non-believer.

✿ ✿ ✿ ✿ ✿

That night the witches' coven gathered in Felicia's lair which, for the moment, appeared as a dream-like glen of giant oak trees with curtains of moss, fragrant lavender bushes, and brooks full of frogs, crickets, and fireflies singing the joy of their holy day. The Ladies Questil and Dori were full and remarkably colorful.

The members of the coven had projected their images into the glen from where they sat, meditating in their own cottages, shops, or lairs. Some sat alone in the safety of their own surroundings. Others sat with their covens, proud to partake in the Queen's Festival on such a holy night. They sat before large ash-colored candles with bluish smoke twisting around their bodies, assisting them in their projections through a magical trance created by the candle-magic of witchcraft.

Witches and warlocks from across Dendür, dressed in white muslin robes that only partially obscured their bodies, sat in a circle around Felicia. Theirs was the largest coven and Felicia, Queen of the Witches, the strongest witch. Thousands of followers surrounded her.

I have so many minions, she thought as she spun slowly, gazing over the coven.

The mumbling of their preparatory incantation sounded like the soft rumbling of distant drums. Felicia smiled. She was happy with the turnout. Even the elderly crone from Theasendür had projected her spirit into the gathering. There were good and evil witches present, young and old, but they were all there, answering her summons, to assist her when witchcraft would be at its most powerful.

Near midnight, Felicia knelt down to start her spell, a divination. She would let the others go soon enough so they could complete their own solstice spells and charms, but she needed the full power of the whole coven to predict the outcome of Amanda's quest and its consequences.

The coven repeated her words as she recited the spell. The pulsating hum of voices chanted in unison. Felicia's body swayed as she fell into a trance, envisioning Jerrod traveling to Theasendür where he intended to rescue Amanda, but as she pressed for more details, a silvery-white light burst out of the air around her, radiating over the coven and knocking everyone to the ground, temporarily blind.

"I'm blind!" Felicia's anger flared.

After her eyesight returned Felicia dismissed her coven. With an aggressive wave of her arm the glamour of the glen faded and she stood alone before her fireplace. Sasha slept nearby on a pillow.

You won't see anything involving Jerrod, the black panther thought openly. *Sasha!* Felicia shot back.

Did you think anything would change from the day he found the sword? the panther questioned as she changed into a large black cat.

Felicia stomped her foot, turned, and stormed angrily away while Sasha licked her paw without care.

The divination was partially effective. At least I learned Amanda would need to be rescued from Theasendür. She paced in her bedroom. *I assume that Jerrod will be successful, but he doesn't realize the power he has gained from the Dragon's Orb. If he had, the coven would more than likely have suffered more than temporary blindness,* Felicia concluded.

One day, you will have to face me, Jerrod. She smiled.

"Hecate can take him," Felicia said aloud, offering Jerrod to the Olympian goddess of witchcraft. "Or Seiðr. I don't care which of you have him once I have the orb." She chuckled, thinking of the Asgardian.

The queen of witches found herself lusting for the company of a warlock. Her heart pounded in her chest. Her breathing was deep and erratic. Frantically, she picked up a gray candle and lit it.

Light gray smoke encircled her as the griffin's feather harvested under a full moon took flame around the wick. Silvery sparkles burst here and there in the smoke. Slowly, Felicia's body dissipated into the smoke and floated away on the air. A continent away, in the bedroom of a powerful young warlock, Felicia reappeared.

☆　　☆　　☆　　☆　　☆

The next morning the Elven guards kept their distance from Jerrod. They stayed as far as they could from him. They avoided making eye contact and quickly found tasks outside of camp. So Jerrod worked with Drin, preparing to depart.

While they worked they shared dreams about what would happen when they returned to Torrence. How they would be received. How their lives would change. But eventually their discussion turned to Rhonda.

"Your girlfriend has quite a temper," Drin said, only partially teasing.

"She's not my girlfriend," Jerrod snapped back defensively without looking at his friend, but in his heart, he questioned the truth of the statement.

"I may only be a couple years older than you, my friend, and I may be bound for the celibate life of holy knighthood, but I still know when two people are in love," Drin responded with boyish over-certainty.

Jerrod looked at Drin, noting his square jaw and cleft chin, the tight curls of his dark hair and dark eyes.

So proud! So sure, aren't you? Jerrod thought. "I have Amanda—" Jerrod started to insist, but Drin interrupted.

"Amanda left you without an explanation. Consider that," he said bluntly.

When they finished packing the wagon with treasure, they joined the others for the evening meal. Afterwards, Jerrod walked Rhonda to her shelter.

"Would you like some tea?" Rhonda asked when they reached it.

"That would be nice. Thank you." Jerrod smiled.

Inside, Rhonda started a small fire and set a pot of water on it. She carefully selected some herbs and, when the water was hot, poured the water into goblets with the herbs.

"Where is Imelrinn?" Jerrod asked.

"I asked him to scout out the easiest trail down the mountain. He won't be back for a few hours," Rhonda answered.

She stepped closer to the young man from Winfred, their bodies nearly touching. Rhonda reached down and pulled his hand to her chest. She looked into Jerrod's azure-blue eyes as she reached into the pocket of her robe, feeling for a soft, braided wristlet. She pulled the bracelet out to show him.

"This is made from locks of my hair. To the druids this bracelet signifies a woman's internal pledge of love. This signifies my lifetime devotion. It is yours if you want it," Rhonda said as she looked down at the braided band. "I am yours if you want me." She looked back up into his eyes as she offered herself.

Jerrod looked into her eyes. He loved her. He reflected on Drin's words as he considered the moment, thinking, *Amanda is gone.*

Rhonda's beauty overwhelmed him. She was strong and spectacular. Her thin, half-Elven body was arousing. She was indeed beautiful, but the druid-power of the princess was just as appealing. He knew that Elves and half-Elves mated for life. That "until death do us part" were more than words. Rhonda had explained it in great detail and he had witnessed it in Lithlillia.

He took less than a moment to decide. Drunk with Rhonda's character, he took her face gently in his hands and slowly leaned forward to kiss her lips. Softly. Gently. Time froze while they kissed. A minute seemed equal with hours and when their kiss ended, Rhonda slipped the wristlet over his right hand onto his wrist. It was done.

Stepping back to allow Jerrod to see her entire body, Rhonda slipped her robe from her shoulders. As it fell to the ground, Jerrod realized Rhonda was only wearing a loin cloth wrapped around her elegant waist. Her small, firm breasts were partially covered by the naturally loose curls of her long brown hair. Otherwise, the druid princess stood before him, as naked as the day of her birth.

"Come. Sleep with me," Rhonda said invitingly as she pulled at his hand.

Jerrod allowed himself to follow, wondering what would happen when Imelrinn and her parents found out. She pulled him down into her bed.

"I must be a virgin when I marry, but we can sleep together," Rhonda said as they lay together for the first time.

In bed she kissed his neck and then his chest. She allowed him to kiss her too, but when Jerrod's excitement pressed for more, she put a finger on his lips.

"I can't," she whispered.

They lay together in the furs with Rhonda's back pressing against Jerrod's nakedness. As his arms pulled her in tighter the world seemed to fade away. He was content. At peace. For the moment Jerrod did not think of fame or fortune. He did not think of Torrence, or Lithlillia. He only thought of the feeling Rhonda's warm body gave him and of her beauty. It was Rhonda's words that eventually broke the timeless silence.

"In nine months both moons will be full again. We can be married in the druid circle north of Lithlillia. Then I can give myself to you. And I will be yours for life," she said softly, snuggling closer to Jerrod.

The words "married" and "life" struck Jerrod like the bell in Trisdale Keep resounding close overhead. A bell that only he could hear. The alarm echoed through his soul as he lay with Rhonda. Panic began to well inside him. What had he done?

He loved feeling her warm body. He pictured her beautiful green eyes, oval face, and pointed ears. He could hear her soft, soothing whisper as it warmed his ear. But he felt some unknown weight in the middle of his chest and a desire to slide his arm from under her head so that he could run away beginning to grow.

But where would I run? How could I leave her? he asked himself.

☆   ☆   ☆   ☆   ☆

If Imelrinn returned to camp that night, he did not return to Rhonda's tent. In the morning Jerrod and Rhonda woke together, naked under the bearskin. When Jerrod felt Rhonda wake he pulled her as tight to him as was comfortable, and then lovingly kissed the back of her exposed neck.

"Good morning, my love," Rhonda said softly.

Somewhere in the night Jerrod's soul had found peace. In the morning he felt they could lay there forever. For the first time in his life he was truly happy, free from his obsession to become a wealthy, powerful hero. He was content.

Rhonda rolled over to smile at Jerrod. She could feel her soul ebbing, wanting out of her body to join with Jerrod's soul. The druid bonding of their natural essence was beginning. The bond would be consummated after their marriage and become eternal when their souls intermixed, becoming one being sharing two bodies.

As they rose together and dressed one another, Jerrod admired the elegance of Rhonda's body. The sight of her nakedness and the soft curls of her long, brown hair began to arouse him again. He stepped to her slowly. Standing before her he laid his hands gently on her still naked waist. Pulling her in, he kissed her lips...a long, deep, passionate kiss of tender love.

"I love you," he said for the first time.

After they dressed, Rhonda sent Jerrod on to the morning meal while she ventured into the forest alone. Her mind reached out, eventually touching two cougars high in the mountains to the east. After speaking with the cats for a minute, the mountain lions consented to pulling the wagon to the closest city, which lay at the top of some waterfalls several days away.

"I would have preferred bears, but I could only reach two mountain lions. The bears are evidently hibernating," Rhonda told the others.

"A city built at the top of a waterfall?" Fraum asked.

"That's the impression I got, why?" Rhonda responded.

"Silandria? The fabled city of Silandria? The scrolls tell of an ancient city with a highly developed civilization where a powerful race lives," Fraum announced.

"Powerful? In what way?" Jerrod asked.

"The scrolls are vague on those details," Fraum answered.

"Can it be worse than a pagan temple to some false gods? The sooner we leave here, the better," Drin sneered.

"Drin, I honor the Olympian gods," Jerrod responded.

"Perhaps our time is better spent on planning our travels than settling religious disputes," Fraum counseled.

The cougars arrived while they were finishing packing the shelters onto the wagon. The Elves, who were accustomed to living among wildlife, did not pay attention to the large cats, but the flatlanders were obviously uncomfortable, even after Rhonda had explained everyone was safe. Fraum, who was very curious and wanted to get close to the animals, helped harness them to the wagon with the rope they had braided from the inner bark of dead trees.

They stood together in the cold winter morning waiting to travel northward while Rhonda and Imelrinn finished a private conversation. They already knew their path would work down out of the mountains. The flatlanders watched and waited.

"Morning is like a new birth. With the sun comes new opportunities and new choices," Fraum commented in reflection, speaking to no one in particular.

"Whether you succeed or fail today, the sun will come again tomorrow. So put your best foot forward and move on." The older man paused, looking at his friends. "Yesterday was just a step we had to take to reach this day."

When the cats began pulling the cart on its skis, they headed northwest as expected, working their way down out of the Anacoztiel Mountains. Jerrod and Rhonda walked alongside the wagon-sleigh holding hands. Imelrinn had disappeared, walking ahead of the group marking the best route, while Drin and Fraum followed immediately behind the cart and the four Lithlillian guards marched stoically behind them.

"I did that," Drin said proudly to Fraum, nodding towards Jerrod and Rhonda.

"Oh?"

"I spoke with Jerrod about his love for Rhonda and Amanda's absence."

"Advising friends on love and war is risky," Fraum commented.

"What do you mean?"

"It's hard to consider everything and easy to be blamed for the outcome."

Drin was happy for his friend, but he still felt conflicted by Rhonda's religious practices. Jerrod was a misguided follower of the Olympians, but at least he believed in some gods. Rhonda believed in what, the earth?

"Love takes work every day. It's a hard and demanding task," Fraum thought out loud.

"Look at them," Drin said, gesturing towards his friends.

"They're young. Love and lust are confusing enough, but she is a druid princess. She is the future leader of Lithlillia. And Amanda just left," Fraumm explained.

"Amanda may not return," Drin interrupted.

"Maybe not," Fraum agreed.

"But young lovers need to give themselves time to determine whether it is love or lust they are really feeling. And even if it is love, they still may not be right for each other," Fraum warned as the wagon started to roll forward.

The first day of travel was long. They were tired by nightfall when they stopped to set up the tents and warm the smoked venison. While everyone else worked, Imelrinn found Jerrod and pulled him aside.

"I know you love Rhonda. She loves you, too. You are wearing her '*esreandrea*,' her braided wristlet of bonding. You understand this is an indication you are betrothed?" Imelrinn finished as he watched for a reaction.

After Jerrod nodded yes, Imelrinn continued.

"You will have to learn our ways. You know I am aware you slept with Rhonda."

"I—" Jerrod started, but Imelrinn interrupted.

"Rhonda's virtue must remain intact until your marriage. Do you understand?" Imelrinn questioned. "All of our lives rest on it." Imelrinn's stark green eyes focused on Jerrod.

✢   ✢   ✢   ✢   ✢

In a dark cave a broad-shouldered man sat reading a large tome. The hood of his dark robe hung down his back, exposing his gray, shoulder-length hair and a short beard that partially covered the pitted skin of his oval face. His black eyes fixated on the text.

Around him were tables full of beakers and vials he had conjured up with his alchemy. The necessary elements he had gathered for the potion were scattered across the table tops. Next to his elbow lay a large, opaque vial and three ordinary, gold rings. Nearby the sounds of sleeping bears and fidgeting wolves distracted him.

"Dragons and scales! Do you have to be animals all of the time?" Nathanial asked himself rhetorically.

Would you like me to chase them off? May be eat a few of them? the large, female dragon laying nearby coaxed.

"Leave them be, Rok-lin. They are our protection now and our allies later," Nathanial answered

The glow from the top of his gnarled staff leaning against the wood table provided him enough light to read the large, leather-bound tome. He flipped the pages past the wish spells into the darkest pages, into death spells. Nathanial wondered how much energy the death spell would demand if he cast it? How much sleep would he need to recover?

"There is so much power here, Rok-lin, but I would sleep for ages," Nathanial mumbled.

Despite their annoying preference for animal forms, he knew the Were-Folk were proving to be good allies. In animal form they seemed to quarrel quite a bit more than in human form, but they were much more alert. In their human form they were rarely as aggressive. The aggressive nature of their animal egos would be advantageous to his plan. Regardless of their form, Nathanial had nothing to worry about. Behind him slept the massive blue-green form of a young adult dragon.

Nathanial sat back a minute, stroking his beard and taking a break from Brendril's Tome to think about the next steps of his plan. The interrelationship between each subsequent step caused him to smile. He could see his success. First the Were-Folk and then the Fendür. The tribes of giants and trolls that were hated by Lithlillia would make powerful allies, but not his most powerful. The final allies would have to wait, but his army was growing and there was nothing the Triad could do to stop him. He chuckled as he thought of Jacob racing towards Cipper.

Next time we meet, my old friend, I will kill you, Nathanial thought.

Rok-lin's snoring comforted him. Her almond shaped, solid black eyes never seemed to close. Her ram-like horns were starting to curl tight around her head, which was more horse-like than cat-like, with a square-shaped jaw and large fangs. Even in her sleep the young dragon was menacing.

Nathanial's attention returned to thumbing through the pages of the tome. Under "W," he found "Wish," "Wish, Three," and "Wish, Ultimate." A spell under "S" caught his attention: "Sleep, Mass."

I must remember that one, he thought.

As he turned forward he found "Revive" and then "Quake."

"Finally," he sighed.

On the page before him was the word, "Projection." Nathanial looked over at the bed of straw he had prepared, and then back at Rok-lin. Looking down at the three rings on the table before him, he stood up and began reciting the words on the page. As he spoke he passed his hand over the rings, causing a fine, dust-like sparkle to fall on the rings as they became magically endowed. Nathanial picked the rings up and put them in a box, which he placed among the alchemy components, candles, vials, and beakers.

Hidden in plain sight, he thought.

He was exhausted. Looking around the smaller cave one last time he picked up the potion he had prepared.

I'm so tired. The down side of magic. I must rest. At least there are benefits to being a bear. No one would think twice if they find a hibernating bear in a cave, he continued as he lifted the vial towards his lips.

"You'll watch over me, won't you, Rok-lin?" Nathanial asked, looking at the dragon before swallowing the liquid.

"That's truly awful," he gasped aloud.

Nathanial walked to the straw bed and sat down, waiting for the alchemy to begin its magic. The pain was tremendous. His body shook as his skin and bones began the transformation. He fell over onto his side, curling up into a ball. When the pain was too much he let out a scream that changed with his body, ending in the roar of a bear.

An old black bear lay on the straw with Nathanial's shredded clothes. A silvery-gray tint grew around the bear's muzzle. The creature rose, circled once, and lay back down to hibernate for the rest of the winter.

Sleep well. I will protect you, the dragon thought.

* * * * *

It had been days since Felicia had observed Jerrod. The Queen of Witches leaned over the table in front of her fire and lit a thin tan colored candle before peering into the basin of oil sitting in front of her. The first image to come into view was of Amanda on a Haithenbeurn ship. Felicia reached over to stir the oil with the long fingernail of her forefinger.

The image swirled out of focus and then, as the oil calmed, a new image came into focus. In the basin before her the image of the druid princess sleeping in Jerrod's arms reflected on the surface of the oil. Breathing the smoke from the candle deeply into her lungs, Felicia focused her thoughts on Jerrod. Concentrating as hard as she could, her mental prowess, enhanced by candle-witchcraft, sought to open his mind, but she failed. She tried again, and then again before giving up.

Frustrated by her inability to open Jerrod's mind and manipulate his thoughts, she fell back on her furs, tossing her head to the side so her long black hair fell loosely down her shoulders. She sensed a new power growing in him, a magical power that was protecting him.

Felicia reached over to stroke Sasha behind the ears. *We will still see what may come. We will see,* she thought.

CHAPTER 3

THE HORN AND DRAGONS

Later that morning the ship pushed away from the Morganwray pier. The vessel set sail under the power of the crew's oars, rowing to the beat of a drum, and the light morning sea breeze that barely filled the sails.

Amanda stood at the starboard rail with the young girl from Ornholtz watching the city and coast fade from view. Amanda was comfortable with her decision that sailing to Theasendür was indeed the safest form of travel, but the captain's amulet raised suspicion in her mind. Had Vendal "acquired" the jewelry from a passenger that had found their way overboard? Was she really safe? And Amanda had not foreseen being befriended by a twelve year old girl. Amanda had limited her interactions with the other passengers, but that could only go so far before her self-imposed isolation started raising questions. And finally, the young girl won her heart.

Kadlin was cute and loving. Like all the local girls Kadlin braided her hair and wore a big smile that lit up her face. Her nose was covered with freckles and her blue eyes seemed to sparkle now and then. Amanda saw the happy, innocent child in Kadlin that she had never had the opportunity to be.

✢　　✢　　✢　　✢　　✢

The next morning Amanda returned alone to the ship's rail to watch the sun rising over the bow. The orange clouds against the pale blue sky painted a beautiful background against the turbulent, gray winter sea. She was standing amidships on the landward side, reflecting on her journey when the captain approached.

"Estrianna, you're up early this morning," he greeted.

Amanda turned and smiled at him as her hand quietly slipped to her dagger. Even in the common clothes of the northern kingdom, dressed plainly so she would not draw attention, Amanda's smile was disarming.

"We are two days from Aegirwick," he said, trying to start a conversation.

"It's a long voyage," she responded, looking back at the horizon over the bow.

"If I can..." He paused, swallowing hard. "If there's anything I can do to make your voyage more comfortable..."

"Thank you, Captain. Will we be able to go into Aegirwick when we land?" Amanda answered, ignoring his innuendo.

They continued to pass pleasantries for a few minutes before the captain excused himself to tend to his sailors. Amanda began wondering what the captain's intent had been before he was called away by his crew as she turned back towards the horizon. The sun was up. It was a new day.

Why is he being so friendly? Too friendly, Amanda reflected as she turned to go down the stairs back to her small, private cabin.

She liked the captain, but she carefully did not offer any more information about herself than necessary. The less she said the easier it was to remember her disguise. It was better that no one knew who she was or where she came from. Although she had already decided her escape would be by a different route, which offered other dangers, she did not want anyone behind her knowing her true identity.

For the remainder of the trip Amanda limited her habit of brief trips on deck for fresh air. During the day she diligently practiced the dance-like exercises that Fraum had taught her. Every evening, after suffering through boastful dinners where the men embellished stories of their lives while ignoring the women, Amanda returned to her cabin with a renewed desire to practice.

The evening meals consisted of fish caught on a line strung out behind the ship. Catching the fish slightly increased the captain's nominal profit. Water or ale and some bread accompanied the fish. Had it been summer the captain would have bought apples, but Vendal explained fruits or vegetables were hard to come by in the winter. The morning meals were even sparser, consisting mostly of bread or potatoes, which seemed abundant, and cold water.

I miss tea, Amanda reflected, thinking of Torrence and Lithlillia.

✻   ✻   ✻   ✻   ✻

Her routine helped the voyage pass quickly and soon they moored in Aegirwick. Estrianna went ashore again. Again she found a city of chauvinists and women who were too scared to stop and talk. They did not gossip or linger while shopping. They did not talk to the merchant or other shoppers. The women went rushing by to shop and then return home with their children in tow.

They don't even know how life should be, she thought.

She returned to the ship in time for the evening meal and, after an uneventful night in port, the ship departed for Theasendür. They had been at sea for five days, with two nights in port. The remainder of their trip would find the ship pulling up to the pier in Theasendür on the morning of the fourth day where she would be face-to-face with her quest at last, the "recovery" of the Horn of Valhalla. Its legendary power to restore the dead was well known, even in Torrence.

A strange sense of panic twisted into the normal sense of calm she typically felt before a recovery. The conflicting feelings were unsettling. She needed to complete the quest for the safety of her friends, but returning such power to Torrence was dangerous. And she wanted to destroy the chauvinism that was oppressing the women of Haithenbeurn.

"Athena, give me guidance," Amanda prayed quietly to the Olympian goddess of wisdom.

The last couple of days, Kadlin's mother invited "Estrianna" back to their cabin after the evening meal. Amanda accepted with all the humbleness of a Haithenbeurn woman.

She would sit on the end of a bed with one leg dangling towards the deck, the other tucked up under her thigh appearing to be relaxed, always careful to put her back towards a wall and face the door. She gained some comfort watching Kadlin's mother, Helga, lovingly tend to her children, but the sight caused her to think of Jerrod, the way his silver hair curled around his ears.

Occasionally, they would ask Estrianna a question, which she answered as quickly and briefly as possible. Amanda found herself becoming fond of the woman and her children. Wistfully, she wondered if her childhood would have been similar had her mother not died when she was so young.

The night before they reached Theasendür, Amanda was sitting on the bed when Kadlin's father, Otkel, came in with his son. He had stayed in the galley drinking with the other men, celebrating the end of the voyage, which only brought him closer to working in the coal mines. He was in a good mood, his chauvinism boosted his ego and the ale obscured his own troubles. In his drunken jubilance, Otkel began ordering the women around. When Helga did not move fast enough for him he pushed her out of his way.

The gentle woman from Ornholtz, who had done nothing to deserve mistreatment, landed sprawled across the bed, unhurt, but Kadlin reacted quickly to protect her mother, jumping into her father's path and drawing his attention.

"What is it? Let me get it for you, Father," she begged.

As Otkel drew his hand back to strike the young girl, months of aggravation resulting from helplessly watching chauvinistic abuse, beginning in Dorindril, the southern fishing village on the Fjord of Menduran, exploded in Amanda's mind. Her soul erupted in fury as her mind blanked out. She leaped forward, slapping his large hand upward as he started his swing towards his daughter.

When Otkel regained his balance, Amanda stood defiantly in front of him. Her long blonde hair fell out of her cap. Amanda could see the rage in his eyes. His bearded face was red with anger as she reached up to pull her long hair back into a pony tail.

"Estrianna?" Helga yelled, frightened for Amanda's safety.

"What's this?" Otkel demanded. "How dare you! By Odin, I am going to teach you a woman's proper place!"

The large burly man lunged forward, his rage overcoming his drunken swagger as he swung his fist wide around towards Amanda's head. She ducked his blow easily, jumping towards his exposed side and punching his exposed ribs.

The whole room could hear the snap as two ribs broke. Amanda turned her hip, snapping the ball of her foot parallel to the floor and driving through Otkel's knee, causing him to collapse to the floor. Then Amanda hopped up to kick him in the back of the head with the other foot. Otkel's massive body flew forward, landing face first on the deck.

Amanda's breathing was calm as she pictured her hatred of the chauvinistic abuse. She stood motionless. With her feet slightly wider than her shoulders and her knees bent, Amanda appeared to be almost sitting as she watched Otkel.

The large man labored a moment before he began to stand. As he stood up he turned towards Estrianna and drew his sword.

"Now, you're going to die," he stated coldly.

Amanda watched him advance, waiting for his attack. The ceiling was too low for him to swing his sword over his head. She watched for a horizontal swing or a thrusting lunge.

When Otkel swung his sword around, Amanda jumped in towards his chest and spun around, placing her back against his stomach. First catching his wrist as it came around, Amanda twisted it, pulling him off balance, and then ducked under his arm, flipping him onto his back.

Otkel looked up into Estrianna's glare, his sword in her hands with the tip pointing at his chest.

Amanda glanced at Kadlin and Helga before she slowly turned her gaze back towards the helpless man at her feet. The sight of his father lying helplessly on the floor, awaiting his death, caused Kadlin's brother to instinctively step towards Estrianna.

"Varin!" Helga yelled.

Amanda's head snapped around to focus on the boy, who stood as still as the statue of Sir Michael before the cathedral in Torrence. When she was comfortable the boy was not a threat, Amanda looked back down to Otkel. She did not want to kill him, particularly in front of his family.

"Please!" Otkel begged.

"Odin will not help you this day," Amanda said coldly. "If I let you live, will you promise to never lay an angry hand on Kadlin or Helga again?"

Otkel responded quickly, nodding his head slowly in agreement as he held his breath.

"If you don't change your ways," Amanda paused, "I will come back and finish this. You will never see me coming. Do you understand?"

He nodded again.

"Don't make me regret my decision," Amanda warned.

Amanda drove the point of the sword down through the floor next to Otkel's ear. Then she backed out of the room with her hand on the crimson pommel of her golden dagger, shutting the door against the wood of the ship's walls.

"Thank the Fates for thick wood and noisy ships," Amanda muttered.

✳   ✳   ✳   ✳   ✳

The next morning Kadlin went to Amanda's cabin but the room was empty. The young girl searched the ship, but Estrianna was nowhere to be found.

By mid-day the ship was tied to the pier in Theasendür. Kadlin looked again for Estrianna as the passengers offloaded, but was not successful in finding her friend from the Ragnaugh Mountains. Sadly, she rejoined her family and followed the gangplank down onto the peir without looking back.

"Estrianna's gone, isn't she, Mother?" Kadlin said as she looked over her shoulder at the ship.

Amanda could not risk saying goodbye. If Otkel raised a complaint, she might never see the end of her quest and her friends would suffer for her failure. So, instead, Amanda stowed away out of sight while Kadlin walked away and the crew began offloading the cargo.

The crew hoisted the cargo onto the pier, where merchants came to collect their shipments. After the merchants paid Captain Vendal, he went into the city to buy merchandise and barter for new shipments to fill the hold on their return voyage. In his absence, the crew loaded the merchants' wagons and then went into the city for the evening. By dusk the pier was empty and only the captain and two crewmen remained on board to watch the ship.

In the darkness of night a silhouette dressed in black leather slipped over the side of the ship, across the pier, and into the shadows of the city. Amanda moved swiftly into a nearby passage with stealth and agility. In a moment's time she disappeared, leaving nothing more than footsteps in the snow to indicate she had ever been present.

Behind her, the harbor was full of vessels, many of which were merchant ships like Captain Vendal's ship, but most were like Captain Grogan's two-decked ship with its single mast. And there were as many military ships as there were merchant ships. The military ships also varied in length and the number of decks, but each was wider and set lower in the water for greater stability. They were adorned with large round shields and were prepared for war. Like the merchant ships, large carvings meant to scare away demons protected each end of the military ships.

Amanda realized that, despite its peaceful setting, this kingdom was prepared for war. She reflected on the men she had observed, how every one was armed. Their weapons were built for battle. There was always a shield close by. Even the merchant vessels were built so they could be used in war.

They are a seagoing kingdom, but I'll bet they would do just as well on land, Amanda throught to herself.

At first glance Theasendür was the same as the other coastal cities. No walls surrounded the city. The buildings were made of logs and stones, with thatched roofs. Poles were placed over the thatch to counter the strength of the coastal winds. Doors were typically on the east or west side of buildings to avoid the coastal wind from the north and direct summer heat from the south. The winter streets and alleys that were heavily traveled were deep mud, but the others were covered with thick, undisturbed snow over a foot deep.

The few soldiers Amanda saw seemed to patrol the streets more for public peace than out of concern for attack. When an army was needed all of the men in Haithenbeurn would respond. It was a citizens' army ready to respond in an instant, but the king had his own forces surrounding him.

Commerce and shipping companies crowded close to the pier with inns frequented by sailors and dock workers scattered nearby. Several clusters of merchant shops could be found throughout the city. The further they were from the wharf the nicer things seemed to be. There were very few stables, which were all built on the outskirts of the city, and no fortress to support any sort of standing army.

It was still early when Amanda slipped her local attire back on to wander through the streets, poking her head into inns and taverns as she sought temporary lodging. The establishments appeared to be like those in Torrence in some ways. Men drank heavily, but unlike Torrence the patrons did not sing and the food and drink selections were more limited. Like Torrence, the condition of the buildings outside appeared to be a good indication of the clientele inside, but unlike Torrence the clientele was less distinguishable. They all carried *langsax* or Haithenbeurn axes, with daggers on their belts. The primary difference of the clientele was the chauvinistic manners that sickened Amanda.

Finding an inn in one of more the run down areas with a little less light and no noise, Amanda went in. Several large heavy tables with bench seats littered the tavern. To the side of the stone fireplace, which was built in the center of the tavern, was a door leading back into a room where she could hear the occasional clanging of cast iron pots. Across the room was a dark hallway leading back into what she assumed were guest rooms. She could not see any other entrances or exits from the inn.

The innkeeper in his wool shirt and thick pants was just like every other man in the northern kingdom. Concern that her powers of observation were dulling, Amanda pushed her perception further.

What haven't I noticed? she quizzed herself.

Unlike most men, the innkeeper had wide leather wrist bands that laced halfway up his forearms. Some of the tavern maidens' clothes were nicer. Their skirts were shorter, they did not wear leggings, and their blouses dropped more, showing more cleavage to the male patrons. Those that were better dressed hung on the men they encouraged to drink.

That's better. Even the slightest variance could be valuable, she thought.

The innkeeper watched the patrons intensely as he barked orders to a young tavern maiden that went quickly back and forth from the kitchen to the guests carrying tankards of ale and an occasional plate of chicken. She raced between tables trying to please the inebriated men who poured half their drinks down their beards.

"What can I do for you?" the innkeeper growled.

"I need a room with a window," Amanda paused, looking around the room. "With no questions asked," Amanda said more boldly than her disguise would suggest.

The innkeeper scowled at Amanda, considering her request as he glared, sizing her up.

A single woman traveling alone. No one wants this one, he thought instinctively, devaluing her status further than an ordinary woman.

"We have one in back. I assume you will be eating as well." He didn't wait for an answer as he doubled his normal rate. "It will be four dürn a night."

Amanda opened her coin pouch and paid him for a week.

"Grittel," the innkeeper called to the young maiden. "Show our guest to the back room. The one on the right."

Grittel slammed the tankards she was carrying down on the table, nearly spilling the contents so she could more quickly respond to the innkeeper's summons. She raced across the tavern floor to turn quickly down a passage, not looking to see how close Amanda followed.

"What is your name?" the innkeeper asked Amanda as she began to follow Grittel down the dark hall.

"Estrianna," Amanda replied more humbly.

*   *   *   *   *

Near the center of the city was a large common lodge with a big attached building where their king lived. He was the chieftain, strongest of six families.

He sat in the windowless lodge dictating the affairs of the kingdom as he saw fit.

His single story lodge stood above most of the other buildings in the city. Two dwellings were attached to the lodge. The smaller building, which appeared to be his private residence, was two stories and built of stone. The larger building was round and appeared to be some sort of indoor arena with a roof that peaked in the middle. Nearby were the only army barracks Amanda had seen in the kingdom. The king's men came and went freely between the buildings.

The center of Haithenbeurn's power, Amanda thought when she saw it.

She quickly learned locals believed the private residence of King Randver was impenetrable. There were always guards and heavy wood doors with iron hardware. With only one door and few windows, the residence was easy to guard. There was little challenge to protecting it.

The king, who had the reputation of being a barbarian, lived alone. His rule was quick and harsh. There was no appeal and seldom any mercy. The citizens spoke openly of the king's favorite penalty, a pit full of hungry wolves.

Valiant warriors condemned to death might be given a sword so they could die honorably when they were thrown into the pit, but most went in empty handed. Without a sword in their hand when they died in battle, the Haithenbeurn warriors would not reach Valhalla. They would not reach the afterlife of honored warriors. When mercy was shown it most often amounted to being drug to death by horses. The most fortunate might be slain by a thrown axe or crossbow bolt.

Amanda spent weeks watching the common lodge and king's residence from a distance. King Randver was as big as any man in the kingdom. He had little reason to leave his residence, and spent most of his time sitting alone in his lodge, where he was often visited by an old crone, the king's witch.

Witchcraft was the only magic in the kingdom. Amanda had not yet seen the old hag-witch, who was described as being nearly blind, having long fingernails that curved and twisted, and unkempt white hair. When she foretold the future, the crone pulled small bones from a pouch and cast them upon the floor, but to read the bones she had to press her nose almost to the floor.

The Horn of Valhalla hung above the King's stone throne in the lodge. The citizens of Haithenbeurn were able to come and go from the lodge under the watchful eyes of several guards, but at night, only four guards were allowed in the lodge.

Most often it was the six Chieftains from the other Houses of Haithenbeurn that visited the king. They gathered each night with the king, eating and drinking while political decisions impacting the entire kingdom and verdicts for criminals were spontaneously presented. Randver seldom asked for or accepted their advice. He ruled with a tight fist, making his own decisions that quickly became law. Envoys would be sent out to notify the kingdom, but more often than not the king's edict would pass by word of mouth faster than the envoy could reach the other cities.

Other decisions, such as which daughter would be betrothed to which son, which house had certain shipping rights, or which house was in charge of the Southern Gate, were made just as impulsively. Consequently, the Chieftains did not dare miss a dinner that would jeopardize their standing.

It was immediately apparent to Amanda that even in the height of the drunken festivities she would be unable to steal the horn. The recovery would need to take place in the early morning when she would only have to deal with the four guards, and from the moment she put her hands on the horn she would become the focus of an intense manhunt ending in the pit if she were caught.

After carefully considering the options, fleeing south by horse across the snow covered land seemed the only rational choice. Fleeing by ship would confine her to a single vessel that was on a specific route. Furthermore, going back the way she came not only increased the chance she might be recognized but also required her to pass over the Crispten Mountains again, a feat she was not sure she could accomplish alone. Riding south through the open countryside offered flexible options, increasing her chance of escape.

The tavern gossip gave Amanda more information. A large city, Dalset, was about two weeks ride to the south. The countryside along the southern road was reportedly unpopulated, save for an occasional hunter's cabin or logging camp. And finally, Haithenbeurn had been at war against a race they called the "Rakenholtz" for as long as anyone could remember.

War is good. Anyone tracking me might be thrown off on the battlefield, she thought.

During the last week of her observations, Amanda began purchasing the things she would need on the winter ride. She purchased two heavy yak-wool blankets, a heavy canvas tent with a low ridge that would minimize the area she needed to heat, candles, oil, a pot, and some dried food, which she stuffed into a new pack.

To avoid arousing suspicion she carefully bought a few items at a time. Shopping at different times of day and in different neighborhoods, Amanda carefully presented herself as neither too rich nor too poor. She waited until the last day to buy the horses, selecting a large dapple-gray gelding, young enough that it still had plenty of strength but old enough not to have too much spirit, and a large pack horse.

On the afternoon of the recovery, Amanda went to the southern road, and finding a small, seemingly abandoned shed on the southern edge of the city, she stabled the horses and stowed supplies inside. While she waited she pulled the black leather that served as her thieves' armor out of her pack to change.

"This feels better," she said aloud as she pulled the tight leather pants on.

Her black shirt felt smooth against her skin. Attaching her crimson-pommel dagger to her belt that fit snuggly against her athletic waist gave her a feeling of security. Amanda knelt, pausing ceremoniously over her bedroll before she began to unroll her sword.

"With the blessings of Ares," she gave homage to the Olympian god of war.

She had been dedicated to the single objective of recovering the horn since leaving Cipper, but on the eve of the recovery she felt a renewed sense of purpose. The weight and balance of her sword empowered her deep within her psyche.

No more Estrianna, she thought.

With plenty of time before the recovery, Amanda drew her sword. The sound of metal scraping as she slowly pulled her blade out of the scabbard sent shivers of joy up her back. At first she held the sword point straight out, angled slightly upward, and then twisted her wrist to catch the reflection of the dim light down the length of her blade. She paused a moment, embracing the feeling of utopia.

Amanda exploded into a quick series of slashing and spinning movements, ending with a deep lunge, thrusting the point of her sword forward. It whistled through the air as she attacked and parried and, after a moment, she stopped to look at the sword again. She knew what she had to do. She knew her actions should not be lethal. They could not be lethal. If they were and she was caught later, even Hermes, the Olympian god of thieves, would not have the power to save her from the Asgardians' wrath.

She picked up the scabbard and walked to the corner where her pack leaned against the wall as she reflected back to the night she had accepted the blood-debt. Rhonda would have died if she had refused. The Olympian priests were not going to heal her without the persusion of the guild. Amanda began to re-sheathe the sword.

"Did I accept this task for Rhonda's sake or because she seemed to mean so much to everyone else?" Amanda questioned herself aloud.

The metallic snap of the sword closing tight in its scabbard drew her attention back to the shack. Amanda reluctantly leaned the sword in the corner behind the pack where it might be obscured if someone entered. After pulling her hair back into a ponytail, Amanda looked around one more time before slipping out into the cold winter night.

The walk back to the lodge was longer than she remembered. The late-night air bit at her face and numbed her hands. When she stopped in the shadows across the street from the lodge, all seemed quiet. The Chieftains had left the lodge and the patrons of the nearby taverns had gone home, leaving the streets empty.

It was well past midnight, closer to dawn, when Amanda crossed the snowy street to enter the hall. She knew this recovery was not a typical theft, sneaking in to carry something away unnoticed. It would rely upon brute strength, which was the worst kind of recovery. She leaned her forehead against the heavy wooden doors as she pictured the guards inside and prayed.

"Hermes, may I be successful this night so that I might see Jerrod again. Athena, goddess of heroic endeavors, may I be successful this night without bloodshed. By the Fates, I lend myself to your care," she whispered under her breath.

Pushing against the doors, she entered the hall. As she had anticipated, her entry was challenged immediately.

"Halt! Who are you?" the closest guard commanded.

Amanda smiled at him coyly as she swaggered towards the center of the room. The two guards at the far end of the room started walking towards her with their spear tips pointing in her direction. The guards who had been in the corners closest to the large doors fell in behind her.

"Halt," the trailing guards echoed, slightly less alarmed. Amanda stopped in the center of the hall as the guards approached. She spun slowly, batting her blue eyes flirtatiously at each as she turned around to rest her attention on the guard who first confronted her.

"What are you doing in here, woman? And what are you wearing?" he asked in a demeaning tone.

Thrusting her knee upward, Amanda snapped her foot outward, kicking him in the groin. The guard collapsed to his knees, gasping for breath. Amanda leaped forward, chopping down on the back of his neck with the outside of her hand, causing him to fall forward. The guard lay unconscious at her feet.

Amanda grabbed his falling spear and, after standing up straight, she began spinning it over her head. Before the remaining guards could react, Amanda swung the spear downward, striking the closest guard on the jaw. The blow flipped him over to land on his back, unconscious. Continuing to swing it until the spear rested behind her back, parallel to the floor, Amanda crouched down on one leg, the other out straight and her free hand extended towards the two remaining guards.

Watching the failed attempts of his comrades, the closest guard tossed his spear aside to draw his sword. The strange woman crouched in a defensive stance, the spear tip pointing away from him. The guard stepped forward, swinging his sword across his body, but Amanda's jumped back too swiftly, evading his sword.

The guard continued forward swinging his sword around, over his head, and slashing down at Amanda's head. Grasping the spear-shaft with both hands she used it to block the sword, but the blade cut through, separating the spear into halves. The tip of the blade arched downward, barely missing Amanda as she rolled backward out of the sword's path.

As Amanda rolled up onto her feet, the guards lunged forward. The tip of a spear thrust by her as the sword blade swung down again, but she was able to jump aside, avoiding both attacks. Amanda countered with the spear-halves hitting the closest guard's wrist, which caused him to drop his sword. Amanda stepped in, and thrusting her knee higher, she snapped her foot outward. The ball of her foot drove through his chest, sending him flying backward, landing on the floor several feet away.

Amanda spun to face the remaining guard as he thrust his spear towards her again. Swinging a spear-half down across her body, as the tip thrust past her side, Amanda stepped towards her attacker and then swung the closer half-spear upward, delivering a backhanded blow across the guard's face. The man's body spun and fell.

With the third guard unconscious, Amanda heard the guard behind her struggling to get up off the floor. He looked for a weapon as he regained his composure. Amanda turned to see him pick up the spear he had previously tossed aside and start stumbling towards her as another guard began to stand up.

Barely more than two spears' length apart, the two guards circled Amanda, trying to find an advantage, jabbing their spears at her. Instinctively, Amanda encouraged the guards to attack, taunting them with false attacks. When a guard lunged, she stepped quickly aside, allowing the spear to thrust past her, and driving in towards the guard, Amanda punched the heel of her hand into the bridge of his nose.

The man stumbled backwards, landing on his back, but immediately began struggling to rise, blood gushing from his nose. Wasting no time, Amanda rushed forward to kick him in the head, leaving him sprawled out upon the floor, and then she turned to face the last guard.

"Give up?" she questioned, cocking her head to the side with a smile.

"Not in the name of Thor. Justice will be done and the king will have you for his pit," the guard said, spitting blood on the floor.

The guard jabbed his spear at Amanda twice, but she just stepped back, turning her body to let the spear thrust by her. When he thrust again, Amanda slid forward to kick his legs out from under him. The guard fell backwards, hitting the back of his head on the wooden floor.

As the guard twisted up onto his knees, Amanda brought her leg up parallel to the floor, and then snapped it around again, striking the last guard in the jaw. He spun and fell, but still squirmed, trying to get off the floor.

This one just doesn't want to go down. I have to end this before others come! she thought.

He stood up and reached for a spear again. Amanda leaped forward, swinging a broken shaft down, breaking his wrist. He hunched over, moaning in pain, grabbing his wrist as Amanda brought the other half-shaft down on his neck, breaking his collarbone, followed immediately by another strike to the opposite collarbone.

The guard went limp, falling to his knees. Amanda snapped her foot upward, kicking the guard under his chin, propelling him backward through the air. The last guard landed on his back, unconscious.

Finally! Amanda thought.

She stood for a moment, trying to catch her breath as she gazed down at the last guard to fall. Tossing the two parts of the spear-shaft onto his chest, she turned towards the throne.

They might not feel too good when they come around, but at least they're alive, she reasoned silently, ignoring what she knew of their king.

"Thank you," she said aloud, giving the gods praise for her victory.

Picking up a fallen spear, Amanda used the point to lift the Horn of Valhalla off its rafter hooks. Tossing the spear aside as the horn fell, she caught the horn with both hands.

It was heavier than she had imagined. Made of a hollowed out, circular horn of a mountain sheep, the horn was too large to hold with one hand. Thick cowhide bands of leather wrapped around the horn where hands would grasp it when it was blown. A gold trim, fashioned like braiding, covered the wide, open end of the immense horn and a golden mouth piece was inserted at the narrow end.

"Now if Hermes will just be gracious enough to let me escape, I might be successful in getting this back to the guild," she thought aloud.

Before escaping into the cold night, Amanda removed her jacket to wrap the bulky horn away, out of sight, hoping that no one would see her leave the lodge with the artifact. At the door she paused to listen before she cracked it open and slipped back into the shadows of the winter night.

"Hermes, let this night pass with ease. Watch over me as I use the skills you rule over. Lend me your thievery and cunning that I may be successful and my friends may live," Amanda prayed.

Outside her shirt was useless against the night's cold. Amanda moved quickly through the alleys, cautiously obscuring herself in the city's shadows. When she reached the shed, she threw the door open to dart inside. She was freezing and the unheated shack offered very little comfort as she saddled her horse and packed the draft horse as quickly as she could manage. With the horn hidden in her pack, Amanda put her riding robe on over her leather jacket, wrapped herself in her bearskin, and opened the shed door before mounting her horse to depart the city on the southern road as though she was on a normal errand.

As she left the city, Amanda pulled the hood of her riding robe down over her forehead and her bearskin as tight around her shoulders as she could manage. The horses walked out of the city, a dark silhouette against the winter snow. She knew it would be hours before the sun rose and the falling snow would cover her tracks.

The luck of thieves. Thank you Hermes, god of thieves.

*   *   *   *   *

Jacob rolled over in bed as he struggled with a dream of Rok-lin and Drok-na. When he had left with Nathanial for the Isle of Dragons more than two years ago, he had no idea what lay before them. The High Master of the Triad had thought a trip together would be a good bonding experience for his two most talented wizards. Someday one of them would be his replacement and, whoever was chosen would desperately need the other's support.

Jacob and Nathanial had joined the Triad about the same time, both as very young boys. They were about the same age and both possessed remarkable connections to magic. Wizardry was by far their strongest area of ability. Nathanial was the stronger wizard, but in the eyes of the High Master, Jacob was the better alchemist, which tormented Nathanial no end. Nathanial was driven to be the best at everything.

On their journey, Jacob and Nathanial had ridden together to Semanie Point, where they caught a ship sailing south. Neither of them particularly liked being on the ship. Nor did they particularly like the sea. The lapping waves beating against the vessel's hull caused a rocking motion, making them seasick, which became worse as the wind filled sails. The ship's hull lumbered through the waves of the open gulf causing its masts to pitch and sway in unison like three needles scrapping erratically at the sky.

Neither of the young wizards were interested in the commerce that sent the ship south to Abiduran, the port city east of the Dunes of Rahfinnidalh. They spent much of their passage in their cabin quietly studying the notes they kept in small, leatherbound spell books. When they were not studying they talked of the future, of their plans and dreams. And the fact that no wizard from Torrence had attempted to attract a dragon familiar in over a hundred years dominated the conversations.

Jacob was content with life. He was content with the Triad continuing on as it was, a place to study three of the magics all at once, protected from the ancient king's edict outlawing studying multiple forms of magic, but Nathanial was already unhappy with Triad life. Nathanial wanted more, much more.

"The Triad has so much potential for true power. They could rule the world," Nathanial would say.

Nathanial was careful not to expose the extent of his disdain for the scholarly organization. In his mind no king's edict or king's army should be allowed to arbitrarily limit their purpose. More dangerously, Nathanial was quickly losing respect for the High Master. The aging man would not exert his influence on the king or the kingdom, and Nathanial resented his master for that. He knew Jacob would always be a loyal follower. He was certain that Jacob would report his thoughts if they became apparent. So, Nathanial remained quiet, keeping his plans buried deep in his mind, allowing the High Master's puppet to remain blissfully happy.

Abiduran was beautiful. Most of the buildings were built of thick, sand-colored walls with thatched roofs, but the large religious buildings and palaces of the tribal leaders had red tile roofs. The men, who were darker skinned with black hair, wore flowing robes. Many carried large curved swords they called "scimitars." The women, who also wore flowing robes that hid their figures, wore thin veils across their faces that concealed all but their mysterious, alluring eyes. Yet, all the beauty was lost to the eyes of the obsessed wizards.

The markets sold strange fruits called "figs" and "dates." Some of the fruits were dried to last longer in the desert heat. Fish was the predominate meat sold in the port city, but there was also lamb covered with exotic spices and roasted on spits. Cheese and honey were plentiful. The bread was flat, unleavened, but not always as plentiful. The flour and rice were imported, so availability depended on trading. But like the beauty, the experience was lost on them.

In their haste and against Jacob's protests, Nathanial asked about the rocky peninsula the locals called Sinawee while they were buying horses for the trip. The stockman quickly warned them about Sinawee.

The locals considered it a dark, evil place plagued by giant, featherless creatures of flight that could sweep down out of the sky to carry riders off without warning, or swallow a horse and rider whole. No one journeyed out onto the peninsula. Even traveling nearby was considered a reckless act, tempting the wrath of theirgod.

Jacob had wanted to hire a guide who would know the safest route, but Nathanial insisted they could not miss the peninsula if they rode south along the beach. Jacob gave in quickly to Nathanial's domineering personality.

On the morning after their arrival in Abiduran, they found themselves departing on horseback, ill-equipped and unprepared. By mid-morning they shed the gray traveling cloaks of Torrence, which they had found too heavy for the desert heat. They carried a desert tent, bedrolls, and several days of local food they had bought in Abiduran, but had failed to buy enough vessels for water. Being wizards, who did not typically carry swords, they appeared unarmed and helpless in an inhospitable land.

"Two stupid foreigners riding into the desert, merely carrying sticks like a couple of sheepless herders," one guard at the southern gate of the walled city commented.

His comment had caused the guards around him to laugh, but a quiet man standing nearby watched as he stoked his goatee. The man watched Nathanial and Jacob ride out of sight of the city gate before he turned and moved swiftly into the city without greeting anyone.

By the time they were out of sight of Abiduran they had already realized Nathanial's vision of traveling down the coast was shortsighted. The coastal wind blew constantly, making traveling miserable. Riding in the softer sand out of the surf tired the horses quickly, but riding in the surf, where the waves pulled back into the ocean exposing harder sand, covered them in sticky sea water and wet sand kicked up by the horses. And, there was still the relentless wind. No matter where they rode the desert sun baked their skin.

At night the light desert tent gave them some protection against the coastal winds. The first night they built a small fire in the tent, warming their tea as they ate figs, dates, and lamb jerky. They spoke briefly of future opportunities and dreams, but the sound of the constantly flapping tent became deafening. Exhausted by the weather conditions, they gave in and quickly lay down to sleep, but the agitated horses, shackled outside, kept interrupting their sleep.

At dawn they woke with little rest. Tired as they were they broke camp to get an early start. At first they loped through the thin water that drained back into the surf as the sun rose in the east over the sea, but as the day began warming, they slowed to a walk.

Jacob did not voice his opinion that Nathanial had been wrong to discard the suggestion of hiring a guide. Nathaniel obviously liked being the leader and it was becoming rapidly apparent that he hated being wrong.

*   *   *   *   *

Before sunrise on the third day, two men in white flowing robes and colorful turbans snuck quietly into their camp. When they reached the horses they began cutting the bindings around their hooves as Nathanial climbed out of the tent to witness the sunrise. When he stepped through the opening of the tent and stood up, Nathanial heard a shrill, resonating yell from somewhere in the nearby sand-dunes. The two men near the horses drew their massive scimitars and charged.

"Azranik!" Nathanial yelled, thrusting the palm of his hand towards the thieves.

The two thieves flew backwards through the air as though they had been catapulted by some unseen war engine, tumbling several times in the sand before coming to a rest.

"Jacob! My staff!" Nathanial screamed as a dozen men began rushing out of the dunes.

Jacob responded quickly, emerging from their tent with both staves in his hands. He tossed Nathanial his gnarled, knotted staff as stepped out of the tent to stand next to his friend.

Grasping his staff two-thirds of the way up, Nathanial jetted the top end towards the sky.

"Mespheric trasnip," he shouted.

A small sphere of intense white light burst upward out of the gnarly top of his staff. Fifty feet above the sand, the sphere burst into dozens of separate bulbs of white light that shot outward in every direction. A split second later each of the smaller bulbs burst into brilliant stars of light, lighting up the entire beach as if it was mid-day.

"Lepsearree," Jacob shouted as he drove the bottom of his smooth, polished ebony staff into the sand.

Like the ripple caused by a pebble falling into the still waters of a pond, the sand heaved upward, radiating out from where Jacob stood. The shockwave knocked many of the horses and all of the bandits off their feet.

As the desert thieves struggled in an attempt to retreat, Nathanial turned towards the closest group of bandits. His dark eyes seemed to sparkle with joy as he thrust the end of his staff towards them.

"Maga-mesphere," Nathanial shouted.

"Wait!" Jacob screamed.

Immense bursts of reddish light shot into the bandits like molten, metal quills shooting from Hephaestus' crossbow, burning as though they had been stoked in the fires of the god of metalworking's own forge.

"Nathanial! Stop!" Jacob yelled.

"Daznakdra," Nathanial commanded.

A thick bolt of lightning leaped from his staff, striking bandits that were

further away and then smaller bolts arched out to strike others nearby. The solid
stream of lightning crackled as their attackers began to smolder. Screams of the
dying surrounded them.

The center of Nathanial's face his eyebrows dropped to the bridge of his
long, skinny nose. The flames of the burning bodies reflected in his dark eyes.

"Wait," Jacob asked again, his voice falling off to a softly spoken plea. '

Nathanial stopped and turned his head to look at Jacob. The expression on
his face was stoic.

"I'm not sure they are worth your pity," Nathanial said softly as he ducked
back into their tent.

✻   ✻   ✻   ✻   ✻

At the end of the crescent shaped coastline they found the Sinawee Peninsula,
its coast lined with immense boulders. Unlike the Desert of Rahfinnidalh, the
ground was firm and covered with short, moss-like grass that seemed to thrive in
the sea-spray. Where the grass did not grow there were bushes with woody stems
and thick, hardy leaves with purple-blue, yellow, or white flowers. Another short
ground cover with meaty, triangular shaped stem-like leaves grew at the base
of the boulders. A few mound-like hills interrupted the otherwise flat ground.
Everything seemed wet from the moist sea breeze.

The peninsula stretched eastward out of their vision. As they started
eastward, their horses became skittish. By nightfall they saw dragons occasionally
flying high in the sky, causing both Jacob's and Nathanial's hearts to pound in
their chests.

"Just think what lies ahead," Jacob muttered aloud.

They had decided to sleep out under the stars without the tent, which
exposed them to something else. Throughout the night Jacob thought he
heard the beating of large wings flapping through the air. In the morning they
released the unruly horses before continuing on foot carrying a few necessities
in small packs.

As the peninsula narrowed, the constant wind became even more prominent
with nagging gusts that tormented them like a child's kite being twisted about
by too heavy of a wind. A salty mist relentlessly sprayed across the thinning
stretch of land. Several days later they stood at the eastern end of the peninsula
as the sun set behind them.

Across a hundred feet of angry sea water, with ten foot waves beating against rocky shores, was the Isle of Dragons. The high point of the island rose up out of a dense forest somewhere near the middle of the isle. Short rock pinnacles jetted up here and there in the open area surrounding the deciduous forest. Mounds of large rocks, where only the moss-like grass would grow, pushed up through the forest intermittently.

Large winged serpents with lizard-like bodies curled up on the rocky mounds, absorbing the sunrays like sea lions on a rocky beach. They had a variety of head shapes, horns, and tails. There were massive adults and cubs no bigger than cats, and every size in between. Occasionally a larger dragon would push up and then jump into the air to fly off over the ocean just before another would return with a large fish to feed the cubs.

"They're magnificent," Jacob whispered.

Jacob and Nathanial stood motionless, breathlessly in awe of the sight. The sands of time went unmeasured as they watched dragons of every color. Most had scales that were a primary color, red, blue, or yellow, with complementary colors accenting around the edges, but there were a few green, purple, and orange scattered about. The yellows and oranges were noticeably the less common. Other colors such as brown, gray, or black were even more uncommon.

That night they withdrew away from the coastline to sleep. After casting a protection spell blocking out the wind, they curled up in their bedrolls. Throughout the night they heard dragons flying overhead. When they rose in the morning they were consumed with anticipation and approached the isle again without taking time to eat.

They did not know how the dragons would react to their presence. Impressing a familiar was never easy, even with simpler animals like cats, owls, or wolves. A wizard had to place themselves where the animal would hear their thoughts and then be able to go to the wizard. Once they were physically located with the potential familiar, the wizard would have to imprint his or her thoughts upon the responding animal, creating a mental bond. If the imprinting did not work, the responding animal often grew angry, which was not much of a problem with smaller species, but larger, more extravagant creatures were more dangerous. Angered bears, poisonous snakes, or lions were one thing, but dragons!

"Brendril's beard!" Nathanial exclaimed after seeing the surging waves beating against the rocky shoreline in the morning's light.

Standing silently, they stood side by side for a moment. They could smell the salty sea spray. They looked briefly at each other and then back at the isle. In unison they struck the bottom of their staves against the rock they stood on and vanished. In an instant they reappeared across the water on the rocky shoreline of the Isle of Dragons.

Nearby a large green dragon with metallic blue around the edge of her scales raised her head to look at them with dark, empty eyes. She had long spiral horns which went straight back over her neck, long, catfish like whiskers, and tremendous fangs. Her tail with its multiple, whip-like ends wrapped around her body, lay motionless. After taking a deep breath through her nostrils, smelling the two older men, she had put her head back down with a sigh and closed her eyes to sleep.

"They know we don't mean them any harm," Nathanial had said.

"Or they're really confident in their ability to protect themselves," Jacob responded.

They walked towards the high point near the center of the island, where they found a rim circling the center of the island. As they approached, a large male dragon crossed in front of them to scratch his side against an unusually large boulder and then moved on towards the coast. Beyond the rim was a bowl. Without pause they stepped over the rim and descended into the bowl.

Around the inside edge grew massive trees with vines running between the limbs. The overgrowth and tree canopy blocked the sun. Inside the shadows there seemed to be continual movement.

"We are being watched," Jacob commented.

As they had continued towards the center of the bowl the overgrowth thinned. Younger dragons about the size of ponies chased each other around and over boulders, occasionally disrupting a sleeping elder. A group of four or five baby dragons, or cubs, tumbled about in a ball, obscuring exactly how many were playing.

"How many are there?" Jacob asked as he tried to count.

"Who cares? Let's move on," Nathanial said, dismissing him.

Mothers lay nearby watching their cubs while the rare male slept with no regard of the young-ones and their mothers.

Jacob was surprised the females were bigger than the males. The female dragons appeared to parent as a group rather than individual mother-child pairs.

In the center of the bowl they discovered a stone floor, thirty feet in diameter with an etching of a dragon rearing back on its legs, its wings spread as it readied for flight. At the edge of the stone etching they stopped and watched. Jacob stood in awe at the marvel of the isle and its great beasts, trying to take everything in. Nathanial, on the other hand, paced slowly around the center of the stone floor, impatiently trying to peer into the surrounding forest, as if his gaze alone might cause the dragons to acknowledge their presence.

"Dragons and scales," Nathanial exclaimed for the first time.

"Relax. They will come. Sit down and cast your spell," Jacob said, gently coaxing his friend to relax.

Jacob sat right in the middle of the etching, but Nathanial sat down a couple feet away. With their legs crossed they closed their eyes and began mumbling the incantation to summon a familiar. Each wizard concentrated on their own spell, putting the activities around them out of their minds while they mentally searched for the one dragon that might answer their call. Simultaneously they sought to form magical bonds with the most prestigious of familiars, dragons.

At first nothing happened. The first to appear was a tiny greenish-blue dragon. The baby dragon stopped at the edge of the vegetation, looking around for danger before trotting a few steps forward. It stopped again, looking around before heading towards the middle of the clearing.

Halfway across the rock etching the little dragon saw Jacob, causing him to pause again, but it only took a moment before the dragon-cub bolted towards the wizard. As the cub's weight got ahead of its body the baby tumbled, rolled on its front shoulder, and then onto its back, causing the adorable creature to squawk as it kicked its legs in the air, squirming off its back onto its side, and then back over onto its feet. When it regained its composure, the creature lowered its head and then shook itself as though it was throwing water off its back.

Jacob laughed at the sight as he held out his hands to catch the small male dragon that tumbled into his arms.

I am Drok-na! the cub thought.

Drok-na's appearance interrupted Nathanial's concentration. As he looked over at Jacob holding the baby dragon, anger filled Nathanial's heart.

Jacob, that insufferable fool, has beaten me!

Nathanial concentrated harder, ignoring the sounds of Jacob bonding with Drok-na. Then he heard two voices far away. The closer one was moving slowly, but the further one was coming fast.

A small brown cub exited the forest first. Its legs were a little shorter. Its weight was a little heavier. As it began crossing the stone etching, Nathanial saw another greenish-blue dragon bolt out of the forest. The brown dragon had only taken a few steps when the second dragon overtook it. The greenish-blue dragon lashed out with its front talons, scratching the brown dragon cub across its left eye. The heavier creature drew back on its hind legs, hissing as the larger greenish-blue dragon passed by with greater speed and agility.

Nathanial reached down and grabbed the small female dragon around its stomach, pulling her into his arms. Nathanial picked up his staff and then placed the cat-sized dragon on his shoulder as he turned to look north. He struck his staff on the rock etching and disappeared with the greenish-blue dragon cub.

Jacob looked down at Drok-na, who snuggled into his arm, and then around the edge of the forest again before he stood up.

Jacob and Nathanaial had come to the Isle of Dragons together and, once there, had both selected greenish-blue dragons. For a moment their lives had come closer than they had ever been before, and then Nathanial had disappeared without a word.

Drok-na looked around nervously. Jacob paused a moment. He could sense the cub's apprehension.

"Don't worry little one. I will take good care of you. I have seen your home and we can come back any time you want," Jacob encouraged the cub as he tapped his staff on the stone etching.

✿　　✿　　✿　　✿　　✿

Jacob rolled over in his restless sleep, Drok-na watching him from across the room.

That's where it began to go wrong, he thought in his dream.

CHAPTER 4

THE ESCAPE

T he trip south from Theasendür was the coldest Amanda had ever undertaken. As the snow continued to fall, the road became harder and harder to follow. The edges began blending into the deepening fields of snow, obscuring the wagon path and its southerly direction. Only the meadow between the tree lines, like the shore of some white river lost in an icy winter, lay before her.

Large snowflakes blew into her eyes, but they also covered her horse's hoof prints behind her, eliminating the proof she had ever gone south, so she chose not to complain. The bad weather slowed her horse, as it had to search for sure footing while she froze in the saddle.

Amanda could barely see the gray silhouettes of evergreen forests hundreds of yards to either side. When she could no longer stand the frigid ride and was barely able to hold the reins, Amanda turned her horse towards the forest on the eastern side of the Meadows. Inside the tree line, where the breeze decreased slightly, Amanda turned south and continued riding until mid-day.

By early afternoon, when she could hardly feel her limbs, exhaustion took hold. Amanda stopped to set up the tent she had bought. It was low to the ground, minimizing the space she needed to heat, good for such a storm. After digging a trench on one side of the tent floor to catch the colder air, she laid evergreen branches on the higher portion of the floor to keep her bedroll off the snow. She put her saddle at the foot of the bed and used her pack as a pillow. She lit a candle and set it on the higher part of the snow-floor for heat, quickly changed into drier clothes, and then crawled into the bedroll. Moments after pulling her bearskin over her body, her eyes closed and she began a satisfactory sleep that brought dreams of a fireplace and hot, spiced wine.

The next morning she began her day with hot tea made from melted snow and dried food. Warmed by her shelter and food, the thought of crawling out into the cold day was not overly appealing. When she did finally pull the flap of her tent back she found nearly a foot of new snow covering the tent. Her horses were still tethered to a nearby tree.

By the Fates, things are looking up this morning. There will be no trace of my departure, Amanda thought as she stretched her arms above her head and took a deep breath welcoming the new day.

Once she repacked her draft horse, Amanda began riding south through the forest again. It was not long before she passed log cabins built by woodsmen and camps of foresters who cut trees for a living. There were piles of tree trunks and large wagons full of raw lumber, waiting to be shipped. Cutting had apparently stopped for the winter. She did not see any men wandering around the camps or through the forest nearby, but she decided to ride deeper inside the forest line to avoid any encounters.

The forest terrain was not much hillier than the meadow as she rode south across the gentle slope of the lower foothills. Under the bearskin and riding robe she stayed warm. Her sword and dagger with its crimson pommel were attached at her hips, where they dangled from her belt. The thought that if she were seen from a distance she would be mistaken as a hooded warrior riding in solitude among the countless columns of tree trunks comforted her.

* * * * *

Although the guards in the king's lodge regained consciousness before they were found, it did not comfort them. They had been beaten by a strange woman in black. And more unfortunate for them, their injured pride would not be their punishment.

Realizing immediately that the horn had been taken, they sounded the alarm. Other armed soldiers who responded immediately filled the lodge. To the disgraced guards, the minutes it took for the king to arrive seemed like hours.

"What's this? Who's taken my horn?" the king demanded as he stormed into the lodge from the connecting hallway.

The four guards who had been on duty were pushed towards their king.

"Who was in charge?" the king questioned.

"I was, Sire," one of the guards answered meekly.

"Well?" The king focused on the man.

"It was a woman, Sire. A woman dressed in tight black leather with a long blonde ponytail."

"A woman!" A woman beat four of Haithenbeurn's guardsmen? Four of the sons of the House of Aumont?"

"Yes, Sire. She may as well have been Tyr's sister. She was unstoppable."

"Tyr? The god of war doesn't have a sister!" And you four couldn't stop her!" the king yelled.

"Send that one to the pit. No sword. He doesn't deserve a warrior's death. And cut him so he bleeds. It'll excite the wolves more when you throw him in!" The king paused.

"Keep one of the others to identify the woman when she is returned to me," the king commanded.

As the king looked around the lodge, anger boiled inside him. Large men with steel weapons surrounded him.

Warriors all! And a woman, less than the weakest man of my house, has stolen my prize. She has stolen the Horn of Valhalla. They're useless! the king thought.

"A bag of gold to the man who brings her to me alive! I'll watch my wolves eat her flesh! And she had better have my horn or don't come back until you find it! Go!" the king commanded.

The king flopped down on his throne and dropped his chin to his fist as he contemplated the theft. Four guardsmen against a female?

"Bring me the crone! I will know where this woman has gone," he ordered.

The king's men scrambled to fulfill his orders and the crone was notified immediately, but she was old, older than any remembered. It took some time just for her to gather herself up. She hobbled as quickly as she could into the lodge and sat on the floor before the king's feet. Her twisted fingers fumbled with a pouch, dumping a number of small bones on the floor. As she leaned forward, squinting to read the bones, the lodge filled with fog.

The ceiling and walls disappeared as the figure of a beautiful woman appeared next to the crone. The woman, dressed in long white muslin robes that partially revealed her voluptuous body, looked down at the crone with compassion, and then turned the focus of her deep blue eyes on King Randver. Her unsettling look caused the king to look away.

"Your Majesty," the crone said, throwing herself on the floor at the woman's feet.

"You have done enough," the witch-queen said compassionately to the old woman at her feet.

Felicia turned her attention back towards the King Randver.

"If you are so intent on finding the thief that stole your horn, watch your southern gate, but beware the consequences of your decision," Felicia warned.

"And who are you to enter my lodge as if you were a Valkyrie?" the king demanded.

"I am Felicia, priestess of witches and all their covens. I have been watching and waiting. I am here to warn you about meddling in things that are larger than you can comprehend," Felicia answered, choosing her words carefully.

"You are not Odin's messenger." The king glared at her. "Your thief has stolen my horn and I will have it back! Not even Odin himself will deny the Horn of Valhalla from me. It was his trophy to me and I will have it back!" the king demanded.

"You may retrieve the horn briefly, but it is no longer yours," Felicia cautioned.

"It is mine! And it will be returned to me or so help me, Odin!"

"So be it. You have been warned, King of Haithenbeurn," Felicia replied softly as she began to fade into the fog, the whisper of her last words echoing through the lodge.

Randver brooded a moment before he turned to the crone.

"Send word to the southern gate. I will pay the weight of the thief's head for the return of my horn, but I want her alive."

"My lord?" the crone said as she struggled to rise from the floor.

The king glared down at the old witch.

"No woman is going to tell me what to do in my kingdom. Beware, crone. You are a valued advisor, but I am king. You are neither man nor warrior. You exist because I seek your advice. But the horn is mine and I will have it again!"

The king stood up and walked away, leaving the crone still struggling to get up from the floor. None of the guards moved to help her. When the crone finally hobbled back to her nearby cabin she took a light blue candle, about eight inches in diameter, from one of shelves and went to sit near her fireplace.

Taking a long, thin stick and placing it into the fire, she used it to light the candle. When a thin line of bluish smoke twisted as it began rising up before her, she closed her eyes to concentrate, sending her mental message to the priestess.

"The king has commanded me to send word to the southern gate, my lady. He continues to meddle in your affairs."

"Then do so with my blessing. Your king condemns himself to death," Felicia said dismissing the old woman.

While Felicia sat back on her pillows, thinking of what had transpired, Sasha came to her. The larger than normal black cat circled twice before it lay down and placed its large head in Felicia's lap.

Felicia thought of Jerrod as she petted the cat. She was proud of her masterful manipulation. She had coaxed a young, innocent miller's son to change his path, leading to the discovery of Lord Trisdale's remains. The boy had instinctively picked up the Sword of Trisdale, and in it, the Dragon's Orb. But Felicia had almost as quickly lost control of his mind. She recalled the vision of Jerrod holding the sword skyward and then discovering the amulet.

"The amulet! He put on the amulet. That's what is protecting him!" Felicia said to her familiar. "But why wasn't the Dragon's Orb radiating power? How did Jerrod activate the orb, Sasha?" Felicia asked the feline purring in her lap.

Sasha rolled over on her other side as she changed into her panther form, her massive head filling Felicia's lap.

More importantly, how will the power change him? Sasha answered.

Felicia considered for a moment that Amanda had gone on alone to Theasendür to acquire the Horn of Valhalla. Felicia could no longer see Amanda's future, either. Everything that involved Jerrod was dark, unreadable. Felicia knew Amanda would escape with the horn and that Jerrod would save her, but she could see nothing beyond that point.

And what of the prophecy? Sasha asked.

The prophecy. 'A second hero is coming and from his death another would bring splendor to a new kingdom.' Could that be Haithenbeurn? she thought more to herself.

"A second hero is coming, Sasha. But who? And when they fall, who will rise to bring 'splendor' to what kingdom?" Felica said softly as she stroked the panther's ears.

The queen of witches paused.

"And when will I get the orb?" Felicia asked, looking down at the wild creature.

"The end is coming."

✿ ✿ ✿ ✿ ✿

In the week she traveled south, Amanda's provisions dwindled. The winter dusk came early and dawn late, limiting the time she had to ride, extending the time it took to travel towards Dalset.

At night she cuddled under her bearskin in her small tent. Amanda worried about the intense cold and the fact that if something happened to her horses she would be left to walk out of Haithenbeurn on foot. Despite concerns over being pursued and the harsh, winter environment, thoughts of Jerrod continually recaptivated her mind.

Amanda pictured his smile, his azure blue eyes, and the lips that had kissed her goodbye at Terrace Xul. She pondered when she had started loving him. Was it when they had wandered through the streets of Torrence exploring the city or when he had saved her in Lord Trisdale's Keep? She recalled the moment at Chelles when she first realized she loved him, when she had awoken in his arms with tears in his eyes.

To distract herself, Amanda began playing with the jeweled dagger she had collected from Tilhem Keep. She appraised the value of the semiprecious gems as ordinary. It was a decorative piece. The *quillon* was short, barely covering her hand and there was virtually no *ricasso*. It would be very little use in a fight. She spun the ornamental weapon by turning the point on her glove and, as she watched the reflections in the blade and the sparkle of the colorful gems, she forgot momentarily about Jerrod.

One night, as she played with the dagger, the horses began neighing wildly. Amanda barely had enough time to crawl out of her bedroll before a bear's roar deafened her. It was close. She heard the snapping of trees as a huge bear knocked them out of its path. With a single swipe of its massive paw the bear broke one horse's neck, leaving deep cuts that bled openly, partially melting the snow.

But the beast did not stop. Crashing forward, the bear landed on the tent and began biting and ripping through the canvas. It tore at the bearskin which protected Amanda as she squirmed out from under the remnants of the tent. When she cleared the wreckage the only thing in her hand was the ornamental dagger.

In desperation, Amanda quickly used her free hand to throw part of the tent back over the bear's head and then jumped past the entangled beast, pulling the tarp back over its head, but the unnaturally large bear ripped through the tent and threw its giant head upward.

Amanda leaped onto the bear's back, driving its massive body forward to land back on its mighty forepaws. While the bear pushed back against Amanda's weight, she plunged the jeweled dagger into the bear's neck just below its skull and, using both hands, she embedded the blade to the *quillon*.

The bear's body collapsed, causing Amanda to tumble forward. She ducked her head to roll onto her shoulder and then up onto her feet. Spinning around empty handed, she turned to face the bear as it struggled to its feet in obvious pain.

That blow would have killed a normal bear! she thought.

Amanda ran back several paces and swung herself up into a tree before looking to see if she was being pursued. The bear was rolling in the snow, pawing at the back of its head, trying to dislodge the dagger from its neck. Amanda watched as the bear finally freed the dagger and ran off. After a few minutes, Amanda lowered herself out of the tree.

A Werebear! Sarric said there were Werebears in Lithlillia, but how did one get here? Is this just by chance? she questioned.

The remnants of the tent lay scattered over the snow. One horse was dead and the other one was gone. Amanda grabbed her sword first and then began searching through the snow for her boots. After putting on her boots, she wrapped herself in her bearskin and threw her pack over a shoulder.

This is going to be a long trip, my love, she thought as she took her first step southward.

✻　✻　✻　✻　✻

It was not until mid-afternoon the next day that Amanda found a woodsman's cabin. Cold, almost frozen, she decided to risk buying a horse from the woodsman. Before approaching the cabin she changed clothes and hid her pack with the horn and her sword in the woods. Amanda was wearing Haithenbeurn attire when she approached the cabin, hoping a local woman wandering alone in the forest would raise fewer questions than a foreigner armed with a sword..

Initially, the woodsman had been cautious, surprised by her appearance at his door, but he quickly became compassionate to her apparent misfortune. When he was comfortable that she was not some beast from the wild, he insisted she sleep near his fireplace, adamant that it was not safe in the forest at night. He appeared genuinely scared of something, but she did not fully trust him either, no matter how nice he appeared. Life had taught her to be wary, particularly of men. So she slept with her hand on the hilt of her crimson pommeled dagger.

In the morning Amanda paid the burly man a couple of gems for a large draft horse with huge hooves. The woodsman used the gelding with a team to pull a wagon of lumber to market, but the horse was old and would soon be unable to pull the heavy wagon. In addition to the horse, Amanda was also able to purchase some warm food, which she ate on the spot, and some dried venison and bread for her journey.

"Estrianna, you shouldn't travel alone. Let me take you," the woodsman offered.

"Theasendür isn't that far. I am used to the woods, but thank you," Amanda lied.

Amanda climbed onto the gelding, then turned the draft horse to plod off westwardly into the open valley. When they were out of sight of the woodsman's cabin, Amanda circled around to pick up her belongings before loping south towards Dalset.

She pushed the horse hard, wanting to put as much distance between her and the woodsman's home as quickly as she could. She knew her only advantage was that the woodsman lived a life of isolation. Her best hope was that he would not travel to Theasendür or Dalset for months, but she knew there was a greater chance that someone searching for the horn would happen across his cabin soon.

*   *   *   *   *

After several days traveling in the harsh environment, Amanda found herself on the edge of the forest staring west into the southern city of Dalset. She waited for dark before approaching the city and, with another storm threatening, Amanda gained the advantage of almost complete darkness.

From a distance she could see the city's lanterns glowing behind the few windows of wooden buildings and from where they occasionally hung in the streets. Like the northern Haithenbeurn cities, no wall surrounded the city. In the darkness of the pending storm, the city streets were bare.

"If they are truly at war, why are there no protecting walls?" Amanda mumbled to herself.

Amanda had not given particular thought to this part of her journey. Her goal had been to first reach Dalset and then disappear through the battlefield to the south. She knew very little about Dalset and its continuing war. She hoped to stay no longer than necessary, just long enough to purchase a map and buy supplies.

After assuming the role of Extrianna again, Amanda entered the city. She went first to a stable to board her horse, and then she found a nearby inn with a small room on the second floor. The elderly innkeeper and his wife, who were happy to have the dürn, allowed her to pay by the day.

Hopefully the second floor will dissuade meddlers, Amanda thought as she closed the door to her room.

The private rooms were small, furnished with a small rope bed, a pitcher of water, and a basin on a small, bedside table. The small size of the rooms reminded Amanda of the passenger cabins on Captain Vendal's ship. After tossing her pack and bedroll onto the bed, Amanda returned to the tavern for a warm, hearty meal.

The small inn only had a few visitors staying and a few local patrons drinking in the tavern. It was clean, but in need of repair. The condition suggested that they did not have enough patronage to maintain the inn. She was cold, tired, and beyond hungry. Taking a seat near the fire in hopes of warming her long chilled body, Amanda waited for her meal. When the food came she ate quickly and then returned directly to her room.

A bed. Finally! It has been too long, she thought as she lay down to sleep without undressing.

The night passed too quickly and, even though she rose well after sun up, Amanda awoke tired. Her sleep had not been restless. There were no bad dreams bothering her through the night. She had not tossed and turned out of worry. The weeks of traveling through a chauvinistic society of barbarians and fraught with bad weather had finally caught up with her.

When she went into the tavern for a morning meal she found herself alone. The elderly woman was slow to wait on her, but the food was good. As the woman dallied about she took a moment to sit with Amanda when she served the meal. The intrusion made Amanda feel uncomfortable.

Amanda was cautious, and not only about answering the old woman's questions. She avoided giving her any name and only said it would be best to kept her business to herself, but the information Amanda gained from the lonely old woman was invaluable for planning her escape.

Haithenbeurn's war had been going on as long as anyone could remember. A giant wall, built from tree trunks sharpened to a point along the top and backed with an earthen mound along the northern side of the wall, spanned the entire southern border of the kingdom. The wall protected the kingdom from the Nogrondal, a race of giants and trolls. The Nogrondal, who lived in the mountains and forests to the south, randomly attacked the wall, which was in constant repair and was always guarded.

This must be the Wall of Haithenbeurn that the mountain men spoke of and the Nogrondal must to be the Fendür, Amanda reasoned.

The innkeeper's wife also told her of a small shop owned by an elderly friend who sold scrolls of history and legends, and maps of other kingdoms. The shop was not far from the inn and only slightly off the beaten path. It no longer attracted many patrons. Then the innkeeper's wife was on to another subject.

"I'm sorry. I really must take care of some family business now," Amanda interrupted.

✻   ✻   ✻   ✻   ✻

The shop was indeed off the beaten path. It took Amanda a little work to find, but when she finally did she chuckled upon entering the doorway. It was a messy little shop, full of dusty scrolls strewn about in apparent disarray, exactly what the innkeeper's wife had described.

The owner was nearly blind, but somehow seemed to know exactly where each parchment hid. He spoke slowly, distracted by his knowledge of each topic. When Amanda asked for a map of the south lands he raised one eyebrow.

"I am interested in the lands beyond the Wall of Haitenbeurn and no questions," Amanda pressed.

The old merchant scurried off as quickly as he could to bring back an overly dusty scroll. He laid the scroll on top of several other parchments and began unrolling it with his shaking hands for Amanda's approval.

The map depicted the eastern mountains she had followed south and the Wall of Haithenbeurn. The eastern mountains continued on south of the wall, but another range beyond the wall ran east and west. On that range was a forest and further south, a great plateau. As Amanda ran her finger across the line depicting the edge of the plateau a smile crossed her tired face.

The Black Forest and the Plateau of Kronese. Trisdale Keep. Lithlillia, she thought as her finger came to rest on the spot of the druid village just below Limerin Falls.

"The Brisbanes Mountains," she mumbled as she moved her finger closer to the Wall of Haithenbeurn.

"What? What'd you say?" the old man asked.

"Sorry. Nothing," she answered as she leaned forward to study the map.

The merchant watched her closely. Maybe it was his blindness. Maybe more, but Amanda would not chance it.

"I will take the map and I will pay you double, but if you share my business with anyone, it will be the last thing you ever do. Do you understand?" Amanda warned coldly.

The man nodded his head affirmatively.

"In my days I have sold more maps for more secret purposes than I care to count. You have nothing to worry about from me."

I can't afford to have the map found in my room while I am out, Amanda considered silently.

"I will come again in a day or two. No more than a week. Keep the map safe and out of sight until I return," Amanda commanded.

* * * * *

Her next ventures out of the inn were to observe the wall. Amanda was amazed to find the log wall was over twenty feet high. She was even more amazed to find a small dwelling built on top of the berm every five hundred feet, but it was the large double gate that barred the southern road that broke her spirit.

Amanda watched for days, hoping for some weakness she could exploit, but the southern gate never opened. The mound behind the wall was never left unguarded. Her escape would not be as simple as riding out of the city. The best she could hope for was to slip over the wall on a dark night and walk through the snow to Torrence. Any pursuit would surely catch her, if she were not shot off the wall trying to escape.

And if I survive that, what about the Fendür? she thought.

Each evening Amanda went out to collect small amounts of supplies and to learn more about the wall and its soldiers. The first supplies she purchased included wire, spikes, and other instruments needed to create traps to protect the horn.

Slipping on her black leather, attaching the scabbard of her long sword to her belt, and pulling her hair back into a ponytail, Amanda slid out in the middle of the night to observe the wall. Moving in her typical, agile manner, Amanda freely passed through the empty winter streets to a suitable spot where she could observe the guards from a place out of the weather. She watched the patrols and the gate guard change, and the citizen-soldiers marching back and forth across the berm, but she could not find a weakness.

The guards, dressed in pants, shirts, and furs common for all the local men, carried great round shields and long spears, and *langsax* hung from their wide leather belts that wrapped around leather vests covered with large, metal rings. They were formidable men, loyal to king and kingdom.

✳   ✳   ✳   ✳   ✳

Days before three bearded men had observed a single woman bartering for lodging while they drank in their favorite tavern. A single woman traveling alone was an easy target and if she were to disappear, who would miss her? They had taken turns watching her eat her evening meal before retiring to her room alone. They planned their attack, figuring it would be easy to enter her room at night, overpower her, and take whatever valuables she had.

It was only a few nights later when they snuck in the back of the inn, up the stairs, and down the hall to Amanda's room. They turned the latch on the door quietly and then pushed gently. The door moved inward slowly without as much as a creak, allowing them entrance into the darkness of the room.

The first man had just passed completely into the darkness when the trip wire released a spring, hurling a spike towards the door and impaling the naïve thief deep into his thigh. The man dropped to the floor in agony, grabbing his leg and murmuring in pain, trying not to yell. He was rolling about the floor as his two accomplices jumped through the doorway.

The last man closed the door quickly, leaving them in almost complete darkness. Only the dim light through the second floor window illuminated the room. He fumbled around the room before finding a lamp to light. He turned the wick down as low as it would go, keeping light to minimum. When he turned around his two friends were in the middle of the room.

"I'll live," the leader said as he pulled the spike from his leg, groaning in pain.

"You sure? A warrior like you. It's not much more than a nail, is it?" the man kneeling next to him badgered.

"Get to it!" the leader responded angrily.

Both the uninjured thieves glanced around the room while their leader wrapped his leg with cloth he tore from his shirt. A pack and a bedroll were all that appeared to be in the room.

"Turn it over! You don't leave a trap in a room that doesn't have some sort of treasure. Find something!" the man sitting in the middle of the floor commanded.

It took a while before they discovered a hidden compartment in the floor under the pack. It had not been obvious that the floor board had been pried away and replaced until they stepped on the plank. A little movement and the plank rising in one corner gave away the hiding place.

The two men knelt down near the corner to look at the floor board. One of the barbarians ran his finger around the edge of the plank and then looked at his companion. After a moment he took a deep breath, sighed, and used his fingernails to carefully slide the plank out of the floor. He looked down into the hole and then slipped his large, burly hand into the darkness. As his hand passed out of sight his fingers tripped a wire, causing three spikes to pierce his wrist, pinning his hand to the floor joist.

He screamed in pain and began tugging at his arm. Unable to free himself, his companion had to pull the spikes out of the wood before the man could raise his hand out of the hole with the spikes still piercing through his wrist. The injured man fell backwards, landing on his butt, and then slid himself towards the center of the room where their leader still lay.

The final thief knelt above the hole, stunned. Amanda's traps had been so well constructed that they had not been detected. She had deterred two of them from stealing from her. Only one remained fully capable of completing the task.

"Hurry! Someone may have heard the scream," the leader said.

With the two injured thieves encouraging him, the remaining man laid on the floor, trying to look deeper into the hole. He paused momentarily before running his fingers all the way around the very edge of the hole. He repeated the observation several times, each time lowering his large hand a little farther into the hole until he could feel the bottom of the floor joist. Taking a deep breath he slowly lowered his hand to reach beyond the joist into the hole.

The blade of the gemmed dagger shot forward, instantly severing part of his wrist. The pain overwhelmed him as the dying man pulled back his arm, his wrist dangling, half attached, and blood surging everywhere. His face turned pale-white with shock as his eyes circled once before the whites turned up and he toppled over, bleeding to death on the wood floor.

The other two watched as the man's body quivered a little before he took his last breath. When the horror of their companion's death finally passed, the remaining two men crawled to the hole together. They could see blood dripping from the blade that had been thrust forward by a heavy spring. Before feeling in the darkness for another trap, they probed it with their own dagger. When they did not find any more traps, the leader reached into the hole.

His arm was nearly elbow length into the hole when his fingers touched a smooth sack tucked back away from the opening. As he slowly pulled a satin bag out of the hole, the contents shifted. Using both hands, he set the bag on the floor and opened the top so that the two men could peer in. In the bottom of the bag were several large rocks that he dumped onto the floor.

"In the name of Loki," one of the thieves exclaimed, calling on the trickster god of Asgard.

✿　　✿　　✿　　✿　　✿

Earlier that night Amanda had followed her routine to observe the wall. She was tired and just wanted to sleep, but as she approached her door she saw the small needle that she had wedged between the door and the doorframe when she had left on the floor. Someone had opened her door. Listening at the door, Amanda could tell someone was still in the room.

I can't be discovered at this point. I don't want this to be bloody. Her thoughts were conflicted.

The cold, metallic sound of her sword clearing the scabbard seemed to fill the hallway outside her door. Slowly, quietly, she pushed the door inward. From the doorway she could see a dead body lying in the middle of the room. The gear and the supplies from her pack were scattered across the room. A burlap sack of food, which had leaned against the far wall, was tipped over, spilling some of the contents out onto the floor. In the far corner two men were staring at some rocks they had dumped on the floor.

Amanda leaped forward, slashing her sword downward on the neck of the first thief and then swinging around to come down on the last thief. It was over quickly, leaving all three men dead.

"Barbarians," Amanda said with disdain.

After wiping her sword on the back of one of the dead men, she stood up to sheathe her sword. Going immediately to the burlap sack, she toppled more food onto the floor and then she reached into the open sack with both hands to pull out the Horn of Valhalla.

As she raised the horn with both hands, admiring the gold and leather clad artifact, her door opened again. The innkeeper's wife, who had heard the screams, stood alone, trembling as she stared at the bodies on the floor. She raised a frail hand to her mouth. Her gasp sent chills down Amanda back.

I can't kill the old woman, Amanda thought.

First, she grabbed her pack to stuff the horn into and then the bearskin off the floor, then Amanda ran towards the window and leaped, crashing through the opaque glass. She landed on her feet and tumbled to avoid injury, rolling head first onto the back of her shoulder and back up onto her feet. Behind her the innkeeper's wife began screaming.

That will bring the soldiers, Amanda thought with a thief's sense of calm.

Amanda looked around for the darkest part of the alleyway. She faded into the night shadows as she began working her way towards the stable. She could hear men running through the snow all around her. Citizen-soldiers on every side were calling for reinforcements. At the alley wall Amanda reached for a grip and began climbing the uneven surface.

It was an easy climb that she made quickly. Swinging her legs up onto the thatched roof, she rolled back from the edge a moment to listen. There were more calls, more shouts, and many more footsteps running towards the inn. Careful not to stand above the ridge of the peaked roof, Amanda began moving in a crouched position, away from the alley. She jumped from roof top to roof top until she had distanced herself from the clamor around the inn.

When she was close to the stable where her horse was boarded, Amanda lowered herself down onto the street and began walking towards the livery, still dressed in her thieves' leathers. As she passed a tavern, two men stepped out into her path.

Before they realized she was there, Amanda kicked the closer man's knee, causing him to collapse, and then stepped past him to punch the other man three times, first in the chest and then twice in his side. She could hear the ribs snapping under his coat. As the man behind her scrambled to his feet, Amanda drove her heel into his face with a mule kick, propelling him back onto the snow.

Twisting her hip, Amanda spun around to face the man, who remained on his feet. With a small hop as she spun, snapping her leg across her body to plant the ball of her foot squarely on the man's jaw, the power of the strike flipping him so that he landed on his back.

As Amanda started running towards the stable she could hear the men behind her calling for soldiers. By the sound of it, the response was coming swiftly. As she approached the stable doors, five soldiers came around the corner.

Throwing her pack and bearskin towards the stable doors, Amanda leaped forward, landing between the five soldiers in a crouched position. Spinning around backward with one leg extended out straight, Amanda swept two of the five soldiers off their feet. As she hopped up, one of the men swung his sword overhead, intending to cleave her in half. Amanda stepped aside avoiding his sword, but was stuck by his large, round wooden shield when he thrust forward. She fell over backward, but rolled over to rest on her knees.

Amanda drew her sword and crimson dagger to face the three standing men. Behind them the other two were standing up as the street filled with soldiers. She stood up, gazing through the crowd of militia, contemplating her life. In her head she recalled Felicia's beautiful voice.

You shall go through great adversity, but the one you love will save you.

Amanda dropped her dagger. Taking her sword in her palms, she set the sword in the snow before her, stepped back, and dropped to her knees.

Several guards raced forward to grab her by her arms. They were not gentle, hitting Amanda several times before she was dragged to the center of the street, where she was forced to her knees again. Her face already bloody, Amanda knelt, looking up at a military officer who did not hesitate to backhand her.

"Lower your gaze, woman," he commanded.

"Here is her sword," a soldier said as he presented the weapon.

Taking the sword, the officer tested its balance and then examined the blade as he contemplated what to do with the woman in black leather. She had killed three men in an inn and assaulted several soldiers while trying to escape. He drew his sword arm back, preparing to sever Amanda's head from her neck.

"In the name of Odin!" one soldier exclaimed.

"The Horn of Valhalla!" another shouted.

Several soldiers standing near the stable looked at the horn in the man's hands. The large, beastly leader looked around the group and then down at Amanda.

The king wants her alive, he thought.

Without warning, he kicked Amanda in the chest hard enough to break the grasp of the men holding her, sending her toppling over backwards. Two more guards pulled Amanda off the ground by her arms, forcing her back onto her knees. The officer walked forward to face her.

"Who are you?" the officer demanded, pulling Amanda's head back by her ponytail to stare into her defiant eyes.

Amanda did not respond. Nor did she avert her eyes.

"You are the thief who stole the horn from King Randver," he commented.

"Sir," a soldier said as he handed the horn to the officer.

The officer looked at the horn and then back at Amanda before flipping his free hand to indicate for them to drag her away.

They dragged Amanda off to a large cell where they stripped her leather jacket off before chaining her wrists, neck, and waist to a large wooden platform. The chains were so short that Amanda could not sit up or raise her head. Her arms were stretched out to the side. She knelt, hunched over, unable to see anything or anyone around her. Amanda heard another man enter the room.

"Who are you?" the new man, the man with the deeper voice asked, but he did not wait for her answer.

Amanda feared that if she provided the name "Estrianna," the kingdom might trace her back to Captain Grogan, who had done nothing but given her passage. She certainly did not want to be traced back to Kadlin.

The leather whip cut through her leather vest, black shirt, and leather pants as if Amanda wore nothing at all. There were no more questions. When the whipping stopped, they punched her head and face, and when they tired of punching her, the whipping began again until Amanda could no longer feel the sting of the snapping leather.

"Jerrod," she whispered just before she passed out.

Blood oozed from her wounds. The cuts on her back were open as though a knife had cut her skin. The blood on her face mixed with the tears of pain that ran down her check as she remained chained and unconscious.

CHAPTER 5

CRUELTY OF MAN

From the night of their betrothal Jerrod and Rhonda slept together. Rhonda consistently limited their nightly love to kissing and cuddling. She was committed to her religious belief that a druid princess must be a virgin when she married and Jerrod was determined to honor her beliefs, but it was impossible for him not to want more. Each night they held each other, the warmth of their partially naked bodies pressing together was both calming and exciting, giving rise to an assortment of conflicting emotions, but they reverently adhered to the druid beliefs.

Like all young lovers, Jerrod and Rhonda had different visions of their relationship. For Rhonda, their relationship offered tranquility. She already envisioned ruling Lithlillia with Jerrod as her king. He was young, handsome, compassionate, and already a warrior proven in battle.

For Jerrod, the relationship was an emotional ecstasy that complemented his dream of fame and fortune. Each night he lay next to a beautiful and powerful half-Elven druid-princess. Her love was exciting. Her power intoxicating. It was not that he overlooked her kindness and compassion. It just was not asstirring .

Jerrod worked hard with the men as they broke camp to start the long, homeward journey. He noticed Rhonda's presence, but did not obsess over her, but she doted on him. When the morning meal was ready, she would bring him food and drink, lingering long enough to touch his forearm or play with the curly hair around his neck, none of which registered in Jerrod's mind. Once they

were on their way, Jerrod held Rhonda's hand or put his arms around her waist
as they walked, but that intimacy ended the moment they stopped to make camp.

✻   ✻   ✻   ✻   ✻

One night, Jerrod sat up suddenly, waking Rhonda in the process. An
expression of panic was on Jerrod's sweating face.

"What is it?" Rhonda asked as she pushed up onto her elbow, the long curls
of her hair gently falling over her shoulders.

"A dream. A bad dream!" he responded, rubbing both eyes with the heel of
his hands.

"What was it?" Rhonda repeated as she began to play with his silver hair
on the far side of his neck.

Jerrod looked at her as the warmth of her breast against the back of his
arm teased his senses. Even after sleeping half the night she was still beautiful.
Her eyes, which had changed to the color of warm, golden honey, gazed deeply
into his soul.

The druids' connection to life? he wondered.

Rhonda was an exquisite creature of nature, in touch with the natural forces
that bound everything together. She had told him that as their souls began to
intermix he would become part of her world.

"It's Amanda. She was... She's being tortured," he replied slowly, watching
for her reaction.

Rhonda sat up, pulling a bearskin over her shoulders in alarm. Her eyes
returned to their green color.

"Go on."

"She was being tortured. I dreamt she was chained down to the floor by her
wrists and neck. She had a leather strap around her neck. She couldn't sit up
straight. Her clothes were cut. Her back bleeding from where they whipped her.
Her mouth and nose bleeding from where they had repeatedly hit her."

"Who?" Rhonda asked, almost in a whisper, somehow knowing it was more
than a dream.

"The sons of Odin. She is in a city behind a great log wall somewhere to
the north."

"How do you know?" Rhonda asked, afraid of the answer.

"How do I know anything?" Jerrod answered in frustration. "I dreamt of this on the Steps of Terrace Xul, but I knew it was a dream. I knew it wasn't real. The next morning I had a premonition that Amanda would continue on without us. I know last night's premonition was not a dream, just like I knew Amanda's voyage was not a dream. It was as real as this is."

"You must go to her, my love," Rhonda responded, looking down. "You must save Amanda."

*　　*　　*　　*　　*

The bucket of cold water crashing across her back shocked Amanda into consciousness. Instinctively, she jumped from the shock, but the chains holding her down jarred her body when it pushed upward. All she could see was a pair of man's boots on the stone floor in front of her. She could not see the puzzlement on his face.

Out of Amanda's sight the man motioned for the chains holding her neck down to be removed. She heard the rattle of the chains first and then the heavy, metallic sound of iron hitting the floor, echoing through the room.

For the first time in days Amanda sat up straight. She had lost count of how long she had been chained and tortured. She tried stretching to relieve her aching body of some of its stiffness, but with the movement came searing pain from where the whip had cut her skin.

Amanda looked up. Before her stood a soldier with a square chin and broad shoulders. Unlike the other men of Haithenbeurn, he was clean shaven and wore a solid metal chest plate over his broad chest.

"Who are you?" the soldier asked.

When Amanda did not answer the man took her chin in his hand, gently lifting her head. He stared at her bruised, swollen face. The dried blood still soiled her cheeks, lips, and chin. The smell of feces and urine choked him, causing him to let go of Amanda and take five or six steps back, where he sat down on a three legged milking stool.

"So, I will ask you again. Who are you?" he asked softly.

"Estrianna. I am known as Estrianna," Amanda whispered. "

"You are the thief who stole the Horn of Valhalla?" the soldier said slowly.

"Yes," she whispered in a raspy voice.

"I am Lief Frothisen, of the House of Gounouf. The king, my uncle, has sent me to collect you," the soldier introduced himself.

For a moment Lief looked at the thief on the floor before him. Her black shirt, shredded by the jailer's whip, barely covered her shoulders and would have fallen off if not for the remnants of her leather vest. The dozen open wounds crossing her back still oozed blood. Her long, tangled hair, which was brown with dirt and blood, obscured much of her face and chest as her head hung slightly to the left, her eyes cast down to the floor.

You might be beautiful once you're cleaned up. Maybe worthy of being a wife. Pity really. You are bound for the wolves and I doubt you will be given a langsax, Lief thought.

"You will be returned to Theasendür where you will undoubtedly face the wolves," Lief said, before turning towards the door of Amanda's cell.

"When?" Amanda choked the question out in a whisper.

Leif stopped and turned to look at her.

"We will leave in the morning. It will be a two week ride back to Theasendür," Lief replied.

"Shackle her hands and feet and then clean her up. Give her a loin cloth but no shoes. I want her vulnerable to the cold. She will be less apt to run away," he barked at the closest guard.

"I want five men watching her. Always!" He paused. "She is not to be harmed! Let the king condemn a living corpse."

"Five, Lord Frothisen?" one of his men asked.

"She beat four of the king's guard and fought off a dozen soldiers here before surrendering. What do you think!"

✿   ✿   ✿   ✿   ✿

In the morning Amanda was loaded into a wagon with iron bars that went around three of the four sides with a solid roof overhead. Caged like a wild animal, her only protection from the weather was the wooden wall at the front of the wagon and a pile of bearskins, which she quickly slid under.

Two men drove the four horses pulling the wagon. Supplies were stored on the roof behind the drivers. Six guards rode in front of the wagon with a dozen following behind as they left Dalset. Lief rode near the wagon, but did not engage Estrianna in conversation. He stared forward as they departed, regal in the great helm adorned with two horns that curved down along his jaw line that covered the well-brushed red hair that rested on his shoulders.

Out of Dalset the wagon rolled. Each time the muleskinner snapped his whip over the heads of his team, Amanda flinched. Like a rabbit burrowed into the ground for warmth, she lay in the middle of the blankets until she called out for a crumb of bread or small cup of water. As soon as the wagon stopped in the evening she was all but drug out and pulled toward a tent where she was just as quickly chained to the center pole. And the next morning, everything would start as it had the day before.

Dawn and dusk came early in the winter days of the northern kingdom. Each day they rode until after dark, when they would stop to set up four tents in the deep snow. They set up a smaller tent for Lief's personal quarters and a larger tent for the soldiers. A third tent was Amanda's prison, where she was always guarded by three soldiers.

At night she was left sitting with her hands chained behind her back and around the center pole, whichwas not much more comfortable than the chains in Dalset had been. The ache in her shoulders from her arms being overly extended behind her back blended with the pain from being beaten in Dalset. There was little opportunity to adjust the way she sat. When Amanda slept she leaned against the pole, partially leaning to her side. The only time her hands were freed was during the evening and morning meals. Even then her sword hand remained chained to the pole and the shackles around her ankles were never unlocked.

One night, early in the second week, Amanda slipped the key for the shackles and chains off the soldier who brought her the evening meal. He had grown careless, which made it easy for her to lift the key from his belt.

Amanda worked quickly under the bearskin to unlock her wrists and then the shackles around her ankles. The complacent guards continued to talk, oblivious to her efforts. The closest man stood with his back to Amanda while the other two stood on either side of the entrance, leaning on their spears.

"A couple of days and we will be home," one man said.

"Good. I'm tired of the cold. I could do with some hot food in a warm room followed by a warm bed," another responded.

"It's more than that one will get," one of the guards commented as he gestured towards Amanda.

They all chuckled.

Amanda was halfway to them before the guards realized she was free. They were unable to react before she grabbed the closest man's shoulder, pulling down and back as she kicked the back of his knee.

Amanda jumped over the falling soldier, landing between the other two, her loin cloth flapping wildly as she continued her attack. Grabbing the *langsax* from the sheath of one guard, Amanda swung around. Turning her back momentarily on the man she had stolen the sword from, she slashed the blade across the upper thighs of the other standing guard. The slash caused his legs to give out and he fell to his knees.

As Amanda turned to face the guard from whom she had taken the sword, he thrust the tip of his spear at her. Amanda parried the spear outward and, as she swung the sword back around in a tight circle, she slashed down across the man's neck. The dying guard stumbled back, dropping the spear to grab at his own neck. Blood flowed through his fingers and down his arm and chest.

Behind her, the first guard she had attacked grabbed a spear and lunged at her back. Stepping aside as she spun to avoid the thrust, Amanda swung the *langsax* down on the wood staff, severing the metal tip. Swinging it up and across her body, Amanda slashed across the guard's chest, but the blade struck the ring-covered leather armor. The force of the blow knocked the guard off balance, causing him to topple over backwards as he tried to retreat.

The guard with wounds on his thighs rushed her with his sword over his head, but Amanda reacted instinctively. Lunging forward, she drove the tip of the sword she held towards the advancing soldier as she threw her empty hand backward. The sword penetrated deep into his throat just above the ringed armor, causing blood to begin pulsating out across the tent floor. The second guard fell dead. Behind her the last guard drew his sword.

"Alarm! Alarm!"

"For the sake of Ares," Amanda sighed.

They circled each other, trying to find that moment when an advantage presented itself. Amanda played with the man like a cat toying with a mouse. When she feigned vulnerability, the guard swung downward at her head, but Amanda parried and then stepped in to smash the back of her elbow into the bridge of his nose. As he stumbled back, Amanda twisted her body, swinging her sword in a downward arch and following through to swing the sharp blade of the *langsax* up into his groin. When he fell to his knees, Amanda took a big, outward swing. The blade easily separated his head from his shoulders.

A formidable weapon, Amanda thought as she looked down at the sword.

Amanda found her pack and pulled out the remaining clothes and fur boots she had bought in Ornholtz. She slipped them on as fast as she could and then grabbed the bearskin and the rest of her belongings. Using the crimson dagger to cut a hole in the back of the tent, she slipped into the winter night and began running towards the forest. Behind her she could hear the shouts as soldiers reponded to the guard's plea for help.

Amanda did not make it to the trees before one of the riders, using the pommel of his sword, knocked her unconscious as he charged past her. As she lay in the snow, more soldiers ran up to drag her back towards her tent. Amanda awoke with her wrists chained to the tent pole and Lief looking at her.

"Do that again and I will kill you myself," he warned.

She committed to memory how calm and cold-hearted Lief's reactions were. He had been decent to her in Dalset and during the trip, but there was no question in her mind that he would kill her without hesitation. Amanda resigned herself to the fact that Lief would deliver her to King Randver.

By the Fates. I hope you are right, Felicia. Where are you, Jerrod? Amanda thought.

*   *   *   *   *

After Jerrod's dream, Rhonda rose to go alone into the woods, where she once again sought to send message, this time to Farris, leader of the herd of winged horses. The message went from a hawk to a giant eagle and then on to the winged horses. It was Farris himself who answered the druid princess's call, arriving days later in their camp.

What can I do for you, young priestess? Farris asked after greeting her.

"My friend, Jerrod, my betrothed, must go north to rescue our friend. She is in great danger so we must act quickly," Rhonda explanation.

Betrothed? Congratulations. This is great news, Farris complimented her.

"It just happened. We have not announced it yet, but he wears my *esreandrea*," Rhonda responded.

And this friend your betrothed goes to rescue, is she one of the flatlanders you traveled to Terrace Xul with? Farris asked.

"Yes. She is the one who saved my life in Cipper. My mother declared her a Friend of Lithlillia," Rhonda responded.

I will carry Jerrod north to find your friend, Farris agreed.

Jerrod went to say goodbye to Rhonda before they departed. After Jerrod kissed her goodbye, Rhonda laid her head on his chest, gently holding his hips.

She could not feel Jerrod's body warmth or hear his heart beat through the layers of robes, armor, and clothes, but his arms round her felt soothing.

Rhonda feared his confrontation with the Sons of Odin, but she feared him being with Amanda even more. Rhonda understood better than Jerrod that Amanda was his first love.

"Come back to me quickly," she begged softly.

✻   ✻   ✻   ✻   ✻

Nearly two weeks after his dream-premonition, Jerrod mounted Farris to fly north. The weather was miserable. The snow was bitter cold. Jerrod found the chill from the wind as they flew north nearly unbearable, even when he was wearing a riding robe covered by a bearskin, the metal armor grew cold, chilling his body. He could not see where they were flying and tucked his head down close to Farris's neck, pulling the hood of his riding cloak down over his face. After a long day's flying they landed in the woods east of Dalset.

The wall from my dreams, Jerrod pondered for a moment.

Landing in the city would cause too much commotion. I will have to walk in, Jerrod thought.

As if Farris understood Jerrod's thoughts, the winged steed landed in the forest east of Dalset. The walk was short and nobody was looking for a traveler in the dark of the winter night. Inside the taverns the men were still talking about the apprehension of the thief who stole the Horn of Valhalla. Jerrod listened while he ordered hot food and drink. The gossip was about a strangely dressed, blonde thief who had stolen the king's prized possession and had been apprehended nearby. With a small ruby Jerrod bought ale for everyone, encouraging the drunken gossip about the strange female thief to continue.

"She must have killed a dozen people," one soldier claimed over his ale.

"But she was no match for our men," another bragged.

"But who are you?" someone challenged Jerrod.

"Just a traveler. I didn't arrive until today and I have been hearing all these stories of a woman being apprehended and deadly battles. What is this about?" Jerrod answered coyly.

With unlimited ale, the men in the tavern told him many stories of their heroism. Jerrod learned that the Horn of Valhalla belonged to the King of Haithenbeurn. It was a legendary artifact believed to have the power to summon the dead heroes who resided in Valhalla, the hall of heroes. Once the horn was blown, the fallen heroes would come to fight for the person who possessed it. Everyone described Amanda perfectly. Her height and busty shape, even her black leather armor, was described without question, but from there, the stories varied.

They had left Torrence together to find a treasure that would have made her rich for life. She did not need anything more, particularly a king's horn from a distant kingdom. The one remaining detail he was able to discern from all the stories was that Amanda had been taken under guard to Theasendür by wagon.

What was it she said at Terrace Xul? I can't go with you because I have a promise to keep, he remembered. He shook his head as if trying to clear the thought. *She had a promise to keep that involved Theasendür?*

When it seemed appropriate, Jerrod left the tavern and returned to Farris. There was no one to notice him walking out of the city in the early morning darkness as the snow began to fall again.

"They have taken Amanda north to a city called Theasendür. It is far to the north, on the coast. I don't know if you can understand me, but we need to fly there as quickly as possible," Jerrod told the leader of the flying horses.

Farris neighed, shaking his head as though he agreed.

As he stood with Farris, Jerrod began feeling a strange sensation. Not like the sensation of heat he had felt when he healed Imelrinn. This was more of a tingling throughout his body, like he had felt when he woke from dreaming about Amanda's torture. It was as if his entire body was aware of his surroundings.

Is it my imagination or did you just say something? Did I really hear you say 'Yes, I understand? Jerrod thought, looking at the winged steed.

"We will have to hurry, Farris. But it is too cold to fly right now and we both need some rest before we continue," Jerrod said aloud. "We leave at first light."

There was little protection from the storm in the forest. Jerrod gathered what he could to start a fire. He found small dead branches, twigs, and some bark and tried to use his flint and steel to ignite the wet kindling, but nothing would catch flame. Jerrod grew colder as he struggled to create even a little smoke that might indicate a fire was trying to start, but nothing. His hands were numb. His mind was beginning to shut down as it became harder to formulate thoughts. He quit striking the flint and steel, and pulled himself into a ball to try and stay warm.

This time he knew a sensation was coming before he felt it. As he looked at the unlit pile of kindling, a niggling of warmth started to pass through his ears and nose, and then in his fingers. The sensation quickly spread up his arms and legs. As the sensation washed over his body, the kindling in front of him flashed into open flame, burning with the intensity of a tiny bonfire.

I don't know what caused it, but thank Hephaestus for the fire. Jerrod thought of the Olympian god.

You'll be warmer now.

"What? Who's there?" Jerrod said, looking around, finally resting his eyes on Farris.

After putting more wood on the fire, Jerrod sat back on a stump to watch it grow. He found he was already warm, too warm. He slipped the bearskin off his shoulders and put it on the snow to lie on and then he took off his riding robe to pull over himself like a blanket.

The woods around the fire seemed to glow. The falling snow melted in midair, never making it to the ground. Jerrod lay on his bearskin, pulling his robe up to his chin, and slept. It was a restless sleep full of dreams of Amanda being hauled north in an open wagon, shivering under a pile of bearskins. She was scared and felt alone.

After the sun was up, Jerrod mounted Farris to fly northward along the locally Ragnaugh Mountains. By dusk they could see the Nasdrawuen coast in the distance. They turned westward into an extraordinary orange sunset, highlighted with reds and painted against a cold, medium-blue sky. Pure white clouds with pink linings broke the splendor with a brilliant contrast of beauty that even Jerrod appreciated. Far below them further to the west lay the log city of Theasendür, the king's city, and Amanda's doom.

As they descended, the world below reminded Jerrod of the view from the terrace before the Lost Kingdom of Terrace Xul. The world had seemed so small as he stood on the terrace, looking at the fjord far below the mountain lair.

It was cold then too, he thought.

From the clouds Theasendür looked like a toy town made of wood blocks, with pinpoint spots of little lights where lamps lit doorways and windows. Jerrod could not see the people yet, but there were two large compounds. One of the compounds had a large hall-like structure that reminded Jerrod of the great Pavilion in Lithlillia.

His thoughts went first to Lady Lieisa, the druid-priestess and queen of Lithlillia, and then to Rhonda before returning to Amanda. The tingling sensation did not surprise Jerrod this time. He felt it starting as his mind went from Rhonda to Amanda. His senses came alive, as if he were reaching out for Amanda. Jerrod could feel her panic. He knew she was safe, but somehow he sensed that her safety was coming to an end.

Farris landed east of the city, avoiding again any unwanted commotion. In a rush to find Amanda, Jerrod turned towards the city before thanking Farris. Realizing what he had done, Jerrod stopped and turned back towards the winged horse.

"Thank you, my friend. You don't need to wait. I'm not sure how long this will take or how it will end. Thank you for bringing me this far," Jerrod said aloud.

There was no doubt in Jerrod's mind that Farris understood him.

It must be my time with Rhonda, he thought, realizing he was much more aware of animal thoughts than he had ever been before.

☆ ☆ ☆ ☆ ☆

The last days in the wagon had been bitter cold. Lief had allowed her to put on the Theasendür clothes before he entered the city, but Amanda shivered under the bearskins. The temperature of the northern coast combined with the cold of the pending storm made it unbearable.

The sight of Theasendür brought conflicting feelings. The ominous view offered her momentary warmth, thinking of escaping the storm, but a feeling of emptiness at the thought of being brought before the king and that meant her death.

Where are you, Jerrod? The thought kept throbbing in her mind, pounding like a drum as her anxiety began to give way to panic.

Word of her capture had been passed by witches' messages, reaching the king's city weeks earlier. And word of her pending arrival, passed by word of mouth, caused the citizens to gather in the streets just to catch a glimpse of Lief Frothisen, destined to rule the House of Gounouf, and the woman who had stolen the Horn of Valhalla.

When the wagon rolled into a stable, Amanda's wrists were unshackled long enough for her to put on a hooded robe. After the guards shackled her wrists again they pulled the hood up over her head, covering her tangled hair and much of her face. As they began to walk to the king's lodge, Amanda held her head up, refusing to subordinate her pride to her captors.

Eight guardsmen surrounded her as they walked through the crowded, snow-covered streets towards the lodge. Amanda tried to observe the streets out of the corner of her eyes, but the hood limited her sight too effectively. When they reached the king's hall, the soldiers had to push through the mob that blocked the great doors. Lief led the column as they marched Amanda through the crowd.

When the column stopped they were standing inside before King Randver. To either side were warriors from the Houses of Haithenbeurn. In the back, women and older children pushed in to see the strange female thief sentenced to her death.

The king leaned forward from his throne, in anticipation of Estrianna's arrival. His fingers tapped on his axe, which leaned against the side of his throne. Lief stepped up to address his uncle.

"Sire, this is the thief, Estrianna," he stated as he gestured towards Amanda.

From behind, one of the guardsmen stepped forward to roughly pull the hood from Amanda's head, revealing her dirty blonde hair and swollen face. The crowd gasped.

"What shall I do with you?" Randver asked rhetorically as he rose to look at Amanda.

"You're not worthy of the pit. Your death should be slow. More painful than being eaten by hungry wolves, but I have no time to waste on you."

"And the Horn?" he asked as he turned away from Amanda.

Lief handed his uncle the Horn of Valhalla. Taking the horn in a massive hand, the king turned back to Amanda.

"Who do you think you are, stealing what is mine?" the king demanded angrily.

Amanda looked at him in defiance, her chin up, resigned to what would surely come. Somehow she had found inner peace, but her calmness angered the king further. He drew his hand up and backhanded her, knocking Amanda to the floor.

Amanda sat up on her side immediately, leaning on her shackled hands and then pushing up onto her knees. Blood began to run down her nose to her lips, causing Amanda to smile.

I've won, she thought.

"Who is this bitch?" the king shouted at Lief.

"We know nothing about her, Sire. She was caught in Dalset. We believe she was trying to escape to the south," Lief responded.

"Who are you?" the king demanded again.

"No one," Amanda's voice was strong and confident.

"We'll see. Cut her right hand off. Maybe she will answer then," the king commanded.

Amanda turned to look at the approaching guard, who was drawing his sword. Two soldiers held her tightly by her upper arms. She tried to stand, but they pressed her towards the floor, their size was too much to overcome as she knelt, shackled and held tight on either side. Amanda tried rolling forward, attempting to cause the guards to lose their balance, but she could not gain the leverage against the two of them.

Seeing Amanda struggle to get free, three more guards were on her immediately, knocking her to the floor on her stomach and pinning her down. As four of them held her down, the fifth unlocked the chains around her wrists and pulled her arms out in front of her.

"Take them both off!" the king commanded, angered by her consistent defiance.

Amanda closed her eyes as the guard with the sword began to swing the heavy blade down towards her wrists.

"Jerrod," she whispered.

It was as if he drew power from some inner place, anger boiling up out of his soul with fury. He could feel the heat, the rage, as the power intensified. He was ready to destroy whoever stood in his path.

From the midst of the crowd a robed figure jumped forward, drawing the Sword of Trisdale as he bounded towards Amanda. Jerrod's attention focused on the guard swinging his *langsax* towards her wrists. The ends of his frowning eyebrows dipped down hard against the bridge of his nose. His eyes burned crystal clear as Jerrod pushed his empty hand towards the object of his focus.

In that instant the guard's body ripped in half at the waist, casting blood around the room. Jerrod stood between the king and crowd with his hood back and robe open, as menacing as any warrior or wizard.

Everyone stood, stunned by the instantaneous attack. Even Jerrod was caught by surprise, unaware he possessed such power. Before anyone else could react, Jerrod stepped towards Amanda, causing the guards to roll away. He bent down and pulled Amanda up into his arms. They stood together, Amanda tucked safely under Jerrod's arm as he rested the tip of his sword on the wooden floor. The nearby guards that had held Amanda down stumbled to their feet.

"Who she is does not matter," Jerrod said calmly as he turned to face the king, his eyes still glowing.

Jerrod looked around the room. The barbarian warriors of the north, from the six Houses of Haithenbeurn, stepped away from his gaze. He looked back to the king. "She is with me and that's enough."

"And who are you?" The king glared at Jerrod.

"I am Jerrod of Winfred," he answered.

"Jerrod of Winfred?" the king mimicked, trying to comprehend the situation. "Jerrod? What does that mean? Who do you think you are and what do you have to do with this thief?"

"The only thing that matters is that I am here to barter for her freedom."

The king looked at the young man before him, and then at the guard's body that had been torn in half in front of him. The crowd, sensing danger, began to push towards the lodge doors as rapidly as possible. The soldiers standing around the hall began circling as far from Jerrod as they could without appearing weak. They waited for the king to give the word, knowing that when the word came they would have to attack a man who was more dangerous than any they had encountered before.

"She will die for stealing my horn," the king said coldly.

Jerrod's thoughts reached for that place where the fury had been before. Amanda could sense the power growing inside Jerrod as she stood next to him. At first it was like the vibrating twinge of a large muscle, but then his whole body felt like it was vibrating. She could not see anything, but she felt the sensation anywhere their bodies touched. As Jerrod's anger intensified, the wooden floor and walls of the lodge started to tremble. The room became warmer. Within seconds the walls burst into flame.

Several soldiers rushed forward. Jerrod let go of Amanda and stepped forward, swinging his sword with sweeping slashes. As the blade cut through the armor and flesh of the closest soldier, silvery white light flashed through the burning room.

With great clarity, Jerrod saw the soldier disintegrate as the sword passed effortlessly through his chest. Time seemed to freeze as he looked calmly around the room. The other soldiers stood like statues, reaching out with their empty hands, trying to find what was around them. The king stood in the lodge, spinning slowly, uncertain what was around him. Even Amanda stood helplessly blind.

"Come on," Jerrod said, pulling Amanda towards the door.

"Wait!" Amanda pulled back. "We cannot leave without the horn!"

Jerrod was puzzled, but gave in without question.

"Wait here," Jerrod instructed.

He walked up to the king and grabbed him by the forearm to lead him forcefully back to his throne.

"Your throne is here. The blindness is temporary, but you must leave your hall or you will burn," Jerrod leaned forward to whisper into the king's ear.

Jerrod yanked the horn from the king's hands and turned to walk away. When he reached Amanda, he stopped and turned back to address the king.

"If you pursue us I will not be as merciful."

Jerrod returned to Amanda and began to lead her to the door, but she resisted again.

"My pack!" she said. "We must have my pack."

"Where is it?" Jerrod said, remembering how much he loved her as he looked at her amidst the chaos.

"I don't know. I think one of the guards was carrying it when they led me into the lodge."

Jerrod looked around to find her pack lying on the floor near the corner of the room. He led her over to the pack and picked it up.

"I have it. Can we go now?" Jerrod asked softly.

Amanda nodded yes.

Outside, the snow covered streets were nearly as chaotic as inside the burning hall. Citizens and soldiers ran through the streets, some escaping the fire while others were bringing buckets of water to fight it. Finding their way through the chaos, Jerrod and Amanda slipped into an alleyway and began working their way east.

"Where are we going?" Amanda asked.

"Towards the mountains east of here," Jerrod answered.

As they scurried through the streets and alleyways, Amanda's eyesight began to return.

"We can't escape by horseback," Amanda thought out loud.

They stopped to look at each other and then up and down the alley. Jerrod had not thought beyond the rescue and escaping was turning out to be a different matter. They were in a quieter part of the city, but both knew it would only be a matter of time before they were found. Shouts could be heard from soldiers in the distance.

"Give me my pack," Amanda insisted with a sense of urgency in her voice.

Jerrod looked at her, confusion painted across his face.

"Give me my pack!" she repeated.

Jerrod slipped the pack from his shoulder and handed it to her.

"And the horn," Amanda spoke quickly.

When Jerrod complied, Amanda squatted to set the pack and the horn on the snow. She pulled the top open and started rifling through the contents. Her hand found the box that Lady Lieisa had given her. After stuffing the horn and everything else back into the pack, Amanda opened the box and withdrew the long, thin golden whistle inside.

She put the whistle to her lips and blew, but they did not hear a sound. Amanda paused a moment and then looked at Jerrod.

"What is it?" Jerrod asked as he looked frantically about.

"Lady Lieisa said this would call the Friends of Lithlillia whenever I am in peril," Amanda answered, looking back down at the whistle.

The long, thin tube was pinched at one end with a cut across the length of the tube. The other end was open. Amanda put the pinched end to her bruised lips and blew it a second time, but no "friends" appeared out of the shadows to come to their aid.

"How's it work?" Jerrod asked after a moment.

"It's a whistle," Amanda glared at him.

"I know it's a whistle. When is it supposed to work?" Jerrod responded in a higher tone, the adrenaline coursing through his body.

The sounds of men shouting and running through the streets were getting closer.

They stood looking at each other when Farris landed at the end of the alley. Running to reach Farris, Amanda and Jerrod jumped on the winged horse's back. The stallion bolted into a gallop before jumping into the frigid night air. He flew straight down the alleyway as he slowly ascended before turning over the rooftops.

Carrying two riders was harder for Farris. He lifted them laboriously into the air to climb slowly away from Theasendür. The stars glistened in the dark night. The large moon was almost new, offering little light, and the smaller moon was not quite half. Their view of the mountains and snowy fields far below was shades of colors, shapes without details. In no time the frigid night air chilled them to the point that they could no longer endure the flight.

Amanda pulled herself into Jerrod's back, not just for the warmth they both desperately needed, but trying to consume the love she felt for him. She knew this, her gallant knight who carried her away to safety on a flying steed, was her life.

CHAPTER 6
LOVE'S ENTRAPMENT

The only thing protecting them during the frigid flight was their cloaks. Under his cloak, Jerrod's chain mail began growing as cold as it had in the icy snow on Mount Thoradan. He was so chilled that his body had begun shivering and Amanda's cloak was not even suitable for riding a horse on a winter night, let alone flying through the sky. Wrapping her arms around Jerrod as much to keep warm as to avoid sliding off Farris's back, Amanda held on with all the strength she had left, but burying her head into his back failed to keep her warm.

Less than halfway through the night, Farris, sensing his riders were in desperate need of protection, decided to land and seek shelter. As he descended, he found a break in the forest canopy where he could land, hoping the trees might offer a wind break. Once on the ground, it became apparent how numb Jerrod and Amanda had become.

Jerrod was barely able to collect the wood necessary for a fire while Amanda fumbled through her pack, searching for her flint and steel. Her limbs were so numb she could hardly move, let alone manage to hold the flint with her fingers.

"We are going to die if I don't get this started," Amanda said as she frantically tried striking the flint against the steel again and again.

"No, we're not. Sit back," Jerrod whispered as he summoned his inner strength and emotions.

Taking a thick branch in his hand, he stared at the wood without desperation. He had done this before. He was familiar with the power. The tingling started in his chest. Spreading rapidly, it passed through his body before the branch burst into flames. After dropping the burning limb onto the kindling pile, Jerrod turned to see the stunned look on Amanda's face.

"I don't know why," Jerrod answered the unasked question. "The first time I created fire was on my way to find you. The biggest fire was when the lodge erupted into flames. I just concentrate and things burn."

"Is there anything else?" Amanda asked, looking at him. *Where is the innocent boy I love?*

The look on Amanda's face as she contemplated Jerrod's power seemed fearful. While feeding the fire with wood, Jerrod told her of the fire in the treasure room of Terrace Xul and how he had healed Imelrinn in Agganon. He also told her of the winter solstice, but he stopped there. Looking into her chilling blue eyes, he could not bear telling her about Rhonda.

"Now, let's see your wounds," Jerrod said compassionately.

Amanda slipped her clothes from her back. Jerrod stood a moment, stunned by the wounds caused by the whip, which marred her back like a tighty woven fishnet.

The pain must be tremendous, Jerrod thought. His heart felt like it was being crushed by some Fendür's fist.

Even with those deep cuts and oozing blood, she's beautiful, Jerrod thought.

Amanda's long blonde hair covered her bare chest. Her captivating blue eyes were turned down as she gazed at the grass exposed from under the melted snow, lost in the twilight of her memories. When Jerrod stepped slowly towards her to kneel down, Amanda looked up.

"Trust me," he said softly as he put one hand on top of her nearest shoulder and the other gently on her wounds.

"I do, with my life," Amanda answered softly.

Amanda felt warmth as her wounds slowly diminished. Jerrod kept his head down and his eyes closed as he concentrated. When she felt healed, she turned to him just as he was looking up. She smiled, holding back the urge to kiss him.

Before they slept, Jerrod removed his chain mail, tucked it into as tight a roll as possible, and placed it in Amanda's pack. Amanda saw the amulet Jerrod had found on the skeleton knight still hung around his neck. Jerrod paused a moment and then, removing the amulet from his neck, he slipped it gently over Amanda's head.

"Perhaps this will bring you luck," Jerrod whispered.

"It's beautiful. What is it?" she asked.

"I found it with the sword. When we entered Trisdale Keep it grew warm, but I have no idea what it is," he answered, revealing more truth than he would have to anyone else.

When they were ready to sleep, they curled up next to a large tree root protruding from the base of the trunk, instinctively seeking protection from a wind that would not come. With the fire close in front of them, they slept warmly wrapped in each other's arms, protected by the force that had started the fire, melted the snow, and blocked the wind through the night.

In the morning they woke sore and hungry. There was nothing left in Amanda's pack to eat and Jerrod had not brought any supplies. After eating a little snow to moisten their mouths, they mounted Farris again to continue their southerly journey. From Farris' back high above the frozen landscape they could see the Wall of Haithenbeurn running as far as they could see to the west and disappearing into the forest to the east. The gates of Dalset remained close.

They lost track of time as Farris fought the wind. When Farris turned eastward towards the Alfarakenloria, Jerrod did not know what to expect, but he sensed Farris was taking them to safety. As they began to descend, Jerrod was not sure if he really saw the ice-colored dome rising out of the forest, but it became more real as Farris continued to fly directly towards the unnatural shape. Jerrod and Amanda began to panic that they were going to collide with the dome, but the winged horse passed through the frozen mist without a problem. Inside the dome the air was as warm as a spring day.

Druids? Jerrod wondered.

A brook, bordered by lush grass, ran between the green trees while deer and smaller animals grazed without a care and songbirds chirped their tunes. As Farris's hooves planted in the soft meadow soil, a solitary Elve dressed in white robes with silver embroidery stepped out from the deciduous forest.

"Greetings," the Elve said as he nodded towards Farris.

"I am Olendorn. Welcome to Asenthia."

How do you come to bring non-Elves to our kingdom, Farris? Olendorn thought to the leader of the winged horse herd.

They are friends of Lithlillia and the saviors of Princess Rhonda.

"Excuse us if we are intruding," Jerrod said aloud, greeting Olendorn.

Olendorn stared at Jerrod a moment before stepping forward to shake his hand, grasping the young man at the elbows with one hand while laying the other over his forearm in Elven fashion. Olendorn's eyes turned to rest on Amanda.

Is she unwell? Olendorn asked Farris.

She was a guest of Haithenbeurn, but Jerrod healed her in the forest, Farris explained.

"Come. You can rest and refresh yourselves in my father's home," Olendorn welcomed them.

"What is this place?" Amanda asked.

"We are the Elves of Asenthia," Olendorn answered.

"And you are the prince?" Jerrod asked.

"Of all of Alfarakenloria that is not Dwarvish," Olendorn said over his shoulder as he began to lead them away.

"Dwarves?" Amanda asked, but Olendorn igorned the question.

It was a short, uphill walk through the pleasant forest. Jerrod put his arm around Amanda's waist, helping her as she stumbled along, trying to keep up with Olendorn while Farris remained in the meadow. The close embrace was comforting, causing Jerrod to reflect on the days in Torrence that now seemed so long ago. He felt Amanda pressing against him, melting into his side as though they were momentarily one being, Amanda drawing more strength from Jerrod's aura.

In the brook along their path, large boulders created rapids and tiered pools of water behind stone dams. Small waterfalls as tall as a man spilled over the dams to race downstream. Tree limbs shaded the brook and pools, and offered perches to colorful songbirds. The rhythmic sound of the water lulled them towards sleepiness.

Jerrod and Amanda could see the splendor of the Elven village through the forest as they approached. The buildings were made from wood with high-peaked, green roofs and great windows overlooking the valley. Fireplaces made from rounded river rock rose along the sides of the buildings. Trees grew between the buildings, creating more privacy and a sense of serenity. Here and there stepping stones created winding paths through the spacious community. Unlike Lithlillia, all the homes were built above ground on flat-stone foundations.

The few Elves they passed were going about their daily chores, seemingly oblivious to Jerrod's and Amanda's presence. The lack of children playing among the trees was unsettling, but the soft, lingering sound of Elven harps and light, crisp, metallic flutes eased their souls. Time seemed to pass without notice in the tranquil forest.

"Olendorn, what race of Elves are you?" Jerrod asked as they walked.

"Our ancestors were Mountain Wood Elves, but we came to live in this forest long ago," the prince answered without looking back.

"Aren't there any Forest Elves?"

"There are some in the Alfarakenloria Valley. The Pavilion is just up ahead."

When they approached the Pavilion, surrounded by trees, Jerrod and Amanda could not tell whether it was in the middle of the village or on the edge. The Pavilion was built very much like the Pavilion of Lithlillia, with a long, oval roof that was rounded at each end and a ridge down the middle of the roof. Like in Lithlillia, smoke rose through the roof in three spots and two large doors at the narrow end of the building welcomed their arrival.

Inside the large room was quiet except for the faintest sound of distant music. The Elves sitting on the tiered seats around the long, oval fire pit had serious looks on their faces as they spoke quietly among themselves, but they stopped their whispering when Amanda and Jerrod entered. At the far end of thePavilion an Elven man and woman sat on the dais.

Olendorn led them down the stairs and around the pit to stand before the dias where his parents sat. The Lord and Lady wore elegant Elven robes of white and silver. A single silver band of soft metal encircled their heads.

"Mezanarani na Fazanarani, quan naprani alip Lithlillia islanorn halistar," Olendorn addressed his parents.

Olendorn's father answered with a quiet tone, using the ancient tongue of the Mountain Wood Elves, notglancing once at Jerrod or Amanda. Olendorn turned to look at the two needy travelers, and then turned back to his father.

"Farris brought them here for sanctuary," Oldendorn answered.

The king barely said a word, ending the short conversation with a flip of his wrist that was obviously meant as a dismissal. His gesture was rude, even without understanding what had been said. Olendorn turned towards them again, spreading his arms, ushering them out of thePavilion as though her were herding unwanted animals.

Without a word, the Prince of Asenthia led them directly to a magnificent cottage near a tall waterfall, where the water from the mountain fell hundreds of feet into a nearby lake, from which a brook rushed down over cascading boulders. The cottage had wood steps up to a front porch. There was a large door, beautiful windows of clear and colored glass, and silver and glass lanterns hanging from the ceiling of the porch.

Olendorn did not wait at the door, but went straight inside to a sitting room with a stone fireplace that was so large that Jerrod could have stood inside it. Two padded leather chairs were placed near the fireplace and a bearskin rug rested on the wooden floor between the chairs and the fireplace. Near the window was a round table with a pitcher of Elven wine and a wooden tray of bread and cheese resting in the middle of it. A hallway led back to two bedrooms.

"Please make yourselves welcome," Olendorn offered quietly.

"I need to clean up and see if I can find anything to wear," Amanda stated.

"I will return later," Oldendor said, dismissing himself.

"Thank you," Jerrod and Amanda responded.

Jerrod poured himself a goblet of wine and then went to sit by the fire while Amanda went off to bathe. He took a knit blanket folded over the back of the chair and spread it on his lap as he sat down. After sipping some wine, he placed his goblet on the floor next to him and stretched out to watch the fire.

I wonder what Rhonda is doing? What do I do with Amanda? By Aphrodite, even at her worst she's the most beautiful woman I've seen, Jerrod thought.

Amanda followed the hallway back to the bedroom. It was large room with a brass tub almost large enough to lie in. Two Elven women dressed in green robes with colorful embroidery were pouring hot water into the tub as she entered. Next to the tub were a bowl of rose petals and a jar of lavender crystals.

"We will return later with fresh clothes," one of the women said as they departed.

Amanda could barely move as she struggled to strip off her shredded clothes. She felt the warm water as she stepped into the tub and lowered herself carefully to lie down in the bathwater. Very slowly the warmth began to overcome her cold bones and wash away the numbness. She added some lavender crystals to the water as she soaked. The aroma of the lavender was relaxing.

This is nearly as soothing as the hot pools in the Black Forest. Those were more pleasant days. I've never been this cold before. And the beatings!

Sitting alone, naked in the hot bath, Amanda wept for the first time since her torture.

✻   ✻   ✻   ✻   ✻

Amanda did not know how long she wept nor how long after that she rested, but the water was becoming uncomfortably cool when one of the Elven women returned with folded clothing.

"Here are some clothes for you. We will take your other clothes and wash what is not ruined. Dinner will be served soon in the Pavilion. You're invited to attend."

"Thank you," Amanda answered softly.

When she emerged from her room, Amanda found Jerrod asleep in the chair.

"Hey." She nudged him. "They're pouring fresh water for your bath. I'm afraid you will have to hurry, the evening meal is not far away," she said, leaning forward to whisper lovingly in his ear.

"You're beautiful," Jerrod blurted as he woke.

"They're Elven clothes," she responded.

With a coy smile, she spun slowly, making the bottom of the sheer dress lift a little.

"Aren't they wonderful? The Elves brought them. There're clean clothes for you, too. Now hurry. We are invited to dine with them tonight." Amanda smiled.

Even though the warm water soothed his soreness, Jerrod did not linger. After cleansing and drying off, he quickly put on the dark pants and a silvery shirt left for him. The clothes were soft and very comfortable. There were also cloth shoes that slipped comfortably onto his feet.

"Not too bad yourself," Amanda teased him when he came out.

When the herald came, Amanda and Jerrod followed him back through the forest to the Pavilion and, like earlier in the day, they only saw a few Elves along the way, but the enchanting music still drifted through the air as if the entire forest was celebrating. The music, composed of deep, full-bodied harps and whimsical flutes, was lighthearted, nearly as refreshing as the bard's magical music.

As they walked, Jerrod noticed Amanda's dress shimmering in the evening light. The dress did not fit tightly against her busty, athletic body, but that only excited him more as he could not help but imagine her figure under the silvery cloth. Captivated by her beauty, Jerrod did not notice their surroundings until they stood before the Pavilion.

Entering through the wide doors they were greeted by Olendorn. Sitting with Olendorn at the bottom of the stairs nearest the door, far across the long fire pit from the Lord and Lady of Asenthia, they began to eat. The Elven fruits, cheese, and wine were intoxicating. Olendorn did not speak to them as they ate, but spent most of his time watching his parents. Not even the women serving the food and wine spoke to them. When they were done, the herald came immediately to usher them back to their cottage.

Jerrod and Amanda did not speak until the herald left them on the porch of the cottage.

"I think they resent our being here," Amanda said.

"They weren't very welcoming, were they? Did anyone say anything to you? They aren't like the Elves of Lithlillia," Jerrod responded.

Amanda immediately thought of Rhonda. Her expression went blank. Her eyes, which had seemed uncommonly warm, like the warmth of a blue sky, turned cold, like light blue ice, at the mention of Lithlillia.

"Good night," Amanda said, turning and walking away.

Jerrod watched the swing of her hips as she walked into the cottage. Amanda's reaction shocked Jerrod. Slowly, he followed her into the cottage. As he walked by her door, he paused to look at the latch.

What was that all about? he thought before continuing to his room.

Jerrod was nearly asleep when his door opened. Amanda was dressed in a sheer Elven sleeping gown that left very little to his imagination. She walked to the edge of his bed, where she stood for a moment, looking at him without saying a word.

"What is it?" Jerrod whispered as he pushed up onto his elbows to partially sit up.

Slipping her gown from her shoulders, she allowed it to fall to the floor, revealing her naked body. Her long blonde hair swayed slightly as she lifted the blankets and slid into bed next to him.

"I have to tell you..." Jerrod started to say.

"Sh sh sh sh," Amanda hushed him as she took his face in both her hands to kiss his lips.

Jerrod rolled onto his side and looked into her sparkling blue eyes. She was beautiful. Jerrod felt the warmth of her body against his body. The touch of the inside of her leg as she slid it over him and the pressure of her breast against his chest was unbearably pleasurable, but Jerrod pushed back gently.

"But I have to tell you..." Jerrod started again.

"It can wait until morning. I love you, Jerrod."

Amanda leaned into him to kiss his ear while she reached around his body and pulled him closer. Her arms tightened. Then she kissed him deeply, passionately.

"I love you," Amanda repeated.

✻   ✻   ✻   ✻   ✻

As she lay in bed trying to go to sleep, Felicia felt the magical pull of her crystal. An irrepressible urge to gaze into the globe overcame her. She got out of bed and slipped on her thin muslin robe to go into her front room.

"Come, Sasha. Let's see what's calling me," she said to the black cat that had been sleeping at her side.

As the cat rolled over to ignore her, it changed into a large black panther that spread its body out across the empty bed. Felicia shook her head and left the bedroom to go to the fireplace, where she swung the teapot on its hook over the fire. Then Felicia sat down on the floor pillows in front of her low table, where a crystal globe on a golden stand and a tall, thin candle rested.

Felicia lit the tan candle to help her meditate. As dark brown smoke began to rise from the candle, a white mist formed inside the crystal. Blurred images formed in the mist, but as she concentrated, the images came into focus. There, together in bed in the eastern Elven kingdom of Asenthia, were Jerrod and Amanda.

Felicia leaned back against a pillow as the panther came into the room, changing back into a black cat as she walked towards the queen of witches. Sasha curled up in Felicia's lap so Felicia would gently scratch her head just in front of the ears. Sasha began to purr as she rolled over on her back to allow the witch to pet her stomach. Felicia looked down at the cat.

"Well Sasha, what do you think the druid princess will think of this?" she whispered rhetorically.

Scratch me.

Felicia smiled and surrender to the feline's request.

✻   ✻   ✻   ✻   ✻

Rhonda watched Farris fly away, thinking of her love and what might come of his journey. She had sent him to rescue their friend from an apparently violent and angry king. It was a trip for experienced wizards and warriors, far more than a boy.

Jerrod has become so much more than the naïve dreamer he was when we met, Rhonda reassured herself.

But it's not the fighting I fear. Amanda is your first love, Jerrod. Come back to me, my love. Her thoughts began tormenting her.

Each day Rhonda and the remaining members of the small company pushed farther northwest. They chose a path above the lower mountains, searching for a route down out of Alfarakenloria, the mountains of the Elves and Dwarves. Imelrinn walked quietly alongside Rhonda as she stared down out of the shadows of the highest peaks of the mountain range, looking towards the great basin beyond the Metamesterrian River. Somewhere, far beyond that, was home.

Rhonda assured them that the mountain lions pulling the sleigh were taking them to the closest city. She assumed the cats knew the best route, putting a great deal of faith in the animals, which had not seemed to bother the Elves, but Drin found them very troubling.

Fruam walked with Drin behind the sleigh. As they walked, Drin spoke about the influence of the Order of One in the small villages of Torrence and the future it had for the king's city. It became evident to Fraum the Order had no acceptance for other religious beliefs.

"One day there will only be the One," Drin concluded.

"And yet you wear the friendship broach of Lithlillia," Fraum remarked.

The young Initiate looked at the much older sage. Fraum's round face was expressionless, but his brown, almond-shaped eyes seemed somehow calming.

"We are," Drin was a little unsure of himself. "The Order accepts all people," Drin protested.

"Life is like a target. You stand in the center because, for everything else to work, you must come first. You must be mentally and physically strong, ready to work for the betterment of the outer rings. The next ring is your family and, perhaps, your religion you share your life with. These things come before personal desires. Desire and the friends who support and protect you, are in the next ring. They share your joys and your troubles. This ring involves personal choice," Fraum stopped seeing the bewilderment on Drin's face.

The older sage put his hand on Drin's shoulder. The young man seemed almost lost. He had a dazed look on his face and was not responding to Fraum's voice.

"The Order comes before everything. To obtain knighthood I must be devout." Drin's voice trembled.

"Which provides greater service to the Order, the fanatic disciple who pushes until he drops, or the devout at heart who takes care of all the elements in his life in order to better serve?"

Drin did not respond.

"To provide the greatest service to the Order you must nurture all the circles in your life. That includes accepting your friends for who they are," Fraum said softly.

Drin spoke very little the rest of the day. His square jaw seemed tense, almost locked in place as he considered what Fraum had said. As they neared the camp site that night, Drin turned to Fraum again.

"Thank you for your words of wisdom today. I understand your point, but how can the teachings from your monastery be compatible with what the Order teaches?"

"There are very few absolutes in life, Drin. You will have to determine how your circles work best for you. No one can tell you that, but I can tell you one thing. Always be honest with yourself."

As they continued to travel, Drin's passion for the Order irritated Rhonda. She started eating her evening meals in her tent with Imelrinn while Fraum and Drin continued to eat with the Elven guards around their campfire. After the meals, the Elves found duties to attend to, leaving more and more times when Fraum and Drinn were alone. During their separation from the others, Fraum and Drin spoke more about the Order.

"What are the Order's intentions and why do you want to be a knight?" Fraum asked.

"The Order will spread the word of the One throughout the kingdoms of Ak'ron and eventually all of Dendür. I want to be a knight so I can be promoted to Cavalier to better serve the Order," Drin said humbly.

"You want to be a knight?" Fraum asked.

Drin smiled as he nodded his affirmation.

"Spreading the word throughout the world is ambitious. What if someone doesn't want to follow the One?"

"All will eventually come," Drin responded, his eyes staring into the distance.

For several days Fraum continued to question the younger man, sometimes asking about the accomplishments he must complete to be eligible for knighthood. Other times they spoke of religious theology, the differences between the druids, the followers of the Olympian gods, and the One. Fraum began understanding that the Order had no room for either magic or the gods and goddesses of the other religions.

He found the manner in which the Order moved into villages, took control, and drove out the other religions concerning. Each time the world as the villages knew it changed. Not only did the gods and goddesses of Olympus disappear, but interestingly, during each conquest magic also disappeared. What was causing the disappearance of magic?

In the couple of weeks it had taken to pull the sleigh to the hilltop overlooking the point where the Metamesterrian River backed up behind the waterfull, Fraum had a good understanding of the Order of One.

The river water waiting to spill over the waterfall created a large lake. In the middle of the lake was a city perched on the edge of the cliff, surrounded by water spanning hundreds of feet in both directions along the waterfall-cliff.

In the setting sun the walls of the city's buildings seemed golden and the high pitched roofs and hilly streets burned bright red. The buildings, many of which were several stories high, were built side-by-side, without yards. Numerous outdoor stairs led up to second and even third floor doorways.

Two long bridges spanned the wide lake of of dark blue water. The stone bridges ran diagonally from the northern quarters of the lake to the hilly island, which seemed to teeter on the very edge of the waterfall cliff. The island, centered like the hub of half a wagon wheel, was taken up entirely by streets and buildings.

As they left the foothills to cross the short plain before the bridge, littered with thesnow covered fields of small farms, all the Elves stopped to regain their balance. Each complained of dizziness, as though something buzzing in their pointed ears had caused them to lose their balance. Even Rhonda felt it, though not to the extent of her full-blooded kinsmen. Fraum and Drin looked at each other and then at their companions.

After the momentary pause to overcome the dizziness, they pushed onward, reaching the eastern bridge into the fabled city of Silandria by nightfall. The city lights glowed softly in the falling snow of the new storm. At the edge of the bridge the large cats said their goodbyes to Rhonda.

"Thank you for bringing us this far," Rhonda said as she detached their harnesses one last time.

You're welcome, Princess, one mountain lion responded.

May your cubs always find you in a warm den, the other added.

There were no guards posted. No one to greet them. Leaving the wagon-sleigh with the four Elven guards, they began to cross the long bridge over the dark waters of the lake under the night's sky. As they crossed, Imelrinn stopped to lean against the smooth masonry walls in order to regain his balance.

"The dizziness is getting stronger," he said, barely able to look at Rhonda.

"I feel it too," she said quietly.

A herald met them near the city side of the bridge. Other than his bald head, which was overly oblong, making him taller than the average man, he seemed to have an average build. His pillowed jacket and straight-legged pants were made of gold and red cloth. At first the herald just stared at them. After Imelrinn winced in pain the herald spoke.

"Welcome to Silandria."

"Thank you. We seek boarding and we need to purchase some horses and rebuild our wagon," Rhonda replied.

"Come. I will take you to the city's common home where you can rest. You can arrange your business tomorrow," the herald explained.

The herald led them through winding streets paved with red tile to a large inn, where they each received separate rooms assigned by a clerk.

"We have companions on the other side of the bridge with our wagon," Rhonda asked as the herald began to leave.

"We will bring it across the bridge tonight and your compains can have rooms, too."

"There is a fair amount of treasure. Not to be rude, but leaving it unguarded seems a little risky," Rhonda responded.

"Your treasure will be safe. We don't have any crime in Silandria," the herald explained.

"Would it be an insult to leave one of our men with the treasure?"

"If you wish. No, it's not insulting, but it really isn't necessary," the herald's said dismissively.

"I will see to this," Imelrinn said softly.

When Rhonda was out of earshot, Imelrinn turned to the herald. "She is the Lady Rhonda, Princess of Lithlillia, and a druid priestess. I would ask that you show her the respect suited for her position." Imelrinn looked into the man's eyes.

While Imelrinn went out to take care of the other Elves, Rhonda went to her room. It was spacious, nothing like she had ever seen before. There were couches, chairs, and a table in a large front room. A basket of fruit, bread rolls, and a wedge of cheese sat in the middle of the table. Double doors with large, clear windows exited out onto a second story balcony.

Stepping out onto the balcony, Rhonda concentrated. Her mind searched for a bird that would start the message chain back to her mother. From the storm filled sky, a blackbird responded to her call, landing on the stonewall surrounding the balcony.

We are safely in Silandria. Fraum tells me we are east of the Plateau of Kronese. Jerrod has gone north to rescue Amanda. I fear for them. I will send word again when we leave for home, Rhonda thought to the bird.

Stepping back inside, Rhonda found the other door leading from the large room went into a room with a large bed, covered with fine linens, and a copper tub. There was a large mirror hanging on the wall.

I'm filthy, Rhonda thought when she saw the image of herself in a mirror attached to the wall nearest the tub.

A few minutes later there was a knock on the door. A woman stood in the hallway with hot water for the tub and fresh clothes.

"We thought you could use these until your clothes were cleaned," one woman said.

Rhonda was surprised by the women's baldness of their overly large foreheads, but she did not stare. She appreciated their timely delivery of hot water and clean clothes, but thought little more of it.

"Our heads are more oblonged due to the size of our brains and all Silandrians are bald, male and female. I'm glad the hot water and clean clothes make you happy," the woman continued.

"Thank you," Rhonda commented as she reflected on the woman's incredible insight.

After the women filled the tub and departed, Rhonda stripped off her clothes and stepped into the perfectly warm water.

Just to my liking. Rhonda relaxed in the bath water.

The temperature reminded her of the hot pools in Kronese, what the flatlanders called the Black Forest, but her mind could not help consider their brief time in Silandria as she soaked. All seemed pleasant enough, but she was becoming more uncomfortable. Not that something dangerous seemed to be lurking nearby.

There is something ominous here, Rhonda thought, then let her head slide under the water to soak her hair.

That night Rhonda dreamt about Jerrod. In her dream she never saw Amanda, but she seemed to feel her presence prying deep into her mind. When she woke, Rhonda was exhausted. The memory of her dream did not feel right. Why had she not seen Amanda? She had barely dressed when there was a knock on the door.

The innkeeper delivered warm bread and boiled eggs along with a message that they were to have their mid-day meal with the City's Master. After eating alone, Rhonda met the others in a large indoor patio. She was still dizzy and became a little suspicious when she learned Imelrinn and the other Elves were also dizzy.

The ceiling of the patio was high, supported by thick wooden beams. Large windows allowed them to see into the city's snow covered streets. Around them green shrubs and small trees in large metal planters and white tables were scattered across the red tiled floor. Wide steps provided passage through the multiple tiers of the patio down to the lowest level, where a stone fireplace dominated the decor.

Outside, the citizens of Silandria wore winter robes with hoods pulled up over their heads and ankle high boots as they wandered peacefully through the streets, shopping and doing other business. They did not carry weapons, not even a knife to cut their food.

Walking through the city to meet the City Master for the mid-day meal, they passed several religious symbols, all of which honored the gods and goddesses of Olympus. As they walked, Drin glanced about and walked a little faster as he sought to distance himself from the symbols. When they reached their destination he still fidgeted, uncommonly nervous in his surroundings.

The tavern where they met for the mid-day meal was large, with a split level floor and several small, circular fireplaces with metal chimneys. There were a lot of tables gathered around the fireplaces. Women bustled between them to service patrons. The meals appeared to be fish or poultry with potatoes and warm bread. On the far side of the room was a short bar.

The City's Master was an older man of modest size and no distinctive markings beyond his overly oblong head and some wrinkles around his eyes and mouth, distinctive of his age. His mannerisms were similar to those of the other Silandrians they had met.

"I am Rupaul, the City's Master. Welcome, Lady Rhonda." The older man's voice was higher than expected.

"Greetings, Master Rupaul, thank you," Rhonda replied, as dignified as any matriarch.

The city's manager turned towards Fraum, pausing as he stared at the monk. For a moment nothing happened, and then he spoke again.

"You are not Elven," Rupaul stated.

"No. I am from the White Fist Monastery in Torrence. A kingdom south of the Elven Kingdom of Lithlillia," Fraum answered, standing with his arms crossed and his hands tucked inside the tan sleeves of his robe.

"You are bald yet you do not hear us?" Rupaul asked.

Fraum looked at him a bit puzzled.

"I hear what you are saying," Fraum assured Rupaul.

"Curious," was all the City Master had to say.

Imelrinn looked at the city's master a moment. The words "do not hear us" reverberated through his mind. Hoping he was wrong, he closed his eyes, relaxed his consciousness, and listened. As they stood talking with Rupaul, Imelrinn's knees buckled and the ancient Mountain Wood Elve fell on his side, unconscious.

*　　*　　*　　*　　*

Imelrinn woke with Rhonda sitting on his bed as she sponged his forehead with a moist towel. Rhonda's long brown hair, tucked behind a pointed ear on one side, hung down over her shoulder. In her high cheekbones and narrow lips, he pictured her mother.

"Lieisa?" he murmured.

"Shhh. No. It's Rhonda."

"The voices. All those voices," Imelrinn said as he pushed up to rest on his elbows.

"I know. They've stopped. We will talk in a little while. Rest now. We're having the evening meal with Rupaul," Rhonda finished as she rose from the bed.

"But—" Imelrinn protested.

"Later! We will talk in a while. Rest now," Rhonda instructed her guardian. She smiled once and then departed Imelrinn's room. She knew Drin and

Fraum waited for word of how the Elve was doing. She knocked twice on the door before Fraum answered.

"Come in."

Drin stood with Fraum in the center of room. They both stepped towards her as she entered the room.

"How is he?" Drin asked.

"He's fine. He's awake. A little shaken, I think. I'm sure he will join us shortly."

Rupaul had told them the citizens of Silandria were telepathic. The news disturbed Rhonda but fascinated Fraum. When Rupaul promised they would avoid using telepathy in their direction, Rhonda relaxed a bit, but she was still suspicious. While the three discussed the potential danger of telepaths, a knock came on the door. Fraum rose and opened the door. After Imelrinn entered, Fraum looked down the hallway and then closed the door to rejoin the group.

"I had a dream last night about Jerrod and Amanda. It seemed like Amanda was prying into my mind, but I never envisioned her. And she was searching for things Amanda would have known. I think it was someone else trying to get information." Rhonda glanced between her friends.

"Before I collapsed I felt a constant prying to access my mind, but it's gone now," Imelrinn added as he watched his ward.

"That was the Silandrians. They have promised to stop. It should be over now. In the dream, though, it was more like someone or something was trying to pull information from me." Rhonda focused on the ancient Elve before looking at the others as she explained further.

"Not like the feeling from the Silandrians?" Fraum furrowed his brow.

Rhonda shook her head.

"Is there someone else we have offended?" Drin asked, bewildered.

"Not that I am aware of," Rhonda answered, her eyes wide open, innocent as a forest animal searching for food.

"We can confirm with Rupaul at tonight's meal that none of the Silandrians are connecting with your mind, but I don't think that's the answer. There must be someone else prying into your thoughts." Fraum's focus rested on Rhonda.

Their evening meal with the City's Master was splendid, more than they would have expected. They had several trays of warm meats, fruits, and breads, which servers brought around for their personal selection. Their goblets were constantly filled with their selected beverage. Drin and Fraum drank water, but Rhonda and Imelrinn selected a wine with a light, tingling sensation from soft bubbles.

The City's Master was not overly excited to talk about Silandria, but did take some time to explain that the city was built when Agganon was still an active place of worship. Caravans traveling up to the temple to worship would stop to rest and replenish. But when Rupaul suggested that the Olympians came and went from Agganon, Drin scoffed at him.

"You aren't really suggesting gods from Olympus, that Zeus, came from Aggannon?" Drin challenged.

"Yes, I am. My great-grandfather traveled to Agganon. We are not followers of Zeus or his gods, but my grandfather wanted to witness the event for himself," Rupual responded.

"It is not Olympus you should turn your attentions to," Drin started.

"Our devout friend is a follower of the Order of One," Fraum interrupted.

The man closed his eyes for a moment before responding.

"It is clear now. Thank you. One of our citizens has heard of your Order."

As they ate they also talked about history and topography, which led to further discussions of Silandria and the Gap of Dillandria. Then they spoke of Torrence and Lithlillia, but eventually they ended up on the politics of Silandria.

"I was elected to master the city's affairs nearly twenty years ago. I will hold the post until I am no longer able to conduct the city's business, at which time all the citizens of the city and the farmlands to the north will elect my replacement," Rupaul explained.

"This election, each person receives one vote?" Fraum questioned.

"It is the old way for us," the master responded.

"How do you cast your votes?" Fraum's curiosity was raised.

"Through our collective minds. You see, master sage, we are all connected mentally. That is why we do not worry about your treasure as you do. Everyone knows the instant anyone even thinks about stealing something. It is a great deterant to theft and violence."

*　　*　　*　　*　　*

In the secret labyrinth of the Triad, deep under the City of Torrence, the winter was dragging on for Jacob. He worried about Nathanial and his company companions who had escaped their grasp at Limerin Falls and disappeared north, into the woods. More concerning, he had not heard from the group that had used the High Master of the Triad's artifact to project from Torrence to Terrace Xul in hopes of surprising Nathanial before he entered the Lost Kingdom.

As if worrying about you was not enough, Drok-na. Jacob smiled as he sat back in his chair.

You needn't worry about me. The dragon's thoughts felt a little confused.

I know, my friend, Jacob responded.

Drok-na had grown far too large to sleep in the rafters of Jacob's room and was uncomfortable on the floor which seemed to shrink a little more each week. Jacob had found a second chamber in the labyrinth that he could use. It had been a vacant storage room with higher ceilings and more room. That room was more bearable for Drok-na, but the adult size dragon could no longer comfortably pass through the labyrinth halls. It was a lot of mental work projecting a full-bodied dragon from one room to another, so Jacob found a cave on the eastern slope of the Wild Mountains where Drok-na could spend some of the time more comfortably, but moving the dragon from the labyrinth to outside the castle caused Jacob to sleep for a day.

Drok-na would spend days curled up in one of the rooms before he was magically returned to the night sky above Torrence or, on rare occasions, to his cave in the Wild Mountains. The distance between the sky and the cave did not seem to tire Jacob more, but he enjoyed riding back in the dark and Drok-na needed the exercise. A simple warming spell would keep him warm on the cold winter nights. Once they arrived at the cave Jacob could sleep until the next day.

The cave was on Mount Torrence, just a few minutes' flight time away. It overlooked the Torrence River and the castle-city, built on the river's island for protection in more dangerous times. Now, there was no one to bother them when Drok-na sunned himself on the mountainside.

Jacob found the thrill of being on the back of the giant beast exhilarating. The powerful beat of Drok-na's wings against the air and the sensation of soaring through the night sky unseen was nearly beyond description. The pull on his body as Drok-na's wings pounded against the night air to gain altitude and speed. The weightlessness he felt in a motionless dive. Nothing he had experienced came close to the thrill of flying on a dragon's back. Sheer power and unmatched speed.

But lately most of Jacob's time was spent with more troubling matters. After Nathanial's departure, Jacob had become the Master's senior protoge. He out ranked the other two masters by many years. Jacob knew he would most probably be the Triad's future leader. He spent more time with the High Master, taking on more responsibility and easing the burdens of their aging leader. The fact that more students were disappearing worried Jacob. The ranks of the Triad were nearly half the size they were before Nathanial's departure.

Jacob was uncertain why the students were leaving. There was no sign of violence and all of the students' possessions disappeared with them. The exodus meant students, who had unlawfully studied multiple forms of magic, were finding another place to gather.

The number of defectors is alarming, he thought.

When he brought the matter to the High Master's attention, the ancient wizard seemed unconcerned. Sometimes the High Master's wisdom mystified Jacob. He had learned to take his master's reactions with humility, relying on the ancient wizard's wisdom without question.

"I fear that we are headed for trouble," Jacob confided to the High Master.

"What will come, will come," the High Master said softly.

"Isn't there something we can do to prepare?" Jacob asked.

"We are. We are preparing by strengthening our resolve with those who chose to stay. Those dedicated to the intent of the Triad. We will achieve nothing by worrying about what 'may' come. We must focus on bringing our abilities to their greatest potential," the High Master guided the much younger wizard.

✻   ✻   ✻   ✻   ✻

After Amanda's rescue, King Randver had rallied the families of Haithenbeurn for battle. He planned to send patrols in every direction to find the thief and her rescuer and, if they were being aided, he promised to lay waste to whatever kingdom might be helping them. He was a man possessed, trapped in a single thought, *vengeance.*

It was the night after the great hall had burned to the ground when he called for the crone. She was wasting no time. She knew the king was impatient and walked as quickly as she could, arriving at his personal chambers late in the evening.

"What took you so long, crone?" the king demanded.

"These old legs are far beyond hurrying, Sire," she answered as she dropped to her knees and began fiddling for her sack of bones.

"By Odin, old woman! Tell me what I need to know or the wolves can have you," the king's deep voice thundered through the room.

Failing at her effort to hurry, the king backhanded the crone, driving her crippled body to the floor. The old woman pushed herself up off the floor, looking up at the barbaric king.

"Please, Sire?" Her body quivered as she finished gathering the bones.

"Now, with no more delay!"

"But Your Majesty, didn't the Queen of Witches warn you not to pursue the thief?" the old witch warned.

The king hit the old woman again. It took her longer to get up, but as soon as she could manage, the crone's arthritic hand cast the bones out on the floor before her. Trembling, she leaned over, squinting to see the signs. The king stood over her, pressing for an answer.

"Well?"

"South, Sire. They sleep in the forest to the south. Just the two of them." The crone's voice cackled as she spoke.

"I'll send patrols south in the morning," the king stated as he turned to leave.

"Sire, if you do it will be the end of your reign and maybe your life," the crone advised.

"You have told me one too many times what I can't do," King Randver responded, staring down at the witch with contempt.

Randver picked up his axe and glared at the crone as he walked towards her.

"Beware the witch's moon, Sire. She will come. She will come to avenge her humble servant and the Ladies will give her such power that your reign will end," the crone said rapidly, cowering on the floor.

The king's axe was swift. With a single stroke the crone's head rolled across the floor.

"No one will tell me what I can do in my own kingdom. Let the wolves have your carcass and your head shall go on a pike. Guards!"

In the morning the king summoned his captains to order patrols to the south, and then called for the six leaders of the Houses of Haithenbeurn. Among them was his nephew, Lief Frothisen, who stood next to his father, Frothi, head of the House of Gounouf.

"Haithenbeurn has been robbed of its greatest treasure, the Horn of Valhalla. The thief who took it and her rescuer travel south. I will have the horn and their heads!" the king declared.

"Why are you so set on retrieving the horn?" one of the family leaders asked.

"It was a gift to me from Odin. Delivered to me by the Valkyries. I will have my gift back!"

"This sounds like a personal matter for the House of Gounouf," another added.

"You don't get it, do you? The wielder of the horn can summon an army of dead heroes right out of Valhalla. They would be invincible!" The king spat his anger at them as he spoke.

Frothi stepped forward to question the king. "What is it you want from us?"

"Ready your houses to march south. Warn the gate. We will catch her between our forces. Anyone who has helped the thief will be destroyed. We march in the morning."

✧　　✧　　✧　　✧　　✧

It has been a month and I still don't have my horn back. What does the year have in store for us? the king thought as he prepared for bed.

Randver looked out the narrow window of his private chamber into the night's sky. The light from the moons was obstructed by clouds. The power of Questil, in her full-moon state, and Dori, which was only a quarter-moon, cast a darker green tint across his room.

The witch's moon. Hel can take you to her underworld for all I care.

Shortly after the king crawled into his bed and began waiting for sleep to overtake him, a gray mist began forming in mid-air near the center of his chamber. It quickly grew as silvery sparkles began to burst in the mist and the transparent figure of a voluptuous, middle aged woman formed. As the smoke dissipated and her robust body, covered by a sheer, muslin gown became solid, Randver sat up in bed.

"I know you," the king said as he stared into her golden-honey colored eyes.

"Yes, you do," Felicia answered coldly.

"You're that priestess witch that invaded my hall, telling me what to do. What are you doing in my chamber?" Randver demanded.

"You ignored my warning and then you killed my minion," Felicia's voice was emotionless.

"Who do you think you are to 'warn' me, King of Haithenbeurn?"

Felicia's eyebrows bent down at the bridge of her nose as her skin turned dark blue and her eyes began to glow bright gold. In her outstretched palm was a small semi-opaque vial with a black fluid swaying back and worth. The king started to get out of bed as she threw the vial, just missing his head. The glass shattered into pieces against the wall behind him, casting the fluid everywhere.

The king began to chuckle, happy at Felicia's misfortune, but the broad smile of Felicia's full lips caused him to stop.

"Good bye, King of Haithenbeurn," Felicia said as her figure faded from view.

The echo of Felicia's evil laugh resounded through the bedchamber. Alone in his room, the King of Haithenbeurn began choking on the black fog of lethal poison rising from the liquid that engulfed his bed.

CHAPTER 7

THE REUNION

The morning sunbeams shone down through the window onto the bed, warming Jerrod's and Amanda's naked bodies as they lay entwined under the thick feather comforters. Amanda's head rested upon his shoulders, her busty body still snuggled against his side, and one leg wrapped over his loin. Her breath-taking beauty and the splendor of what they had shared in the secret shadows of the night's moonlight still possessed Jerrod's thoughts.

Amanda lifted her head slightly to look into his azure-blue eyes. After pausing a moment, she stretched to kiss him tenderly on his lips.

"Good morning, my love," Amanda said just above a whisper.

"Good morning," Jerrod answered.

I do love you. Rhonda! The thought surged into his consciousness.

Jerrod forced a smile before they rose and dressed together. He put on his own clothes, which had been cleaned by the Elves, while Amanda put the Elven clothes back on. Her beautiful face bore a continuous smile on her full lips as they dressed. When he had put his shirt on, Amanda danced over to help him button it up.

Her long blonde hair seemed to fly as she spun around, pulling her dress over her head. When they were done, they came together again and Amanda, wrapping her arms around his back, pulled him close and then rested her cheek on his shoulder. After a moment they separated, but Amanda clung to Jerrod's hand as they walked towards the large front room, where they found the fire lit and fruit, cheese, and warm bread on the table. They could smell the tea brewing in a pot that hung over the fire.

"Want some?" Amanda asked coyly as she removed the pot from the fire.

Jerrod was not sure whether Amanda was referring to the tea, but nodded from the overstuffed chair he had fallen into. The thought of Rhonda was almost unbearable as he sat watching Amanda pour a cup of tea for him, desiring her as much as he ever had. After carefully crossing the room to hand him the cup, Amanda slid her finger down his wrist, running it through the braided wristlet, and playfully twisting it around her finger.

"What's this?" Amanda asked.

Jerrod leaned forward to place his tea cup on an end table. Taking both of Amanda's hands in his, he gently pulled her around in front of him, where she knelt down on her knees, her blue eyes looking up into his own.

"This is what I tried to tell you last night," Jerrod stopped to take a deep breath.

"What is it?" her voice was soft and playful.

"It is Rhonda's braided hair. She made it." He paused, staring into her eyes, knowing he was about to hurt her. "It's their symbol of betrothal," Jerrod finished.

Amanda did not move. She did not even seem to breathe until she rose and slowly turned away, walking back to her room without saying a word or looking back.

Behind the closed door of her room Amanda fell to her knees, burying her face in her unused bed, her arms stretched across the mattress. When she could finally manage it, she looked upward.

"Aphrodite, the Fates have left me on your doorstep. Is this where my love is to end? Am I not worthy of Jerrod's love?" she questioned.

Her tears flowed freely without sound as she wept herself back to sleep, sleeping through the soft knock at her door. When Jerrod quietly entered her room, he found her on the floor next to the bed. Jerrod pulled the feather blanket from the bed to cover her before he left her room.

Jerrod? He heard in his mind as he walked down the hallway.

What? What is this? Who is this? Jerrod thought, uncertain whether he was hearing something or imagining it.

It is Farris. Will you meet me where we landed? the stallion answered.

Jerrod had no trouble finding the winged steed. The meadow was empty except for the leader of the winged horses, looking majestic in the morning sun.

How am I hearing you? Jerrod thought.

How? I thought you were a druid? Farris asked.

No.

I sense magic in you. Deep, old magic, Farris told him. *The Elves will take you to the city were Lady Rhonda and your friends wait,* Farris explained.

Why? What's wrong? I thought you were flying us back.

You will be warmer if you travel with the Elves, Farris responded thoughtfully.

Are you okay? Where will you go? Jerrod asked.

I will return to Lithlillia and tell the Lady what I have witnessed. You are safe and will be with Lady Rhonda and the others very soon. I have spoken with Olendorn and he is willing to take you to Silandria, Farris finished.

As Jerrod and Farris parted company, Jerrod thought briefly of how much he would miss Farris. He valued the winged horse's friendship. When Farris thought back, *thank you,* Jerrod chuckled to himself self-consciously.

When Jerrod returned to the cabin, Olendorn was already waiting at the foot of the front steps. The Elven prince smiled at him for the first time.

"I have spoken to Farris. Did he explain things to you?" Olendorn asked.

"Yes. You have offered to take us to Silandria."

"My parents are waiting at their home. Come, let's go see them," Olendorn walked away from the cabin.

Jerrod walked slightly behind the Elve, just enough to follow him to his father's home, but the new friendliness of the Elven family confused him.

"Olendorn, why the sudden interest?"

"You wear an esreandrea?"

"It is from Princess Rhonda of Lithlillia."

Olendorn gave him a puzzled look but said nothing.

His parents' home was beautiful. It was built of polished wood with high peaked green roofs and marvelous windows. Ornate wood carvings lined the rakes and fascias along the roof's edge. A porch protected the southern face of the residence from the sun and there was a double door entrance in the middle of the southern wall. Inside, Olendorn's mother and father waited for their guest.

"Mother, father, this is Jerrod, betrothed to the Princess Rhonda of the western clan," Olendorn introduced Jerrod again.

"Welcome," they greeted.

"Thank you."

"Come. Sit and tell us of your journeys."

Jerrod limited the explanation of his travels to the effort of freeing Amanda, careful not to mention the horn. Once Jerrod brought the story up to his morning meeting with Farris, Olendorn spoke up to explain that he had offered to take Jerrod and Amanda south.

"I will take them by wolf-sled," Olendorn concluded.

After the decision of how Jerrod and Amanda would leave, Olendorn and his father went into another room for a private discussion. Jerrod remained briefly before he said good morning and left graciously.

Thoughts of Rhonda and Amanda tormented Jerrod as he walked alone through the forest towards the cottage. When he got back, Amanda was up, standing at a large window near the table, looking at the waterfall with her back to the door. She still wore the suggestive Elven clothes. The image caused Jerrod to recall the exquisite time they had shared the night before.

"Amanda?" Jerrod said when he saw her, but she did not answer. "Amanda. I tried to tell you last night," Jerrod said as he crossed the room.

"I know," she whispered, just loud enough for him to hear.

"I love you. I didn't know if you were coming back," Jerrod continued.

"I know," she repeated.

"Can we talk about this?" Jerrod said, encouraging her to open up.

"No. It's done," she answered before returning to her room and shutting the door behind her.

Amanda stayed in her room until they were called for dinner. For the first time since her mother's death she had lost her self-confidence. She had let Jerrod into her heart and when she left on the blood quest, she had lost him to the woman who was responsible for the quest in the first place. And for the first time in her life, she had been captured and brought to judgment.

As they walked to the Pavilion they could hear the Elven harps and flutes playing, but the music did not ease Amanda's torment. She was numb. The evening filled with talk about the Kingdom of Haithenbeurn and its war with the Fendür, and the differences between Lithlillia and Asenthia, but Amanda's mind was a whirl of undefined images, like looking at objects in a snowstorm through a frosted glass window. And like those images, somewhere beyond the protected boundaries of Asenthia was a cold, brutal winter and Rhonda.

Amanda's mind cried, the numbness taking hold as though she were walking in her sleep.

It was all Amanda could do to return to her room and fall asleep without a tear.

Never again, she swore before slipping into a restless sleep.

Amanda rose slowly in the morning and, after putting on the Elven dress, went out to the table in the front room, where she found Jerrod already eating. He looked worn, tired, sitting at the windowside table staring out. Amanda pulled back the second chair to sit down without saying a word.

Why do I have to love you? she thought.

They ate the morning meal in silence, averting their eyes by watching the water falling into the nearby lake or staring into the small fire in the cottage's fireplace. When they had eaten enough, they separated to go pack their belongings. There was little to pack. Jerrod wore his own clothes, but kept his armor rolled up, which he returned to Amanda's pack with the remnants of her belongings.

They said their goodbyes to the Lord and Lady of Asenthia before mid-morning and followed Prince Olendorn to the edge of the kingdom. Just beyond the magical barrier that kept the winter out they could see a long, skinny sled sitting on skies. It was low to the snow with two thick wooden beams rising up in the back of the sled. Six wolves were attached to the front of the sled with long leather tethers that allowed them to fan out as they pulled. The two center leads were the longest and the two outside leads were the shortest.

Inside the barrier, Prince Olendorn handed them fur jackets with fur hoods. The jackets nearly reached the ground when they put them on. The fur was warm and thick. Amanda pulled the coat tight around her, snuggling into the fur inside the hood.

"It's bear," Olendorn commented as he watched her.

"Jerrod, you're in first. Heavier weight in the back of the sled, and it will be more comfortable for Amanda." Oldendorn smiled. "She won't be squished."

Sitting in the back of the sled with his back against the wooden risers, Jerrod made room for Amanda to sit between his legs with her back pressed against his body. Once they were comfortably in place, Olendorn placed the pack on the front of the sled between Amanda's legs, laid a bear skin over them, and then strapped everything into the winter sled. Amanda sat very still, keeping her arms crossed over her chest to avoid hugging Jerrod's knees.

Standing on the back of the skis and holding the bar at the top of the wooden risers, Olendorn said a single word, causing the large wolves to jump into a run.

"Mush!"

At sunset they stopped along the edge of the shallow valley just inside the forest line. Olendorn brought one small tent to share. While he began setting up the tent, Jerrod noticed Amanda clinging to her bearskin as if she were cold.

"Oh, enough of this!" Jerrod said, realizing the discomfort of winter was weighing upon him as well.

As Jerrod waved his arm in an arc over his head, spreading his fingers wide apart, the air around them began growing warmer and the snow on the ground began melting, swamping the grass around them. The water soaked in quickly, leaving lush, green grass for them to rest upon.

"There is more to you than being a swordsman. Farris told me you possessed the old magic," Olendorn commented.

"The old magic?" Jerrod questioned.

"Long before wizards and druids, the only 'magic' was the Fairy-Folk. They are our kinsmen. The 'old magic' is a direct link to the powers that make the world what it is. Other forms of magic only use a part of the 'magic,'" Olendorn explained.

"Then you can use magic?"

"Only in part. It varies with each person. Most Elves are limited to being part of nature, which allows us to do such things as going unseen, passing without a trace, or conversing with animals."

"Is he in danger?" Amanda interjected.

"It depends on how attuned he is to the 'old magic' and whether he can control it," Olendorn said in candor.

Amanda looked at Jerrod as her eyes grew moist.

Noticing the crystal orb in the talon at the end of the hilt of Jerrod's sword, Olendorn cocked his head to one side, trying to get a better look.

"That's an interesting sword," Olendorn commented as he went back to setting up the tent.

"An heirloom of sorts," Jerrod deflected.

✻   ✻   ✻   ✻   ✻

After a warm night in the tent heated by Jerrod's magic, they made an early start when morning came. The wolves ran with power, easily pulling the sled across the snow. The day was warm, making their ride beneath the furry hoods of the traveling cloaks pleasant. Amanda allowed herself to melt into Jerrod's embrace, bringing a smile to her face. She could not help being comforted by his touch.

They raced along the edge of the eastern woods, traveling south over the Meadows. Stopping at mid-day to eat chicken, cheese, and Elven bread, and to drink some wine, they spread a blanket out on the snow before sitting down to a relaxed meal and conversation. As Olendorn became more interested in Torrence, he began opening up about the histories of Asenthia. When he spoke of Alfardoria's long histories and its ancient kingdoms of Dwarves and Elves, he seemed to yearn for the past.

The next day was similar to the first. The wolves sped along pulling the sled, bringing a breeze into their face, which caused Amanda to smile. Occassionally the sled bounced as it skied across the uneven ground, causing her to press tighter against Jerrod. It was comforting to know no one could see her blush each time it happened.

The second night was equally similar to the first as they sat in Jerrod's magical sphere of protection, eating food warmed by the small camp fire. Although Amanda would not speak, Jerrod and Olendorn were getting to know each other better. They did not bother with the tent, sleeping in their bedrolls that night. As they had before they rose early to get an early start.

On the eve of the third day they approached a golden city from the north. Olendorn drove the wolf-sled through scattered farms until a young, half-Elven woman appeared, standing in their path.

Olendorn jumped from the sled before it completely stopped, walking towards her to greet her in the formal Elven language.

"I won't say it again, but remember that I will always love you," Amanda whispered so only Jerrod would hear.

With Amanda's back to him and Olendorn and Rhonda walking towards the sled, Jerrod could not respond quickly enough to continue the conversation in privacy. Olendorn unstrapped the sled, freeing Jerrod and Amanda.

"The Elven clothes complement your beauty," Olendorn commented as he extended a hand, helping Amanda to stand up.

When Jerrod stepped off the sled, Rhonda took both hands and pulled him to her before he could act. Pulling Jerrod's hand close to her chest, Rhonda stared into his eyes.

"I was worried about you," Rhonda began, turning her head towards Amanda as she spoke.

"Both of you," Rhonda finished, turning back towards Jerrod.

Amanda forced a slight smile as she watched Rhonda with Jerrod.

"Where is everyone?" Jerrod asked, looking from Rhonda to Amanda and back.

"I felt the wolves and Prince Olendorn coming, but I did not tell anyone. It is better you arrive quietly. How is it you came from Asenthia?" Rhonda asked.

"Farris could not carry both of us and we were freezing. They were good to us," Jerrod said, complimenting his host.

"Come. You can tell me over warm food. Prince Olendorn, will you join us in Silandria?" Rhonda offered.

"Unfortunately, I must decline. We need to return immediately. Clan business," the prince answered politely.

As Rhonda helped Amanda gather their belongings, Prince Olendorn pulled Jerrod aside.

"Be careful, my friend. The Silandrians can control your mind. They're telepaths. And it is not just thoughts that you need to beware of. Their minds are powerful. There is a reason why they don't need armies," Olendorn warned.

After warning Jerrod, Olendorn took Amanda by the hands before giving her a hug. Jerrod watched him lean in to speak softly in Amanda's ear.

"You are delicate like a flower amoung thorns. I sense something in you that most of your kind do not have," he said, pulling back as he finished so he could look into Amanda's eyes.

Amanda smiled innocently at the prince, batting her eyes in a fashion that she had learned long ago. Taking her hands again, Olendorn slipped a round, disk-shaped object wrapped in cloth into her hands and then pressed her hands closed over the small package.

"Think of Asenthia when you look at this," he whispered.

"Thank you, Lord Olendorn," Amanda said, looking at the snow.

"Have a safe journey home, Prince Olendorn," Rhonda said.

"May your return to Lithlillia be pleasant, Lady," Ollendorn responded.

The prince watched as Rhonda, Jerrod, and Amanda began walking back towards the city. They were not halfway to the eastern bridge when Olendorn stepped onto the ends of the skies and said "mush."

In the distance, Amanda, Jerrod, and Rhonda could hear the wolves howling as they ran northward into the night.

Beware the tall brains, the wolves howled.

Amanda watched Rhonda pulling her bearskin tight around her shoulders and Jerrod glancing back over his shoulders at the wolves' howl.

"What is it?" Amanda asked.

"Nothing. It's nothing," Jerrod answered as Rhonda began to walk faster.

"Come. Let's hurry," Rhonda pushed.

"What is it?" Amanda stopped to ask again.

Jerrod turned to face her and then walked back to her.

"It's the wolves. They are warning us about Silandria," Jerrod explained.

"A warning?" Amanda said, hopping a little to adjust her pack.

"Would you like me to take that?" Jerrod nodded at the pack.

"No. And what warning? Against who?"

"The Silandrians are telepathic. They can read minds. Now, come on," Jerrod said before turning to follow after Rhonda.

The walk was longer than Amanda would have liked, but they were at the bridge soon enough. It was a long walk across the red-tiled bidge and then up the hilly streets before the three companions were at their lodge. Once inside, they were met by Fraum, Drin, and Imelrinn in the tiered patio.

Rhonda turned to Jerrod, throwing her arms around his back and holding him tight before she relexed her grasp to kiss his lips, and then hugged him tight again with the excitement. When Rhonda was finally able to push herself away, she looked at Amanda.

"It was true? The dream. Was it true?" Rhonda asked, taking a couple steps towards her.

Amanda nodded in affirmation.

"I healed her wounds on our way to Asenthia," Jerrod answered.

"Imelrinn, would you please take her to her room and see that she has a warm bath," Rhonda requested.

"You'll find the water soothing, Amanda," she added.

"Thank you," Amanda responded, avoiding eye contact.

As Imelrinn escorted Amanda to her room, Rhonda turned her attentions back to Jerrod. Hugging his upper arm between both of hers, she pulled him close to kiss his cheek. Her pleasant green eyes seemed to twinkle as they turned a golden honey color. Her thin lips drew up into a pleasant smile that captivated her oval face.

"Fraum, could you please show Jerrod to my room? I need to collect herbs for Amanda's bath," Rhonda asked.

✦   ✦   ✦   ✦   ✦

When Amanda got to her room, a hot bath was wiating. She set her belongings aside, stuffing the object Olendorn had given her into the bottom of her pack. The two women, who were laying out new clothes as Imelrinn and Amanda entered, offered Amanda tea, and when Amanda indicated she did not need any more assistance, they left her with her Elven escort.

Imelrinn spoke with Amanda briefly, just long enough to assure she was comfortable, then departed, leaving Amanda alone to slip into the tub. By the time Rhonda reached the room, Amanda was already soaking in the warm water.

"I have brought you some herbs for your bath. They will help you rest. I will stay until you are ready for bed," Rhonda said with a smile.

"Thank you." Amanda managed a smile.

"May I ask what they did to you?" Rhonda asked softly.

"The beatings and whippings lasted for days," Amanda said, staring into the bath water.

"I am sorry," Rhonda responded, looking down at her hands, unable to look at Amanda.

"Rhonda," Amanda started.

"Yes?" The princess finally looked up.

"I... I couldn't have made it any longer. Jarrod rescued me as I was about to lose my hands." Amanda stopped to swallow hard. "And then I would have lost my life," Amanda choked out.

"I know," Rhonda empathized.

"It's just... I was so grateful. So..."Amanda stopped.

"Shhhh. It will wait 'til morning."

The words echoed in Amanda's mind, *"wait 'til morning"*. She had said the same thing when Jerrod was trying to tell her about their betrothal.

How can I blame you, Jerrod? Amanda was surprised by her toughts.

✳   ✳   ✳   ✳   ✳

Jerrod was also in a hot bath when Rhonda came to their room. Rhonda sat down behind him and began scrubbing his back. She was in a talkative mood, so Jerrod let her go on, responding only when necessary.

When Rhonda began speaking of Lithlillia and their wedding in a few months, Jerrod sunk down into the water until the water rose to his neck. Listening to her as he tilted his head back and closed his eyes, the stress grew, pushing down on him as though it was trying to push his head under water.

The turmoil was incapacitating him. As Rhonda caressed his shoulders, he fought to control his thoughts. When they went to bed and Rhonda snuggled up to him, sleep did not come. Jerrod could only stare restlessly at the ceiling, thinking about Amanda and Rhonda and their wedding.

A month had passed since the first of the year and the Great Solstice. It had been a special solstice with both moons full, something that only happened every third year, and even more special with the announcement of their betrothal. He had not fully rested. He had not fully slept. Outside, the winter was starting to show signs that it would soon be submitting to spring.

As the days are slowly starting to grow longer, the date of our wedding is slowly drawing nearer, Jerrod began to dread.

Lying in bed, Rhonda pulled at Jerrod's arm to hold her tighter, but Jerrod hastily rose to put on clean clothes. Rhonda scurried to catch up and, before they had even kissed good morning, they were heading down a hallway towards the large patio where they found Imelrinn, Drin, and Fraum sitting at a heavy wood table near a window having tea, fruit, and warm bread.

"How do you suppose they have such fresh fruit in the winter?" Fraum was asking.

While they sat, Jerrod noticed the great, arched beams that held the knotted-wood ceiling up high over their heads The sight was a pleasant distraction from his entanglement. As he scanned the décor, his nose began picking up the wonderful aroma from the indoor vines wrapping around the wooden beams and hanging down like moss from a tree, the vines filled with white flowers.

The discussion at the table buzzed in his ear relentlessly. While Rhonda and Fraum contemplated the homeward journey, Jerrod's eyes caught sight of the street through the beautiful window next to the table. The falling snow took on a different luster. The large flakes drifting slowly down out of the sunny sky were playful rather than menacing like the blizzards they had been through.

The tan stone of the city warmed quickly in the morning sun, melting any residual snow and ice off the streets. Snow slid off the steep peaks of the red tiled roofs as they collected warmth from the winter sun and the patios and terraces invited on-lookers to sit outside as if it were already spring, but the outside vines that grew over the trellises were still dormant.

"Jerrod, are you even listening?" Rhonda interrupted his thoughts.

"I'm sorry. What is it?"

"Drin wants to go directly to Torrence," Rhonda repeated the gist of the conversation.

"Well, I think it is best we return swiftly and a direct path is better than the Black Forest," Drin commented.

"We have kin in the Black Forest," Imelrinn explained.

"Fairy-Folk," Fraum added.

"I really think we should go straight to Torrence," Drin insisted.

They stopped talking and rose when Amanda joined them at the table. Hanging from her shoulder was the knitted bag from Ornholts.

"How did you sleep?" Rhonda asked.

"Well. Thank you."

"Come, sit," Rhonda said, pulling out the chair next to her.

"Thank you."

"You look good," Drin complimented earnestly.

"Food and rest does wonders," Fraum added.

"Master," Amanda greeted the monk, her voice quivering.

"What is it?" Fraum asked.

"It was bad," Amanda choked out.

"Come, come. You can tell me later. For now, remember that each day is like a new birth. It offers a new beginning," the older man consoled her.

"The last time we were together was on the ship under Mount Thoradan," Drin commented.

At first their discussion was awkward, but as Amanda began recounting her journey the awkwardness disappeared. She left out small points, like how she had disappeared in the forest the night she left the ship, and when they asked, she smiled and fell back on it being a trade secret.

Amanda told them of Kadlin and their trip to Theasendür. She even boasted a little about her theft of the Horn of Valhalla, but she said very little about her capture and nothing about the events that followed until Jerrod's rescue. As much as she tried, her eyes eventually came to rest on Jerrod, causing him to shift in his seat.

"How did you end up arriving on an Elven sled?" Drin asked.

"Farris landed us in the Elven kingdom of Asenthia, north of here," Jerrod answered.

"Asenthia?" Fraum asked.

"Yes," Jerrod confirmed.

"Your knowledge of Elves always amazes me, Master Sage. Someday I would like to visit your library," Imelrinn commented respectfully.

"I would love to show you our scrolls."

"And the Horn of Valhalla that you stole? Why?" Rhonda asked.

"I owed a blood debt," Amanda answered, looking directly into Rhonda's eyes.

"A blood debt? For what?"

"I promised my thieves' guild that I would 'recover' the horn if they would pressure the priests in Cipper to heal you," Amanda confided.

"For me?" Rhonda questioned.

Amanda nodded her head slowly.

"So that's what changed their mind," Imelrinn thought aloud.

As Imelrinn spoke, Amanda reached into her bag and pulled out the ram's horn. She did not look at it but placed in immediately in the middle of the table.

"That's the legendary horn you went to steal?" asked Drin.

Amanda glared at Drin.

"Legend has it that the possessor of the horn can summon heroes from Valhalla, an Asgardian land of dead heroes," Fraum explained.

"From the dead? I doubt it. Dead is dead," Drin proclaimed.

"Each religion offers its own beliefs, leading to multiple possibilities," Fraum countered diplomatically.

"If I don't deliver the horn to the guild within the year they will send assassins to kill all of us. And there are more than enough assassins to get the job done," Amanda offered, looking towards Fraum for support.

"Assassins! You're an..." Drin protested.

"No, I am not an assassin! I am a thief. I am the guild's greatest thief," Amanda interrupted.

"And now you are the possessor of a legendary horn that has great power," Fraum pointed out.

After the tense discussion over their morning meal, Amanda and Fraum went for a walk while Jerrod, Rhonda, and Imelrinn met with the Elven guards to work out the details of the return trip. Drin, who was happy to be left alone so that he could pray, return to his room. The discussion about summoning the dead had shaken his resolve. He spent the remainder of the morning on his knees seeking guidance.

While he attempted to pray, Drin was tormented by Fraum's statement about multiple religions with multiple options for the living and the dead. The thought of multiple worlds for the dead pried its way deeper into his mind, disrupting his ability to pray.

There was but one answer, the Order of One. And that the dead belong to heaven, hell, or purgatory. These are the only spiritual kingdoms. Drin considered his thoughts a moment. *The One will come,* Drin concluded.

☼   ☼   ☼   ☼   ☼

While Drin prayed, Amanda and Fraum walked through the city. Amanda found the morning cold somehow refreshing. As they walked, the citizens of Silandria did not seem to intrude in their thoughts. Nor did Amanda and Fraum speak with anyone, not even between themselves.

A world of silence, Amanda thought.

"Master?" Amanda said, breaking that silence.

"What is it?" Fraum's soft voice encouraged her to continue.

"I don't know where to start," she mumbled.

"As always, at the beginning," Fraum smiled.

When Amanda started it all seemed to spill out like a child's confession, rambling and unable to stop. She spoke of her mother's death and growing up in the house of an unknown thief. How he had mentored her. How she had protected herself from attachments to others and her manipulation of men's feelings to get what she desired. Things had changed for her when she met Jerrod. She spoke of the months in Torrence before their journey, of her love for the stable boy from Winfred, and finally, of Jerrod's betrothal to Rhonda.

"Does Jerrod know how much you love him?"

"Yes. I gave myself to him before I knew he was betrothed to Rhonda," Amanda whispered, her eyes cast down at the red tiled street.

"I know that Jerrod thought you were gone, if that helps," Fraum responded.

They walked on silently for a few minutes before Fraum spoke again.

"A lot can happen between now and their autumn wedding. Look what we have been through in the months we have been together." The gentle scholar paused to look at the young thief.

Fraum took her hands in his, bouncing them up and down gently until he had her attention. When Amanda finally looked into his almond shaped eyes, Fraum continued.

"It may not feel like it but things will change. It's like the spring that offers new life. Things will turn out okay."

Amanda collapsed into his chest.

"But what do I do?" Amanda said as she began to cry.

"Come with me to Torrence and I will show you our library. We can practice more on your training while we figure the rest out," Fraum encouraged her as he put his arms around her. "You are very special, my child," Fraum finished.

✳   ✳   ✳   ✳   ✳

After meeting with the Elven guard, Jerrod and Rhonda returned to their room. While Rhonda went to change, Jerrod found a seat near the large window where he could watch the wet snow as it began to fall in big flakes. He did not realize Rhonda was approaching, and jumped when she put her hands on his shoulders. Taking her hands, Jerrod pulled Rhonda around in front of him and then enticed her to sit.

"We need to talk," Jerrod started.

"What is it?"

"I need to tell you about our trip back from Haithenbeurn."

"Haven't you told me everything already?" Rhonda questioned.

"On the first night, after we landed in the forest, I healed Amanda's injuries," Jerrod began to explain.

"You used your magic?" Rhonda asked, confirming what he had already told her.

"Yes, but that is not what I need to talk about right now," Jerrod said, looking into her green eyes.

"Amanda was a mess. She was in a lot of pain and very grateful to be alive. On the second night we landed in Asenthia. They gave us warm food and dry clothes. Amanda was very emotional." Jerrod stopped.

I hurt Amanda when I confessed my betrothal, but it was the right thing to do. How am I here again? He swallowed deep.

"After we said good night, Amanda came to my room. I tried to tell her about us."

"You slept with her?" Rhonda interjected.

"Yes," Jerrod answered truthfully, his heart breaking again.

"You slept with her!" Rhonda repeated as she jumped up, pulling her hands free.

"It was wrong. I know it. But can you forgive me? Will you forgive me?" Jerrod's soft voice trembled.

"Jerrod! If I could…" Rhonda started.

A breeze began to rise in the room, lifting her hair away from her body as her eyes began to glow green. As Rhonda grew angrier, a silvery white light seemed to wash over Jerrod before Rhonda turned and stomped away.

Jerrod was once again alone. And once again his thoughts bounced between Amanda and Rhonda.

I love them both. Now I may have lost them both. How stupid can I be! Now what? Jerrod's mind seemed to explode with emotion.

Jerrod felt something pulling at his mind, like something or someone trying to touch his consciousness.

Who is it? Jerrod thought.

Ah, Jerrod, it is Rupaul. I'm the City's Manager.

I remember you. Why are you trying to get into my mind? Jerrod demanded.

Ah, well, I wanted to talk and I understand you are leaving in the morning. I wasn't sure we would have time to meet in person, Rupaul answered awkwardly. *I'm sorry. I don't know where to start,* Rupaul stumbled through his thoughts.

The conversation rambled on for a while but really didn't seem to focus on a particular question until the end. *"What is this Asgardian horn you have brought into our city?*

It is an artifact from the north. Payment we owe for services we received in Torrence. It will be gone in the morning, Jerrod answered.

When Rupaul tried to say goodnight, Jerrod captivated his thoughts, holding the mental connection open. The feeling of captivation began to panic Rupaul.

While you were trying to read my thoughts without being noticed, I read yours, Rupaul. Stay out of my friends' minds. While all this is new to me, I promise you that I will use everything within my power to protect my friends, Jerrod warned.

Troubled by yet another issue, Jerrod decided to take a walk. The walls of the building went right to the edge of the city, beyond which was either water or a cliff. Around the city a street would occasionally find the city's edge where a beautiful patio was built for others to enjoy the view. There was a grand view along the southern cliff, overlooking the Metamesterrian River far below the city, the Elven-Dwarven mountains known as Alfarakenloria of the east, and the U'thra Basin, a great plain further south. The ice on the Metamesterrian River and the lake surrounding the city was beginning to break up. Yet, the days were still cold and the nights were even colder.

Amanda found him sitting on a patio taking in the panorama, but Jerrod's mind was empty. He was trying to let go of all the turmoil in his life, contemplating nothing as he sought the answers to his life.

Where it all began, Jerrod thought to himself as his eyes came to rest on the sunset.

Jerrod was envisioning Torrence's walls, the king's castle, and the cathedral of the Order of One in the evening sunlight. He did not hear Amanda walk up behind him. The thief's voice startled him.

"May I join you?"

"Please," Jerrod responded as he sat up quickly.

"Where's Rhonda?"

"I don't know."

"Are you okay?"

"Yes," he lied.

"You are going to Lithlillia with her, aren't you?" Amanda asked.

"I think so. She's not talking to me at the moment. And you? I suspect you are returning to Torrence?" Jerrod's voice was distant.

"I have to take the horn to the Grand Thief of the Crimson Pommel Guild and then I'm going to the White Fist Monastery. I don't know after that."

CHAPTER 8
PARTING OF WAYS

Rupaul watched from the city walls as the group crossed the western bridge. Humans rarely sensed the mental probing, but when they did they had never been able to block it. Fraum and Drin had been open books. The Elves had been a little tougher due to their "sensitivities." To his surprise, Amanda had been unreadable. He had not sensed anything extraordinary about her. In fact, he had not sensed anything about her mind at all. It was as if her mind was not present. Jerrod, on the other hand, had entrapped his mind.

The travelers from the west departed Silandria with a wagon full of treasure, ten riders, and a number of mules purchased at a premium price. Rupaul watched Jerrod and Imelrinn leading the caravan across the bridge, followed by Rhonda, and then the large wagon with a trail of riders.

Farewell. May your minds be trouble free, Rupaul thought to himself.

Amanda rode with Fraum, withdrawing from the others as she sat high up on the wagon bench, protected by the physical barrier between wagon and horse. She did not want to join any of the conversations or listen to the ramblings that had become customary on long rides. Riding west across the Meadows for the entire day, they found themselves setting up camp on the eastern edge of the Gap of Dillandria just before dusk. They rested between the cliffs of Kronese to the west and Metamesterrian back to the east. This was where they would split again.

There was little talking during the evening meal, but there was one thing on their minds that needed to be addressed.

"And what of Nathanial?" Jerrod finally asked.

No one had spoken of the wizard since Terrace Xul, which had left deep marks on all of their souls.

"We have no idea where he is," Rhonda pointed out, the tone of her words sharp.

"He is gone. Isn't that good enough?" Drin stated firmly.

"What was the book he took from the altar?" Jerrod asked.

"All that wealth and he only grabbed that book," Imelrinn spoke of his observation aloud as he watched the fire. "Why?"

"I am concerned about his intentions," Rhonda reflected.

"I believe it was the legendary Book of Brendril. The most powerful tome of spells in history," Fraum added.

"You couldn't have told us this before?" Imelrinn asked.

"I didn't know who might be in league with him and who was merely being used. As it turned out we were all his puppets."

"Is this why you sought to join our group? It wasn't to learn about the mountains or to draw pictures for your library as you suggested, was it?" Jerrod asked.

"Our journey is almost at its end. I must confess. My monastery was watching high ranking members of the Triad. Our Master had grown concerned. It was my responsibility to watch Nathanial, and when he went to leave, I had no choice but to join you," Fraum explained.

"Master?" Amanda spoke up, momentarily drawing the monk's attention.

"You lied," Drin accused him.

"No. It is true that our monastery collects and studies the mountains and plants. But I did fail to fulfill my responsibility. I go home in disgrace," Fraum concluded.

"For hundreds of years I have watched the struggles of Elves and man. There is no shame in what you have done," Imelrinn countered.

"We must part in the morning," Rhonda changed the subject.

"Those going to Torrence will descend the Gap of Dillandria to cross the U'thra Basin. The rest of us will cross the Meadows and enter the Black Forest," she concluded.

After a troubled night's sleep, they woke to have a last meal together and, when they were ready to resume their travels, to say their emotion-filled goodbyes. Jerrod and Amanda said their goodbyes to each other from a distance, avoiding eye contact.

"I want to thank you again for enduring what you did to save all of us," Rhonda said quietly to Amanda in private.

"You are my friends. What else could I do?"

Rhonda looked at the thief, her savior and her betrayer.

"Rhonda, I didn't know," Amanda pleaded.

"I know. It's just too soon."

Amanda stood there in her Elven dress, wrapped in furs from Lithlillia, and without a weapon. Rhonda considered how vulnerable Amanda appeared. Her eyebrows were raised, her pupils dilated. Rhonda watched her a moment.

"Perhaps in time. I know I owe my life to you," Rhonda finished as she gestured for a hug.

"Take care of him," Amanda whispered.

When all was said and done the wagon separated from the mule train and the two groups began their separate journeys home. Jerrod looked back over his shoulder to watch Amanda sitting on the wagon as it disappeared down the slope towards the basin below the gap, but Amanda never looked back.

The westward ride across the wide Meadow was long and cold. The shallow valley between the tree covered mountains was barren, open to the winter breeze, but it was not long before the tall trees of the Black Forest came into view.

"I remember the first time we entered the Black Forest. Nathanial seemed to fear it," Jerrod commented.

"You don't know the forest. It's not black at all. Our name for it is Ruhenmiur. It is part of Effenlia. The fairy place," Rhonda finished.

"And the Fendür?" Jerrod asked.

"The Fendür are always a concern, but we will be safe in Effenlia."

"The Fairies are an ancient race. They control the eastern end of Ruhenmiur," Imelrinn added.

They rode together in a loose group, two or three abreast. Sometime Imelrinn joined Jerrod and Rhonda. At other times he rode back with the guards, giving Jerrod and Rhonda time together. It was a straight path across the Meadows towards the bluish-gray silhouette of the treeline. They did not pause or falter at the border of the forest, but rode in, ignoring the barrier as a rider might ignore the gate in a fence.

Jerrod had expected to see some forest animals, but there were none.

Occasionally he heard birds chirping off in the distance, but they flew away before the riders got close. Even the rabbits scurried away before they approached. The absence of forest animals in the pines bothered him a little, reinforcing his concern about the Black Forest.

They rode in single file until mid-day, the path twisting around small hills of granite with steep sides that were higher than a rider could see over. Manzanita bushes blanketed the hillsides, growing around boulders that protruded from the hills and the tall pine trees that grew from both the hills and ravines creating the forest landscape.

At first the pine trees were as Jerrod remembered from the year before when they entered the Black Forest from the south, pursued by mercenaries, but the trees began to change. The trunks grew much thicker, as thick as a street in Torrence was wide, and the brown bark was replaced by a thicker, reddish bark. Rather than the smoother bark of pine trees, the long grooves that ran up the sides of the trees were deep and rough.

"These trees are spectacular," Jerrod commented.

"They're redwoods," Imelrinn explained.

"I have never seen anything like them."

"They are special, sacred trees. Hundreds of years old," Rhonda added as she reined in her horse.

Sliding from her saddle, Rhonda stood a moment with her head down, eyes closed, connecting with nature's energy. Reaching out mentally, she raised her arms up, turning her palms towards the sky. Her mind touched the mind of the closest Fairy, a Forest Sprite who lived in a nearby tree.

After a moment the small female sprite appeared on a tree branch at the height of Rhonda's head. The sprite, who wore a brown button down jacket with green pants and a brown chaperon cap, poked her head out from behind the tree trunk. Her pale skin contrasted against the reddish bark of the tree, making it easier to distinguish her features. Jerrod marveled at the fact she was no taller than the length of a fighting dagger.

"Good day," Rhonda greeted the sprite.

"Good day," the creature answered with a nervous giggle.

"We're returning to Lithlillia from the Alfarakenloria. We would like to visit Effendoria, if your queen will have us."

"Who are you?" the sprit asked coyly.

"I am Rhonda, daughter of the Lady of Lithlillia, druid of E'fretté, and protector of the forest realms. These are Imelrinn, my protector, the Elves of Lithlillia, and Jerrod of the flat-lands, who travel with me," Rhonda answered.

"Are there many of you?" the tiny sprite replied as she tucked her blonde hair behind her pointed ear.

"Just those you see. Will you inform your queen of our desire to visit her realm?"

"I will. Do you know your way?"

"I do, thank you. We did not want to surprise Her Majesty by showing up in her realm unannounced," Rhonda said politely.

Rhonda turned to the others to indicate they would rest for a while. While they rested they passed out some unleavened bread, cheese, and smoked meat to eat, and wine to wash it down. Imelrinn slid a harp from a mule's pack and began playing an Elvish song. The music was enchanting. His long slender fingers delicately picked the strings with unmatched grace as he stared into the forest.

"I didn't know you played. Where did you get the harp?" Jerrod asked.

"I bought it in Silandria. I thought it would be nice as we traveled," Imelrinn explained.

Jerrod listened as his friend created mystical music. The Elvish sound reminded him of Lithlillia and Asenthia as he allowed his mind to drift pleasantly with the music. He watched the ancient Elve play with his eyes closed, his body swaying with the rhythm as he plucked the harp.

"It seems like your mind is in another place," Jerrod said when the Mountain Elve finished.

"It has been a long time. I suppose the Fairy Realm is encouraging me. I haven't wanted to play since Rhonda was young," the ancient Elve answered.

"I remember," Rhonda commented. Her eyes seemed to sparkle a little as she smiled.

"Are we close to their realm?"

"We will be there in the morning if we travel through the night," Rhonda responded as she reflected on Imelrinn's music.

"Traveling through the night?" Jerrod asked.

"There are things in the forest we do not want to meet. The sooner we are in Effendoria, the better we will be," Rhonda explained and then walked away.

"I thought we were headed to Effenlia?" Jerrod asked.

"*Effenlia* means 'fairy place.' *Effendoria* means 'fairy kingdom.' It shows respect for the Fairy Queen," Imelrinn explained.

"Who is in Effendoria?"

"The Fairy Kingdom is made up of different races of Fairy-Folk. Fairies, Brownies, Pixies, and Sprites. They are all cousins. Sprites are small creatures who are often associated with the elements of nature, such as Water or the Forest Sprites. They are high spirited and nervous, quick to react, and somewhat untrusting." Imelrinn paused to sip his wine.

"Pixies, on the other hand, are mischievous little creatures, as small as the Sprites. They live underground, often in ancient ruins. They love to dance and are easily distracted by music."

"And Brownies?" Jerrod asked.

"They are larger, nearly the height of a rabbit standing on its back legs. Brownies are the largest of the Fairy realm. They are also the most secretive. They live in the rocks along the cliffs and riverbanks, but prefer stone bridges and abandoned buildings. They seldom speak with anyone or anything other than other Brownies. They barely even speak to their Fairy and Elven kinsmen."

"Is that all?"

"Other than the Fairies themselves?" Imelrinn chuckled. "Fairies are regal, soft-spoken, intelligent creatures with translucent wings. Their size varies with magic, but their true size is about the size of a songbird. Fairies glimmer when they're happy," the ancient Mountain Wood Elve's voice trailed off to a whisper as he fondly recalled past memories.

"Rhonda said 'things.' I remember our unpleasant encounter with the Fendür trolls. What other 'things' lurk out there?" Jerrod asked.

"Imps, colossal bears, tree snakes, the Fendür... and worse," Imelrinn turned to look at the young man he called a friend.

"And worse? Like Vespree?"

"No Vespree in the Ruhenmiur. They like higher elevations, like the Crispten and Brisbane Mountains," Imelrinn explained as he watched Jerrod.

"Don't worry. We are less than a day from Effendoria. We will move as quickly as we can and we will soon have the Queen watching over us."

"She's that powerful?"

"Powerful may not be the word for it. She is a Fairy. Fairies have a natural connection to the magic. It is hard to imagine. Their personal 'magic' may be less powerful than a druid, but their connection to E'fretté is direct. Reality is quickly lost in the presence of angry Fairy-Folk."

After the mid-day meal they mounted up and rode northwesterly, deeper into the eastern end of the Ruhenmiur. As evening fell and the dim light of the afternoon gave way to the darkness of the night, they unpacked more bread and wine to pass around as they continued to ride. Very soon after dark they were forced to dismount and lead their horses.

During their dark journey, somewhere deep in the sands of time, Jerrod thought he saw a small, glowing sphere of light darting around between the tree trunks and lower limbs, like a firefly playfully dodging through cattails over a still pond.

In the forest there was no way of telling how much time had fallen. The moons were not visible through the canopy that extended far above their heads. But in the consuming darkness the number of fireflies grew, hovering nearby. They were more of a glow than a spot of light, as though they were not quite in focus. The tiny spheres came in blues, and greens, and yellows. And on a rare occasion, there would be a silvery, white sphere that floated slowly by at a distance.

As dawn rose over the redwood canopy, the glowing lights surrendered their luster to more prominent figures. In place of the lights were small men and women dressed in silky, sheer clothes, with nearly translucent wings. Were it not for the longer hair, at a distance Jerrod would not have been able to tell between the men and the women. They hovered like hummingbirds before darting away.

"Fairies?" Jerrod whispered to Imelrinn.

His ancient Elven friend just smiled at him.

As the morning light crept into the redwood forest, they mounted their horses for the remainder of the trip. It was still early morning when they could see in the distance a stone wall with an arched stone gateway wide enough for the horses and mules to pass through. Moss-like vines hung from the trees and stone wall. There was no snow on the ground or the archway. Beyond the boarder of Effendoria lush, green grass covered the forest floor.

Magic like Asenthia, Jerrod thought to himself.

Elves are our kinsmen, came the tender thoughts of a female mind.

Rhonda and all the Elves were looking at him.

"I meant no disrespect," Jerrod offered.

"When did you start reading minds?" Rhonda looked puzzled.

"It is something I have slowly started doing. It started on the flight to Theasendür and has grown stronger since," Jerrod said innocently.

"That was the queen who contacted you," Rhonda said.

"The queen? Have I done something wrong?" Jerrod asked as Rhonda began to ride ahead with anticipation of greeting the queen.

"The queen seldom talks to anyone. And never to anyone who is not Fairy-Folk," Imelrinn explained.

When they stopped before the entrance, Rhonda dismounted and stepped forward. She stood alone before the wall for a moment while the air above them quickly filled with hundreds of fluttering fairies. On the ground and the stone wall there were twice the number of Fairy-Folk wearing pants, overcoats, and dresses. Some were climbing up from behind the wall while others simply faded into view as if they had always been there.

"I am Rhonda, druid princess of Lithlillia, the Alfardoria to the west beyond Kronese and the Ruhenmiur. We come as friends of Effendoria. May we enter?"

A fairy with a silvery aura flew slowly forward. As she landed, she transformed into an Elven sized woman with long silvery white hair that fell straight beyond her hips. Her oval face with its high cheekbones, narrow nose, and thin lips resembled the Elven features with which Jerrod had become so familiar. The appearance of her pointed ears from under her beautiful, soft hair completed the picture.

"Welcome, Rhonda, daughter of Lady Lieisa and Lord Steffen, druid princess under Limerin Falls. You are welcome here," the Fairy Queen addressed Rhonda, and then turned towards Jerrod.

"Welcome Great One. We have foreseen your arrival."

Jerrod was surprised to be addressed directly, but thought it wiser to do no more than politely acknowledge the greeting. He was taken by the soft paleness of the queen's skin, and was overwhelmed by her beauty.

"Thank you," he answered.

When he looked away he noticed Rhonda smiling at him.

"What?"

"You are incorrigible! I am going to have to keep my eye on you," Rhonda teased.

As they entered the Fairy Realm they left the snow and cold behind. Inside the magical realm the morning fog had lifted, leaving the dew on all the plants. The ground was soft and wet, comforting to their feet as they walked.

Inside the stone wall, Jerrod sensed a calming peacefulness. As they continued they started to hear full, deep-bodied harps and high pitched, metallic flutes being played somewhere off in the distance. The music reminded Jerrod of the enchanting sounds in Asenthia and he felt like he was floating across the ground.

"Careful. Don't give in to the music," Rhonda whispered.

"It's wonderful. Better than Asenthia."

"That's the magic. It could be awful and you would still want to lie down and sleep your life away or wander off as if you were chasing a Will-o'-the-Wisp. Fairies are our friends, but in some ways they are more dangerous than our being alone in the forest."

"Will of who?"

"Will-o'-the-Wisp. They look like fireflies or fairies and lure people into swamps and bogs to drown. They are undead souls that mean you harm."

"Are there any in Effendoria?"

"No."

"Then why bring it up?"

"Jerrod! It was just an example."

"I'm sorry."

"It's okay. There's just a lot of differences in our past experiences. We will work through it. Now, come on."

Taking Jerrod firmly by the hand Rhonda led the Elves to a large lake where they were surrounded by Fairies, Brownies, Pixies, and Sprites. It was as if they were setting up camp in the middle of an ongoing gala, the music and dancing already well underway. The queen entered their camp as they busily unloaded the tents from the pack mules. Again the striking elegance of her Elven size female figure, which seemed almost transparent, caught Jerrod's eye.

"Rest. You are welcome as long as you would like to stay. No one will touch your treasures or bother you." The queen's pleasant voice, echoing softly through the nearby glade, was comforting.

After the queen's welcome, they quickly set out the bedrolls, but it was so comfortable they decided to sleep in the open air. Rhonda and Jerrod laid their rolls away from the others for a little privacy. Nearby they could hear the frogs and crickets at the lake's edge.

It had barely been two days since they left Silandria and Rhonda was already mentally drained. When she finally slept, her sleep was tormented by thoughts of Amanda, who had saved all of them but had seduced her betrothed, and of Jerrod, who had willingly accepted the thief into his bed. The conflict between her anger and her appreciation for Amanda's sacrifice weighed upon her soul, even in the mystic beauty of the Fairy Realm.

Rhonda rose from her bed next to Jerrod. She could see that on the far side of the lake the shore was lined with square stones. A stone wall covered with ivy and secluded by several redwoods would offer privacy for bathing. Under the starry sky, Rhonda walked around the edge of the lake, listening to the fairy music. When she reached the far side of the lake she slipped off her clothes before stepping gracefully down the stones into the lake.

She did not know how long she floated on her back, her pointed ears submerged in the crystal clear water, unable to hear the noises of the demanding world. Her body and mind relaxed. When she was done floating, she moved to the stones to sit in the water along the edge of the lake. When she looked away from the lake she was surprised to see a white unicorn watching her.

His long flowing mane and tail were free from tangles. The spiraling horn in the middle of his forehead was exceptionally long, indicating his many years of age. Rhonda drew in a breath. The steed was one of the most perfect equine specimens she had ever seen.

I am sorry to disturb you, the unicorn thought, sensing Rhonda's embarrassment at being naked.

The mythical steed turned his head away, allowing Rhonda to dress in privacy.

So it's true? Rhonda thought.

True?

Unicorns appear to virgins. Is it only virgins?

Yes, it's true.

But why only virgins?

Virginity represents purity and devotion. We appear in times of need.

But I want him so much, Rhonda's thought desperately.

I know, but you are a druid princess and future priestess. You must be a virgin when you are married or you will not become the priestess. Your powers will diminish.

I know, but I love him so much! Rhonda's thoughts rushed out, repeating her deepest desire.

The Great One loves you, the unicorn comforted her.

Great One? The Queen called him 'Great One' too. Why do you call him 'the Great One'? Rhonda questioned.

He is the one in a thousand years. The one with a true connection to magic.

He is not a simple flatlander then, Rhonda responded, already knowing the answer to her question.

No, and there is more.

More?

You know the prophecy. A second hero will come and fall, and from his blood another hero will bring splendor to a new kingdom. The first hero, Sir Michael, has fallen. The fairies have foreseen Jerrod to be the rising hero. But one must still die.

Who must die? Rhonda quickly responded.

We cannot say. The answer was without emotion.

Will Jerrod succeed? Will I lose him? Rhonda thought slowly, unsure she wanted to know the answer.

He loves you now. Cherish that.

With respect, that is not an answer, Rhonda pressed.

That is the answer. Every time you make a decision you potentially change your own future. You can make your own destiny, Princess of Lithlillia.

After her encounter with the magical steed, Rhonda returned to the camp more troubled than she had been when she first sought a bath. Jerrod still slept where she had left him. She lay down next to him and kissed his forehead before falling back to let sleep overtake her.

When they rose the Effendoria was covered in a refreshing mist, covering the plants with moisturizing droplets of fresh water. The fragrance from the wet flowers filled the air, easing any residual tension from the evening's sleep. The fog softened the morning light as if to ease the morning into daylight.

At the morning meal Rhonda told the others they would spend the day resting and then leave first thing the next morning. It was a directive, not open for discussion, which caused Jerrod to go to her immediately after the meal. Taking her hands in his, he pulled her close.

"Are you okay?" he asked softly as he looked into her green eyes as they turned golden.

"Yes, as long as you are with me," Rhonda answered.

"Your command to leave tomorrow morning was unexpected. What happened?"

"Nothing. We must go," Rhonda answered, her voice raising a little as she spoke more rapidly than normal.

"Of course we must go, but what of the things in the forest?"

"It will be okay. Some Effendoria guardians will accompany us to Trisdale," Rhonda said, unable to continue looking into Jerrod's eyes.

Each of the travelers spent the day relaxing in their own way. Imelrinn played his harp and visited with the other Elves. Rhonda and Jerrod wandered through the forest and visited with the fairies. As they walked Rhonda and Jerrod talked of meaningless things, but spent no time on the thoughts that bothered them.

As evening fell the top of the forest canopy collected the sunlight and passed it down through the trees' veins and out across their lower limbs, causing the trees to glow ever so slightly. The glow from the branches and leaves became more prevalent in the darkness of night, casting a silvery tint around the glen in which they camped. Above them some of the light from the rising moons managed to twist its way through the tree limbs, casting magical hues of green and purple light that changed in waves that illuminated the glen. The Fairies brought golden candles that floated in the air, complementing the other lights in the enchanted forest.

When the Queen came to them her form was solid. Her pale, white skin seemed to glisten in the magical light, her translucent wings softly reflecting at times the silver, gold, green, and purple light around them. Her silvery white gown trailed behind her.

Here, come partake of the Fairies' food. Have the evening meal with me, she invited as she spread her arms over the forest floor.

At her feet a long, red blanket appeared to cover the ground. On the blanket were trays of minced venison with raisins and spice, roast wild boar, and boiled quail eggs. There were other forest foods like potatoes, mushrooms, bowls of fruit, and assorted cheeses from the milk of wild goats.

The queen sat at the end of the blanket, beckoning them to join her. As everyone sat along the blanket, Brownies began bringing them pitchers of a crystal clear liquid they called '*dew*' and kept the guests' tiny tea cups full. The Fairy music floated in from the surrounding forest.

At first Jerrod was offended by the smallness of the cups, but after feeling how quickly the *dew* warmed his body, he surrendered. The drink was immediately intoxicating. The liquid, magically fermented by the fairies, was made from the morning's dew, and after a couple teacups everyone was giggling happily. Even Imelrinn relaxed, allowing his protective guard to relax. Disposing of his usual serious nature, the ancient Elve's laughter was disarming. Once again he picked up a lap harp, his music quieting the laughter.

"You surpass any of the music I've heard, my friend. Whether the bard's near Cipper or the music of the Elven kingdoms," Jerrod told him.

"Thank you, Jerrod, for such a compliment. You're too kind."

Rhonda relaxed, too. Lying on her side with her head in Jerrod's lap, she gazed up at her love as she slowly spun a flower stem between her fingers, picking the petals off one by one. She was intoxicated and intoxicating, so much so that Jerrod could think of nothing else to the point that he almost forgot to breathe.

At the end of the meal the fairies brought a cake covered by a blue flame. The rich cake, warmed by the fire, was sweeter than anything any of them had experienced. The small bits of fruit in the cake tingled with bursts of intoxication when bit. After their first thin slice, they pieced upon small bites that they randomly broke off when they desired more. As they spoke together of what had passed and of dreams to come, Jerrod could envision dimensional images of each topic in his mind.

When the dessert was finished, Rhonda pulled Jerrod up by the hand, dragging him playfully back to their sleeping area. It seemed so much more than a thicket, curtained by moss hanging from tree limbs surrounding them. Their bedrolls lay together on the lush grass. They undressed quickly. The soft forest light caused their naked bodies to glow as Rhonda and Jerrod lay together, ready for sleep, but Rhonda wanted more. She pulled Jerrod onto her, kissing his neck, but he resisted her seduction.

"What is it, Jerrod? I thought you wanted more," Rhonda questioned.

"No. I mean yes, but not like this. You must be a virgin."

"What?"

"You must be a virgin."

"Aren't I good enough? Don't you want me?"

"Yes, but I can't."

"You wanted Amanda! What's wrong with me?"

"Sweetheart," Jerrod pled.

"No! Don't sweetheart me. Get out!" Rhonda demanded.

"But..."

"Get out!"

Grabbing his clothes and boots, Jerrod stood up and walked across the thicket, stopping briefly to dress. He paused a moment to look back at Rhonda before he passed through the hanging moss.

What just happened? he thought.

Unaware of how long or in what direction he walked, Jerrod's thoughts jumped from Rhonda to Amanda and back again. He was unable to concentrate on either of them. Here and there Fairies fluttered through the trees and scantily-clad Tree Sprites jumped around the base of large trunks in games of hide and seek. When they saw Jerrod they giggled and quickly disappeared into the forest. Their presence annoyed him as he kept walking further into the fairy forest.

When Jerrod came upon three Brownies sitting on some small rocks he tried to address them, but they got up to scamper away.

"Wait! Please," Jerrod begged.

"What is it?" One stopped to face him.

"Why do you run?" Jerrod asked, but the Brownie turned to walk away.

"I'm looking for your queen. Do you know where she is?"

"Up ahead. Follow the path," the Brownie responded before fading into the air like fog burnt off by the morning sun.

It was only a few minutes' walk. More than a dozen fairies were floating nearby when he approached the queen. Their bodies glowed, bright with happiness.

"Excuse me," Jerrod said, trying to be polite.

One silvery-white fairy flew slowly towards him.

"What is it, Great One?" the queen asked as she took Elven shape.

"I wanted to thank you for your hospitality."

"You are welcome," the queen's voice was soft.

"May I ask, why do you call me Great One?"

"Don't you feel it?" the queen responded.

"Feel what?"

"The magic. You have magic in your being."

"I have felt something. It is a... a power. It seems to be growing, but I don't know how."

"Once in a thousand years a human is born with the link to our world."

"A link? A mental link? What do you mean?" Jerrod asked as politely as he could, but the tone of his voice disclosed his concern.

"It is neither mental nor physical. It is both. The fabric of your body and your soul are part of the magic. They are part of the natural force the Elves have named E'fretté."

Jerrod spoke with the queen for a while, but when he left he seemed to have more questions than answers and the intoxicating effect of the evening meal had worn off. He walked as if he was in a trance, without focus or purpose. Slowly he began to realize he simply wanted to get back to Rhonda.

The Fairies gave him directions to get back to the camp that seemed easy to follow and the route seemed more direct than his wanderings had been. As instructed, when Jerrod reached the large lake he turned left to follow the shoreline around to the camp. Walking at night along the shoreline, the lake seemed to call to him, causing him to linger.

Questil and Dori reflected on the still water. Crickets and frogs sang a night-song, but there was something more. Losing his thoughts to the magical night, Jerrod picked up a flat, oval stone and flung it across the lake's surface. While he watched, circles radiated out from each spot where the stone skipped off the water, and several soft female voices came into focus. Jerrod looked up, startled to see several naked women in the middle of the lake. The Water Sprites' bodies were ghostly white, their silver hair glistening in the moonlight as they sat upon some large boulders protruding from the middle of the lake.

"Come swim with us," they pled in unison.

Jerrod looked into their cold, grey eyes that, even from the distance, seemed to look into his soul. They giggled when Jerrod began to strip. He sat down and, as he was slipping off his second boot, dark clouds rolled over the lake. When a deafening clap of thunder struck close overhead, the sprites dove under the water, escaping the bolt of lightning that burst across the dark sky. Behind him, Rhonda stood with her green eyes glowing, her light brown hair floating in the air, as the wind created waves across the lake.

"Do not tempt my betrothed," echoed across the surface.

Jerrod turned to see Rhonda standing behind him, unsure of what had happened. As Rhonda relaxed, the storm dissipated. The lake returned to its smooth, glass surface and the skies above the lake once again became bright and clear with glimmering stars.

"You can't swim with sprites, Jerrod. At best you will never return," Rhonda said with a smile.

"And at worst?" Jerrod asked as he began to dress.

"You will drown when they lose interest in you," Rhonda answered calmly.

The lack of tone in her voice made Jerrod uneasy. He finished dressing as quickly as he could. When he was finished he turned to tell her he loved her.

"I know," Rhonda said before he could speak.

* * * * *

Amanda had not looked back as the wagon started down the long, snow-covered slope of the gap. The snow was wetter and the ground underneath was not as frozen as it had been. The wheels sunk into the moist sod as they rolled through small white flowers that pushed up through the snow. The flowers hung down from green stalks like white drops. Spring was coming.

"The snowdrops are sprouting," Fraum said to himself.

Amanda did not comment. She sat thinking of the wheels rolling through the moist ground and the tracks they were leaving behind them. She could see Drin riding in front of the small wagon while the two Elven escorts rode behind. The wagon creaked and groaned under the weight of the treasure as it lumbered down the hill towards the U'thra basin.

"Change so soon," Fraum continued without looking at Amanda.

Change? My love rides away with his betrothed, Amanda thought.

"It's not just the weather that is changing, is it?" Fraum pressed, turning his head to look at the young woman sitting next to him.

Amanda looked away. Her eyes fixed on the horizon over the long, gentle hills of the otherwise flat basin. A steady winter breeze blew across the plain.

They traveled south for many hours before stopping to eat and then continued on until nightfall. The open plain of U'thra was harsh. The blowing wind made it seem colder than a late-winter night ought to be. They started burning some wood they carried for campfires and struggling to set up their tent. Even on the leeward side of the wagon there was no relief from the wind. As they struggled to prepare their camp, three tall men covered with wolf furs walked out of the dark plain into the edge of their campfire's light.

Amanda noticed the strange bows they carried. She cautiously slipped away from the fire and onto the wagon, reaching for her bedroll. She rested her hand on the hilt of her sword, waiting for what might come.

I wish I hadn't had to leave my bow with Grogan, she thought.

"May we enter your camp?" one man shouted out.

At the sound of the man's voice, Drin stood up and drew his two handed sword from its sheath. Fraum also stood up and stepped towards the three men as he played with his rope belt, feeling the weight of the balls on the end of the three braided leather cords.

"Greetings. What brings you to our camp?" Fraum answered.

"We saw the fire and wondered who would be traveling across the basin on a winter night?"

"Come in. We are brewing some tea. Join us," Fraum invited.

Still resting on the wagon bench like an eagle watching its prey, Amanda observed the exceptionally tall men as they approached out of the darkness. They carried a freshly killed antelope and several wolf skins. Large quivers holding many arrows rested on their shoulders. The limbs of the bows they carried seemed to curve strangely forward at the grip, away from the shooter, and then back towards the string near the tip of the limbs. Even under the pressure of bowstring, the tips bent forward again.

"Why do you build your fire like this?" one of the men asked.

"We are making camp for the night," Drin answered as he resheathed his sword.

"What would you suggest?" Fraum asked.

The men looked around and then at one another.

"Come. Put out your fire and come with us. You'll stay at our village tonight, out of the wind. This is no place to be on a winter night," they insisted.

After agreeing to follow the hunters to their village, Amanda and Drin packed quickly while Fraum put out the fire with snow and some sod where the snow had melted. They hitched the mules again and were following the hunters within the hour. It was a couple more hours before the fires of the U'thra village came into view.

Their village was built near a brook that bubbled up out of the ground, creating a natural springwater pond. About half of the pond was surrounded by tall bushes. A single tree stood nearby.

The village huts were oblong, constructed of stone and vegetation, and covered by sod dug up from the plains. The small huts were clustered together in a tight group far enough from the pond that nothing from the village would contaminate their water source. In the center of the cluster was a much larger, round building with a peaked roof. The only animals visible as they approached were dogs and chickens.

"I know the Order teaches that theirs is the only religion, but don't they also teach respect for others, particularly those who are helping you?" Fraum asked.

"Yes."

"These plains people will undoubtedly follow another religion. They are offering us sanctuary from the cold and have asked for nothing in return. Let's not be judgmental," Fraum cautioned.

"That seems to be a contradiction, being devoted to the Order of One and accepting other religions," Drin said, looking up at the monk from the saddle of his horse.

"Do you live a life of absolutes? Things are seldom purely right or purely wrong, one way or another. If you listen to your heart you will hear what should be done," Fraum counseled the younger man.

The villagers came out of their huts to see the strangers and the large wooden wagon pulled by strange animals. They were particularly interested in Drin's metal armor. The old man in his robes carrying a red mahogany staff and a young woman wrapped in strange fur drew far less attention.

Out of the crowd stepped an old man assisted by a teenage girl. One of the hunters accompanying the travelers went to the old man for a private discussion. The other two hunters laid their harvests down, causing some village women to scurry forward and then carry off the meat and furs towards the village..

After their discussion, the old man walked with the first hunter to greet Fraum.

"Welcome," the old man said.

"Thank you," Fraum responded, bowing at the waist.

"I am told you were camping on the plain. Come, come to our village. You must be cold and hungry," the old man invited before turning to walk back into the cluster of huts.

They group of villagers parted, allowing the travelers and their wagon to pass, and then followed closely behind, but the wagon could not fit between the buildings and had to be parked outside. Leaving their horses tied to a wagon wheel, the five travelers continued following on foot.

When they reached the larger hut at the center of the village, the woman pulled a flap made of several furs aside so the old man could enter more easily. Furs hung from thick walls made from dirt and vegetation. Passing through the walls beyond the flap, there was a small room that collected the colder outside air, keeping it out of the inner part of the building. Another flap covering the far end of the room protected the warmth of the inner room, which was dark, lit only by torches and the glowing embers of a log-less fire.

The old man went around the embers to sit on a woven mat on the far side of the round room. Men and women of the village began flowing in to sit on the ground nearer to the pit. Around the outer wall were some tall woven baskets.

"Please, sit." The old man gestured to the ground where Amanda and the rest of the travelers stood.

Amanda noticed that the villagers had knives on their belts and there were several of the strange bows nearby, but there were no other weapons apparent in the hut. Her senses relaxed a bit as she sat down next to Fraum while Drin already sat uncomfortably on the sage's other side.

"We are U'thra. I am the Chieftain of our village. We will eat and talk," the old man stated.

The U'thra offered meat and potatoes roasted over the fire while Fraum answered questions about their journey. Most of the discussion was between Fraum and the older villagers, but occasionally a younger villager would interject a question.

"We have a vacant hut you and your men shall share. In our tribes single women stay together in one hut. Amanda can stay there," the Chieftain insisted.

After the meal a woman offered to lead Fraum, Drin, and the two Elves to the vacant hut. Several young women gathered around Amanda to show her to the hut where they all slept. Drin watched as the women surrounded her like a litter of kittens vying for the attention of their mother.

"I'll be fine," Amanda told Drin as they parted.

Like the lodge, the huts had small entry rooms. There were pegs in the walls for their heavy winter coats and stools to sit on. Several pairs of boots lined the wall around the stools.

"Sit. You can take your boots off here," one of the women said.

Inside the second flap bedrolls were laid out on a woven mats that covered all of the ground. The half dozen U'thra women that had accompanied Amanda to the hut took turns brushing each other's long straight black hair as they gossiped between their many questions.

The women openly welcomed Amanda without any noticeable concern, as if she were already one of their family, but her presence caused a mild excitement. They were curious who was Amanda? Where had she been? Where was she headed? What were other lands like? And so on. The questions did not seem to stop, one asked after another.

The Elven clothes under her furs created an even greater commotion. The soft, smooth texture of the Elven material caught the women's attention first, but Amanda's crimson dagger quickly became a topic of discussion. And there were questions about the metal clad warrior with dark curly hair and a square jaw whom several thought was adorable.

Answering their questions as quickly and directly as possible, Amanda felt like she was spinning in the center of the lodge, getting dizzy as she looked up. She was careful not to mention Haithenbeurn nor the contents of the bag she kept close to her side.

"Where are your horses?" Amanda asked.

"Horses? We don't have any horses. Just a few goats for milk, some chickens, and the dogs," one of the women answered.

"How do you get around?"

"We walk or run."

"I didn't see a lot of weapons. Do you have swords?" Amanda asked.

"No swords. A few axes for chopping. Mostly just knives and our bows."

"How do you protect yourselves?"

"From what? What can a sword do that a bow cannot do quicker? The men are great shots and our bows are strong. On the U'thra you see things coming in plenty of time to protect yourself."

"May I ask you something," another woman shyly asked.

"What is it?"

"What is the strange fur you wear?"

"It's a bear skin."

"A what?"

"A bear. They are large beasts that live in forests and mountains. They eat berries, tubers, insects, and sometimes other animals."

"It's a large skin."

"Normal bears are about the size of a horse, but I have seen much bigger ones."

When they were finally content, the women crawled into their bedrolls, but the conversations continued. The feminine banter made Amanda uncomfortable, so she quickly slipped into her bedroll, pushing her pack with the horn into her side and closing her eyes.

Before they slept, the women prayed to Utu that the sun would rise in the morning and Nanna that the moons would watch over them through the night. They prayed together, asking for simple things that would benefit the entire village.

No one can be this innocent. I wonder what they are hiding? Amanda thought as she pretended to sleep.

When the women were sleeping, Amanda pushed her pack with the horn to the bottom of her bedroll and then crawled out. She moved back into the entry to find a dog watching the flap. The animal looked up at her briefly and then went back to sleep. Slipping on her boots and fur, Amanda stepped out into the cold night.

From outside the huts, Amanda could not tell whether there were dogs sleeping just inside of the huts, so she decided to explore the lodge first. A quick check revealed that some baskets contained potatoes and others were full of peat collected from the plains to be burned in the fire pit. Amanda decided that her observations during the evening meal had been correct. There was nothing interesting in the lodge.

Slipping back outside, she paused to look up at the stars. They were beautiful, full of luster contrasted against the black emptiness of the night sky.

The last time I looked at the stars was on Vendal's ship. So much has happened. Where are you taking me, Zeus, father, god of fate? Has Hermes left me to you then? Amanda thought.

Amanda resumed her search. Going to the nearest hut, she paused to listen at the flap. Amanda could hear the light breathing of a dog just inside. The next hut had a guard dog as well, and the one after that.

This just isn't worth the trouble, Amanda thought.

Amanda was mildly amused by her willingness to give up the search. She wandered towards the pond for no reason other than to absorb comfort from the night's sky. Between the village and the pond she saw a single figure sitting cross-legged on the snow in meditation.

"Did you find what you were looking for?" Fraum spoke without moving.

"I found nothing, Master," Amanda answered as she sat down next to the monk.

"Ah, but did you find what you were looking for?"

"I don't understand."

"These are humble people. Did you really expect to find something or was your search more about you?" Fraum asked the legendary thief of Torrence.

"I have no interest in stealing from them, if that is what you mean," Amanda confessed.

"Perhaps you found what you were looking for. Perhaps you found you are no longer a thief."

Amanda looked at the older man a moment and then turned to watch the stars until her master was finished meditating. When she returned to her hut she checked for the horn before curling up to sleep. As she lay there, trying to go to sleep, Fraum's final words echoed in her mind. It had not been a question. It was a statement.

"If I am not a thief, what am I?" she pondered.

The village rose at dawn. Amanda was surprised to learn there was more to be done in the village each day than she had imagined. In addition to tending to the village children, cooking, and cleaning and mending clothes, the women gathered and processed the village food. They were responsible for picking berries and nuts, and tending to the potato gardens, but most importantly they cared for the hunters' harvest, which occurred at dusk or twilight.

During the winter especially, the village survived on hunting. The women cleaned and skinned each day, tanning hides while the men smoked and salted the meat to preserve it until it was completely consumed. When the hunt was good, the village prospered. When the herds of antelope and deer moved away, village life became more difficult.

The basin stretched from the mountains far east of the Metamesterrian River to the raised plain far west of the village. The northern border was the waterfall and cliffs of Silandria. The southern border was a delta that led into a great sea. Small ponds fed by water bubbling up through the ground littered the basin, providing for the only bushes and trees other than those along the river bank. Tiny villages were built near the ponds. The size of the basin and the plentiful water encouraged the herds to move. When they did, hunters had to travel further to feed the village.

Amanda helped with the chores while she talked with the single women. She learned more about the village life and the U'thra. The U'thra respected the elders and rejoiced in their children. Although the women had different chores than the men, they were perceived as equals, which Amanda found refreshing. Here it was a matter of what chores they were best suit for in order for the community to survive rather than an egotistical dominance based on sex.

After Haithenbeurn, this wouldn't be a bad place to spend some time, she thought.

When it was time for the morning meal, Amanda rejoined her friends in their hut. The single women brought them nuts, dried berries, thinly sliced strips of meat, and herbal tea. After eating they began to load their personal belongings back onto the wagon, but the hunters approached them to demonstrate the power of their bows.

"I know you were interested in our bows," one of the hunters said as he pulled out a coiled object.

"That's your bow?" Amanda asked.

In the center of the bow, on either side of the handle, was a thick limb that tapered off towards the tip, allowing the unstrung bow to curl into a circle. The limbs were made of three layers, wood with bone on the inside and sinew on the outside of the wood, allowing for flexibility over the length of the limb.

The man strung the bow and pulled a longer than normal arrow from his quiver. The arrow was almost another quarter shaft longer than an arrow from Torrence. Nocking his arrow the man shot at a nearby basket of potatoes, embedding the arrow deep into its target, to demonstrate its strength.

"Impressive," Fraum commented politely.

Potatoes aren't the densest target, Amanda thought, considering whether to take the weapon seriously.

The hunter offered him the bow. Fraum fired two shots at the basket and then turned to hand it to Amanda.

"Our women can't pull the bows back," the man said respectfully.

Amanda smiled for the first time in days. Nocking the arrow as it pointed towards the ground, she pulled back the string as she raised the bow towards its target and then released the arrow, splitting the hunter's in half.

"Rahhhh!" the village cheered.

"It's a fine bow," Amanda complimented the hunter as she handed it back to him.

"It's yours," he said, gesturing for her to stop.

"I can't," Amanda protested.

"It's yours. I give it to you."

"Only if you will accept something in return."

Amanda went back to the wagon and withdrew her sword, and then returned to where the hunter and Fraum stood.

"Here. From one hunter to another."

The man took her sword graciously.

When they were ready to leave the village, one of the single maidens who had shared the hut with Amanda came running up and placed a small stone idol on a leather strap in Amanda's hand.

"It is Inanna, goddess of war, passionate love, and female fertility. We want you to have it," the woman blurted out.

Amanda looked down at the small stone carving of a well-endowed woman with an overly thin waist and wide hips. Then she looked into the maiden's innocent eyes. The woman had no idea who Amanda was, the suffering she had endured, or what she was capable of. It was a simple gift meant to help Amanda achieve what all the women of the village hoped for, love and children.

Amanda thought a moment and then reached for her pack. Pulling it open, she sifted through the contents, taking a bag from the top of the contents. In the bag were coins and gems that she had personally collected during their journey. Mixed in with the other items was the large ruby she had acquired in Cheerin. Pulling the fist-sized gem from the bag, Amanda gazed at it for a moment and then handed it to the woman.

"Here. It isn't much, but please take it. It is rather valuable in my world. Maybe your village will have a use for it," Amanda said, placing the red gem in the young woman's hands.

"Thank you, Amanda. It's beautiful," the woman responded.

"What do you call your village?" Amanda asked.

"What do we call it? It is our village. Why would we call it anything?"

Amanda looked back over her shoulder as the wagon rolled away. The woman had watched briefly but then gone quickly back to her chores. Things had already returned to what they were before their arrival.

Survival, Amanda thought.

"That was a kind gesture," Fraum said when she turned back around.

"It's all I have left," Amanda responded.

"You have your portion of the treasure. You are wealthy," Fraum reminded her.

"And what will that buy?"

Fraum simply smiled.

CHAPTER 9
HOMECOMING

The plain had been cold and barren, covered with snow as the third month of the year began, but it melted away and the rains came. Their camps were uncomfortable at best and seldom dry. Amanda still spent much of her time thinking of Jerrod. She felt empty, betrayed by a love she had happily given.

Would I do it again? Yes, she concluded.

For whatever reason, to whatever end, she loved Jerrod. She had given herself to him freely, willingly, but in that moment she had lost herself. The king of Haithenbeurn had taken her resolve. She had never been caught and certainly never been tortured. There was nothing left.

She despised the Guild of the Crimson Pommel for their threats on her friends' safety, but it was the guild that had provided her a living after her mother's death.

Is there anything in my life that I regret? That I would not do again? The questions tormented her each night they camped.

But Amanda was not tormented alone. Each night seemed to irritate Drin a little more. He began pacing around the fire and fidgeting in the tent when they went to sleep. He spoke more and more of the Order and the dedication required to be a devout knight. Drin increased his prayer time, apparently in an effort to comfort his anxiety, spending more time on his knees before lying down to sleep.

Fraum, in his usual fashion, took things as they came. As Drin prayed, Fraum sat cross-legged to meditate and Amanda sat motionless, facing the older man while she tried to meditate. Years of thievery conditioned her to wait quietly. She watched, seemingly without breathing.

When he was done meditating, Fraum went out of the tent to begin his exercises, often in the rain. Without fail, he practiced the series of very slow movements designed to strengthen his arms. As he moved his arms slowly from side-to-side, over his head, and then back down to his waist, his muscles and arms vibrated with the rippling of his muscles. Amanda flawlessly mirrored his every movement.

Amanda's muscles did not shake with the fierceness of Fraum's, but Fraum was impressed by his student. As he observed Amanda, Fraum reflected on her ascent of the cliff near Sismen Summit. The climb had been easier for her than it had been for him. He knew she had strength. Her flawless execution of the mirrored exercise reminded him that Amanda's strength and abilities were deceiving.

When they were done exercising, they faced each other, practicing punching and blocking techniques. As they traveled, Fraum increased his speed to challenge Amanda.

"How long have you done that?" Drin asked one night when he finished his prayer first.

"As long as I have been a member of White Fists," the sage-monk replied.

"Why don't you use a sword?"

"I haven't needed one, but we are trained on swords, too. We are monks, not priests," Fraum answered.

"You haven't needed a sword? Not even against the vespree?" Drin teased.

"It might have been better to have a sword then, but I was on another errand at the time. An errand that did not allow for a sword, if you recall."

They talked a while before Amanda sheepishly asked a question that really did not need to be answered. She shifted her position, pulling one knee up to her chest, her other foot tucked between her ankle and her seat.

"It won't be the same when we get back to Torrence, will it?" Amanda said, looking down at her foot.

"What's bothering you, Amanda?" Fraum asked thoughtfully.

"We left seeking fortune. My share is more wealth than I will ever need, but I have lost everything. Everything except this," she finished as she pulled the horn out and set it on the ground to look at.

"And what will you do with it?" Fraum asked.

"It goes to the guild or we will all die," Amanda's voice was stern, but quiet. She resented the guild for forcing her to recover the horn.

"Perhaps," Fraum said, watching her until she looked up.

"You could take it to the Order and seek sanctuary," Drin offered.

"There are no walls that will protect any of us if the guild does not receive the horn soon."

"The future is never certain. You can decide your own destiny," Fraum's voice was soft and compassionate.

"Not Jerrod..." her voice trailed off as she looked back down, staring at her foot again.

"That is my fault, I'm afraid. I told him you were gone. I encouraged him to go to Rhonda," Drin confessed.

Amanda snapped her head up, looking at Drin as she considered what he had said. Her broken heart could not stomach the words. Already having cried her last tear for Jerrod, her head fell. Her dry eyes resumed their lost stare.

"It is no one's fault," Fraum interjected.

"Our choices have consequences. Whether you chose to do the right thing, or the wrong thing, each has consequences. You chose to save your friends no matter the consequence to you. I think that is admirable," Fraum added.

"But look at the cost."

"You have to be true to yourself. Not to a momentary desire. Where would you be if you had done otherwise?"

Amanda looked up at him.

"You are not the type that could have abandoned Rhonda to die in Cipper when you had the power to save her, just as you cannot doom all of us to be hunted down by your guild. I have always known you are a good person." Fraum encouraged her like a father consoling his daughter.

"I never would have thought I would find an honorable thief, but you are as honorable and virtuous as any knight I know," Drin added.

Fraum looked at Drin and smiled.

In the morning they continued their westerly ride in the rain. For days they continued the soggy trek until the wagon rolled up a slope onto the Plain of Demeter. From there they were a week away from Torrence. The weather changed as they rode up out of the U'thra basin onto the Plain of Demeter. Although the air was humid and cool, they were pleased the rain had stopped.

It was none too soon when Drin sat upon his horse with Amanda and Fraum on the wagon behind him as they started for Torrence. As the river surrounding the island castle and the banners flying from the castle towers came into view the feeling of being "home" swept over them.

Finally, Drin thought, relieved to be so close to returning to the Order of One.

He reflected on the time he had spent on his quest. It had been the better part of a year. And upon his friends. They had vanquished several seemingly impossible opponents and were returning with a great treasure. Drin had achieved both parts of his quest while enduring magic and religious superstitions.

Soon I can pray in the Cathedral and cleanse my soul, Drin thought.

"What is it, Drin?" Fraum called out.

"We're home, my friends. We're home," Drin responded.

✻   ✻   ✻   ✻   ✻

The Queen of the Fairies had walked with Rhonda, Jerrod, and the others to the stone arch that marked the edge of her kingdom, but her subjects had stayed behind in the shadows of the Fairy Forest. Word of Rhonda's anger at the Sprites had apparently spread through the realm. Only the dozen Fairy-Folk that had volunteered to travel with the Great One as far as Trisdale Keep could be seen.

"May E'fretté watch over you, Rhonda, Princess of Lithlillia," the Fairy Queen blessed them.

"May spring be forever on your realm, Lady, Queen of Fairies and friend of Lithlillia," Rhonda responded.

The band of magical creatures leaving Effendoria consisted mostly of Brownies, but three Pixies, a couple of Fairies, and a Forest Sprite were also going along. The Brownies and Pixies scattered themselves around the company of riders while the Fairies fluttered in and out of view like hummingbirds darting through a spring flower garden. Jerrod seldom caught sight of the Sprite. She was quick and altogether untrusting, but he could sense she was there.

"Can they keep up?" Jerrod asked Imelrinn.

"The fairies or us?" Imelrinn chuckled.

Within the first day's ride after leaving the Fairy Realm, the Black Forest reminded Jerrod again of his first day with Rhonda and Imelrinn. The redwoods were gone. Surrounded by the natural pines of the Black Forest, the forest seemed darker and less friendly. Their ride took them around the small hills of rock again. But with that realization, came other memories.

"Imelrinn, what of the colossal bears or the Fendür trolls?" Jerrod asked.

"We will know if they come and we have sufficient strength to fight off any aggression. Don't worry," the Elve's eyes twinkled as he answered.

"You're enjoying this."

"We are on the edge of the forests we protect. Now, if there were only jagged mountains," Imelrinn teased.

Their campsites continued to be cold, the snow lingering into spring within the forest where the forest canopy prevented lighter rains from reaching the forest floor. Their tents were cast upon the cold, wet ground, but the fairies would not have anything to do with the harsh weather. Before Jerrod could act, the Pixies cast colorful magic spells that dried the ground while the Fairies lit the lower branches with spots of colored lights that appeared like candles dangling from the tree branches. The Brownies went about cooking a meal while the Elves began to set up tents.

Jerrod watched as Rhonda went into the forest, away from the lights and the commotion in the camp. As he followed her she stopped, standing with her back facing the direction of the camp, to meditate. Jerrod could hear her thoughts.

Come to me, giant one. Come so that I may speak with you, her thoughts broadcast through the forest.

"It's all right, Jerrod. Join me," she said without turning to address him.

They had not had a chance to speak any more when they heard heavy breathing. Jerrod was standing right behind her, his breathing shallow in anticipation of what was coming through the forest when Rhonda sent her thoughts out again.

It's all right. Come. Come out of the forest so we may greet you.

Out of the darkness the furry face of a colossal black bear slowly pushed through the pines. His jowls and eyes appeared first, surrounded by a giant head with large, pointed ears that were half hidden by his fur. Then his tremendous body that dwarfed the size of a large horse appeared. Even through the thick fur coat Jerrod could see the rippled muscles of the bear's body.

Why do you call me from my sleep? the bear asked.

It's the third month.

Maybe, but there are still a couple of weeks I could sleep, the bear's thoughts responded as though he was muttering.

We travel through Ruhenmiur with the fairies, but we could use more protection, Rhonda admitted.

I will come, priestess, the colossal bear responded sleepily.

✳   ✳   ✳   ✳   ✳

In the morning they packed quickly to get on their way early. The forest canopy created a dark shadow which pressed upon their spirits, but the trees also blocked most of the wind. Although the spring air was not quite as cold and the wind not quite as strong, they still needed to wrap themselves tightly in their furs to fight off the rain that eventually made it through the trees.

I do not like your furs, Princess, the bear informed Rhonda.

We take only what we need and we honor the gift, Rhonda responded.

Druids, Elves, and forest-warriors of Lithlillia I understand, but who is this man-boy you travel with?

I am Jerrod.

He is the Great One and you will show him respect or you will have no trees to scratch your back upon, the Forest Sprite interjected.

My mistake, the bear snorted.

While they traveled the Pixies played throughout the entire day, dancing between the horses' hooves. The Brownies, on the other hand, were constantly trying to climb onto the back of one of the horses to avoid walking. Eventually, they settled for riding on the pack mules, snuggling into the packs, but the ones riding on the treasure bags complained that they were uncomfortable. The enormous bear and the Forest Sprite paralleled the group just out of sight.

By afternoon Jerrod started seeing the heads of snakes hanging from lower tree branches here and there. They appeared one at a time and when the Fairies chased them the snakes quickly wound their way back up the trees. Jerrod found himself relaxing and when they decided to stop for the evening, his spirits lifted despite the ominous reputation of the forest.

They slept well, Jerrod and Rhonda in one tent, and Imelrinn and the guards in another. The Fairy-Folk found their own accommodations in the nearby trees and foliage. The morning was pleasant, sitting around a small fire that warmed their legs and some water for tea.

Like a swarm of bees angrily descending upon an animal that had swatted at their hive, the snakes began swarming their camp. The snakes' wings buzzed, moving so fast that their wings could not be seen. Their long tails hanging down, swaying side to side, as the flying reptiles struck with sharp fangs and hissing breath.

As Jerrod and Imelrinn drew their weapons, the Brownies and Pixies began casting magical spells upon the flying vipers. It was not the colorful magic spent on pleasant moments. They cast dark blue gases that burst around the snakes' heads, causing them to fall paralyzed on the ground. The Elves' arrows pierced the snakes as the Fairies buzzed in and out, distracting the vipers' attention while Jerrod made great, open swings with his sword, easily slicing though the dangling bodies of the confused serpents.

The battle was done in a moment without anyone being bitten. It had been little more than an irritation, briefly interrupting their morning tea. While Jerrod and Rhonda stopped to talk about the path they needed to take, the Brownies and Pixies around them were laughing, slapping each other on the back, and rolling on the ground, bragging about their heroism.

"We are still days away from Trisdale Keep," Rhonda said cautiously.

"The walls will provide some protection and then we can take the western path off the plateau," Jerrod offered.

"Do you want me to ride ahead to scout the way?" Imelrinn asked.

"No. The trees and our guardians will warn us if danger approaches," Rhonda concluded.

The next couple of days were uneventful, but on the third afternoon the Forest Sprite appeared to Rhonda. She seemed hurried, glancing around rapidly from side-to-side as if she were trying to spy something.

The Fendür. They're here! she cried out.

They saw the giant trolls at a distance. The trolls were three times the size of a man, their hands resting on large hammers made of tree trunks and large stone blocks. The beasts were watching them, deciding whether to charge or pick up boulders to throw at them.

Only a moment lapsed before the trolls charged. The Elves fired a volley of arrows, but the Fendür trolls continued charging through the next volley until Rhonda and the fairies beckoned the tree roots to grab and hold them. One by one the giant trolls were pulled down, but one escaped the twisting tree roots to continue its charge.

Jerrod drew the Sword of Trisdale and stepped forward. The vision of his first troll battle, etched in his mind, pounded back into his mind like

Hephaestus's hammer striking the god's anvil. Jerrod assumed a defensive stance as the first troll closed the distance on him. With the troll a dozen feet away, he raised his sword over his head to strike.

Suddenly, out of the forest the colossal bear bounded in from the side, pouncing on the startled troll. The black bear began mercilessly ripping the troll into dozens of pieces. It took only a minute, a horrific minute that stunned everyone. In a moment the bear stood amidst pieces of troll, its jowls and paws drenched in hot, black blood.

"In the name of Ares," Jerrod whispered.

I think your praise would be better suited for E'fretté, Rhonda's thoughts responded.

As the remaining two trolls were struggling to free themselves, the sound of trees being snapped in two resounded through the forest. Almost immediately a giant, twice the height of the trolls, lumbered into view. His footsteps echoed like the popping sound a small earthquake makes when the shock wave rumbles by. The giant, pushing full grown trees out of his way as though he was walking through willows, was on the bear in two steps.

They faced off, but the struggle began immediately as the two collided, twisting and turning, fighting for an advantage. The giant's fists struck at the clawing, biting bear. They fell and tumbled, snapping trees, and rolled up to face each other again, both bleeding. They circled at arm's length before the giant began to back away.

The bear rose on his back feet, letting out a long roar that drowned out all the sounds of battle. The sound hurt everyone's ears. The remaining two trolls broke free of their entrapments to scurry off into the forest as the Brownies and Pixies threw harassing spells at them as if they were small boys throwing dirt clods at unwanted playmates.

Jerrod stood watching the troll pieces a moment, expecting the pieces to regenerate and renew the attack. As he watched, Imelrinn walked up behind him.

"Come, let's finished setting camp," the ancient Elve said calmly.

"Will they rise again?" Jerrod asked, not taking his eye from the troll's remains.

"No. Fire is not the only thing that kills the Fendür trolls," Imelrinn answered.

After the attack the stay in the forest was unsettling. No one slept well between the weather and thoughts of the forest creatures. In the morning they set out again and much to their liking, the snakes and Fendür stayed away. Several evenings later, they left the Black Forest to cross the grassy plain covering the edge of the Plateau of Kronese. From the edge of the forest they could see a needle-like silhouette pointing up against the dark horizon.

"Trisdale," Jerrod announced.

"We return to the ruins again," Imelrinn said reflectively.

"Again?" Jerrod asked.

"The rangers and druids of Lithlillia often stop at Trisdale for shelter when they are pursuing the Fendür," Imelrinn explained.

"I was wondering if you meant our visit a year ago?" Jerrod asked.

"That was only one of many visits," Imelrinn smiled.

They nudged their horses on but, halfway across the plateau, Jerrod stopped to look upon the ruins. Imelrinn stopped next to him.

"Do you see that?" Jerrod asked.

"What? That green glow?" Imelrinn asked.

"Yes, the glow. Do you see it?"

"Yes," Imelrinn answered.

"Did you see it last time we were here?"

"No. It's new." Imelrinn looked puzzled.

"Not to me. And now the glow is constant instead of the single wave I saw last year."

Rhonda led the riders and mule train towards the remnants of Trisdale's Keep, unaware of the three foot tall Imp with tattered clothes that watched them from the edge of the forest.

Turning back towards the keep, Rhonda rode up to the two large, square towers that were the remains of the gatehouse.

"The last time I saw these walls was a few nights before we met you," Rhoda said, turning towards Jerrod.

"You were unconscious the last time we were here. The structure hasn't changed, but the glow is new. I don't like it," Imelrinn responded.

"Is it the glow or the memory of what happened to us here?" Jerrod asked.

"Both, and neither. I don't like the feel," the ancient Elve looked uncommonly nervous.

"The green glow has always been here to me. It's just more constant," Jerrod said as he looked over the ruins.

Rhonda and Imelrinn looked at him as the wind blew across the plateau and over the lowest points of the wall like the cold waters of Limerin Falls tumbling over the spillway at Tilhelm Keep. The height of the outer walls still varied from twenty feet down to a height where a man could step up onto the ten foot wide foundation. Within the confines of the outer wall, the five-foot high terrace rested in the southwest corner, completely intact. On the terrace the foundation of the main house pressed up to surround a square tower that rose into the sky from the corner of the keep.

"We came here after fighting the trolls. This is where you fought the ghoul? Under the keep?" Rhonda said, trying to envision the battle.

"There are stairs down under the house," Jerrod explained.

"We should leave the tomb alone," Imelrinn insisted.

Imelrinn directed a guardsman to take up a position in the needle-like tower. The tower steps were exposed to the weather, but offered the best vantage for a lookout. He directed the other guardsman to take a position on one of the gatehouse towers.

"You know the best protection is down the stairs," Jerrod said, looking at the corner of the ruins.

"That is not my choice. I would rather stay in the stable," Imelrinn responded without a second thought.

"It was that bad?" Rhonda questioned.

From the look both men gave her she concluded it was so. She knew the ghoul had nearly killed them, but she did not know the particulars. No one would speak of the fight. Nor had she realized the impression it had left on their souls. Rhonda watched as being so near to the crypt visibly intensified their anxiety.

"We will pitch the tents over there near the well," Rhonda said, pointing in the direction of the stables.

✻   ✻   ✻   ✻   ✻

The fairies departed the next morning after wishing the Great One, the princess of Lithlillia, and the Elves a safe journey. As they walked towards the two towers that formed the gatehouse, they disappeared like they had walked into a waking dream, leaving those who watched feeling as if there may not have been anyone there in the first place.

"That's convenient," Jerrod said, turning to Rhonda.

"What's that?" Rhonda asked.

"To walk about invisibly. No one would even know you were there."

Rhonda took his hand and smiled. Her eyes twinkled green as they headed back to the others, holding hands. Rhonda swayed playfully as she stepped. When they reached the horses, they mounted up to lead the others out of the keep.

It must have been a glorious keep in its day, Jerrod thought as they rode through the gate house.

"In days of old when the signal light burned atop the tower in Trisdale Keep. I remember," Imelrinn reflected out loud.

They had decided to skirt the rim of the plateau north and take Pewton's Ledge down around Limerin Falls, rather than descend immediately and travel through Cipper. Either way, they were still more than a week from home. As they passed the steep, downward path towards Cipper, Jerrod looked down the trail.

And that was the beginning of Amanda's quest, he thought, carefully blocking the others out of his mind.

I hope she is well.

✻   ✻   ✻   ✻   ✻

Drin led the wagon and its Elven guard across the bridge into Torrence as Questil rose into the night's sky. Both moons were waning and their colored light was dim. The guards at the gate just watched them roll into the walled island city. When Drin suggested taking the wagon to the Cathedral, Fraum insisted the treasure be taken directly to the monastery.

"The wagon holds three shares of treasure for those who are not members of the Order and only one share that is. We will take into the monastery," Fraum directed.

Their arrival caught the monks by surprise, but the gate swung open quickly to move the wagon into the courtyard. By the time everything was settled the Master of the White Fists arrived to see what all the commotion was. He leaned on his golden staff as he watched.

"Master," Fraum greeted him.

"You return to us with a wagon of gold, but what of your assignment?" the Master asked.

"I have failed, Master. Nathanial was the one we feared. He escaped with the tome, leaving us trapped inside Mount Thoradan."

"And yet, here you are." The oldest monk smiled. "You can tell us about it in the morning. See to your friends. It appears you have had a long journey."

Once Drin was satisfied the wagon was safe, he took his leave to ride on to the Cathedral. Amanda watched until he was out of sight while Fraum arranged for the two Elves to stay at the monastery that night.

"Amanda, you can stay here if you like. You are welcome here," Fraum invited.

"No, Master, but thank you. I must go," she replied quietly without turning around.

"Where will you go?" Fraum asked.

Amanda turned around and smiled at the sage.

"All I need is this," she responded, holding up a large bag.

All Fraum could do was watch her walk away in the Elven clothes she had received in Asenthia. In her arms she carried a bag containing the legendary artifact that would save them all. She did not even wait to collect her possessions. Fraum watched her walk down the cobblestone street until she passed out of his view.

Amanda did not look at the shops along the road on her way home. The dull feeling of a lost routine slowly washed over her as if her feet remembered the path that her mind refused to follow. She walked without thought, but as she approached the turnoff to her home, she refocused.

When she stepped off the street into the secrecy of an alley and then up onto the roof, only part of her was the legendary thief from the Guild of the Crimson Pommel. The other part of her felt like a stranger, observing a third person as if to deny this was once her life. When she was on the roof she wound her way over a series of buildings until she came to an unusual flat roof. Amanda carefully side-stepped the plank leading up onto the roof and jumped to the ledge. When she was on the other side she looked down to confirm the trap under the plank was still set.

On the far side of the unusual roof, the walls of the next building extended upward. There was a build-out from the wall near the back of the adjacent building. Behind the build-out, out of sight from the world, was a subtle doorway visible only to someone standing directly in front of it, where they could see the outline of the otherwise flush door. Inside the doorway was a very small closet with just enough room for brooms and shovels. Hidden in the tool room was a secret doorway.

Amanda checked to see that her warning device had not been displaced.

Before opening the door, she locked her trap so she could pass through safely. After sliding the hidden latch, she opened the secret door to slip inside her home.

Her small room did not have any windows. The walls were lined entirely with wood panels. In the center of the room there was a single chair next to a small table with a half-full wine bottle, its cork stopper partially sticking out of the top. A rope bed with a feather mattress and comforter filled the far corner of the room along the wall where she had entered. At the end of the bed was a large trunk. On the far wall hung climbing gear, a couple long swords, and some thieving tools. There were empty pegs for another sword, a bow, and another set of thieving tools. The room, devoid of normal pleasantries, seemed to sum up Amanda's existence.

Who have I become? Amanda thought as she looked at the contents of her tiny room.

After walking to the far corner beyond the trunk, Amanda ran her hand down the wood panel until she touched a hole where the knot had fallen out. Inside the hole, Amanda's finger found the latch, releasing a secret door. She listened for the soft sound of a click and then pushed the wall gently inward, opening a doorway into a large, walk-in closet with shelves. At the other end of the secret room was a moderate size treasure chest.

She pulled the Horn of Valhalla from the bag, placing it on a shelf. Amanda turned and walked back to her bed, collapsing on the mattress. After unlacing and kicking her boots off, she pulled her feather comforter over herself and rolled over to go to sleep. It was a restless sleep tormented by visions of Jerrod. In the morning she woke to find the door to her secret treasure room open.

"In the name of Hermes, I never leave that open," she said aloud as though she was explaining herself to someone else.

After shutting the treasure room door, Amanda went to the chest at the foot of the bed to pull out a set of leathers. The black leather pants were skin tight, and slipping into a silky black blouse felt strange. Returning to the trunk, Amanda removed a pair of knee high, black lace-up boots and a wide leather belt. When she was dressed, she grabbed a leather jacket, closed everything up, and left her home to return to the monastery.

Amanda walked uncharacteristically down the center of the street. She did not watch the sides of the street or the alleys, but walked with deliberate purpose with quick steps and a solid gaze on the road ahead. Within a short period of time the monastery came into view.

The buildings were made of stone, covered by a smooth surface that had been painted white. Above the high walls that were meant to close the world out, Amanda could see red tiled roofs. In the center of the wall a large, wooden gate hung on iron hinges, splitting in the middle open wide enough for a wagon to pass through. A solitary man in brown robes with a black leather belt holding a white staff stood in front of the closed gate.

A student? Amanda thought.

When she approached, the young man about her age, greeted her.

"I would like to see Master Fraum," Amanda requested.

The wait was not too long. When Fraum came out in new brown robes, Amanda chuckled to herself. It had been nearly a year since they departed Torrence together and in that year he only had one change of clothes.

"You clean up real good, Master," she greeted.

"And you. But you're wearing black again."

"Yes. There are things I must finish," she answered, her face as serious as ever. "I need my belongings."

"The dagger?"

"Yes. It's a necessary token. They know who I am but it is still protocol."

"Will I see you again afterward?"

Amanda did not answer. Nor did she use her feminine guile on him. She knew it would be insulting. She simply turned and walked away with her pack and bedroll.

When she was back at home, Amanda took the bag of gold and gems from Trisdale Keep out of her pack and placed it in her secret treasure chest. When she removed the treasure bag, she saw the small disc Olendorn had given her. After looking at the wrapper for a moment, Amanda unwrapped the present. Inside was a disc the size of her palm made of a silver colored metal she did not recognize.

"What was it Olendorn said? 'Think of Asenthia when you look at this,'" Amanda recalled.

As she did a colorful, egg-shaped orb appeared. Amanda could hear the harps and flutes of Asenthia as the colors washed through the translucent image. Watching the colors and hearing the music, Amanda thought of the waterfall behind the cabin they had stayed in. As the thought of the waterfall came to mind, the image changed to translucent trees, falling water, hills, and the pond.

It's beautiful, she thought as she set it on her shelf.

When she let go of the disc, the image and music faded. Grabbing the Horn of Valhalla off the shelf, Amanda closed the door. Pulling her dagger out of her backpack, she latched it to her belt and departed for the Guild of the Crimson Pommel carrying the horn in the burlap bag like a bag of potatoes flung over her shoulder.

It was after dark when she approached the warehouse district. Squeezed between the warehouses were the city's most disreputable taverns, a few of which had rooms to rent, but not for anyone with honorable intentions. In one of the darkest alleys, Amanda stopped looking down the cobblestoned street at a wooden sign hanging from the roof near the entry. The picture of a crimson rose was carved in the wooden sign.

Outside the entry a single man stood, leaning his back against the wall. Amanda was in no mood to tolerate stupidity. As she walked towards the doorway the large man pushed off the wall and moved in front of the door.

"What do you want?"

"You know who I am. You know I am a member. Get out of my way," Amanda demanded as she pulled her dagger from its sheath to push the crimson pommel close to his face.

"Well, maybe," the man started to say as he reached to brush the hair away from Amanda's face.

With the speed of a panther, Amanda reached up, grabbing his wrist and pushing it in towards his inner arm. They could hear the wrist snap. The man instantly grabbed his wrist as he fell back against the wall and slid down to sit on the ground. Amanda stepped by to push the door open.

It was dark inside, lit by candles, lamps, and the fire in the fireplace. A long bar ran down the side wall across from the fireplace At the far end was a doorway without a door. One large man leaned against the end of the bar, another stood at the doorway. Several patrons clustered at the bar near the entry.

Amanda could see through the doorway that the guild master of the Crimson Pommel was sitting alone at a table in the adjoining room. An extremely large, husky man stood to either side of the table, guarding him in what seemed to be an otherwise empty room.

Amanda did not look at the man at the bar or at the doorway as she crossed the room. Her eyes fixated on the Grand Thief. The guard at the doorway pushed off the wall to stand straight before her, looking at the man at the table

for direction. With a simple nod from the guild's master the door guard knew
to step away.

She did not wait for the Grand Thief to acknowledge her or to direct her to
approach. She walked straight up to the table where he sat. When she stopped
in front of him, the chubby old man leaned back and looked up into her eyes.

In a flash Amanda withdrew her dagger, raised it above her head and threw
it down so hard that she drove the tip of the blade deep into the table. Standing
defiantly before the guild master, her feet shoulder-width apart, Amanda slipped
the burlap sack from her shoulder. She leaned over to drop the bag on the table
in front of the old man. Without saying a word, she pulled the large ram's horn
from the bag, placing it in the middle of the table for the man to see, and then
she stood back and waited.

"So, this is it," he said, his eyes fixed on the horn, his mouth salivating, as
he pulled the artifact towards him. "You have done well, Amanda. You have a
great future with the guild," he said finally, looking up at her.

"I've done my last recovery." Amanda's voice was hard and cold.

The man stopped to stare at the young thief of Torrence.

"We will say when it is the last." His voice was louder, his tone rising.

Amanda leaned forward on the table with both hands, bringing her face
close to his. Her azure eyes stared intensely into the old man's eyes. Deep in the
dark of his pupils she could see the fear.

"I will say when you are done," he said, a little less certain.

"I am done, old man. I owe you nothing."

With a nod from the guild master, the two nearby guards jumped towards
the table. They drew swords, which they began swing as they rushed forward, but
Amanda spun around to kick the first man in the chest, the blow sending him
backwards as the blade of the second man swept forward.

Amanda ducked the blow and then stood up to plant the heel of her open
palm in the back of the attacker's sword arm just as she kicked out the back of
his closest knee. As he fell, Amanda caught his sword, flipping it around to drive
the point through his chest, impaling the dying man to the floor.

Regaining his footing, the first man charged forward with his sword over his
head. As he swung down, Amanda leapt forward, grabbing his wrist and spinning
until she stood next to the large man. Driving her shoulder into the armpit of
his sword arm and throwing her hip into the man's side as she pulled down on

his wrist, flipping him head first onto his back. Amanda stood above the guard with his sword in her hand. She stood above him as she breathed calmly.

Before anyone could react, Amanda leapt towards the Grand Thief of the Crimson Pommel. With the tip of the guard's sword at his throat, Amanda watched the old man for a moment. The master barely dared to breathe.

"You can send your assassins if you wish, but if the first one misses me, if I hear of an attempt on one of my friends' lives, if one of my friends dies, I will come for you and you know there is nothing I can't find my way into," Amanda said slowly, not taking an eye off the old man. "Do you understand? A move against me or my friends and you are a dead man."

The old man nodded slowly.

Amanda stepped back and looked around the room. Several of the patrons stood with the two guards at the doorway, watching. Amanda tossed the sword onto the guard who was still lying on the floor.

"Don't ever let me see you again or I will finish this," she said to the guard.

Amanda turned towards the door, leaving her crimson dagger stuck in the middle of the table. The men in the doorway stumbled over each other attempting to get out of her way.

"Enjoy your life, Amanda," the Grand Thief said as he stood up. *Whatever time you may have left,* he finished in thought.

Passing through the doorway, Amanda saw a single man clenching his wrist as he pressed his back against the bar, trying to stay as far away from her as he could. Amanda looked at him as she walked to the front door. When she stepped out into the street no one dared follow her.

Amanda walked calmly away from the Crimson Rose into the darkness without looking back. Within a block she disappeared into the shadowy back alleys of Torrence.

✵   ✵   ✵   ✵   ✵

It is done, Amanda thought as she sat on the rooftop overlooking Torrence.

The city spread out below her. The thatched roofs of the inn district lay ahead of her and the warehouses beyond rested in the dark. The Cathedral and the king's castle lay to the north. The markets and residences lay to the south. There were no sounds rising from the cobblestone streets. Amanda sat reflecting on her past in the dark, moonless night. She was completely alone and completely free.

Somewhere in the night while everyone slept, Amanda's silhouette left its high perch over Torrence to climb down into a community that shared life. At dawn she found herself sitting cross-legged in front of the plain gates of the White Fist Monastery, still dressed in black leather. It was as if she was in a dream, walking as though she slept, unaware of the places she passed or her eventual destination. In the early morning none of the monks had come out to stand before the gate yet. When the first to arrive found her sitting motionlessly in front of the gate, they approached Amanda, respectful of her choice to meditate.

"May I see Master Fraum?" Amanda asked without looking back at the approaching monk.

The monk left without saying a word and, in time, Fraum came to greet her.

"You've returned. I am glad to see you. Come in," Fraum welcomed her.

Inside the four rectangular buildings that joined at the corners to create a square compound with an open court in the middle, Amanda saw the wagon had not moved. It cluttered the tranquil nature of the courtyard with its single tree that shaded a small pond, three small hills, rocks, and well-groomed sand. She smelled the slightest scent of burning sandalwood. The sound of a wooden flute filled the air with a low, haunting melody. Amanda's soul stirred deep inside her, calming her spirit as she thought again of the Elves.

"Master?" Amanda asked.

Fraum turned and looked at her.

"The wagon? It's here in the open, full of gold?"

"No one here has any need for the treasure. It is safe from all of us and no one will enter the compound without our knowledge."

"There is perhaps one that could," Amanda teased.

"Yes, but you are already here." Fraum laughed.

He had a deep, wholesome laugh that lightened Amanda's heart. She could not remember the last time she had heard him laugh, if ever. Amanda looked around again. There was a covered patio lining the inside wall of the courtyard. Across from the entrance was a large, brass gong hanging from a beam that supported the patio terrace. A single monk, dressed in their common attire, stood motionlessly next to the gong.

"The music sounds so wonderful," Amanda commented.

"Yes, it soothes our minds nearly as completely as the bird's song."

"It reminds me of Asenthia. I wish you could have heard the music."

"Was it so different from Lithlillia?" Fraum asked.

"Asenthia was more mystical, as if the Elven kingdom were not part of this world. They did not seem to be as attached to their forest, more that they created their surroundings. It was beyond beautiful and the music was wonderful."

"I would like to visit them so I could add their history and culture to our library," Fraum answered.

When Amanda stared at the brass gong, Fraum stopped.

"We strike the gong to call the brothers for exercise periods, quiet periods, for mealtime, prayer time, and bed time," he explained as he stood with his hands tucked into the opposite sleeves.

"Who do you pray to?"

"For such an easy question, that is a hard answer. Athena is the Olympians' goddess of wisdom. Ares is their god of war. Apollo is the god of music and healing. Demeter of agriculture and Dionysus of wine. We accept all these gods for who they are, but the monastery believes in an internal balance. We pray for enrichment and perfection. For harmony. We don't pray directly to any god, but to our inner being for personal enlightenment, if that makes sense."

Amanda looked at him, reflecting on his words.

"I left the guild. It's all I've ever been. There is nothing left for me," Amanda confessed.

"Our libraries, mental training, and physical exercise offer a great way to discover yourself. You are welcome here for as long as you wish."

✵ ✵ ✵ ✵ ✵

It was late when Drin rode up to the gates of the Cathedral the night of their return. When he was presented to the senior knight on duty, Drin genuflected, bowing his head until his chin rested on his chest. The Cavalier came over to him and grabbed him gently by the arm to help him from the tile floor.

"Come. Off the ground, Drin. You have returned to us," the man said softly.

"Thank you, Sire. I bring back treasure for the glory of the Order."

"I'm sure. And great deeds too, I imagine, but you look tired and could use a bath," the knight empathized.

Squires were called to lead Drin to a hot bath where he could soak. Bread, cheese, and wine were brought to him while he bathed in a less familiar part of the Cathedral. He had been there once or twice to clean the room for the Cavaliers, but it was generally off limits to the Initiates and Squires. It was adjacent to the sacred chambers where Initiates stood their vigil, praying alone for a day, before taking their vows of knighthood.

Clean clothes were brought for Drin and his armor and dirty clothes were carried away. One squire accompanied him back to his private room, which was a privilege held only for senior Initiates. His room had not changed in his absence. As he heard the door close behind him, Drin allowed himself to fall to his knees next to his bed and cry.

Thank You for the strength and fortitude through all that I have endured so that I might return in Your glory, Drin prayed in silence.

He was up with the sound of the morning bells to dress and eat with the other Initiates. Word of his return had already gone through the Cathedral. The junior Initiates and Squires moved quickly out of his way as he walked towards the hall for the morning meal. As he entered, the senior Initiates, those waiting for the next chance to take a quest, got as close to Drin as possible. They all hoped that being in Drin's presence would draw the Prophet's attention to their devotion.

All of the ranks had assigned seating; the higher the rank, the closer they were to the front of the hall. The Acolytes, who had not yet chosen whether to follow the Protector or Prophet path of the Order, sat nearest the doors. The Protectors were the knights who protected the Order with might and devotion. The Prophets were the priests who guided the Order with prayer and sermon. Like everything else in the Order, there was a specific place for everyone.

When an Elder rose to say the morning prayer, they all bowed their heads. At the end of the long prayer of thanks, another Elder officially announced that Drin had returned from his quest. The applause was nearly deafening.

Near the end of the meal an Acolyte brought Drin a message. He was to meet with the Lord Marshal, leader of the Protectors, in the private temple after the meal. Drin finished up, went to wash his hands, and then went directly to the private temple. As he entered he was greeted at the door by one of the Field Marshals.

"Come, Drin. They are waiting for you," the Field Marshal started.

"They?" Drin stopped.

"The Elders and the Lord Marshal."

"The Elders? All twelve?"

"Yes, now come on," the Field Marshal responded as he turned to walk into the temple.

"Is something wrong?" Drin asked, still standing in the same spot.

"No. Now, come on!"

Once he was presented to the leadership, Drin recited the story of their trip, including healing Rhonda, fighting the vespree, and being trapped under Mount Thoradan, but he was careful when speaking about Agganon, avoiding the name of the Olympian temple entirely. Moving on as quickly as possible, Drin spoke next of Silandria, a beautiful city built on the edge of a waterfall that was surrounded by a lake, and finally of their final days traveling across the U'thra Basin and Plain of Demeter.

They made Drin repeat the stories of fighting trolls and vespree, but they were most intrigued by Silandria and its apparent lack of religion. They asked about the city and its citizens several times, each time prying a little deeper into the details of the society. In the end the discussion focused on the money.

"I cannot tell you how much each share is worth. The treasure has not been appraised and the coins have not been counted, but four shares filled an entire wagon," Drin reported.

"And one quarter of the load is to come to the Order?"

"Yes. It is at the White Fist Monastery now."

"You must go collect our quarter share at once. I will inform the Prophet," an Elder directed.

That afternoon Drin led a small group of Initiates with an empty wagon to the monastery. Wearing a new royal blue cape over a white tunic and polished chainmail, Drin already appeared knightly.

"Drin! Welcome! Come in! Come in," Fraum greeted him.

"I can't stay, my friend. The Order has sent to collect my share of the treasure," Drin finished with a smile.

"It's all here, in the back of this wagon as it was when you left, but it hasn't been appraised yet," Fraum responded, throwing back the canvas covering the wagon so the much younger man could see the treasure.

"I must return with my share. Can we settle on a quarter of the load?"

"A quarter is fine. I will make up for any concerns Jerrod or Amanda might have out of the monastery's portion. We have little need for it."

"Awfully trusting, aren't you? Leaving it out like this." Drin's smile broadened.

"The one person able to sneak into a monastery full of monks and steal some of the treasure without being seen is already in the monastery. I think we're safe."

"Amanda is here?"

"Come say hi."

"Why is she here?"

"Her whole world has changed. She is seeking a new life, a new beginning, without any indication of which step to take next. Come say hi. It would do her good."

"I really can't stay. I have been directed to return quickly. Please tell her hello for me," Drin answered as the Initiates finished loading their wagon.

When they rolled through the gates at the Cathedral, the Initiates were directed to unload the wagon into the treasury. While the wagon was unloaded under the supervision of a Cavalier, a Cleric led Drin back to the private temple behind the Cathedral. The Cleric seemed to scurry through the hallway, making Drin walk a little faster than was comfortable.

Odd that a Cleric is sent for me, Drin thought.

When they reached the private chambers, the twelve Elders, the Lord Marshal, and the Field Marshals were waiting for him. The Elders stood together on the far side of the room. Drin was astonished by how immaculate their silver robes looked, clean beyond clean. Their hoods hung halfway down their backs and white robe belts identified their senior positions. Only the Prophet himself was more senior. The Marshals stood to the side, with the Field Marshals nearer the door.

"Drin, you've done well, my son," the eldest Elder greeted him.

"Thank you."

The Lord Marshal stepped forward, his silver shoulder braid indicating his rank draped under his left arm, hanging from the shoulder under his royal blue cape. He also wore the royal blue shoulder braid indicating the honorary title of Lord Paladin.

He has done something extraordinary, Drin thought, looking at the blue braid.

"Drin, it is my privilege to tell you that you have been selected for Knighthood if you are willing to take the oath."

"Yes, thank you, my lord. It would be an honor. It has always been my dream to serve in such a capacity."

They mingled for the next hour, encouraging Drin to retell his adventure. It had been many years since an Initiate had been knighted and joined the Cavaliers. Eventually, they turned to the issues of the Accolade, the ceremony of knighthood.

"Who would you like to attend?" an Elder asked.

"My family from Semanie Point and my friends, Jerrod, Amanda, Fraum, Princess Rhonda, and her guardian, Imelrinn. And if I could, Elder, I was declared 'a Friend of Lithlillia.' I would like to invite the druid queen, Lady Lieisa, and her husband, Lord Steffen."

"Druids and Elves?" the response was slow.

"Yes, your worship."

"Fraum is from the monastery that you visited, is he not?"

"Yes, he is a master and teacher in the White Fist Monastery. Amanda is there as well."

"And the others?"

"They traveled to Lithlillia."

"It isn't common to invite non-believers to our ceremonies and even less common to include pagans," an elder commented.

"These are people I have spent nearly a year traveling and fighting with. The Order has profited from the friendship I share with them," Drin explained.

"Word will be sent at once," the eldest Elder replied before departing to talk among some of his fellow spiritual leaders, leaving Drin to talk with the Marshals.

✻   ✻   ✻   ✻   ✻

Rhonda and Jerrod rode side-by-side until they reached Pewton's Ledge. Listening to her as she spoke more of Lithlillian history and how they would live was overwhelming him. Rhonda had a home picked out and was speculating on how they, as a couple, would fit into the kingdom's leadership. When the ledge forced them to travel single file, Jerrod took a deep breath of joy. As much as he loved Rhonda, he needed the break.

Pewton's Ledge wound down the cliff face of the narrow box canyon, and near the base it passed behind the falling water of Limerin Falls. Built under an outcropping of rock, Tilhelm's Keep was not visible during their descent, and the misty vapor from the waterfall obscured everything in the bottom of the canyon.

Jerrod could hear the water falling into the lake he knew was there. The lower they rode the louder the sound was, deafening every sound before they reached the bottom. As they rode behind the falling water, the mist gave way to a thick sheet of water falling into the pond with tremendous force.

At the bottom of the falls they moved quickly to cross the small, flat area of moist grass between the lake and the canyon walls to the thick, wooden door of the keep. They passed through the moss covered door and, closing it with a thud, the thundering sound of the falls suddenly ended, leaving them in a dark, quiet room.

"Jerrod, I'm sorry. You can't see in the dark. Let me get a torch," Rhonda said.

She heard him mumble and a small ball of fire appeared, hovering above Jerrod's palm. The fire lit up most of the semi-circular room.

"I'm learning to control it," Jerrod said sheepishly.

After they all dismounted, Rhonda, Jerrod, and Imelrinn gathered together while the Elves checked the mule packs.

"Lithlillia is a day's ride. We would have to ride all night, but we could be there by morning," Imelrinn offered.

"I really wanted to get home," Rhonda added.

Jerrod could hear the disappointment in her voice.

"We will be there soon enough, my love."

"It's been almost a year since we were there," Rhonda commented.

Rhonda took Jerrod's upper arm and pulled it in. She looked towards the oversized doorway in the rock wall and then began to lead her horse towards the door.

"So we stay here again," Jerrod reflected as he looked around the room.

"Someday we should find the Dwarves and hire them to restore the keep," Imelrinn commented.

"Dwarves?" Jerrod looked at him.

"It was the Dwarves of Frausnaugh who built the keep long before the Elve-Dwarve wars."

"Elve-Dwarve wars?"

"That is a story for another time, but the Elves and Dwarves stood together against the Dark Elves."

"What happened?"

"We were vanquished. The woods of Lithlillia are not our original home," Imelrinn said before he turned away.

Jerrod turned towards Rhonda with bewilderment on his face.

"Imelrinn is a Mountain Elve. His family, all of our ancestors, came from the mountain range that you call the Wilds," Rhonda explained.

"And the Dwarves?"

"They vanished after we were vanquished. We don't know where they went."

After stabling the horses in the wooden stalls of Tilhelm Keep and drawing water from the well in the center of the room, they built a small fire in the corner to warm their food and to brew tea. They laid out their bedrolls on the stone floor and, despite the discomfort of sleeping on the stone, slept soundly wrapped in the protection of Tilhelm Keep.

In the morning, Rhonda rose early, anxious to be home. She pushed them to pack and eat quickly so they could start the final ride early. They did not stop to eat a mid-day meal, but passed cold food while they continued the ride, and by early afternoon they approached Lithlillia. Winding out of the path towards the village, they found Lady Lieisa and Lord Steffen standing at the edge of the village, waiting to greet them.

"Can you ever surprise a druid?" Jerrod leaned over to joke with Imelrinn.

"Not in their own forest."

They both chuckled.

The evening of their return became a celebration with a great feast in the Pavilion. The large, oval room was filled with clan members while venison turned over the three fires and Elven music lingered in the background. After Rhonda and Imelrinn spoke briefly with Rhonda's parents, Rhonda returned to sit with Jerrod during the festivities. After the celebration, Rhonda led Jerrod to a little cottage.

"Aren't you staying with me tonight?" Jerrod asked when Rhonda turned to leave.

"I must go speak with my mother," Rhonda explained.

"Will you be back? Tonight?"

"I'll see you in the morning, my love."

Jerrod watched as Rhonda walked away, subconsciously playing with the esreandrea around his wrist.

Rhonda was not looking forward to the conversation she knew her mother intended to have.

You're a princess of Lithlillia. How can you choose a flatlander? Rhonda imitated her mother as she entered her parents' home.

Lady Lieisa was standing in the center of the room while her father paced about. When things settled down so they could talk, the conversation did indeed start with the question Rhonda had anticipated. She quickly found herself defending her love for Jerrod and her decision to marry him.

"I fell in love with him a long time ago. Somewhere between our first meeting on the plateau and our arrival here. I don't know when, exactly."

The discussion seemed to go around in circles, repeating itself several times, each time a little less emotional than before. When it seemed settled, Rhonda told them of her experience in Effendoria

"The Queen of the Fairies called Jerrod the 'Great One,'" Rhonda reported.

"Great One?" her mother repeated.

"Are you sure?" Lady Lieisa asked.

"Yes, it was the queen herself that called him the 'Great One' first."

"First? Were there others?"

"Yes. All the fairies. And a unicorn."

"You saw a unicorn!"

"Yes."

"No one has seen a unicorn in thousands of years."

"He appeared to me as I bathed in the lake in Effenddoria. My thoughts were tormenting me," Rhonda explained.

"Do you understand what this means, the full meaning?" Her mother's voice was slower and more deliberate than normal.

Lady Lieisa's chin dropped to her chest, her head tilting a little to one side as she watched her daughter's reaction.

"Yes. One flatlander is born every thousand years with a direct connection with magic. I know, Mother, but I loved him long before I knew he was the 'Great One.'"

"That's only part of it, honey," Lieisa said, taking Rhonda's hands and pulling her to sit.

"What is it?"

"At the time a druid priestess marries, she bonds with her life partner, sharing her force with him. It has always been the priestess who was the stronger of the pair." Lieisa paused. "Always."

"And if Jerrod is the Great One?" Rhonda whispered.

"If he is the Great One, he is far more powerful than anyone either of us has ever met."

"Can we be together?" Rhonda pled.

Lady Lieisa said nothing. She sat next to her daughter, looking into her green eyes for a moment before pulling Rhonda into her arms.

"I don't know," she whispered as Rhonda began to cry.

In the week that followed, Jerrod sensed an unhappiness in Lady Lieisa and Lord Steffen, but Jerrod had been accepted. He was treated respectfully. He ate with the Lord and Lady, and with their daughter, but he slept alone in his own cottage. No one other than Rhonda spoke of the wedding.

The morning and mid-day meals were taken in a variety of places. Jerrod's favorite was in the forest near the path to the flatlanders' mill. The evening meal was always in the Pavilion where the Lord and Lady sat on the dais and Rhonda and Jerrod sat nearby. Still, with all the politeness and hospitality, Jerrod felt like an outsider.

One evening while they ate, two riders approached the village from the south. An Elve came onto the dais behind the Lord and Lady to whisper into the Lady's ear. After receiving the report, Lady Lieisa turned towards Jerrod.

"Are you expecting visitors, flatlanders?"

"Me? No, my lady. I don't know of anyone. Why?"

"Two riders are approaching from the south. One is armored, carrying a sword. The other one is unarmed."

"What are they wearing?"

Lady Lieisa turned towards the Elven guardsman.

"The hawk did not say."

"Why do you ask what they wear?" Lady Lieisa asked.

"In Torrence the King's Guard wears a purple cape. His Legion wears red or black. All of the soldiers from the Order wear royal blue. It is how they identify the armies and their soldiers."

When the riders reached the Pavilion, the squire stayed outside with the horses while the armored emissary followed an Elven guardsman in to be presented. Dressed in polished chain mail, covered by a white tunic and a blue cape, the soldier descended the steps to walk around the fire pit towards the dais. He stood straight as he walked and did not look around, but focused on the dais where Lord Steffen and Lady Lieisa remained seated. When he reached the foot of the dais, the soldier genuflected.

"Please, stand," Lady Lieisa asked.

"I am from the Order of One in Torrence," he reported.

"Welcome to Lithlillia. To what do we owe this honor?" Lord Steffen said, stirring in his seat.

"I come with an invitation from the Order of One and the King of Torrence," the emissary said as he handed a scroll to Lady Lieisa.

Lady Lieisa unrolled the scroll to skim over the writing, and then handed it to Lord Steffen before turning to Rhonda and Jerrod.

"It seems a 'Friend of Lithlilllia' is to be knighted."

"Come. You will eat and stay with us tonight. Bring your servant in. You can start your return trip in the morning. You can tell them Lithlillia is coming," Lady Lieisa concluded.

"They can stay with me," Jerrod offered.

"Then it is settled," Lord Steffen announced.

"May I ask, what is your position in the Order?" Jerrod spoke up.

"I am an Initiate. Are you Jerrod and the Princess Rhonda?" the young man asked.

"We are," Rhonda responded.

"Word of your deeds is already spreading across our kingdom, my lady. You are all heroes."

When the time came to travel to Torrence, Lord Steffen and Lady Lieisa rode side-by-side at the head of the column. Jerrod and Rhonda followed next, with Imelrinn close behind. Behind them came one hundred of Lithlillia's forest-warriors dressed in green with brown robes clasped by silver pinecone brooches. Their hoods fell down their backs exposing their blond hair and pointed ears.

✲   ✲   ✲   ✲   ✲

Far below Torrence, Jacob sat in his room reviewing his book of alchemy. As he flipped the pages he leaned over, staring intently at the parchment, looking for the potion-spell. Near the middle of the book he stopped to read the delicate pages, hand printed in multiple colors of ink, "Memory Loss." He ran his finger along the words as he read, coming to the last word.

"Powder of dragon's talon," Jacob said aloud as he sat back in his chair.

He envisioned trimming Drok-na's talons. He could grind the clippings into powder for the last ingredient in the potion-spell. Jacob relaxed, realizing he had all the other necessary elements for the potion to restore memory to be completed.

The High Master was getting old. He allowed Jacob to secretly brew the memory potion to aid him in warding off the symptoms of his age. The last batch, which had lasted nearly a year, was almost gone and Jacob was working quickly to replenish the supply.

After latching the bolt on his door, Jacob stood alone in the middle of his room. Uttering the ancient words of magic, Jacob was engulfed in spinning white lights, each the size of a diamond. As the lights spun faster, his body faded from his room and reappeared in a cave southwest of Torrence. In the back of the cave was a large, greenish-blue bull dragon.

Good evening, my friend, Jacob thought.

Good evennning, Jacob, Drok-na answered quickly.

The adult sized dragon jumped to his feet and spun once. His body shuddered like a puppy as he lowered his head in submission. His eyes focused on Jacob.

"I am sorry it has been a while, my little friend," Jacob said teasingly.

Can we play? Drok-na thought back.

The year old dragon had grown to full size, but he was still young at heart. His thoughts and emotions were innocent. Drok-na loved to play. Jacob would use his magic to create a glowing red sphere that would float or hover in one part of the cave then dart across the cave, moving up or down, while Drok-na swiped at it with his fore-claw, batted at it with his tail, or snapped at it with his jaws. When the dragon hit the sphere, pieces of tiny red light would fly in every direction. Ripples ran down Drok-na's back from his wings to his tail when it happened and the image made Jacob burst out in laughter.

Drok-na also seemed to favor a sort of hiding game. Jacob would begin projecting himself around the room. As he appeared in a new location, Drok-na would try to lick him with his long forked tongue. As soft as Drok-na's tongue was, when he did catch Jacob, the lick typically sent him sprawling on the ground. But even with Jacob's experience, the continual use of the spell quickly wore him out. So that game was short and seldom played.

Jacob spent as much time with Drok-na as he did studying magic, illusion, and alchemy. Their relationship was strong, based on positive affection, creating a solid bond between master and familiar. As familiars go, the bond was as resilient as any other, but the nurturing environment Jacob provided helped the growing dragon develop into a happy, good spirited creature who was more interested in the prosperity of man than ravaging the countryside.

After they played, Jacob explained his need for the talon clippings. Drok-na allowed the trimming and, in fact enjoyed the extra attention. Afterward, Jacob returned to his room to grind the clippings into powder in order to complete the potion. The potion fizzed a little as Jacob picked it up to hold over a small candle, heating the liquid slowly to a boil. When the color changed from a watery blue to a fluorescent green, Jacob took it off the heat and poured it into a large vial, which he closed with a cork.

It had been a long day and he was tired. He could give the memory potion to the High Master in the morning. Lying down on his cot without disrobing, Jacob sent a thought to Drok-na before rolling over to sleep.

Good night, my friend.

Good night, Drok-na responded quickly.

CHAPTER 10

ACCOLADE

W ord had spread through Torrence that the Elves and rangers of Lithlillia were coming. When the column of forest warriors was spotted from the walls of Torrence, a fanfare of trumpets sounded to announce their arrival. By the time they reached the bridge into Torrence, the walls were lined by the flatlanders anxious to see mythical Elves.

The fanfare sounded again as Lady Lieisa and Lord Steffen's horses stepped onto the stone bridge. At the gate they were met by a man wearing a black cape with red fringe. Three braids looped around his shoulder, under his arm, and back to his shoulder. One black and red braid, one red and silver braid, and one red braid identified his position.

He is the General of the Cavalry for the King's Standing Army, Jerrod thought to Lady Lieisa.

Do you know him?

No, not personally.

Then how do you know who he is?

The colors indicate his position. The red and black cape and braid indicate he is in the Standing Army. The red and silver braid is his rank—general. The red braid is his unit—the Fourth Army, who are cavaliers."

"Lord Steffen, Lady Lieisa. Welcome to Torrence. I am General Noland. I will escort you to the king's castle."

"Thank you, General," Lord Steffen acknowledged.

Is there anyone between the General and the King? Lady Lieisa asked.

The Commander of the Armies. He would wear a silver braid instead of red and silver. There is also the Commander of the Guard, but that is a separate army, Jerrod answered.

Thank you, Jerrod.

To Jerrod, the ride through the cobblestone streets of Torrence seemed surreal. His first visit to Torrence was in a rainstorm at night. He had walked many days and was tired and hungry when he crossed over the bridge. He had been a nobody, but now he rode with the Lord, Lady, and Princess of Lithlillia. He was wealthy and betrothed to the princess.

My dreams are complete, he thought.

What dreams? Imelrinn asked.

I wanted to be somebody. To be someone important.

I fought in the Elven-Dwarven War and I have been the guardian for three of Lithlillia's princesses, but I have always been Imelrinn.

Now you are starting to sound like Fraum.

But Fraum is so young, Imelrinn jested.

What does that make me?

That makes you Jerrod, the ancient Elve joked.

Not the Great One? Jerrod bantered back.

Are you? Imelrinn asked.

Jerrod started pondering the question, but caught himself. Not wanting to be "overheard," he immediately stopped thinking about it.

You will learn to block others out better, Imelrinn encouraged him.

As they rode through the streets, Jerrod glanced at Lord Steffen, Lady Lieisa, and Princess Rhonda, who all wore smooth golden bands around their heads. Although Lord Steffen looked regal, riding with the legendary bastard sword of the Lord of Lithlillia strapped to his belt, Lady Lieisa and Princess Rhonda's beauty as they rode sidesaddle in their forest green riding robes overshadowed them all. The ladies of Lithlillia were magnificent.

I'm blessed to be in such company, Jerrod thought.

Thank you, Jerrod, Lady Lieisa responded as Rhonda's thoughts seemed to giggle.

Jerrod took a deep breath and held it as he looked at Rhonda. Her long, open curls of brown hair fell almost to the seat of the saddle. Both of her hands rested in her lap, holding the reins, as she sat up straight, her legs elegantly wrapped around the saddle's pommels.

She looks more a princess than a druid priestess, Jerrod thought.

Amidst the Elven royalty, Jerrod wore a common brown, almost caramel colored jacket, a knife stuck down his knee high boots, and a brown cape that hung over the Sword of Trisdale. Behind them were the Elves and rangers in their black leather bodice jackets with metal rings. White Elven longbows rose above their heads. Each carried a quiver of arrows and an Elven longsword.

Magnificent, Jerrod thought.

Jerrod shifted in his saddle, surprised when a hand extended from a brown sleeve, reaching out of the crowd to touch his boot.

"Fraum! How are you?" Jerrod exclaimed, looking down at the monk as he rode.

"Good. Good."

"And Amanda? Is she here?" Jerrod asked as he looked rapidly over the crowd.

"She is good. She's at the monastery. She's not here."

Jerrod frowned as he looked down at the reins in his hands.

"I can't continue to walk through the crowd like this. Let's meet later. Come to the monastery this evening," Fraum said as he patted Jerrod's rein hand.

"I'll try," Jerrod promised.

"And welcome home, Jerrod," Fraum called out as the crowd forced him to let Jerrod ride by.

As the column approached the Cathedral they could see great white banners flying from the walls and towers of the complex. On the banners were two silver hands cupped as though they held something. The giant statue of Sir Michael stood in the middle of the street as it had when Jerrod first came to Torrence.

"Is this the great hero that Drin spoke of?" Imelrinn asked.

"Yes. Sir Michael is the greatest knight of the Order."

"And he came back from the dead to fight again?"

"That is the legend of Sir Michael, if you believe it."

"Why do you doubt the legend?"

"Sir Michael was not a god. He was mortal. No mortal man has come back from the dead. Not even Brendril."

King Derik of Torrence, and his wife, Queen Isabelle, and their son, Prince Garrett, awaited the arrival of Lithlillia on the steps of the king's castle. The king and queen wore colorful clothes with long purple capes and golden crowns, but the prince's cape was much shorter, his clothes more like those of the citizens, and he did not wear a crown.

When the introductions were made, Jerrod and Imelrinn stood behind the royal family of Lithlillia, but Rhonda turned and called them forward to meet the royal family of Torrence.

"This is the Lord Jerrod of Winfred, my betrothed, and Lord Imelrinn, Guardian of the Royal House of Lithlillia, Your Majesty," Rhonda introduced them.

"Our Winfred?" King Derik asked, turning his head to look at Jerrod.

"Yes, Your Majesty," Jerrod answered.

"How did you come to be part of Lithlillia?" the king asked him.

"It is a long story, Your Majesty," Jerrod answered.

"One I will enjoy hearing, I'm sure. Come, come, everyone. Let's go into the castle."

Together the royal families retired into the throne room where other guests were waiting, including a king, queen, and princess of Greenlands who had arrived earlier in the week to arrange a marriage between their daughter and Prince Garrett. The princess was beautiful, but younger, just barely the age of marriage. She stood with her parents, her eyes cast down as she fidgeted in her gown, unable to stand still.

"So you are friends of the knight apparent?" King Derik asked when he stood with Jerrod again.

"Yes, Your Majesty."

"I have been told you carry the Sword of Trisdale. Is that it?" the king asked.

"Yes, it is."

"The sword that was lost when the Lord of the Keep disappeared. I was just a child," the king commented, looking down at Jerrod's side.

The moment that Jerrod had feared had arrived.

Will the king take the sword from me? he thought.

You have nothing to fear, Lady Lieisa answered.

"It is one of many things I have encountered over the last year, Sire," Jerrod responded.

"The Keep of Trisdale is abandoned, is it not?"

"It is, Your Majesty. The beacon between your kingdom and ours was abandoned long ago," Imelrinn added.

"It might benefit both of the kingdoms if Trisdale were rebuilt," the king responded after watching Imelrinn a moment.

After introductions were finished, the kings and queens ate and talked together, speaking of their kingdoms. There was a great deal of interest in Elves, druids, and rangers, leaving much of the talking to Lord Steffen and Lady Lieisa. But the coastal kingdom of Greenlands, a kingdom to the southeast along the Coast of Semanie, held some strategic importance to Torrence, so King Derik encouraged the king's participation in the discussion and showed an encouraging amount of interest in Greenlands. The queens became bored with the politics and quickly focused on the unique traditions of each kingdom.

With their parents involved in separate discussions they considered boring, the prince and princesses stepped away. Both the prince and princess pulled at Rhonda to join them. Prince Garrett, who was older than Rhonda, was far less experienced and became interested in her stories of travels and fights. The younger princess craved Rhonda's reassurances. When Rhonda realized that Jerrod was being cut out, she looked at him briefly.

Go *on. I have an errand to run, anyway*, Jerrod thought to her and then kissed her cheek gently, causing the younger princess to blush.

✳   ✳   ✳   ✳   ✳

After the parade of Lithlillia, Fraum returned to the monastery, where he sought out Amanda. He found her alone in the large prayer room near the front gate. She was sitting cross-legged in the brown robes of a monk as the sound of a wooden flute played nearby. Her wrists rested on her knees, her palms up, deep in meditation. She stared through the smoke of the incense in front of her, her eyelids open, unmoving, revealing her chilling blue eyes.

Fraum did not make a sound as sat down in front of her to stare back through the smoke.

"Did you see him?" Amanda asked without the slightest movement.

"Yes."

"And he looks well?"

"Yes. And yes, he knows you are here."

"Your head looks good without hair. When did you cut it?" Fraum continued when Amanda did not answer.

"It's the custom of a monk, isn't it?" Amanda reminded her master.

"All the monks shave their heads." Fraum smiled.

Amanda was the best student he had ever seen. During their travels she had learned physical abilities some monks practice for a lifetime, but become only marginally successful. Her success was undoubtedly due to the combination of her warrior and thieving training, but Amanda also had an undying internal resolve. She was already lethal when they had met, before she started studying the empty hand techniques.

Now, she was in advanced training. In addition to teaching her new weapons and techniques, Fraum was teaching her philosophy and religion. They studied philosophy to balance life, to see the bigger picture. They avoided the teachings of Zeus, who was too self-important, Apollo the war-god, and the mischievous Hermes, god of thieves and luck. Although they studied Athena, the goddess of wisdom, their studies focused more on the spirituality of nature, all things being connected. It was less a study about what was right or wrong and more a study of knowledge and wisdom.

"Always follow your heart," Fraum often said to end a lesson.

Amanda had spent all of her free time over the last month in the library. After her prayers, meditation, chores, and exercise she followed the stairs down to the large room full of scrolls beneath the monastery where she had read history, ecology, astrology, anthropology, and poetry. But when the poetry she had been reading unexpectedly turned to romance, she quit reading entirely.

"Come. It's time for exercise. It will ease the pressures of the world. What will it be, sword or throws?" Fraum encouraged her.

"Can't we do both?" Amanda asked as she stood up, a smile growing slowly on her face.

"Your ability to influence a man's heart is still your greatest weapon," Fraum teased.

*   *   *   *   *

On the eve of the accolade, Drin was taken to the private room behind the Cathedral. The Acolytes had prepared a warm bath for him to soak in. When he emerged from the bath, the Acolytes anointed him in oil, which had the pleasant smell of sandalwood.

Drin dressed in a white cotton shirt and soft deerskin pants that had been laid out for him, and then went to an adjoining chapel, where knight apparents typically await the Accolade. He was expected to spend the entire night alone in prayer.

Reflecting on his life, Drin prayed for strength to fulfill the knightly commitment he would take in the morning. Thinking back to his childhood, when he played in the surf and helped his father with the fishing nets, he reflected on happiness. Then thinking of his later youth, when he took on more responsibility for fishing, he reflected on responsibility. He had loved sailing with his father and pulling in the fish. He even loved cleaning and delivering the catch to the market in Semanie Point.

How can I, a boy from a small fishing village, become a Knight of the Order? Drin questioned.

When he first started fishing, Drin was a follower of Pontus and Poseidon, the gods of fishing and the sea, just like his father. Local fishermen praised the gods when the fishing was plentiful and questioned them when the fishing was slow. Drin remembered being happy when he was young, but the Order of One had moved into his small fishing village when he was a teenager.

He had become mesmerized by the clerics and their teachings. Very soon afterward he had joined the local cleric's following, abandoning his father's faith. He remembered how hurt his father had been. How his father had turned his back on him, deciding his son was a waste to humanity, lost in the abyss of a heretic religion. In despair, Drin had snuck off to become an Acolyte and traveled to Torrence with the Order. He had not seen his family since.

The cleric had arranged for Drin to go to the Cathedral, where he worked as an Acolyte before choosing between his paths. They were difficult years full of hard, menial tasks, like hours of scrubbing stone floors on his hands and knees, and other even less appealing tasks. When the chance finally came, Drin chose the path of the Protector. He became a Squire, replacing the stone floors with soiled stables.

Like everyone who became interested in the holy knights, Drin was particularly interested in the legend of Sir Michael, who had reappeared years after his death to save the Legion of the Order. The legend was that Sir Michael, wielding a two-handed sword, had reappeared near the end of a battle the Order was losing. He had stood at the apex of the Legion's defensive line, which vanquished a superior enemy. Behind him the remnants of knights stood their ground in an arrowhead formation as the enemy repeatedly attacked. The few that survived the battle retold Sir Michael's story.

The Order encouraged chastity for its knights. Through hours of work followed by hours of training, Drin had learned commitment and dedication. He had no time to pursue impure thoughts. Squires had no childhood friendships.

They did not run and play or lay on their backs staring up at the clouds. They did not linger over thoughts of girls. There was no time for them to be boys. Since leaving his village, every moment of his life had been dedicated to the Order and achieving knighthood.

As he prepared for his prayer vigil, a Priest came to the room.

"Who would you like to vouch for your valor?" the Priest asked.

Drin considered Fraum a mentor of sorts, but it was Jerrod, who had become his friend, that he ultimately selected.

"My friend and brother-at-arms, Jerrod," Drin answered.

"He is not a follower," the Priest responded.

"He knows me better than anyone. We have stood side-by-side in battle. He can vouch for me better than anyone," Drin answered.

"So be it," the Priest said as he turned and shut the door, leaving Drin alone.

Drin knelt on the marble floor in prayer, preparing for his Accolade, but his prayers were disturbed. He was preoccupied with hope that his father would attend, and that his father would forgive him and recognize his achievements.

✻   ✻   ✻   ✻   ✻

Jerrod left Rhonda in the throne room with the prince and princess. He was not altogether comfortable socializing with royalty. Feeling like an unwanted cousin trying to become popular through his relatives' lives, Jerrod preferred to wander through the castle for a while, eventually finding himself on the wall watching the sun setting over the dark silhouette of the Wild's mountains. Jerrod could only imagine what lay beyond. Thoughts of home and then highlights of his journey drifted into his mind.

Has it really been a year? he thought.

A year? A year since what? someone thought back.

Imelrinn? Jerrod thought.

Who is Imelrinn?

Aren't you? Jerrod demanded.

No. I'm Drok-na. A year since what?

A year since I left home.

It's been more than a year for me, but I am with a good friend now.

Where are you?

In my cave.

Cave? What cave?

In the mountains where I live.

The mountains? Who's your friend? Jerrod questioned.

Jacob.

The wizard?

Yes, do you know him?

The name gave Jerrod chills like ice water being poured down his back. He broke the link off immediately and locked Drok-na out of his mind. Shaking his head slightly as if he had just been punched, Jerrod turned and walked quickly down the wall and up the steps to an entrance back into the king's castle. Finding his way back to his room as quickly as possible, Jerrod slipped through his door before encountering anyone.

His hands trembled slightly as he started to untie his boots. His breathing was rapid. His nerves were still a little raw when someone knocked on his door, causing him to jump.

I'm becoming unnerved, Jerrod teased himself.

Jerrod went to the door to find a boy his age wearing the uniform of an Order's Initiate. He handed Jerrod a scroll and waited as Jerrod opened and read the message. Quickly lacing up his boots, Jerrod grabbed his brown cape and sword, and followed the Initiate. The evening was growing late when they departed the castle for the Cathedral.

Jerrod had meant to go to the monastery, but had not found the courage. He wanted desperately to see Amanda, but could not imagine facing her. The urgent note to visit Drin was all he needed to delay the visit even longer, but it was nice to be out of the castle. The thought caused Jerrod to laugh at himself.

All my life I have dreamt of being in the king's castle and now I can't wait to get out. He considered the paradox.

"You are an Initiate of the Order, right?" Jerrod tried to strike up a conversation as a diversion to his thoughts.

"Yes."

"So, you haven't taken your Oath of Knighthood yet?"

"No."

"Is Drin a friend of yours?"

"Not particularly. We are both Initiates, but when he is knighted in the morning he will become a Cavalier."

When they reached the Cathedral, a holy man in a tan robe with a hood hanging down his back and a white rope belt met them.

"I am Friar Jon," the man greeted Jerrod as he dismissed the Initiate.

"Good evening, Friar," Jerrod said quietly.

The Friar looked down at the crystal pommel sticking out from under Jerrod's cape and then he looked up into Jerrod's blue eyes.

"This way." The Friar turned to walk away.

"Have I done something to offend you, Friar?" Jerrod confronted the older man.

"No." The Friar stopped, turning back to answer Jerrod.

"You are not a knight, are you?" The Friar's voice was sharp.

"No. I have not been knighted."

"Your sword does not appear to be typical. Is it magic?"

"Yes," Jerrod answered as his hand shifted to the pommel of the sword.

The holy man looked down to watch Jerrod's hand and then back to the young man's face.

"You have nothing to fear from me," the Friar stated plainly.

"Then what?"

"We do not condone the use of magic."

"So I have been told. You'll like me even less if I grow angry. Where is Drin?"

The Friar showed Jerrod to the small room where Drin was on his knees praying. At the sight of Jerrod, Drin rose to his feet. They grasped each other's inner elbows in a warrior's greeting before Drin embraced him for a moment.

"Jerrod! Thank you for coming," Drin said, broaching a smile that crossed his face over his cleft chin.

"Couldn't miss it. Look at you. Cleaner than I have seen you since the hot pools."

"Not any more rested, I'm afraid." Drin's forced laugh sounded tense.

"You look good. What can I do for you, my friend? Your note said you urgently needed to talk to me."

"Come, sit down. The Order has granted me an unusual request. During the Accolade I need someone who will speak for my valor. Typically it is a follower of the Order, but I have requested permission for you to speak on my behalf. It is my choice."

"It would be an honor."

Jerrod cocked his head slightly, listening to the soft music playing in the background before turning his attention back to Drin. They spoke for a little while before Jerrod departed, leaving Drin to return to his haunted prayers. On his way back to the king's castle Jerrod had to pass the monastery. There was no more avoiding it. It was late into the night when he asked at the gate for Fraum. It took a while for the monk to come to the hall where Jerrod waited.

"I'm sorry. Would you like some tea?" Fraum offered.

"That would be fantastic. It would be nice to sit quietly for a while."

They spoke a while, telling each other of their return journeys and what had happened with their friends since they had departed Silandria. Jerrod also spoke of his experience with Drok-na.

"Jacob must be the wizard Nathanial feared," Jerrod concluded.

"Drok-na is in a cave? Drok-na must be Jacob's dragon. But just because Nathanial betrayed us, doesn't mean we can trust Jacob or Drok-na. Enemies of our enemy are not necessarily our friends," Fraum reasoned aloud.

"The Triad?" Jerrod asked.

"And will they consider us friends or foes?" Fraum added.

They spoke a little more before Jerrod stood up to leave. The late hour was weighing on him, but he had one final question.

"She is here?"

"Yes, but she doesn't want to see you."

"I understand. I don't blame her. You are a good friend to all of us. More importantly, to Amanda. Thank you," Jerrod said as he turned to walk away.

"Jerrod, love is always confusing. Do you even know what you want? Don't expect her to know how to feel," Fraum counseled.

Jerrod did not respond. His eyes stared into the distance somewhere far beyond his friend's shoulder.

"Give it time, Jerrod," Fraum comforted his friend.

"Time? I have two absolutely marvelous women that I love and I have ruined both relationships," Jerrod confessed.

"You can't press. Let things be, let the tension relax. Life works its way out."

Jerrod looked at the old man, his almond shaped eyes seemed to smile as much as the smile on his lips. Jerrod paused a moment reflecting on what Fraum had said, and then turned to walk away without another word.

Jerrod took his time walking back to the castle. He intended to return to his room, anticipating he would be up early to eat the morning meal with Rhonda and her family, but when he returned to the castle he was greeted by a herald.

"There you are! Where have you been? I have been searching the castle for hours," the herald spoke quickly.

"I had business out of the castle," Jerrod started to reply.

"No matter now, come! The king has been waiting. We must go, now!"

The herald walked so quickly through the castle that Jerrod was almost in a trot to keep up. They wound through the halls until they stood in front of the doors to the king's private chambers. The guards at the door opened it as the herald and Jerrod approached. The king was standing alone in the middle of the chambers.

"Come in, Jerrod," the king greeted him.

"I'm sorry for your wait, Your Majesty. I just returned to the castle," Jerrod explained.

"You didn't know I wanted to see you. Thank you for coming at this late hour."

"Anytime, Your Majesty. What can I do for you?"

"We spoke of the Sword of Trisdale earlier?" the king said.

"Yes, Your Majesty."

"I assume that's it?" the king asked, nodding towards the sword on Jerrod's hip.

"Yes, Your Majesty. Would you like to see it?"

"Certainly."

Jerrod drew his sword and held the blade and *ricasso* in his hands, holding the sword parallel to the floor, for the king to inspect and take if he wished to do so. The crystal pommel and brass *quillon* reflected the light from the lamps. The king looked at the three-fingered talon and dewclaw holding the crystal in place before taking the sword in his hand to inspect the multicolored gold inlay and inset emeralds on each side. The king ran his finger along the distinctive flower pattern inlaid in the *ricasso*.

"It's a fine sword," the king said as he handed it back to Jerrod.

"Thank you, Your Majesty."

"I had heard the pommel was dark blue with energy like lightning dancing around inside it?"

"It was when I found it."

"What happened?"

Jerrod recounted the story of fighting the ghoul beneath Trisdale. How the ghoul had attacked Amanda, but when Jerrod had used the sword against it, the ghoul had vanished.

"After the ghoul disappeared the crystal was clear, Your Majesty."

"How did the sword end up in your hands?" the king asked.

"I found the remains of a knight holding the sword. I can only assume it was Lord Trisdale."

"You found his remains?"

"Yes, Your Majesty. He had been crushed by a tree. I buried him."

"The sword rightfully belongs to the Lord of Trisdale, or his heirs," the king pointed out.

"You could command it, Sire, but other treasure belongs to the finder," Jerrod countered politely.

"How did you become friends with the Elves?"

"We met on the Plateau of Kronese. The Princess Rhonda and Lord Imelrinn led us through the Black Forest," Jerrod answered.

"And now you're betrothed to the druid Princess?"

"Yes, Your Majesty."

"And you are from my kingdom? Winfred, wasn't it?"

"Yes, Your Majesty."

"Jerrod, I must be blunt and come directly to the point. I want to rebuild Trisdale. There are a hundred lords, knights, and accomplished warriors with more experience that would ride out tonight to start rebuilding the ruins," the king said, watching for a reaction.

"Not one of them even knows an Elve," the king paused again as he paced the room.

"I want to strengthen ties with Lithlillia. You already possess the Sword of Trisdale. What do you know about the keep?"

"It was once a warning beacon for both kingdoms," Jerrod acknowledged.

"Yes. Lord Trisdale was master of the keep until his disappearance. It was a great responsibility to warn two kingdoms."

"It must have been, but what does that have to do with me, Your Majesty? Are you asking for the sword back?"

"What do you think about rebuilding the signal tower at Trisdale?" the king asked, studying his reaction.

"It is a monumental task that could take two lifetimes. The keep is in ruins."

"It will take builders, stone masons, carpenters, and much more. There are no subjects to support it. I will finance the rebuilding of the keep and pay whatever tithing is needed until such time as the keep is self-supporting. Do you think you could manage the rebuilding of the keep?" the king asked.

"I can be your builder, Sire," Jerrod answered quickly.

The king went to the door and asked the guard to show the Commanders of the Armies and of the Guard in, and then turned to a table, where he picked up a small box. The two men entered as the king turned around with the box and walked back to Jerrod.

"Commanders, thank you for joining us. I believe you both met Jerrod, Friend of Lithlillia, earlier this evening."

"Jerrod, I don't want you to be my builder. I want you to oversee the rebuilding while you strengthen Torrence's relationship with the Elves. Can you do that?" the king asked as he opened the small box.

"This is a ring of lordship. Both of the other lords of Torrence have similar rings signifying their position and authority. Trisdale is the third territory in the kingdom. It has been vacant since I was a boy. Trisdale is yours, if you will have it."

Jerrod looked at him, momentarily stunned.

"Yes, Your Majesty. I will," he answered when he could.

"Then you, Jerrod of Winfred, Friend of Lithlillia, are now the new Lord of Trisdale. It is not a knighthood, but in some ways it is so much more," the king said as he handed him the ring.

"Congratulations, Jerrod," the king concluded.

"Congratulations," both commanders offered after looking at one another in disbelief.

*   *   *   *   *

Unable to sleep, Amanda rose and went to the front of the monastery, where she followed the winding stairwell down to the basement. The stone walls of the library were cool. It had been a while since she was interested in reading. She pulled a scroll from the shelves and sat at the table to read about the Order of One's knighthood.

Knights generally vowed to serve the people, but knights of the Order answered an unspoken expectation to serve the One. Amanda read on. The knights were ordained during an Accolade ceremony after which they became members of the Order of Cavaliers, mounted warriors who charged into battle with lances and swords.

Amanda read until the morning bell summoned the monks to eat. Rolling up the scroll, she joined the other monks. Afterward, she prepared for the Accolade. She and Fraum were the only ones from the monastery attending the ceremony.

It was a short walk to the arched stone doorway of the Cathedral. Inside they found seats against the wall opposite from the Clerics, Priests, and Friars where the few guests were directed to sit. In the middle of the hall were rows of knights, members of the Order of Cavaliers, who stood in well-polished plate armor. Behind them, closer to the door, were the Initiates in polished chain mail. Both groups wore white tunics with blue capes. Among them were a few who wore royal blue shoulder braid.

"I read last night that the blue braids are for the title of Lord Paladin. They have done something of extraordinary valor that qualified them for the honorary title," Amanda whispered to Fraum.

The Squires, in their best clothes, stood nearest the doors, leaving the Acolytes outside.

The Elders and Marshals stood at the front of the hall, and between them sat the Prophet, dressed in his gold hooded robe with a white rope belt. The Elders attended to him as the celebration waited to begin.

Near the front of the Cathedral hall, the kings, queens, prince, and princesses sat in honor. There was a group of chairs set nearby where a woman sat alone, but there was no room for Imelrinn to sit with his Lord, Lady, and Princess, so he worked his way through the seated guests until he saw two monks sitting near the door, their bald heads and brown robes sticking out in the crowd.

"Fraum, my friend," Imelrinn greeted the monk as he walked up behind him.

When the monks turned around, Imelrinn found himself not only greeting Fraum, but the other monk had strangely familiar blue eyes.

"Amanda?" Imelrinn questioned.

She nodded as the brass fanfare started the ceremony.

The crowd quieted and sat down as a single knightly figure walked into the hall and up the middle aisle between the columns of Cavaliers and Initiates. His plate armor seemed to glisten in the candle light of the Cathedral chandeliers. On his shoulder he wore a silver brooch to clasp his royal blue cape, the pinecone brooch indicating his title as a Friend of Lithlillia.

The metallic sound of his boots striking the stone floor echoed through the silence as his cape fluttered behind him. Reaching the head of the Cathedral, Drin stopped, standing directly in front of where the kings and queens sat on the side. As the eldest Elder stepped forward to face him, Drin genuflected.

"Who will vouch for this Initiate's valor?" the Elder asked.

From the far side of the Cathedral, Jerrod walked forward with a purple cape and golden *aiguillette* circling his left arm before draping across his chest. The pointed tips of the golden braid hung down his right side almost to his belt. Jerrod walked forward to stand behind Drin.

"I, Jerrod, Lord of Trisdale, Friend of Lithlillia, will vouch for his valor." Jerrod's voice filled the Cathedral.

All the attention focused momentarily on the young man claiming lordship. A new lordship that had not been announced. The quiet rumble of whispers erupted in the Cathedral.

Jerrod could feel all the eyes upon him until the attention shifted back to Drin, kneeling before the Elder. Slowly the Prophet rose and walked forward. Another Elder walked forward, carrying a beautiful sword in a diamond encrusted sheath. The Prophet drew the sword and, holding it upright, the tip point towards the ceiling, kissed the blade. Then he stepped closer to Drin.

"Repeat after me," the Prophet directed.

"I shall:

Stand with virtue and purity that all may see.

Have integrity in all your affairs.

Place honor and trust unto all you meet until they prove unworthy.

Take all obligations of fellow Knights as your own.

Adorn yourself with valor in the face of danger.

Protect all life with the same value, that one life be not made more important than any another.

Uphold your oath, even to your own end.

Serve with faith that this oath and all who take it will defend what is good and just to this end.

So is your charge."

When Drin, having said "I" and "my" in the proper place as he repeated each line the Prophet spoke, concluded the Oath of Knighthood, the Prophet tapped Drin on each shoulder with the tip of his sword.

"I pronounce you a Knight, Cavalier of the Order," he said as he tapped Drin a third time.

"Do you vouch that this knight has exhibited extraordinary valor in completing his quest?" the Prophet asked, looking at Jerrod.

"I do."

The Lord Marshal stepped forward to stand next to the Prophet.

"Then I award you, Sir Drin, the title of Lord Paladin for your extraordinary valor in the northern Wilds and for the tithing you bring back to the Order," the Prophet pronounced.

The Lord Marshal stepped up to Sir Drin and slid a royal blue braid around his left arm, attaching it to his shoulder. Drin slowly bowed his head, humbly acknowledging the recognition.

"Arise, Lord Paladin, Sir Drin, Knight, Cavalier of the Order of One," the Lord Marshal commanded.

Drawing his sword as he rose, Drin held it aloft a moment before bringing the *ricasso* to his forehead. He held it there a moment before re-sheathing the sword.

Jerrod watched as Drin turned and marched down the center aisle. As he passed by, each row of Cavaliers turned and marched out behind him, creating two columns of knights, their metal footsteps echoing through the Cathedral as thunder had over Mount Sismin. Then the Initiates followed in similar fashion. As Drin reached the doors of the Cathedral, the brass fanfare announced the departure of the Order's newest Knight and Lord Paladin.

"The Prophet and the Order of One invite all attendees to the dining hall for food and wine," the eldest Elder announced as the Squires began filing out of the Cathedral.

On the way to the dining hall, Rhonda pulled Jerrod aside.

"When did you accept a lordship?" she started.

"I was summoned by the king late last night."

"Are you crazy? Now, to be together, one of us will have to abandon their responsibilities!"

"It was barely a choice!" Jerrod responded, his voice growing louder.

"There is always a choice."

"The king asked if I would rebuild Trisdale and strengthen the bond between Lithlillia and Torrence. I didn't know this was going to happen," Jerrod finished as he passed his hands in front of himself.

"You chose to accept the appointment without thinking of the impact it would have on our betrothal. You wanted fame. You were impulsive and foolish. Isn't being Lord of Lithlillia good enough for you?"

Rhonda's eyes were beginning to glow, her hair trembled as if it were trying to lift from her shoulders. She turned abruptly, storming off, and leaving Jerrod, Lord of Trisdale Keep, standing alone.

She's right. I have always wanted fame and fortune. Did I forsake her for personal desire?

*   *   *   *   *

In the back of a dark cave, a single bear, silvered with old age, stirred. The old bear slept alone. Only a table, tossed on its side, and broken vials and jars littered the room. The bear stirred again and then lifted its head to look around the cave.

Alone? it thought.

The bear slowly stood up and stretched as hunger took hold. From the main part of the cave, the bear heard wolves and other bears stirring.

Where is Rok-lin? That fool, Nathanial thought, still in his bear form.

One has to eat, the dragon thought back.

Ah, there you are. Did anything enter the cave?

A few of the wolves looked in, but nothing special. No one suspected and there was nothing I couldn't have handled.

Why is everything tossed about then?

It was too cramped for me to move in and out. I had to eat. I wasn't hibernating, resting without eating.

Magic sometimes requires rest. Nathanial was defensive.

Nathanial stretched one last time in bear form before starting the change. His changing bones and muscles caused him to roar in pain, ending as a man's scream. When it was done the wizard stood naked in the dark cave. He stumbled as he reached for the robe he had discarded months ago.

CHAPTER 11

WIZARDS AND KINGS

The reception was full of knights, generals mingling with the kings and queens, and hundreds of Initiates hoping for the day they would be granted a quest. The generals spoke on about military strength and a long history of peace, boring the kings while the queens snuck off to sit away from the male egos. Lady Lieisa took hold of Rhonda's upper arm, gently pulling her along, as the queens and the young princess from Greensland sought their escape. Prince Garrett watched enviously as the women skillfully left him to the torment of his position.

Nearby a couple of stout men with broad shoulders and muscular arms were watching over the royal family of Greensland. Their masculine frames filled their shirts, spreading the v-necks and exposing their chests. Their kilts, which covered their thighs to their knees and provided long blanket-like bolts of cloth which they draped over their shoulders, pinning the remnants with large, jeweled brooches, were a blue and green plaid. Wide broadswords hung from their thick leather belts.

I think I would rather have them as friends than enemies, Jerrod pondered.

Jerrod learned the coastal kingdom of Greensland lay east of Torrence along the Sea of Semanie. The king's castle was built on the delta of the Metamesterrian River. Apparently, the *kilted* warriors were from coastal mountains they called the "Highlands." The Highlands were west of Greensland, from the point the range rose up to overlook Greensland to where two ranges came together.

Could he be speaking of the area east of where the Inner Range and Coast Range meet? Jerrod wondered when he heard the description of their home.

"Is your home like Torrence?" Jerrod asked, trying to strike up a conversation.

"Naw. The Highlands have high, rocky hilltops with greener than green grass and rock faced cliffs and promenades. You can see the world from there, and overlook the delta to the east and the great plains to the north."

"Sounds beautiful. Why did you leave it to come here?" Jerrod's interest rose a bit.

"Long ago, we were in a great battle with Greensland which had lasted generations. To settle the dispute, Greensland offered the Highland Clans the right to govern ourselves and asked only that we serve to protect their king. Our ancestors formed the treaty and we honor it."

"You are self-governed?" Jerrod asked.

"Aye. Many years before our fathers' fathers, the truce was made, creating our debt to the King of Greensland. They have honored their word. We honor ours, but it's not as if they could force their will in the Highlands, is it?"

"In what sense?" Jerrod asked.

"The clans are spread throughout the Highlands. The only castle is Innesril, which would withstand any attack that might be launched against its steep hills and stone walls. It's large enough to protect all the clans within its walls, if we so choose."

"It sounds nice. I would like to visit there someday," Jerrod reflected.

"Aye, it is. But why go there? You should visit our family homes. There are stone walls and sod roofs with gardens and rock walls lining the pastures. Cold water from a well or spring which will quench your thirst better than any on a warm day. And the *galas*. That's the beauty of the Highlands. You should come to the Highlands," the kilted warrior said, looking at him.

It was evident that under the watchful eyes of the highlanders, the farmers of Greensland had prospered. The farmers grew great crops and raised herds of cattle and sheep on the fertile flatlands around the delta. Their fishermen brought in great catches from the Semanie Sea. Long ago the kingdom traded with miners from the Anacoztiel Mountains and farther east into the Elven-Dwarven Mountains, but those days had passed, leaving the agriculturally rich kingdom with less trade.

Finishing his conversation with the kilted warriors, Jerrod began looking for Rhonda. When he saw her still sitting with the queens, Jerrod sought Drin out.

"Congratulations, my friend, or should I say, Sir Paladin?" Jerrod teased, grasping Drin's inner elbow in friendship.

"Thank you, Lord Trisdale. And when did that happen?" Drin smiled, understanding Jerrod's deep desire for fame and fortune.

"I was called to the king's chambers after leaving you last night. Rhonda isn't happy about it."

"Is she ever happy about anything?"

"Not lately."

"What are you going to do now?"

"I don't know. Return to Lithlillia, I guess. The king wants me to oversee the reconstruction of Trisdale Keep and to remain friends with Lithlillia. I thought I was getting a castle out of what I already planned, but Rhonda doesn't see it that way."

"Of course not. What about Amanda?"

"She isn't talking to me, either. What's in your future?" Jerrod asked, hoping to change the topic.

"Serve the Order. Is there anything else?" Drin answered, causing them both to chuckle.

Being interrupted by a line of well-wishers who wanted Drin's attention, Jerrod stepped away and began wandering through the crowd again. Near the door he saw two monks he recognized immediately.

"Congratulations," Fraum greeted him as he walked up.

"Thank you," Jerrod answered as he turned to gaze at Amanda's head for a moment before looking into her eyes.

"Brown robes, I see. I take it you have joined the White Fists. Are you done with the Guild?" Jerrod asked, trying to divert his attention from her baldness.

"I have 'resigned.'"

"How did they take that?" Jerrod asked lightheartedly.

"It took a little persuasion," Amanda said, actually smiling.

"And what of Lord Trisdale? Are you leaving?" Fraum asked.

"Yeah. Not sure where I fit in yet, though. Should I go to Lithlillia or Trisdale?"

Amanda looked down without commenting.

"I am sure all will become clear with time," Fraum responded.

*   *   *   *   *

Nathanial stretched again, pulling his robe tighter before he began righting the tables. As he did, he found the box where he had placed the rings months before. He slid open the box.

Ahh, still there, Nathanial thought.

I told you no one entered. I wouldn't let them.

Thank you. You are the only one that I can count on.

After arranging the table, vials, burners, and other alchemy equipment, and tucking the box with three rings back into a nook, out of view of anyone's meddlesome curiosity, Nathanial went to the old were-bear, leader of the Were-Folk.

"Raznik?" Nathanial called to a large bear.

The bear slowly transformed into an old man, who struggled to pull a robe on before answering.

"Why do you insist on communicating in human form, wizard?" the old man protested.

"I have business to attend to. I am going to strengthen our alliance."

"Strengthen? With whom?"

"Another group that shares our common enmity against the Elves. Make sure no one enters my den. I go to the Fendür."

Nathanial mounted Rok-lin to fly out of the Were-Folks' cavern. She was much bigger than she had been when they burst out of Terrace Xul, which gave Nathanial a great sense of comfort. As Rok-lin stumbled towards the cavern entrance, preparing to leap into the air, Nathanial looked at the scores of were-wolves and were-bears.

So insignificant, he thought.

The wolves? Rok-lin asked.

The Were-Folk, but they will help us accomplish our goal.

How?

They will strengthen our army, no one will suspect them, and if they die in battle, there is little lost.

Nathanial rode towards the Fendür who lived in the Crispten and Brisbane Mountains overlooking the Plateau of Kronese and its Black Forest.

He knew they were a loosely organized tribe of trolls and giants held together by one common point. They hated the Elves who guarded the forests. The Elves who hunted and slaughtered them whenever and wherever they could.

I hope to use the Fendür's shared hatred of the Elves to encourage them to join my army, Nathanial explained.

Are they smart enough to understand? Rok-lin questioned.

I don't know. It's a risk, Nathanial reflected.

Nathanial pulled his robes tight, trying to stay warm as he peered ahead, ignoring the scenic beauty of the land below.

How pompous. Won't Lady Lieisa be surprised to learn I have joined with the Fendür. Nathanial marveled at the thought.

The flight over the Crispten Mountains, along Lake Almandee, to Mount Sismin was quick. What had taken them days to travel by horseback took little more than an hour on Rok-lin's back. Her power and grace, and the feeling of flight on the back of a dragon were always exhilarating.

Closing his eyes, Nathanial took a deep breath, enjoying the sound of the cold wind as they soared across the sky. Only the occasional beats of Rok-lin's giant wings broke the tranquility of the rushing air.

The sight of Rok-lin approaching the giants' cottages on Mount Sismin alarmed the Fendür. Her massive wingspan blocked the sun, casting a shadow over the village as they approached. At first she seemed to hover, her wings beating against the air as she held her position, just out of range of the Fendür spears and boulders. When the giants' hands were empty, they landed.

Nathanial quickly slid off her back to approach the large, ugly giant he assumed to be their leader. He had not been present on Sismin Pass when Rhonda battled the giants so he did not know how they might react.

"Greetings, brothers. I mean you no harm," Nathanial said, using his magic to speak in Fendür.

But the giants were not eased by his greetings. When they raised their stone hammers to renew their attack, Nathanial brought his staff up, sending out a pulse of blinding white light, stunning the giants into submission.

"I mean you no harm! Listen to me. I come to offer you an alliance against the Elves." Nathanial paused, letting the meaning of his words sink in.

"The blindness will pass in a moment. While we wait, listen to my offer. Lithlillia is our common enemy, but together I can free you from their hunters," Nathanial persuaded.

After talking for some time with the tribal leader, Nathanial gained the alliance he sought. It had not been easy. The Fendür were untrusting of man and Elve, and simple of thought. They did not care about power and cared little about treasure, but Nathanial had been able to use their desire to be free from persecution, no longer hunted and killed, to his advantage.

An envoy from the first tribe went with Nathanial to the second village to help foster the alliance. At first, Nathanial had gone from fortress to fortress to enlist each tribe into his army, but soon they were sending their own envoys out to the various villages. Within days Nathanial had an agreement with all the giant and troll tribes of the Fendür.

He had chosen to approach the giant-trolls last. They were the unwanted offspring of the other two races, from rare relationships and after battle conquests resulting in crossbreeding. Long ago the giant-trolls had been a rare breed, but as the savagery between trolls and giants continued with their inevitable fighting, the breed grew more common. Now, there were enough giant-trolls to be a legitimate third race of the Fendür.

On the northern slope of the Brisbane Mountains, at the east end near the Meadows and south of the Wall of Haithenbeurn, Nathanial's army began assembling next to one of the larger Fendür villages, one of the few where all three tribes already cohabitated. Hacking away the trees to build a log wall, they began clearing the field they could use for practicing army tactics.

As construction of the camp began, wizards who had deserted the Triad began arriving. With their use of magic to help speed the construction of the camp, a log wall surrounding the large practice field was erected in little time. With the wizards came mercenaries from Torrence, rogue warriors always looking for power and coin.

One of the first to arrive was a tall skinny man with dark, scraggly hair who answered to Sescious. He always seemed in need of a wash. He still wore the black onyx ring with rubies inset in the corners, the symbol of one of the sixteen lower Masters in the Triad. Sescious did not look into the eyes of anyone with whom he spoke as he played with his ring.

Nathanial would not normally have put up with Sescious's ego, but he got things done and Nathanial quickly identified him as second in command. Gesturing with his ring hand so all would see his symbol of authority, Sescious gave direct orders with an expectation for immediate action. With Sescious firmly in place and the alliance with the Were-Folk and the Fendür complete, Nathanial started the next phase of his plan.

Nathanial mounted Rok-lin the next morning and departed. Flying to the west over the Brisbane and Crispten Mountains, they flew until they were above the steep, jagged peaks of the Wilds. Misty clouds wrapping around the terrain obscured the mountain tops. Soaring high above the range, where the air was much colder, they reached the eastern slope of the Wilds.

As they crossed the Wilds ridgeline, another mountain range stretched westward. Following the east-west range they began flying westerly. Gliding close to the barren, rocky ridge, they floated down across the tree-line, skimming the top of the forest. Continuing down the slope, they flew like an eagle searching for its prey, ready to swoop through the trees to break the back of an unsuspecting creature with powerful talons and carry it off for a meal.

As the slopes began to level out, the evergreens gave way to thick, deciduous trees with massive trunks and branches that spread out. The deciduous forest was entangled with thick vines that wrapped around the trunks of the trees and branches, passing from tree to tree, creating net-like walls of tangled vegetation with thick leaves that obstructed any view through the entanglement.

Rok-lin slowed, pulling her head and upper body upward and extending her wings to break the speed of their glide. With a couple mighty beats of her wings, Rok-lin began a slow, circular flight, searching the nearly impassible woods for a place to land.

Slowly, slowly. They will hear us, Nathanial thought.

I saw them as we flew over. They may already know we are here.

If they knew I'm sure we would be fighting them now. Dragons may be rare, but they are not unheard of and I'm sure the Dark Elves aren't going to let one land in their forest without a fight.

The warm, humid air of the deciduous valley made it harder to breath as sweat beaded on his skin and began rolling downward to be absorbed into Nathanial's heavy clothes.

By Hades, it's warm, Nathanial thought as Rok-lin landed in a small break in the canopy.

You don't follow the Olympians. You have said so many times, Rok-lin challenged.

Not everything can be caused by dragons and magic, Nathanial retorted.

I saw a few of the Elves you seek as we came down the mountain, but they were moving the other direction, away from here, Rok-lin reported.

Dragons and scales! They will be miles from here now, Nathanial responded.

Tear up that tree and place it in the middle of the meadow, Nathanial ordered.

Rok-lin effortlessly ripped the tree from the ground and dropped it where she had been directed. She watched Nathanial point his staff at the once living tree.

"Magaraknic!" Nathanial exclaimed, causing the tree to burst into flames with a loud, booming sound.

"That should draw some attention." Nathanial chuckled aloud.

It was not an hour before a group of tall Elves with bluish-gray skin stepped into the light of the bonfire. They came from all sides, surrounding Nathanial and Rok-lin. With two dozen Elven archers aiming their bows at Rok-lin, a single Elve walked towards Nathanial, his Elven long sword drawn.

His yellow eyes, peering out from under the hood of his sleeveless black leather vest, seemed to glow in the dark. Nathanial glanced at the thinner Elvish sword, with its edge on one side and the slight curve near the point. The reflection of the bonfire's light down the side of the blade made it even more menacing.

"We mean you no harm," Nathanial said softly.

"Why are you in our forest?" the Elve demanded.

"I am Nathanial. I'm looking for your king."

"What business do you have with him?"

"My business is with him, not his henchman."

The Dark Elve looked at Rok-lin and then back at Nathanial, sizing up the situation. He knew they were ill-prepared to fight a dragon, but they were not eager to invite one into their kingdom, either.

"It would be better if the dragon waited on the mountain," the Elve suggested.

"Wait for me on the mountains above the forest, but be ready to come if I call," Nathanial said aloud to Rok-lin so the Elves would hear.

It was hard to follow the Dark Elves through the forest at night. Their dark clothes hid them in the shadows. Occasionally, a glimmer reflected off a crease of a sleeve from a silky shirt, giving a ghostly sense to their dark silhouettes. They led Nathanial through the dense forest down paths only they knew. Anyone else traveling the forest, day or night, would most surely have lost their way.

Imelrinn is the best tracker I have ever seen. I don't know that he could discover the hidden paths of these Dark Elves. His thoughts of the Mountain Elves surprised him.

Nathanial was lost. He could no longer tell which direction they were traveling. He could not see the moons, so there was no hope he might regain his east-west orientation. His first indication they had arrived at the Dark Elven

Kingdom was an arched doorway in a wall of vines and tree trunks, but without knowing where he was, there was nothing to do but enter. Carved into a wooden archway was a symbol of a black leaf over the two moons of Dendür.

As they continued single file through the gates, drums began to beat, deep, heavy drums. In the trees above them several levels of lanterns became visible. Nathanial began making out cabins from which the lanterns were hung. In the dark the tree-cabins were camouflaged by the leaves and bark and vines as though they were part of the trees.

The higher cabins were smaller in construction. The lower cabins were not only larger, but they were more elegant with more windows and lanterns, and had balconies that wrapped around the tree-cabin structures.

Marching towards the center of the kingdom, they occasionally passed under a wooden bridge supported by vine-rope, which spanned between branches where the wooden paths that joined the cabins would not otherwise connect.

They stopped at an open fire pit where a pig was roasting. The pit was lined with stones and a series of stumps circling around the fire. In the two large wooden seats on the far side of the fire sat a Lord and Lady of the Dark Elves. They were dressed in black cloth with silver stitched highlights. Around their heads were black metal bands.

The leader of the Dark Elven guard that had escorted Nathanial into the realm pulled back his hood revealing his dark hair and pointed ears. His hair was cut short due to the heat of the forest. The man bowed his head to the Lord and Lady.

"Your Majesties, we found a traveler in the large meadow. He came by dragon. He says he has business with you," the guard finished and turned towards the wizard.

"You are a flatlander, are you not? What business do you have with me?"

"Your Majesties, I am Nathanial. I am a high Master of the Triad, a wizard from Torrence," Nathanial greeted them. He genuflected, leaning on his staff to help lower himself.

The Elves stirred.

"Of Torrence? Of men and Mountain Elves! That's not the best reference you could bring to us."

"Yes, Torrence, but I don't hold alliances to Torrence or Lithlillia."

"And you say you are a wizard?"

"Yes, Your Majesty."

"I imagine anyone can say they are a wizard and some may even be. And the fact that you rode in on the back of a dragon is impressive, but a dragon can be dispatched. So, what it comes to is how powerful you are. No jester's tricks will save you," the king warned.

Pulling back their bows at the king's remark, the dark warriors of the forest aimed at Nathanial as the wizard leaned against his staff to get off his knee. Nathanial looked at the king a moment. With a quick movement of his forearm, Nathanial raised his staff and struck the ground with the bottom as the archers released their black shafted arrows.

In an instant everyone except the king and queen found themselves floating twenty to thirty feet in the air. The black arrows were also floating, stopped in mid-flight. The king gazed at Nathanial, his chin resting on his loosely clenched fist.

"I can be more persuasive, if you like?" Nathanial warned.

"Why are you here, wizard? What is it you want so much that you would risk entering our kingdom?"

"I have an army, my lord. Small and marginally trained by your standards, I'm sure..." Nathanial paused to judge the king's reaction as he released the spell.

The on-lookers fell from where they were floating. Some were injured as the landed on the ground below where they floated, causing moans and protests, but Nathanial ignored them.

"I'm going to make war upon the men and Mountain Elves, as you put it," Nathanial said, focusing on the Lord of the Dark Elves.

"How big is your army? Who are your allies?" the Lord of the Dark Elves asked as he looked about at his followers.

"May I approach and speak more privately?" Nathanial requested.

"Come closer if you must, but I don't think the trees will retell your story. And I am sure none of my men will," the Dark Elve added.

Nathanial revealed to the king his intention to overthrow Torrence. After listening to the wizard, the Lord and Lady invited him to stay with the Dark Elves while they formed an alliance. Over the next few weeks Nathanial stayed in a higher cabin with a sitting room and a bedroom. It had a small porch and a single window, both in the front of the cabin. The Elves showed him the long path of ropes, stairs, and bridges he needed to manage to get to the cabin.

"Dragons and scales!" he exclaimed as he projected from the ground to the porch.

"I am a Master wizard of the Triad. I don't need to be climbing through ropes and bridges," Nathanial said as he looked around, then went quickly into his cabin.

The Dark Elves became accustom to Nathanial popping in and out as he went from his porch to the ground or to the training area where the Elves practiced. Each night, he ate with the Elves around the fire pit, where he was provided an honorary chair to the right of the Lord. Occasionally he took a goblet of Elven wine to finish in his cabin after the evening meal. It was made from a strange berry that grew plentifully on vines in the Wilds. It was sweet, almost nectar. As he finished the drink alone on his porch, he would smoke a pipe of Elven leaf harvested from the top of the canopy where the sun made it grow rich.

Much of his time was spent in consultation with the king, but when he could, Nathanial would project himself to his own training camp on the slopes of the Brisbane Mountains to learn how things were progressing. During his trips he retrieved some personal belongings, including the Tome of Brendril. Nathanial also visited the Were-Folk and Rok-lin, who was growing impatient.

We can't communicate while I am with the Elves. Some may be able to read thoughts. You will have to be patient and wait alone. It won't be much longer, Nathanial explained.

You stay alone in a mountain cave, Rok-lin thought defiantly.

I need the Elven army, and more importantly... Nathanial stopped.

What are you planning now, wizard? Rok-lin asked.

I have to train some of the Elves for a special task, Nathanial responded.

Nathanial spent hours reading the large, thick leather bound book of Brendril's spells. Legend held that Brendril had been able to create his own magical spells and that he had seemingly inexhaustible powers. The tome was the only known remnant from the legendary wizard.

The pages were hand cut parchment with painstakingly printed letters. Large icons started each spell followed by smaller lettering, each imprinted in colorful inks. Some spells seemed peculiar, with strange consequences and apparently limited power. But other spells, darker spells, were obviously much more extraordinary, the worst of which could cause massive destruction or death. After each spell incantation was the number of hours, or days, or weeks that a wizard should anticipate needing to rest or sleep.

Alchemy is so much easier on the body. You don't need to sleep after mixing a potion unless you've been up all night, Nathanial thought, chuckling.

When he could not slip away Nathanial communicated with Sescious by oil, flame, or smoke. The army grew slowly at first, gaining strength in numbers as hundreds of Were-Folk and Fendür arrived. With the promise of thousands of Dark Elves, their strength was becoming significant. Still, Nathanial knew Torrence had 800 men in the King's Guard and another 3,000 in the Standing Army, and the Order could offer at least 500 more.

But I have a surprise for you. He chuckled, carefully protecting his thoughts as he planned his assault on Torrence.

It was Rok-lin's impatience that created the problem. Although there was an abundance of food to pick from near her cave, she was demanding more and more attention. It was to the point that her thoughts interrupted Nathanial several times a day, often while he was in the middle of important conversations.

What is it! he snapped.

I'm not meant for cave dwelling and certainly not alone. Hunting for food is boring. Let's do something! How about a flight?

Can't you be patient!

I have been patient for months! I want to kill something. And no, I don't mean another wild animal. When do I get to kill Drok-na?

Despite his stress, Nathanial enjoyed life in the tree kingdom while pulling his plan together, making final arrangements. He slept when he wanted and there was always peaceful music. The forest air was fragrant, a mixture of moist bark and rich soil with a hint of some unseen flowers. But he enjoyed hearing the consistent banging of the blacksmiths' hammers against countless anvils most of all.

War, he thought.

The pounding of the metal to forge swords and shape armor echoing through the tree city set the pace like drums beating cadence. Archers, practicing their marksmanship, sent flights of black arrows into targets hundreds of feet away. Their aim was flawless. The black metal tips embedding deep into the targets caused the shafts to vibrate. Swordsmen, practicing deadly slashes and thrusts with the thin, slightly curved blades of the Elven long swords, kept cadence with the metallic drum sounds of the anvils.

At first Nathanial was oblivious to the differences between the Dark Elves and the Mountain Elves of Lithlillian. He had always heard it was the malevolence of the Dark Elves that caused the Elven-Dwarven War, but he had not been mistreated nor was there any apparent threat. He had expected to be threatened with his life, and to find torture chambers and public executions at the whim of some grotesque tyrant, but none existed.

Perhaps it is because I'm a wizard, he thought carelessly.

What's because you are a wizard? Rok-lin responded.

They are treating me well.

Perhaps it is because you have a dragon guardian. Ever think of that, wizard?

Perhaps.

I'm past bored! Maybe I should fly down there and cause some excitement. Rok-lin's thoughts were intense.

Rok-lin!

The Dark Elves' strict laws benefited their king, but he was smart enough to realize his need for his subjects, which impressed Nathanial. The king took care of the kingdom and his subjects in the manner he saw fit with quick, decisive rule. His subjects took care of the needs for the kingdom, food, security, and countless other things that came up.

I am trying to earn their trust! What do you think will happen when they realize you are eating their hunters? Nathanial scolded Rok-lin.

I'm bored and they were good sport. Not so good of taste, though. When do we get to go? Rok-lin said, ignoring Nathanial's warning.

Dragons and scales! You oversized lizard!

I'd watch it, wizard.

You weren't my equal before I obtained the Tome of Brendril and you certainly aren't now. It would merely take a wave of my hand for you to disappear, Nathanial thought back coldly.

And years of sleep afterward. You are stuck with me, Nathanial, like it or not.

While the Dark Elven army trained, Nathanial began training six of the king's best warriors to become his bodyguards, and three more for special "assignments." Nathanial provided long stiletto knives for the special training. The narrow knives were all black with thin blades that went straight to a point and sharp edges on both sides. They were design for one purpose, killing.

Only the king knew Nathanial's intent for the three Dark Elves and the secret gifts Nathanial bestowed upon them, three magical rings. Unlike the spells spoken by wizards as they thought of projecting to some familiar spot within their range, Brendril's spell enabled the rings to project the wearers to places they had never seen before. While the others trained for physical combat, the three Dark Elves became comfortable with projecting themselves into strange places.

Nathanial practiced too, reading wizardry from the tome. Currently he studied the summoning of Demon Cats, Harpies, and Succubi. He read late into the night, learning new magical words. It was a serious spell, not one that could be practiced in its entirety. He knew he would have to say the words precisely. In order to concentrate on the new spells, Nathanial projected himself to Rok-lin's cave which, after Rok-lin finished complaining, was very productive. Studying in the back of a dragon's cave generally assures undisturbed thoughts. And when he accidently summoned a Harpy or Succubus it was a single bite for Rok-lin to correct his oversight.

You seem to enjoy that, Nathanial thought.

Rok-lin looked at him.

I didn't realize dragon's could smile, Nathanial continued as he petted her neck.

✻   ✻   ✻   ✻   ✻

In the short time following Drin's Accolade, Torrence and Lithlillia renewed their forgotten alliance while Torrence and Greensland solidified a new one that would be finalized with a wedding between the prince and princess. During that time Lord Steffen and Lady Lieisa had quickly grown restless for their forest.

When the time came for Lithlillia to depart, Jerrod kissed Rhonda goodbye before helping her into the saddle. Rhonda's feelings were deeply hurt that Jerrod felt obligated to remain in Torrence to fulfill his Lordly responsibilities.

"I wish you were coming with us. It's not right for you to stay here rather than accompanying me back to Lithlillia," Rhonda mumbled.

"I have things here that I must attend to before going to Lithlillia. You must understand that."

"I understand that I am the Druid Princess of Lithlillia, that we are betrothed, and you are the future Lord of Lithlillia. What else is there to understand?"

"In time all that will be true. Right now the king has asked for my aid."

Rhonda looked at him.

"He is my king."

"And what of my father and mother? What are they to you?"

"They haven't asked me for anything. I'm not even sure they accept me as their future son-in-law, let alone the heir of Lithlillia. What do you want of me?"

"I want you at my side."

"I want that too."

"Just not today."

Jerrod walked next to her as the column of Elves rode towards the gate. In front of the gate, Rhonda stopped her horse briefly to look down into Jerrod's eyes. Running her fingers through his silver hair, pushing it out of his eyes, she smiled briefly. Then she nudged the horse with her heel and she was gone.

Imelrinn stopped to lean over from his saddle to clasp Jerrod by the elbow.

"She didn't even look back," Jerrod commented.

"Give her time. By the time we arrive home she will miss you and will want to work things out. If I send a message will you come?" the Elven guardian from the ancient mountains asked.

"Always, my friend. Always."

"Then, Lord Trisdale, I take my leave of you."

Imelrinn nudged his horse a little harder, causing it to jump slightly before trotting away.

"May your home be blessed by the forest!" he yelled back over his shoulder as his horse broke into a gallop.

"And yours, my friend. And yours," Jerrod whispered as he watched the Mountain Elve ride away.

What splendors you must have seen in your hundreds of years, Jerrod thought.

Jerrod saw the king several times to discuss the future of Trisdale Keep. They also met with the two other lords before they returned to their own keeps in the south.

One lord was from Semanie Point, the second largest city in Torrence and the largest harbor. Akkian Keep guarded the mouth of the Torrence River. He was an older man, set in his ways, comfortable with years in his position. The lord spent most of his time managing the city's affairs.

The other lord was from the keep on the Inner Range. In years long past, Rizendür Keep had protected the kingdom's southeastern region by overlooking the Plains of Demeter, which was to the north of the pass where the keep stood. Now, the lord sent out patrols just to keep his men mindful of military maneuvers.

The king wanted Trisdale Keep rebuilt. The keep, overlooking the Lithlillian Valley to the northwest, Cipper to the West, and the Plains of Demeter to the south, stood on the edge of the Black Forest. It could provide warning to all of the northern regions. Unlike the other keeps, Trisdale was in a region that was still hostile. Once it was rebuilt, it could guard against the Fendür should they ever decide to leave the Black Forest and descend from the Plateau of Kronese into the other regions.

"Jerrod, I will send builders, a herdsman, a baker, a cook, and a blacksmith to Trisdale to help you rebuild. I will send a train of mules twice a month to supplement whatever you can't forage from the plateau's forest. I will also send you a monthly stipend of gold coins for each warrior who pledges service to Lord Trisdale. The soldiers in turn will pay the merchants and the region will start to grow," the king finished.

Jerrod did not see the king again before the royal family from Greensland departed. He spent his time with the prince, often accompanied by the Princess until her departure. The prince was in his mid-twenties and ten years the princess's elder. On a couple of occasions they practiced with swords together, but Jerrod was not impressed by the prince's level of swordsmanship.

The Order's training is better than whatever the prince received. Drin taught us well, Jerrod observed.

He took the prince hunting once, but the accompanying guards made it impossible to approach any game. So they rode together, learning more of each other's dreams and a friendship grew.

"I'm not happy about the engagement," Prince Garrett confessed on one ride.

"Not happy? Why?"

"Neither of us loves the other and I am nearly twice her age." The prince paused.

"Would you be happy?" He turned to look at Jerrod.

"She's pretty."

"Pretty for a girl, you mean." The prince watched for his reaction.

"For a girl?"

"For a girl. She isn't a woman yet. She's barely old enough for marriage."

   ✳ ✳ ✳ ✳ ✳

Jerrod also spent time with Fraum, partially in hopes of seeing Amanda. They took long walks often on the walls of the castle, where Jerrod continued to stay, or on the outer city walls, but occasionally they strode through the streets, watching the citizens of Torrence as if they were passing through a theater. The behavior and concerns of citizens who knew nothing of Dendür other than their lives in Torrence had become amusing to Jerrod.

"They really don't understand what they have, do they?" Jerrod asked without thinking.

"Many of them haven't been beyond the walls," Fraum responded.

They spoke of philosophy, history, and life. At the end of each discussion Fraum encouraged Jerrod to visit the monastery to read their scrolls, and each time they parted, the last thing Jerrod would ask was about Amanda.

"She's adapting to the life of a monk at her own pace, as anyone would," Fraum always answered.

"She's going to live her life as a monk then?"

"She is living the life of a monk now," Fraum repeated. "But tomorrow is a new beginning, Jerrod. Who knows what may come." Fraum smiled at him.

It had taken more time than Jerrod had wished, but a message from Imelrinn had finally come. Jerrod said his goodbyes to Drin first and then went to the king to get permission to leave. Afterward he spoke with his friend, the prince, before going to the monastery.

Fraum was in the library. Following the stairs down, he found the older sage sitting at a table reading a scroll. He was startled when Jerrod spoke.

"I wanted to let you know I'm going back to Lithlillia."

"Rhonda?" Fraum said, looking up.

Jerrod nodded.

"You need to know Amanda still loves you," Fraum disclosed quietly.

"Why won't she see me then?" Jerrod questioned, his frustration evident.

"She will in time. But pushing her at this point would be unwise. You know her better than any of us. Right now she would rather sacrifice her happiness to ensure yours."

"Augh!" Jerrod groaned.

"It will pass, but when it does, when she is ready, you need to know your own heart. Do you know who you really want? Rhonda or Amanda?"

"Both." Jerrod paused. "Neither if it means losing the other one!" he continued.

Fraum looked at him.

Jerrod sat down on a nearby chair. Putting his forehead in his hands, he took a deep breath.

"I love them both. The king appointed me Lord Trisdale. I wouldn't have accepted had I realized the consequences. Oh, who knows if I even had a choice." Jerrod paused again.

He stood up and paced away several steps before turning around to look at his friend and counselor.

"So here I am. Rhonda will be the Lady of Lithlillia. She can't denounce her responsibility. Amanda has shaved her head to become a White Fist monk. She won't even talk to me. And my destiny is the ruins of Trisdale."

He took another deep breath. "They are complete opposites. I love them both and I can't have either of them."

"Young love is always a desperate thing," Fraum answered, the expression on his face serious.

"You will find that as love matures it changes from the raw heat of the blacksmith's fire overwhelming you as you approach, to the low, steady heat radiating from forged metal that billows steam when the smith tempers the steel with his loving hand."

Jerrod looked at the monk in his monkly robes. Fraum sat calmly, watching Jerrod's reaction.

"I think I understand, but I'm not sure how understanding will help," Jerrod said, reaching down to grab Fraum's elbow as the older man stood up.

"I had Aphrodite's blessing in finding their love. Perhaps I will have Zeus' wisdom to help me decide which one I should love." Jerrod tried to smile.

"The answer is deep in your heart. Take time to listen, to find the pure feeling."

"Pure feeling?"

"The purity of your heart's committed love, not influenced by spontaneous desire or emotional lust."

"Thank you. You're a cherished friend," Jerrod said, finally able to smile.

"All will come in time if you are true to the feelings in your heart. Don't get swayed by the moment," Fraum concluded.

When they parted, Jerrod knew it would be the last time that they would see each other for a long while. Riding out alone the next morning, he crossed the city bridge eastward until he reached the north-south road, where he turned north for the river crossing. As he rode he reflected on the past year's experience.

I was so naïve, he admitted to himself.

When he first left Torrence he had felt powerful, strong, able to overcome any foe. Now, as Lord of Trisdale, possessed with magic, he felt less sure that he could overcome such challenges, and was much more aware of the demands of the world.

Two dozen troops and several merchants would arrive at Trisdale Keep soon to begin the rebuilding. They would begin to secure the ruins and clear the debris. Builders, paid by the king, would follow. It was Jerrod's responsibility to meet them and oversee the rebuilding, but Lithlillia awaited. He felt the weight of the dilemma on his chest.

Jerrod rode north until the sun began to fall, then he stopped to pitch a small tent along the road. He built a fire using only dead wood he found on the ground.

I have been with the druids too long. Only dead wood. No need to chop a live tree, is there?

Starting the fire with a flick of his forefinger, small sparks like those off a flint and steel jumped onto the twigs he had placed under small, dead branches. In a moment he had a fire which he fed with larger limbs of dry wood.

It wasn't this easy when I walked from Winfred to Torrence, he thought.

After he finished eating, Jerrod rolled onto his back to stare at the stars. He thought of his mother, but then visions of Amanda and Rhonda swirled back into his consciousness.

The next night he spent in an inn at Torrence River Crossing, but the feather bed did not provide any more comfort than his tent had offered. Dreaming troubling thoughts, he tossed and turned through the night and woke from a shallow sleep, un-refreshed.

He rose and ate quickly, eager to renew his journey. Crossing the only bridge spanning the Torrence River, Jerrod followed the road to Cipper. Two nights later he was in the city surrounded by a logged wall, staying at the inn they had visited the year before and, much to his pleasure, they did not recognize him. After spending the next night in the forest, Jerrod found himself at dusk the next night riding up to the stone mill south of Lithlillia.

Everything was as he remembered. The two story inn lay just beyond the mill, the barn across the small meadow, surrounded by trees, and the mill house by the stream. The miller and his family did not recognize Jerrod at first, but when they did, the questions did not stop and their first questions were about Drin.

Jerrod spent the evening answering and re-answering their questions. He told them of the battles they had encountered on the road to Terrace Xul and of Nathanial's treachery, but he avoided mentioning Amanda after she left their group. When he finally told them of the Accolade, Jerrod had to reveal his Lordship.

Jerrod watched the change in their posture after hearing of his Lordship. He sensed an increase in tension.

"I am still Jerrod to you. Please, just Jerrod," he said, his voice trailing off.

The spring air was pleasant the next morning when Jerrod mounted his horse to ride north towards Lithlillia. He smelled the forest dew, fresh and clean, and when he rode into the cluster of stone cottages that made up Lithlillia without warning, everyone was surprised. Word passed to Rhonda quickly, causing her to go to him. She did not run like a young lover overwhelmed by a reunion might, but walked towards him with all the dignity of her station. It was her smile and the sparkling of her green eyes that told Jerrod she was happy to see him.

"You are here." Rhonda was surprised.

"Didn't the forest or the animals tell you I was close?"

Rhonda shook her head slowly.

The day filled Rhonda's heart with love. She looked at Jerrod constantly as she clung to his arm, all his transgressions forgiven, but Jerrod's heart twisted in his chest. They ate the evening meal in the Great Pavilion with Lord Steffen and Lady Lieisa, and then went for a walk in the forest.

"It's strange the forest did not warn us of your arrival," Rhonda was saying.

Jerrod took a deep breath. He knew what he had to say.

"Are you sure you want to marry me after I slept with Amanda?" Jerrod started.

"This? On your first night back with me, you ask me this?" Rhonda stopped walking to look into his eyes.

"I just want to..." He paused, not knowing how to continue.

"Yes. I thought we were working through that?"

"What about my Lordship?"

"What about it? We will work through that, too. I was angry, but I know we can work these things out."

"I love you, but I don't know if getting married so quickly is wise," Jerrod confessed.

"What are you saying, Jerrod?"

He looked at her. She was beautiful standing in the light of the rising moons with her long hair pulled back behind one of her pointed ears. Her eyes looked innocent, but Jerrod had seen them change with her emotions. There was no expression on her oval face. No anger stirring up a wind or causing the clouds to converge overhead.

"I think we should wait," Jerrod continued.

Rhonda turned away.

"We need to be sure," he encouraged her.

"Have you been with her while you were in Torrence?"

"No. She won't see me."

"But you tried?"

Jerrod nodded.

"But you tried?" Rhonda repeated after turning around.

"Yes."

"Is it me? Don't you want me?"

"No. I mean, it's not you."

"Then it's her?"

"No." He paused.

"In truth, it's both of you, and probably more me."

"I still love you," Jerrod said as he slipped the esreandrea from his wrist.

Rhonda took the braided wristlet and turned away as the tears began to roll over her high cheek bones.

✤   ✤   ✤   ✤   ✤

Amanda was sitting at the table in the library, engrossed in her reading, when Fraum approached. He watched her a moment, reflecting on the turmoil both she and Jerrod had confided they were feeling. When she looked up, Fraum sat down.

"Good morning. Have you been up all night reading again?"

"Most of it. I couldn't sleep. Do you think they are married?" Amanda answered.

"There are a lot of things that neither of them are happy about."

"And if they are married?" Amanda asked, her eyes swollen and watery.

Fraum smiled gently.

"Let's concentrate on what we know has happened, not what may have happened. We will handle that if and when it comes," Fraum encouraged his protégé.

"I'll try, master."

"Sometimes the only thing harder than asking for help is accepting it," Fraum said softly.

"Master?"

"If you need to talk, I am here for you."

"Thank you. I'm okay. Has something new happened?" Amanda asked, trying to change the subject.

"Jerrod said that Drok-na touched his mind. We can only assume that Drok-na is Jacob's dragon. It is time to find out whether the Triad is our enemy," Fraum said as if he were thinking aloud.

"What can I do to help?"

"Do you know how to enter their labyrinth?" Fraum asked as he turned to look at her.

"I heard stories through the Guild. The entrances are reportedly well guarded."

"Do you know anyone who could get through?" Fraum teased.

"There are three entrances. The first is a small shed attached to a stone house with direct access from the alley. The owner of the home was paid not to ask questions and to keep anyone without a ring from entering. The second is in the back of an inn where a similar arrangement has evidently been made with the innkeeper. The last is from a magic shop in the merchant district. The owner is a member of the Triad who practices at night after his shop closes. No one really understands what he is selling. This entrance is protected by magical spells, both illusory and physical."

"Well, the third entrance is probably out. How do you feel about the other two?" Fraum asked.

"I prefer the open alleyway. But the inn is manageable."

✻　　✻　　✻　　✻　　✻

Amanda led Fraum to the small stone house where they sat watching the front of the house and the alleyway for a while, but nothing seemed to move. When Fraum was satisfied he began to stand up, but Amanda gently grabbed his sleeve to hold him down. She pressed a finger to her lips and then pointed to a shadowy corner of a roof that overlooked the alley before she leaned into him.

"See him on the roof, in the shadow? Wait a moment. It won't take long," she whispered in his ear.

Fraum watched Amanda walk away from the house, back up the alley they had taken in order to observe the entrance.

She never ceases to amaze me, Fraum thought.

It was only a couple of minutes before he saw Amanda hop over the roof line, surprising the sentry. After two punches she guided his motionless body down to lie on the roof, out of sight from the street. Fraum walked across the street directly into the alley as Amanda jumped down.

"You didn't kill him, did you?" he hoped to confirm.

"No, master. This is not his fight and I don't kill unless I have no other choice."

Inside the shed they found a square stairwell that wound down through the rock below the river and its island. Amanda quickly searched the first steps, but when she didn't find any traps they started down the wooden stairs. Thick lumber and beams lined the walls as they traveled downward, deep into the square shaft. At the bottom of the stairs they startled a man in a robe standing at the door.

"Stop!"

Before the man could react, Amanda leaped forward into a roll, coming up on one knee in front of the wizard. Striking his hands and causing the wizard to let go of the staff, Amanda spun backwards with an outstretched leg. Her heel hit his legs just above the ankles, causing him to fall over backwards. Amanda popped up as the young wizard struggled to get off the floor, jumping to the man's side, and then driving her clenched fist into his jaw, rendering him unconscious.

"I think I'm starting to like punching wizards. They all remind me of Nathanial." Amanda giggled.

They wandered the halls, listening and observing as they went, but nothing seemed noteworthy. Passing a door here and there, they continued on, looking for something that might indicate someone of authority. They turned into a larger hallway, where they quickly found a set of double doors.

"This appears to be something. First set of double doors," Fraum commented as he opened the door just wide enough to see.

Behind the doors was a large pentagon-shaped room where three men in robes sat around a pentagon shaped table in the center of the room, apparently waiting for someone else to join them. There were two empty chairs, resting side by side.

"We don't get visitors very often," one of the men greeted. He rose with confidence from the table.

"Please excuse our intrusion, but we have urgent business to discuss with the leader of the Triad," Fraum responded.

"I am Jacob. Perhaps I can help you?"

"You don't seem alarmed by our presence?" Amanda commented.

"Surprised, yes. Worried? Not really. We are three Masters of the Triad. I don't think you're here to fight," Jacob reasoned.

He was not what Amanda had expected. She had a dark image of an ominous wizard whose men had chased them across the Plateau of Kronese, into Cipper, and north out of Lithlillia etched in her mind. Jacob was taller and thinner than she had imagined. His well-kempt, sandy-brown hair and short beard with strands of grey seemed pleasant, but a ring like Nathanial's, the ring of a Triad Master, hung loosely on the knuckle of his bony finger.

He is a formidable wizard, Amanda thought.

"We have some friends in common," Amanda spoke up, her voice harsh.

"Does that make us friends?" Jacob asked, turning towards Amanda as he realized she was a woman.

"Maybe," Fraum answered.

The other two wizards began to stand up.

"We mean you no harm or disrespect," Fraum stated as he removed his hands from his sleeves and opened his arms.

"What can we do for a couple of monks that so easily found their way into our home?" Jacob responded. "Come, sit. I don't mean to be rude."

Fraum and Amanda told the three Triad wizards of Nathanial's treachery, but did not mention anything about the horn. They also relayed Jerrod's story of the discussions with Drok-na, causing Jacob to chuckle.

"So that is who Drok-na was talking with," Jacob chuckled. "If Nathanial has the tome, it's not good." Jacob sat back in his chair.

"According to our archives, Brendril's Tome is the book of ultimate magic. How he created magic. It is obviously a significant find, but why were you chasing us?" Fraum asked.

"It is our belief that Nathanial wants the tome for himself and may have, shall we say, 'ominous' reasons for it," Jacob said, picking his words carefully.

"Your mercenaries would have killed us," Amanda added sharply.

"We consider Nathanial dangerous. We considered all of you a danger by association. Your presence here suggests we may have been wrong," one of the other wizards explained.

"Fortunately, we were not harmed by the misunderstanding," Fraum interjected.

"We sent a group of men to Terrace Xul. Did you kill them?" Jacob asked, his eyes fixated on the old sage.

"There were no men in Terrace Xul. It was full of Rahjin, who were very unfriendly," Fraum explained.

When everyone was comfortable that they no longer were a threat to one another, Fraum and Amanda said their goodbyes. Nathanial still remained a concern to both groups, so they agreed to meet again in the near future. When they stood to depart, Jacob called for a young wizard to escort them back to the stairwell.

"And why are we forgiving their hunting us across Torrence and Lithlillia with the intent of killing us?" Amanda asked again as they climbed the wooden stairs out of the Triad.

"Which is more in need of forgiveness, the hunters or the hunted who killed the hunters?" Fraum asked, without looking back at her.

"It was self-defense."

"Yes, it was."

"And if we forgive those who attempted to kill us don't we condone their behavior?" Amanda asked.

"Yes, but you can let the grudge consume your life or let the forgiveness free your soul. It's your choice. The real question should be, which is better for you, not how to hold someone else accountable."

✳   ✳   ✳   ✳   ✳

Late at night, Nathanial projected himself into a shadowy alley of the warehouse district that he was well acquainted with. There was no one there to observe him projecting into Torrence or to see him walking through the streets in his robes with his gnarled staff in one hand, the bottom snapping against the

cobblestones as he moved it with every other step. He did not have far to walk
before he saw the inn with the crimson rose hanging above the door.

Nathanial stepped inside, but stopped momentarily inside the entrance a
moment as his eyes adjusted. A number of men drank in small groups in the
front near the door. Peering through the darkness of the inn, he spotted a single
man through a doorway at the back of the room. The man was sitting alone at
a table eating his late night dinner. The noise in the inn was the soft rumble
typical of a late-night tavern until Nathanial stepped towards the doorway.

All of the patrons stopped what they were doing to watch Nathanial. As he
approached the doorway two men step away from the bar to stand in his path.

"Can we help you?" one of the men asked.

Nathanial leaned a little to his side to see around the guard and then stood
up to face the man directly. He peered into the guard's eyes for a moment before
looking at the other man.

"I wish to see the Grand Thief."

The guard looked back at the older man with a round belly from years of
comfortably collecting money from the work of others who nodded once. The
large guards stepped aside allowing Nathanial to pass into the second room. As
he approached the table, two tall, muscular men, intimidating on their own even
without the long swords that dangled on their sides, stepped up to the table.
Nathanial noted their daggers with crimson pommels on their sides.

Nathanial stopped to look around the room. All their eyes were watching
him. Striking the bottom of the staff on the wood floor, the top of his staff
instantly glowed as bright as the sun, flooding the room with intense light.

"There is always someone who wishes to interfere. Who will it be?"
Nathanial said loudly as he turned to look at the crowd in the room behind him.

"Relax, we've had some trouble lately. Nathanial, come and sit," the solitary
man said. "Bring our guest a chair."

"Do you have it?" Nathanial demanded.

"Yes, of course," the guild master responded.

"Bring our friend a goblet of wine," he commanded the innkeeper. "And
bring the bag," he continued, turning to one of the large henchmen.

"Do you have the gold?" he asked Nathanial.

"Plenty, once I see the horn."

Nathanial sat across from the Grand Thief, waiting for the bag to be delivered. As soon as the bag was set in front of him, the portly man pulled the horn out and slid it to the center of the table for Nathanial to see.

"And the coin?" His bushy eyebrows rose.

"Double what you asked," Nathanial said as he tossed a large bag of gold coins to the guild master as he stood up.

"What are you going to use the horn for?" the man asked as Nathanial leaned forward to pick up the horn.

"It's a surprise that will soon benefit both of us."

CHAPTER 12
WALLS OF TORRENCE

Rhonda watched Jerrod walk away as she twisted her *esreandrea* between her fingers. When she knew she was out of his sight, Rhonda walked aimlessly towards the forest.

I can't face them, she thought as her parents came to mind.

Lost in time and the shadows of the moons, Rhonda found herself standing between the stone obelisks on the plateau above Lithlillia. She collapsed in the center of the circle. She wept, she prayed, and she slept.

While she was gone, Jerrod rode his horse back to the miller's inn. When he got there he went straight to his room. The innkeeper's wife came to his room shortly after he returned to ask if she could bring him something to eat or drink.

"No, thank you. I have eaten and I am tired now. Thank you," Jerrod said politely.

"Just call if you need anything."

"You're very kind. Thank you," Jerrod said before turning to his empty room.

Zeus? What do I do now? he thought, praying to the father of the Olympian gods.

In the morning he was up and gone before dawn, before anyone was up. He left a small bag of coins on the table in his room, far more than was necessary.

Jerrod chose to take the easiest, most direct route towards Trisdale, riding south through Cipper and then turning east to follow the trail up onto the plateau before skirting the edge southward towards the ruins. The lonely ride seemed much longer than it had seemed when the brought Rhonda off the plateau the year before, but it was more than just traveling alone. Jerrod felt empty.

I have all the wealth I can imagine, but to what end? I have lost everything I care for, he thought.

☆   ☆   ☆   ☆   ☆

A message had been delivered to the merchant who watched one of the entrances to the Triad. A strange man in a hooded cloak that partially hid his bearded face delivered the scroll. The stranger appeared older, unable to stand straight as he walked, dragging a knotted walking stick behind him as he crossed the floor one step at a time. The long sleeve of his gray cloak covered his extended hand as he gave the scroll to the merchant.

"This is for someone named Jacob. I believe you know him," the stranger said without looking up.

The scroll was carried from the merchant, down the stairs, where the journeymen at the bottom received it, and on to Jacob. Jacob examined the scroll, noting the wax seal as he sat at his desk.

Still soft. This was sealed recently, he thought as he broke the seal.

Unrolling the scroll to reveal the message, Jacob recognized the handwriting immediately.

> Jacob,
>
> By now you should know that I have the tome. It is no longer a test of who will get there first. Can't we settle this amicably? Meet me on the west wall tomorrow at mid-day so we can talk this out. Let's be reasonable.
>
> Nathanial

Jacob put down the scroll and sat back, contemplating the message.

☆   ☆   ☆   ☆   ☆

The next morning promised a fine summer day. It was still comfortably warm, before the baking heat of summer really set in. By mid-day the citizens were out enjoying the weather, filling the market with leisurely shoppers and those who just wanted to look. Inside his castle, the king was in the main hall with his normal court. The daily religious services had just ended in the Cathedral of the Order of One and far beneath the city the High Master of the Triad sat near his fire, warming his old bones in the cool labyrinth carved from bedrock.

Nathanial had given specific orders to his three Dark Elve assassins before leaving them unexpectedly. They were to attack simultaneously, each killing their targets at precisely the same time. Unbeknownst to anyone, while his orders were being carried out, Nathanial and Rok-lin circled high above Torrence, so high the city walls looked like two rings lying on a blue ribbon.

The first assassin, dressed in black, projected in behind the king in his hall, immediately plunging his black stiletto into the king's back as he appeared, angling the pointed blade up into his heart. The mortal wound was finished before anyone could move and, withdrawing the bloody dagger from the king's back, the Elve with bluish gray skin sheathed his dagger before disappearing as though he was never there.

Prince Garrett leapt forward, trying to catch his collapsing father. Landing on his knees, Garrett struggled to support the weight of his father's upper body as the king fell into his arms. The king rolled over to look into his son's eyes as the queen rushed forward.

"Derik!" the queen screamed as the king's head rocked back.

As though he was lost in time, Garrett rose slowly, staring down at his father's body, trying to reject the events that had unfolded. Then he turned to his mother, intending to console her. As they came together, the Captain of the Guard knelt over the king. That moment, as the queen looked at the captain, seemed to last indefinitely.

"His ring," the queen whispered, drawing everyone's attention.

"His signet ring. It's Garrett's now."

The captain slid the ring from the king's dead hand and handed it to the prince.

"I am sorry, my prince."

At that precise moment when the assassin had appeared behind the king, another assassin appeared behind the Prophet. His blade went deep into the Prophet's back before the Elven assassin disappeared. The Prophet's knees buckled, causing him to land on them before falling face first to the floor, his warm blood beginning to cover the tile like an artesian well springing out of the ground for the first time.

The Elders around him ran to his aid. Several meditated momentarily and then they all laid hands upon their religious leader, healing his wounds. When he regained consciousness, they carried him quickly back to his private chambers as Cavaliers and Initiates responding to calls of alarm swarming through the hall with their swords drawn, and spreading out through the compound, but there was nothing but air to defend against.

And at the same time, the third assassin appeared deep in the bedrock below Torrence. He had timed it perfectly. Nathanial knew the High Master's habits, allowing the assassin to appear behind the oldest and wisest wizard where he sat next to his fire, but the High Master had felt the magic forming. As the Dark Elve projected into the room, the High Master disappeared into a swirl of black smoke. The Dark Elve stood helplessly, looking around anxiously.

"Only a fool openly attacks an experienced wizard," the High Master's voice filled the room.

On the far side of the bed chamber the High Master re-appeared. He stood there watching the Elve. When the assassin stepped forward, the wizard whispered a single word. Across the room the body of the Dark Elve burst into thousands of tiny, golden spheres that burned intensely for a moment before burning out.

Not knowing of the assassins' attacks around Torrence, Jacob waited patiently on the western wall just north of the river harbor.

I wonder what Nathanial will offer? The message was very strange. Why send a physical scroll? Why not send it magically? he thought as he watched the current of the river.

Will Rok-lin be there too? Can I come? I haven't seen Rok-lin for so long, Drok-na plead.

At that moment Rok-lin dove out of the sky like a hawk dropping down on an unsuspecting field mouse. Her wings and legs folded back, increasing her speed. She focused on Jacob, but Nathanial would not let her attack.

Land on the wall, he thought carefully, focusing his thoughts so just Rok-lin would hear.

But I can kill him now, Rok-lin responded carelessly.

I want that opportunity, Nathanial started.

You leave him alone! Drok-na's thoughts screamed. *Jacob, they intend to kill you!* Drok-na screamed to his wizard.

Rok-lin pulled her head back and extended her wings, beating against the air as she extended her back legs towards the top of the wall. She landed with a thud that shook the masonry. Nathanial slipped quickly down her foreleg with his staff in his hand.

Far to the southwest, Drok-na burst from his cave, flying at full speed just above the tree tops. The walls of Torrence were minutes away. Drok-na was panicked by the vision of Jacob on the wall, facing both Nathanial and Rok-lin. His short, straight horns lay back on his neck, his panic exploding in his mind as he disappeared from the sky.

"Have you come to kill me, Nathanial?" Jacob asked, his staff raised in defense.

"You and your dragon, you wretch! Where is Drok-na?"

"On his way."

"Great. We will kill you and then tend to Drok-na when he gets here."

The nearby citizens, startled to see a dragon perched on the outer wall, began screaming and running away. Fraum and Amanda, who were walking through the city at the time, emerged from an alleyway to find chaos in the streets of Torrence. Instinctively the two monks raced towards the commotion.

"Megalas!" Jacob yelled as he pointed the palm of his right hand towards Nathanial and Rok-lin.

A burst of fire erupted towards them, engulfing them both as the fire impacted on Rok-lin's chest, but the large dragon instinctively wrapped her wings around Nathanial, protecting him from the flame. She held tight until the burning heat dissipated.

As Nathanial stepped towards Jacob, Rok-lin roared. When Nathanial pointed his gnarled staff at his opponent, a thick beam of green light pulsed out of the top of the staff, hitting Jacob in the center of his chest, knocking him backward, causing him to hit his head on the stone floor.

As Jacob rose to his knees, Nathanial was holding his staff in both hands, parallel to the stone floor and began raising it. When his arms extended the staff above his head, it began to glow.

"Metlock!" Jacob yelled, shielding himself from Nathanial's pending attack.

Rok-lin began marching forward across the wall towards the dazed wizard who was still on his knees.

"Dazrik!" Nathanial yelled, causing lightning bolts to strike and deflect off Jacob's spell.

Surrounded by sparks, Jacob sank down on his one knee until he was sitting on his other leg. Pushing back against the impact of Nathanial's attack, he clenched his staff in a tight grip.

I don't want to kill you, Nathanial, Jacob thought, but he knew time was running out.

"Azranik," Nathanial said, causing him to smile.

The force of Nathanial's staff drove Jacob to the floor again as Rok-lin pulled back her head and opened her jowls to snap.

From under the skyline of the city wall, Drok-na instantly appeared, flying at full speed, soaring upward over the wall with his forelegs stretched out. His talons dug deep into Rok-lin's back as he flew over the larger female dragon, pulling her off balance. Rok-lin fell from the wall, landing on her back on the cobblestone street in front of Fraum and Amanda.

"Chiz'nardak!" Nathanial yelled, unaware of Drok-na's arrival.

Dozens of small meteorites launched from Nathanial's staff towards Jacob. A fiery rock hit Jacob's shield, bursting into tiny, burning particles and expending the last of the shield-magic, allowing several of the burning stones to strike Jacob.

Jacob jumped up, turned, and spun, trying to avoid the searing impact of the magical rock, and then fell to the ground. Stepping forward quickly, Nathanial stood above him, gloating.

"Always trying to be the hero," Nathanial taunted.

"Darasma!" Jacob yelled.

Nathanial dropped his staff to grab his head with both hands as he began feeling the crushing pressure of Jacob's spell.

On the street below the wall, Rok-lin roared again, twisting in a frenzy to get back up to protect Nathanial. As she put her front legs under her and began pushing up, Fraum removed his black belt, made of braided leather straps, and began spinning it above his head. The black balls on the end gained speed rapidly until the belt was a blur. When Fraum released the bola-belt towards Rok-lin's legs, the spinning balls and cord wrapped around her feet, causing her to stumble. By the time the bola wrapped Rok-lin's legs, Amanda had already started spinning her belt and on her release, the belt wound around Rok-lin's mouth.

Behind them Fraum and Amanda could hear the faint sound of running footsteps as soldiers responded to the attack, but they were still far away. On the wall above them, Nathanial, screaming in pain as the bones in his legs splintered, fell to the floor. Pushing up on his elbows, Nathanial began crawling towards his staff. Behind him, Jacob stood up.

"Why?" Jacob asked as he wiped his face on his sleeve. "We were friends. Darasma!"

Nathanial curled up in pain from the second spell, quivering as he lay on the stone floor of the city wall. Stepping towards the inside edge of the wall, Jacob looked down to see Rok-lin's front legs and mouth bound. He watched a moment before turning back to Nathanial.

"Rok-lin can't help you," Jacob said as he looked back towards Nathanial.

"This wasn't necessary, Nathanial."

Come! Help me, please, Nathanial pleaded to Rok-lin.

"Metlock," Jacob said, blocking the spell Nathanial was trying to conjure.

After circling around, Drok-na beat his wings against the air, landing on a nearby roof.

You should have left my friend alone, Drok-na thought to Rok-lin as he looked down at the helpless dragon below him.

Pulling his head up, Drok-na took a deep breath, and then spit fire downward, engulfing Rok-lin's body in flames. Rok-lin squirmed wildly as the dragon-fire burned her scales. When her tail hit the building Drok-na was standing on, the building collapsed under Drok-na's weight.

As Drok-na began to fall, the bola-belts restraining Rok-lin burnt in half. Pulling her body up the wall, gouging the stone with her talons as she climbed upward, and raising her head over the wall, Rok-lin peered down on Jacob. In an instant she spit fire down at the wizard.

"Taknu'num," Jacob uttered, encasing himself in ice.

Pushing up with her back feet, Rok-lin climbed out of the fiery street and back onto the wall as Drok-na dug his way out of the burning rubble of the fallen building. Rok-lin swung her tail around, batting Jacob against the crenellations in the outer wall. His body hit the low point with such impact that he nearly fell off the wall. The edge of the stone nearly snapped his back before his body slid to the floor.

"Metlock," Jacob mumbled as Rok-lin put her forefoot down on him.

"That won't help against the physical force of a dragon," Nathanial sputtered, laughing under his efforts to talk.

A bluish light radiated from Rok-lin, exploding into a wave of energy that knocked everyone off their feet as Jacob's body disintegrated into a glowing yellow vapor. Only the shadowy silhouette of his body etched into the floor remained under Rok-lin's forefoot.

From the street below, Drok-na bellowed, his roar shaking nearby windows and street lamps.

Rok-lin reached out, gently lifting Nathanial off the floor with her forearms. Standing momentarily on her back legs, she jumped and beat her wings to lift off the wall. Just as she took flight, Drok-na pounced like a cat leaping into the air to catch an unsuspecting bird. His talons dug deep into her back, ripping into her flank as his weight pulled Rok-lin down towards the wall.

Rok-lin began spinning in a roll, wing over wing, pulling Nathanial in to cradle the wizard in her arms as she tried to shake Drok-na loose. She twisted, trying to use her back legs to rake at Drok-na's chest, trying to push the smaller dragon off.

Drok-na fell away before they collided with the wall. As Rok-lin began beating her wings against the air again, Drok-na quickly caught flight and turned a tight circle to fly under the larger dragon as she attempted to gain altitude. Rolling over to fly upside down, Drok-na swiped at Rok-lin's exposed stomach. His talons cut deep through the larger dragon's thinner underbelly scales.

They fell again. Rok-lin's back landed against the city wall's merlons, causing the large blocks of stone between the crenellations to fall into the river. Rok-lin rolled up to stand on three legs, still cradling Nathanial with her fourth. She carefully kept her head and chest towards Drok-na as he flew circles around her. Each time Drok-na darted by, swiping at Rok-lin's head, Rok-lin ducked and countered, rearing up to use her free fore-claw and snap her jaws at the male dragon, but Drok-na had already moved beyond her reach. They turned and twisted like alley cats swatting at each other in some territorial struggle.

As the dragons fought, journeymen from the Triad appeared on the walls and in the streets. They materialized out of small, twisting clouds of dark smoke. At the same time the soldiers arrived on the streets, armed with spears and bows, but none of them knew which dragon to attack.

Unable to gain an advantage and tiring from Drok-na's repeated attacks, Rok-lin leaped into the air. As her wings spread Drok-na struck, embedding the talons of both his forearms on each side of Rok-lin's hindquarters. Drok-na wrapped his hind leg talons around her body to embed them into her stomach, inside her legs.

Rok-lin beat her wings even harder, attempting to fly with Drok-na hanging from her body, but she was losing altitude.

"Fas na re'al!" Nathanial exclaimed, pointing his long bony fingers at Drok-na.

The smaller dragon froze where it hung and, with a little twist, Rok-lin freed herself from his grip. Exhausted from the battle, Nathanial fainted. Rok-lin quickly climbed out of the city and away from the city.

Drok-na fell towards the ground, motionless. His wings collapsed against his body, flapping in the wind as he fell. When he landed on the roof of a nearby store, the impact caused it to cave it in and knocked down two adjacent walls, scattering rubble into the cobblestone streets.

Fraum and Amanda reached the store first. They began pulling rubble off Drok-na as the soldiers arrived. Some of the soldiers aided them in uncovering the dragon while others started moving the citizens of Torrence back, away from the devastation. When they reached Drok-na, his breathing was slow and erratic.

"He's still alive. Send for..." Fraum stopped and looked at Amanda.

"Who do you send for to cure a dragon?" Amanda asked.

"A druid," answered Fraum.

✦   ✦   ✦   ✦   ✦

It was an unusually dark evening for summer. The evening meal had been wonderful and the music lingered, soothing the listeners into a trance of dreams. The music brought them a shared dream of tall mountains with great forests, waterfalls, and brooks that sang like watery chimes, but everyone stirred from the dream when dark smoke began to form before the dais, twisting in a column that rose towards the ceiling of the Pavilion. In a moment an old man in flowing white robes stood before them, leaning on a long, white staff.

Lord Steffen rose to stand between the old man and his wife and daughter. Nearby Elves grabbed longbows and nocked arrows as Lady Lieisa and Princess Rhonda stood up to watch.

"How dare you appear in such a manner!" Steffen demanded.

"Please forgive my intrusion. I have great need of a druid," the stranger said in a soft, gentle voice.

"What is your need?" Lady Lieisa asked.

"A dragon has been injured. We want to save its life. I can take you to it if you are willing," the old man offered.

"Where?" Lady Lieisa asked.

"Torrence."

Rhonda's head snapped back to focus on him.

"Torrence? What dragon?" Rhonda asked.

"It is Drok-na, Jacob's dragon."

"Jacob?"

"Yes. Jacob and Nathanial fought on the walls of Torrence. Jacob was killed and Drok-na is mortally wounded. Fraum asks you to come. I am his messenger."

"Are you a wizard or warlock?" Lady Lieisa's question was guarded.

"I am the High Master of the Triad."

For a moment Lady Lieisa thought his eyes flickered to slit pupils as his face became that of a white dragon, but the old wizard still stood in front of her.

I must be hallucinating, Lieisa thought.

Mother? Rhonda thought.

Nearby, Imelrinn watched protectively, his hand resting on his sword.

Nothing. I thought I saw something that cannot be. It died with the old magic, Lady Lieisa answered.

"I will go. If Fraum calls, I must answer," Rhonda answered.

✻　　✻　　✻　　✻　　✻

After talking with the wizards who sent word of Jacob's death and Drok-na's injuries to the Triad, Fraum looked about. An adult-size male dragon in a ruined building in the middle of Torrence was not going to do. He could neither drag the beast nor load it on a wagon to transport it. The wagons in Torrence were simply not big enough.

As wizards came and went, checking on the circumstances and letting Fraum know that the High Master would travel to Lithlillia himself, it was finally suggested that a group of journeymen could work together, levitating the unconscious dragon and, step by step, moving him to safety.

"But what would be a safe place for Drok-na and for the citizens of Torrence?" a younger wizard asked.

"We can't carry him back to his cave," another added.

"The White Fists could provide some safety within their walls," Amanda suggested.

Fraum shot a look at her.

"They already have a wagon full of gold and me." She smiled.

"What am I going to tell the Master?" Fraum wondered aloud.

"Tell him having a dragon for a friend is lucky." Amanda laughed.

With a dozen wizards surrounding Drok-na, they slowly levitated the dragon inches off the ground and, step by step, moved him up the gentle slope towards the monastery. Even the typically detached monks were surprised by the sight of a dragon floating through their front gate. All of the brown robed bald men who studied writings and martial exercises, devoid of emotion, scampered to the gate to see Drok-na lowered into the open courtyard.

"What's this?" the Master questioned, looking directly at Fraum.

A dragon, Amanda thought, knowing she had better not say what she was thinking.

"Our studies teach us to preserve all life, do they not?" Fraum responded.

"They do," the master admitted with hesitation.

"I don't even know when the last dragon was seen," Fraum commented.

"These beasts have faded into legend, or so it seemed. Will you have us heal it and protect it from dragon hunters, if there are any left?" the Master questioned, already knowing what the response would be.

"Yes. It would be good to have a dragon as a friend," Fraum smiled. *Amanda, you should get a kick out of that,* Fraum thought.

*　　*　　*　　*　　*

Rhonda and the High Master of the Triad left Lithlillia that night rather than waiting for the morning. In a swirl of smoke they departed, reappearing instantly at the gate of the White Fist Monastery. Rhonda grasped the High Master's forearm tightly as they reappeared.

"Dizzy?"

"Yes."

"Everyone is the first time. You've done better than most." The High Master looked at her with his eyebrows raised above his innocent eyes.

"Thank you."

"Would you mind if I stay and watch? All forms of magic interest me and I don't know a great deal about druid magic."

"I don't mind, but I'm not sure you will see much magic. Drok-na needs healing, which we do with herbs, and a little power we gain from E'fretté. We don't consider our work magic."

Amanda hesitantly crossed the courtyard to greet them. When Rhonda opened her arms for a hug, Amanda was relieved.

"You look well. How is the life of a monk suiting you?" Rhonda said after stepping back, still holding on to Amanda's elbows as she spoke.

"I'm not sure. How is your life?"

"We are good. Mother and Father are home. Imelrinn is watching over them. I can't believe I got away without him." Rhonda smiled.

"A lot has changed since last year. We have all grown. And Jerrod? Is he with you?" Amanda asked coyly.

"No. He went to Trisdale to oversee the rebuilding of his keep," Rhonda said as her gaze dropped to the ground.

"Are you okay?"

"No, but I'm not sure we should talk about it."

"I understand. I will go get Fraum. As you see, Drok-na is there," Amanda gestured towards the dragon as she started to walk away. "I'm sure Fraum will come right away."

Rhonda watched as Amanda walked quietly away. She did not seem to have the agile nature or playful personality she once had. Amanda walked methodically, as controlled as their surroundings.

"If an old man may, that seemed a strange greeting," the High Master commented.

"We love the same man," Rhonda said as she headed towards the dragon.

"I imagine that is awkward," he responded.

"Not as much for us as you might think."

"Really?"

"Amanda saved my life and then she saved all of our lives. She sacrificed a great deal for us," Rhonda stopped to explain.

Ronda looked at Drok-na's cuts and burns. She listened to his shallow breathing and the beat of his heart, and then, pulling back his eyelids, looked into the slit pupils of his unconscious eyes. Touching the dragon's head gently, she concentrated to find his thoughts. When she was finished she sat back and looked at the High Master.

"How did he get injured?" Rhonda asked.

"I was not there, but from what I was told Drok-na was clinging to Rok-lin when he suddenly fell, lifeless. It was a terrible fight and Rok-lin was trying to fly away with Nathanial."

"Nathanial?"

"Rok-lin was carrying him away. I am told Jacob almost killed him."

"When I was injured, Nathanial cast a spell on me that made me appear to be dead. He may have used the spell on Drok-na," Rhonda commented.

"That would explain a great deal. Welcome Rhonda," Fraum said as he walked up.

"Fraum, how are you?"

"Good. What do you think about Drok-na?"

"Some of the wounds are very serious, but he will be fine, especially if the wizards keep him sleeping. I can make ointments for the cuts and burns, but there is another way if you need the dragon well sooner rather than later," Rhonda suggested.

"Drin? We tried, but the Order won't let anyone leave. The Prophet was attacked. A lot has happened today," Fraum explained.

"There is another."

"Jerrod?"

Rhonda nodded her head affirmatively.

"We thought he was with you."

"He went to Trisdale."

"I will discuss it with the Master," Fraum answered.

"I can make up some herbal ointments that you can apply once I'm gone, but I will stay two or three days to make sure Drok-na responds to my..." Rhonda stopped to look at the High Master.

"My druid magic," she finished, smiling.

"You are welcome to stay with us," Fraum offered.

☆   ☆   ☆   ☆   ☆

The death of his father in his arms within the royal family's own throne room was devastating to young Prince Garrett. Afterward, his mother had wept in his arms until she slept. The generals of his father's armies were pressing him with their advice and his father's advisors were even more relentless. Everyone seemed to know what was best for him, but the only thing the prince was sure of was he needed to recall the three lords of the kingdom.

He had immediately sent the fastest riders out to all three keeps. The lords were Prince Garrett's hope for unbiased opinions. He weighed the experience of each lord. Lord Francis, Lord of Rizendür Keep in the Inner Range, had been in some minor skirmishes when he was young. Lord Edward, Lord of Akkian Keep on Semanie Point, was older with many years of experience guarding the mouth of the Torrence River. There too, raiders had attacked the city and wharf. Some had been by land, but most were from small ships trying to sail into port to loot the warehouses in hopes of escaping before the guard could respond.

In his father's days, the Lord Akkian held more authority due to his age, the importance of his post, and out of their friendship. Lord Rizendür resented the matter. To add insult to his position, the Rizendür Keep barely had three hundred men, and half of those were squires. They had been reduced to quiet marches through the peaceful countryside where no one noticed the complacency of their military maneuvers.

By the time the messenger reached Trisdale, Jerrod had already departed for Torrence. When Rhonda had learned of their need for Jerrod's healing abilities, she sent a message asking the leader of the flying horse herd to find Jerrod and bring him to the White Fist Monastery. While she waited, Rhonda tended to Drok-na's wounds, but there was still a lot of free time.

On the first night Rhonda and Amanda sat with Fraum eating the evening meal. Very little time had passed before Fraum excused himself to go manage monastery matters.

"It appears we're meant to talk," Amanda stated as she watched Fraum walk away.

"Apparently," Rhonda retorted.

Amanda could not tell if it was anger or hurt feelings creating the harshness in Rhonda's voice.

"I'm sorry for my part in all this." Amanda's voice was soft and gentle, her eyes looking down at her hands.

"We all hold a share of the blame," Rhonda confessed, looking at Amanda, reflecting on all the flatlander had done for them. "Jerrod and I are no longer together," Rhonda added.

Amanda looked up.

"I thought you should know. He broke off our betrothal. He still loves you," Rhonda confessed.

"He loves both of us," Rhonda spoke slowly.

"I don't know what to say. I'm sorry," Amanda said as a teardrop began rolling down her cheek.

"Me either. Don't cry. It may be better this way," Rhonda said as she reached up to wipe away the tears.

Amanda was lost in her emotions. She had never felt for others. She had never let anyone in. Overwhelmed by her feelings, tears began cascading down both cheeks. Rhonda pulled her in, hugging her as they wept openly together.

*   *   *   *   *

Jerrod had been reluctant at first, but when Farris explained Rhonda needed him in Torrence to heal a dragon, they had left immediately. As Farris and Jerrod approached the city, they could see the walls were manned by guards. Jerrod could not remember hearing about the walls of Torrence being guarded since the kingdom was first established when the Plains of Demeter had been cleared.

What happened? Why are there guards on the walls? Why are the masons doing repairs? Jerrod asked Farris.

There was a great battle between two dragons, Farris answered as he began his descent into Torrence.

Farris set down in the street near the monastery. Still in fear of dragons returning to the city walls, the citizens ran at the sight of a flying horse. Once they landed, Jerrod slid from the steed's back and turned to thank him.

Again you have delivered me. Thank you, my friend.

I am always available to help the Great One whenever needed.

Jerrod walked towards the monastery gates as Farris leaped into the air. The steed was surprisingly quick and was out of sight before Jerrod reached the gates. Jerrod could see Drok-na through the gateway. As he walked into the monastery, Amanda and Rhonda stepped from behind the dragon's head.

"Um, hello," Jerrod stammered.

Rhonda stood with her arms crossed in front of her chest, her hip pushed to the side. Behind her, Amanda stood straight, her hands folded into the sleeves of her monk's robe.

I may be in trouble, he thought, carefully concealing the thought from Rhonda.

"This is a bit of a surprise," Jerrod said, regaining his composure.

"Thank you for coming so quickly," Rhonda answered.

"How did Drok-na get injured?" Jerrod asked.

"It was Nathanial," Rhonda began. "But we will explain later. Drok-na needs healing."

After Jerrod looked at Drok-na and healed his worst wounds, Amanda and Rhonda filled him in on what had happened.

"The king was killed?" Jerrod repeated what he had been told.

"Yes. And the Prophet was attacked," Rhonda confirmed.

"We haven't heard anything else," Amanda added.

"I must go to the castle," Jerrod responded.

"I think I will fly home tomorrow. There is little more I can do. You are here and Fraum has the recipe for the healing compresses," Rhonda stated as Jerrod prepared to leave.

"Take care and send my regards to everyone. I'll miss you," Jerrod said as he stopped, taking her hands as he looked into her eyes.

When Amanda and Fraum turned away to give them privacy, Jerrod leaned forward to kiss Rhonda but she turned her face away. Jerrod looked at her a moment, and then turned and walked away without looking back. Rhonda rejoined Amanda and Fraum without saying a word.

"It has to be awkward saying goodbye when both of you are together," Fraum commented.

"For whom?" Amanda and Rhonda asked in unison.

✳   ✳   ✳   ✳   ✳

At the castle Jerrod was quickly rushed to the prince's chambers. Inside the prince paced back and forth.

"Ahh, Jerrod, my friend. Of course you would be the first to arrive," the prince greeted him.

"I was already on my way by flying horse on another matter. I was here when I heard what happened. I'm so sorry for your loss, Garrett," Jerrod replied.

"Mother is sedated by the alchemist and I am left with the kingdom. I wasn't ready for this, Jerrod."

Jerrod sensed it was his friend who turned to look at him, not the young king-to-be. Garrett's eyes swelled with tears as he swallowed hard.

"How can I help?" Jerrod asked softly.

"Stay by my side. Help me decide what I need to do next."

"I am your friend. You can always call upon me."

The next few days were in turmoil while the prince put the business of the kingdom in order. The other lords arrived quickly and competed to always be in Prince Garrett's company. After years out of the life at court, the king's cousin, Count Rieslane, persisted in making himself constantly present.

During the week the prince, Count, and Jerrod met with the Elders and the Lord Marshal of the Order, and with the religious leadership for the Olympian gods. The Commander of the Academy and several city leaders also requested an audience with Prince Garrett. Through all the chaos, Jerrod stood nearby.

At the end of the week the priests of Zeus wound their way through the streets of Torrence leading a long funeral procession for their fallen king. Immediately following the priest was a riderless horse, a pair of empty boots turned backwards sticking out of the stirrups. Queen Isabelle, dressed in black, rode next to her son following the white steed. Behind them came the dead king, carried by eight of the King's Guard and accompanied by the Commander Beals, Commander of the Guard, who was riding to the side of the king's litter.

The king lay on a litter that rested on the shoulders of his guard. He was well groomed and wore a shiny gold breast plate, his purple cape beneath him. His hands grasped the sword that lay on the length of his body. On his head was the Crown of Torrence.

Following behind the king came the Count, dressed in brilliant colors as though he were going to a royal ball, along with his family, including his son, Roger, who wore the uniform of the Academy. The three Lords of Torrence followed next. Further back the Commander of the Armies and Lord Marshal of the Order were riding side by side ahead of one hundred of the King's Guard and one hundred of the King's Fourth Army with their Generals, all in freshly polished armor.

The first one to come behind the precession of military was the eldest Elder. The Prophet had decided not to attend a non-believer's funeral, but the

Elder went as a sign of respect. After the Elder and his escorts, a long line of the citizens of Torrence followed their beloved king.

A group of bards playing soothing music gathered on the eastern end of the bridge. Nearby, a pyre had been built for the king. Wooden steps leading up through the pile of wood offered access for the King's Guard to easily place the king upon the very top.

The torch in Prince Garrett's hand burned wildly as he ascended the steps to stand with his father. With his free hand he removed the Crown of Torrence and tucked it under his arm. He looked at his father for a moment, then closed his eyes. When he opened them, he reached out to grasp his father's sword. As he lifted the sword he gently pushed the torch into the dry wood.

The skies were clear when Prince Garrett lit his father's pyre. The flames burned high, radiating heat out into the already warm summer day. They could smell the heavy gray smoke that billowed into the sky, partially obscuring the sun. Privately saying their goodbyes to their beloved king, the audience tolerated the nearly unbearable heat.

Perhaps it was the magic of the bards' music or some potion offered by the royal alchemist, but Queen Isabelle did not cry during the ceremony. It would not be until she returned to her room that she would break down and cry herself to sleep. For now, she stood as solemn as a statue watching as her husband's body turned to ash, and no one chose to leave before the queen-mother.

At the end of the day, as Prince Garrett spoke privately with his lords, a herald interrupted.

"Your Majesty, there is an old man here to see you. He does not walk well and carries a white staff. He says he is the High Master of the Triad."

"Show him in," the prince responded after a pause.

Garrett looked at Jerrod, who gently shook his head as he offered a slight shrug.

"Good evening, Prince Garrett. I hope I'm not intruding," the old man greeted the king.

"No. Come in. Let's sit over here," Garrett invited, motioning to a nearby table.

"Thank you. That is kind of you," the old wizard said as he hobbled towards the table and chairs.

"And you are Jerrod, the Great One, as you are called by the Elves and Fairy-Folk. Lord Trisdale to the kingdom, I believe," the High Master acknowledged.

"I am. And you are Jacob and Nathanial's master."

"I was at one time," the High Master said as he sat down with the prince.

"How can I help you?" Garrett asked.

"For a long time the laws have outlawed the study of multiple forms of magic. We can debate the reasonableness of this decision at another time, but I foresee a need for us to work together."

"Why? What do you foresee?" the prince asked cautiously.

"I suspect the assassins were Nathanial's henchmen. And as Jerrod can attest, Nathanial now has the Tome of Brendril, the most powerful artifact I know of," the High Master explained.

"What are you suggesting?" the prince asked.

"We might all survive together, but standing alone we will surely fail. Did you get a good look at the assassin that killed your father?"

"A blue skinned Elve dressed in black. A black dagger. Nothing more." The young prince looked down at his hands.

"They were Dark Elves. I suspect Nathanial has an alliance with them. Why else would Dark Elves, who have not been heard from for hundreds of years, suddenly attack the leaders in Torrence?"

"Dark Elves?" Jerrod interrupted.

The High Master nodded.

"You cannot withstand an alliance of wizards and Elves alone. What happens to Torrence impacts the Triad. We offer our help."

"Nothing more?" the prince pushed.

"Perhaps some gratitude."

"Amnesty?" Jerrod interjected.

"You want the law repealed?" the prince looked at the old wizard.

"It seems fair," the High Master shrugged.

"How many wizards do you offer?" the Lord Akkian demanded.

"I have less than a hundred now."

"And what can your wizards do for us?" the lord persisted.

"It is much easier to fight magic with magic. When was the last time you fought a dragon?"

"Never. No one thought the beasts still existed," the lord protested.

"You need us. Like us or not, you need us."

"I will consider your offer. Please, allow me to talk it over with my council," Prince Garrett responded.

When the High Master departed, the lords' protests escalated.

"You can't trust him!" Lord Akkian argued.

"Whether I can trust him is not the question. Whether we can survive without him is," the prince responded.

"We have over three thousand men just in Torrence. Our armies will do fine without them."

"Really? What leads you to that conclusion?" Jerrod interjected.

"Oh, the boy from Winfred speaks," the Lord Akkian glared at him.

"Hold out your sword," Jerrod said with confidence.

"What?"

"Draw your sword and hold it in an attacking position."

"Okay, now what?" the lord said as he raised his sword above his head.

"Swing."

"What? Are you crazy? I'll kill you."

"Swing," Jerrod responded calmly.

As Lord Akkian started to move his sword, Jerrod twisted his wrist slightly, concentrating on the sword, causing it to grow as hot as a blacksmith's forge. Lord Akkian dropped his sword, his hand burning as he screamed in pain.

"Understand? Now, come here. I will ease your pain," Jerrod commanded.

"Your Majesty, it was the Dark Elves who drove the Elves and Dwarves out of the Wilds in the Elven-Dwarven War," Jerrod counseled Prince Garrett.

"That settles it. Jerrod, let the High Master know we accept his alliance," Prince Garrett decided.

*   *   *   *   *

Soon afterward the citizens of Torrence gathered again, this time in celebration. The throne room was cleaned and polished. Prince Garrett was sitting on the dais with the Queen Mother behind him. His much older first cousin, once removed, stood to the side, scowling as he observed the passing of the crown from father to son.

Lord Trisdale was the only other person standing on the dais with the royal family. The other lords, marshals, and the generals standing in the front row were expressionless at best. There was some mumbling between themselves as they fidgeted like young children impatiently waiting for the end of class. Also in the front row stood the Lord Paladin, Sir Drin, in his shining plate mail with the other Paladins and military leadership from the Order.

Behind them the citizens of Torrence, from merchants to dock workers, packed the throne room. Engulfed by the crowd, two monks stood watching Zeus's priest place the crown upon Prince Garrett's head, causing the crowd to cheer.

"Long live King Garrett!" the priest proclaimed.

"Long live King Garrett!" cheered the crowd and then echoed in the streets.

*　　*　　*　　*　　*

It was nearly dusk when the shadowy figure appeared at the edge of the forest surrounding Cipper. A thin smile spread across Nathanial's lips as he began to speak the incantation, his eyes fixated on the vertical logs forming the wall surrounding Cipper. Inside, the spell agitated all of the cats, who began to stir.

The spell was rhythmic, almost pulsating, as he spoke in the language of magic. Nathanial could sense the cats' adrenalin rising as he completed the words. When he finished he waited, listening for some indication the spell had worked.

Why not just kill them? Rok-lin questioned.

Dragons and scales! Because I want to test this spell. I want to see how it works.

At first, all the cats in Cipper just became irritable, and then they started gathering in a long line that stretched from the center of the city to its gate. Some sat on rain barrels, crates, or rooftops while others paced the streets in tight circles, almost spinning in one place. All of their eyes turned red, glowing like the sun behind a cloud of dark smoke. In unison, they all began to move in a clockwise direction, rotating around the center of Cipper like the spoke of a wagon wheel around the hub, clawing and biting everything in their path.

Attacking in packs, they dragged people and animals to the ground as they piled on each victim, shredding the victims' skin before moving on. When Nathanial heard the screams he projected himself to the roof of the council's hall. He watched, laughing to himself, as the demon cats victimized whatever they met on the streets.

What's so funny? Rok-lin thought from where she stood in the forest.

No one is fighting off the cats. They are intimidated like little mice, not knowing what to do. They are completely defenseless.

Have you seen what you wanted to see?

Enough. Let the beasts go.

The howls started when Rok-lin burst into the night sky, her wings beating against the summer night air. The werewolves and werebears were a lot slower than Rok-lin, who landed almost immediately on the stone hall next to Nathanial. Drawing her long neck back, raising her head upward as she landed, Rok-lin lunged forward to spew fire across the rooftops of Cipper.

"Magaraknic!" Nathanial yelled, his voice reverberating through the fortress as the front gate of the forest city exploded.

Scrambling to pick up their bows and swords the forestmen rushed out of their homes to defend the village. With cats pouncing, scratching, clawing, and biting at them, they struggled until they were overwhelmed, dropping their weapons to run or being pulled down by a frantic horde of demon cats. In the midst of the chaos dozens of werewolves and werebears rushed through the open gate, descending upon the living.

Climbing onto Rok-lin's back, Nathanial sat in front of her powerful wings before the year old dragon leaped into the air and began circling Cipper. The wood structures in Cipper were burning. The villagers who had not tried to escape through the streets were trapped inside, burning alive. Those that had tried to escape were first torn apart in a gruesome manner, and then ravished by the hungry Were-Folk.

When all was done, there was nothing left of the northernmost city in Torrence. Nathanial grinned and turned Rok-lin east towards the Plateau of Kronese.

That was done well. And there's nothing left, no one left to warn Torrence, Nathanial thought.

You know who I want, Rok-lin answered.

Soon, Rok-lin. Soon enough.

✻   ✻   ✻   ✻   ✻

Walking the street alone, Fraum retraced the path he and Amanda had taken to the labyrinth of the Triad. At the bottom of the stairs he met the wizard on guard and asked to see the High Master. He was quickly ushered into the octagonal room and soon afterward the High Master entered, assisted by a young magic student.

"Welcome, Fraum. What brings you back to our school?" the High Master greeted.

"I seek your guidance," Fraum answered.

"Guidance? How can I assist such a well-studied monk as yourself?"

"You are too kind. It's about Drok-na," Fraum started.

The High Master whispered to his assistant, sending him scurrying out of the room before turning back to Fraum.

"We will have some tea while we talk. Now, what about Drok-na? Is he all right?" the High Master asked.

"Yes. He's doing well. In fact, that's why I have come. Drok-na is feeling well enough that he's starting to move around and there is not much room in the monastery, but he's not fully healed. I don't know what I can do for him or what he may want," Fraum admitted.

"Ahh, I think I have something that can help. While we wait, tell me more about your journey with Nathanial," the old wizard said.

When the young wizard came back with the tea, the High Master whispered to him again causing the boy scurried away a second time. The wizard poured tea and then sat back in his chair.

"I have known Nathanial since he was a boy. I mistook his determination to learn magic for a thirst for knowledge. In hind sight, I'm afraid it was just a thirst for power."

The boy returned with a square box in his hands. Pointing at Fraum, the wizard flipped his fingers a couple of times. The boy obeyed without a word, placing the box on the table in front of the monk.

"What is it?" Fraum asked.

"It's a gift. Open it."

Fraum leaned forward and opened the lid, exposing a metal band the length of half his forearm. Each side of the band raised up with golden metal. Between the bands was smooth metal that shifted and changed color, cold to the touch.

"This is beautiful." Fraum paused. "Why are you giving it to me?"

The High Master smiled.

"It's enchanted. Non-magic folks cannot hear dragons. Only a very few wizards can." The old wizard paused, watching Fraum's expression.

"The wrist band enables the wearer to hear the magic. To hear dragons."

"To hear dragons talk?" Fraum repeated.

The High Master nodded.

"Enchanted to hear the dragons?"

"It focuses the dragon's thoughts so you can hear them. The purity of the magic enables the connection," the High Master explained.

"Thank you. It's a wonderful gift," Fraum answered as he slipped the band over his forearm above his wrist, under his sleeve.

"This is the sister-piece. There is another like it, with different properties."

Fraum felt the chill of the metal on his forearm, but the feeling was strangely calming.

"I have something else to show you. Something no one else knows, but I think you need to see."

The wizard sent the boy away and then walked slowly to the far side of the room. Fraum watched the man moving into the shadows, his skin seemed to glimmer with a white aura. The old wizard stood staring at him as he transformed into an ancient white dragon, his extremely long tail coiled about the room. Fraum could feel the wrist pulsating as he stood in the presence of the magnificent creature.

Now you know my secret. It's the magic. Dragons are tied to the magic and once you have studied as long as I have, you become part of the magic. It is the destiny of each High Master.

CHAPTER 13
PAWNS OF WAR

The weeks of numbness were wearing off and life in Torrence was cautiously returning to its normal state. The new king was putting business in order, the markets were filling, and the soldiers were once again visiting the taverns in the evening. Here and there the music of a wandering bard could be heard floating on the summer air. And on such an evening, Jerrod stole out of the king's castle to visit the Axe & Bow again.

I need some peace. A night where my mind doesn't think about Amanda, Rhonda, or Trisdale, Jerrod thought as he walked the cobblestone street.

When he entered, the tavern maiden recognized him immediately.

"Jerrod, welcome. I haven't seen you for a year. Come, Roger and Thomas are at their regular table," Tabatha said taking his arm and pulling him towards a table near the fireplace.

"Jerrod!" they all yelled as the two approached.

"Tabatha, do you know who you have by the arm?" Roger asked.

"Yeah, Jerrod," she answered in her superior tone.

Tabatha continued bouncing across the floor, leading Jerrod by the arm as if he was her more innocent little brother.

"That's Lord Trisdale's arm you're hugging," Thomas chimed in.

"Lord?" Tabatha's eyes widened as she turned to look at Jerrod.

"You're buying, my Lord," Roger teased.

Tabatha stopped and turned to look at Jerrod as if she had never seen him before, letting his arm fall from her grasp.

"Is a count's son higher than a lord?" Jerrod gabbed back in fun.

"I'm no longer certain about the royalty, but definitely not poorer when it comes to money. But you came back to us with a treasure, did you not?" Roger countered.

"A small one. Drinks are on me," Jerrod answered loudly.

"I'm sorry for the loss of your cousin, Roger," Jerrod said quietly as the drinks were being served.

"Thank you. We weren't close. My father was not, ahhh, welcome in the king's court. Let's drink and forget politics for the night," Roger concluded.

"Just what my heart needs," Jerrod said, putting his arm around Roger's shoulders.

They were drinking and singing when they heard some commotion outside. Screams somewhere in the dark streets of Torrence filtered into the tavern. Beyond the screams came some drum-like sounds.

"What in name of Olympus?" Thomas questioned.

It sounds like the trolls' boulders being thrown into the city, Jerrod thought.

The small group ran out of the inn together. In the streets groups of two and three cats were attacking citizens where they found them, but since the attack on the king almost everyone in Torrence was armed and the demon cats were finding the opposition quite a bit more intense than Cipper.

As the men from the Axe & Bow worked their way towards the louder, drum-like sounds, occasionally having to slash through an enchanted cat, the sounds of the boulders hitting buildings became more identifiable. The softer sound of boulders rolling down streets after the initial impact and soldiers calling for help grew louder with each step. When they came to the gatehouse at the bridge they found a dozen werewolves and werebears with two giants killing all the soldiers fighting against them.

As the reinforcements grew, the raiding force quickly withdrew, causing the soldiers to pursue them back across the bridge.

"Wait!" Jerrod yelled, but it was too late.

The soldiers chasing after the band were slaughtered, mostly crushed by large boulders flung onto the bridge before they reached the halfway point while the soldiers on the walls watched helplessly. A captain of the armies stopped more soldiers from following.

"Stand your posts! We don't have sufficient forces to deal with the marauders right now," the captain yelled.

"You. I need you to follow them. Let me know where they go, but don't get close. Just follow them," he said to a soldier on horseback.

"Close the gates! Double the guard," the captain commanded.

Jerrod, saying a quick goodbye to his friends, went straight back to the king's castle. King Garrett, the two lords, and the Commander of the Armies were already discussing battle tactics when Jerrod arrived.

"It's just a small band of rabble. We should send the cavalry to trample them at dawn," Commander De'Ran, commander of the standing armies, stated.

"The Legion can handle a few wild animals and a couple of giants," Lord Akkian concurred.

"Are you serious? Did you see what happened? Our swords were cutting the wolves and bears, but they hardly flinch and we were barely able to touch the giants," Jerrod urged.

"Those were unprepared foot soldiers and citizens from Torrence, not cavalry," the commander said, dismissing him.

"We can't rush into this," Jerrod insisted.

"What do you know? You are a boy from where, Winfred? You went on an adventure and brought back a lot of gold, but you have never fought in battle. You are not a soldier. You bought your title," the commander rebuked.

"Commander," King Garrett interrupted. "Lord Trisdale's title was bestowed by my father and you will honor it."

"The cavalry are trained soldiers," Garrett said turning to Jerrod.

"This is a matter for the military, your Majesty," Lord Akkian encouraged.

King Garrett looked between his lords and the commander of his armies as he considered their advice. He knew Jerrod was much more than a boy from Winfred. He had seen some of Jerrod's magic and heard of far greater feats, but in his mind, the others were right.

This is a military matter, the king reassured himself.

"Commander, I will leave it in your hands."

By morning the soldier who had been sent to follow the raiders came back. There were more wolves, bears, and giants than those that had raided Torrence. The report suggested a hundred giants with some trolls mixed in, and about two hundred wolves and bears roamed around the area. Once he heard the report, the Commander of the Armies convened a military council with the Commander of the Guard and the Lord Marshal of the Order of One.

"One battalion of the army's cavalry and a company of the Order's Cavaliers should be sufficient. That's five hundred trained Cavaliers," the Commander of the Armies commented.

"We'll send the Fourth Army, Sixth Battalion, along with the Order. That's nearly two-to-one in our favor," he continued, thinking aloud.

"The General of the Fourth Army will lead the charge. The Field Marshal from the Order will be second in command," the commander stated, looking at each of the other leaders present. "Now, I must go tell the king."

Jerrod was with Garrett when Commander De'Ran reported his plan.

"We can't do this, Sire, please," Jerrod begged.

"And why not? Over five hundred mounted soldiers with one hundred lances against three hundred unorganized beasts," De'Ran retorted.

"These have to be Nathanial's forces. What about a wizard and dragon? What if they show up?" Jerrod argued.

"Then we will kill the dragon as well. And yes, I remember your argument on how strong magic is, but he can't use magic against all five hundred."

"And our swords didn't hurt the wolves and bears, did they?" Jerrod tried to remind them.

"Oh please! More werewolf stories."

"You have to take this seriously..." Jerrod began to argue.

"Do we have your blessing, my King?" De'Ran interrupted.

"You have it. And may Ares and Athena watch over you," King Garrett responded.

In the morning, when Jerrod went out to wish the troops luck, he saw Thomas in the army's column. Thomas looked happy. Jerrod knew he was ready for an opportunity to finally serve.

"I didn't know you were with the Sixth Cavalry," Jerrod greeted him.

"I was just assigned. The army asked the Academy for soldiers and I was chosen. Barely appointed to the Fourth Army and here I sit, riding out to battle. It's the first time an army of Torrance has fought in generations. The Fates are with me, Jerrod. It's my time to prove myself. Wish me luck." Thomas smiled.

"May Hermes be with you. Stay alert. The swords may not hurt the wolves or bears. It may be better to be cunning and lucky than to stand toe-to-toe with one of them," Jerrod counseled his friend as he clasped Thomas's elbow.

"Well met, my friend. Thank you, Lord Trisdale," Thomas replied, grinning like a young boy with a piece of candy.

Thomas's parting comment bothered Jerrod as he walked down the column, reflecting. Along the line he saw faces here and there that he recognized from the Axe & Bow and from his wandering about the castle. Thomas had never been so formal with him. Was Thomas changing or was he? Why had Thomas felt the need to be formal? As Jerrod started back up the other side of the column, offering his best wishes to the Cavaliers of the Order of One, he spotted Drin.

"Look at you, Lord Paladin," Jerrod greeted him.

"Lord Trisdale," Drin mocked him in jest. "Thank you for coming to wish us off my friend," Drin added.

"Everything a knight should be. Take care. I fear the wolves and bears are worse than the trolls we fought in the Black Forest."

"It's not like you to worry." Drin's eyebrows dropped as he spoke.

"This does not feel right. Take care of yourself."

"And you too. Fare thee well, my friend. May your gods care for you, always," Drin said sincerely.

"And you yours, brother," Jerrod responded, reflecting on the past year he had spent with Drin and their comrades.

Jerrod stood watching as the columns rode away from the castle through the streets of Torrence. By the time he reached the top of the eastern wall, the column could barely be seen in the pre-dawn light, the Fourth Army's Sixth Cavalry Battalion leading the march.

"Zeus, watch over these men that they may see far beyond tomorrow's dawn. It is not their decision to rush off so quickly, throwing their lives to the Fates," Jerrod prayed.

After leaving sight of Torrence, the column rode east until reaching the north-south road, which it crossed over before sunset, and continuing on to the Plain of Demeter, making camp where the grass was still mostly green, barely starting to turn brown from the summer heat. The squires came up from the rear with wagons and immediately began scurrying about setting up tents and tending to the knights' horses. The camp cooks followed close behind, hurrying to provide warm food for the force.

Services were held after they ate their evening meal. Scouts had returned to tell the General that the enemy was nearby and no one wanted to miss the blessings bestowed the night before battle. On one side of the camp Zeus' priests gave the offering of a sacrificial lamb. On the other side, the Clerics and Friars of the Order burned smoke and chanted blessings. By nightfall all had dispersed to their tents, hoping for a good night's rest in preparation for battle, but as is common to battle forces, particularly for untried troops, most lay awake in expectation.

In the morning the armies of cavaliers and knights rode off as the squires and cooks packed the camp into the wagons. The armies rode southeasterly across the plain with the lances of the Order's Cavaliers pointing skyward, swaying like saplings in the wind. The morning air smelled fresh when they started, but the dust from five hundred horses quickly spoiled the air, choking those in the rear. Still the soldiers' spirits remained high in anticipation of a quick victory.

"A bunch of wolves and bears with a couple of giants," one of the Fourth Army soldiers commented.

"They'll all run off at the site of our column, I'll wager," another soldier responded.

"And we'll be stuck chasing them all afternoon," someone else chimed in.

Each soldier knew the armies of Torrence outnumbered their opponents, not including the squires that followed, who would provide support in a time of need. The squires had been trained to protect the horses and then the knights with their lives, if necessary.

The battle plans had been drawn with confidence. The Order's Cavaliers would be the center of the mounted charge. Their lances would drive down their enemy and the Sixth Cavalry would ride over the broken ranks, hacking with their swords as they bolted through, and then they would turn inward, surrounding the animals they hunted. It was a well-practiced maneuver they could not wait to implement. Even the horses seemed eager for the attack.

Before the sun was halfway to mid-day, they found their objectives. They could see giants and trolls wandering about a make-shift camp, surrounded by hundreds of wolves and bears. Some of the animals paced through the camp while others circled the outer perimeter, but most were curled up, sleeping in small groups. A sense of reassurance swept over the combined force as they looked upon the chaotic nature and small numbers of their opponent.

The General of the Fourth Army sat with his Captain and the Order's Marshal watching their opponent. The column of the combined armies waited for orders.

"Well, gentlemen, here they are," the general said, looking from the battlefield to his comrades.

The Captain shifted in his saddle, looking back at the column, and then back to his superior officer.

"The men await your order, sir."

"Marshal, we shall leave you to lead the charge as discussed. Captain, you take the north end of the line and will take the south. On my command then, gentlemen," the general ordered before turning his horse to make room for the line to form.

As the two officers of the Sixth Battalion split from the center the Cavaliers rode forth to form a single line spanning north and south. Behind them the cavalry split to join their leaders at each end of the field. The Marshal of the Order of One sat alone in the middle of the field.

When he reached the southern end of the line the general spun his horse, taking a last look at his enemy before coming to rest his sight on the Marshal. Drawing his sword and raising it over his head caused all the cavalry to follow his action.

"For Torrence! Charge!" the General of the Fourth Army yelled.

A roar of approval rose into the air. With the signal the line of Cavaliers burst forward in full gallop, their lances still raised as they rode forth side by side, their plate mail gleaming in the morning sun. To either side hundreds of cavalry charged with their swords raised above their heads point towards the Fenür and the animals surrounding them.

At a full gallop the Cavaliers lowered their lances, pointing the deadly metal tips of the long poles at the enemy in front of them. The cavalry leaned forward in their saddles as the speed of the horses increased, lowering their sword tips to point directly at their adversary, ready to slash when the horses trampled through their battle line. In all, five hundred men of Torrence speed across the Plains of Demeter, intent on destroying their foe.

Over the heads of the giants and trolls, wolves and bears, came volleys of black shafted arrows striking horses and riders as they charged into doom. Knights, horsemen, and horses falling from their wounds were trampled by those charging behind them, causing more to stumble and fall. Horses broke their necks. Fallen riders were crushed by stumbling horses. The army's line began falling apart as a third of the army faltered.

Behind the Fendür and Were-Folk, hundreds of Dark Elves stood up from the long grass of the plain, launching volley after volley into the charge. Black-metal arrowheads struck deep into the horses' flesh and pierced the protective armor of the charging soldiers, quickly cut the ranks of Torrence. The black shafts and feathers of the deadly arrows vibrated as they drove deep into the flesh of their targets.

The wolves jumped out of the way of the lances, allowing the remaining Cavaliers to rush through their line, inflicting very little damage. The bears swatted the lances, snapping them as if they were twigs, ripped open gashes into the horses' necks, and batted riders from their mounts. Then the slower giants and trolls waded into the battle. Their blows knocked horses off their feet, sending riders tumbling to the ground before the remainder of the gallant army scrambled to its feet.

Here and there a blade from a Torrence blade cut deep into its target, but to no avail. The giants were so large that the wounds from the remaining warriors quickly became insignificant. When the trolls and Were-Folk were struck they momentarily withdrew from the battle, recovering from the momentary pain, and then immediately renewed their attacks with greater anger. The most injured retreated to heal their wounds with rest. Meanwhile the Dark Elves were circling the battle without resistance, picking off soldiers with deadly accuracy.

Those few men of Torrence who gained their footing instinctively moved into a tight circle as the wolves, bears, giants, and trolls surrounded them. Their armor tarnished with dirt and blood, they drew together, desperate to form a defense, slashing at the Fendür and Were-Folk when they pressed within reach. In the midst of the group Drin and Thomas stood near each other, swinging their swords with all the energy they could muster.

The wounded began crawling towards the army's defensive circle, but most were killed off as they crawled, smashed by a stone weapon of the Fendür or ripped apart by the Were-Folk. Their screams of pain mixed with the groans of struggling warriors who continued to swing heavy weapons as the strength in their arms failed.

The number of those standing their last ground quickly dwindled. Thomas never even saw the archer whose arrow pierced his neck. The Cavaliers and cavalry fought side by side to the end. All around them hundreds of giants, trolls, Were-Folk, and Dark Elves clad in black pressed inward. The ring grew tighter until the hundred surrounded one lone survivor.

A single knight stood in the middle of the circle. Around his feet were scores of fallen soldiers who had stood with him to fight to their death or who had crawled towards him for protection. Each time a foe moved within his reach, Drin swung his great two handed sword, cutting deep into his opponent, momentarily staying off another advance. He was exhausted. His armor was stained by the blood of his foe, and his friends. With every ounce of energy he could find, Drin strove to fight the hundreds off.

"I have done what you asked of me. I have done my best to protect my brothers. I commend my soul unto you," Drin gasped his final prayer.

From behind Drin a large giant stepped in, swinging his axe down and cleaving the knight's helmet. Drin dropped to his knees, momentarily balancing as he leaned on his sword before falling face first on the blood soaked ground, his body covering Feorn Fang, the gifted sword from Lithlillian. The Battle of the Sixth Battalion was lost.

All of the Order's squires who had waited to witness the charge had raced forward to protect the horses and offer what aid they could to the knights, but they had been killed quickly before reaching the battle. Some of the Dark Elves circling the perimeter of the battle broke away to intercept the misguided attack of stable boys. They took great pleasure in their sword play as they cut down the far less experienced squires. In the end, only one muleskinner survived to be taunted by the "small band of rabble" as he drove away.

"Let that one go. He will tell Torrence they cannot defeat us," a Dark Elve commanded.

The muleskinner had seen the entire battle. In less than an hour five hundred soldiers and a hundred squires had died. And the other muleskinners were slaughtered by wolves. Only a few of the Fendür giants were dead and none of the Were-Folk or Dark Elves. As the skinner's wagon rolled out of sight the Were-Folk began feasting on the bodies of the dead.

What is that? the muleskinner thought. *A dragon?*

The ride had seemed so short on the way out, while they were full of excitement and dreams of victory. Just a day's ride, but the hours dragged out for the muleskinner on his homeward trip. He watched and waited for someone to attack, but none came. Pushing through the night, his wagon crossed the bridge into Torrence by mid-day. He was tired and hungry. What he had witnessed plagued his mind. Returning alone, when he reached the gate he was ushered directly to the Commander of the Armies.

"It was horrible. They didn't stand a chance. In the end the new Paladin stood alone trying to protect the others. There were hundreds of them. They didn't stand a chance," the muleskinner repeated.

At first no one spoke. There were no questions. No requests for more details.

"Thank you. Show him out and pay him for his troubles," the Commander finally spoke up.

The Commander called for a captain to send word to the Order that all had been lost. Then he rose to report to the King. To his dismay, the King was not alone.

"Your Majesty, word has come from the battle. It's not good."

"What is it?" the King asked.

"All were lost, your Majesty."

"All? Everyone?"

The Commander nodded his head in affirmation.

The King looked at Jerrod and then back to the Commander. He grew pale as he placed his hand on the back of chair for support. He stood for a moment, staring at the floor before speaking.

"I suppose it's my fault, really. We raced after them." The King paused and then looked at Jerrod. "You warned me not to be hasty. What now, Commander?" the King asked.

"Honestly? I don't know."

"Lord Trisdale, any thoughts?" the King said, looking back to Jerrod.

"Let me consult with some friends, Your Majesty. What of the bodies?" Jerrod asked.

"We will have to go in force to retrieve whatever remains. When we reach the battlefield we will collect the dead. I suspect we will need a mass burial," the king answered without looking up. "We can't possibly bring them all back."

✳   ✳   ✳   ✳   ✳

Word of the defeat went racing through Torrence like a wildfire through dry grass. The horrific description of the battle terrified everyone who heard the story. Some went home and closed their doors and windows as though it were already winter, seeking safety in the shadows of their seclusion. Others went immediately to the temples to pray to the Olympian gods for protection. A few went to the Cathedral.

Fraum and Amanda were sitting in the library when Jerrod brought the news. Before they reached the bottom step, Jerrod waved off the monk leading him down to the library. He was halfway to the table before Fraum and Amanda realized he was in the room.

"I bring hard news." Jerrod's voice was soft, it trembled slightly.

"Here, sit. What has happened?" Fraum asked.

"You know the King's Army and the Order rode out to meet the Fendür and some wild animals on the Plain of Demeter. Wolves and bears, to be exact. There were Dark Elves waiting." Jerrod paused. "And there's rumor that a dragon was heard after the battle."

"Drin?" Amanda asked.

Jerrod took a breath before meeting her eyes.

"And Thomas," he added.

"No one survived?" Fraum asked.

"No one. It is said that Drin was the last to fall. He fought gallantly," Jerrod reported.

Amanda looked at Fraum as a tear began to roll down her cheek. Jerrod watched.

"He was kind to me... Kind when I needed a friend. After you left us at Gap of Dillandria..." Amanda stammered as she tried to explain.

Jerrod swallowed hard and nodded.

"Oh, no. By Athena, no. We were only friends. I swear," Amanda stammered.

Jerrod looked up at her and then to Fraum.

"He was a good man. Like a brother to me."

"He will be missed," Fraum sympathized.

They sat a moment in silence, each reflecting on what Drin had meant to them. They recalled his square jaw, curly black hair, and devout stubbornness. After a moment, Amanda looked at Jerrod.

"Did you say wolves and bears?"

"Yes."

"When we were staying at the miller's inn in Lithlillia, Nathanial snuck out one night to go find some wolves and bears. I tracked him part of the way." Amanda stopped, looking at them with glazed eyes. "They were werewolves."

Jerrod and Fraum looked at each other and then back at her.

"Nathanial has made an alliance with the Were-Folk," Amanda said to confirm what she had thought had become obvious.

"In Hades' name. How do you kill a werewolf?" Jerrod asked.

Fraum and Amanda went to the shelves and began searching through the scrolls until they located the section of histories and legends referencing Were-Folk. As they searched Amanda told them the story of the bear she had encountered on the road to Dalset.

"It was a mortal wound and the thing just got up and ran off. Unless we find the answer, the best we can hope for is to hurt them bad enough to drive them off," Amanda concluded.

"Don't forget the trolls. They weren't any easier to kill," Jerrod reminded them as he watched them sifting through the monastery's library.

They all selected a scroll and began reading. Fraum read the quickest, leafing through one and then another scroll while Jerrod and Amanda worked slower. Each unrolled a scroll to review the text and then rolled it back up to select another. The scrolls varied in length, some incredibly long, so long they need to be rolled out on the library table to read.

"Silver! A silver weapon," Amanda exclaimed.

The witch's dagger. She knew, she thought.

Fraum took the scroll from her, turning the bars to advance the parchment.

"Magic also kills them. And some beasts may be powerful enough, or pure enough, to kill the Were," Fraum added.

I'll bet Drok-na could kill a werewolf, he thought.

Jerrod turned towards him and smiled.

"I'm not sure what this means, but I will let the king know. Thank you," Jerrod said as he rose from the table. "Do you need help re-shelving these?"

"No. We have it. You go. Tell the king. It may be important to his plans," Fraum urged.

"Thank you," Jerrod finished before turning and ascending the stairs out of the library in order to return.

Jerrod's path back to the king's castle took him by the Cathedral where the statue of Sir Michael stood poised in battle, his two-handed sword forever held back over his head. How magnificent? Sir Michael had inspired them all, especially Drin. When Jerrod looked upon the statue, the vision of Drin's final moments flooded his mind. His eyes eventually refocused and he looked down to the words etched in the obelisk that held the statue.

THROUGH DEDICATION WILL COME GLORY
THROUGH PURITY ANYTHING CAN BE ACCOMPLISHED

Oh Drin, what have we done? You died doing what you always wanted, but where are we now? What have we gained? Jerrod thought.

I have fulfilled my dream, brother. Don't fret. I am content, Jerrod heard Drin's voice in his mind.

Drin?

There is so much for you to learn, brother. I do not lie in death's eternal sleep.

What? Where are you?

Remember the prophecy, Jerrod, Drin's voice said as it faded away.

Jerrod fell to the ground, sitting for a moment while he regained his breath. Then he slid over to lean his back against the obelisk. He put his forehead in his hands, resting his elbows on his knees, attempting to regain his composure. When at last he stood up, a ghostly woman appeared before him.

"Hello, Jerrod."

"Who are you?" he questioned.

"You know me. I am Felicia. You visited me in my cottage near Cipper."

"The witch?" he said slowly.

"Yes. Does that bother you?"

"No, not really. You warned us that Jacob was coming."

"Yes."

"Why are you here? And why now, of all times?"

"I watch you and your friends from time to time. Does that bother you?"

"A little."

"You know it was Nathanial," she continued, her ghostly image turning away teasingly.

"I suspected it," he said as he stood up.

"You know he has been plotting this for a long time?"

"When did you find out?" Jerrod asked.

"I suspected it when you were in my cottage. I warned Amanda about him."

"She told me."

"See? I want to help." Felicia's vaporous face smiled.

"How can you help?" Jerrod asked, suspicious of Felicia's intentions.

"The bears and wolves were Were-Folk. Did you know that?"

"No. Were-Folk? Like werewolves?" Jerrod lied, luring her to be over confident.

Felicia nodded.

"And what's in it for you?"

"You have the Dragon's Orb. I want it." Felicia smiled as she looked down at the pommel of the Sword of Trisdale.

Jerrod's hand slid to his sword handle, causing Felicia to laugh.

"And if I don't feel like giving it to you?"

"You will, Jerrod. You will," Felicia's voice faded with her body.

"Zeus, don't let the Fates bring anything else on us this night," Jerrod prayed aloud.

When he finally returned to the castle, Jerrod went straight to the king's chamber and directed the guards to wake him. Apologizing for the late hour, he proceeded to describe his evening. The news had seemed important enough to pass on to the king before they departed in the morning for the battlefield.

"Nathanial is gathering an army," Jerrod concluded.

"With Trisdale Keep incomplete we have nothing to warn us if the Were-Folk or the Fendür come out of the north," King Garrett thought aloud.

"We have our alliance with Lithlillia. Nathanial won't attack the druids and Elves. Not yet," Jerrod counseled.

Jerrod left the king and returned to his room. Before falling asleep he reached out to a nearby bird. The tiny animal's thoughts were simple and changed rapidly, but Jerrod was able to convey a short message to be carried to Rhonda.

"Drin died. Funeral tomorrow. Southern side of the Plain of Demeter."

❖   ❖   ❖   ❖   ❖

With the King's Guard and the King's Standing Armies', Third Army and First Army's Archer Battalion, and joined by the remaining company of Cavaliers from the Order, King Garrett departed Torrence for the battlefield on the southwestern edge of the plain. Over two thousand men in all, they traveled with the intent to bury their dead, but were prepared for war.

Riding in a carriage with several Elders, the Prophet's traveling with the armies was highly unusual. He never ventured from the Cathedral, but he deemed the burial to be of such great importance that he had selected to accompany the force. Priests of Olympus were also traveling to the site with the procession. The prominent citizens from Torrence and others, wishing to witness the burial, rode farther back on horses or in wagons. A troop of bards spread themselves through the caravan, playing music to ease the pain of Torrence's loss.

They did not stop to make camp that night, but rode through and, before morning's light, reached the battle site. Despite the carnage that littered the field, the carrion birds left the bodies alone. On the south side of the field a large white dragon lay watching for the fallen.

The sight of the magnificent beast alarmed the Commander and his Generals, causing the armies to stir. The white dragon, its immense tail wrapping nearly all the way around its body, soaked in the sun as twilight began burning the dew off the ground.

Welcome, Jerrod, the dragon thought.

Who are you and why are you here? Jerrod challenged the old drake.

I am a friend of Torrence, and a friend of Fraum's. I did not want the bodies desecrated further or the funeral parade to be attacked. You are safe to bury your dead.

"The dragon pledges to protect us, Your Majesty," Jerrod stated as he turned to the king.

"The dragon pledges. Really? What nonsense is this?" Commander De'Ran protested.

With a glance the young king quieted De'Ran, but despite the pledge, the Comander and Lord Marshal posted sentries around the battlefield while the soldiers worked to dig two long, massive graves. The Prophet, who had heard of Drin's last stand, requested that his body be separated and buried alone.

"We will place a statue over his gravesite," the Prophet declared.

"Another statue. How appropriate," Commander De'Ran's voice was hard and slurred with sarcasm.

The Prophet turned and looked at him, and then turned back to the Lord Marshal.

"Find Drin and his sword. They will be buried here," the Prophet's declared.

"See that it's done Commander," the king commanded.

When the Cavaliers found Drin, two monks were already cleaning his body, preparing him for burial. The Cavaliers watched them until they finished, but then the monks sat down cross-legged next to him to stand a vigil.

From a distance Jerrod could see the small gathering watching the monks, but he could not see for certain that the monks were Fraum and Amanda. When the Cavaliers reported that they did not dare take Drin's body and a Priest complained, Jerrod interjected.

"Leave Drin to his friends. They know him well and honor him. Besides, there is no one here who can forcibly remove them," Jerrod warned.

The Priest withdrew, leaving Jerrod to socialize with the King, Count Rieslane, and the other lords. He found their conversation heartless, dwelling on implications of losing the battle rather than the tragic loss of life. As they spoke, Roger walked up dressed as a count's son rather than an Academy student.

"Your Majesty, my lords, Father," he greeted them.

"I have not seen you in years," the young king greeted his second cousin.

"No, Your Majesty. We have not visited for quite a while," Roger answered before glancing at his father.

"We should change that. You're my age, aren't you?"

"A bit older, but yes, Your Majesty."

Jerrod took the opportunity to excuse himself.

Perhaps I am too close to Drin and they are not being callous. I'm just too sensitive, Jerrod tried to reassure himself.

You are right to be offended, Jerrod. The dead deserve their recognition and respect, the white dragon responded.

✼   ✼   ✼   ✼   ✼

"Is this all there is to life? To struggle and die?" Amanda asked Fraum as they watched over Drin's body.

"Measure your life by the impact you make on others' lives, not on your possessions and achievements. Drin was a good friend to us all. He fought alongside us without reservation. He charged the vespree without concern for his own well-being. More than once he laid his healing hands on one of us, giving us the care we desperately needed. His was a life of selflessness spent in devotion to the Order of One."

"He was kind to me when I needed it most." Amanda turned away to hide her swelling eyes.

"Dawn brings a new day and each day offers a new beginning."

"But there is no new beginning in death. Drin's days have ended." Her voice sounded angry as she looked back at him, a tear running down her cheek.

"Perhaps, but maybe something will come out of his death."

They sat their vigil throughout the day as the soldiers worked. At dusk they lit a candle, remaining at Drin's side without food or water. Nearby the soldiers continued digging two long pits for a mass burial. One side of the grave was for the remains of the four hundred soldiers belonging to the king's Legion. The other was for the uneaten pieces of the two hundred Cavaliers and Squires of the Order. Between the two pits they dug a single grave.

When morning came six Knights from the Order brought a litter to carry Sir Drin, Lord Paladin, to his gravesite. Each Knight was spotlessly groomed with shining armor and brilliant, royal-blue capes. Each wore the royal blue shoulder braid of Paladin. They picked Drin up gently, placing his sword on his corpse, and carried him to his grave, where others stood guard waiting for the burial ceremony. Fraum and Amanda followed slowly and remained with the Knights of the Order of One.

In the field, soldiers were picking up the fallen by their arms and legs to carry them to one of the two mass graves. The smell was nearly intolerable. Flies were buzzing throughout the carnage while the soldiers tried to lay each of the fallen carefully into the graves.

At the end of each massive grave was a pile of armor and weapons that had been stripped from the dead and picked up off the battlefield. Wagons were waiting to load the cold metal remnants of the dead to take back to Torrence.

Is this all that remains for them? Jerrod thought as he looked over the burial site.

A solitary gravesite on the field of battle is not so bad, the white dragon responded.

And their families? What of them?

They are safe.

Nothing more? Jerrod questioned.

Perhaps something will come of their sacrifice. The dragon's thought was somber.

While the last of the bodies were being placed in the mass graves, four flying horses descended upon the field. Many of the soldiers picked up their bows as Jerrod walked out to greet them.

"You made it," he said.

"We had some trouble finding you," Rhonda answered as she slipped off a winged horse.

"I didn't know the location when I sent you the message."

"No matter. We are here. We would not miss the burial of a Friend of Lithlillia. We are sorry for your loss." Lady Lieisa's soft voice was soothing.

"These flies are awful," Lady Lieisa said, waving her hand towards the sky.

The annoying insects scattered while Jerrod led them towards Drin's grave, where the leaders were gathering for the ceremony. While they walked, Jerrod recited the report of the battle. When they reached the site, the new king seemed genuinely happy to see them, but the Prophet and other members of the Order seemed agitated.

"We are not altogether comfortable with druids at a burial ceremony of the Order," the Prophet announced.

"And yet I understand the ceremony is to be led by the Priest of Zeus, is it not?" Lady Lieisa asked, causing the Prophet to frown.

"We will erect a statue over Sir Drin's grave to honor all the fallen and protect his tomb. It is to be a depiction of his last stance," the young king interjected, trying to overcome the growing tension.

"And you won't forget the pinecone brooch on his shoulder when you sculpt the statue, will you?" Lady Lieisa commented as she looked at the Prophet. "Your Paladin is also a Friend of Lithlillia." She smiled.

"The approved uniform would be more suitable," the Prophet offered.

"Drin wore the brooch at his Accolade."

"So be it," the Prophet relented.

More people from Torrence were arriving to witness the burial. The crowd included all the more affluent citizens of Torrence as well as family and friends of the fallen. The mothers, sisters, and daughters of the dead sobbed. Even the fathers, brothers, and sons could not swallow easily, their eyes swelling with unfallen tears. Nearby a group of bards played harps and flutes, trying to ease the pain of the audience. Amanda heard a dove cooing in the distance.

As the others were negotiating over the ceremony, Imelrinn stepped away to clear his mind of some of the pettiness. He walked along the massive grave for the Sixth Battalion looking down at the bodies.

I have not seen such carnage for hundreds of years. Not since the Elve-Dwarve Wars, he thought, careful not to share his thoughts.

A single tear lingered on the Mountain Elve's cheek as he walked to the end of the pit. Wiping the drop away with the tip of his long finger, he looked away from the bodies. At the end of the grave, he stared a moment at the pile of weapons and armor and then turned to walk back across the field, but something caught his attention.

There, on top of the pile, lay an arrow. Its shaft, feathers, and metal tip were all black. Kneeling down, Imelrinn picked it up to examine closer. In his wildest dreams, he hoped beyond hoping that what he saw did not really exist.

Standing up, he looked at the pile of metal more carefully, spotting more and more of the arrows.

Dark Elves, he thought without guard.

What! Lady Lieisa asked, panicked by the word.

Dark Elves battled here, my Lady. I have an arrow.

It can't be, the queen of the Elves protested.

I'm afraid it is. They have come out of the Wilds. We will soon be at war, Imelrinn advised.

Dark Elves? The ones from the Elve-Dwarve War? What are you talking about? Jerrod thought in alarm.

Yes, the same Dark Elves that defeated the Dwarves and Mountain Elves and drove us out of the high mountains into Lithlillia. They are more formidable than anyone in Torrence can imagine. And if they know we are here, there will be war, Lady Lieisa explained.

✳   ✳   ✳   ✳   ✳

After the Priest of Zeus completed the ceremony, the Prophet spoke briefly, focusing on the gallantry of those who had been lost, particularly on Drin's last stand. He spoke of the muleskinner who had witnessed the battle, but his last comment was less tolerant of the Olympians.

"And in time, those who do not yet follow the One shall come to know his light, and such losses will become legend, for under the protection of the One we shall be saved."

As a quite murmur passed through the crowd, Lady Lieisa stepped forward, joining the religious leaders who had presented the burial ceremony. She looked at both of the religious leaders and smiled. Then, lowering her head for a moment in concentration, Lieisa raised her arms, pointing to each side of Drin's grave.

Looking at the two mass graves stretching away from the central point where Drin's grave lay, she pointed at each. When her hands dropped to her side, the white dragon pushed up on his forelegs, lifting his head towards the sun, and let loose a prideful roar.

"A small grove of pine trees will grow to either side of Drin's grave and the mass graves will be covered with white flowers that will bloom every year," Lady Lieisa said as she smiled at the priests.

Then she turned to the crowd and opened her arms wide.

"Any who are troubled may come here to the grove and the trees will calm those with honest hearts," she finished before looking back at the priests defiantly.

When the ceremony was done, the citizens of Torrence began their trip home. It may have been closure for many of them, but only a few departing the field of battle did so with a lighter heart. Here and there a family stopped, recognizing the sword of a fallen loved one lying in the heap of discarded weapons, asking if they could have the only memento that remained. Together the elite and the pauper, the soldier and the merchant, began their homeward journey as the bards played magical music to lighten their burden.

Amanda and Fraum were returning with the crowd when she saw a tall bard with curly, sandy brown hair playing his mandolin. As he played the sun reflected off his gold dragon ring.

"Fernando," Amanda exclaimed, nodding towards the bard as she pulled Fraum's sleeve.

Leaving the road to greet the bard, Fraum extended his arm to shake. Looking at Fraum and smiling as they grasped arms, Fernando turned to look at Amanda. His eyes squinted a bit before the corner of his mouth, partially covered by his goatee, turned up.

"You probably don't remember me. When we met near Cipper I had long, blonde hair and dressed in black leather," Amanda said.

"Amanda, right?"

She nodded and smiled.

"I could never forget that smile. But why the...ahh?"

"I'm living in the White Fist Monastery."

"That's a little odd, isn't it?"

"She has a remarkable knack for learning our teachings. I have taken her on as my fulltime student," Fraum interjected.

The golden figure of a dragon cradling a tiger's eye gem that wrapped around the bard's finger caught Amanda's eye, momentarily distracting her.

"I'm sorry. I was admiring your ring."

"It was given to me by a very old friend," Fernando said, subconsciously reaching over with his other hand to twist the dragon tail-band of the ring a bit.

"I remember it. It is very nice," Amanda complimented him.

"Thank you. What brings you out to the battlefield? Did you have a friend with the army?"

"A couple," Amanda answered.

"You may remember Drin. He was with us in the forest when we met," Fraum added.

"The Paladin?"

"Yes," Fraum confirmed.

"A shame. He was a nice young man. I understand he fought valiantly."

"It's all he wanted," Amanda said softly.

"I shall have to write a song for him then," Fernando offered.

"Thank you. That would be wonderful."

Amanda and Fraum left the bard to play for the long procession as they returned to Drin's gravesite. The dust rose, choking the travelers as thousands of feet trudged homeward while the King remained on the field watching his subjects.

After Lady Lieisa and Lord Steffen took their leave of him, they turned to join Rhonda and Imelrinn. As they passed Jerrod, Lady Lieisa stopped.

"Are you well?" she asked.

"Yes, Lady. It is kind of you to ask. Thank you."

"She truly misses you, Jerrod, but I think the decision not to marry is for the best. Thank you. Come say goodbye." The queen pulled her husband lovingly by the arm.

They met with Rhonda and Imelrinn briefly, but Lady Lieisa pushed to mount her winged horse and return to Lithlillia. Rhonda began to follow her mother and then stopped, standing in front of Jerrod, the point of her ear pushing through her fine hair. The softness of her face and high, thin eyebrows made Jerrod's heart ache for a new reason.

"And how is Trisdale?" Rhonda asked as her hand pulled her hair back to rest behind her ear.

"Me or the keep?"

When Rhonda looked at him he felt like he had shrunk several inches.

Of course the keep, Jerrod thought, blocking Rhonda from his mind.

"I was there too short of a time to really know, but things seem to be going slowly. There will be a lot of stone work to be done and only a few soldiers to manage it."

"Perhaps I could contact the Fairy-Folk to see if they will help transport the rocks necessary to rebuild."

"That would be helpful. Thank you." Jerrod paused. "And us?" he asked hopelessly.

"Has anything changed?"

"No, I guess not," Jerrod admitted.

Rhonda smiled.

"Perhaps we can spend more time together next time and talk about it?" Jerrod suggested.

"We'll see."

The departure of Lithlillia left the king with his military leadership, Count Rieslane, and the priests of both Olympus and the Order. Jerrod joined the group as the priests were departing and the king was reflecting on their loss.

"All this for nothing!" King Garrett's voice broke as he spoke, still staring at the battlefield.

"Who could have known, Your Majesty?" Commander De'Ran responded.

"As the Commander of the Armies, you should have." The young king's voice was hardened.

"But Your Majesty..." De'Ran began to protest.

"Lord Trisdale knew. You should have," the king interrupted, turning away from the field to shoot a look at the Commander.

"He tried to warn us. What is it you said? He's a boy with no battle experience?"

The king turned back to gaze silently on the grassy field.

"Next time I will go with them. Better that I share their fate," the king whispered.

"It is worse than we knew, I'm afraid," Jerrod interjected.

The young king turned to look at him. His face already appeared sad. Jerrod knew the sincerity of the young king who had befriended him.

"What else?" Garrett spoke just above a whisper.

"I am told that the Elves who partook in the battle were Dark Elves," Jerrod explained.

"Dark Elves? What in Hades' name are Dark Elves?" Commander De'Ran demanded.

"A formidable group of Elves. They defeated the combined army of Dwarves and Mountain Elves."

"What do you know about any of this?" the commander mocked him.

"I have spent a year in the company of Elves and druids. King Derik asked me to grow my friendship with the Elves so Torrence would benefit, and they tell me Dark Elves are responsible for this." Jerrod spoke fast, the tone of his voice slightly elevated, showing his youth.

"Dark Elves, giants, and trolls. Is that what you are saying destroyed the Sixth Battalion?" the commander pressed.

"The giants and trolls are called the Fendür. The Elves have fought them for hundreds of years. It's why Trisdale Keep was built. I have fought them myself. They are almost impossible to kill, and yes, with the help of the Dark Elves and some Were-Folk, they killed your men."

"Were-Folk?" the king asked.

"Skin changers that can only be killed by silver and magic, Your Majesty," Jerrod explained.

*   *   *   *   *

As the others departed, Jerrod went to visit Drin's grave one last time. Standing next to the gravesite were two monks.

"This is a sad meeting, my friends," Jerrod said as he approached.

Amanda and Fraum turned around to greet him.

"Jerrod?" Amanda responded.

"Hello."

Amanda simply smiled.

"And how is the Lord of Trisdale?" Fraum's asked sincerely.

"In truth, I'm not sure."

"Not sure? Agh!" Amanda exploded before stomping off.

Jerrod watched her and then turned to Fraum.

"I just don't understand?" Jerrod shrugged.

"She is bound to have some frustration. You denied her for Rhonda and then left Rhonda. And now you're a lord. She doesn't know where she fits in or how to react."

"Neither do I."

"For a simple feeling, love is very complicated," Fraum acknowledged.

"And where does that put us?" Jerrod asked before looking at the battlefield again.

"She still loves you Jerrod. All will come in time. Today we must focus on this tragedy," Fraum said as he pulled Jerrod by the arm towards the battlefield.

"I tried to warn them," Jerrod began. Jerrod told Fraum the whole story, starting with his desperate plea to the king for caution.

"This isn't your fault," Fraum reached out to grab Jerrod's shoulder, staring into his eyes as the spoke.

Jerrod looked at him like a child who had been left with nothing, lost in the world of adults.

"Heroes aren't invincible," Fraum consoled him.

CHAPTER 14
THE TRUE QUEST

The ride back to Torrence had been humbling, leaving more to be desired, like a cold winter morning without the sun. Fraum's words were echoing in Jerrod's mind. *Heroes aren't invincible.* Jerrod had not thought of his mortality when he rushed into battle with the vespree, but now it was staring him in the face. And the weight of the funeral was pressing him down further into despair.

As he rode, his mind sought an escape from the numbing pain. He thought of home and his hike to Torrence, which had started his adventure, and he thought of Amanda. His escape ultimately led him to the skeletal remains of the former Lord Trisdale.

I need to return his bones to the keep, he concluded.

When Jerrod reached Torrence he rode to the Monastery of the White Fist. Dismounting at the gate, he asked to see Amanda, who agreed to walk with him back to the stable where Jerrod had worked and now stabled his horse.

"I have seen a lot of death this week," Jerrod said, not much above a whisper.

"What?" Amanda responded.

"I'm considering taking Lord Trisdale's bones back to the keep. I may even visit my parents. I would like you to go with me," Jerrod invited.

Amanda hesitated. The love inside her was erupting, twisting her heart with agony and joy. She did not know how to answer. She could see the compassion in Jerrod's azure-blue eyes melting her like honey over warm, buttered bread. She could taste her love for him.

"What about all that has happened? There's an army out there somewhere," Amanda questioned.

"Perhaps it's all the loss, but I need to return Lord Trisdale's bones to the tomb in the keep. Winfred is only a two-day walk from where I found Lord Trisdale. I would like to show it to you. We can pick up his skeleton on the return ride."

"What about Rhonda? She should be the one to go with you. She should be the one you introduce to your family."

"I don't know. If war is coming I want to see my family before the battle. Rhonda is in Lithlillia and I don't want to travel alone. You are my first closest friend. Please go with me."

Jerrod turned away in frustration as his hands slapped his side.

"I will go," she whispered after watching him for a moment.

After they left Jerrod's horse at the stable, Jerrod walked Amanda back to the monastery. They agreed to meet back at the stable in the morning to start the journey and then said an awkward good night.

"Thank you for accompanying me," he told her, taking her hand gently in his own before turning to walk back to the castle.

There was neither kiss nor hug before they parted. Amanda watched him walk out of sight and then entered the monastery. The soft music did not sooth her troubled heart as Amanda retrieved the U'thra bow before searching for Fraum.

"I have decided to leave the monastery. It has been a wonderful experience, but I don't think this is the life for me," she told the sage.

"Still hiding," he confirmed.

"I'm not sure," Amanda answered.

"Where will you go?"

"I have agreed to accompany Jerrod while he returns Lord Trisdale's bones to the keep. We will go to Winfred first."

"A noble act. How do you think it will help your quest?"

Amanda looked at the old monk.

"Your true quest has not been about retrieving the Horn of Valhalla. It is one of self-determination."

"I don't know how or if it will help me. It just feels right."

Amanda hugged the fatherly monk and turned to walk away.

"Wait here a moment," Fraum asked.

Amanda watched Fraum walk towards the back of the monastery where the sleeping quarters and the armory were located.

What is he up to? she thought.

When he returned he was carrying a long wooden box made of polished walnut. The shiny brass hinges and latches caught her eye. Fraum carried it as though the contents were fragile.

"We want you to have this," Fraum announced.

"What is it?" she asked as she took the box.

"That is easier to find out if you simply open it," Fraum teased.

Balancing the long box in one arm, Amanda opened it carefully. Inside were two matching Elven swords and a scroll with a gold ribbon tied around it.

"It's in Elven. They are sister swords. We think they're magical." Fraum looked at her with his soft, almond-shaped eyes.

"I will miss you," Amanda said as she reached to hug him with her empty arm.

"Remember, follow your heart. Abandon momentary desire. It's a fine line, but it will keep you true to yourself."

✻   ✻   ✻   ✻   ✻

After he left Amanda, Jerrod went to the king to explain his plan to relocate Lord Trisdale's remains and to request soldiers to escort him on the journey. The king approved and insisted on sending an Olympian priest with them.

"Choose whomever you wish for the soldiers. I will send a priest to the stable in the morning," King Garrett said.

"Thank you, Your Majesty."

"Be careful. We don't know where that army is or what they intend," Garrett cautioned.

"I appreciate the king's concern and friendship," Jerrod answered.

"Jerrod, you are my friend. One of a very few. Take care of yourself."

When they were finished, Jerrod went directly to the Academy to find Roger, but the officer on duty informed him Roger had been appointed to the King's Guard. Returning to the king's castle Jerrod found his way to the Guard's barracks and to Roger's room, which he shared with several other guards.

"How are you?" Jerrod asked.

"As well as can be expected," Roger answered.

"Thomas was a great friend. I enjoyed our nights together at the Axe & Bow," Jerrod responded.

"Thank you. And I have gained a post in the King's Guard because of it. I'm not sure how I feel about prospering from our friend's misfortune," Roger admitted.

"Your father's influence?" Jerrod asked.

"Probably. Keeping me safe, out of the regular army, I imagine."

"I have a position for a leader and four soldiers. It would be a posting to the army, but not in Torrence," Jerrod explained.

"Where would it be?"

"It is a positing at Trisdale Keep as part of my force. My soldiers will still be part of the army, like the other lords' armies. Would you be interested?"

"Definitely. When do we start?"

"We leave in the morning. We'll meet at the stable where I used to work. You will be in charge. Pick out four men you trust and meet me there at dawn."

"Thank you, Lord Trisdale. We will be there."

"Here's the king's appointment. Just add the appropriate names," Jerrod said, handing Roger a scroll.

When he finally lay down, Jerrod did not rest easy. His sleep was plagued with memories of the last year and dreams for the future. He knew his station and the king's expectations, but he was no longer Jerrod. Worse, he no longer appeared to have the love of either of the women he loved. He rolled over again in his effort to sleep.

Jerrod was pleased to find five soldiers and the priest already waiting for him when he arrived at the stables in the morning. Eight horses were saddled and ready to go, including one for Amanda and his own. Just as he was about to ask about her, a woman wearing a gray scarf wrapped around her head and neck walked up. Her black bodice, which pulled her white pillow sleeved blouse tight against her busty chest, and tight pants disclosed her athletic body.

"Amanda?" Jerrod asked.

Amanda smiled as she leaned against the barn door a moment, one leg crossed over the other, resting the point of her toe on the ground. The others turned to look at her.

"Hey Roger," she responded, ignoring Jerrod.

"Amanda!" Roger yelled in typical fashion before running over to give her a hug.

The larger, somewhat older man joyously lifted her off the ground as he spun around until he was done giving her a bear hug.

"I left the monastery. There must be something more to life," she said, looking back at Jerrod as she moved towards the horses.

Kicking her knee high boot into the stirrup of her saddle, Amanda swung herself up onto her horse.

"Ready?" she asked, reining her horse around and trotting out of the stable barn without waiting for a reply.

"Now that's Amanda," Roger said to Jerrod.

The first day's ride was steady. They stopped to eat the mid-day meal, but quickly resumed their journey. As they rode on, Jerrod looked over at Amanda and reached out to gently pull back her scarf, exposing Amanda's bald head. Amanda looked down at first, but then looked back at him, smiling.

That smile that has disarmed so many, Jerrod thought.

"This won't do," he said, touching her head with his finger.

Amanda's blonde hair began to grow, continuing until it reached her waist. The soldiers and priest behind them stared.

"What was that?" Roger demanded as he rode up beside Jerrod.

"Magic." Jerrod looked back calmly.

"Magic! Since when did you start studying magic?" Roger asked.

"I don't study magic." Jerrod paused. "I am the magic."

"What?" Roger persisted.

"Apparently, once every thousand years a child is born with a direct connection to magic. I'm still learning about my abilities, but I don't need to study."

"This has happened before?" Roger asked as the others listened.

Jerrod nodded his head and then looked back over his shoulder glancing at the group that rode behind them.

"I think the last time was a wizard named Brendril," he finished.

On the first night they camped near the road, sleeping on their bedrolls under the stars. With Amanda lying next to him, Jerrod looked up at the moons.

Are you watching these moons tonight, Rhonda? Jerrod thought, not really wanting her to answer.

The next morning offered another pleasant day of riding, but it was a much longer day, allowing them to ride in two days the distance it had taken Jerrod several days to walk. When they reached Oakwood, they found rooms at an inn.

While they slept, word passed quickly that a young lord was traveling with his soldiers to Winfred. Travelers between the villages passed word to Raven's Claw and then on to Winfred.

In the morning they gathered in the inn's tavern for their meal together.

"Will you bless our morning meal?" Jerrod asked the priest.

After the prayer they ate together. The tavern maid brought warm bread, hard boiled eggs, and cheese. The tea was a local herb, plentiful in the summer and stored dry for the winter.

"Were you at the burial?" Amanda asked.

"Yes, I was there to witness the passing on to Hades," the priest answered.

"He was our friend," Jerrod commented.

"The Paladin? He was a good man, I hear. He died a hero," the priest acknowledged carefully.

"Yes, he was. And there was another, a merchant's son, Thomas," Amanda answered before looking away.

"Perhaps he is in Elysian Fields with the other heroes. Or Asphodel Meadows with those who lead common lives," the priest offered.

"Elysian Fields, I think," Amanda whispered.

"He was not bound for Tartarus to be tortured at least," the priest added.

"The one realm of the underworld that I would rather not see," Roger chimed in.

"The underworld? Like Valhalla?" Amanda looked at them.

"If such a place exists, it would be part of Hades' realm, but that is an Asgardian teaching. Why?" the priest asked.

"What do you know of it?" Amanda demanded.

"The Asgardians believe that fallen heroes who died valiant deaths go there as a reward."

"The good?" The words came out of Amanda's mouth slowly.

"And the bad. Each hero is a hero to someone, good or bad. Asgardian gods would make the decision."

"And what of our friends who died on the battlefield with the Sixth?" Roger asked.

"Each man would go to his god."

"What if there was a way to get them back from Valhalla?" Amanda pressed.

"You don't get it. Valhalla is a place where heroes go to be rewarded for their heroism. They become braggarts. Their egos out of control. They would not be happy to return to Dendür. The dead are best left to the dead."

"I was an orphan. My mentor taught me how to pick pockets and steal. He spoke of Hermes, god of thieves, and the Fates. I learned about Zeus, and Athena, and all the rest of them, but I'm sorry, I don't know about the realms of the underworld!"

"It's okay, Amanda. I don't know much about Hades' realm either," Jerrod said calmly before turning towards the priest.

"I think the question is whether the realms of the Olympian underworld could be accessed from Valhalla?"

"I don't know." The priest shrugged.

After the morning meal as the others were preparing to mount up, Jerrod pulled Amanda aside. In his hand was a silver dagger.

"You gave this to me last winter. Take it so you don't ride without a weapon," Jerrod said to Amanda as he handed her the dagger.

"The witch's dagger," Amanda said, quietly taking the dagger, which she slid into her boot.

On horseback the trip to the bluff was shorter than Jerrod expected. He led them first to the lake where he had camped and then they rode single file up to the site of Lord Trisdale's shallow grave. The stones where he had buried the knight remained untouched. Sliding off his horse, Jerrod knelt at the gravesite.

"In the name of Zeus and Hades, for all that you have given me, I have come to return your remains to your keep," Jerrod said over the grave.

Jerrod lingered over the grave a moment before standing up.

"We will leave you here, priest, to make the necessary preparations to move the remains. Two of the soldiers will stay with you. We will return in five or six days," Jerrod ordered.

You have found your place, Amanda thought as she listened to Jerrod.

As they rode on towards Winfred, Jerrod reflected more and more on his life.

I left a poor miller's son and now I am returning not only rich, but a lord. Who will believe this? How will my family react?" the thoughts ran through Jerrod's mind.

Amanda, who had been watching him, realized he was fidgeting more and more as they approached Winfred.

"What's bothering you?" Amanda finally asked.

"A lot has happened over the last year. Will they still see me as the boy I was?"

"I imagine your mother will always see you as her boy. As for your father and brother, that may depend more on how you present yourself," Amanda tried to comfort him.

"My father always wants more of me. He's always pushing," Roger interjected.

"Great. So my father will either be disappointed because I am not a king or because I am not a miller."

"At least you have family that loves you," Amanda said, ending the conversation.

It was after dark when they approached Winfred. Recalling some of Jerrod's childhood stories, Amanda found the silhouettes of the deciduous forest intriguing. Envisioning Jerrod's friends charging at each other with wooden swords and shields, she connected with his past, understanding a little more about the man she still loved. The night sounds, filled with cricket songs and an occasional hooting owl, soothed her soul, easing her torment.

What would it have been like if I were returning with Jerrod before he became the Lord of Trisdale? If we were not rich, before the magic, Amanda mused. *It would have been wonderful,* the thought drifted into her mind.

Amanda looked at Jerrod, wondered if he had whispered something sweet into her ear or if she had just imagined it.

"My mother is going to like you," Jerrod said to Amanda as they dismounted outside the only inn Winfred.

Roger went inside to pay for the rooms while Jerrod and Amanda spoke with the soldiers about caring for the horses. Inside, it was immediately apparent to the villagers in the tavern that Roger was the henchman of Lord Trisdale. It only took a couple of minutes to make arrangements before Roger found himself following the innkeeper up the stairs towards the rooms. Outside, Jerrod and Amanda stood together with the hoods of their riding cloaks pulled over their heads as the remaining soldiers led the horses towards a stable.

"I don't want to be seen. I might be recognized and I don't want word to get to my family before we visit them in the morning," Jerrod confessed.

"What do you want to do?"

"Come here," Jerrod said as he put his arms around her.

In an instant they were in the second floor hallway behind Roger. Jerrod paused, looking into Amanda's eyes to see how she reacted to projecting into the inn. She did not push him away, but leaned in as close as she could.

"What?" Roger exclaimed, causing Amanda to giggle.

"Sorry. I didn't want to be seen coming up the stairs," Jerrod explained.

"What are you going to do next?" Roger asked a little shaken.

After they went to their own rooms, Jerrod was undressing when there was a knock on his door. When he opened the door, Amanda stood before him with two tankards of ale.

"I thought you would enjoy a drink." Amanda smiled.

By Aphrodite, you are so beautiful, Jerrod thought.

"And the company," Jerrod answered.

They drank and talked about the events leading up to Terrace Xul and remembering happier times with Thomas and Roger at the Axe & Bow before they left on their adventure. But their fondest memories included Drin.

"Will you stay?" Jerrod asked when Amanda rose to leave.

She reached out with one hand to gently touch his jaw, looking down into his azure-blue eyes.

Follow your heart, not momentary desire. Isn't that what Fraum said? She looked into his eyes.

I truly love him, she admitted to herself.

"Yes," Amanda whispered. She took him by the hand and led him to the bed.

"But only to sleep," Amanda said as she pulled him gently into the bed.

✻   ✻   ✻   ✻   ✻

When Amanda woke early she put on a long skirt rather than her normal tight leather pants, and then brushed her hair. The feeling of the brush and then her hair resting on her back was comforting. Jerrod rose as she finished. His smile warmed her heart.

"I thought I would wear this to meet your family. Do you like it?" Amanda said as she stood up for him to see.

"It's very nice, thank you. I love the skirt."

Roger was already downstairs when they approached the table for the morning meal. The smell of the warm bread, eggs, and crispy bacon served on wooden plates heightened Amanda's senses. She stretched, enjoying the morning just a little more.

"It is going to be a wonderful day," she said, smiling at Jerrod again.

"You remind me of the fun we had at the Axe & Bow," Roger commented.

Jerrod returned her smile, appreciating the beauty of her full lips and fair skin. For a moment they sat like a young couple in love, drinking in the spirit of their relationship. Then Jerrod turned to Roger.

"We will be gone most of the day. We may not return until after dark. These are wonderful people. Get to know them, enjoy the village, but please don't let on that I am Lord Trisdale. They all know me as Jerrod," he requested as he stood up.

Pulling his gray travel cloak over his shoulders and his hood up over his head, Jerrod turned to walk towards the door.

"A little warm for a cloak, isn't it?" Amanda teased, batting her heavy eyelashes as if to entice Jerrod to stay.

You're too beautiful, Jerrod thought.

"You're in a good mood," Roger commented.

"I got a good night's sleep," Amanda answered, her smile broadening.

Amanda and Jerrod rode east down the path of the wagon wheel road. The morning was already growing hot. The shade from the trees seemed to do little to lower the heat, so once they were out of the village, Jerrod slipped his riding cloak off, laying it back over his horse's rump and tying it to the saddle as they rode.

"It was just over a year ago that I set out on foot down this road to meet you," Jerrod thought out loud.

"For me? And I thought you came to Torrence for fame and fortune," Amanda teased.

"Were you in Dionysus's wine last night?" Jerrod said in jest.

"I feel like I did before we left Torrence with Nathanial. Everything was good then. Do you remember our days together?"

"Yes, fondly. Life was much simpler then," Jerrod reflected.

"And much cheaper, but we got by." Amanda laughed.

"You have accomplished a lot, Jerrod. You dared to chase your dream," Amanda said more seriously.

Do I have the courage to chase mine? she thought.

As she finished her thought Jerrod's face went blank. He continued watching her.

"What?"

"I'm sorry. It's nothing. Amanda, what is your dream?" Jerrod answered.

"I left the monastery to answer that question," Amanda answered before looking away.

Down the wagon trail the high peak of a thatched roof cradled in the trees came into view. A thin line of smoke rose out of the stone chimney from a fire, cooking the morning meal. As they approached the cottage they could hear the grinding of the nearby stone mill.

"Already at work," Jerrod commented.

Amanda looked at him.

"The donkey is turning the mill. My father will be filling the fifty pound sacks and my brother stacking them."

"What will your family think of me?" Amanda blurted out.

Jerrod looked at her; Amanda's long blonde hair and disarming smile.

Those eyes. A woman who could have anything she wants and she's worried about what my family will think of her, Jerrod thought briefly.

"They will like you, especially my mom. But don't take any of the utensils," Jerrod said as he began to laugh.

Joining in the laughter, Amanda backhanded him on the shoulder.

"Are they silver?"

Before they had the chance to enter the clearing around the home two young voices shouted out.

"Jerrod!" Jason and Tracie yelled as they ran to greet him.

"My brother and sister," Jerrod said to Amanda.

Sliding off their horses to greet the two enthusiastic siblings, Jerrod knelt to one knee. Jason and Tracie nearly knocked him over as they dove into his outstretched arms. For a long time they did not let go.

"We missed you!" they exclaimed.

"Who is this?" Tracie asked when she finally let go.

"This is Amanda. She has been my closest friend since I left. Amanda, this is Jason and Tracie," Jerrod finished the introduction.

Friend? What else would he call me? Amanda thought.

I can't say 'lover' to my family, Amanda thought she heard Jerrod say.

She looked at him, trying to decide if he had said something, but he was immersed in the reunion and hardly seemed aware she was even there.

"You're pretty," Tracie said, taking Amanda by the hand.

"Thank you. So are you." Amanda blushed.

"That's a pretty amulet," Tracie complimented.

"Yes it is. Jerrod gave it to me," Amanda explained.

"He must really like you."

They had not reached the front of the cottage before Jerrod's mother saw them. She took a couple slow steps and then ran to throw her arms around Jerrod's neck, tears rolling freely down her cheek as she held him tight. Jerrod waited patiently, enjoying his mother's embrace, until she was ready to let go.

"Your hair? It's silver," his mother asked as she touched the same curl she always played with, and then she looked at Amanda.

"I'm sorry. Who is this?"

"Mother, this is my dearest friend, Amanda. Amanda, this is my mother, Annalisa," Jerrod said formally.

"W-Welcome to our home," Annalisa stammered out.

"Your father and Marc are already in the mill. Go see them. He has missed you," Annalisa turned from Jerrod.

"Come, Amanda, let me show you our home," Annalisa added as she took Amanda by the arm.

The short walk to the mill offered little time to prepare himself to see his father. Jerrod stepped through the mill door with his hand on the crystal orb inset in the pommel of his sword. He watched his father and brother working hard to fill flour sacks with the wheat they had ground on the mill stone. Marc was tending to the donkey as his father sewed up a sack.

"May I help you, Sire?" Andrew said, startled by the presence of a soldier in the doorway.

Jerrod smiled.

"Jerrod? Jerrod!" his father exclaimed.

"Hey Marc," Jerrod answered, stepping forward.

"Son, wow. It's great to see you. Marc! Your brother is here. How've you been? By the Fates, you look good."

"Life has been tough, but the reward has been worth it," Jerrod opened up.

"Life usually is, son," Andrew responded as he put down his sewing needle and stepped away from the flour sacks.

"Does your mother know you are here?"

"Yes, we saw her when we rode in."

"We?" Marc asked.

"I'm here with Amanda. She is…" Jerrod stopped.

"Amanda? Sounds serious. Coming home with a woman." Andrew looked at his son.

"Well, it is. Actually she's one of two women that I love."

"Two?" his father's eyebrows raised a bit.

"They are both wonderful. Rhonda is a half-Elve druid princess. Amanda is, well, Amanda is Amanda. She's wonderful. She is everything." Jerrod paused as his father looked at him.

"She's here. If we can go inside you can meet her," Jerrod suggested.

Andrew looked around the mill and the work that still needed to be done.

"Sure. I'd love to meet her," he said, taking off his gloves and laying them on a nearby bench.

When they entered their home, Amanda was sitting in the middle of the room, surrounded by Jerrod's family, with the largest grin Jerrod had ever seen on her face. Her eyes seemed to twinkle as Annalisa filled her in with all sorts of stories about Jerrod's childhood. Gabrielle was watching and listening, learning many things about her brother-in-law she had not heard before. Jason and Tracie were lying on the floor listening intently with the hope of adding something about each story as it was told.

After the childhood stories Jerrod told them about their adventure to retrieve the secret treasure from Terrace Xul. He described the battles with exciting detail and emphasized the severity of Rhonda's wounds. He was short and factual when describing Nathanial's treachery and avoided everything after Agganon until the group was reunited for Drin's accolade.

"Actually, it was Amanda who introduced me to Nathanial, which started our quest. She's the reason for our good fortune in more ways than one," Jerrod concluded.

"Have you heard that Lord Trisdale is visiting Winfred? Did you meet him when you came home?" Gabrielle asked, changing the topic to the local gossip.

"Tell them." Amanda giggled, raising her head to look at Jerrod. "Tell them or I will," Amanda insisted.

"Tell us what?" Annalisa asked.

Jerrod looked around the room of the meager countryside cottage.

"I am Lord Trisdale. King Derik appointed me when we returned from Terrace Xul."

Everyone seemed to stop breathing as time was lost in the moment. Only the quiet crackle of the small cooking fire that lit the inside of the cottage could be heard as Jerrod's family stared at him in disbelief.

"You're Lord Trisdale!" Jason exclaimed, looking first at his brother and then at Amanda.

Amanda nodded her head.

If I had a family like this, Amanda thought.

You will, Jerrod's thought intruded again.

What? Athena, who am I? she thought again to herself.

Amanda felt odd praying to the goddess of wisdom. She had sought the guidance and protection of Hermes most of her life and relied on the Fates as a thief must, but now she needed something more, but felt nothing from the Olympians.

Just as you left me in Haithenbeurn, without an answer, Amanda's anger flared.

They finished the evening meal, washing it down with wine in celebration of Jerrod's return and his new position with the young king of Torrence.

"I am rebuilding Trisdale Keep. It's isolated, but I could use a good miller," Jerrod offered his father.

"We are well established here, son. Perhaps we could visit," his father replied.

"You're always welcome," Jerrod answered as he handed his father a modest sized pouch and used his other hand to close his father's hand around the gems.

"If you ever have need of anything, send for me," Jerrod finished.

"I am proud of you, son. You made your dreams come true," his father stated.

After saying their tearful goodbyes Amanda and Jerrod mounted their horses. Andrew lingered at the side of his sons horse.

"Don't forget where you came from," Andrew said, looking down and patting his son's knee.

"I... I love you, son," he stammered, choking back the tears.

"I love you, Father. Thank you." Jerrod responded, his heart bursting with joy.

Annalisa stepped up to take Andrew's hand as they watch Jerrod and Amanda ride away.

"That's our boy," Andrew whispered causing Annalisa to lean into him and rest her head on his chest.

The ride back under the green and purple moons of Dendür was enchanting. The weather was not too warm and the wine had lightened their spirits.

Jerrod and Amanda repeatedly glanced at each other, flirting like they'd just been introduced.

"You have a wonderful family, Jerrod. I would give anything to have a family," Amanda reflected.

"I am not a great lord. I am a miller's son. It's not really much," Jerrod told her.

"It's everything," Amanda answered.

Jerrod looked at her. Her chilling blue eyes seemed to shine in the moonlight. He loved how her long hair hung straight down her back and the voluptuous curves of her athletic body.

It's not her beauty I love, it's the things she does, her joy in life, her ability to overcome anything. And she can kick my ass, his thoughts making him laugh to himself.

"What is it?" Amanda asked.

"I am a fool. You're wonderful," Jerrod said, stopping to look at her in the moonlight.

"This has been a wonderful evening. Thank you."

"You're welcome. You know I wanted fame and fortune, but it's not what I expected," Jerrod added.

"What did you expect?" Amanda asked.

How do I answer that? I'm not sure I even know, Jerrod thought, speechless.

"I don't know, but not this."

When they got back to the inn, Jerrod reached up to grab Amanda's waist and help her off her horse. Her body slid down next to his as he lowered her slowly to the ground, falling into a deep kiss.

"Will you stay with me again tonight?" Jerrod gasped.

Amanda looked up at him, her arms around his waist. They were both breathing hard, excited by their lingering contact.

"Just to sleep," Jerrod reassured her.

"I don't know if I can do that tonight."

"We can. I will protect you." Jerrod grinned.

"You are my protector."

Resting her forehead on his chest, Amanda relented. They lay down together in Jerrod's room and, without even a button of her bodice undone, Amanda waited patiently until Jerrod's breathing slowed before she rose.

Fraum's right. I need to know who I am before I can know who we are, my love, she thought.

"I love you," Amanda whispered before she departed.

✻   ✻   ✻   ✻   ✻

When Jerrod awoke alone in the morning and Amanda's room was empty, he sat down in the middle of the room to concentrate. Using his mind he reached out, trying to use the magic to find her.

Amanda? He concentrated his thoughts, but there was nothing.

Jerrod slowly admitted to himself that she had left. All he could do was finish his mission, to return to Lord Trisdale's gravesite and collect his bones.

By the Fates, I hope that I'm not destined to the same end, Jerrod thought.

Roger met him in the stable, the two soldiers with them were mounted and waiting outside.

"Amanda's horse is gone," Roger stated when he saw Jerrod.

"She apparently left last night."

"What happened?" Roger asked.

"I wish I knew."

"She has always had a mind of her own," Roger pointed out.

Jerrod looked at him, nodding in agreement without saying a word.

"Jerrod, may I ask something as an old friend?"

"What is it?"

"You two have always been close, ever since the Axe & Bow, but now you seem affectionate?"

"I saved her life."

"Is that it?"

"No, but that's all I can talk about."

When they arrived at the mound of rocks the priest was ready and they began their journey back to Trisdale Keep. They followed the north-south road past the turn to Torrence, and continued northward to the western edge of the Plateau of Kronese. Taking the pass up the plateau, they turned back south towards Trisdale Keep, where they intended to inter Lord Trisdale's bones in his empty crypt.

The priest's ceremony was brief and the lid of the large, glossy-black

obelisk was quickly slid back into place. When it was done, the others left
Jerrod standing next to the crypt below the ruins of Trisdale.

"Sleep well. I don't know if you rest in the underworld with Hades. Perhaps
the Asgardians are right and there is a place for heroes. All I know is that this
lonely act is far less than any man deserves," Jerrod said quietly as he looked
upon the smooth surface of the stone.

The next day Jerrod began overseeing the long process of rebuilding the
keep. All the soldiers worked with the stone masons and general laborers side-
by-side, fostering a society of equals instead of the more common monarchy.
Jerrod had seen the benefit of the Elven approach to leadership. If he could be
close to those he commanded and still retain his authority, things would be done
better and people would be happier. Loyalty would grow in place of resentment.

*   *   *   *   *

What was it Fraum had said? My true quest may be discovering who I am,
Amanda thought as she nudged her horse out of the Winfred stable.

It had been easy for her to slip away in the night, even dressed as she was
with only a dagger in her boot. Traveling alone allowed her to set her own pace.
The only stop she made was to stay a night at Drin's burial site. White flowers
were starting to bloom on the burial mounds and pine saplings were sprouting
around his grave.

"You died a hero, which is what you always wanted," Amanda whispered to
Drin's grave. "Rest easy with your brothers of the Order. Rest in the care of
Sir Michael."

Even for being exhausted from the relentless riding, her sleep was
uncommonly restful and in the morning she rose with a renewed sense of
energy, feeling vibrant. There was no residual effect of the days of riding, half
sleeping in the saddle. Even her horse seemed rested. After a quick bite, Amanda
mounted her horse to continue northwesterly across the Plain of Demeter.

There was nothing out of the ordinary as she trotted across the bridge
before Torrence or entering the island city. The city still had increased soldiers
at the gate and on the walls, but she did not appear to be a threat and passed
through without questioning. At the stable where Jerrod had worked the old
man did not ask about their trip or where Jerrod was. He just took her horse and

went back to his other business. Even the moderate temperature left Amanda with a feeling of loss.

It's like nothing has happened, but it's somehow different. They go about their days without seeing anything. This is not my city. I don't belong here anymore.

Amanda's walk through the city towards home was dream-like. At first she wasn't really sure that it was happening, but as she approached the secret entrance to her home she slipped back into consciousness.

Passing through her secret door she immediately smelled the dry dust that had accumulated in her absence. Inside everything was exactly where she had left it. Her rope bed with the feather mattress and comforter was still in the corner. The wine bottle was still on the small table near the middle of the room and, next to it, the long wooden box that Fraum had given her. But the room and its belongings no longer felt like hers.

Spinning slowly in the middle of the room, Amanda looked at the things hanging on her walls. Her emotions still lost, Amanda went to her treasury. The moderate size chest and items on the shelves were untouched. The sight of the shelf where the Horn had rested made her think.

Valhalla.

Amanda closed the secret door to the treasure room behind her and looked at her room again in silence. Nothing drew her attention.

I don't want to be here, she thought.

It did not take her long to work her way back to the cobblestone streets in the upper part of Torrence, away from the wharf area. After blindly following her footsteps she found herself standing in front of the Axe & Bow. She stood staring at the wooden sign above the door before finally entering.

Inside Tabatha was carting drinks to tables surrounded by armed men who were drinking and singing, the volume of their songs drowning out all conversation. Signaling for a pint, Amanda found a dark corner from which she could sit with her back to the wall and watch. She knew the innkeeper and barmaid very well, though they did not recognize her dressed in a bodice and skirt, even with her long blonde hair hanging down her back. Neither the surroundings nor the ale offered any comfort.

It's the same, but somehow different, she thought.

As she drank the men began a new song, one she had not heard before.

Beyond the reach of care, you lie in quiet rest,
Our hearts recall your deeds, the last your very best,
Oh sons, oh fathers all, depart without protest,
So now to your valor, in song we shall attest.

Answer'd the call to battle march'd the kingdom's brave,
Swords sharp and shields held high, fearless both knight and knave,
Your king has called, to arms, to arms, your foe threatens,
And for Torrence glory assured, our King's army depends,
Kissing wife and child's face, fall in to soldiers' ranks,
and save our lives with blood, you all deserve our thanks,
So full of pride our men marched out without concern,
We waved them off awaiting their heroes return.

Beyond the reach of care, you lie in quiet rest,
Our hearts recall your deeds, the last your very best,
Oh sons, oh fathers all, depart without protest,
So now to your valor, in song we shall attest.

They rode onto the field, while letting banners fly,
with sword and lance they rode to war, their heads held high,
Their foe seem'd weak, their numbers appear'd far too small,
Charging into waiting ambush they all did fall,
Valiantly they gather'd upon the bloody plain,
The last to die stood guard while he endure'd their pain,
Evil forces sprung forth, from the shadows they creep,
In death their souls delivered to Hades to sleep.

Beyond the reach of care, you lie in quiet rest,
Our hearts recall your deeds, the last your very best,
Oh sons, oh fathers all, sent into crypt too soon,
All that's left in memory is to sing this tune.

Drin. Thomas. What has become of you? Amanda questioned as she looked into the half drank tankard of ale in her hand. *At least Fernando did you well.*

Amanda rose from her seat, leaving the tankard on the table. With her eyes cast upon the floor she made her way directly to the door. No one asked why she was leaving. No one called out her name.

The inn was not far from her home and, after taking her normal precautions, she was back in the familiar room, sitting at her table. After pouring some wine into a clay mug, she sat down and began taking off her boots.

What did the song say? Evil forces? she thought as she slipped her first boot off. *Evil forces? Nathanial!*

After finishing the wine and removing her bodice she let her skirt fall to the floor before climbing into bed with her blouse on. The thoughts of Nathanial and Drin faded when the thoughts of her life washed into her consciousness like the waves of the fjord crashing over the bow of Grogan's ship.

"Athena, don't abandon me. Give me the wisdom to answer my quest," she prayed as she closed her eyes and rolled over to sleep.

✳   ✳   ✳   ✳   ✳

In Olympus, far from Dendür, Athena watched the image of Amanda falling asleep in her orb. Turning to her owl, Athena stoked the creature's head with the back of her fingers as she thought a moment.

"Hermes has abandoned her even though she was one of his best thieves. Or, perhaps, she abandoned him. No matter." Athena looked away, out between the marble columns into the starry sky.

"She could be a devout follower. This is a wonderful opportunity, but the witch could be a problem. She won't like my being involved so close to her prize," Athena pondered aloud.

"Should I torment Felicia a little?" the goddess of wisdom asked her owl.

✳   ✳   ✳   ✳   ✳

In the morning Amanda awoke less refreshed than she had on the battlefield, but she was rested, nonetheless. Although she felt some attachment to her surroundings again, she still struggled with the feeling of no longer belonging.

This is not the place for me. I am no longer this person, but where do I go from here?

Amanda rose and, after putting on her skirt and bodice, began packing. Pausing a moment to consider her selection, she took a black shirt, jacket, and pants, and a white blouse from the trunk at the foot of her bed. After retrieving a bag of gems from her treasure chest, she began filling a small pack. From the weapons hanging on her wall she removed the recurve bow and tied it to the pack. Taking one last look at her small, windowless room, Amanda stopped to touch the rope belt from the White Fists.

"The monk's belt. A simple weapon," Amanda said as the balls clacked together.

I will never forget your compassion, Fraum.

After stuffing the belt into the pack Amanda headed out, but at the door she paused. Turning back around she went to the table, where she flipped open the walnut box.

Amanda looked down at the pair of Elven swords for a moment before picking one up.

Sister swords. Light. Balanced.

Spinning the sword around a couple times and then slashing across her body, she tested the Elven sword. She peered down at the slightly curved silver blade.

This feels right. I am still a warrior, but for whom? Where do I belong?

Amanda gathered her hair up and braided it as she had in Haithenbeurn as she considered whether to take the swords. When she was done she looked at the weapons resting in the box again and then at her pack.

I'll tie them into the pack, she decided.

She set a trap on the door then crossed the roof and returned to the streets of Torrence. Walking the cobblestone streets without a purpose, she ended up in one of the finer markets. As she walked by a tailor's shop, a brown suede forester's jacket with long sleeves, two pockets, a flap that surrounded the shoulders, and a hood to keep the rain off caught her eye.

That reminds me of the Elves' jackets, Amanda thought as she found herself buying the jacket. *The Elves of Lithlillia, and the herd of centaurs. I miss Sarric.*

Walking towards the stable where her horse was kept, Amanda stopped briefly at the smithy to buy scabbards for the Elven swords and a quiver for some arrows. She found a leather frog and scabbard rig with straps that would allow her to attach a sword on each side of her hips. She also found a tubular quiver that held more than a dozen arrows. She filled up the quiver at a nearby fletcher before continuing on for her horse.

When she reached the stable, she saddled her horse, carefully tying the swords and quiver to her saddle. With her backpack strapped behind the saddle's cantle, Amanda stepped into the stirrup and swung her leg over the horse. Just as unceremonious as her arrival had been, her departure went without notice.

A young woman in a hooded riding robe, only the heels of her knee-high boots showing, departing across the bridge alone, left nothing for anyone to remember.

CHAPTER 15

ASSEMBLY OF ARMS

Nathanial had returned to the Dark Elves' kingdom to celebrate their victories. The death of the king was good. It would have been better had they also been successful killing the Prophet, but the Crimson Pommel had informed him of the failure. He realized that killing the High Master had always been an issue of luck. But the death of Jacob!

That arrogant ass got his, Nathanial thought.

If only we had killed Drok-na too, Rok-lin responded from his cave.

Dragons and scales! We'll get him in good time. All in good time, Nathanial answered sharply.

I want to feel his neck snap between my teeth.

With news of the massacre, the king of the Dark Elves fulfilled his promise, releasing twenty-five hundred Elven warriors to Nathanial's command. They were packed with gear and weapons, ready for a long march. They left in single file, all in black, starting out of the Wilds Forest eastward towards the mountain range. Marching out of the deciduous forest up the slope through the pines and on towards the jagged, barren ridge where they intended to cross at the Wilds Mountain range, they would march through Sismen Pass and continue east along the Brisbane Mountains until they reached their destination, the newly constructed encampment on the northeastern slope of the Brisbanes.

Hunting parties killed fresh meat, slaughtering every deer and elk they saw and at the top of the ridge they killed mountain sheep, but there was not enough game to feed the army. As much as she objected, Nathanial tasked Rok-lin to hunt for the army, causing her to fly many miles before finding fresh herds or swooping down on cottages in Torrence to steal cows at night.

As the army began to cross the ridge of the Wild Mountains, Nathanial mounted Rok-lin to fly on to the Fendür village at Sismin Pass. When they got to the village they found only females, children, and very old male giants remained in the village. The men had gone on to join Nathanial's army.

Very soon, Rok-lin, very soon, Nathanial thought.

Very soon? the young adult dragon responded.

The Dark Elves will rest here before moving on to join the waiting army. And then we march on Torrence in full force. I will sit on the throne in Torrence very soon.

*   *   *   *   *

The victorious army crossed the Plain of Demeter and descended into the U'thra Plain, leaving a wide path of destruction before reaching the Gap of Dillandria. The U'thra bows had held off the giants, but the arrows only delayed the trolls and the few Were-Folk that traveled with them. The Dark Elves, watching as the more primeval creatures ravaged each village, marched onward, leaving the others to follow along their path.

Lumbering north towards the eastern end of the Brisbane Mountains, they passed between the Black Forest and the Meadows far west of Silandria. The giants, trolls, and giant-trolls of the Fendür still straggled along behind the single file of Dark Elves, the remaining Were-Folk skirting the army as though they were patrolling for trouble. Even a child could track the trail they left behind them. When they arrived at the new fortress on the northern slope of the Brisbane Mountains, the raiding army was tired and worn down.

The Fendür village, on the southern edge of the fortress, was overwhelmed by the new construction. The village was uphill from the crude log buildings and thousands of tents that provided temporary lodging to the growing army. The trees had been cut away to form a practice ground. The field was enclosed by logs, cut from the forest that grew in the Brisbane Mountains.

When the army returned, the encampment was already swelling with the Dark Elven army and more wizards, nearly half the wizards of the Triad. The sight of a bluish-green dragon sleeping on its belly with its chin resting on a foreleg in the middle of the compound concerned the arriving troops.

They were directed to the main cabin where Nathanial was waiting. When the leader of the Dark Elves reported, he lay a large red ruby on the table before Nathanial.

"We exterminated five hundred horse-warriors and a hundred foot-warriors from Torrence before we started our return. On our way here we raided villages on the grass plains. Nothing in are path remained. This is the only valuable treasure that was found. Your Fendür allies are strong and will follow simple battle orders, but they are not soldiers," the Dark Elven archer leading the raiders reported.

"I know, but they serve my purpose. Thank you." Nathanial smiled as he picked up the ruby.

✳   ✳   ✳   ✳   ✳

I don't know what I may find with the centaurs, but Sarric has a unique perspective. A non-human perspective that may enlighten me, Amanda thought as she turned her horse north onto the north-south road that skirted the western edge of the Plain of Demeter.

It was nearing mid-summer and the weather was no longer just warm. By mid-morning she had removed her new jacket, carefully strapping it down over her pack behind the saddle. Mid-day brought the real heat, making the plain more than just uncomfortable.

Amanda continued north for a few more days before arriving at Torrence River Crossing. In place of the inn that had been built on the plain side of the river was a stone chimney standing in cinders and the remnants of wooden beams, blackened by fire. Two stone columns that had been used to support the wagon-bridge rose out of the river, ghostly markers of what had once been the river crossing. Amanda got off her horse to kick over some of the rubble from the inn.

By all the Fates, what's happened? Where's Imelrinn when you need him? she thought as she looked around, amused by the realization of how much she missed the Elve. *I may as well cross tonight. I'll be dry in the morning and can continue the journey more comfortably.*

Leading her horse into the water, Amanda waded out until the river was deep enough she had to swim. Holding onto the saddle as she swam next to her horse, she let its body block the river current, allowing them to go almost straight across the river as the sun set over the Wild Mountain range, casting a long shadow over the river. On the other side she turned south, away from the road to find a secluded camp site.

After pitching her tent and building a small fire for cooking, she removed her wet clothing and grabbed her riding robe to cover herself while she laid all her clothes out to dry. Cleaning and oiling her gear as she ate, Amanda sipped on warm tea and glanced at the river from time to time until she finished. Afterward she sat, staring at the river as though she were meditating in the monastery. At last she rose from her seat near the fire to walk to the river's edge.

Dropping her robe off her shoulders, Amanda waded into the river to bathe under the light of Questill and Dori. The foliage glistened in green and purple tints of the moonlight. With crickets and frogs singing under the crisp starlight of the summer night, Amanda fell back, letting herself drift on her back, allowing the cool river water to wash over her face, but that feeling, that sixth sense developed by thieves that protects and guides them through their "recovery" efforts, began tingling across her skin.

Something's wrong.

Wading back to the river bank, Amanda reached for her clothing but froze, standing as still as the statute in front of the Cathedral instead of picking anything up.

I am a warrior. Am I left for you, mighty Aries, or you, my Lady Athena? Hermes has abandoned me.

Her hand moved slowly for the black leather pants she typically wore as thief. She quietly wormed into the pants and then reached for her black shirt. It took more time to dress than she wanted, but when she was done she reached for the circular shape of the U'thra bow. Taking care to quietly restring the bow as she had been shown, she pulled the quiver closer and relocated the two Elven swords and the silver dagger to a spot within her reach.

She could hear the heavy breathing of nearby animals. Slinging the quiver over her shoulder, Amanda picked up a sword and moved to her horse. She listened quietly until the breathing faded and then moved back to her tent.

In the sleepless dreams that followed Amanda envisioned six riders pulling a travois crossing the river on their way to Cipper. An odd group it was, consisting of a wizard, two warriors in chainmail, a female warrior dressed in tight black leather, a sage in tan robes drawing in a book, and an Elven guardian. On the travois was a motionless, half-Elven druid. The vision of the group that she had been part of the year before haunted her throughout the night.

Morning came too early. Moving slowly from fatigue after a night of worries, Amanda gathered her belongings. Instead of mounting her horse once it was saddled, Amanda leaned on the horn for a moment, pondering her choices.

The Fates set me on this course. My mind sees the ghosts of my past. My heart pulls me north. Why? What is happening to me?

She was neither aware of nor concerned about the time. It was not the issue. In that sense, she was free, but her future plagued her, creating a conflict that was nearly unbearable.

Zeus, this will be my time! she demanded from the god of order and fate.

Her prayers for self-determination took more than a moment's pause as time passed unnoticed. Her head pressed to the saddle leather as she contemplated life and love. When she calmed her mind and lifted her head, she pulled up and kicked her leg over the saddle. Sitting solidly in the saddle she felt the movement of the horse under her.

Riding northward on the road to Cipper, Amanda enjoyed the shade of the deciduous forest. The little breeze cooling the summer heat made her ride bearable and as the elevation began to rise the temperature slowly dropped, but despite the pleasant conditions she continued looking side-to-side, trying to see something that did not appear to be there. She strained to see the threat her thief's sense told her was there.

Before reaching Cipper, Amanda turned westward, off the road, towards the Wild's Mountain range. Winding through the forest and around the small, gentle hills, she easily found the cottage made of rounded river stones with its thatched roof. A light smoke rose out of the chimney.

Why does this feel comfortable? Was I meant to come here?

Tying her horse's reins to a tree, Amanda walked across the open area directly to the front of the house and knocked on the door before entering. Nothing had changed. It was still dark inside the witch's cottage. The opaque windows still limited the light coming into the rooms and only a small fire and a couple of lamps lit the room. The shelves and tables were still crowded with nick-knacks.

As she had before, the old woman sat on the floor pillows in front of a short table where a crystal orb rested in its gold stand. Behind her the fire burned just enough to warm the tea pot that hung from an iron arm, resting where it had been pushed over the fire. Next to the witch lay the large black panther.

"Welcome back, Amanda," Felicia greeted her.

"You knew I was coming, didn't you? You always know."

"I saw you here," the witch answered, reaching out to touch the orb with the tips of her long fingers.

Inside the crystal a fog stirred. The panther yawned, showing its large fangs, and then turned to look at Felicia.

"Have a seat. I will pour some tea. Sasha wants to know about the battle."

"I see you still have the silver dagger I gave you. And what a pretty amulet," Felicia added.

Looking down as her fingers instinctively reached for the oval cut gem, Amanda took a moment before responding. The old woman had helped her, but still, she was in the witch's lair.

"It was given to me by a dear friend."

"Ahh, how is Jerrod these days?"

"You remember Jerrod?"

"Yes. He visited me that day just before your visit."

She is in pain. Lost. Don't torment her, Sasha thought in a whisper.

"And the wizard? What happened to Nathanial?" the witch asked softly.

I can't read her mind. It must be the amulet Jerrod found, Felicia thought to Sasha.

"He betrayed us all." Amanda looked at the witch as her eyebrows dipped to the bridge of her nose.

"I feared he might. Tea?"

They drank tea as they sat talking about the trip to Terrace Xul, of Ornholtz, Theasendür, and Asenthia. When Amanda mentioned Silandria, Felicia shifted awkwardly.

"What is it?" Amanda asked.

"Nothing, nothing. So you returned the Horn of Valhalla to Torrence," Felicia stated.

"I did not mention the horn," Amanda challenged her.

"Child. King Randver's witch belonged to my coven," Felicia said as she changed into a beautiful woman with long black hair.

"Of course I knew," Felicia patted the panther's head as the beast turned into a large house cat.

"Belonged?"

"Randver beheaded the old woman. But that was his last mistake."

Deciding she did not want to know the answer to the question of what had happened to the king, Amanda finished her story. By the end Sasha was lying in Amanda's lap, purring as Amanda scratched behind the cat's ears.

I like this woman. She needs a good friend. I think I will travel with her for a while, Sasha thought.

Good. Maybe then I will learn what I need to know about Jerrod's intentions and the Dragon's Orb.

I go for my own reasons, mistress, not as your spy, the large cat corrected her.

"I think she likes you," Felicia said as she looked down at the defiant animal.

It will be better for us both if you keep me informed, Felicia warned.

"Will you stay for dinner?" Felicia asked.

"No. I must go."

"Where are you going?" Felicia asked.

"Cipper," Amanda's answer was, at least, partially true.

As Amanda rose to leave, Sasha changed back into a panther.

"I will send Sasha with you. She can travel as fast as any horse and is a fierce companion. She understands commands, but doesn't always choose to listen. I am afraid she has a mind of her own sometimes," Felicia said.

Send? Sasha looked at the witch.

How else do you want me to explain it to a thief?

"No, I couldn't take your pet," Amanda protested.

"I'm afraid there is very little choice. Sasha will follow you anyway."

Amanda reached down to scratch the panther behind her ears.

When they departed, Amanda went to her horse alone at first. She found the creature was skittish and tried to comfort it by patting its neck while the large cat hung back. Taking each side of its head and looking into its eyes, she watched his ears until he rotated them forward, upright, off of his neck.

"I don't know if you understand me, but we have a new friend traveling with us. I'm not sure you will like her, but it will be okay."

When Sasha walked slowly into view the horse pulled back, twisting its hindquarters away from the large cat, but not so much as to pull away from Amanda. Throwing the reins around her horse's neck and throwing her foot into the stirrup, Amanda swung effortlessly up onto the horse's back and turned north towards Cipper.

"What am I going to do with you when we get to Cipper? The Elders will undoubtedly have a problem with you," Amanda asked, looking back at the cat.

It was near sundown when they approached Cipper. Amanda sat in the forest watching for the torches being lit by guards taking their posts on the log walls, but none came. When it was dark and nothing had stirred, Amanda looked at the weapons tied to her saddle.

"Sword or bow, Sasha?" Amanda thought aloud, smiling at the large cat when no answer came. "Let me guess, cat's got your tongue?"

Drawing one of the Elven blades from its scabbard, Amanda turned to walk across the meadow surrounding Cipper. As she crossed the meadow she could see the gate was missing. In the dark it was hard to see into the quiet village. Ten paces behind her the large cat sauntered towards the village.

When she reached the entrance, Amanda peered into the burnt ruins. Squinting in the growing darkness Amanda began making out the charred remains of the villagers scattered through the streets.

"What in Hades' name?"

The panther looked up at her and then back to the streets. Sasha let out a challenging roar.

Amanda made her way towards the center of the village. The eerie sense of the dead was troubling. Stopping to look closely at a body, she knelt down. Drawing the dagger from her boot, Amanda used the blade to lift the charred remains up and examine the under layer, the long Elven blade pointed off to the side, ready if needed.

"Look at these gaps where the flesh was torn away before it was burned. This must be a bite and this gash across the chest looks more like claw marks." She paused. "The Were-Folk?"

Sasha roared again. Amanda stood up and looked around. A light smell of burnt flesh lingered on the structures.

"We must go now. I must find Sarric."

Amanda turned and ran out of the village to her horse with Sasha bounding after her. She did not hesitate, leaping into the saddle to turn the horse northward and kick the steed into action. They started at a gallop, but when they were clear of the village, they slowed to a walk. Amanda knew the journey would be many days and the horse would not be able to run the entire way.

After a day's ride north, Amanda found the small open hilltop with its crowning boulders where they had slept before. After taking the saddle off her horse, Amanda staked its reins to the ground inside the ring of the large boulders. Then she withdrew her black shirt from her pack.

"Someone is following us, Sasha. I don't know if it's man, or beast, or both," Amanda said to the panther.

I am not a thief anymore, but it appears I must set a trap again.

Amanda built a large fire near the center of the boulders. After dark she stepped into the shadows to strap on the double sword scabbard and frog rig. Leaning her bow and quiver in the shadow of one of the large boulders, Amanda returned to the light of the camp. She filled her bedroll with her pack and spare clothing, making it look as if she slept near one of the tall boulders.

"I need you to be a cat until the attack. They must think we are sleeping. We need one survivor. Do you understand? One survivor. I need to send a message to their leader," Amanda said, looking into the panther's eyes as Sasha changed into a large, black, housecat.

"Thank you."

The attack did not come until long after dark when three assassins crept into the encampment. On the far side one drew his bow, looking for the panther they had watched enter the hill's stone crown. Not seeing the panther, he decided to shoot Amanda where she appeared to be sleeping. As he released his arrow, two more assassins entered from opposite sides with their swords drawn. As the arrow struck the bedroll Amanda stepped into the circle from behind the nearest boulder and Sasha became a panther.

"Kill the archer," Amanda directed.

Leaping from where she had been sleeping, Sasha landed her outstretched forepaws on the archer's chest, digging her claws deep into his body with a death grip. Biting the man's head and driving him to the ground, Sasha's tail whipped from side to side. The fierceness of the attack stopped the others in their tracks, glancing between Sasha and Amanda.

"Didn't they tell you who I am?" Amanda asked.

"They said you betrayed the Guild and not to underestimate you," one answered with a shaken voice.

"I am Amanda of Torrence," she stated defiantly.

"The thief who stole the Horn of Valhalla?"

"Yes. I'm tired of thieves and death threats," Amanda warned.

"You can't threaten the Guild Master and expect to walk away. No one quits," the other responded.

"Don't push me. I'm done. I won't be part of this anymore."

One assassin stepped more cautiously towards Amanda, circling around the perimeter of the stones, trying to choose the best attack. His sword wavered a little from his trembling hand. Drawing his dagger as he walked, his eyes never leaving Amanda, he inched forward while the other assassin watched Sasha, glancing briefly towards Amanda and his partner.

When the attack finally came it was quick. The first assassin thrust his dagger towards Amanda's chest, holding his sword back to follow with a slashing attack. Stepping to the outside to avoid the thrust, Amanda grabbed his dagger hand at the wrist and spun, turning her back towards the assassin, and then twisting his elbow over his shoulder, causing him to land on his back before he could swing his sword. The two swords on her hips bounced against her thighs as Amanda maneuvered through the fight.

At first the assassin was just rocking on the ground, moaning. Struggling to get to his knees, he pushed off the ground but his left shoulder was dislocated and he fell back to the ground, unable to withstand the pain.

"You should have brought more men if you were unwilling to leave me alone," Amanda said emotionlessly as she stepped back.

Struggling to his knees again, her assailant's left arm hung motionless. He picked his sword up off the ground with the other hand and began circling again. Amanda glanced at the second assassin. When he took a step to join the attack, Sasha attacked, dragging the man to the ground with her strong paws. Sasha's claws tore through his chest ripping it open. Sasha's large yellow eyes fixed on the dying man for a moment before she let out a triumphant roar.

Turning back to face the man in front of her, Amanda paused with her feet shoulder width apart, ready for his attack. The tip of the assassin's sword pointed directly at her face as he seemed to weigh the situation.

Twisting his wrist to sweep his sword over his head and slash across his body, he lunged forward with resumed confidence. Jumping to the side, with her two swords dangling awkwardly from her sides, Amanda blocked the assassin's sword hand outward with the heel of her hand and, using her other elbow, struck the man under the chin. As the assassin's head flew back Amanda brought her knee up above her waist and snapping her foot outward, struck the assassin in the chest, sending him reeling backward.

The ground jarred the sword from his good hand when he landed on his back, but the assassin immediately began scrambling to recover. Rising up on his remaining elbow and pushing with his heels he started crawling away backwards. Amanda looked at Sasha as the man retreated.

"I have a message for the Crimson Pommel," Amanda commanded, turning back to the crawling man.

"What? What is it?" the man's voice crackled.

Sasha turned to stand behind Amanda, her eyes watching the remaining assassin as she roared again.

"I am coming for them. I tried to quit. I tried to let it be. I warned them. I told them if they came after me or any of my friends they would die." Amanda stared through the man on the ground.

"Tell them I'm coming for them. Now, get out of here!"

"Let him go. He is delivering a message," Amanda commanded.

Sasha responded with a frightening scream.

✳   ✳   ✳   ✳   ✳

Days later Amanda found herself riding up to the miller's inn just south of Lithlillia. His children stopped playing to watch her ride up. At first they did not recognize her dressed in a white blouse with pillowed sleeves and bodice, and carrying a black housecat as she rode, her long blonde hair braided in an uncustomary fashion.

"Amanda!" they yelled when they finally recognized her.

Swarming her like hungry lambs thirsty for their mother's milk, they nearly knocked her over when she got off her horse. Excited to learn from her about where she had been and what she had seen, they dragged her towards the inn.

"Mother! Mother! Look who's returned!" they yelled.

Inside, question after question were thrown at her so quickly that Amanda was becoming dizzy. Most of all they were interested in Fraum and the monastery.

"You seem to know a lot about our travels," Amanda inquired.

"Jerrod visited some time ago. He told us of your adventures and Drin's knighthood," the miller's wife explained.

"Jerrod was here? He told you of Theasendür?"

"He was here, but he didn't say much about Theasendür. You traveled there, right?"

"I was there, briefly. And Drin? Jerrod didn't tell you of the battle?"

"What battle?" they all asked.

It was difficult talking about their travels leading up to Drin's death causing her voice faltered a little when she spoke of his death.

The news of Drin's death ended the questions abruptly. The miller's daughter began crying and leaped into her mother's arms. Her mother carried her away to finish cooking the evening meal. When it was ready they sat in silence eating the lamb, vegetables, and warm bread, but at the end of the meal they spoke a little more before turning in.

Amanda stayed the night in a small room on the second floor. In the morning she came downstairs with Sasha at her side in panther form, the sight causing tremendous commotion at first. After the morning meal Amanda went to the stable for the rest of her belongings. After tying the Elven swords to her pack, she hoisted it to her shoulders. When she emerged from the stable she had the pack and quiver of arrows on her shoulders, and the U'thra bow in her hand.

"What about your horse?" the miller questioned.

"It's yours. It can't go with me where I'm going and you could use another horse. Take good care of her. She was good to me."

"Thank you, Amanda. Take care. I hope you find what you're seeking," the miller responded.

He watched Amanda and the large cat walk northward into the Lithlillian forest.

"It's never safe in that forest. Fare thee well," he whispered to himself.

✲   ✲   ✲   ✲   ✲

Life since Drin's funeral had become mundane for Rhonda. It was as if each day was shrouded in grayness. To her, the sun did not shine as brightly. The forest was not as green, and the two moons offered no comfort. It was Drin's death that overwhelmed her. She liked him, certainly. Did she love him as a brother? Perhaps, in the end. But his death had called her own mortality into question.

Life can be so short. Shorter for men, for Jerrod, she thought.

In the weeks following the funeral Rhonda spent several moonlit nights at the stone altar in the meadow above Lithlillia seeking guidance from E'fretté, the natural forces of nature. She had basked in the moonlight and partaken of the mountain water, collected from a glacier on the highest peaks of the Wilds, to cleanse her spirit and receive the guidance she sought. But the guidance did not come. Her mother's words echoed in Rhonda's conscious thought.

One is born every thousand years. He has a direct connection with magic.

And if he is truly the 'Great One' he is more powerful than me, Rhonda reflected. *I don't want to wait any longer. I can't wait to be with Jerrod,* Rhonda decided as she started back down the concealed steps that led up to the druid temple.

She thought she spent the evening alone in prayer. She did not realize Imelrinn had watched her from the trees, knowing more about what was happening to her than she would ever realize, even without hearing her thoughts.

He had known forbidden love. Love that was barred by the circumstances of life. Circumstances that had not allowed him to express what he had felt for so long. He did not want Rhonda to suffer the same fate. While she had prayed for Jerrod and for their love, Imelrinn stood in the night-shadows of the trees, watching. A single tear rolled down his high-boned, Elven cheek.

✻ ✻ ✻ ✻ ✻

Jerrod's days had become routine. The two dozen men who had left ahead of him had started to clean up the keep. They worked hard collecting debris and placing the rubble in mounds near the base of the terrace. Workmen from Torrence had started to arrive as well. Cooks fed the growing mass as the terrace and walls were prepared for new building. Even the Fairy-Folk Rhonda had promised had begun showing up. And King Garrett had sent a wizard to help speed communications between the Lords of the Keeps. Jerrod noticed that the wizard the king had sent did not wear a ring from the Triad.

Garrett must not trust the Triad yet, Jerrod thought.

In a short period of time the group grew to nearly two hundred. They worked together, the soldiers, the craftsmen, and the young Lord Trisdale. With their shirts off, the men toiled constructing new rock walls with large stone cut from a quarry miles away and magically transported by the Fairy-Folk. The stones were not the quality of the original builders, but they fit into place nicely to form sturdy granite walls.

They built the gatehouses first and then started on the stable. Still others worked cleaning out the well. As the stone walls went up, Jerrod realized that he would need wooden beams from the forest.

We will plan carefully, taking straighter trees that will thin out overgrown areas, but I will have to get approval before we cut anything in the Ruhenmiur, he concluded, using the Elven word for the Black Forest of Kronese.

Jerrod loved the work. It was hard, but it was rewarding to see the gatehouse walls form slowly. From time to time, when he thought about Amanda and Rhonda, he just pushed himself to work harder and those problems disappeared, but there always seemed to be a decision to be made or a squabble to resolve.

Is this what leadership is? Solving others' problems. Things that should be so simple, that mean so much to those involved, Jerrod thought on his way back to his tent.

Like the others, his tent was inside the walls, which offered more mental reassurance than physical protection from the beasts in the Black Forest. However, rebuilding the ten foot wide outer walls was more of a monumental task than he had imagined.

What was it Imelrinn had said about Tilhelm Keep? They would have to get Dwarves to rebuild it, Jerrod thought as he sat down to take off his boots. *We could use a few Dwarves around here.*

A cook brought him some roast boar and wine for the evening meal. Being tired and hungry from the day's work, he ate quickly. Afterward he undressed and lay down to sleep, but in the dark he heard a familiar sound, the beating wings of a winged horse.

Jarrod grabbed his shirt and stepped out of his tent, expecting to see Farris. What he did not expect was to see Rhonda sliding off the back of the steed.

As she walked towards him, her green Elven riding robe swayed with each step she took. The robe seemed fluorescent in the dominant green light of Questil, which was nearly full.

"You're exquisite," Jerrod blurted out, causing Rhonda to smile. "I mean, ahh. You're a sight for sore eyes."

"I've missed you," the princess's voice was soft, her eyes changing to honey-golden.

"You can't imagine how much I've missed you," Jerrod repeated.

Leading her into his tent, he went to his small table to pour two glasses of wine. Taking both glasses in his hands he turned around to see Rhonda dressed in a translucent gown that changed colors as it moved with her breathing. The green riding robe lay on the ground around her ankles. The long, open curls of her brown hair covered her breasts, but nothing else was left to his imagination.

"Aphrodite! If you are not as beautiful as the goddess herself," Jerrod exclaimed, nearly dropping the goblets in his hands.

Rhonda smiled again as she reached for a goblet.

"Do you want me? I can't wait any longer, Jerrod," Rhonda whispered in a low, husky voice.

"Rhonda?" Jerrod said stepping back.

Reaching out, she grabbed his wrists gently. Sitting down on his cot, she pulled him towards her. The sheer fabric of the gown did not mask the shape of her figure.

"Rhonda, Elves mate for life."

"I can't wait any longer. I want it to be you. I want you for my mate."

"But?" Jerrod mumbled as Rhonda pulled at his shirt.

"Leave this to someone else. Come, be with me."

"What?" Jerrod said strongly as he pushed away.

Rhonda rose to lean on her elbows.

"This. The keep. Leave it for someone else to rebuild. I offer you my love and the rule of Lithlillia. Come back with me."

"Rhonda, this is wrong. I learned that lesson."

"Don't you want me?"

"Yes, but not like this." He paused. "And not now."

"Come to Lithlillia with me. We can be together forever."

Jerrod looked sternly at her.

She is exquisite, he thought, forgetting to protect his thoughts.

And I am all yours, forever, Rhonda reminded him.

"You are so beautiful and I love you so much," Jerrod said as he rose from the cot.

"But?" Rhonda glared at him, the golden color of her eyes beginning to bleed away.

"This is not you and this is not the right way," he said as he bent over to pick up her robe from the ground.

"I'm not Amanda, you mean. Isn't this the way she came to you?"

"Rhonda, I love you, and I love her. I don't know where this will lead and I know I haven't been fair to either of you, but you must wait. I respect you too much. You must wait. You have to be a virgin to inherit all the druid priestess's powers."

"I hate you, Jerrod!" Rhonda screamed.

Rhonda stepped rapidly towards Jerrod, yanking the robe from his hands, and punching him so hard Jerrod fell backward. Looking down at him on the ground, a breeze came up and her eyes began to glow green. Rhonda stood above him a moment, looking down to where Jerrod lay on the ground, but she turned and walked out, leaving the wind to beat wildly against the inside of the tent.

Outside, storm clouds were rolling in and lightning flashed across the sky. Rhonda walked straight to Farris and jumped on his back. Jerrod watched as they disappeared into the angry night sky.

A few nights later, with Questil in her full moon position, Jerrod sat on the remnants of the tower stairs looking up at the stars.

I would have been married today, he realized.

While he was in the tower, a plume of black smoke appeared in the courtyard, causing armed soldiers to gather in alarm.

What now? Jerrod wondered as he began to stand up.

From the twisting smoke a beautiful woman with black hair so long it hung to her ankles appeared. Despite her older age, her beauty was seductive. The mesmerized soldiers lowered their weapons and stepped towards the queen of witches.

"Where is the Lord Trisdale?" Felicia asked.

The soldiers looked towards the tower where Jerrod was standing. Walking down the stairs, he grabbed his sword belt off the banister. Buckling the belt around his waist, he walked towards the witch.

"Felicia, welcome," Jerrod greeted her.

"Jerrod, look at you." She smiled, holding out her hands to greet him. "You've been busy."

They sat on the grassy terrace to talk as a cook brought wine and a platter of meats and cheese. Playing with a piece of meat and drinking her wine, Felicia glanced down at the platter and then around the courtyard.

"Did our last meeting upset you?" the queen asked.

"It was a little unsettling."

"Have you had a chance to consider what I said?"

"I have, but I haven't changed my mind."

"Pity. You have come a long way since you visited my cottage."

"I'm glad that I can reciprocate. You were very hospitable," Jerrod said.

"Thank you. It's nice you remember. I've spoken with Amanda. I'm sorry about Nathanial. Wasn't today supposed to be your wedding day?" Felicia asked.

"Amanda?" Jerrod ignored the rest of her comment.

"Yes. She's traveling north. Didn't you know?" Felicia smiled.

"No. What brings you to Trisdale tonight?"

"A partnership."

"A partnership?" The look on Jerrod's face was stern.

"Maybe a little more. You will need help handling Nathanial." She smiled again.

"How well do you know Nathanial?" Jerrod questioned.

"Just from when we met in my cottage, but I know of the battle in Torrence."

"What else do you know?" Jerrod asked slowly.

"He has allies. Allies you are not prepared to handle."

"And what do you offer in the proposed partnership?"

"I will help you find Nathanial."

"And what do you want?" Jerrod asked.

"Nothing more than what I have already asked for. Have you thought about the orb?"

"Yes, but I'm not ready to part with it."

"And when you are?"

"You'll pledge on the Ladies Questil and Dori, your goddesses, that there is nothing else?"

"Lord Trisdale, really. I swear there is nothing else on the goddesses of the moons. Well, maybe your company from time to time."

Jerrod looked at her.

"You've had your fun with your little thief and you have turned down a druid princess. Imagine the pleasure the queen of witches could bring you." Felicia smiled again as she turned her body to let the moon highlight her silhouette.

"I will consider your offer."

"And I will wait for your answer in my cottage." Felicia's voice echoed into a whisper as she disappeared into a twisting column of black smoke. "You know the way."

"Witches," Jerrod exhaled.

Why does a witch want the sword of a fallen knight? Jerrod asked himself as he drew his sword to hold it aloft, twisting his wrist so the light of the moons reflected down the blade. *And why the interest in the orb?*

*   *   *   *   *

Amanda walked towards the forest without looking back. Before her was the patch of aspen trees near the corner of the barn, surrounded by taller pine trees.

The southern edge of Lithlillia, Amanda reflected.

Amanda started north before turning slightly west, walking at a slow pace. Her pack, weighed down by supplies and food, was heavy as she continued up the slope, winding around the small hills covered with manzanita and large granite boulders, circling to the west towards the Wilds and avoiding the Elves and druids.

Listening to the birds and gazing at the flora while rabbits hopped lazily away, Amanda continued hiking towards the mountains before turning north again. The large black panther walking next to her gave her comfort.

It will be good to see Sarric again. He is the only one that knows of the Were-Folk and I need his thoughts, Amanda thought.

"Panthers are a natural enemy of horses. Maybe it would be better if you travel as a cat for a while," Amanda said, looking down at Sasha.

Reaching down, Amanda picked up the cat, carrying Sasha in her arms.

"That's better. We need to be careful not to go too close to Lithlillia. The animals will tell Lady Lieisa that we're in the forest," she said, scratching the cat's head.

It seemed to take longer than Amanda remembered for her to find the herd. Perhaps it was the dark that had obscured the scenery before, causing her to lose her sense of the time as she tracked Nathanial, but in the daylight the distance was easier to measure, making it seem longer.

Just after mid-day she came upon the herd. A young centaur standing away from the group stood guard, protecting the rest. Amanda watched the centaur fidget as though he was nervous, his head turning side to side as if he were looking for something.

The centaur-guard's white coat stood in stark contrast to the vegetation, even with his several brown spots. The short hair covered his entire body, but the top of his head had curly brown hair like a young man's hair. He had the lean body of a three year old horse.

Tallen? Amanda thought.

"This should be fun. No one surprises a centaur. Wait with my stuff," Amanda said to Sasha after deciding to try to sneak up on the young centaur.

She slipped her belongings from her shoulders to lay them on the ground. With every trick she had learned as a thief and her newer abilities as a monk, Amanda snuck towards the lone centaur. She avoided stepping on twigs, approaching into the wind to mask her scent.

"Tallen?" she asked when she was nearly within arm's reach.

The young stallion-man jumped forward and then spun around with a series of short horse steps.

"Who? Amanda?" Tallen responded.

"Hello," Amanda said, laughing softly.

"Amanda! Wow! I didn't recognize you. Your hair! You've tied it up."

"Good to see you too, my friend. How's Sarric and the herd?"

"Good. Good. Everything is good. Come. I will take you to him."

"I need to get my things first," Amanda responded.

Tallen followed Amanda back to where she had laid her belongings.

"What's that?" his hooves pranced a bit as he asked.

"This is Sasha. She's a cat," Amanda answered when she realized the young centaur had never seen a housecat before.

Tallen leaned his upper human body forward in a horse-like manner as he used his human nose to sniff at Sasha. He pulled back quickly as the smell of feline caught his senses.

"What! It smells like a mountain lion, but not a lion. What is it doing here?"

"Sasha is traveling with me. She's my friend. You have nothing to worry about," Amanda picked Sasha up and stroked her back. "Have you seen anyone from Lithlillia?" Amanda asked innocently as Tallen led her towards the herd.

"No, but we rarely do. The Elves keep to themselves. Sarric sometimes goes to see the Lady on the great cliff, but they never come to the herd. They think they are above us. They think they are the best of Alfardoria.'"

They walked a few minutes before the herd became visible. The older horse-men were gathered closer together in a loose group while the fillies and foals played chase nearby. The men still had their swords or two-headed axes strapped on thick belts that wrapped around their waist where their human hips met with the front shoulders of their horse's body. Quivers of light red arrows hung over their shoulders and their great bows were either hanging over the shoulder next to the quiver or carried in their hands.

The year may have been good to them as Tallen suggests, but they are still prepared to fight, Amanda observed.

The mare-women were beautiful. Their human upper bodies were also covered with fine, short horse hair. Both their human and horse bodies were lean and muscular. Their head hair was long and fine, draping off their heads down to their hips as it grew into horses' manes running down the small of their backs. They moved gracefully, and when the children needed their attention, the women stopped to focus on them. When the children did not require attention, the women-mares gossiped.

They are not that different from the women in the market in Torrence, or the ladies in Ornholtz, or those along the Coast of Nasdrawuen, for that matter. Women are women, I guess. Amanda was slightly surprised by the observation.

Amanda appreciated their peaceful existence. She had never been a social person. She had never had the chance. Becoming a thief at such a young age and taking on the role of a warrior to cover her true nature had denied her the chance of being social. She used her beauty and ability to sway men to her purpose, but that alienated her even more from other women who were threatened by her.

The closest I have been to a group was at the Axe and Bow, and Tabatha was the only woman there.

The men-stallions gathered in several smaller groups. A large centaur was in the middle moving slowly between groups. Amanda recognized Sarric immediately. He was magnificent, the largest of the stallions. His satin black hair covered his muscular upper body with large biceps and well defined, rippled abdomen. The short curly hair on his head was also black. Rodnic, with his reddish-brown body, and black head and tail hair, stood next to Sarric. He was not much smaller than their leader. When they saw Amanda they trotted over.

"Manda! I didn't think we would see you again," Sarric welcomed her.

"Hi," Amanda answered sheepishly.

"What have you done with your hair? You tied it up," Sarric asked as he noticed Sasha.

"It's a cat," Tallen interjected.

"It smells like a lion," Rodnic added.

"That's what I said," the young centaur responded.

"Sasha's my friend. She means you no harm, but I need to tell you she can change like the Were-Folk do. In her other form she is a much larger cat. A panther," Amanda confessed.

The centaurs glanced at each other nervously.

"Manda. A panther? This is serious," Sarric said cautiously.

"I know, but I needed to see you and Sasha is traveling with me." Amanda paused. "She is my friend," Amanda repeated.

"As your friend, Sasha is welcome. But she is your responsibility. If there is a problem you will be held responsible," Sarric warned.

"I understand. Can we talk...privately?"

"Of course." Sarric smiled then gave her a hug. "It is nice to have you back with the herd. I remember the friendship you showed us. You are always welcome here," Sarric continued.

"You were right. I have become too involved in magic."

Amanda told Sarric everything that had happened to her since she had left them. She told him of Nathanial's treachery, the brutality of Haithenbeurn, and their journey home. Then she thanked him for coming to their aid at Limerin Falls.

Sarric looked at her as if he did not understand the reference.

"The pale red arrows," she reminded him, causing Sarric to smile.

CHAPTER 16

THE HERD

After setting her tent up along the edge of the herd's meadow, Amanda began stowing all her gear and weapons near the back. The space below the canvas was not even high enough for her to sit up straight, so she had to pack the tent crawling on her stomach.

The low height of the tent made it easier to warm. The tent, with a single pole in the front, was pegged to the ground on three sides. A small fire near the front entrance provided warmth. Although the centaurs were not afraid of fire, they did not like it, even though they used it for brewing tea and cooking.

The herd was largely vegetarian, foraging potatoes, mushrooms, fruits, and nuts from the forest and storing extra in large earthenware jars and baskets that they made. They were very fond of bird eggs, which they boiled and pickled to preserve through winter. Only on special occasions would they roast a wild boar or turkey.

Amanda had heard the bards' songs of the centaurs' knowledge and wisdom. Many of the ballads described centaurs as great instructors, but that they seldom taught anyone outside their herds. And she had learned from her prior visits the herd passed its history and philosophy down by word of mouth, much like the Bards of Torrence. Like the White Fists, they had accumulated a great wealth of knowledge. She had heard them playing beautiful music with their wood flutes, harps, and a flat drum they called *bodhrán,* which complemented their love for dance. Watching them dance in the meadow again, Amanda decided their dancing looked more like horse play as she watched them spinning about wildly.

Living largely without the tools and conveniences that men pampered themselves with, the centaurs had leather and cloth, a variety of beads, and rope made from vegetation. The metal weapons and cooking pots they used were bartered for from Lithlillia, where they provided services in exchange for mercantile. They did not exchange coins or collect precious gems to amass wealth.

Their swords and axes, and their metal arrow tips came from the Elves, with whom they only socialized on very rare occasions. The metal in their weapons was a strange mixture of silver, something Amanda had not seen before. The metal was light and held the sharpest edge. When the forest warriors, the Rangers, had come into the forest with the druids and were accepted into the Elven family, the centaurs had withdrawn further into solitude.

"Why do you avoid men?" Amanda asked Sarric over tea.

"Men are emotional and do not always do what they have promised," Sarric answered. "The ancient ones are much better, but they tend to hold themselves above others."

"The 'ancient ones'?"

"The Elves. The most noble of the Fairy Realm."

"And where do the centaurs fit in?"

"Centaurs are centaurs. We have been on Dendür since the Elves left Alfardoria. Before the Elven-Dwarven War. Before the Dwarves fled Frausnaugh."

"When I was in the monastery I read that centaurs are great teachers. That you particularly love to teach such things as music, medicine, and hunting. But how is it that you have a reputation for being teachers if you shy away from men?"

"Our reputation is from the old days when we tried to teach man civility and wisdom."

"What happened?"

"We also taught them battle strategy when they were faced with an overwhelming opponent. Not long after the battle, the men began using what we had taught them against us."

"Did they become better than you?"

"No, just more numerous. We felt it wiser to fade into the forest rather than continue a confrontation that was dwindling our numbers."

"But you accept me?"

"You have proven yourself. You have shown us loyalty and shared your trust in us when you didn't know us. You are part of our herd now."

"Thank you, Sarric. I need a place to rediscover who I am."

"I think you already know who you are. You just need time to get comfortable with yourself again. Stay with us as long as you like. You are welcome here."

In the days that followed, Amanda watched the herd. She took particular interest in the colts and fillies. They played so innocently, but the stallion-men also took them aside to teach them archery and tracking. When the mare-women took the fillies away to teach weaving and food preparation, the colts practiced their swordsmanship.

One afternoon as they started to gather for archery practice, Amanda approached Sarric.

"Sarric, I was wondering if you would allow me to demonstrate this," she said as she played with the three balls suspended by the leather bands of her belt.

The weight of the falling balls snapped the leather, causing the balls to bounce up, just to come down again, repeating the process. She could feel the weight and the force of gravity as the balls clacked together, colliding again when they reached the extension of the belt.

"What? Is it a toy? Amanda, you know this is the time set aside to learn to feed and defend the herd."

"I think you will find this 'toy' interesting." Amanda smiled.

"Well, if you only take a minute. We have important things to do." Sarric sounded annoyed.

Amanda asked them all to stand to her side. Picking out a tree across the meadow for a target, she began spinning the bolo over her head. As the balls whirled faster and faster, the colts and foals pushed forward with curiosity. Even some of the stallion-men took a step or two closer.

Amanda released the bolo, sending it flying across the meadow. She watched it strike the tree, its balls wrapping until they struck the trunk hard enough to splinter bark from the tree. The young ones cheered with excitement and galloped to the tree. When she looked at Sarric, he had a big grin on his face.

"A toy." He laughed.

"It can be very effective. I trapped a dragon's legs with one," Amanda said when she could quit smiling.

"A dragon? Amanda, what are you going to tell me next?"

"I can teach the herd how to use the monks' weapon," she offered.

"What can we do for you?"

"You have done so much already."

"Isn't there something we could do that you might like?"

"I like your wooden flutes. They remind me of the monastery." She smiled again.

"Then we will teach you how to play them. Can you make more of these rope-balls?"

"Bolos."

"Bolos. Can you make more of these bolos?"

Amanda nodded.

"And they strike hard enough to knock a man unconscious," she added.

Over the next few weeks Amanda continued to become more a part of the herd. Watching the colts and foals playing gave her joy. Spinning, hopping, jumping, and kicking as the young ones played chase. The games also interested Sasha, who moved closer and closer to watch, hoping to become part of the play. The first time she jumped in, they played around the large cat, but Sasha persisted, jumping forward and batting at them with her large paw when the centaurs came closer. Keeping her claws retracted, the power of her paw knocked them off balance, but the young ones lowered their hindquarters and skirted away.

When the young ones got the hang of including the cat in the game they began running in a herd. When they all turned to chase Sasha at once, the large panther was startled, falling over herself before scampering away. Amanda, who had been watching with Rodnic, fell back on the ground laughing as she looked up into the forest trees.

"It's good to see you relaxing," Rodnic commented, looking down at her.

"It's so good to be here. You have no idea."

"The world of man can be treacherous."

Amanda stood up and brushed off her black leather pants and shirt.

"There are many demons in the world, some of which we create ourselves," Amanda answered.

"The herd follows one leader and works to protect all of its members. We don't trifle with the business of other herds," Rodnic counseled.

"Which is why I am here. I have rejected the life I once led in favor of a new path."

"You'll figure it out. I have faith in you, Manda," Rodnic grinned.

The next morning when they gathered for archery practice, Amanda walked towards them wearing a tan backless top made of leather showing her bare midriff, and her long hair braided back along the side of her head to a long ponytail hanging down her back. In her hand she was carrying her U'thra bow, its limbs having a much more pronounced curve, unlike the Elven-like long bows the centaurs were familiar with.

"What's that?" Rondic jested.

"It was given to me by a U'thra village, far to the east across the Plain of Demeter in the U'thra Basin. Would you like to try it?"

Rondic nocked an arrow, pulled the string back to his eye, and let one of his pale red arrows fly. The metal arrow head drove deep into the target, causing the shaft to vibrate on impact causing Rodnic to smile and then to look at Amanda.

"Not bad for an old man." She smiled.

"You're welcome to do better."

Amanda smiled again and then stepped up next to the centaur, her bare midriff, tight pants, and high boots in sharp contrast to the fine body hair of the centaurs. Amanda focused on the target as she drew an arrow from her quiver. Giving Rodnic a smile before re-focusing on the target, she pulled the bowstring back to her cheek as she raised her aim from the ground before her to the center of the target. Gently relaxing her fingers, she let the arrow fly.

The arrow shaft vibrated with the power of the U'thra bow as it impacted next to Rodnic's, but closer to dead center and nearly a third of the shaft deeper.

"What is it?" The deep tone of Rodnic's voice was slightly higher than normal.

"The U'thra called it recurved, because the limbs bend away from you. It's stronger than the longbows, even the Elven longbows."

"May I shoot it again?"

Amanda handed her bow back to the old centaur, standing next to him while he tested it with a few flights. While Rodnic enjoyed the more powerful bow, Sarric joined them. When Amanda turned towards him, Sarric grinned.

"That outfit almost suits you," he said.

"Almost?"

"Black pants. Don't you have anything more like a centaur?" the leader jested.

"No, but I could make some with the hides we have."

Sarric laughed.

"Just a thought. Your aim is excellent."

"Thank you," Amanda simply said.

"Are you as good with a sword?"

"Fraum would have me humbly admit to abilities that I typically hide."

"Deception is a way of life for you, yet you have been nothing but loyal and honest to the herd," Sarric acknowledged.

"When you met me I was the best thief in Torrence. Life has a way of changing you."

"What is it you want, Manda?"

"Jerrod."

"No, deeper than your love for someone else."

Amanda looked at the stallion-man, the leader of the centaur herd, considering his question.

"Fraum said before I can have Jerrod I must know and like myself."

"And who are you?"

"I am no longer a thief and I refused to be an assassin."

"An assassin? Are you trying to surprise me again?"

"No. No. But since I was a young child I have been trained in stealth and deception. I can fight one-on-one, but it was not my strongest method. Master Fraum's training has helped."

"Fraum's training?"

"Both empty hand and an assortment of weapons."

"Like the bolo?" Sarric sought to confirm.

"That is one of the more simple exercises."

"Well. We will focus on your swordsmanship as well as knowledge."

Amanda and Sarric began taking long walks after archery practice, sometimes accompanied by Sasha, discussing philosophy and battle strategy as they strolled. Amanda enjoyed Sarric's tales of ancient wars which he used to demonstrate battle strategy. They even talked about the Olympian gods.

"We do not worship the Olympians, but we were friendly when they visited Dendür long ago. We were actually closer to the Sumerian gods, but we are now closest to E'fretté, whom the druids introduced us to long ago."

"Have you seen her?"

"Not as you would imagine."

"Then how do you know she is real?"

"You can see her. Touch her. Feel her. She is in all of nature and all of us."

Sarric's wildest tales were of Dionysus, who brought wine to the centaurs, wine which made them crazy, but the best tales were of Apollo, the god of music and healing, who's friendship the centaurs favored most.

"They are a colorful bunch," Amanda commented, making Sarric laugh.

After her walks with Sarric, Amanda spent the early afternoon with the mare-women learning about herbs and healing, but their basket weaving and pottery did not interest her, so she would excuse herself to wait impatiently for the evening weapons training with the stallion-men and colts. One evening Rodnic brought out a great two-handed sword.

"Have you seen a sword as great as this before?" he asked.

"Drin bore a two-handed sword given to him by Lady Lieisa."

"By the Lady? Impressive. Did you use it or spar against him when he wielded it?"

"A little."

"Let me show you the way centaurs use the two-handed sword," Rodnic offered.

Picking up a two handed sword, Amanda held it up towards the sky and then slashed with it in several arcs, testing the weapon. Holding it in one hand, level to the ground, she tested the balance.

"Not bad," Amanda said.

"Shall we spar?" Rodnic coaxed her.

"Be gentle," Amanda teased.

Wielding the sword with two hands, Rodnic circled to attack Amanda. They brought the weapons over their heads to deliver blows against each other's sword. The clash of metal rang through the forest as a bell, clear and free. Occasionally they used a sweeping slash across their bodies, causing the defender to jump back, avoiding the attack. But the length and weight of the sword tired Amanda much quicker than Rodnic. When she over extended her attack, stumbling forward with the weight of the sword, Rodnic stopped his blade at the back of her neck.

Amanda stood up and nodded to Rodnic.

"Wait a moment," she asked before turning to trot towards her small tent.

From the back of the tent Amanda withdrew the two slightly curved long swords from their scabbards.

"Let's try again," Amanda said playfully, holding one of the Elven swords in each hand.

"You're as crazy as a foal running through the rain."

"We'll see." Amanda winked at him.

They circled for a moment before Rodnic jumped forward, swinging his sword down from over his head. Amanda parried with one sword, blocking the much larger two-handed sword outward, and countering with a slash across her body with the other sword, causing Rodnic to rear up away from her swing. Bringing his sword around behind his head and over his horse-back, Rodnic came around to slash across his body as his front hooves landed on the ground. Amanda turned to face the coming blow and parried with both swords. Before Rodnic could react, she spun around and stopped the leading sword at his neck, the point of her sword aimed at his face.

Amanda smiled, her eyes twinkling, as she stared into Rodnic's eyes. The centaur relaxed, spreading his arms wide in submission.

"Not bad, Manda, not bad."

They both stepped back, Amanda with one sword over her head, parallel to the ground, and the other extended out, continuing to point at Rodnic. The centaur grinned as he held the two handed sword with just one of his muscular arms.

"One handed?" Amanda teased as she stepped back and lowered her stance.

Rodnic shrugged.

They circled again, watching each other for a weakness. Amanda jumped in, sweeping with a backhanded slash and following with the opposite hand in a cross body sweep. Rodnic parried the first attack, bringing his sword through to parry the following sword, and then rotated his wrist to bring his sword down towards Amanda's head with more speed than he had exhibited using two hands.

Amanda brought both her swords up in a cross block before her forehead. The swords locked in place briefly. Pulling back and downward, Amanda brought her swords over her head in a series of attacks as Rodnic stepped back, parrying, and then stepped to the side to allow Amanda to extend past his position.

When she passed, Rodnic charged from her side, attacking overhead again. Amanda blocked with one sword, bringing the other over her head, but Rodnic swung under her swords and up, knocking her swords upward.

They stepped away, lowering their swords with mutual admiration.

"Impressive," Sarric said, throwing Amanda a water bag.

Amanda drank deeply and then tossed the bag to Rodnic.

"You're about even, I would say," Sarric needled them.

"Ready to go again?" Amanda taunted.

With a smile, Rodnic turned and went to the edge of the meadow to pick up a two sided axe.

"Are you sure you are up to it?" Rodnic teased back.

"Just getting warmed up, but you've got to be getting tired using one hand with that big sword. You sure you want the axe, too? That thing is bigger than me."

"I guess we will see. Don't over extend your attacks." Rodnic laughed.

"This is insane," Tallen commented as he stepped closer to Sarric, watching Rodnic and Amanda attack and parry.

Rodnic leaped forward, swinging with his sword and then his large axe. Amanda parried, but Rodnic's speed was too great and the third attack overtook her. Diving forward into a roll, Amanda rolled up onto her feet, spinning to attack, but Rodnic spun around just in time, parrying with the sword and then countering with his axe. The heavy blade swung over Rodnic's head and down towards Amanda's, but she rolled under the axe, coming up on one knee to parry his sword. Leaping into the air, Amanda swept her foot in front of Rodnic's nose.

Rodnic stopped, startled by the passing kick.

"You guys are amazing!" Tallen exclaimed, running up to them.

"You always amaze me, Manda," Sarric said as he trotted up behind the younger centaur.

"Well done," Rodnic complimented.

"That was a fantastic practice. Thank you," Amanda answered.

Amanda looked at the centaur a moment, and then down at the swords.

"I have an issue with the swords. I was wondering whether you might have an idea?"

"I don't see a problem. That was amazing!" Tallen's voice was racing.

"What's the problem?" Rodnic asked.

"I have a rig to wear a sword on each hip, but when I use weaponless techniques with them on my hips it's awkward. I haven't tripped yet, but the swords bounce around too much. I need something a little more secure. Any ideas?"

"I might just have an idea for you. I will show you later," Rodnic promised.

Their sparring had drawn an audience. Most of the herd had gathered around them. When they were done, the spectators pressed as close as they could to share in the excitement and to congratulate Rodnic and Amanda.

"This has been extraordinary. Two powerful members of the herd, equally matched, showing us their talent. It is time to celebrate their achievement!" Sarric commanded.

"If you only had four legs," Rodnic teased as they ended their sparring.

Retiring to the meadow for an evening meal, several of the centaurs brought their musical instruments out while others brought food from the nearby thicket. The herd was interested in learning about Amanda's rolls and kicks, and about Fraum's teachings. Finally relenting, Amanda demonstrated more of the empty hand fighting she had learned from her master. As the evening festivities slowed, Amanda found Sarric alone.

"Sarric. There is something I must do."

"What is it, Manda?"

"I want to go to the druid temple, but I don't want them to know that I'm there."

"Why do you want to go there?"

"I hope to find answers there to questions I don't even know to ask. It's drawing me to it."

"Then we will go. For now, let's drink the artesian water, play some music, dance to the songs, and celebrate life. You've done well today."

Celebrating until after dark, Amanda went to her tent to lie down. Comforted by her bow and swords that lay beside her, she lay on her back, looking up at her tent.

This feels right, she thought as she began to drift to sleep.

"Are you sleeping, Manda?" Sarric's deep voice came from outside her tent.

"No. No, I'm not. Give me a moment," Amanda said, shaking off sleep.

After slipping her boots back on and lacing them up, Amanda slid out from under the tent and stood up.

"Good. Let's go," Sarric said as he turned to walk away, twisting around to look over his horse's back.

"Where?"

"You said you wanted to go to the druid temple."

"Wait here, Sasha," Amanda said.

The cat's large eyes looked up at Amanda from where she lay in the tent.

What's in that feline mind of yours? Amanda thought.

After Sasha laid her head on her large forepaw, Amanda turned to run after Sarric. She caught up quickly and they continued walking together quietly for a while, weaving between the silhouettes of the boulders, hills, and trees, as they worked their way around Lithlillia towards the hidden steps to the druid temple.

"You know you are a natural warrior, don't you?" Sarric asked.

Amanda nodded her head. Sarric turned to look at her as they strolled through the darkness.

"But for whom?" Amanda asked out loud.

"Does it matter?"

Amanda looked at him, not knowing what to say.

"You're a warrior. You protect your friends and form bonds with centaurs based on trust and loyalty. I'd say you're a champion for what is right and just."

Amanda looked at the centaur, reflecting on their legendary wisdom. She had come back to the herd for their guidance. They walked for a while before they came to the narrow stairway leading up through a narrow gap in the rock face.

"We have circled around the Elven village. This is the stairway to their temple. No one should be up there, but you never know with Elves and druids. Mind yourself. They don't like intrusions. I will wait here."

"Thank you," Amanda said, and then turned to climb the stairs, but stopped, turning back to her friend.

"I don't know what to say, Sarric. You have given me a lot to consider," she finished as she stretched up onto her toes to kiss his horsehair-covered cheek.

Taking the long, narrow stairway slowly in the dark, feeling her way with her toes as she went, Amanda moved up the stairway through the crevasse of the cliff face. The rocks cast night shadows across the steps where they blocked the moonlight, making it even harder for her to see. The top of the stairs ended abruptly at the top of the rock cliff. There was a thick, grassy meadow between the cliff and the woods. In the middle of the meadow before her were the silhouettes of twelve columns.

The columns formed a perfect circle in the middle of the small meadow. Nearby the forest encroached on the silhouettes. The dark shadow of a stone altar in the center of the circle came into view as Amanda approached the druid's circle. Passing between two columns, she walked cautiously up to the altar. A bowl-like indentation was carved out of the otherwise smooth surface of the black obelisk. Even in the dark she could see the veins of lighter rock that marbled the glossy surface.

Walking around the altar slowly, her thief's senses overcoming her curiosity, Amanda looked carefully for secret compartments or traps, but she could not find anything.

Quite a plain block, really. What am I doing here? she thought.

Amanda leaned her back against the obelisk, allowing herself to slowly slide down its side to sit on the surrounding grass. She looked up at the moons and paused for a moment before pulling her knees up to her chest. Wrapping her arms around her knees, she dropped her head to rest in the silence of the forest temple. She was quickly lost in the solitude of the night. When she finally raised her eyes to gaze at the stars again, the back of her head touched the cold, stone altar.

"Why am I here?"

Because you seek wisdom, a calming, female voice answered in her thoughts.

"Who are you? What are you?" Amanda asked, startled by the voice.

I am she who the druids worship. Neither goddess nor Lady of the Moons. Neither mortal nor immortal. I am E'fretté.

"E'fretté? Why are you speaking with me? I'm not a druid or Elve," Amanda asked, looking around for the woman.

Despite all that you have endured, you are pure of heart. You protect your friends and those who can't protect themselves.

The temple began to glitter in soft, white light.

"I seem to do okay for my friends. That is not the problem."

What do you think the problem is?

"My heart is the problem. I know who I am, but I have lost both my love and my purpose."

True love is never lost. It is a moment in time that lasts forever.

"But Jerrod is gone."

The Great One has many things to accomplish and his love is split. That does not mean he loves you any less. You will have to come to terms with that before you will be whole.

Amanda stood up, looking around again for the woman, but she saw no one.

"How do you know what is in Jerrod's mind?"

The Great One is as much a part of me as he is not. His link to nature and to magic is more powerful than Brendril's was.

"Why do you tell me this?"

Your god has abandoned you. Others would use you against your friends, but if you stay on the true path you will accomplish great things.

"The true path? How do I know what the 'true path' is?"

Follow your heart. Do what is just and right. Non-believers are coming, Amanda, and there will be great need for a champion of justice.

Amanda did not know how to respond. The light in the temple began to dim.

"Thank you," Amanda said, looking around again for the woman.

You will be my knight. My defender of what is just and right and pure, the voice said as a bright flash of light filled the temple.

Searing pain centered on Amanda's forehead. She staggered a little, touching her forehead, and then looked around for the source of the light, but everything had returned to darkness.

Go. Go now, daughter of E'fretté.

Amanda went straight to the stony staircase and worked her way back down through the rock face. She was as slow going down as she had been going up, carefully placing her heel against the last narrow step to make sure her next step down was solid. Sarric was still there when she reached the bottom.

"Where have you been? It's nearly dawn." Sarric spoke a little faster than normal as he walked towards her. "What's that on your forehead? Did you fall?" Sarric questioned as he stopped in his tracks.

"No. No, I didn't fall. Why?" Amanda said softly.

"There is a dark spot on your forehead. Come, let me see. Face the moon," Sarric said as he reached out to touch her face, brushing her hair from her forehead.

Amanda smiled as Sarric's hands reached for her forehead, but he quickly withdrew them as he gasped. A round circle with three lines through the bottom part and three dots above the lines began to sparkle with white light as the moonlight caressed her face.

"In the name of E'fretté! What happened?" Sarric exclaimed.

"What? What are you talking about, Sarric?"

"The druid symbol for power is glowing on your forehead. It's the symbol for E'fretté."

"She spoke to me and then my forehead burned."

"She spoke to you? E'fretté spoke to you? Amanda, E'fretté doesn't speak directly to anyone, except maybe the Druid Priestess."

"She said I was her daughter."

"Her daughter?"

Amanda nodded slowly, affirming Sarric's question.

"We must go."

"Where?"

"Back to the herd."

"What's wrong?" Amanda questioned as she started to follow the centaurs' leader.

She could not measure the time they took returning to the meadow. They walked without talking, Amanda struggling to keep up with Sarric's pace. As they approached the meadow, Sarric turned to Amanda.

"The symbol on your forehead will cause a lot of commotion. You are now the most important member of our herd, and maybe in Lithlillia. Tonight we will celebrate. I will send a hunting party out to shoot a boar."

"I didn't ask for this," Amanda said softly, her soft blue eyes reaching into Sarric's soul.

"You earned her blessing somewhere, at some time," Sarric reassured her.

"I am honored to be a member of your herd, but I'm nothing special."

"You are now, Amanda. You always have been. My sword is yours, and my herd." Sarric paused. "We will have to tell the druids," he said, taking her by the shoulders as he looked into her eyes. "Get some rest. We will go to them in the morning."

His tone is different, Amanda thought.

Sasha stood up when she saw Amanda returning. The large cat stared at Amanda's face a moment, and then began rubbing against her until the panther knocked her down. Wrapping her forepaws over Amanda's shoulders, Sasha began using her large tongue to try and clean Amanda's forehead.

"It was E'fretté, Sasha. It's not going to come off."

While Amanda slept, Sasha curled up just outside the opening of her tent. The small band of stallion-men that trotted off to hunt was gone most of the morning while the herd prepared for the evening's festivities. Amanda woke to the sound of horse hooves as the herd gathered around the returning hunting party. On a pole between the shoulders of two of the centaurs was a giant boar.

As Amanda tied the leather strand that pulled the sides of her beaded top tight against her breasts, Rodnic and Sarric approached. Amanda slipped on her boots and began lacing them up.

"A successful hunt, I see. When is the evening meal?"

"We are putting the boar on the spit now," Rodnic answered as he handed her a cup of water.

"Thank you."

"It's true then, your forehead," Rodnic commented.

"Apparently," Amanda responded, reaching up to touch her forehead with her fingers.

"The hunting party discovered something concerning. A pack passed south along the Wilds," Rodnic began.

"A large pack of Were-Folk," Sarric interjected.

"Were they the ones that attacked Cipper?" Amanda asked.

"Undoubtedly. And they did not return."

"Torrence?"

Sarric shrugged.

✣   ✣   ✣   ✣   ✣

Around a small table in the middle of a crudely made log building Nathanial spoke with his leaders. The general of the Dark Elves, the giant leader of the Fendür, the old bear leader of Were-Folk, and Sescious, the rogue leader of the Triad traitors, all listened intently to the dark wizard.

"Gather your troops. We march at dawn. We head south through the Gap of Dillandria. We will cross the U'thra Basin and then turn west across the Plains of Demeter. Torrence will probably ride out to meet us on the plain, but if we make it to the city, all the better." Nathanial stopped to look each one of the leaders in the eye, making sure he had their attention.

"The Elves will lead the march, followed by Sescious's wizards, and then the Fendür. The Were will meet us on the battlefield. I have another task for them."

"You leave tonight," Nathanial said, turning to the Were leader.

"You? Where?" the giant asked in Fendür.

"I will be with Rok-lin observing from the air. Sescious can contact me. Anything else?"

Everyone was quiet.

"Good," Nathanial said, looking around the table one last time. "Assemble your troops."

✣   ✣   ✣   ✣   ✣

Amanda was a sensation at the celebration. They ate the roasted boar, potatoes that they buried in the coals to cook, pine nuts, and fresh vegetables from their garden. They drank cold artesian water and listened to music played on their harps, wood flutes, and bodhrán-drums while the colts and foals were playing chase with Sasha.

When asked to tell her story about talking with E'fretté, Amanda insisted at first that there was not much to tell, but she finally relented. She had to repeat the story several times to satisfy the curiosity of the herd, many of whom sat in for a second or third time.

"I thought you didn't worship gods?" Amanda asked Sarric.

"It is not a matter of worship and E'fretté is not a goddess. We respect her more than we do the Olympian gods. We give the Olympians the respect they deserved, but we do not worship them, not even when they came to Dendür. Whether it is the power of nature or the innate power of a deity, power commands respect."

"And magic?"

"Magic comes from the connection with nature. Some is good, but much of it is bad."

"It always comes from nature?"

"As far as we know."

"E'fretté called Jerrod the Great One."

"You are both eternally tied to E'fretté now. The Great One has a task greater than magic or nature. You only need to worry about E'fretté's needs."

Sarric looked at Amanda.

"I will go to see Lady Lieisa tomorrow. For now, let's just enjoy the evening."

The celebration went late into the night. When Amanda went to bed, Sasha, who usually preferred to sleep with her in the form of a lap-cat, changed into the large black panther to curl up against Amanda, purring Amanda to sleep. Amanda's arm slid around the panther's chest as she slipped into slumber.

In her dreams Amanda walked through a forest highlighted by shimmering light. At first the animals did not run, but after a while things grew dark and the animals disappeared. Before her was a large, dark silhouette wielding a large Haithenbeurn axe and bearing a round shield. The figure's evil laugh was deep, as if echoing up from the deep, dark caverns in the earth.

When Amanda woke, sweat covered her nearly naked body. Sasha was sitting up at the entrance of the tent watching the meadow. The light of dawn filtered through the trees, and the sound of birds singing in the distance beckoned her. The air was cooler and, as she sat up pulling her blanket around her, Amanda's eyes focused on a drop of dew on a blade of grass.

"Fall is coming, Sasha," Amanda said, reaching out to stroke the panther's back.

I see that, Sasha thought in response.

"What in the name of Zeus?" Amanda stopped.

"E'fretté. Nature connects to the animals, doesn't it, Sasha?" Amanda said, looking at the feline.

Of course. And there is so much I have to tell you, the panther thought as she looked back into the tent.

Soon after Amanda had dressed, Sarric came to her tent. She was in the middle of rummaging through her pack as he walked up. After closing her hand around the object she was seeking, Amanda slid out from under the tent wearing the backless top she had made and some new leather pants.

"Brown suits you better," Sarric commented on seeing her.

"It's not as good for sneaking through the shadows." Amanda giggled.

"Do you really need to sneak?"

"No. I don't. But it makes it harder for an assassin's blade to find me. Nathanial still has at least two of the rings the assassins used," she answered, her face expressionless.

"Witches, wizards, Elves, druids, and dragons. And now, E'fretté? This is deep magic, Amanda. I told you, you are far too..."

"I know, I know. I am 'far too involved in magic,'" Amanda said, interrupting as she reflected on the time when Sarric had first helped her track Nathanial.

Was it that long ago? So much has happened and now I have to see the Elves, she thought to herself.

Elves? Sasha interjected.

"I don't know what the reaction at the village will be," Sarric said, breaking the silence.

Amanda looked up at him, ignoring Sasha.

"Lady Lieisa is the most revered and powerful follower of E'fretté in western Ak'ron. She is Elven and the senior-most druid. Her power is, well, the depth of her power has never been tested to my knowledge. I'm not sure what her limits are."

"I am friendly with Lithlillia," Amanda answered confidently.

With the Elves in Lithlillia, Amanda's thought answered the panther.

"You haven't had the mark of E'fretté on your forehead before," Sarric pointed out. "It's hard to know how they will react."

There was no one waiting for them when they reached the edge of the village. Walking in, Amanda felt surprisingly calm, reflecting on her dream as she walked. The image had empowered her. She understood that she was now, somehow, tied to all the natural forces around her. Sarric's acceptance of her furthered her inner tranquility.

"The forest and animals must not have let the Lady know we are coming," Amanda commented.

"They know," Sarric responded, pointing at a small group standing in front of the Great Pavilion.

Just how "friendly" are you with the Elves? Sasha questioned, glaring at the group.

I saved the princess's life and stole the man she loves. We are better now, I think.

You think?

We saved a dragon together.

A dragon! What dragon?

Hush! We're here, Amanda said, shooting a stern glare at the temperamental panther.

As they reached the stairs before the Great Pavilion, the group bowed without saying a word. Amanda nodded to them as Sarric and Sasha, who stood just behind her, watched.

"This is not normal," Sarric whispered.

The group of Elves turned and went to the large door of the Great Pavilion that was being held open by two forest warriors.

"Rangers," he whispered again.

"I remember."

Inside, the Great Pavilion was packed, more than it had been when she last visited them. This time the Great Pavilion was so silent Amanda could hear the embers in the long fire pit crackling. At the far end of the oval building, Lady Lieisa and Lord Steffen stood on the dais awaiting their arrival as if they were awaiting royalty. Rhonda was standing to the side behind her mother.

Amanda walked down the steps towards the fire pit with Sasha at her side. Sarric followed close behind, his bow in his hand. The Elves, half-Elves, and humans all watched intently as Amanda approached the dais. As she walked, the symbol on her forehead began to glimmer softly.

"Welcome, Amanda," Lady Lieisa greeted. "Welcome, Sarric, Lord of the Herd of Lithlillia."

"Thank you, Lady," Sarric's voice was deep and strong.

"Amanda, it's good to see you again. How are Fraum and Drok-na?" Rhonda spoke up.

"It's been weeks since I have seen them, but they were good when I left."

"Amanda, how did you come to have the mark of power placed on your forehead?" Lady Lieisa went directly to the point.

"I sought guidance in your temple," Amanda confessed.

"In the Temple of Lithlillia? In the meadow above the cliff?" the Lady asked calmly as she looked at Sarric and then back to Amanda.

Her voice is stressed, Amanda thought.

No one has ever been approached in this manner, Imelrinn's thought entered her mind like the Elven music drifting softly on a breeze.

"Doesn't the teachings of the druids and Elves say that we are all connected?" Amanda asked after glancing at the ancient guardian.

"Yes, but typically we know when others visit us. It was a surprise to hear from the Mother that you were marked as her daughter. That is a great privilege. More than you may realize."

"So I am beginning to gather. I did not ask for this."

"But you have been chosen. You know you are always welcome here. We owe you so much already." The Elven priestess paused.

"Bring Amanda a chair," Lady Lieisa directed a nearby Elve.

"You will sit with us and tell us more of what has happened," the lady finished.

I'm not sure that is a request, Amanda thought.

Shall I impress her?" Sasha jested.

I think she is impressed enough, Rhonda chimed in.

Is everyone in my mind? Amanda thought.

Pretty much. Imelrinn grinned as his thought answered the rhetorical question.

Instead of music playing and soft conversations between the members of the clan, everything was quiet as Amanda described what happened in the druid temple. The Elves sitting further away moved as close as they could, despite their superior hearing, leaning in, eager to hear first-hand how the flatlander had been marked by E'fretté.

They ate the mid-day meal with the clan. At the end of the meal, Lady Lieisa handed Amanda a hard object wrapped in cloth.

"For me? You are too kind, Lady," Amanda said humbly.

"I should have given you this last year. I should have given you all one."

Amanda carefully unwrapped the cloth and looked down at the silver pinecone brooch in her hand. It too was ornately crafted by skilled hands. Her experience as a thief told her the workmanship of the brooch and the fine metal made it valuable, but it was the significance of the gift that made it invaluable to her.

Poor Drin. I miss you, Amanda thought as she peered at the intricate piece of jewelry.

"The Brooch of Lithlillia. Thank you, Lady Lieisa. I will wear this with honor," Amanda said, overcoming a lump in her throat.

"How many times have you saved the princess and all of your friends? It is we who must thank you."

"Thank you for being such a good friend," Rhonda added.

"There is one thing I need to tell you," Amanda started, looking at Sarric and then back to the Lord and Lady of Lithlillia.

"What is it, Amanda?" the Lady asked.

"I visited Cipper on my return to Lithlillia." Amanda watched them until she was certain she had everyone's attention.

"They were dead. All of them. Everyone in Cipper."

"What happened?"

"It sounds as if it was the Were-Folk, my lady," Sarric interjected.

"The Were?"

Sarric nodded.

"They were ripped apart and burned," Amanda described.

"Steffen, we must post guards in the forest."

"It has been decades since we needed guards," Lord Steffen rumbled.

"All the same, the forest is no longer safe if the Were are actively hunting man again."

"I have another question," Amanda asked.

"What is it?" Lady Lieisa asked.

"Prince Olendorn gave me this, but I'm not sure what it is," Amanda said as she pulled out the round object wrapped in cloth she had retrieved from her pack.

Holding the package out in one hand, Amanda unwrapped the cloth from a glimmering sphere. Whitish-blue light illuminated everyone on the dais.

"Who gave you the power globe?" Lady Lieisa asked.

"Prince Olendorn gave it to me."

"I've never seen one glow this bright. It is a power globe. It provides light based on the power the holder can draw from E'fretté."

Amanda looked down at the globe and then back to Lady Lieisa.

"They are not uncommon and are not overly valuable, but they hold a special meaning to Fairy-Folk. They don't usually pass out of the Fairy realm."

"It was a gift."

"Cherish it."

"Thank you. I am afraid I must beg your leave, Lady."

"Where will you go?" the priestess asked.

"I will stay with the herd a while longer. After that? I don't know."

"Mother, I will walk them out. I will be back shortly."

As Rhonda escorted them out, the members of the clan all parted to allow them through, bowing their heads as they passed.

"Are they paying respect to you? I don't remember anyone bowing their heads when we walked through the clan last year," Amanda questioned, afraid of the answer that might come.

"They always show me the respect of a princess, but they are bowing to you," Rhonda answered.

"Me?"

"Um-hm. With the mark of E'fretté on your forehead, you will be received with reverence in all the Elven and Fairy kingdoms."

"Me? With reverence?"

"You are part of E'fretté now," Rhonda said matter-of-factly.

"And Amanda is part of our herd," Sarric said defensively.

"The herd is a loyal and respected ally of Lithlillia," the princess responded.

"Sarric, may I have a few words with Amanda alone? It's girl stuff," Rhonda requested shyly.

"Certainly. Sasha and I will wait at the edge of the village. Come, Sasha," Sarric said, looking first at Amanda and then back to the princess.

They watched Sarric and Sasha walk out of sight.

"Never thought I would see a centaur and a panther walking side by side," Amanda commented aloud. "I'm sorry, Rhonda, what is it?"

"I went to Jerrod and threw myself at him," Rhonda blurted out.

"But your virtue?" Amanda's spoke rapidly.

"I am not proud of what I did." Rhonda looked at her with tears in her eyes.

"He refused me." Rhonda struggled to continue as the tears began running down her cheeks.

Amanda stopped and hugged her for a moment.

"I'm sorry," Amanda said, taking a step back, sliding her hands down Rhonda's arms until their fingers wrapped around each other's hands.

Rhonda nodded, keeping her eyes cast down.

"We were to have been wed," Rhonda said, finally looking up.

Amanda took Rhonda in her arms again as the princess's body began to quiver.

"Shhhh. It will be fine," Amanda comforted her.

"But he loves you."

"Even E'fretté says his love is split." Amanda stepped back again so she could look Rhonda in the eyes. "He loves both of us."

✾   ✾   ✾   ✾   ✾

Did you know the witch has been watching you? Sasha thought to Amanda when they were alone again.

I suspected as much, but why?

She enjoys manipulating one person against another. It started with Jerrod, but she lost control.

"Jerrod? Why Jerrod?" Amanda said, turning to look into the panther's yellow eyes.

She wants Jerrod to bring her the orb in the sword.

The crystal in the hilt of Jerrod's sword? Amanda asked.

It is the Dragon's Orb.

What is she going to do with it?

Felicia is the most powerful witch on Dendür. It has been foretold that the end of all magic is coming. She hopes to preserve the magic in the orb as it was when Jerrod first found the sword, but stronger.

The lightning? Was that magic? Amanda asked slowly.

Yes. She must have the orb to store the magic before the last day is upon us.

When is the last day?

No one knows, but Felicia thinks it will be soon.

Is this part of the prophecy that one must die so another hero will rise?

No, the prophecy is occurring now.

Drin?

Yes, Sasha confirmed.

Who is the hero?

No one knows that either, or what the hero will do. There have been many ceremonies seeking guidance on the hero and what is to come. The Ladies of the Moons have not seen fit to inform any of the covens on Dendür.

Sasha, why do you tell me these things? Doesn't it violate some loyalty to your mistress?

I am not Felicia's familiar. There is no spell binding me to her. I am not in servitude. I befriended her long ago. We have saved each other's lives many times, but I have free will, Sasha answered as she began licking her large paw.

"Sasha?"

The large black panther stopped her bath to look at Amanda.

"Where does the orb come from?"

The great wizard Brendril made it. The Fairies called him the Great One, too.

✻   ✻   ✻   ✻   ✻

A gray silhouette sat cross-legged on a large boulder in the darkness of the forest. Nearby, the darker silhouette of a large panther sat flicking its tail as the music of a wooden flute filled the evening air. The two moons over Dendür rose above the evergreen forest as she played, casting filtered purple and green moonlight onto the forest bed.

Amanda's hair fell freely down her back, much like the manes of the women-mares in the herd. As she played her mind emptied, allowing the tranquility of the evening to inflate her persona.

I can feel it, Sasha. I can feel E'fretté, Amanda thought.

She is part of you now. You are E'fretté's daughter.

CHAPTER 17

OMEN OF DEATH

S itting on her pillows at the small table before her fireplace, Felicia had let her tea cool to that moment where it was still warm enough to be pleasant, but cool enough that she no longer had to sip the hotter liquid, hoping not to burn her mouth. She took in a long drink, marveling at the taste of the forest herbs.

The evening was quiet and peaceful, as nearly all of them were. They had become even quieter since Sasha had departed with Amanda. Felicia thought a moment about the young woman, the beautiful body and tender heart of the once legendary thief, and of the boy she loved, Jerrod.

He has such a naïve soul. And he thinks he can keep the orb from me. So cute. So misguided.

Felicia sipped her tea again.

The lamps providing light in the small cottage had been turned up. The small window with opaque glass was not enough to light the room during the day, let alone at night. In the middle of the low table a round pinkish candle rested next to the newly formed crystal globe that had been crafted on the night of the last double full-moon, when Felicia's witchcraft had been at its strongest.

The smoke of the pink candle filled the air with the sweet, light hint of native spring flowers. The candle-magic assisted Felicia to slip more easily into the trance-like state necessary for reading the future and for remaining there longer.

It has been too long. I can't wait to meditate, Felicia thought.

As she closed her eyes, she heard the lights of the lamps and candle flickering. Felicia opened her eyes. Before her stood the ghostly figure of a woman in a white toga with a silver headband that resembled a grape vine with small leaves circling the woman's long sandy-blonde hair. Modest curls fell loosely down the side of her face. The queen of witches rose to her feet as the figure became solid.

"Good evening, Hecate. To what do I owe the honor of your visit?" Felicia asked quietly.

"Where's Sasha?" Hecate asked, touching the candles, vials, clay pots, and trinkets filling the shelves and tables with the tips of her fingers as she circled the room like a woman sightseeing in the market, with no intention of buying.

"Is Olympia so boring that you can find nothing better to do than worry about my cat?"

"But I know how precious your familiar is to you," Hecate's voice was arrogant and overconfident.

"Surely you know that Sasha is not a familiar. She chose to go with the thief. I don't remember the last time Agganon was opened. What can I do for you?"

"I didn't come by way of Agganon, this time, but there is nothing you can do for me," Hecate responded, still allowing herself to be distracted by the items laid out for sale.

Hecate paused to look at Felicia.

"And everything," Hecate added.

Felicia did not react, but stood calmly watching the Olympian. She waited patiently to find out why the goddess of witchcraft was visiting her lair.

"It's coming, you know, the end of your magic, and there is nothing you can do to stop it," Hecate declared.

"Are you worried I might save witchcraft?" Felicia asked innocently.

"Stay out of my business!"

Felicia smiled at the goddess's outburst.

"You have been watching him all along. Did you think I wouldn't notice?" Hecate said sharply.

Again Felicia waited patiently, not saying a word.

"He will not survive. Dendür will fall into darkness as other worlds have and there is nothing you can do to stop it," Hecate challenged.

"I don't know about other worlds and I don't care, but Jerrod will survive. More importantly, witchcraft will survive."

Hecate's skin turned blue with purple shadowing, reflecting the color of the smaller moon. Anger burned in her gaze.

"You dare to defy Olympus!" Hecate's voice became shrill as the goddess of witchcraft's body grew taller.

When Hecate stepped towards Felicia, the queen of witches raised her arms then threw them violently towards the floor, igniting a blinding light. Gray smoke filled her cottage instantly.

When the smoke cleared enough to see they found themselves in a wall-less realm with only the pink candle floating in mid-air for light. Felicia's skin was glowing whitish-blue. Her long black hair that normally fell to her ankles blew wildly around as though it was caught in a terrible wind. Her thin muslin robes pressed tight against the front of her body, exposing her beautiful, curved form that would have made Aphrodite stir in competition.

"You dare to come into my lair and threaten me! For a thousand years I have been loyal. I have given you homage as the patron goddess of witchcraft. I have never questioned you or the Olympians. I have not put the Ladies of the Moons before you, nor you before them. I am Felicia, queen of all the covens on Dendür."

Hecate stood speechless, motionless. She looked around, trying to see the edge of the witch's lair.

How dare you! Hecate thought.

"A thousand years ago I may have needed your guidance to draw on the power of the stars and moons, but I grew out of that long ago. I have had a thousand years to study, to learn. This is my realm now and you are my guest for as long as I allow it."

Hecate looked around calmly as her skin tone returned to normal. She was submissive when she looked back at Felicia, but the sound of confidence still filled her voice.

"You are the mistress of your lair, Felicia. Forgive me. I misspoke."

Hecate watched Felicia's hair whipping in the air.

"We sometimes forget there are other forces at work. Olympia has grown egotistical. I understand others deserve our respect. You have made an enemy of Asgard. Do you really want to take me on, too?" Hecate asked calmly.

"I do not want you as my enemy and I value your friendship, but Jerrod holds the future of Dendür, and if I can control him through love or craft, I will," Felicia finished.

Hecate looked at the witch. She had pushed her disciple too far and the student had, for the moment at least, become the teacher. As much as Hecate might deny it, the future of the Olympians rested on Jerrod's action as well. She had lost control of Felicia and now, the queen of the Dendür covens was their only hope.

"What of Odin? And the Order of One?" Hecate asked.

"I will preserve magic in the orb. What that does for Olympia or Asgard is their concern. Mine is the preservation of magic on Dendür."

"I beg your pardon for the interruption, then. If we are through, will you release me?" Hecate looked around again, unable to see the boundary of the witch's lair.

The moment Felicia returned them to her cottage, Hecate vanished into the air. When Felicia sat down on her pillows, a large black dog with a powerful body and broad, deep chest trotted out of her room to lie next to her. The dog's two broad heads, both with rounded foreheads, wide black noses, and almond shaped eyes that burned red, looked around the room. Felicia reached over to stroke the dog's back, avoiding one head, which would cause the other head to become violently jealous.

"It's okay. She's gone. I will have to thank Hades for your companionship," Felicia celebrated aloud. "I've won this battle."

* * * * *

Fraum's daily routine had changed. He no longer had time to browse the scrolls. Instead, he spent the mid-morning hours after his exercises studying about dragons and often returned late in the evening to continue those studies. He had become obsessed by dragon anatomy and lore, reading about the Isle of Dragons and seeking maps to pinpoint the tiny island far to the south.

He was surprised to find such diversity in dragons. The scrolls indicated that most dragons could communicate through thought. The really remarkable histories were of young children who had befriended dragons. Their lives were enhanced by the dragon's mental and physical attributes, increasing their own abilities. What one felt, so did the other. There were even legends that the death of one caused the death of the other.

All dragons had breath that could cause harm, but that also varied greatly. By far the most common was fire, then acid. Others included gas, sticky-spit, freezing frost, and great winds. As Fraum read he learned that many dragons had magical properties, but most of the magic was very minor. A few, like he had seen with Rok-lin, had strong magical ability that could kill instantly.

While the scrolls indicated scale color, horns, and tails varied, Fraum could not identify a correlation between the physical variations and the dragons' abilities. The myth that a dragon's color indicated whether they were good or evil, or had any particular attributes, was apparently no more accurate than predicting a man's actions based upon his physical attributes.

"The morals of the dragons are not related to its color," Fraum thought aloud.

"What's that you say?" the frail voice of an old man came from behind him.

Fraum turned in his seat to confirm the voice he had already recognized.

"Master," Fraum greeted, rising out of his seat.

"Forgive me. I was engrossed in this scroll," Fraum said, waving his hand over the many scrolls on the library table.

"No, forgive me for intruding."

"What can I do for you, Master?"

"What are you reading?"

"About dragons. I am finding a lot about their history and lore, but it is curious," Fraum stopped.

"What is it?"

"I have read about all these colors and abilities, but there is nothing about white dragons."

"White is the presence of all color," the Master commented.

"Exactly. And there are no references to white dragons in the scrolls."

"And that troubles you," the Master stated in confirmation.

"Yes."

"White is also a sign of purity."

Fraum thought a moment before the Master's next question broke his train of thought.

"Your protégé, the thief, has gone and now you spend all your time here, reading the ancient scrolls. The dragon is healed. What troubles you, Fraum?"

"With your permission, I would like to return to Drok-na's cave."

"He is truly a remarkable beast, isn't he? You will need to spend time with him in the Wilds, I imagine. Of course you can go. Come and go as you please, like any of us, but it may be your path is no longer in our monastery."

Fraum looked at the old master.

"You are worldly. You have wisdom beyond those within our walls. The ancient scrolls only offer knowledge, but not experience. We offer you less than the world offers. You can always read. Perhaps it is your time to experience what you are reading about."

✻   ✻   ✻   ✻   ✻

When he was healthy enough to fly, Drok-na had left Torrence with Fraum. Fraum packed a small bag and with the High Master's colorful wrist band, which enabled Fraum to converse with Drok-na, he climbed onto the dragon's back for the journey back to the dragon's cave. They left after dark to avoid panicking the citizens by the appearance of a flying dragon.

Gliding through the cold night air under Dori's purple face, Drok-na flew towards the Wilds' mountain range, southwest of Torrence. The feel of the cold air rushing over Fraum's face had been exhilarating. Experiencing the gravitational weight pressing down on his body as Drok-na's powerful wings climbed upward out of the city and then the floating sensation as the dragon began its descent was indescribable. Fraum nearly forgot to breathe as he gave in to his senses, experiencing dragon flight to its fullest.

The first flight after recuperating had felt good to Drok-na, too. To stretch his wings again! To feel his muscles pulling against the air as he ascended towards the moon with a rider on his back had been invigorating.

I miss Jacob, Drok-na thought, confiding his feelings to the monk.

I know. I'm sorry, was all Fraum had been able to offer.

Fraum spent the first few nights in the cave with Drok-na They spent hours discussing a variety of topics. Drok-na, who was opinionated, always added a thought or two to the conversation.

"What did you and Jacob do with your time?" Fraum asked out of curiosity one afternoon.

Lots of things. He liked to play. I think his favorite game was getting me to chase a bright, glowing ball. It was fun. Jacob could play that game for hours.

Fraum chuckled. Not a full laugh, more of an amusement, but it warmed his heart all the same.

"I don't have a ball that is big enough you wouldn't swallow," Fraum teased.

"It's okay. I chased the ball for Jacob's amusement. Maybe we could play hide-and-seek?"

"Aren't you a little large for hide-and-seek?"

You won't be able to find me.

"Really? Where are you going to hide?"

If I tell you that it won't be much of a game, will it?

Finally, Fraum relented to play and agreed to be the seeker first. Closing his eyes, he began counting. Drok-na got up and moved to the edge of the cave to lie down. When the dragon was content with his position, Drok-na faded from view.

Reaching one hundred, Fraum opened his eyes and peered around the cave. It was a large cave, large enough for an adult-sized dragon to live in comfortably, but not so large that Fraum could not see the entire cave from where he stood. There were no pillars or walls sectioning off a portion of the cave. The stalactites hung so high off the floor not even Drok-na hit his head on them when he was standing up. Nothing blocked his view.

"Where are you?" Fraum gasped in astonishment.

That's the game. You're supposed to find me, Drok-na teased.

"Are you in the cave?"

Yes.

"Then where are you? I can't see you."

I'm right here, but I don't think this is how the game is played, Drok-na thought as he sheepishly reappeared.

"Magic? You know magic?" Fraum asked.

It's not much. Jacob would find me quickly using magic.

"What else can you do?" the monk continued.

I don't know. Jacob was teaching me.

When the games were done, Fraum sat down next to Drok-na, who rolled onto his side, begging the monk to scratch his belly. Scratching the dragon's scales reminded Fraum of the vespree, causing him to shudder as an eerie feeling washed over his body like cold rain falling down his back.

What is it? Drok-na thought.

"I'm sorry. I was thinking of our fight with the vespree, when Rok-lin radiated a bluish light that engulfed the creature and turned it into a glowing, yellow vapor."

Rok-lin? She has magic, too?

"Yes. Powerful, dangerous magic."

✳   ✳   ✳   ✳   ✳

Fraum was amazed at Drok-na's speed and agility. In the labyrinth of Terrace Xul Rok-lin had seemed cumbersome, but she too could move with grace, speed, and power when necessary. Perhaps it was just an awkward age dragons pass through while growing from childhood to adulthood.

"I think you are faster than Rok-lin, my friend," Fraum said, looking at the yearling.

I am smaller and I don't know that I have as great a magical ability. The male dragon's matter of fact answer disclosed a slight lack of confidence.

"I think you will be surprised. Smaller appears to mean greater speed and agility. Your magic may come."

Do you really think so?

"I will ask the High Master for his opinion. I don't know a great deal about magic yet."

You know the High Master?

"We are acquainted."

Of their adventures, Fraum and Drok-na enjoyed the rides they shared the most. They would fly in the afternoon when it was warm. On clear days Fraum could see for miles. Their path typically took them eastward over the Plains of Demeter before circling back around over the Plateau of Kronese and back towards Torrence. They flew south along the Wilds, staying out of sight of the king's city as they continued south, back to Drok-na's cave. The long flight allowed them to talk, sharing ideas and dreams.

Fraum's heavy riding cloak helped him enjoy the flight. Other than the rope belt around his monk's robes, he chose to ride weaponless.

Who was going to attack me on the back of a dragon? he reasoned.

When Fraum returned to the monastery he waited until after dark to paddle a canoe back across the river and into the river harbor, leaving the canoe and the winter riding cloak under a pier. Arriving back at the monastery long after dinner, Fraum ate bread and cheese in his room with a small piece of chicken leftover from the evening meal. Afterward he meditated. Sleep came late, but he was always up early with the rest of the order.

While his days continued with the studies of weaponless and weapon combat, his duties around the monastery, and teaching, Fraum still found time to steal away. Most of the time he visited Drok-na, but occasionally he visited the High Master of the Triad. They had become friends, as friendly as someone who did not study magic might be with the most powerful wizard in Torrence.

I wonder which is greater, his power as a wizard or his terror as a white dragon? Fraum pondered.

It was the High Master who had told Fraum about the curse on the ghoul's possessions. Sharing an interest in knowledge had helped develop their friendship, and both were concerned about Nathanial.

Fraum felt strange each time he entered the catacombs of the Triad. The secret passages winding down into the earth below the island were like an ancient mine. Even stranger, when he was finally surrounded by members of the Triad, they seemed to ignore him. Only the High Master acknowledged Fraum's presence.

"Drok-na appears to have some magical abilities, but he doesn't seem to know how to use it. Jacob was apparently teaching him. Is there anything I can do?" Fraum asked on one of his visits.

"Like many species, male dragons mature slower than females. It is a law of nature that they are smaller and slower to mature. It allows the females to protect their cubs after they are hatched. The females must be more dominant than the males, but Drok-na's stronger powers are inherent. They will come in their own time. We just have to wait and see. Teaching him just initiated the process."

"Jacob taught him invisibility."

"It's a minor spell. Let's see what comes," the High Master reasserted.

"Both Drok-na and Rok-lin are greenish-blue, but you are white. Are there other colors?"

"You know white is all the colors," the wizard teased. "I am a dragon because I have studied magic so long that I am becoming part of the magic. I am white because I was not born a dragon. Each High Master has turned into a white dragon at the end of their mortal life unless they were killed first. But yes, there are many colors," the old wizard explained.

"Do the colors mean anything?"

"No. Dragons have personalities like men. It doesn't matter their color. There are good and bad, magical and non-magical in each color. As a cub they are pure of heart. As they grow older their morality is determined by their life experiences," the wizard answered, confirming Fraum's research.

"Just how old are you?"

"Not so old that I met Brendril," he said as the wrinkles of his smiling face grew wide.

＊　＊　＊　＊　＊

On the eastern edge of Ruhenmiur, the Elven name for the Black Forest, a great army was marching south through the Meadows. A single forest sprite, playfully exploring the forest, saw them as they marched in a long column, beating down the tall grass and kicking up the late summer dust like an endless line of horses moving to greener pastures. The sprite watched, observing all the races of Fendür, some Flatlanders, and the bluish-gray skinned Elves from the Wilds.

Dark Elves from the Fairy realm marching with the Fendür! The sprite was dismayed, her otherwise joyous spirit sinking into depression.

The Queen must be informed!

With great speed, the sprint darted westward, deep into Ruhenmiur towards Effenlia, to warn her queen.

"The Elves of the Wild have come! And they march with the Fendür," the sprite gasped.

"The Dark Elves of the Wilds? Are you sure?" the Fairy Queen asked.

"Yes, Your Majesty. They are marching south through the Meadows towards the Gap of Dillandria. They are well armed. There are even some flatlanders with them."

"How many?"

"Three thousand, more or less."

"But why would such an army be heading towards the Gap of Dillandria and the U'thra Basin?" the queen thought aloud.

"Send out scouts. Don't let them see us, and report back to me immediately if anything changes," the queen ordered.

＊　＊　＊　＊　＊

The dust from the marching warriors was nearly unbearable to the wizards following behind the Elves, but the Fendür were unbothered by the fouled air. The wizards began casting minor spells to create barriers protecting them from the dust, creating visible bubbles of clean air in the dust cloud.

From the front of the column, the general of the Dark Elves watched a single figure in a red and gold pillowed jacket on the horizon to the south between them and the Gap of Dillandria. Looking to the west towards the Plateau of Kronese first, the general turned his head eastward towards the Metamesterrian cliff and the city of Silandria. Nathanial had ordered them to avoid the east.

He must be from Silandria, the general thought as he watched the statuesque man.

"Tell Nathanial we have an observer," the general instructed Sescious, who rode next to him.

The wizard reined his horse away from the army's path, out towards the center of the meadow. When he was far enough from the column that his horse might not be spooked, he dismounted so he could sit down and meditate.

Nathanial?

What is it? Nathanial responded a moment later.

We have an observer. A tall man with an oblong head, I think. He is quite a ways away.

What's he doing?

Just watching.

Dragons and scales! Can't you do anything on your own?

I was instructed to tell you. I have done that. Is there anything else I can do?

No. You've done your part. I will handle it.

From high above the army, Rok-lin began a wide circle, slowly gliding downward. She strained her long greenish-blue neck, stretching it towards the center of her circle, her eyes searching like a hawk peering for its prey. Once she spotted the man, she tightened the circle and increased the descent. In the last moment before landing Rok-lin spread her wings and pulled up, setting herself down on her back legs.

Nathanial slipped from her neck down her foreleg as the talons scratched at the dirt. Guiding himself with his free hand, Nathanial stepped forward, leaning slightly on his staff.

"Good afternoon. We imagine you are Sescious's friend, Nathanial."

"You must be from Silandria," Nathanial commented.

The man looked down at Nathanial for a moment.

"You are taller than your, should we say, 'friends'?" the man observed.

"Who?"

"Jerrod and all the others you traveled with to Terrace Xul."

Nathanial started to raise his staff but stopped, sensing pressure upon his mind.

"I wouldn't," the Silandrian said.

"How do you know Jerrod?"

"We had the pleasure of his company a few months back. He visited Silandria."

"And how do you know my business?"

"Jerrod and the others told us what happened in Terrace Xul. As for your army, their thoughts are easy to hear. They are hungry for Torrence."

"I warn you," Nathanial stopped, realizing to whom he was speaking.

"The Elves are strong, but the others... well, they wouldn't stand a chance against us and you know it."

"We have no quarrel with you. That is why we are on the western edge of the Meadows. We merely seek to pass into the U'thra Basin."

"We know. We will not stop you. Nor will we aid you. We are merely curious."

"Then we have your leave to pass?" Nathanial questioned.

"You face more than you know, wizard. Far be it from us to stop you."

The words echoed in Nathanial's mind as he mounted Rok-lin again. As she jumped into the air and began to flap her wings, pushing the air downward to lift her body further from the ground, Nathanial reflected on the words of the Silandrian, "more than you know."

"*Rok-lin, what did he mean?*" the wizard asked.

"*I have no idea, but I can't imagine anything greater than you and me together.*"

✳　✳　✳　✳　✳

It was dusk after another long, laborious day. Jerrod's days were the same, placing the large, square boulders brought by the Fairies onto the fallen walls of Trisdale Keep. Even with the Fairy-Folk helping them move the square stones that were the height of a man, it was work fitting the stones in place in the outer wall. And despite their efforts, the seams in the walls were much more pronounced than the fittings of the Dwarves, who had built the original walls.

The days were still hot and Jerrod was covered with dirt from work. He was using the water in the wash basin in his tent to clean up before his evening meal when a faint thought came to him.

Jerrod, it's Rupaul.

Rupaul? From Silandria?

Yes. We have news that we think you will want to hear.

What is it? Jerrod responded, puzzled as much by the news as by the distance they were communicating.

Earlier today we observed an army marching south towards the U'thra Basin. They intend to attack Torrence.

What army? Who's army?

Nathanial's. He travels with Dark Elves, wizards, Fendür, and a large female dragon he calls Rok-lin.

They have attacked Torrence before, Jerrod responded.

It's a large army. We thought you would want to know.

Large? How large?

Three thousand or more. We didn't count, the city manager answered.

Thank you. Where are they now, do you know?

They have passed our realm, down through the Gap of Dillandria and onto the U'thra Basin.

Thank you again. I must go, Jerrod responded.

The magical rage of emotion had become familiar. He could feel it beginning to explode within him, but he did not recognize the new sensation accompanying his rage. With a flash of silvery-white light he stood without a shirt or shoes before the dais of Lady Lieisa and Lord Steffen.

"This is not acceptable, Jerrod. You can't just appear in our Pavilion!" Lord Steffen's harsh voice resounded in the room as he leaned forward in his throne.

"Father," Rhonda said as she stood up.

"What's happened?"

"I was standing in my tent, washing, and now I'm here," Jerrod said, looking around the Pavilion for a moment.

"The Silandrians informed me that Nathanial is marching across the U'thra Basin. They intend to attack Torrence again."

"Are you sure of this? Do you trust them?" Lady Lieisa questioned as she rose.

"I am sure of what they told me and no, not entirely," Jerrod answered candidly.

"Effendoria is close by. Perhaps they can tell us more. I will ask Horis to go," Lady Lieisa stated.

"If what Rupaul said is right, we only have days before they cross the Plains of Demeter. I must warn Torrence," Jerrod responded.

"Jerrod, you're half naked," Rhonda interjected.

Jerrod looked down at his feet and then back to the princess.

"Before you go you need to know about Cipper," Lady Lieisa added.

"What about Cipper?" Jerrod asked, turning to the priestess.

"It has been destroyed. Everyone is dead."

"How can this be?"

"Amanda found the city slain. Everyone. Men. Women. Children. All dead," the queen finished.

"Amanda? When?"

"About a month ago."

"What happened?"

"They were attacked by the Were-Folk. Bitten and clawed to death, and then burned."

"All of Cipper?" Jerrod was struggling to accept the fact.

"Yes. Any that survived will probably turn Were. Who knows how many."

"The muleskinner reported seeing wolves and bears in the Battle of the Sixth Battalion. Do you think they were Were?"

No one moved, not even a nod. The Pavilion was silent. They all understood what it meant. Nathanial was in league with the Were-Folk, too.

"As if an army of trolls and giant trolls is not enough!" Jerrod's frustration flashed out.

"Jerrod," Rhonda said stepping forward.

"I'm okay," he said more calmly as he turned to look at the princess.

"And Amanda? Where is she?"

"We don't know. She visited us and then left with the centaurs," Rhonda explained.

"Centaurs?" Jerrod repeated.

"Yes. There is a herd in the Lithlillian forest. She was with them. She was touched by E'fretté. She is part of our connection now."

Jerrod looked at the princess, and then down at his hands before looking back to her.

"Come on. I will get you some clothing." She smiled.

Rhonda led him to her parents' home and found him some ranger's clothes; a green shirt, forester's jacket, and high laced boots. Then she took a brown hooded robe and handed it to him with a silver pinecone brooch. Rhonda smiled again as he pinned the robe closed with the brooch.

"Much better, but throw the robe back over your sword-side shoulder. Now you look like a forest warrior. Would you like a sword?" Rhonda asked as Jerrod arranged his robe.

"No. I won't need one. Thank you."

"Jerrod, I was wrong to push myself on you. Thank you for respecting me enough to say no." A single tear pooled in her eye.

"You're welcome," Jerrod whispered slowly as a smile crossed his face. "I love you, Rhonda."

"I know. And Amanda told me you did, too."

"Amanda?"

"Mother told you she had an encounter with E'fretté."

"Yes, but she didn't really say what kind of encounter."

"Amanda bears the power mark of E'fretté in the middle of her forehead."

"Power mark?"

"We are all eternally bound together now. I am E'fretté's priestess. Amanda is her daughter. And you are connected to her in some magical way. Mother says you are more than the natural power we draw from E'fretté."

"I would love to stay, but I must go," Jerrod's voice was soft.

"I know. Be careful."

Jerrod kissed Rhonda lightly on the lips and then stepped back. He concentrated on the feeling he had in his tent, grasping for his internal power. Looking into her green eyes, Jerrod projected himself out of Lithlillia.

After the accidental trip to Lithlillia, Jerrod found the intentional trip to Torrence easy. He was growing accustomed to the magic. His largest limitation was his lack of knowledge, but he was beginning to sense that, like the accidental projection to Lithlillia, his instinct was showing him the way.

Trial by fire I suppose, he thought.

Jerrod appeared just outside the king's castle within the walled city of Torrence, which surprised the guards, causing them some alarm, but they quickly recognized Lord Trisdale and, at his request, took him directly to the king.

"Your Majesty," Jerrod greeted the king.

"Jerrod, it has been too long. I am glad to see you, but what brings you here so late?"

"It's Nathanial. He will be marching across the Plain of Demeter very soon. He brings an army to attack Torrence."

"How do you know?"

"It's complicated, Garrett. The short answer is that I was told by friends. Please trust in me and our friendship. Call the Lords. Ready the armies."

"Do you know how many?"

"Not for certain, maybe three thousand, but there is a column of Dark Elves and Fendür marching this way and Nathanial is probably allies with the Were-Folk from the north."

"Were-Folk?"

"Everyone in Cipper was killed by wolves and bears. The Lady Lieisa believes they may have been killed by the werewolves and werebears that live in the Wilds northwest of Lithlillia. I believe the same Were-Folk were seen by the muleskinner at the Battle of the Sixth Battalion."

"How many of these Were-Folk are in the army?"

"We don't know and, like the trolls, only silver and magical weapons will harm them."

"The army doesn't have silver or magical weapons!"

"I know. We need the Triad and the Elves."

King Garrett turned away for a moment, his hand going to his chin.

"When will you know how many?"

"Lady Lieisa is contacting the Fairy Kingdom on the eastern edge of the Black Forest, but no one seems to know the number of Were-Folk and if some were bitten at Cipper…" Jerrod paused.

"Their pack may have grown considerably."

"Okay. I will call the Lords to Torrence and put the army on alert. You find the Triad and gain their alliance."

"Yes, Your Majesty," Jerrod said as he turned to go.

"And Jerrod, tell me the moment you get any information."

Jerrod nodded, turned, and walked out of the king's private chambers.

✻   ✻   ✻   ✻   ✻

The streets near the king's castle were barren, but in the distance Jerrod could hear music in the market. Envisioning the bards playing while people danced, celebrating the cooling evenings of late summer, Jerrod allowed himself to daydream a bit as he walked towards the monastery. The sight of the gate brought reality crashing back on him.

"May I see Fraum, please?" Jerrod asked the young sage standing before the monastery.

"May I tell him who is calling?"

"Jerrod. Tell him Jerrod is at the gate." His voice was slow and tired.

It was not long before Fraum came calmly to the gate. A big grin was on his oval face as he reached out with both hands to grab Jerrod's.

"At your scrolls again, I see."

Fraum looked back over his shoulder, reflecting on the path he had taken to arrive at the gate and then back at Jerrod.

"The stairs?"

"Either that or you have taken up praying after dark," Jerrod teased.

"If I prayed for you, would it help?" the monk asked.

"No, probably not. You look well."

"Come in. Tea?" Fraum offered.

"Do you have anything stronger?"

"I have some wine, and a little liqueur if you would like something even stronger?"

Jerrod shrugged.

"I will be right back. I need to go to my room. Go on down to the library. I'll meet you there."

At the top of the stairs Jerrod turned to descend. He could see the large room where the monks gathered to meditate and pray. There were a couple of younger students sitting cross-legged, small sticks of incense burning in front of them. Descending the stairs he quickly found a chair in the library to plop down in.

Fraum's hand gently shook his shoulder.

"Oh, I'm sorry. I dozed off."

"When did you get to Torrence and what is it that brings you to the monastery so late?" Fraum asked as he sat down.

Jerrod took a deep sip of the liqueur Fraum had set before him. The warm burning sensation going down his throat felt good. He let his head tilt back and rest on the back of the chair for a moment before answering.

"Nathanial's coming with an army," Jerrod said, his head still laying back, his eyes still closed.

"How large?"

Jerrod sat up to look at the older monk.

"We don't know for certain. In truth? Massive. Dark Elves, wizards, the Fendür, and the Lady believes there are Were-Folk from the Wilds."

"Wizards? From the Triad?"

"I assume so."

"I must tell the High Master."

"Do you know how to contact him? We need his help."

"Yes. He and I have become friends. And I know where Drok-na is."

"Shall we wait 'til morning?" Fraum asked watching the young lord.

"No. I'm fine. We can go now," Jerrod answered as he exhaled a long breath.

It was well into the night when they reached the bottom of the Triad's stairs. Jerrod looked around at the wooden beams and planks lining the walls.

"How deep have we come?" Jerrod asked.

"I have counted seven hundred fifty steps. I imagine it is about five hundred feet deep," Fraum commented as a math scholar distracted by his own calculations.

At the bottom they were greeted by a young student who led them quickly to the octagonal room where the Triad met. On the far side of the table in the center of the room was the High Master. The only items on the table were three steaming cups of tea and a shallow bowl.

"A visit from the Great One and a dragon riding monk in the middle of the night... what has happened?" The High Master questioned.

Jerrod looked at Fraum briefly and then turned back to answer the wizard.

"Nathanial is bringing an army that may include some of your wizards," Jerrod responded, his voice slow and deliberate.

"You're tired. Come, sit. Drink some tea."

As they lowered themselves into chairs, the wizard leaned over the table and flicked his fingers, causing the oil in the bowl to ignite into a low burning flame. At first heavy black smoke rose from the flame. Then flickering sparkles began dancing through the smoke, which was turning light blue. Motionless, the wizard stared deep into the smoke.

"More than four thousand five hundred troops, but I don't sense the Were-Folk. Animal minds are hard to find. And Fairies. I sense some Fairy-Folk."

"Lady Lieisa was going to ask for their help," Jerrod thought out loud. "What about the wizards?"

"They are the Triad deserters. They have studied wizardry, illusion, and alchemy to varying degrees. Sescious."

"Sescious?" Fraum asked.

"Sescious was a Master of the Triad before he deserted."

"A Master, like Nathanial?" Jerrod asked.

"Nathanial is a Master, one of four. Sescious is a lower level Master. He is next below Nathanial and the two remaining full Masters. Sescious would have taken Jacob's place."

"We are going to need your help to fight the Trolls. We have very few silver weapons and even fewer magical ones," Jerrod explained.

"The Triad will do its part. Pray the boy-king remembers."

"And Drok-na will come, I'm sure," Fraum offered.

"I need you and Drok-na to watch for Rok-lin," Jerrod responded.

"And who will confront Nathanial?" the High Master asked.

"I will see to Nathanial," Jerrod said confidently.

"Are you sure you're ready?" Fraum looked at him.

Jerrod held out his sword hand, his palm up. In a brief moment the Sword of Trisdale appeared in his hand.

"I'm ready."

✻　　✻　　✻　　✻　　✻

Neither Jerrod nor Fraum said a word as they wound their way back up the square staircase, the wood creaking beneath their feet. Jerrod walked with his head down, laboriously watching each step.

"You sound tired," Fraum commented.

"Sound? How do you sound tired?"

"You're breathing is hard and your footsteps are heavy. Your feet are sliding onto each step," Fraum explained.

Jerrod exhaled.

"Yeah. It's been a long day."

"Did you see her?" Fraum asked.

"I saw Rhonda. Amanda had been there but was gone. She is with the centaurs who live in the Lithlillian forest."

"Another teacher. Centaurs are some of the best," Fraum reflected.

They climbed a little more before Jerrod spoke again.

"Fraum, I need you to do something."

"What is it?"

"You are friends with Drok-na, right?"

"Yes."

"And you ride him?"

"Yes."

"I need you to take Drok-na to Trisdale Keep so that when the battle begins, you are in position to find Nathanial and Rok-lin. They are not traveling with the army."

CHAPTER 18

BATTLE OF DEMETER PLAINS

T he citizens of Torrence came out in their finest attire to watch their young king lead the combined forces of Torrence through the gates and across the bridge. Long, pointed banners flew over the armies. Solid purple banners flew over the cavalry of the King's Guard leading the combined army. White banners with royal blue trim flew over the Cavaliers and foot soldiers of the Order of One. Then came the red and black banners of the Fourth Army, Fifth Battalion, and the remaining cavalry of the Standing Army. Scores of bards and wizards mixed in with the archers and foot soldiers marching in the column.

After crossing the bridge the king waited, watching each battalion parade by him. Twenty-four hundred men from the Standing Army and another three hundred from the Order dressed in their white tunics over their armor or chainmail and their royal blue capes. Lord Trisdale, the Grand Marshal of the Order of One, and the Commander of the Armies sat on their horses next to him.

Nearby a company of bards were playing their mandolins and flutes. The magical music made the armies feel strong and the citizens feel happy. They played a soldier's march, the men from Torrence joining in song.

To war, to war, our heroes lost, our brothers slain,
Our swords and arrows kill evil without refrain,
Fight on! The blows of our foes glancing off our shields,
But in the end we shall leave them on bloodied field.

March out, march out, valiant, brave sons to victory,
Your gleaming armor for all of Torrence to see,
Soldiers don't hesitate, when your battles await,
When evil roars, then turn to your courage within.

To war, to war, our heroes lost, our brothers slain,
Our swords and arrows kill evil without refrain,
Fight on! The blows of our foes glancing off our shields,
But in the end we shall leave them on bloodied field.

Beat down the beasts, revenge our dead and slay our foe,
Your sword and lance revenge their deaths, mercy forgo,
And when battle is done, our brothers' souls may rest,
With setting sun their souls can fade into the west.

To war, to war, our heroes lost, our brothers slain,
Our swords and arrows kill evil without refrain,
Fight on! The blows of our foes glancing off our shields,
But in the end we shall leave them on bloodied field.

Hurrah! Hurrah! We march to fight with sword and lance.
Hurrah! Hurrah! We march to deliver their deaths!

As the last of the soldiers marched off the bridge under watchful eyes, trumpets on the walls sounded a fanfare. The citizens once again watched their loved ones, their husbands, their fathers, their brothers, marching off to war.

It took hours for the lances of the Cavaliers and the spears of the soldiers, which bounced and weaved like saplings swaying in a heavy breeze, to pass by the king and his entourage. Before the supply wagons, pulled by teams of four or six mules, passed, the king nudged his horse and began to lope towards the front of the long column. As their four leaders rode by each section, the faithful men cheered.

"Hurrah! Hurrah!"

The foot soldiers marching four abreast rattled their spears against their shields, adding to the thunderous cheers. Nearer the front, the Cavaliers in their columns of two raised their lances straight up, sending a ripple of their salute and respect for the young king forward as the king rode onward.

When at last the wagons had passed, the bards mounted their horses and trotted towards the front of the army. They did not wear armor but instead wore colorful clothes with pillowed shirts, leather jackets, riding cloaks, and high leather boots. Here and there one of the magical musicians fell in with a section of soldiers to play for them as they slowly marched or rode towards their destiny.

The army of soldiers and horses traveled east from Torrence, following the road until it ended at the north-south road, and then they continued, straight across onto the grassy fields of the Plain of Demeter until dusk imposed its will on the weary travelers.

In the camps of the Order, the Cavaliers' squires set up their tents and cared for their horses while the foot soldiers were left to care for themselves, but in the Standing Armies of the king they worked together, mounted and foot soldiers erecting tents side by side while their Captains directed the companies into loosely formed groups.

When the wagons stopped, men and women emerged to cook the meals for the massive army while the muleskinners led the mules away to tether them on the edge of the camp. It was hours before the men and women, who had followed the army out of Torrence to cook and feed the gallant men, began serving the hungry troops.

After the evening meal a large service for the three hundred warriors of the Order was held. A few priests of Olympia wandered through the camp offering prayers for the others. And after prayer, the warriors lay in their tents, searching for sleep while the cooks labored well into the night, long after the camp had retired.

By early morning the army was marching eastward, leaving the chore of breaking down and packing up the camp behind them for the muleskinners and women. The squires were the next to start the march. When the muleskinners began driving the wagons they pushed the mules hard in order to get ahead of the army so the evening meal would be ready upon the army's arrival.

On the morning of the second day, Lord Edward's troops from Akkian joined the parade and by mid-day Lord Francis's troops from Rizendür rode up from the Seimenie Mountains south of the plain. In the early evening the army stopped again to set camp so the king could convene a counsel with his generals, officers, and lords.

Jerrod walked through the camp's chaos towards the king's tent as Roger rode in with all seventy-five of the soldiers from Trisdale Keep. When he saw Jerrod, Roger dismounted.

"I'm sorry we're late," Roger greeted Jerrod.

"You're not late. It's fine. Set up some tents on the north side of camp and grab some food. I'll be there as soon as I can," Jerrod said.

The king was addressing the leaders as Jerrod entered the large tent.

"We are about twenty-seven hundred, including one hundred Cavaliers and four hundred cavalry, facing forty-five hundred Elves and Fendür," the king started.

"Lithlillia brings twenty-five hundred Elves and rangers," Jerrod interjected.

"I don't see Lithlillia at counsel," Commander De'Ran pointed out.

"They will come," Jerrod said with confidence.

"They will come because why? Because the young Lord Trisdale says so. Why would the Elves come to the aid of Torrence?" Commander De'Ran mocked.

"Because they are honorable," Jerrod responded.

"Enough!" King Garrett commanded. "I won't have you fighting one another. Not here. Not now. We must determine how to approach a superior force. The wizards would balance our fight with the trolls, but they can't fight both Nathanial's wizards and the Fendür trolls."

"May I make a suggestion?" the old wizard asked as he stepped into the tent.

"Welcome. Come in and sit. What do you suggest?" the king greeted the High Master.

"Focus some of your archers on Nathanial's wizards to make them cast defensive spells, or to distract them altogether. We can then focus half our wizards on the Fendür and half on the Nathanial's army."

"We are short of archers," Commander De'Ran said, looking at Jerrod.

"They will be here and they will fire twice the arrows of any of our archers."

King Garrett looked at the two lords, the seasoned Lord Akkian, with experience of army battles, and his friend Lord Trisdale, who had proven ingenuity and a special power no one seemed to understand.

"I need you to work together," Garrett started.

"We will trust that to Lord Steffen and Lady Lieisa. Together, we will avenge the Sixth. Let that be our battle cry," King Garrett concluded.

When they left the king's tent, the High Master pulled Jerrod aside.

"We have a great challenge ahead of us, but I fear yours will be the greatest of them all."

"What have you foreseen?"

The old wizard shook his head.

"Nothing. It's a feeling, nothing more."

After bidding the High Master good night, Jerrod went to the north side of the camp to find Roger. As he walked up, Roger handed him a cup of wine.

"Thank you."

"Was it bad? You look tense."

"Commander De'Ran..." Jerrod stopped. "No, my friend, it wasn't bad." Jerrod slapped Roger on the shoulder.

"I am not convinced, my Lord," Roger said slowly.

"Let's drink. Let's drink of friendship. To the Axe & Bow," Jerrod said, taking a long sip of wine.

"And to the dreams of battle that we shared," Jerrod finished after a large gulp of wine.

Through the night a large white dragon slept nearby on the plains, it's incredibly long tail wrapped around it. Around it were the odd shaped tents of nearly one hundred wizards.

✻   ✻   ✻   ✻   ✻

The next morning came too early for the warriors, all of whom rose at sunrise again. Their food was ready. It was warm, soothing to their stomachs, but unable to fill that pit everyone swore was hunger rather than anxiety. They ate quickly so they could start the march before the camp was struck.

The army marched through the day with the king and his advisors at the front. The colorful banners rippled as they rode and the bards continued to mix into the groups playing their magical music, lifting the spirits of the men and extending their march just a few more hours. The members of the Triad walked at a distance, away from the column, out of the dust to avoid using spells. Walking together in small groups, they talked of the spells they might use in the battle they knew lay ahead. High above the army a white dragon ducked in and out of the white clouds, keeping a watchful eye on the horizon.

As they marched in their long column like ants following one another to a point, the muleskinners drove the wagons past them, eager to get ahead of the army. When they arrived at dusk the new camp was already built. Thousands of empty tents waited with cooking fires spread throughout the small canvas city. It was after dusk when the brass horns sounded, announcing the arrival of Lithlillia.

Lord Steffen and Lady Lieisia rode at the head of the column of two, behind them thousands of forest warriors, men and Elves, their hooded forest robes clasped by silver pinecone brooches. The white limbs of their Elven longbows rose above their covered heads as they marched into the camp. Rhonda and Imelrinn were the only others on horseback. Unlike the Elves behind them, they rode with their hoods down, the loose curls of Rhonda's wheat-colored hair covering her shoulders. The chainmail *coifs* were pulled off their heads and resting on their shoulders.

Hooded druids, mostly women, were intermixed with the warriors. They wore no armor. Their Elven long swords hung from their leather belts. Only the hilts showed from under their long cloaks as they walked alongside the column of warriors.

Jerrod and Roger watched Lithlillia enter the western edge of the camp.

"You are a sight for weary eyes, my Lord. Lady Lieisa. Rhonda. Imelrinn, my friends," Jerrod greeted them.

"Lord Trisdale, thank you for your greetings. We bring twenty-five hundred warriors, rangers as you call them, both Elves and men. Where shall we camp?" Lord Steffen asked.

"I would be honored if you would camp next to me, there, on the north side. Roger can show you the way. The king's council meets within the hour," Jerrod answered as he looked between Roger and the leader of Lithlillia.

Rhonda slid off her horse to give him a hug.

"Jerrod, I have missed you."

"I'm not surprised to see you here, but in armor?"

"I come as a warrior, not a druid priestess. Mother can more than handle that. It is my sword that the Fendür will taste." Rhonda smiled.

"And your arrows, I'm sure," Imelrinn added as he kicked his leg over his horse and jumped to the ground.

"If either are half as terrifying as Mount Sismin, the Fendür are in for more than they bargained for," Jerrod teased.

Commander De'Ran scowled when Jerrod walked into the king's tent with Lord Steffen and Lady Lieisa.

"Welcome," King Garrett greeted them enthusiastically.

"Thank you, Your Highness. We bring Lithlillia in answer to the treaties of old," Lord Steffen announced.

"Thank you, Lord Steffen. You honor us in these dark times."

"Our army grows, gentlemen, and Lady Lieisa, your druids are welcome," the king said, acknowledging the druid priestess.

Lieisa smiled at the young king and then at the old man sitting nearby. Her smile faded when she looked, at last, at Commander De'Ran.

Gathering in the center of the tent, they discussed battle strategy as wine was brought in and poured. The king handed Lord Steffen and Lady Lieisa a goblet before turning to take his own. When he reached back for the wine, Commander De'Ran was there to put it into his hand. The king stepped back, crowded by the commander's closeness.

"Thank you, Commander. Now, to the business of battle. Nathanial is on his way west. We will meet him in the next few days," the king explained.

"The morning after tomorrow, if each of us march a full day tomorrow. We will meet him before mid-day," Lord Steffen interrupted.

"How do you know this?" Commander De'Ran challenged.

"Because, Commander, the Fairy-Folk follow his army," Lady Lieisa interjected.

"Your Highness, we should send out scouts. Really, Fairy-Folk?" the commander protested.

"I have seen a large dust plume in the distance. The Fairies are right," the High Master's voice was filled with the softness of an old man.

"With the addition of Lithlillia, we have the larger army. The timing is in our favor," the king surmised.

"How will the wizards react?" he asked, turning to the High Master.

"They are not soldiers. We can tell them now what we want from them, but in the heat of battle they will fight against the targets they deem most threatening."

"Commander, your thoughts?" the king asked.

"Cavaliers and cavalry should lead the charge, followed by foot soldiers. Archers should support from behind. Throw in the druids and wizards where you can, but don't count on them. They are not soldiers."

"Lords, any thoughts?

"I agree," Lord Edward answered.

"And what about the Were-Folk?" Lord Trisdale asked.

They all looked at him.

"The Were that attacked Cipper? Skin changers," Jerrod paused.

"We suspect the wolves and bears in the Battle of the Sixth Battalion were Were-Folk. Cavaliers' lances and the cavalry's swords won't harm them, not permanently." Jerrod stopped.

"Lord Trisdale is right. They won't hurt the trolls either," Lord Steffen added.

"The object is not to kill the smaller forces but to drive through them and attack the Elven archers that Nathanial will have behind them. We will have time to gather up the Fendür later," Commander De'Ran counseled as he stepped forward to stand in between everyone.

The commander spun slowly, stopping as he faced Jerrod.

"The wizards and druids can keep each other in check and help with the trolls. Our objective will be the archers," the commander finished, turning away from Jerrod.

"And Lord Trisdale's concern for the Were-Folk?" the king pressed.

"The 'Were-Folk' are insignificant. A small group of ravenous animals without the ability to plan or follow instructions, if they show up at all," De'Ran challenged.

"Seems you have thought it out, commander. Our archers will support your charge," Lord Steffen said, dismissing himself from the council.

Lady Lieisa and Jerrod turned and followed Lord Steffen out of the tent without a word.

"I am not following that pompous ass," Lord Steffen growled as he turned to walk away.

"It will be the king who leads the army," Jerrod tried to encourage the leader of Lithlillia.

"I have asked the centaurs to track the Were-Folk. They are starting at Cipper," Lady Lieisa commented as they wound their way through the tents.

"Is Amanda with them?"

"I don't know."

In an uncustomary show of affection, Lady Lieisa wrapped her arms around Lord Steffen's upper arm, pulling his arm close to her chest. Not another word was spoken as they made their way towards their own camps. Thoughts of the coming battle consumed their minds. They knew in less than two days' time thousands would die.

"We will go out onto the plain to pray and purify our souls if you would like to join us," Lady Lieisa invited Jerrod.

"I would love to join you but tonight my place is with my men."

When he returned to his camp, Jerrod was met by Roger.

"How did it go?"

"They are fools! Only the Elves understand."

"Commander De'Ran again?"

"Yes, but forget it. Where are the men?"

As the single file line of men and Elves wearing long hooded robes filed out of the camp to worship in secret, Jerrod knelt with his men.

"Very soon we will be asked to charge into battle against inhuman beasts. Giants, many times our height, and trolls that will get up to fight again after we have beaten them down. But Athena will provide us her wisdom for battle, and we will overcome. We will fight as though we carried Ares' bronze spear itself. The Fates have provided us with this chance for glory and we will not fail. Drink up tonight. Spill a little of your wine on the dirt to honor Dionysus and listen to the bards' songs."

Jerrod stayed and drank for a little while, and then rose to go to his tent.

"To Lord Trisdale. Hurrah! Hurrah!" his men cheered.

"Sleep well tonight upon the field of glory," Jerrod replied as he raised his goblet, drank a bit, and spilled the last of his wine upon the dirt.

❊   ❊   ❊   ❊   ❊

In the morning Imelrinn appeared early at Jerrod's tent to invite him to breakfast with the Lady, Lord, and Princess of Lithlillia. Calling for Roger, the two men followed Imelrinn back to the Elves' tent. When they entered, Rhonda was wringing her hands as she paced on the far side of the tent. Her long brown hair was braided and pulled tight to her head to fit more comfortably under her *coif*.

She's beautiful, Jerrod thought to himself.

Lady Lieisa and Lord Steffen sat on a plush bed of green grass. Roger fidgeted a little and glanced around the tent, unnerved.

"Relax, Roger. They're druids. This is normal." Jerrod smiled.

"This is Roger, my second in command and a close friend."

"We want to share a little more detail with you, Jerrod," Lord Steffen said as Jerrod and Roger sat down.

"Your king is young and listens to the wrong advisors," Steffen continued as Rhonda sat down.

"The plan to charge forward will lead to ruin. Not even in the Elven-Dwarve wars did I see such folly," Imelrinn offered as he began handing out warm tea.

"You know Nathanial will seek to surprise us," Rhonda added.

Jerrod nodded his agreement. "Thank you," Jerrod said as he took some tea, and then turned his attention back to the conversation.

"All the more reason for our secondary attack," Lady Lieisai persuade.

"Secondary attack?" Jerrod asked.

"I said that the centaurs are tracking the Were. That's not completely true. We believe the Were will try to outflank us. The destruction of Cipper seems to indicate they are behind us and the Fairies have not seen any wolves or bears with Nathanial's army," Lady Lieisa confided.

"The centaurs are much closer," Rhonda added.

"Their job is to protect our flank," Lord Steffen asserted.

"I have another surprise." Jerrod smiled, watching their reaction.

"Fraum and Drok-na are sitting on top of the tower at Trisdale, searching for Rok-lin. They will find her and when they do, they will attack Nathanial and Rok-lin. I will join them immediately."

As they finished their tea, trumpets blared, sounding the first call to march.

"We march in an hour, my Lord," Roger said to Jerrod.

"See to our men. I will be right behind you," Jerrod instructed.

"King Garrett is a good man." Jerrod's voice was soft when he turned back to Lieisa and Steffen.

"We know. And this war is more than the internal squabbles of one kingdom. Nathanial has allied with the Fendür and the Dark Elves, which makes it all of our problem," Lady Lieisa sympathized.

"It was the Dark Elves that defeated us long ago. We left what you call the Wilds and the Dwarves abandoned Frausnaugh." Imelrinn's voice was distant.

"Jerrod, where does your allegiance lie?" Lord Steffen asked slowly.

"Drin took an oath that seems a good guideline. 'Stand with virtue and purity that all may see. Have integrity in all your affairs. Place honor and trust

unto all you meet until they prove unworthy.'" Jerrod paused. "If I remain true
to myself in all my dealings then I am honest to everyone," he finished.

"But if it comes down to it, between Lithlillia or Torrence, where do you
stand?" Steffen pressed.

"I don't know why I would ever be faced with that decision." Jerrod nodded
respectfully and left the tent.

"I like him. He is a Friend of Lithlillia, but he is not Lithlillian," Steffen
thought aloud.

"Father, he is the Great One," Rhonda protested.

"He told us what we wanted to know. He seeks honor and trust, values
that Lithlillia cherishes. While honor remains, we are in allegiance," Lady
Lieisa finished.

Jerrod excused himself from what had become an uncomfortable discussion
and returned to his men. When he arrived at their camp, Roger had his horse
saddled and waiting. All the men of Trisdale stood near their hoses waiting for
the command to mount up.

The combined armies rode another day and, with the setting sun, they
began to hear the faint sound of drums in the distance. In typical fashion the
followers of the Order of One gathered for one large group prayer while the
Olympian priests visited smaller groups of soldiers to call upon their gods for
support. But unlike the previous nights when the leaders had gathered in the
king's tent, the men paced while they waited for their king. Tension filled the
air as they avoided looking at each other, glancing down to their feet while they
talked. When King Garrett was ready, the commander cleared his throat.

"The Cavaliers of the Order will charge directly east, supported by their
own foot soldiers and foot soldiers from the First Battalion; that's seven hundred
men at your command, Field Marshal. The cavalry from the Fifth Battalion will
circle around, attacking from the north supported by the Third Army's foot
soldiers. That's twelve hundred men from the north. That leaves the Elves with
their bows and swords and the First Army's Archers to hold the middle, nearly
three thousand men in all." Commander De'Ran stopped to make eye contact
with each leader.

"Is that acceptable to Lithlillia?" He looked directly at Lord Steffen.

"We will hold the middle," Lord Steffen confirmed.

"We will hold the foot soldiers from the East Guard cavalry and the Second

Battalion soldiers in reserve. And what will the wizards provide us?" Commander De'Ran asked the High Master.

"We will spread between your ranks and provide what support we can until our strength wears out."

"Are you sure you want to hold eight hundred horsemen and soldiers out of battle, Commander?" King Garrett asked.

"We must see where the battle's weaknesses are, your Highness, then we will use the East Guard and the Second Battalion to reinforce the line."

"And what of Rok-lin?" Jerrod baited.

"Let Nathanial and his dragon come. With eight hundred in reserve, they will die in the middle of this ill-gotten battle," the commander snapped as he glared at the young Lord Trisdale.

"Then I will take the Fifth Battalion," King Garrett announced.

"Your Highness?" the commander began to protest.

"It is done. This is your plan, Commander. I hope it works."

"I ride with the king," Jerrod announced before looking at Lord Steffen and Lady Lieisa.

Once the battle plan was set the leaders quickly disbanded to join their troops, leaving the boy-king with his thoughts. His father had never been on the battlefield. Torrence had been at peace for so long, most had forgotten the days when the Plains of Demeter were filled with beasts. Long before the kingdom had been won by the sword.

May I lead with honor tomorrow, Garrett thought as he looked at his father's sword.

When Jerrod left the king he walked back towards their camps with Lord Steffen and Lady Lieisa. Groups of bards were wandering through the camps, playing magical songs to drown out the relentless drums of the Fendür.

"It's fun to bait the commander, isn't it?" Lord Steffen asked Jerrod, who just smiled.

"Impetuous," Lady Lieisa said when Jerrod left them.

"Jerrod reminds me of me in my youth," Lord Steffen answered.

"Me too," she agreed.

Returning to camp as his men were finishing the evening meal, Jerrod knelt down to share some wine.

"May Zeus, the father of the gods, send the Fates to bless our course tomorrow. We will draw upon his son, Ares, god of war and courage, to fight so well that our names earn a place among heroes. Let no man question our valor nor call us weak, or by Hades himself, I will return from the underworld to release Cerberus, the three headed hound, upon them myself. So drink in the blood of war from Dionysus's wine. Release his madness upon the field of battle, and let it be said, those are the men of Trisdale!"

"Hurrah! Hurrah!"

They drank a while, encouraging each other with boisterous stories, bragging to build their strength. When Jerrod turned to go to his tent, Roger followed shortly.

"I wanted to thank you for all you have provided me," Roger said, stopping Jerrod.

"You are a loyal friend, Roger."

"Thank you, my Lord."

In the morning hours before dawn the servants helped the young king don his armor. A purple cape hung from his shoulders as he held his crowned helm, looking again at his father's sword.

The Fifth Battalion Cavalry and Third Army rose before dawn to start their march towards the northeast. The remaining armies, who did not rise quite so early, would start their march after sunrise. Shortly after the Fifth Battalion started its march, scouts came back to the column with news that they would meet Nathanial's army by mid-day and, with each eastward step, the drums of the Fendür grew louder.

Lord Steffen was right, the king thought.

✳   ✳   ✳   ✳   ✳

Nathanial's army had marched from the Gap of Dillandria, down through the U'thra Basin until they could see the Semanie Mountains in the distance, and then they turned westward to cross the Plains of Demeter. With the gray shadow of the mountains to the south they continued marching westward, camping at night, and continuing the next day until they saw the armies of Torrence. Nearly a hundred wizards carrying staves and other magical devices mixed between the Dark Elves, giants, and trolls. High above the plains Nathanial circled on Rok-lin.

When they finally faced the men of Torrence and Lithlillia, the Fendür stood waving stone hammers the size of ponies, and great metal axes and swords crudely constructed with rough edges hastily sharpened on dry stones. The Fendür spread out in long rows, hundreds standing shoulder to shoulder. Behind the rows of trolls and giants were Dark Elves with their bows in hand and quivers full of black arrows hanging from their shoulders.

The charge of the Order's knights was glorious. Their armor glistened in the mid-day sun as the horses began trotting towards their foe. When they broke into a gallop the holy Cavaliers lowered their white lances, pointing the deadly tips at the Fendür. The hooves of their steeds drove into the grass, throwing up the sod as they raced towards the clash of battle. Their white and blue banners whipped loudly in the wind of their charge.

Simultaneously, the Fifth Battalion's cavalry began its charge on the eastern end of the battlefield. Charging south under their red and black banners, their swords drawn as the King of Torrence led the galloping horses towards the enemy battle line. Jerrod and the men of Trisdale rode with Fifth Battalion.

"Hurray!" the foot shoulders cheered.

Behind the charge the foot soldiers advanced as rapidly as possible, running in a long line several ranks deep. They could not keep up with the horses, nor, under the weight of their chainmail, could they run at full speed. Their battle line staggered by the charge. In the middle of the line the foot soldiers advanced slower, marching forward with spears extending from behind their shields as the outer wings of the line extended past the slower center.

Behind the ranks of Fendür, the Dark Elves released scores of black arrows, striking riders and horses, causing both to tumble to the ground. The Lithlillian Elves answered with volley after volley, their arrows striking deep into the evil forces. Each flight of arrows caused the giants and trolls to spin, swatting at the arrows like humans swatting at a swarm of hornets, momentarily stopping their advance. Here or there a troll fell lifeless on the battlefield, only to get up moments later and resume their fight. Far less often giants fell, not to rise again.

When the mounted warriors of the combined armies collided with the Fendür, the archers began vaulting arrows over the battle line into the Dark Elven archers, carefully avoiding the Torrence forces, but the Dark Elves had little regard for their own troops. They continued firing at the mounted warriors despite hitting their allies. Here and there wizards on both sides began casting deflection spells, creating small pockets where arrows were stopped in flight as though they had struck an unseen wall.

Once the armies collided, Lord Steffen drew his sword with Rhonda standing at his side.

"For Lithlillia!" Lord Steffen yelled as he began to run.

"For Lithlillia and Lord Steffen!" the Elves and rangers answered.

Druids stopped to raise their arms, beckoning black storm clouds to fill the sky.

Somewhere to the north a burning mass of fire lobbed out of the mass of soldiers to land in the middle of the Fendür, causing panic and chaos in their ranks as trolls jumped and rolled away from the fire. Like the flood gates of a dam allowing water to rush over the spillway, the spell signaled all the wizards to begin casting their magic.

Great balls of fire and bolts of lightning shot across the lines, maiming Fendür and killing men and Elves. The winds came up as druids began calling lightning strikes down on the masses of the Fendür. The magical attacks maimed and occasionally killed one of the beasts.

The sky grew so dark from the storm clouds that it seemed like they were fighting at dusk. Warriors on both sides became dark shapes without color. The Fendür, wielding their crude weapons, struck against the chainmail clad warriors of Torrence. The men of Torrance slashed at the exposed skin of the Fendür with little affect. All around them bodies lay on the ground, occasionally causing someone to trip and fall. In the middle of the battle line, the Elves and men of Lithlillia waded into the mêlée.

Slowly the power of the spells began to weigh upon the wizards, causing them to collapse with fatigue. Lady Lieisa, calling gale force winds to beat upon the Dark Elven archers, turned arrows from straight flight and pushed them into the ground short of their target, but many of the druids began feeling the exhaustion of battle.

As the war continued the fronts mixed and the battle line became less apparent as each army struggled to defeat the other. The armies' banners fell when soldiers dropped the banner pole to fight or were struck down by a fatal stoke.

"I think the Fendür on the north side are beginning to fail," Commander De'Ran said to the Captain of the East Guard.

"Take the East Guard to the north to support the king's advance," the commander ordered.

"Yes sir," the captain said as he turned his horse around and galloped away.

The commander watched as the East Guard with its purple banner dancing behind the line of archers wheeled around to join the Fifth, attacking the Fendür's right wing. Nearby lightning hit an archer then radiated out to hit other archers nearby. The commander moved as druids called for counter attacks of lightning.

On the western wing of the combined army, wolves and bears snuck up out of the tall, dry grass of the plains. From the north and south, hundreds of Were attacked each side of the Elven archers' flank. Dropping their bows and drawing their Elven swords, the Elves turned to defend against the Were.

The ensuing battle was ferocious. Werewolves and Werebears bit and scratched at the Elves, who parried as they could, countering blows with silver swords. Even wounds that were not normally mortal began killing the Were, but it was not enough. Behind the overwhelmed Elves a few druids left the main front to gather around their priestess, standing next to the green and gold banner of Lithlillia. The surge of Were began flowing over the Elves like a strong wind through a pile of leaves.

As the Were closed around the Elves for a final assault, a large black panther leapt onto the back of an unsuspecting werebear, ripping the beast's back open. Sasha dug her claws further into the creature's back, riding it until it collapsed, and then leaped to pounce upon a wolf. She rolled onto her back to rip the wolf's belly open with all four claws before rolling up to face more of the Were. Behind her the centaurs galloped into the battle.

The Elves rallied, forming a tight circle that moved slowly back towards Lady Lieisa and the other druids. A burst of lightning struck behind the Elven archers, opening a path for them to reach the druids. Again the Were circled, looking for the vulnerability of the small group of Elves that were greatly outnumbered.

As the centaurs descended upon the Were, Amanda leapt from Sarric's back, drawing both swords from the sheath on her back as she flew through the air. Landing on her feet and springing forward into a roll, she broke through the Were to come up on her feet, slashing at the startled beasts. The power mark in the middle of her forehead burned bright blue like lightning in a black sky. Behind her, Sarric and the man-stallions beat down upon the Were army.

Before Sarric stood the old bear, the leader of the Were. Sarric stopped, circling a little as he threw his bow aside and drew a great, two-handed sword from his back. The old bear roared in defiance, and then bounded forward. The muscles in the bear's arms and back rippled with power as he drove towards Sarric, swiping with a giant paw, but Sarric, reeling around to the side, came back across with the two-handed sword, and cut the bear's shoulder open. The bear roared again.

As the bear lunged, Sarric raised on his hind feet to avoid the bear's paw. Swinging the sword behind his back with both hands, Sarric brought the silver sword down over his head, slashing the bear's back. The force of the blow drove the bear into the ground.

The old bear struggled to push up off the ground and face Sarric. Blood ran from its nose as the he began to circle again. He blew large breaths of air and clacked his teeth in fear. The leader of the Were moaned and then stood on his back feet, standing taller than Sarric, attempting to intimidate the centaur leader.

Around them the centaurs were slashing at the Were with silver axes and swords. Red arrows from the back of the group of centaurs flew through the chaos to imbed deep into the Were. Occasionally, a leather strap and balls rotated across the field to entwine the feet of a Were, rendering it helpless for a closer centaur to dispatch. The Elves took up their bows again and began shooting their silver arrows at the Were, supporting the centaurs' attacks.

Amanda's slashes and cross-cuts of her Elven swords quickly killed the werewolf in front of her. As she turned towards another Were, lightning struck nearby.

With the Were attack drawing the Elven archers into the mêlée, the Dark Elven archers began picking off the soldiers of the combined armies. The battle ground was becoming muddy, soaked with the blood of men, Elves, and Fendür. The middle of the line was beginning to fail as the Fendür and Dark Elves were overcoming the weakened line of their foe.

In the darkening sky Nathanial had lost sight of the battlefield. He pushed Rok-lin into a descent, slowly circling down above the battlefield. The warring factions had merged into one mass, looking like a pile of red and black ants fighting over a mound of sand. As she descended, Rok-lin released a high pitched screech ending in a deep roar that caused both sides to quit fighting, holding their ears as Rok-lin landed amidst the warriors, spitting fire on a line of Elves who combusted in the magical flame.

Many more will roast on the plain today, but where is Drok-na? Rok-lin emphasized her thought with another roar. The roar temporarily deafened everyone within a hundred feet.

"He will come. He will come," Nathanial repeated.

"To the dragon!" Commander De'Ran ordered.

The Second Battalion marched forward with some swords drawn and spears still pointed up. When they reached the Elves' flank, the soldiers blended into the battle, supporting the Lithlillian army, but the battle prevented the Second Battalion from advancing to engage Rok-lin. With the additional push the battle line began to slowly surge south, pressing the Fendür back towards the dragon.

The Elven archers who had remained at the battle line when the Were attacked turned their aim towards Rok-lin as Nathanial slid down her foreleg. Leaning with one hand against Rok-lin's shoulder and his gnarled staff in the other, Nathanial jumped off her foreleg. The long strap of a brown leather bag hung across Nathanial's chest, the thick bag resting on his hip.

"Metlock!" Nathanial shouted as the Lithlillian Elves released their arrows.

In mid-air the arrows seemed to hit a wall, stopping, some splintering, as they all fell harmlessly to the ground. Not a single arrow hit its mark. Rok-lin drew her head up and back before lunging her long neck forward to spit a stream of fire over the soldiers in front of her. The continuous stream burned through the archers like a wildfire in dry grass.

"Lepsearree," Nathanial shouted as he drove the bottom of his gnarled staff into the ground.

The ground near him heaved upward, radiating out in a circle. The shockwave knocked all the horses, soldiers, and wizards off their feet. In the distance, a single Elven woman stood, her long blonde hair blowing back, disclosing her pointed ears, as the wind came up around her. Her Elven eyes fixated on Nathanial as lightning burst down from the sky, striking Nathanial's back and driving him face forward into the ground.

Rok-lin roared as her head whipped around to lay eyes upon the druid priestess. The shrill sound of Rok-lin's roar stopped all the fighting between the dragon and Lady Lieisa as man, Elve, and Fendür covered their ears.

You will die now, druid! Rok-lin's thoughts screamed.

And what makes you think that a worm like you can kill the Priestess of E'fretté, Rok-lin? Lady Lieisa responded as the fighting around them resumed.

✻   ✻   ✻   ✻   ✻

The top of Trisdale's tower was lonely. Both Fraum and Drok-na knew the enemy was coming. Jerrod had asked that they wait and watch, but the armies of Torrence had passed beyond Drok-na's vision.

The sky in the distance is growing dark, but I can't see Rok-lin, Drok-na reported.

How far?

Too far to measure, but only a moment of flying time.

Picking up a double headed spear, Fraum jumped down the stairs and out onto the southern wall of the keep where Drok-na was perched. Running up the dragon's back, he jumped down onto the rough scales, sitting with his legs wrapped around the dragon's neck in front of his wings. Grabbing the edge of a thick scale like he would the fork of a saddle, Fraum encouraged Drok-na into flight.

The powerful male dragon leaped off the wall into the air over the plateau's cliff, soaring quickly over the plains far below as though he were weightless. Drok-na beat his wings against the updraft and, a hundred feet below, the dried grass of the Plains of Demeter fell away as he began pulling them up into the sky.

As the dragon built speed, the air whistled in Fraum's ears and then Drok-na vanished. It seemed to grow instantly cold and then, nothing. No cold. No sound. In a flash Drok-na reappeared over the battlefield.

✻   ✻   ✻   ✻   ✻

Sarric gazed into the bear's eyes as it came forward, landing on his forelegs. Unlike before the bear did not circle, but stood there, breathing hard, blood running from his wounds. Around them centaurs struggled against the Were, but there were many more bodies of Were than the stallion-men.

The centaurs continued to push forward. They were accustomed to hunting the Were and their silver blades and arrows were doing the job. In each direction hundreds of yards of earth was covered with blood and bodies, but hundreds more Were still fought. Nearby Amanda swung her two Elven swords against three wolves that were attempting to circle her.

The leader of the Were stood defiantly against Sarric as the centaur leapt forward, slashing down across his body and then circling the large blade around for a second slash, opening the Were-bear's throat and spilling his hot blood upon the soil. The ancient were-bear fell to the ground and drew his last breath.

Amanda slashed one wolf and then lunged at another, driving the tip of one blade deep into the Were's chest. Holding onto the sword, she turned her back to the dying wolf so she could slash across the face of another, but the move opened her body up to the third wolf that leapt at her defenseless position. As Amanda braced for the impact, a red shafted arrow whizzing by her head imbedded halfway into the wolf's chest. The impact of the arrow drove the animal from its course, causing it to land dead on its side before her feet.

Clearing her sword from the first wolf's body, Amanda spun around with two slashes, nearly cutting the surviving wolf in half. She watched the wolf a moment as she caught her breath and then looked up to see Tallen striding towards her, a new U'thra-style bow in his hand. He was smiling, oblivious to the chaos around them. As Tallen approached, Sarric came up behind her.

"Thank you," she said to Tallen, causing the young centaur's smile to grow even wider.

"My duty here is done," Amanda said, trying to wipe the sweat away with the back of her wrist.

"I need to find Jerrod," Amanda said, turning to Sarric.

"Go. We've got this. Find your love." Sarric's voice was strong.

"Come, lad. There are Were to kill," Sarric said as he slapped Tallen on the back.

He has a right to be proud, Amanda reflected.

As Amanda began working her way towards the middle of the battlefield where she figured she would find Jerrod the power mark slowly dimmed. Winding her way around and sometimes jumping over piles of the dead and dying, she moved towards the spot she thought the dragon bellows had come from. Here and there hands, arms, and legs that had been hacked off, lay in the bloody mud. Death waited for the fallen men and Elves to bleed out and the large gashes that had not killed instantly would certainly get infected, causing an agonizingly slow death for many more.

Perhaps if the druids and healers can get to them quickly enough, Amanda thought as she stopped to look around the field, unaware of the bards' music drifting over the battlefield.

Unconscious wizards and druids also lay about, collapsed from the overuse of magic and covered in mud from the blood soaked soil. Some of the trolls and giant trolls were moaning back to life to go kill more men and Elves, eager to rip their foe apart or pick up a stone and smash them like an over-ripe tomato.

I must find Jerrod, Amanda thought again as she waded on through her horrific surroundings.

* * * * *

Near Lady Lieisa, Lord Steffen, Rhonda, and the forest warriors of Lithlillia beat upon the Fendür with such ferociousness that the giants were beginning to fall. Their bodies, like new hills of bleeding flesh, littered the line. Their large clubs, hammers, and crude swords cluttered the battlefield. But the trolls and giant trolls kept rising again and again, giving Lithlillia constant resistance. The First Army contacted the Elven archers to set fire to their arrows and relieve the hand to hand combat in the middle of the battle line while the soldiers surged forward to engage the deadly Dark Elven archers.

Keep attacking the Elves, Rok-lin, Nathanial thought, his black robes blowing in the remnants of the druids' breeze.

To the southwest the Cavaliers had abandoned their lances, swinging swords against the Fendür, but the non-magical weapons were not causing any permanent harm to the trolls. The giants moved back, allowing the trolls and giant trolls to fight the warriors. When they found a stray horse or large rock, the giants flung it into a crowd of foot soldiers.

The Order and the soldiers of the First Battalion were losing the western flank. The Elves and men of Lithlillia attempted to stretch their ranks to hold the line while they continued to fight with the Second Battalion's support. As the centaurs overcame the Were-Folk they moved to support Lithlillia against the Fendür in the middle of the line.

To the northeast the Dark Elves had taken up their swords and shields. The eastern flank of Nathanial's battle line was beginning to falter as King Garrett pushed forward. The Third, Fourth, and Fifth Battalions and the men of Trisdale were making headway, collapsing Nathanial's right wing.

The bolts of lightning and balls of flame were being lobbed across the field less often as the last of the wizards fell unconscious. Even the howling winds of the druids were calming as the darkened sky gave way to rays of the mid-day sunlight. Near Nathanial one of his wizards was struck by several white bursts of energy, knocking him backwards, blood drooling from the corner of his mouth as the wizard's eyes glazed over.

"Dragons and scales! We are not going to lose this battle!" Nathanial yelled as he reached into the bag hanging from his shoulder.

The leather flap over the top of the bag fell back as Nathanial slowly pulled the curled ram's horn out of the bag with one hand. The Horn of Valhalla was heavy enough that he had to lean his staff against his shoulders and use two hands to lift the golden mouth piece on the point of the horn to his lips. Nathanial took a deep breath and blew.

CHAPTER 19
RISING OF A HERO

The sound of the horn was deafening, even more so than a dragon's roar, but the warriors fought on in an awkward deafness. The hard metallic sounds of battle, the grunts and groans of men and beast struggling to exert themselves, all became momentarily silenced, replaced by the ringing in their ears. Not even the moans of the dying could be heard.

Slowly, a frigid mist, as cold as death itself, formed on the battlefield. It did not roll in like the fog off the ocean. Nor did it rise up like a fog over a lake on an early fall morning. The mist simply appeared, eerie and gray.

At first only the soldiers' sight seemed to be affected. The archers were no longer able to see across the field. The few remaining druids in the middle of the turmoil called for the wind to push the mist away, but the fog was relentless, unaffected by their wind. Then, out of the gray mist, shadows began to appear randomly across the battlefield.

Slowly the dark shadows took shape, the detail of their beings becoming evident. They were men dressed in breast plates, wearing great helms. They carried large round, wooden shields. Some came with spears. Some with Haithenbeurn Axes. *Langsax* swords were strapped to all of their wide leather belts.

"E'fretté help us! The Olympians have forsaken us," Amanda gasped as she took two steps forward and stopped.

Stepping around a mound of fallen bodies, Amanda found in her path a large Haithenbeurn warrior who jabbed his spear at her. Parrying it with one of her swords, she knocked the shaft of the spear outward. The power mark burned bright again as Amanda feigned an attacking blow with the other sword, causing the warrior to extend his shield in defense and expose his chest. Amanda quickly slashed upward through his chest, splitting him open. The warrior fell over backward, his body turning to black crystal before falling to the ground like a forgotten shadow.

"Sons of Valhalla," Amanda whispered, looking down at the remnants of the Haithenbeurn warrior.

Stepping past the spot where the body had fallen, she picked up her pace.

"In the name of Apollo, who curses us now?" she asked aloud.

Nathanial has blown the Horn of Valhalla. All who are summoned will follow him, a female voice resounded through her thoughts.

"Jerrod?" Amanda whispered.

Amanda jogged in desperation towards the center of the battle, ignoring as much as she could as she rushed onward.

✻   ✻   ✻   ✻   ✻

To the east, King Garrett and the cavalry from the Fifth Battalion had charged forth, supporting the Third and Fourth Battalions. Jerrod rode next to the king as they charged south, but the battle separated them more and more as they pushed forward through the Fendür. As the king's horse drove into the opposing line, a giant troll swung a large stone hammer into its neck and shoulder.

The horse stumbled sideways and collapsed, sending the king tumbling forward. Garrett rested face down in the mud as the beast lumbered towards him, but as the vile creature drew close, the king pushed up, his hands slipping a bit, and stood. In his hand he held his father's bastard sword.

With his free hand Garrett removed his helm and tossed it aside. As he faced his massive opponent he brought his free hand around to grip the hilt with both hands. The giant troll raised the stone hammer and swung down on the king. Facing his own opponents, Jerrod only caught a glimpse of the overwhelming attack.

The stone hammer came around with surprising speed. King Garrett ducked under the path of the hammer and sliced at the troll's leading knee, causing it to fall to its knees. In Garrett's hand his father's sword burned in wild flames.

Garrett looked down at his father's sword while the troll, frightened by the flame, began pushing away from the king.

Recovering from his surprise, Garrett seized the opportunity, jumping in and slashing down upon the troll's bare head. His father's sword cut deep, causing more steaming, black blood to spew out upon the ground. Garrett stepped back, taking a deep breath, expecting the creature to fall and die.

To his astonishment he watched the troll's wounds slowly stop bleeding, but the open gash remained. Stepping backward, the king was amazed to see the troll begin to stand. Garrett rushed forward, slashing at the beast while it reached for the hammer. Everywhere the sword struck, the troll's hide began to burn.

Jerrod caught another glimpse of the king's desperate battle, but from the distance he could do nothing and another troll stood before him. Jerrod turned back to his own fight. The king was alone.

Garrett slashed again and again, keeping up the fight as he tired until the troll's hammer finally struck his side, sending him reeling several feet to land in the mud. Again the king stood up, leaning on his now extinguished sword, resting as he watched the massive troll dauntlessly pursue him. He raised his sword over his head, unyielding, preparing to attack again.

"The King!" a nearby soldier yelled.

"To the King!" another shouted over the deafening sounds of the battle.

Across the field Jerrod killed his opponent and glanced towards his friend, the young King of Torrence. The soldiers of the Fifth Battalion were rallying to their king's side as Garrett led the charge to slay his beast. As much as any man can pause on the battlefield, Jerrod watched the gallant struggle, the king's sword bursting into flames again.

With all the power of Ares and the support of your men, my friend. I must find Nathanial, Jerrod thought.

✳   ✳   ✳   ✳   ✳

Traveling across the sky in a flash, Drok-na and Fraum reappeared over the battle. The black clouds began to dissipate as the remaining druids fell unconscious upon the ground, unable to call upon E'fretté' to continue the storm.

"There! In the middle," Fraum yelled over the rush of wind and the beat of the dragon's wings.

In the middle of battle Rok-lin tore at the forces of Torrence. She ripped most in half, sometimes with a single swipe of her talons, sometimes using both forepaws to grab and rip an opponent apart while she swatted at the soldiers like a cat batting at a mouse, enjoying the game of death. Occasionally, her neck extended to swallow a soldier whole.

I see them. Rok-lin. On the ground, Drok-na acknowledged.

Drok-na twisted in the air, bringing his wing over his body to roll and turn downward, wasting no time descending towards Jacob's killer. His mind burned with anger, with hatred. A searing pain began to burn in Fraum's mind, throbbing with each beat of the dragon's heart.

Drok-na, they will pay, but don't make this about revenge, or hatred, or other evil thoughts. We fight for what is right. We fight against the evil.

Drok-na roared in agreement as he plunged downward towards his prey, his wings back like a falcon. At the last moment he pulled up to land on all four paws. Soldiers on both sides jumped out of his way to avoid being crushed. Nearby, the object of Drok-na's focus stood with her belly just off the ground, her front shoulders slightly lower than the back hips, as she whimsically hunted the soldiers.

Drok-na immediately exhaled a stream of fire upon Rok-lin while Fraum leaped from his shoulders to land upon his feet. Pitching forward into a roll, the monk come up on his feet again, pointing one end of the double headed spear towards the female dragon. The sharp metal heads of the spear were split in the middle, with three large barbs extending perpendicular form each side of the spear-head.

The larger female dragon was briefly engulfed in flames. Raising her head, she roared as the fire subsided and she spun partially around to look back at them. Fraum quickly removed his belt and began twirling it over his head. When Rok-lin's head came down to spit back at Drok-na, Fraum released the bolo, sending it whirling across the field and wrapping around Rok-lin's neck so tight she began choking. Rok-lin's forepaw immediately came to her neck, her giant talon clawing at the leather bands.

Drok-na lunged forward to pounce on the larger dragon's back, his forepaws digging deep into her shoulders between her wings. Drok-na's teeth bit into Rok-lin's neck as Fraum raced forward.

Nathanial watched the attempt to overcome his dragon. He was confident in her magical abilities, knowing she could vaporize them in an instance, if it came down to that.

What a meek, foolhardy attempt. You didn't die in Terrace Xul, but I have you now, Fraum. Nathanial's thought caused him to chuckle.

Drok-na released his bite to look up at the wizard in the distance. He saw Fraum running towards them, but it was too late. He could hear Nathanial's laughter as the wizard pointed his staff towards the unsuspecting monk.

A great force hit the ground they stood upon, the unseen shock caused it to shake and a powerful wind to rush across the battlefield. Elves and men, Fendür and Dark Elves, the Heroes of Valhalla, were all knocked from their feet. Before Nathanial had cast his spell against Fraum the impact threw him from his feet. Even Rok-lin and Drok-na rolled apart, struggling to maintain their balance.

Jerrod stood nearby with the Sword of Trisdale in one hand, the fist of the other held downward and away from his body. Silvery white light radiated from him and his silver hair glowed. He stood, staring at Nathanial.

While the warriors on the battlefield regained their footing, Jerrod began walking towards Nathanial. His stare focused on his nemesis. Nothing caused him to look away. The wizard, whose breath had been knocked from him when he hit the ground, leaned on his staff, using both hands as he struggled to stand.

✳   ✳   ✳   ✳   ✳

All around Amanda, Elves and men fought the dead Heroes of Valhalla. With the battle lines eroded like a river bank overrun by the flooding waters of a storm, Amanda passed through the chaos with a single purpose. Wielding one sword then the other without care whether she struck flesh or parried a sword away, she marched forward, intent on reaching her objective. In the distance she could hear Rok-lin and Drok-na screaming insults at each other in dragon tongue.

Suddenly, the monstrous shadow of a man with a large Haithenbeurn Axe and round shield loomed before her.

"You!" Randver's deep voice boomed.

By E'fretté I will see Jerrod one last time! Amanda swore to herself.

"The King of Haithenbeurn? I was told you were dead." Amanda looked at him, puzzled.

"A witch's trick, but now I will have the pleasure of finishing you myself!" the king spurted out as he swung his axe over his head towards Amanda.

Amanda stepped back with one foot, allowing the king's swing to over extend, and then she stepped forward and placed a hard kick in the king's side, knocking him to the ground.

"You? Kill me? You have no idea who I am," she said, standing defiantly in one place.

"You are a thief who would be dead already if it wasn't for your demon-friend," Randver said, regaining his feet.

He was faster than his size suggested. His axe came from the side, almost without warning, but Amanda parried with a sword. Randver stepped forward, attempting to strike Amanda with his shield, but she brought her other sword around to meet his shield and then countered with a slash across his face, cutting deep into his flesh, but no blood oozed from the wound. Amanda stepped back, startled by the sight.

"What do you expect? I'm dead. I was summoned from Valhalla," Randver laughed.

"I don't care whether you are living or dead. Where do the dead go when they are killed again? They can't return to Valhalla." Amanda smiled.

Randver rushed forward, swinging his axe over his head and in front of his shield in a backhanded slash. Amanda parried, but before she could counter, Randver butted her with his shield, knocking her backward. Amanda fell into a back roll and came up, slashing across her body, but Randver had not advanced. He laughed at her again.

"You are nothing more than a thief. And not a very good one, either."

Amanda feigned an attack, causing the king to swing his axe and open up part of his body. She stepped forward, slashing at his chest, cutting him deep, and then glancing a blow off the shield before cutting the king's forward leg with the third slash.

The king stepped back and glared at Amanda a moment. His breathing was heavy, his chest rising and falling under his labored breath. Throwing the round wooden shield aside, the king drew the *langsax* from his belt.

"Okay. We will do it your way." The king's voice was labored.

They stepped forward into mêlée, their weapons trading blows in rapid succession. They circled, advancing and retreating, trying to gain an advantage as they beat upon each other. Metal rang like a blacksmith's hammer on the anvil as their weapons took the impact of each attack. They did not break, striking at each other relentlessly.

Eventually the king over extended his axe, swinging at Amanda's head. She spun, turning her back to the king before coming down on the king's wrist with her leading sword arm. The king's hand dropped the axe as it fell to the ground, severed from his body. After it came to rest the already dead flesh turned to black crystal before vanishing.

Behind them lightning struck, illuminating the field. Amanda looked down where the hand had fallen and then back up at the King of Haithenbeurn. The king did not show any sign of pain, but simply glared at her.

"I will take you apart one piece at a time if need be," she promised.

Randver turned to keep his remaining sword arm towards Amanda. He parried with the *langsax* blade as best as he could, slapping Amanda's Elven blades outward as she began to play with him, tiring him as they circled. When he finally lunged again, Amanda swung low and separated his leading leg at the knee.

Randver, the dead King of Haithenbeurn, knelt on the ground before her, trying to turn and face her as Amanda circled slowly.

"So this is what it comes down to, fallen Hero of Valhalla. Who declared you a hero, coward?" Amanda asked as she disappeared from his sight.

Her stroke was swift, decapitating his head from his shoulders.

"Where will your spirit go now, King?" Amanda mused as his body scattered across the ground.

✼   ✼   ✼   ✼   ✼

The battle waged on as the Fifth Battalion cavalry pressed south with the soldiers from the Third and Fourth Battalions. They were holding the eastern end of the line, but most of the archers from the First Army were dead, leaving Lithlillia and the centaurs to keep the middle. The appearance of the Heroes of Valhalla broke the resolve of the combined army causing the line faltered and break into fragments.

Wizards on both sides lay unconscious, some were dead from trying to cast more powerful spells than their bodies could withstand. The bodies of giants and trolls were strewn about the battlefield.

Very little magic was being cast as the dead warriors from Valhalla set upon the men and Elves. Lightning and heavy rains beat down on the battlefield as the druids and forest warriors struggled to hold back the Fendür and Dark

Elves. Occasionally, the faint music of a surviving bard drifted into earshot, momentarily lifting the hope of the valiant warriors from Torrence and Lithlillia.

For a while the armies stagnated on the blood and rain soaked battlefield. The middle line continued pushing with Lord Steffen leading the resistance against the Dark Elves. Rhonda and Imelrinn were in the midst of the foot soldiers following their king. Lady Lieisa and a few conscious druids encouraged the rain to keep beating down on the Dark Elven archers, desperate to minimize their archers' ability to shoot their deadly black arrows through the lingering fog.

In the clash a sword from a Dark Elve cut King Steffen's leg, causing him to fall forward. As he fell, the Dark Elve slashed him across the chest opening a deep, mortal wound, and then again across his back as Steffen hit the ground. As the Dark Elve prepared another blow, an archer's arrow impaled the Dark Elve's neck, but the shot came too late for the king.

Seeing Lord Steffen stumble, Lady Lieisa ran towards him. Lithlillian archers shot arrows to clear a path. From the sides warriors rallied, gathering to run alongside her as she raced to reach her husband. At his side, Lieisa knelt down and gently turned Steffen over to look into his eyes. Lieisa held him, gently stroking his hair from his head as she watched him dying in the rain.

"I..." Steffen coughed. "I may have failed you my love." He paused, looking deep into her eyes.

"Don't talk, Steffen."

"I love you so much. You have been my life," Steffen struggled.

"Steffen," she whispered.

"I could not have been happier, my love," he whispered.

"Nor I," she whispered as she leaned forward to kiss him.

Steffen died in her arms. Slowly, gently, she lowered him to the ground, oblivious to what continued around her, and then red washed over the priestess's eyes. The ground, the sky, and all the warriors around her where tinted in red. From where she knelt, the priestess of druids reached down with her hand, her fingers outstretched as she drove her hand into the soil.

"Hasnatak Roknireil!" Lieisa screamed.

The earth instantly began to rumble. As the ground around her split open with Lady Liesia in the center, the earth began to rise violently. Lieisa knelt at the highpoint on the growing hill with Steffen in her lap. Red, molten rock began spewing out of crevasse in all directions like hot streams of death, burning everything in its path.

"No! My Lady!" Imelrinn yelled as the hill continued to rise.

"You mustn't!" he exclaimed as he started towards her.

When Imelrinn reached Lieisa, her eyes were glowing bright red. Hot air swirled around her, lifting her hair off her shoulders. Imelrinn took both her hands in his as he knelt down in front of her, with Lord Steffen's body between them. He pulled her arms towards him, causing her to focus upon his face.

"You mustn't," Imelrinn whispered. "You will destroy the world."

Slowly the ground quit rising as Lieisa's eyes returned to normal and the wind subsided. The sound of the rain hissing on the rivers of hot rock was deafening. Lieisa fell forward over Steffen's body and began sobbing uncontrollably while the battle raged on all around them.

At the foot of the mound a giant-troll regained consciousness. The beast rolled over and picked up a giant spear lying nearby. As he regained his footing, he saw the queen of the druids at the top of the stone capped hill. With three steps he cast the deadly weapon towards her chest.

Imelrinn saw the giant hurl the spear toward the Lady of Lithlillia. He knew the deadly course on which the spear had been cast. The queen of the druids knelt helplessly in its path. From his knees Imelrinn leapt forward, placing his body between Lieisa and the deadly spear. The spear impaled his shoulder, entering the front and protruding out the back. The guardian fell over Steffen's body.

"No! Not you too!" Lieisa screamed as lightning burst down on the giant, leaving nothing but ash that quickly washed away in the rainwaters.

She looked down at Imelrinn and attempted to pull him towards her, but the spear kept from rolling over. Imelrinn turned his head to look at her, his stark green eyes looking into hers as he attempted a smile. Lieisa looked up into the rain.

"E'fretté, please, no!"

*　*　*　*　*

Mòr stood with one foot up on a small boulder in front of her as she looked down the steep, rocky hillside onto the distant battlefield where the embattled forces of Torrence struggled. Her long, dark hair and green kilt blew in the breeze. Just behind her stood her younger brother, Ròidh. He was taller, even for a highlander. His long hair, more red than hers, was unkempt. His cheek bones and square jaw were strong, as were his deep brown eyes. A falcon sat on his gloved hand.

Mòr looked over her shoulder at her brother and nodded. With a subtle but quick flick of his wrist, lifting his hand, Ròidh coaxed the falcon into the air. The raptor flew directly towards the battle, soaring high above.

Mòr leaned on her own two-handed sword, contemplating how the lowland king of Greensland had pledged the support of the Highlanders to Torrence. It did not set well with the Highlanders to do the lowland king's bidding.

"It is a fine place we find ourselves on this morn, brother," she said, turning to Ròidh.

"Aye, and none of our own choosing."

"Be that as it may, none we meet today shall avoid our wrath," she responded with a coy smile.

The Highlanders who stood behind them, carrying bastard swords and round shields, many of whom also had longbows or halberds, waited, intensely watching for her command. A few of the men and less of the women carried the legendary two-handed swords of the Highlands.

Mòr's brown eyes twinkled mischievously as she turned towards the highland army. The sun gleamed on their polished breast plates and the metal ends of the long halberds. She walked back towards the men and women who had long ago pledged to answer the call of the King of Greensland.

"We find ourselves on this foreign battlefield to fight an evil that may threaten our own lands if left unattended. It is not for the lowlands that we fight. Think of the valor of the highlands. We fight for Beinn Caladh!" Mòr yelled as she raised her large sword over her head with one hand, pointing the tip skyward.

"Beinn Caladh!" the army responded.

Behind the army the bagpipes moaned into a full volume with a screeching whine that quickly became the marching song of the highlanders as hundreds ebbed over the rocky crest of the coastal range down towards the battle like waves over a rocky reef.

The Highlanders rushed into the flank of the Dark Elves, cutting down the first ones they encountered, causing the Elves to rush to form a second battle line splitting their troops. The fighting intensified as Dark Elves raced to reinforce the flank against the southern assault. The great swords wielded with two hands and long halberds of the Highlanders met Elven swords and the black arrows of keen archers as the forces clashed.

The Battle of the Demeter Plains had grown to five fronts.

✵ ✵ ✵ ✵ ✵

Rhonda stepped and parried with her sword, knocking the clumsy swing of the troll's club aside. Swinging her sword over her head, the blade sliced open the troll's chest. When the club came back around, Rhonda braced with her shoulder, her legs planted beneath her, and blocked the club with her shield. Bringing her sword around, she severed the troll's club hand from its body.

When the creature reeled back, looking to the sky, screaming in pain, Rhonda lunged forward, driving the point of her sword into its chest. Before she could clear her sword, the troll grabbed her and threw her across the battlefield. Landing against a boulder, Rhonda lay unconscious.

The angry troll lumbered forward, focusing on Rhonda's lifeless body. As he reached out with his remaining hand, Amanda rushed him from behind, slashing first with one and then the other sword, cutting deep into the troll's back.

The bleeding creature turned to backhand Amanda, but she rolled under his swing and came up on one knee, crouching in front of the beast. Again, the troll swung. Amanda leaped over the troll's arm into a front roll that finished next to the beast. Lunging a sword into its armpit, Amanda attempted to pull away, but the embedded sword stuck and as the troll moved away, she lost her grip on the sword.

Attempting to grab her, the troll reached out its remaining hand, but Amanda jumped to the side. Bringing her second sword down across the troll's wrist she cut deep, but the troll pulled back and then backhanded her, flinging its hot blood everywhere. Amanda flew across the field, tumbling on the ground.

Nearly unconscious from the loss of blood, the troll crawled towards Amanda as Rhonda awoke. She staggered to her feet, blood from her soaked hair trickled down the side of her face as she looked with blurred vision for her sword.

The troll reached for Amanda's head just as a clap of thunder with an immediate strike of lightning hit the troll in his back. Burning pieces of troll flew in every direction.

When Amanda regained her conscious thoughts, she was covered in warm, brown blood and bits of troll flesh. Her ears hurt. Above the spot where

Rhonda had fallen, the druid princess floated in mid-air, spinning very slowly. Rhonda's arms were spread outward, her hands about waist height, her toes pointed downward, but inches off the ground.

Amanda got to her feet to stumble towards the floating princess. Other than her hair, which was drifting like lilies upon the glassy surface of a quiet pond, Rhonda appeared to be a glass figurine dancing on top of a table. As she approached, Amanda looked deeply into Rhonda's burning, bright green eyes.

"E'fretté," Amanda whispered.

Rhonda's glowing eyes returned to normal as her limp body fell to the ground. Amanda could feel warmth growing first in her chest and then in her arms and legs. For a moment it was as though her fingers burned, but then everything went normal. Amanda ran to Rhonda's side. She felt her chest rise and fall under her Elven chainmail.

"Blessed E'fretté, you're alive," Amanda exclaimed.

Rhonda looked up at her.

"Let me help you sit up."

"Thank you," Rhonda whispered.

"No. Thank you. You saved me," Amanda's voice was soft and the power mark was once again dormant.

Rhonda smiled. Around them the sounds of metal striking metal and grunting men and Elves pushing against their foe filled the air. Deep guttural sounds of the Fendür responded. In the distance a dragon roared again.

"We must go," Amanda insisted as she pulled Rhonda up and wrapped her arm over her shoulders.

"It's Drok-na," Rhonda whispered.

"I know. Come on," Amanda answered, her words rapid and her tone elevated.

As they headed towards the sound of the dragon, Amanda stopped to retrieve her second sword. While she picked up the sword they heard a dove cooing. A single white dove sat on the ground before them. Amanda stood up slowly watching the bird, and then she looked at Rhonda. They paused, silently sharing the sign before continuing towards the center of the battle.

✳   ✳   ✳   ✳   ✳

You are going to die now, Drok-na! Rok-lin roared.

The smaller male dragon lowered his chest closer to the ground, his hind legs crouched, ready to drive forward as he stood at an angle to the larger dragon.

I should have stayed and finished you in that castle, but your time is at its end, Rok-lin thought, beginning to circle.

Rok-lin rushed forward, but Drok-na drove up from his lower position. He wrapped his neck around Rok-lin's as he pulled her to the side and began digging his hind talons into Rok-lin's exposed stomach. The two dragons fell to the side, twisting in battle like a couple wild ferrets.

Fraum ran towards the ravaging beasts. The men, Elves, and Fendür moved away from the battling monsters as they fought their own struggles. Crossing the open space quickly, Fraum leapt onto Rok-lin's back. When he reached the point between Rok-lin's wings, Fraum raised his spear and drove a point straight down, impaling her halfway up the shaft of the spear.

Hot, bright red blood flowed out of the wound as Rok-lin reared up on her back legs, lifting her head skyward, roaring in pain. Fraum jumped off her back as she extended upward, landing on his feet behind her. He could see the blood from the wound and the spear still stuck in her back as she turned to glare at the monk.

Landing on her front feet, Rok-lin lowered her head to the ground, gazing at the old sage. Fraum began to move towards a sword lying on the ground. Rok-lin watched him for a moment and then, with remarkable speed, twisted her body, bringing her tail around and batting Fraum across the battlefield.

Drok-na leapt on her back again, biting her neck just below the head and locking his jaws. Rok-lin twisted again, but Drok-na held on as Rok-lin brought her rear paws around to scrape at the smaller dragon's belly. They tumbled and rolled until Rok-lin ended up on top, her forelegs pinning the smaller male dragon to the ground. Driving her head towards the base of Drok-na's neck, Rok-lin sunk her fangs into his neck, causing his bright red blood to run into her mouth.

Your hot blood is sweet, Rok-lin thought as Drok-na squirmed to get free. *It won't be much longer, little one.* Rok-lin was careful not to loosen her death grip.

The ancient white dragon dove recklessly downward, his wings tucked tight against his body. He did not slow as the ground approached. Colliding with Rok-lin at full speed, the two dragons rolled across the ground.

"Fas na re'al," the High Master thought as they came to a stop, still intertwined.

Rok-lin felt the paralysis constricting her muscles as if she were turning to stone. Panic erupted in her mind.

"What's happening?" Rok-lin's mind screamed out as she became motionless.

"No!" Nathanial yelled in the distance where he faced Jerrod.

Energy exploded from Rok-lin's body, radiating a wave of bluish light. The white dragon's talons disintegrated into yellow vapor. The ancient white dragon's flesh glowed red as it burned away. In an instant the High Master was gone. He had not understood the full power of Rok-lin's touch.

"Fas na re'al nakdraznic." Nathanial cast the spell towards Rok-lin in the distance.

Rok-lin felt her legs tingle as the paralysis ebbed away. Slowly, she rolled off her side and stood up. Looking around the clearing where the battle had given them a wide berth, she saw Drok-na lying partially on his back as blood drained from his neck wound. His chest moved slowly up and down as he struggled to breathe.

It won't be long now, little brother, Rok-lin snarled again as she limped towards him.

A small ball of white light with sparkling bursts formed, floating in front of the fallen dragon. As Rok-lin stumbled closer, the light grew until it was the height of a man. Rok-lin stopped and watched. Before her stood a knight, shimmering in white light. His plate armor glistened. The white plume rising out of his helmet swayed slightly in a breeze that was not quite strong enough to ruffle his long white cape.

The knight did not move as Rok-lin approached. He stood defiantly with his wrists resting over the *quillon* of a great, two-handed sword. Because his visor remained down, she could not see who this new adversary was and the mystery made her wary. She did not go straight at him but walked partially sideways, allowing her tail, head, and fore-claws to be ready for an attack.

Rok-lin lunged at the knight, who stepped aside and swung down on her forearm, causing a deep gash. More hot dragon blood spilled onto the mud. She countered, snapping her teeth at him, opening her forehead up for attack. The knight circled the great two-handed sword over his head and down upon Rok-lin's head, splitting the scales between her eyes and cutting her to the bone, causing blood to run down her nose.

Rok-lin pulled back violently and hissed, unsure of her next attack. The two circled a moment, looking for an advantage. With startling speed, Rok-lin leapt forward to grab the knight with both fore-paws. He just stood there as a bluish light engulfed them before radiating outward. Rok-lin held the knight tightly, willing her magic to work, but the knight still stood in her grasp. She tried harder, but nothing.

Why won't it work? I killed the white one. Rok-lin's thoughts were panicked.

Rok-lin, leave him. I am coming, Nathanial ordered.

The glimmering knight swung his sword, cutting halfway through Rok-lin's claw. The pain forced her to release him. As he stepped away, Rok-lin's jaws struck out again. The knight took one step back and with the blade of his sword coming over his head, he separated the dragon's head from her neck. In the distance, Nathanial fell to his knees from the pain of Rok-lin's dying breath.

"Get up," Jerrod ordered the fallen wizard.

Anger swelled in the young warrior, Lord of Trisdale. As he marched towards Nathanial, Jerrod threw his hand out in the wizard's direction. A sphere of swirling blue with lightning dancing across the surface burst towards Nathanial, exploding on impact, causing Nathanial to fly backwards.

Nathanial was struggling to his feet as Jerrod pursued him. Still on the ground, Nathanial picked his staff up off the ground and pointed it at Jerrod.

"Megarizna!" Nathanial yelled.

A steady stream of fire flowed from the staff, hitting Jerrod on the chest. The flame wrapped around him, burning at him, but Jerrod pushed back, waving his empty hand forward, causing the flame to be extinguished.

"You did not burn me in Terrace Xul, either," Jerrod mocked the wizard.

"Dazrik!" Nathanial shouted.

Massive lightning struck down from the sky, blanketing the spot where Jerrod stood, causing rocks and soil to be thrown everywhere. The blast completely obscured Jerrod from view.

Nathanial watched a moment, then shook his head and leaned forward on his staff, using both hands. He took a deep breath as he watched the spot where Jerrod had stood. His sight was unfocused. He was tired, barely able to stand. As he regained his full sight, Jerrod stood before him. In the moment that Nathanial realized Jerrod had survived, Jerrod swung the Sword of Trisdale, sweeping across Nathanial's body. The instant the blade touched Nathanial, a silvery white light flashed across the battlefield.

Time seemed to freeze. Around Jerrod, the Elves, men, and Fendür stood motionless like statues sculpted into a massive battle scene. The ones closest to him dropped their weapons to cover their eyes. Beyond them, swords seemed to freeze in mid-swing or in contact with an opposing weapon. Their struggle to overcome an opponent, to push through in order to advance the attack, was frozen in the moment. A single band of thin, black smoke drifted upward from where Nathanial had stood.

At first, nothing moved except a shimmering knight who walked towards him. As the knight reached his side and the last of the black smoke dissipated, the battlefield came alive again. For just a moment the sounds of swords clashing together and the groans of struggling warriors continued, but as Nathanial's army realized he was gone they dropped their weapons, turned, and ran.

The Dark Elves, Fendür, and Were fled in any direction they could, mostly northward back towards the Plateau of Kronese and its Black Forest, or towards the sunken plains of the U'thra Basin. Some went south towards the coastal range. Behind them the battlefield was littered with the injured, the dying, and the dead. Horses, men, Elves, and half-Elves. knights and squires, wizards and druids. Occasionally, the body of a bard, swept up by the waves of battle and carried off to death, rested on the battlefield. The battle had not discriminated between the young and the old, men and women. All lay upon the bloodied soil.

Jerrod looked around. His soul was empty. He felt sick. Then he turned to the knight.

"Who are you?" Jerrod asked quietly.

The knight raised his gauntlet to lift his visor. Beneath the helm Jerrod saw the knight's thick eyebrows, dark eyes, and high bridged nose. Jerrod looked at the man's dark, almost olive colored skin a moment. Still recovering from battle, it took Jerrod a second to recognize the white knight.

"How can this be? We buried you," Jerrod exclaimed as he threw his arms around the knight, patting the man on the back several times before releasing him to step back and grasp his elbow.

"All the power of E'fretté and the Olympian gods, Drin!" he exclaimed.

His friend smiled.

"My brother," Drin responded. "My time is short, Jerrod. I am with the One. It is magnificent. There is so much I want to share with you."

"Too short?" Jerrod repeated.

"There are thousands of worlds, Jerrod. And each is at a different level of acceptance. Some don't even know of the One yet. There is a lot of work for me to do."

✳   ✳   ✳   ✳   ✳

Rhonda and Amanda were helping each other limp towards Jerrod. In the distance they could see him standing with a white knight. As they approached, the knight removed his helm. They immediately recognized his short, curly dark hair and square jaw.

"Drin?" Amanda gasped.

"In the name of E'fretté," Rhonda whispered.

Picking up their pace as much as they could, they hobbled, supporting each other as they struggled towards Jerrod and Drin. When they reached their friends, they interrupted at the same time.

"Drin! Is it really you?" Amanda exclaimed.

"How is this possible?" Rhonda questioned.

"My truest friends. It is good to see you, all of you," Drin said as his eyes came to rest on Rhonda.

The others gazed at him, speechlessly pondering what they saw.

"There is so much that you don't know. Life is so much more mystical than I ever imagined. Cherish what you have," Drin said, looking between them.

"I owe you an apology, Rhonda. You were so accepting of me and I was so judgmental. Can you forgive me?" Drin asked.

"Yes, of course. We have all missed you." Rhonda smiled.

"Where is Fraum? He should be here for this," Amanda suggested.

"He is over there, past Drok-na," Drin said, pointing to a spot in the distance. "Jerrod, he is dying."

Amanda did not wait for the others. She raced across the ground in the direction Drin pointed. She could see his light brown robes covered in reddish mud, lying on the ground. Amanda fell to her knees and gently pulled the monk over onto his back. His almond shaped eyes opened to look up at her.

"Amanda, you've come. Look at you. Brown leather and beads," Fraum coughed as Jerrod and Rhonda ran up to stand behind Amanda.

Behind them the figure of the white knight faded into existence, standing next to Jerrod, just as a ray of sunlight slipped through the clouds to shine upon the group. Fraum smiled as he looked up at Drin. Holding Fraum in her arms, Amanda looked back at Drin.

"Can't you lay hands on him? Can't you save him?" she asked as tears began to roll down her cheeks.

"I cannot. This is the will of the One. I cannot change that," Drin replied. Drin removed his gauntlet as he knelt down next to Fraum and touched his head with his bare hand.

"You are a remarkable man. You have done us all well. All you need do is ask to join me," Drin whispered, just loud enough for Fraum to hear.

Fraum smiled one last time and closed his eyes. Amanda fell upon him, wrapping her arms around her master. Drin waited a moment before standing up.

"I cannot spare him, but Jerrod can," Drin said as he looked down on the sage.

Jerrod and Rhonda looked at him.

"It is not my place to change what the One has done." Drin paused. "For the magic to work I must leave. Magic cannot exist in the presence of the One. But Jerrod, after I am gone, you will have the power again. You are the magic," Drin finished.

"I know," Jerrod muttered.

Drin stepped to Rhonda and gave her a big hug, kissing her cheek when he released her. Then he knelt down and grabbed Amanda gently by the shoulders to lift her up. She turned around and fell into his arms. The hug seemed to last an eternity. It was somehow warm and comforting. When they parted, Drin kissed Amanda's cheek as well. Putting his arm on Jerrod's shoulder, he smiled before stepping back.

"It is not time for the One to come to Dendür, but He will come." Drin smiled. "I love you all. Goodbye, my friends."

As they watched, white wings appeared on Drin's back. Flapping his wings, Drin lifted himself off the ground, steadily climbing into the dark sky. Twenty feet above the ground, the Paladin of the Order of One faded from sight. Jerrod stood quietly, gazing at the spot Drin had disappeared. When he was done he turned to see Amanda and Rhonda watching him, tears running from their eyes. Then Jerrod knelt slowly to Fraum's side.

Concentrating, Jerrod felt his body get warm. His hands passed the warmth onto Fraum's body, but he sensed nothing. He focused harder, but nothing changed. He refocused again. Suddenly it was like his insides, his mind, burst with energy and desire. He felt a surge of power flow into Fraum and suddenly, everything went black.

Amanda and Rhonda watched as Jerrod fell over on top of Fraum, who suddenly gasped for air and opened his eyes.

"Jerrod!" Amanda screamed.

CHAPTER 20

IN THE SHADOWS

The king of Haithenbeurn was dead, killed by the queen witch for his arrogance. He had been wrong to kill the crone. He had been laid on his ship to be set adrift in the wind. Flaming arrows had arched from the shore, striking the ship and setting it aflame, ushering him to Valhalla.

Ironic. He died over a horn that could call him out of the very place we are sending him, Leif thought at the funeral.

A new king had not been named until three days after the funeral. King Randver's bastard son, who lived with his mother and was the only direct heir to the throne, had been expected to succeed to the throne, but Haithenbeurn laws allowed anyone to challenge for the throne and challenges were always to the death. It was a brutal right of succession, but it had always been done that way for as long as the histories had been recorded.

Succession always resulted in the strongest leader being selected. Haithenbeurn did not believe that one man was divinely destined to be their leader. They believed in might. Unfortunately, the strong were not always the brightest or most compassionate.

On the third day everyone had gathered for the mid-day meal to pay final homage to King Randver. Minutes after his son had been presented, the king's cousin, an older, fouler man, had killed the would-be boy king. With the death of the king's son and the succession of his cousin, the house of Fingard continued to reign.

The first thing the new king had done was to call the six houses of Haithenbeurn together for a War Counsel.

"There is a matter to attend to," the new king started.

"Somewhere to the south, a kingdom harbors the thief that stole the Horn of Valhalla. We will find that kingdom and along the way we shall bring back spoils that our rightfully ours," the king commanded.

✳   ✳   ✳   ✳   ✳

When the Dark Elves, Fendür, and Were-Folk had retreated, King Garrett had ordered the soldiers to break off any pursuit. He focused his forces on the last of the Heroes of Valhalla, who fought until all the abominations from Asgard fell and withered to ash. The trolls, giant trolls, and Were that had not been slashed down by weapon or magic, scattered across the plain. Vanquishing the last of their assailants, the King of Torrence declared their victory.

After the battle ended, the armies' injured were carried to large tents in the middle of the camp where priests did what they could to heal those that would live and to comfort the dying. The few remaining bards played on, easing the pain, allowing the injured to sleep, and giving more endurance to the priests who comforted them. There were so few survivors of the Order that they shared resources with the king's army, the priests of both religions working side by side in the same tent to do what they could.

While the valiant warriors were tended to, King Garrett stood in his tent with Lady Lieisa, Commander De'Ran, Lord Edward of Akkian, Lord Francis of Rizendür, and the highlanders' leaders, Mòr, and her brother, Ròidh.

"I am sorry for your loss, Lady," the king empathized.

"Thank you, Garrett. We have all sacrificed this day."

"Still, your husband is dead and Princess Rhonda's guardian is unconscious. So many of the men and Elves of Lithlillia fell today." The king paused.

"They fought an evil that threatened us all." Lady Lieisa tried to feign a smile.

"You have honored our treaty. Thank you," the king acknowledged.

"You're welcome."

"What of Lord Trisdale?" Garrett asked politely.

"The Great One will be carried back to Lithlillia with all the surviving followers of E'fretté."

"With all due respect, my Lady, I am not sure that Lord Trisdale is a follower," Garrett pushed carefully.

"No, he is part of E'fretté and part of what you call 'magic.' He will be carried back to Lithlillia," Lady Liesia left no room for argument.

"So be it, but I wish you would reconsider. Jerrod is also part of our kingdom," Garrett pushed.

"I understand, but no. I must see to my wounded," she answered as she turned and began to walk away. "You know, he is greater than both," she said over her shoulder before ducking out of the tent.

King Garrett watched her walk out of the tent before turning to Mòr and Ròidh. "You have also done us a great service. Thank you," Garrett said honestly.

"It was but a wee task that we were obliged to do," Mòr answered.

"I don't know about your arrangements with Greensland, but you had no obligation to Torrence. We called upon Greensland, not the Highlands. However, we are eternally grateful."

"Thank you for your kind words, Your Majesty, but we were bound by our pledge to Greensland. It was a matter of pride," Mòr answered.

The young king found her soft accent alluring.

"You would be a good ally, if I may offer you the friendship of Torrence. Will you come to Torrence so we can draw up articles of alliance?"

"Aye. We will come," Ròidh's deep voice answered.

"Give us a bit. Perhaps a month," Mòr added.

"Done. We will see you in Torrence in a month." Garrett extended his hand to them, the signet ring of his father fitting loosely on his ring finger.

After the Highlanders departed, Garrett turned to Commander De'Ran and his Lords as a servant brought in goblets of wine. The king fell into a chair, leaning into the back and extending his legs in exhaustion. Cradling his forehead in his hand for a moment, he rubbed his forehead before looking up again.

"How many have we lost?"

"About half, I would imagine," the commander answered.

"Half? So many? What's left?"

"The Order has a handful of Cavaliers and Squires, but they are done as any sort of army. All their foot soldiers are dead. We have less than a hundred cavalry and very few archers. The Third Army has about four hundred soldiers left between the Third and Fourth Battalions, and there are less than two hundred soldiers left in the First Battalion," Commander De'Ran reported.

"I have about one hundred eighty men," Lord Edward added.

"And I have about a hundred," Lord Francis jumped in.

"So few. Can we hold Torrence?" the king asked, staring at the Commander of the Armies.

"Commander Beals remained in Torrence with half of the King's Guard. We can also call upon the training school, but..." Commander De'Ran stopped.

"But what, Commander?"

"I'm a simple soldier, your Majesty. These dragons, wizards, and magic. I don't know," he responded, shaking his head.

"Has anyone seen the old wizard? How did the Triad fare?" Garrett asked.

Those remaining in the room just shook their heads.

✻　　✻　　✻　　✻　　✻

Rhonda learned of her father's death after Jerrod collapsed. When she heard the news, Amanda was the only one there for her. She fell into Amanda's arms and wept openly while litters were brought to carry Jerrod to the druid camp. Amanda and Rhonda followed as quickly as they could, helping each other walk.

On their way to Lady Lieisa's tent they saw Sarric in the distance, standing with a group over the body of a fallen centaur. At first they could not see who lay on the ground or who stood with the leader of the herd. As they hobbled closer, they could see that one of the centaurs standing with him had chestnut body hair and long black mane and tail. A handsome bay.

"I think that is Rodnic standing with Sarric," Amanda said.

"Can you see who they are standing over?" Rhonda asked.

"Uh-uhm," Amanda responded in the negative.

The centaur on the ground appeared gray, but in the mud it was hard to tell from a distance. Sarric and Rodnic looked towards Amanda and Rhonda when they came close enough to be noticed. The centaurs parted to let them into the ring. Drawing close, the grayness changed to a white body with several large brown spots. When she reached the centaur's body, Amanda knelt down in the mud to stroke the hair out of the young one's eyes.

"Oh, Tallen. Why you?" Amanda whispered, all her tears already spent.

"He fought gallantly," Rodnic offered.

"He took on several Fendür alone. When he died, he was fighting next to me," Sarric added.

"He saved me," Amanda added, her voice barely a whisper.

Standing up, Amanda turned to face Sarric and Rodnic, who had a gaping wound across his chest.

"You're hurt," Amanda said, reaching out towards the wound.

"It's nothing. Well, maybe it stings a little," the proud centaur admitted.

"I will send some of the druids to heal you, and the other centaurs who have been injured," Rhonda offered.

"Thank you. We would appreciate it," Sarric answered.

"How many did you lose?" Amanda asked.

"Fifty. A hundred. We are not really sure yet," Rodnic answered.

"We are still gathering the herd," Sarric added, looking at the older centaur.

"We fought the Were and the Fendür. Very few of the Dark Elves and fewer of those creatures. What were they?" Sarric looked back at Amanda and Rhonda.

"They were the Heroes of Valhalla. The dead, gone to the Asgardian Hall for dead heroes. Nathanial summoned them with the horn I stole," Amanda confessed.

"This is not your fault, Amanda. It was not your choice to steal the horn. You only did it to protect your friends. You did not blow it," Sarric argued.

"But all the dead," Amanda choked out in a whisper.

"You are a member of the herd and the daughter of E'fretté. You have nothing to explain," Sarric insisted.

"And a friend of Lithlillia," Rhonda added.

After saying their goodbyes, Amanda and Rhonda hobbled towards the druid-Elve camp. Sarric and Rodnic watched as they left, arm-in-arm, leaning on each other for support.

"She fought without armor like a true centaur," Rodnic commented.

"And she waded into the depth of the battle where the fighting was at its worst, and returned," Sarric acknowledged.

*   *   *   *   *

Amanda and Rhonda stood outside Lady Lieisa's tent while the druids who were tending to Jerrod and Imelrinn came and went. Inside, Roger insisted on standing watch over his Lord and friend. Nearby, other druids in a larger tent cared for the injured forest warriors of Lithlillia.

"They will be fine, Amanda. They just need rest," Rhonda said, hoping to encourage herself as much as she did Amanda.

"How do you know?"

"We will take them back to Lithlillia, where my mother will care for them. There is nothing better that can be done for them. Have faith."

Amanda looked at her. She understood. She had felt the power of E'fretté. It was a leap of faith Rhonda was asking for, and life had taught Amanda to only rely upon herself.

"I will," Amanda answered as Fraum walked up.

"What's happened?" the monk asked.

"Shouldn't you be resting?" Amanda scolded him.

"I'm fine. The priests released me. What's going on?"

"Jerrod is still unconscious. We won't know any more until he wakes," Rhonda explained.

Amanda shot a quick look at the monk as Lady Lieisa joined them.

"How are they?" Lady Lieisa asked.

"They are being cared for, but they haven't woken," Rhonda answered.

"I saw King Garrett and told him we are returning to Lithlillia with Jerrod. I have ordered our dead to be buried around the rock knoll that formed when your father died," Lady Lieisa said, her words trailing off as she looked aimlessly towards the hill. "Let's go to the site. I want to create an artesian well at the top of the knoll and we can plant pine trees," Lady Lieisa voice faltered.

"We can plant white flowers on the grave like you did where Drin fell," Rhonda suggested.

"That would be pretty, wouldn't it?" Lieisa commented.

Amanda and Rhonda glanced at each other and then back to Lady Lieisa.

"Are you okay?" Rhonda asked.

"Yes dear, I'm fine," Lieisa said as she started to walk off alone.

"Excuse me. I hate to burden you, but has anyone seen to Drok-na?" Fraum asked.

"A group of druids have mended his wounds. As soon as he has enough strength, he will be able to fly again," Amanda answered.

As Amanda finished directing Fraum towards Drok-na, she turned towards Rhonda and saw, limping through the camp, the large black panther. Sasha had scrapes and claw marks on several parts of her body, but the large gaping wound on her front shoulder oozed blood.

"Sasha!" Amanda yelled.

Lady Lieisa and Rhonda turned around to see the noble cat making its way slowly towards them.

Are you okay, Sasha? Rhonda thought.

I survived, but it hurts. You look well, Sasha responded as Amanda knelt down next to the panther.

I guess I survived too. My father is dead. Jerrod and Imelrinn are recovering in my mother's tent, Rhonda let loose in excitement.

I am sorry, princess of Lithlillia, the cat responded in earnest.

Sasha, go lay down in my tent and I will see to your wounds when I return from the druid hill, Lady Lieisa thought as she took Rhonda's arm again.

Sasha looked up at Amanda.

It's okay. I will be there soon, Amanda thought.

"Go with your mother. I will be along in a moment," Amanda said to Rhonda.

"Did anyone tell you that Drin appeared?" Amanda lingered behind to ask her master.

"No. How could Drin be here?"

"Through the One, apparently. But it wasn't Drin who saved you. It was Jerrod."

"Jerrod? He's become that powerful?"

"While I was with the centaurs I connected with E'fretté. She gave me the mark on my forehead. I felt her power, but Jerrod is way beyond even E'fretté. It scares me."

"Amanda, do you love him?" the monk's almond eyes looked at her softly.

"Yes, I do."

"Then go to him. He's a good man. Let it become whatever is in store for you both."

"Thank you, master," she whispered, looking down at her hands.

Fraum reached out to gently touch her chin, lifting it up so he could look into her blue eyes.

"No, thank you," he said.

Amanda looked at him, cocking her head a little to the side.

"You are my greatest student and the daughter I have never had. I love you as though you were my very own."

Amanda leaped towards him, throwing her arms around the older man as tears began to run again.

"I love you too." She paused. "Father."

✻   ✻   ✻   ✻   ✻

Fraum watched the Elves and men of Lithlillia ride away from the battlefield with Lady Lieisa leading the column, with her daughter, the Princess of Lithlillia, and Amanda, Friend of Lithlillia and the daughter of E'fretté.

Perhaps you have found yourself, Amanda, or at least you are well on your way, he thought.

Immediately behind the three women was a rider carrying a rectangular banner hanging down. The golden pinecone of the clan on a green field did not waver in the windless morning. Behind the bearer eight warriors carried Lord Steffen on a litter, taking the honorary position between the banner and the king's rider-less horse.

Imelrinn and Jerrod lay in the first wagon following directly behind the king's honor guard, and then a column of forest warriors and druids followed. Fairy-Folk fluttered over the wagon or sat on the side, observing the Great One. Some played music which Imelrinn, who faded in and out of consciousness, thoroughly enjoyed.

At the end of the column wagons full of the injured being tended by the druids were rolling across the field. Some of the injured sat up. Others lay down, and still others slept. Fraum watched the stiff wagons bouncing slowly westward.

It may take them more than a week, but they will be well cared for, Fraum reassured himself, reflecting on the injured and dead behind him.

Why don't they fly? I could carry them, Drok-na suggested.

I don't think either Jerrod or Imelrinn are well enough.

Well? Do they have to be "well" to fly?

We'll leave in the morning, Fraum answered, ignoring Drok-na's question.

Fraum sat down to watch the caravan creaking and moaning as the horses lumbered on, kicking up a dust cloud. The druids were bustling around casting spells to keep the dust off the wagons. The sight caused Fraum to chuckle.

Why do you laugh?

It's sometimes funny the way men do things. Don't the druids look funny scurrying around the rolling wagons?

Beyond the column Fraum and Drok-na could see a small group of centaurs watching the column moving towards their position.

I imagine the centaurs will escort them all the way home, Fraum thought.

Why? There is nothing to worry about. Nathanial and Rok-lin are dead. The Dark Elves and Fendür have been driven off.

It's loyalty. The bond between Lithlillia and the centaur herd has been strengthened.

          ✻   ✻   ✻   ✻   ✻

The island castle of Torrence faded into view as though appearing from nowhere. There were no trumpets on the walls to welcome them. Word of the considerable losses had already reached the city's residents. The citizens did not rush out to line the bridge. Instead, they waited inside the walls, happy the army was returning, but afraid their own loved one might not be among the survivors.

King Garrett had ordered a massive grave at the battlefield, which they modeled after the grave site at the Battle of the Sixth Battalion, but this time there was no statue to mark the sacred ground. And there had not been a parade of citizens to witness the burial. Only the brothers at arms had witnessed the final act of laying the fallen to rest. North of the gravesite for the men of Torrence, the druids and rangers of Lithlillia had been buried around the steep rock hill that had formed during the battle.

So many dead. Too many families will mourn their dead tonight, the king thought as the armies began crossing the bridge.

One riderless horse with a pair of boots stuck backwards in the stirrups led the armies through the gates of Torrence. Ahead of everyone else, a foot soldier led the stallion by its reins. Then came the king's standard followed by the king with the remnants of the once magnificent army following silently behind. The surviving priest of the Order of One followed next, painfully aware none of their troops had survived. The muleskinners waited at the entry to the bridge for the valiant warriors to pass through the gates before then started across.

On the other side all the loved ones waited along the street in hopes of greeting their returning heroes. The fortunate greeted their loved ones with an embrace and quickly went to their homes, allowing the less fortunate to meet their grief with some privacy. Too many were left standing alone in the empty street after the army passed them by. The sounds of women wailing could be heard into the night.

The street of pain, Garrett thought. *My people will never forget this day.*

✳   ✳   ✳   ✳   ✳

The trip to Lithlillia was long but proved to be uneventful. Rhonda and Amanda fretted over Jerrod while Lieisa tended to Imelrinn. The Lady barely left the Mountain Elve's side. When the ancient guardian woke they were camped along the upper Torrence River. That evening Lady Lieisa insisted on feeding him herself.

"Thank you," Imelrinn whispered, managing a smile as he looked into her green eyes.

"Shhhh. Take care. Drink your soup." Lieisa returned a slim smile.

Days later the column twisted its way into Lithlillia. The families came out to greet the men and women, the druids, Elves and forest warriors who were returning from war. Two thousand five hundred had ridden out behind the green banner of Lithlillia. Nearly a thousand would not return.

The honor guard carrying Lord Steffen on their shoulders went directly into the Pavilion and placed him on the dais before his throne. Most of the families and the surviving heroes followed them in and filled the seats. Others tended to the clan's grieving.

While Lady Lieisa, Rhonda, and Amanda moved towards the dais, the wounded were helped to bear rugs near the fire. Families whose loved ones had been lost on the field of battle sat close to the more fortunate, drawing from their strength.

There was no wailing or crying as Lady Lieisa turned to speak.

"Once again the clan and forest have been protected. Once again we have driven off our ancient enemies, the Fendür. And once again we faced our ancient enemy, the Dark Elves of old. This time we were victorious and it was the Dark Elves that retreated." Lieisa paused.

"We have sent our fathers and husbands, our brothers and sons on to E'fretté. We have buried the fallen at the base of a hill with a pine tree growing nearby that will bear pinecones in the spring and white flowers will grow year around upon the burial mound. At the top of the hill, out of rock, an artesian well bubbles in honor of E'fretté and our heroes." Lieisa paused again, looking at the faces of the clan.

"There were too many to bring them all home." Lady Lieisa stopped, looking around the giant oval room.

"But tonight we bury Lord Steffen who represents all those who journeyed with him to E'fretté. We will go to the temple and stand naked to bathe in the moonlight and we will drink the water purifying our souls in remembrance of the fallen. As the clan lives, so does their memories."

✻   ✻   ✻   ✻   ✻

Jerrod and Imelrinn were carried to Lady Lieisa's home, where it would be easier to tend to their conditions. Imelrinn was conscious and coherent, but Jerrod still had not awoken. While Jerrod was laid in the bed of the second room, the Mountain Elve moved laboriously with some assistance to a comfortable place in the main room of the queen's home.

"He still sleeps. E'fretté can sense him, but she cannot reach him," Lieisa said as she touched Jerrod's brow.

Rhonda twisted her hands in front of her as she glanced between her mother and Jerrod.

"He will wake, right?" Rhonda pled.

Lady Lieisa looked at her daughter.

"Let me try," Amanda interjected.

Kneeling down at the side of the bed, Amanda took Jerrod's hand in both of hers. Leaning over so she could touch the marks on her forehead to his hand, she began meditating. She could feel the marks on her forehead growing warm as they began to glow.

"I feel him," she whispered.

Come back to me, Amanda thought privately towards Jerrod.

"His body is recovering from channeling the power in order to save Fraum," Amanda stated when she looked back at Lieisa and Rhonda.

✻   ✻   ✻   ✻   ✻

When Imelrinn was able to move about he asked for a chair and a blanket in order to sit with Jerrod. He spent hours watching over his motionless friend, but he never sat too close. Occasionally he played his harp, filling the home with wonderful Elven music, but most of the time he seemed to sit motionlessly as if he were in a trance.

Amanda and Rhonda constantly fretted over Jerrod, oftentimes together. One would fetch something or adjust a blanket while the other held his hand or softly stroked his brow, and then they would switch roles. When they were not fussing over Jerrod they sat together watching him from a distance as they gossiped. At first they focused on Jerrod, his favorite foods or funny little things they loved about him, but as time went on they began talking about anything and everything, though they never talked about the battle or their love for Jerrod.

On one very rare occasion when Imelrinn was sitting alone with Jerrod, Lady Lieisa came up behind the ancient Elve and put her arms over his shoulders to rest. Imelrinn leaned his head back as much as he could and rolled his eyes upward to catch Lieisa's green eyes looking down at him. Slowly, Lieisa leaned over and kissed the Mountain Elve's forehead, and then she turned and walked away. A thin smile crossed the much older Elve's face.

✻   ✻   ✻   ✻   ✻

In the dark the small light of a pale blue candle flickered in front of him. As his vision focused, the light expanded, allowing Jerrod to perceive there were no walls around him. Nor did he sense a ceiling above him. He sat on a black bearskin in the middle of a smooth, flat floor. Through the bluish smoke he recognized the beautiful woman with silky black hair sitting across from him. Next to her lay a two-headed dog, sleeping.

"Hello, Felicia," he said, unafraid to look into her deep blue eyes.

"You've done well."

"Thank you."

"Do you have something for me?"

"Not now, not today," Jerrod answered, watching her eyes grow darker.

"I told you, you don't have a choice," her voice was stern.

"Where's Hecate? Isn't she your mistress?" Jerrod countered.

"The goddess of witchcraft can do what she wishes. I haven't answered to her for years," Felicia responded with a chuckle.

"There must be someone for you to answer to?"

"Not any more, Jerrod. I want the Dragon's Orb."

"As you can see, I don't even have the sword. Where are we? Am I dreaming?"

"It's not really your sword, is it?" Felicia pushed.

"Who's dog?" Jerrod asked, avoiding her question.

"Hades."

"A hound from the underworld. That's impressive. I thought hellhounds had three heads?"

"This is Orthrus, Cerberus's brother." She paused.

"Jerrod, I want the orb."

"Why?"

Do I tell him? she thought as she watched him, trying to decide.

Yes, tell me.

"You can read minds now?"

Jerrod smiled as he nodded.

"I still have the vial you gave me. What is it?" Jerrod tested.

"After you drink it, you are temporarily impervious to spells. I am not sure you still need it." Felicia shifted on her pillow as she reached out to rub the dog's back.

"You can't pet one head, you know," she said, looking down at the sleeping dog.

"They get jealous and try to bite each other. Look, how about we share? Let me use the orb and I will share the benefit with you," Felicia bartered.

The Queen of the Witches' eyes had softened. They had turned a golden honey color, warm and loving. Felicia smiled. The robust nature of her elegant body beneath her semi-translucent muslin robe was infatuating. Jerrod took a deep breath as the long fingers of one of Felicia's hands played enticingly with her robe.

"Let me think about it," Jerrod answered, trying to ignore her.

"I won't wait long," he heard Felicia's soft voice echo as he faded back into the darkness.

☆   ☆   ☆   ☆   ☆

Jerrod woke in a softly lit room with several lamps burning a small flame. As his vision came into focus he could see Imelrinn sitting in a chair with his legs propped up under a blanket. The guardian was quietly watching him.

"Now that is a sight worth waiting for. Welcome back," Imelrinn said softly.

"How long?"

"Two months. It's fall." Imelrinn smiled.

Jerrod pushed up on the bed with his elbows, moving up just enough that his head could see more easily over his body. Then he looked around the room.

"Are we in Lithlillia?"

Imelrinn nodded.

"My cottage?"

"No. You are in Lady Lieisa's home."

"Where is everybody?"

"Amanda and Rhonda are here. They are safe. They do everything together now, including fretting over you nearly every minute of every day. They are inseparable."

"Really?"

"Those two together are more trouble than any one man deserves." Imelrinn laughed.

Jerrod looked at his friend, laughing like a young Elve.

"Where are Lady Lieisa and Lord Steffen?"

"Lady Lieisa is here. She has been overseeing your care. Lord Steffen was killed."

"I'm sorry. What about Fraum?"

"Fraum returned to Torrence with their king." Imelrinn paused. "Roger has taken your men back to Trisdale Keep, if you were wondering." Imelrinn watched for a reaction.

"He survived. That's good," Jerrod reflected.

Imelrinn filled Jerrod in on the losses that Torrence and Lithlillia had incurred. He also spoke of the homeward journey and the centaurs. He even spoke a little about the Highlanders.

"Are you aware of the white dragon's death?" Imelrinn asked.

"I saw his body on the field near Fraum." Jerrod looked down at his blanket. "I don't know where I fit in anymore. I don't know that I want to return to Trisdale."

"Leave it for now," Imelrinn said as Lady Lieisa entered the room.

She walked over to stand behind Imelrinn, reaching down for his hand as he instinctively moved it to his shoulder. Jerrod could hear footsteps scurrying towards his room.

"You should have told us he was awake!" Rhonda said, appearing at the door.

When Jerrod turned to look, Amanda and Rhonda were standing together in the doorway, an arm around each other's waist. A large black cat ran around their feet and across the floor to leap onto his bed. The cat swaggered as she made her way along the side of the bed towards Jerrod.

"You look familiar," Jerrod said as he reached to pet the cat and looked up at Amanda and Rhonda.

"She lived with Felicia." Amanda smiled.

"The witch?" Jerrod said, pulling his hand away.

Yes, but now I travel with Amanda, Sasha thought for everyone to hear.

✻   ✻   ✻   ✻   ✻

Deep in the rocky depths of a mountainous cave, the dark figure of a naked man slept coiled around a large, black egg. His unkempt hair partially covered his short gray beard and pitted face.

EPILOGUE

The last chord of Amanda's Quest floated through the air of the Minstrel's Inn unlike any song before, even those magical songs sung by bards of old. The brethren were completely silent. The eyes of even the hardest bard welled with tears while the more emotional brethren wept openly. The applause started softly, growing quickly to a roar.

"Hurrah! Hurrah!"

"Thank you, my brethren, thank you," Reginald said, raising his hand.

"He has surpassed last year's song, *The Legend of Jerrod*. Can you believe it?" a bard in the crowd praised their master.

With the last chord, James scurried from the bar towards the Master of the Bards with a goblet of water. He did not look up, his long, dirty blond hair obscuring his slightly deformed face. Lawrence stepped forward to take the drink and then turned, handing the cup to the Master.

"Reginald Rhinestone," he announced as Reginald sipped from the cup.

The applause roared again before quieting slowly. Looking around the crowd, Reginald made eye contact with as many of the brethren as he could. They were his inspiration.

Such young bards with so much before them, but they will never really know what it is like to be a wandering bard, he thought before taking another sip of the water.

The bards of Torrence moved closer to their Master, each hoping to just shake the legend's hand. Lawrence stood just behind his shoulder, ready to protect him from excessive pushing and shoving if it became necessary, but the crowd remained respectful.

While the brethren focused on Reginald, Lawrence toyed with the hilt of his sword under his purple cape, frustrated by what he perceived as a boring life. He was one of the few bards that still carried the weapons of the ancient bards, a sword and a musical instrument. Comfortable with the crowd's behavior, he withdrew towards the bar.

There is no need for worry. Nothing is going to happen. Why am I here? What am I learning? Lawrence thought.

"Be patient, your time is coming," James said softly.

"How in the name of the One do you know what I am thinking?" Lawrence questioned.

"Lawrence, I am not a bard. I do not want to be one. I chose to care for our Master for my own reasons, but I am not just a servant. I see and understand," James said, looking into Lawrence's eyes.

"What reasons?"

"They are my own, like your desire to be the next great bard is yours. Your father cannot take that from you."

Lawrence looked at the thin, old man as though it was the first time he had seen him.

"The Master looks tired," James said, looking at Reginald. "He is very old and I am afraid the glamour of his position is taking its toll."

"Let's take him back to the hotel," Lawrence responded.

Together they went back towards the Master, who was still talking with the entire group. The younger bards were quiet, leaning in to hear the strained voice of the bard. They yearned for any of Reginald's mastery and wisdom of the art that he cared to share.

"You will have to return next year to sing the next song of the Torrence Ballads," several encouraged him.

"I am old. There are not so many Bards' Festivals left in me."

"Master, you are not that old," someone said, causing Reginald to smile.

"Won't you return next year to sing the next ballad? To sing the *Light of Ak'ron?*" another chimed in.

"That's a long way off. Perhaps my protégée will sing next year," Reginald answered.

"But you are the Master. You should be the one to close the festival," someone in the crowd pressed.

Reginald looked into their eyes again and then he glanced at Lawrence. He took another deep drink of water.

"Perhaps, perhaps, but every king eventually turns his crown over to his successor. I have had a long and happy life, many years more than most, but it is coming to an end," Reginald said as he played with his tiger's eye ring.

The touch of the golden dragon and its tail, which wrapped around his finger, gave Reginald comfort. As the Master finished, James handed him his jacket. He put it on and pulled the heavy jacket tight around his leather tunic before putting his floppy hat comfortably over his head.

"Thank you. It's going to be cold tonight," he said, smiling at James a moment before turning back to the crowd.

"But you have always been the Master of the Brethren, for as long as I can remember," a female voice pled.

"Like all bards, your love and appreciation inspires me. Thank you all, but we must go. I am tired," Reginald concluded.

Lawrence turned and led the Master and James towards the door. The brethren parted quickly to make a clear path for the legendary bard to pass. A soft applause started as Reginald moved towards the front door and continued until he reached the foyer.

"Mesphere," James whispered.

As they approached the door of the tavern, the light in the entryway seemed to increase a little, allowing them to more easily as they passed into the street. Outside was dark and cold, and the cobblestones slowed their walking speed. Reginald and Lawrence walked together as James followed carrying the Master's beautiful mandolin.

"How old is James?" Lawrence asked.

"I don't know. He was old when I first met him, and I was young then," Reginald answered.

"And how old are you, Master? You have never told me," Lawrence pushed.

"Older than any other bard."

"I'm not sure that answers the question, Master," Lawrence teased.

Reginald smiled at the youth.

"There are some secrets I still choose to keep. I will tell you soon."

The walk seemed exceptionally long to Reginald. As tired as he had been after singing *Amanda's Quest*, he was completely exhausted by the end of their trek back to their hotel. When they reached his room, Reginald disrobed quickly and slid under the thick down comforter on his large, king size bed. James left the room, scurrying off to prepare some herbal tea.

"Lawrence, I have lived a long time. Soon you must take my place," Reginald counseled his protégée.

"Master, I have nowhere near your experience."

"No, you don't. You have your own experiences. I don't want you to be me."

"I am not as good as you are."

"Perhaps not yet. Next year you must compete in the bard competitions."

"Me, compete?"

"It's your time, Lawrence. You are ready," Reginald insisted.

"And the closing song? Who will sing *Light of Ak'ron* next year?" Lawrence asked.

"We will see," Reginald answered as James entered the room.

"Did you put some of those special herbs in the tea?"

"Yes. Sleep," James responded softly as Reginald took his first sip.

"We have been together a long time, my friend."

"Yes, Master Rhinestone, we have."

"Wouldn't it have been nice to have known Jerrod and his friends?" Reginald said after taking another sip.

"They are your great-grandfather's songs. Be contented in that," James responded as he took the tea cup from the ancient bard.

"Your grandfather? That was hundreds of years ago," Lawrence questioned.

Reginald yawned as he snuggled down into his bed.

"Yes, maybe more. And can't you imagine fighting the vespree or ascending Terrace Xul? Or flying on the back of Horis, escaping Haithenbeurn with beautiful Amanda behind you," Reginald said as closed his eyes.

"I can see Lithlillia and Asenthia in my dreams..." Reginald's soft voice faded away.

Lawrence and James moved towards the door of the Master's bedroom. When they passed into the living room of the suite, Lawrence turned to James.

"How long have you been with the Master?" Lawrence asked inquisitively.

"I knew his father. Let's let him sleep now," James whispered as he pulled the bedroom door shut.

"His father? How old are you, James?" Lawrence looked at him.

"Older than anyone you will ever meet," James looked at him through the unkempt curls that partially covered his face.

HISTORIES AND ARMS

T he Histories and Arms provide some of the background for Amanda's
Quest. It includes some of the events and details of the kingdoms Amanda
and her friends travel through. The histories of the regions, which are in
alphabetical order, are followed by two maps and the arms, or organizational
structures, of the groups they encounter.

HISTORIES

Dendür: Dendür is the name of the world. Two moons circle the world, Questil
and Dori. Questil, the larger of the two moons, emits green moonbeams. The
smaller moon, Dori, emits purple moonbeams.

Ak'ron: Ak'ron is the continent with Torrence, Lithlillia, Heithenbeurn,
Asenthia, Silandria, Greensland, the Beinn Caladh (the Highlands), the U'thra
Basin, Plains of Demeter, Plateau of Kronese, Effendoria, the Wilds, and the
Eastern Realm.

Eastern Realm

Agganon: Agganon is the portal to Olympus. The octagonal temple, constructed
of marble with doors to the north, south, east, and west, is built on a lower
peak of the western slope in the Alfarakenloria (Mountains). From the steps of

Agganon, in the shadows of the jagged Alfaraenloria, the U'thra Basin and great Metamesterrian River can be seen.

The priests' and followers' pilgrimages to Agganon have long been abandoned.

Alfardoria: Alfardoria is the legendary land of Elves and Dwarves. It includes all of the Alfarakenloria range that runs north and south along the eastern edge of Ak'ron. In the middle of the mountain range is the Alfarakenloria Valley. Some of the highest mountains on Dendür can be found in the range.

Asenthia: Asenthia is an ancient eastern kingdom of Mountain Wood Elves, which is nestled in a valley on the western slope of the Alfarakenloria (Mountains). The kingdom is protected by Elven magic which controls the weather and hides the Elven kingdom from the world. Legend has it that the protection even prevented enemies from entering the kingdom.

Long before the histories were recorded the Elves of Asenthia fled the Alfarakenloria Valley and traveled to Asenthia, where they found a lush green valley full of trees, lakes, waterfalls, and brooks. After they began building their new kingdom the protective power was put in place.

Outsiders, those who are not Elven, are rarely allowed to enter Asenthia. Preferring their solitude, the Elves of Asenthia do not leave a trace of their existence when, on the rare occasions, they travel outside the protected realm. Like the entire Fairy realm, Asenthia and its king and queen draw their "magical" power from E'fretté, the power of nature.

Fjords of Menduran

Terrace Xul: Xul was the kingdom of five kings who went together into the mountains above the Menduran Fjord to mine gold. On the upper slope of Mount Thoradan they found gold, silver, gems and other riches, which caused them to hire miners. They generously shared the wealth with the miners and the subjects who followed. The five men who found the wealth decided to rule together. Their kingdom became known for its hospitality.

Before the entrance to their underground kingdom, the kings built a large patio terrace overlooking the fjord, which Terrace Xul is named after. No one knows why the kingdom vanished. One day the kings and their subjects were gone.

Mount Thoradan: The peak of Mount Thoradan is on the western side of the Fjord of Menduran, south of Terrace Xul. It is the highest peak in the Wilds Mountain range. It is one of the legendary homes of an ancient white dragon.

Ornholtz: Ornholtz is the northern most city on the Fjord of Menduran. It was built on the northeastern coast, southeast of the Cape of Bestla. Ornholtz is the causeway between the other cities on the fjord and the Kingdom of Haithenbeurn. It has a chauvinistic culture that values men and boys before women and girls. Ornholtz is governed by a governor and has a small army that polices and protects the city.

Haithenbeurn

Haithenbeurn was the original leader who discovered the northern lands, but his family died out in the struggle to establish a kingdom. The surviving six men who sailed with their families to the northern coastline where they landed and fought the Nogrondal (also known as the Fendür) for every inch of land they settled. The kingdom is constantly at war with the Nogrondal, a race of giants, trolls, and giant-trolls who live in the Brisbane Mountains.

The men of Haithenbeurn, who worshiped Asgard, reached the coast in long, wide ships with a shallow draft, and both masts and oars.

The ruling Houses of Haithenbeurn are: Aumont, Brúdmaðr, Fingard, Gounouf, Turdard, and Varanger. Additionally, there is Quétel, which is a small coven of witches and warlocks who provide magical communications and glimpses into the future.

Morganwray: Morganwray (*n.* Morgan's Remote Place) is named after its founder. It is the most western city in the Kingdom of Haithenbeurn. The city is the first or last stop for ships rounding the Cape of Bestla, depending on whether they are sailing east or west, respectively. It has a chauvinistic culture that values men and boys before women and girls. Morganwray is governed by a governor and has a small compound or fort in the middle of the city.

Aegirwick: Aegirwick (*n.* Aegir Bay) is named after its founder. It was built on the coast of Nasdrawuen, closest to Morganwray. It has a chauvinistic culture that values men and boys before women and girls. Aegirwick is governed by a governor and has a small compound or fort in the middle of the city.

Theasendür: Theasendür is named after its founder and is the seat of the Ruling House of Haithenbeurn. The largest city in the kingdom, it was originally built away from the coast to guard against sea attack, but growth expanded the city to the water's edge. It has a large harbor and three roads leading out of the city: the eastern road leading into the mountains where coal and ore mines are worked; the southern road leading to the southern city of Dalset; and, the western road leading to the coastal cities. The roads are seldom passable during the winter.

Also known as the "King's City," Theasendür has a large log hall where the ruler sits to govern the kingdom and attached buildings where the ruler and his guards reside. One of the attached buildings has a vault that keeps the king's treasure, but the greatest treasure, the Horn of Valhalla, hangs from a wood peg above the king's throne and is guarded day and night.

Dalset: Dalset (*n.* Dal – valley, -set – shielding) is the southernmost city in the Kingdom of Haithenbeurn. It is responsible for manning the Wall of Haithenbeurn and guarding its only gate. It has a chauvinistic culture that values men and boys before women and girls. Dalset is governed by a governor and has a larger military compound or fort in the middle of the city. Dalset is the only city in Haithenbeurn with an active army, but the posts on the wall are manned by the men of Dalset on a "voluntary" basis.

Coast of Nasdrawuen: The Coast of Nasdrawuen is the northern coast of Ak'ron.

Wall of Haithenbeurn: The Wall of Haithenbeurn, which protects the city from the Nogrondal; that runs the length of the kingdom's southern border.

It is the perception of Haithenbeurn that their kingdom is the center of Dendür.

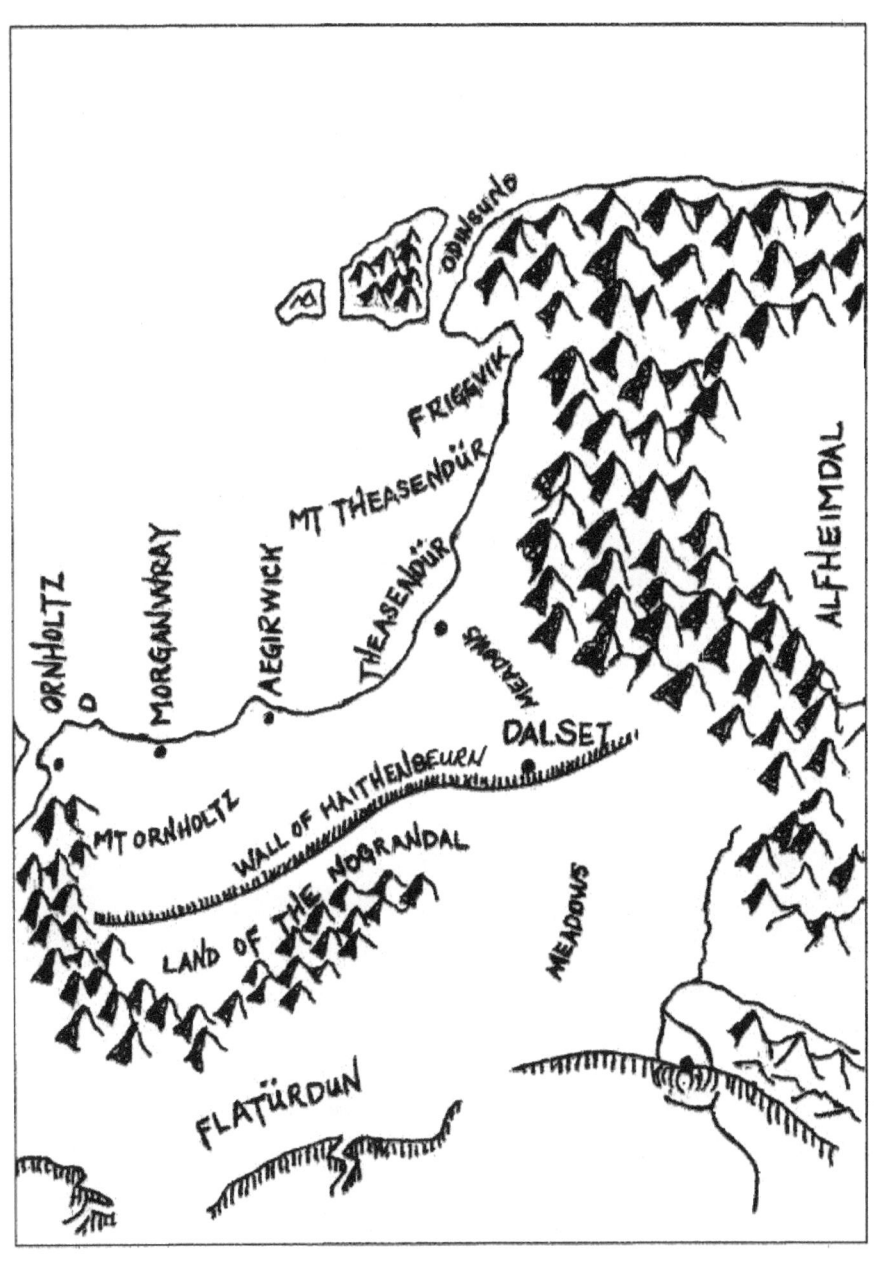

Lithlillian: Lithlillian is the ancient western kingdom of Mountain Wood Elves. The Mountain Elves fled the Wilds Mountains after the Dark Elves defeated the combined armies of the Mountain Elves and the Dwarves of Frausnaugh. The Mountain Elves took refuge below the Falls of Limerin.

As the world aged, human druids and rangers joined the Mountain Elves in Lithlillia. Together they created a clan that protected everything in the south from the creatures in the Black Forest. The symbol of their clan was a golden pinecone. The kingdom has a small village, but many of its subjects live independently in the surrounding forest. Lithlillia and its druids draw their "magical" power from E'fretté, the power of nature.

Plateau of Kronese: The Plateau of Kronese, also known by the Fairy Kingdoms as the Ruhenmiur, runs easterly from the Wilds along the northern and eastern borders of Lithlillian and then easterly along the northern border of Torrence to the Gap of Dillandria. There are three narrow passes off the plateau: one under Limerin Falls, another into the Torrence River valley, and the last onto the northern edge of the Plains of Demeter. The Black Forest covers most of the plateau and provides protection for its inhabitants.

On the eastern side of the Ruhenmiur, Effendoria (*n.* Fairy Kingdom) is hidden deep in the forest, protected by fairy magic. The Fairy Queen's magic is almost unlimited within her realm, which is inhabited by Fairies, Brownies, Pixies, and Sprites. Effendoria and its queen draw their "magical" power from E'fretté, the power of nature.

Giant bears and other magical creatures also inhabit the Black Forest. A loosely formed community of giants, trolls, and giant-trolls, called the Fendür (Elvish) or Nogrondal (Haithenbeurn), who live in tribes north of the forest in the Brisbane Mountains, raid each other and the forest.

Keep of Trisdale: Trisdale Keep was built on the southwestern promontory of the Plateau of Kronese when lycanthropes joined the trolls and giants raiding

Kronese, Lithlillian, and Torrence. A signal fire was lit on the top of this tower to signal Lithlillian and Torrence when raiding parties were spotted in the forest. It is rumored that it was the legendary masonry work of the Frausnaugh Dwarves that built the keep after the Elven-Dwarven War.

Southern Ak'ron

Gap of Dillandria: The Gap of Dillanddria leading down into the U'thra Basin between the Plateau of Kronese (the Ruhenmiur) and the cliffs of the Metamesterrian River. The gap is wide and the grassy ground is smooth, but the slope is somewhat steep towards the top.

Greensland: Greensland is on the southern side of the U'thra Basin at the mouth of the Metamesterrian River where it flows into the Semanie Gulf. The kingdom is largely agricultural with farmlands along the river and its delta. Some fishing also supports their commerce and some mining in the very southern edge of the eastern mountains they call the Blue Mountains (southern end of the Alfarakenloria) for the dark blue silhouette.

Long ago Greensland and the Highlands were at war, arising out of the Highlands asserting its autonomy. The war ended in a truce, the king of Greensland agreeing to Highland independence for an eternal pledge that the Highlanders would protect Greensland.

Highlands: The Highlands, called Beinn Caladh (*n.* Mountain Haven; safe place) by its inhabitants, is a small kingdom at the eastern end of the Semanie Mountains where one castle stands to protect all the clans in time of need. Normally, clansmen live loosely in groups across the rocky ridge, their families spread over miles of rocky terrain. They farm fields cleared of rock and herd sheep. They wear kilts and play bagpipes for enjoyment.

The greatest clansmen and women wield great two-handed swords called *claymores*. They hunt with long bows and falcons.

Silandria: Silandria is a city built on a cliff surrounded by a large lake where the

Metamesterrian River spills over a hundred foot waterfall. It is governed by an elected mayor and inhabited by a race of highly intelligent telepaths.

Torrence

Torrence: Torrence is the castle-capitol of the kingdom named after its first ruler. Lord Torrence was an adventurer who sailed up the Torrence River to conquer the savage land and rid it of wild beasts. He landed on an inland island where he began building the castle and started his campaign. When the lands were tamed, people came to build farms and open trade. They named Lord Torrence the first king.

Torrence allied with Lithlillian who still protects Torrence's northern border. A small amount of trade is shipped by horse or wagon from Torrence to Lithlillian including grain, wool, cotton, wine, ale, metal, mirrors and other personal items, but few people of Torrence know about Lithlillian or its subjects.

Although the king is the leader of Torrence, the most influential group, having the king's ear, are the priest and clerics of the gods and goddesses of Olympus. Two secret societies have equal influence through threat and manipulation: a powerful magic school called the Triad that was outlawed by the first king, and Crimson Pommel, a thieves and assassins guild. In Jerrod's time a new religious sect is growing. They are known as the Order of One. Lastly, there is a group of scholarly monks, symbolized by a white fist, that secretly watches over the kingdom.

Plains of Demeter: The Plains of Demeter are named after Demeter, the goddess of harvests. The grassy plain is due east of Torrence and south of the Plateau of Kronese. The south side of the plain is the flat and the north side has small, gently rolling hills. The soil is fertile, but no trees grow there. The eastern border slopes down into a great grass basin known as the U'thra Basin. The Elven-druid clan calls the Plains of Demeter, Hesperis.

The Wilds

Wilds: The Wilds start at the mountain range that runs along the western border of Torrence, Lithlillian and the Fjord of Menduran and extend westward into the mountains. It is the home of the Dark Elves and many vile beasts. Creatures from the Wilds encroach upon the bordering kingdoms. That encroachment caused the end of merchant travel between northern cities on the Fjord of Menduran and Lithlillian.

A map of Ak'ron is found on the next page, including the Eastern Realm, the Fjords of Menduran, Haithenbeurn, Lithlillia, Southern Ak'ron, Torrence, and the Wilds.

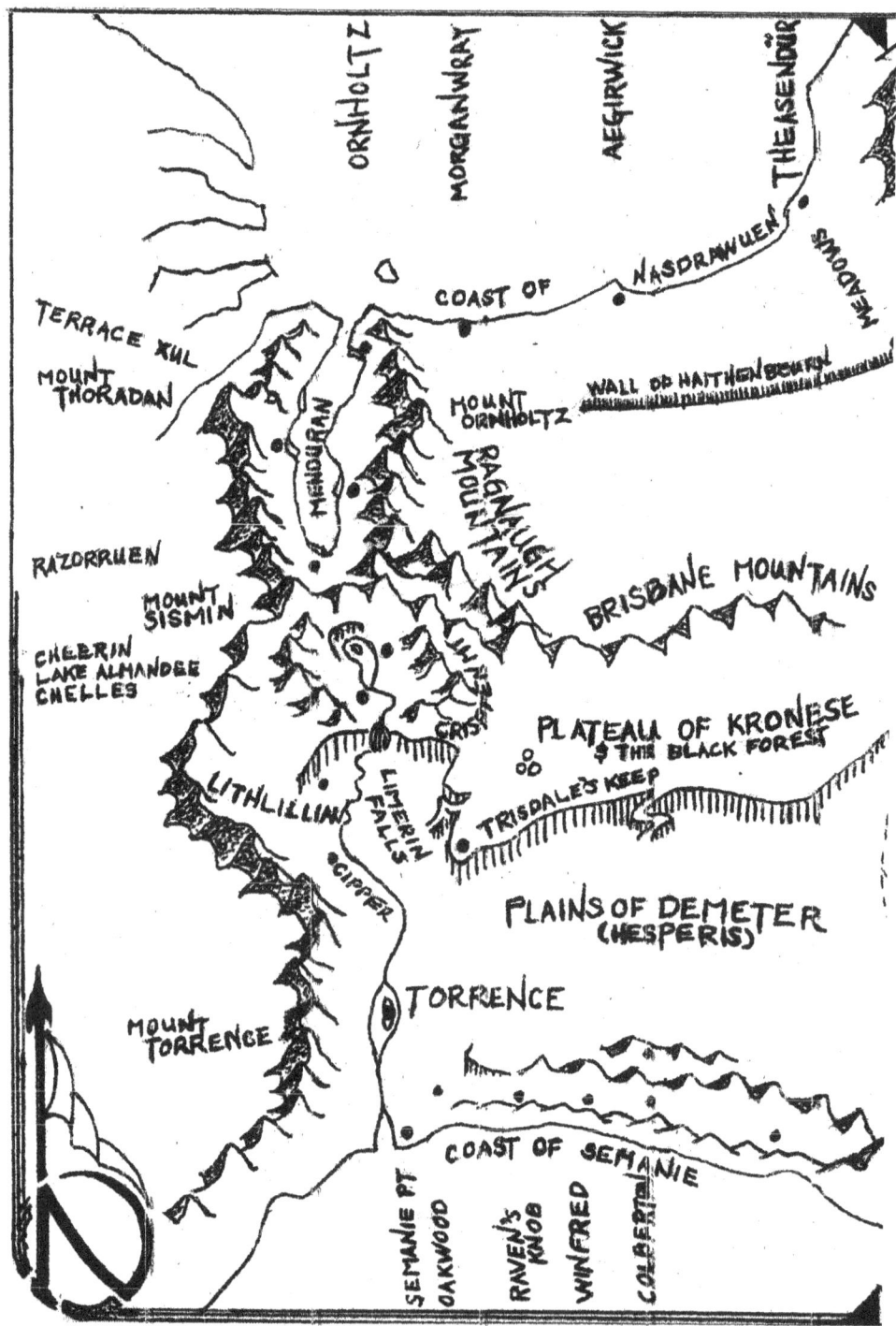

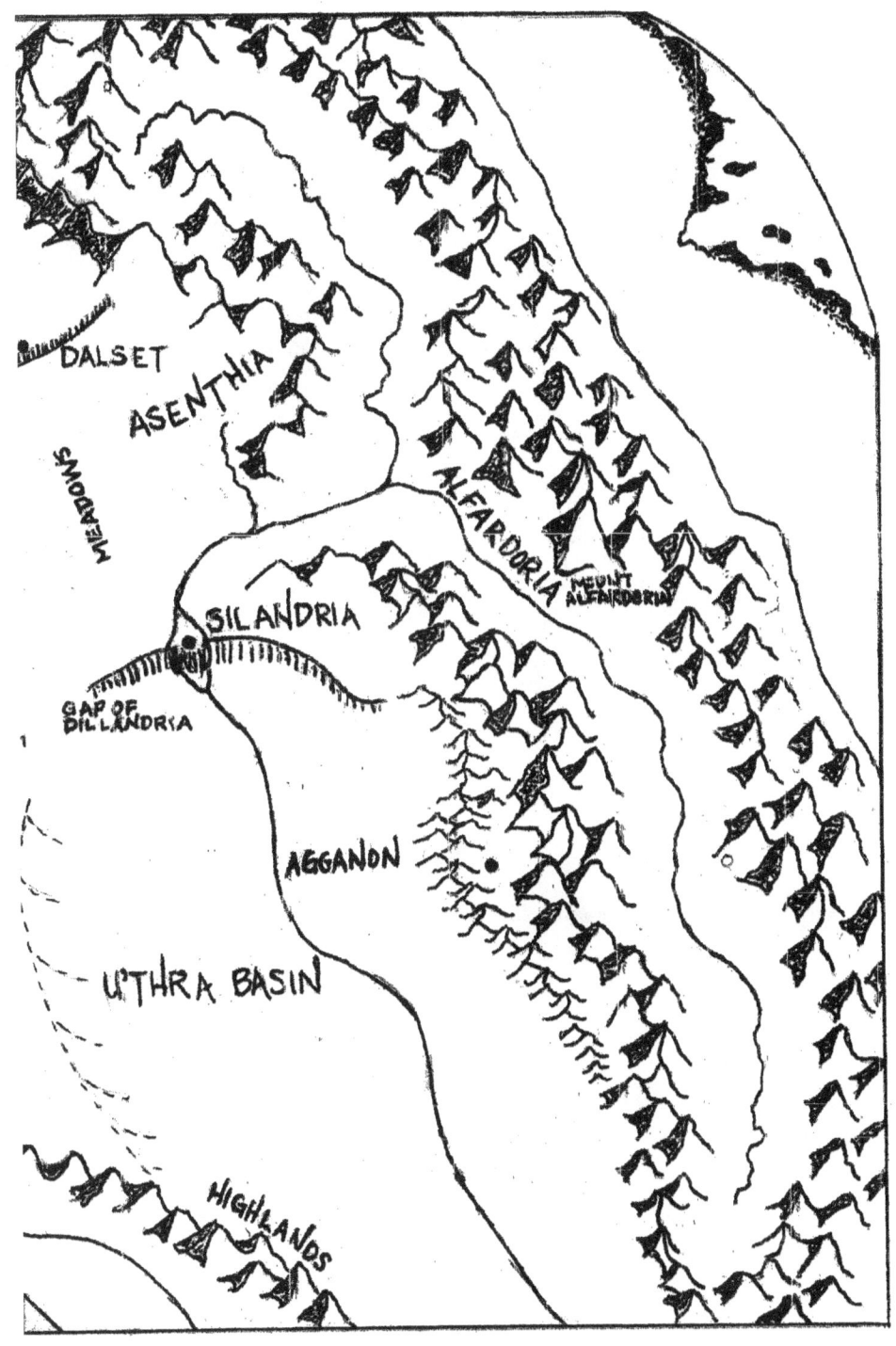

Mountain Ranges

Alfarakenloria – (Alfaraken: *n* Elven and Dwarven, - loria: *n.* mountains).the northern mountain range bordering the Eastern Realm.

Anacoztiel Mountains – southern mountain range bordering the Eastern Realm where Agganon was built and up to the Metamesterrian River. It is a lower range than the Alfarakenloria.

Brisbane Mountains – northern border of the Black Forest, south of the Wall of Haithenbeurn.

Crispten Mountains – surrounding Lake Almandee.

Plateau of Kornese (the Ruhenmiur) – plateau between Lithlillia and the Gap of Dillandria.

Ragnaugh Mountains – The eastern shore of the Fjords of Menduran.

Rhinefjell – The Haithenbeurn name for the upper portion of the Alfarakenloria range.

Semanie Mountains – northern coastal hills (inland) along the Coast of Semanie.

Semanie Hills – southern coastal hills (coastal) along the Coast of Semanie.

(The) Wilds – range running north and south from the Coast of Nasdrawuen in the north to the Coast of Semanie in the south. The range is on the west side of the Fjord of Menduran, Lake Almandee, Lithlillia, and the Torrence River. Peaks include Mount Thoradan, Mount Sismin, and Mount Torrence (north to south).

ARMS

Armies

King's Legion: The King's Legion is led by the Commander of the Armies. The Legion consists of five armies and one training army. The structure includes:

> General of the First Army (600 men)
> > Captain of Archers – four companies
> > Captain of Catapults – two companies

> Generals of the Second, Third, and Forth Armies (800 men per army; 2,400 men total)
> > Captains of the 1st through 4th Battalions (foot soldiers) – four companies each
> > Captains of the 5th and 6th Ballalion (cavalry) – 4 companies each

> General of the Guard (800 men)
> > Captain of the East Guard (cavalry) – four companies
> > Captain of the West Guard (castle guard) – four companies

> Commandant of Training
> > Captain of Cadets (foot soldiers) – two companies

The Armies total 3,800 men and 400 horses in the standing army, with an additional 200 men in training. There are two squads for each company consisting of 50 men per squad, or 100 men per company. Each catapult squad is responsible for two engines, either a catapult or a siege engine. Additionally, the cavalry may have a squire for each horse.

In the time of peace there is little movement in the ranks of the armies, leading to lower morale, but enlistment is coveted because of the benefits: room and board are paid, as well as a small pittance to spend in the local shops and taverns. The Guard, who protects the king and his castle, is considered the most prestigious posting.

Order of the One: The Order is led by the Prophet. There are two sides to the organization: a priestly side who guide their followers' religious growth and a protecting side who battle in the name of the Order of One to protect the Order and its followers.

The priests have twelve Elders, twenty-four Priests, and an unlimited number of Clerics, Friars, and Scribes. The protectors have two armies led by a Lord Marshal. Each army is led by a Field Marshal and is composed primarily of two companies of ordained, mounted knights. The structure includes:

Field Marshals (1 per company)
Cavaliers (mounted knights) – one hundred
Initiates (foot soldiers) – two hundred
Squires – one hundred

The Army of the Order totals 1,600 men and 400 horses. Additionally, the cavalry has a squire for each horse. Squires tend to the mounted knights and their horses.

The title Lord Paladin is the highest honor given to a member of the army. It is given to acknowledge extraordinary valor, independent of a soldier's rank.

Acolytes are followers of the One who have not yet been selected for priesthood or the army.

Order of the Triad: The High Master leads the Triad, which was started as a school that studied multiple disciplines of magic: wizardry, illusion, and alchemy. Members wear a large, gold ring worn on the left hand identifying their position.

The ring is a square piece of black onyx with a stone inset on each corner. The color of the stones indicates the level of expertise the member has:

Diamond – High Master (1)
Blue Sapphire – Master (4)
Ruby – (Lower) Master (16)
Dark Green Jade – Journeyman (32)
Light Blue Aquamarine – (Lower) Journeyman (unlimited)

New student-members of the Triad are indoctrinated apprentices who receive a ring without its corner stones. Those hoping to become students are pledged apprentices. They have not been fully accepted by the Triad as students and do not wear a ring.

Swords and Axes

The warriors of these Histories and Arms used a variety of swords and axes that was partially dependent on their race and kingdom.

Short Sword: A two-sided blade about twenty-four inches long with a handle large enough for one hand. The blade is about two inches wide. The taper of the point is very short. It is relatively heavy and is used for cutting, slashing, and thrusts.

Long Sword: A two-sided blade about thirty to thirty-six inches long with a handle eight to ten inches long. The blade is about two inches wide. The taper of the point is very short. It is relatively heavy and is used for cutting, slashing, and thrusts.

Elven Long Sword: A single or two-sided blade, but the blade is thinner than traditional long swords. The single-sided blade is slightly curved. The double-sided blade has a longer taper of the point. It is lighter than a normal long sword, resulting in quicker attack capabilities.

Broadsword: Similar to the long sword, but with a wider blade, causing the sword to be heavier.

Two-handed Sword (Claymore): A two-sided blade at least forty-eight inches long with a handle at least twelve inches long. The blade is at least two inches wide. The taper of the point is very short. It is a heavy sword used primarily for slashing and crushing blows, but can cut and thrust.

Bastard Sword: A sword that combines the characteristics of two types of swords. The most common combination is the long and two-handed sword, resulting in a thirty-six to forty-eight inch blade with a ten to twelve inch handle. This combination is sometimes called a "hand and a half" sword.

(Battle) Axe: An axe with one or two blades six to twelve inches long with a handle about three feet long. Single-sided blades may have a pike or spike on the opposite side. The battle axe is heavier than a woodsman's axe. It is used for slashing and crushing, but the blades can cut.

Dwarven Axe: Two opposing blades at least twelve inches long with a handle twelve to eighteen inches long. The Dwarven axe is a heavy weapon for strong warriors. It is used for slashing and crushing, but can cut.

Haithenbeurn Axe: A single blade about eight inches long with a handle twelve to eighteen inches long. The top extends straight out from the handle to the blade, which arches down and back towards the handle. The weapon is built for speed and throwing. It is used for slashing, cutting, and crushing.

Haithenbeurn Longsword ("Langsax"): A shorter two-sided blade about twenty-six to thirty inches long with a handle eight to ten inches long. The blade is about three inches wide. The taper of the point is very short. It is relatively heavy and is used for cutting, slashing, and thrusts.

BATTLE OF DEMETER PLAIN

Battle Maps

▨	Standing Armies of Torrence	⊡	Combined Armies of Dark Elves and Fendür
⦀	Elves and Rangers of Lithlillia		
⊞	Cavaliers of the Order of One	☐	Were-Folk
☐	Centaurs of the Lithlillia Forest	⠿	Heroes of Valhalla
⊟	Highlanders of Greensland	$\mathcal{D}$	denotes a dragon

Figure 1.

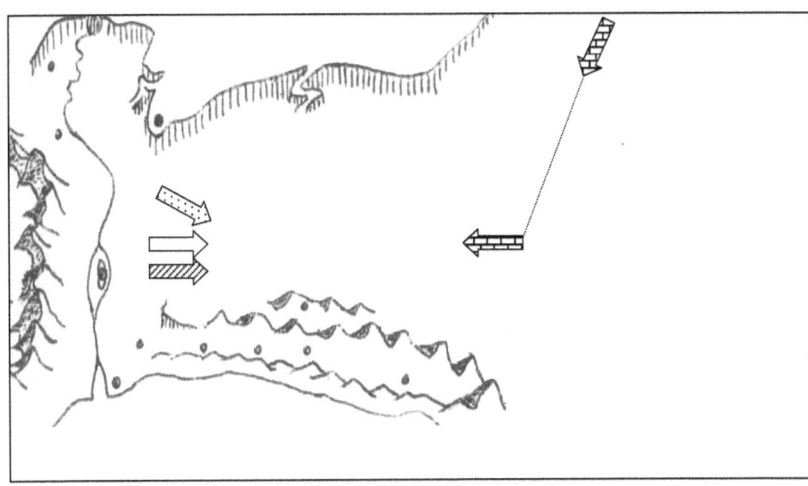

The allied forces of Torrence march eastward across the Plain of Demeter as Nathanial's forces march westward out of the U'thra Basin.

Figure 2.

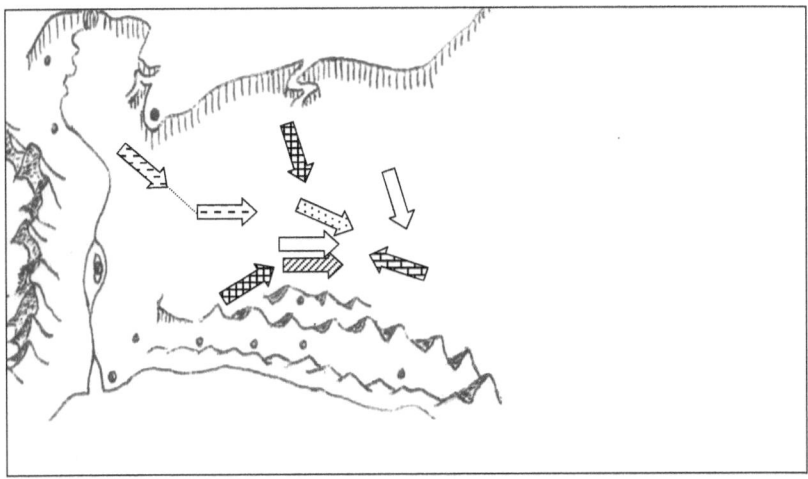

The Standing Armies of Torrence drive around to attack the Fendür from the north; and the combined armies of Torrence and Lithlillia's archers and foot soldiers hold the middle, while the Order of One strikes from the east with support from the Standing Armies. The Fendür are supported by Dark Elven archers. Were-Folk launch a surprise attack from the western flanks.

Figure 3.

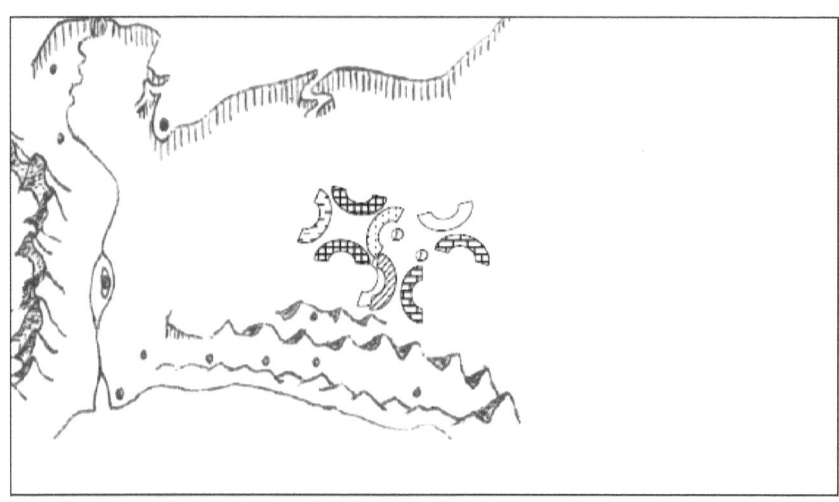

The Army of Lithlillia turn to fight the Were-Folk as the Centaurs attack the Were flanks. The Standing Armies of Torrence and the Order continue to drive forward against the Fendür causing the Dark Elves to join hand-to-hand combat. Rok-lin lands in the battle line of the Fendür and Dark Elves. Drok-na lands between the Standing Armies of Torrence and the Cavaliers of the Order of One.

Figure 4.

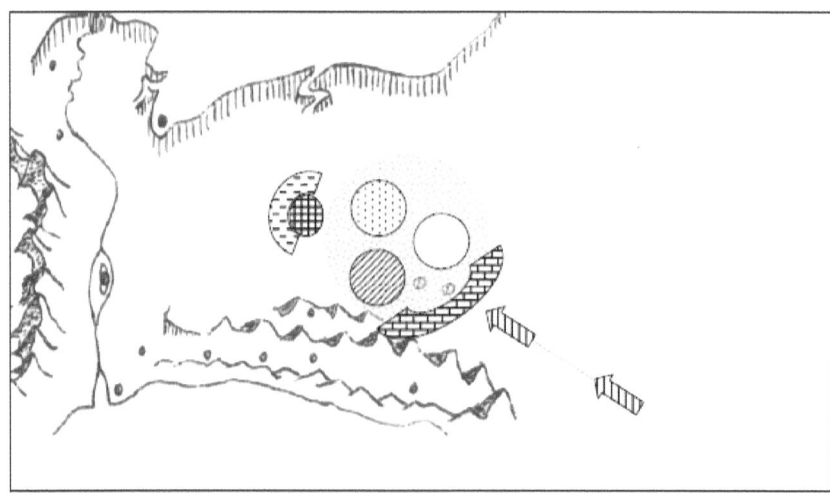

As the Centaurs overwhelm the Were-Folk, the Heroes of Valhalla are summoned into battle and quickly surround Torrence, Lithlillia, and the Order of One. The Dark Elves begin to provide support from the southeast, but the Highlanders from Greensland run into battle from their flank.

Men at Arms

Standing Armies of Torrence – foot soldiers	1,600	Dark Elves	2,500
Standing Army of Torrence – archers	400		
Standing Army of Torrence – Cavalry	400		
East Guard Cavalry	400		
Elves and Rangers of Lithlillia	2,500	Fendür	2,000
Cavaliers of the Order of One	100	Were-Folk	800
Initiates of the Order of One	200		
Centaurs of the Lithlillia Forest	500	Heroes of Valhalla	5,000
Highlanders from Greensland	2,000		
Wizards of the Triad	100	Rogue Wizards of the Triad	80
Bards	100		
Lord Trisdale (100), Akkian (250), Rizendür (150)	500		
Total...	8,800	Total...	10,380

AUTHOR AND SERIES

ABOUT THE AUTHOR

D.M. Stoddard, author, artist, and composer.

D.M. Stoddard actively seeks to provide an interesting and enjoyable story for fantasy readers. His love for storytelling began when he was a pre-teen, writing fictitious stories that ranged from football games to modern war battles. In his twenties he wrote poetry and was introduced to fantasy role-playing games. After years of being a game master where he developed worlds and designed fantasy campaigns for players to enjoy, DM studied creative writing and Greek mythology at the University of Maryland. Later, while telling improvisational stories of whimsical forest creatures to his children at bedtime, he became hooked on storytelling.

D.M. Stoddard has been exposed to a variety of athletic experiences that he relies upon in the Kingdom of Torrence series. When he was young he rode horses, shot bows, fished, and camped with his family. In college he began studying martial arts. Through his outdoor activities, DM learned to track and is currently returning to backpacking and archery. He incorporates his knowledge of these activities into his writing to enrich his stories.

D.M. Stoddard has a Master's degree and has studied Chinese, Spanish, and Tagalog, although English is now his only functional language. He is retired from the United States Navy and works for the State of Nevada. He and his son wrote and published *Lost Kingdom of Terrace Xul, The Bard's Song*© for the song in chapter nine of *The Legend of Jerrod*. D.M. used watercolors to paint the sword on his first book and the face on his second. He did the maps in pen and ink.

As an author, the most influential quote D.M. Stoddard heard was from his creative writing professor: "Just keep writing."

KINGDOM OF TORRENCE SERIES

Amanda's Quest is written so the reader can read it as an individual novel, but it is the second book in the Kingdom of Torrence series. Amanda has left her comrades behind to pursue the completion of a "recovery" quest arising from a blood-debt she promised to fulfill in order to secure Rhonda being healed. Amanda must venture into the barbaric northern realm where the gods of Asgard are followed. With less than a year to return the Horn of Valhalla to Torrence, she races against time while the only man she has ever loved travels with Rhonda, the druid Princess of Lithlillia.

The Legend of Jerrod is DM Stoddard's debut novel and the first book of the series. Jerrod, who wants more from life than following in his father's footsteps to become a miller, seeks fame and fortune that leads him on an adventure quest for lost treasure. Traveling with a two other warriors, a wizard, and a sage, they meet Rhonda, druid Princess of Lithlillia, and her Elven guardian. While being pursued by mercenaries, they fight creatures intent on their distruction. During the journey Jerrod realizes he is in love with the female warrior, Amanda, and the druid princess while he struggles to survive.

The Legend of Jerrod received awards and recognition from:

Next Generation Indie Book Awards – 2014 Finalist
for First Novel (over 80,000 words)
San Francisco Book Festival – 2013 Honorable Mention in Science Fiction